The Blackbird of Kirthgarran

Susan Brown

Fenalla Books

Published by Fenalla Books

First Edition 2011

Copyright © 2011 by Susan Brown

This book is a work of fiction. Names, characters, places, and incidents are products of the author's imagination or are used fictitiously. Any resemblance to actual events or locales or persons, living or dead, is entirely coincidental.

Bible quotations are from the King James Bible. The excerpts from the poetry by Robert Burns and William Blake, as well as the song lyrics from Scottish and Irish folk songs of the eighteenth century, may be found in the public domain, except for "Wheesht, Wheesht," written by the author.

Book design, cover, and graphics by Susan Brown.

ISBN-13: 978-0615530420

ISBN-10: 0615530427

Dedicated with love to Robbie and Jamie,
who grew up calling this *Mama's Castle Book*

I turned to leave, but my eye caught on the bed. My feet came to a halt. I felt my scalp contract as my hair lifted. My clarsach had been placed on the forest-green coverlet, on its side. I had not put it there. And there was something wrong with it.

I stepped forward and stood at my bedside to view it better. With a shaking hand I brought the candle closer. Someone had hacked at the taut strings and broken the highest, thinnest ones; someone had struck again and again at the honey-colored wood, scarring and splintering and permanently disfiguring the polished surface. The medieval designs inspired by the Books of Kells and Durrow and lovingly carved into the oak were now chipped and sliced. The dragon, or dog, on the bottom was now neither, only a welter of notches and punctures.

Embedded in the sounding box, abandoned by the hand that had wielded it, was a plain, heather-wood-handled knife from the kitchen of Kirthgarran.

The sight took the life from my limbs.

That someone could have harmed an instrument meant for giving pleasure was mystifying. That someone had meant the knife to lie in my throat and not the clarsach's was a possibility that was terrifying.

It could not be, I told myself. But there it was in front of me, and with cold clarity, fear crept into my soul, and stayed.

I've seen Tweed's silver streams,
Glitt'ring in the sunny beams,
Grow drumlie and dark,
As they roll'd on their way.
    The Flowers of the Forest (Cockburn)

Chapter One

I was convinced of two things as I lay in the grass listening to the tale of Thomas the Rhymer. One, that The Fairies had again stolen one of Mamma's bairns. And two, that as much as I'd loved the wild strawberries we had scavenged by the River Tweed that afternoon, I had never in all my eight years been hungrier.

The evidence of the first was Mamma's teary eyes and the visit, several days earlier, from Mrs. Dundas with her customary offerings of lemon pudding and hartshorn jelly. I had learnt long ago that when the two instances occurred together they meant The Other People had whisked away another one of my siblings.

The second conviction required no thought at all. My stomach was hollow and wanting cake.

"Mamma," I interrupted, throwing my bracken-stuffed rabbit high into the air and catching him again. "I'm hungry."

She stopped her storytelling in mid-sentence, but I did not think she was surprised by my declaration. "Time for tea, is it?" she asked. She hugged her knees and squinted lazily at the June sun.

Thomas the Rhymer and The Fairies forgotten, I scooped up the wilting wildflowers I had collected and leapt to my feet.

Mamma brought her smiling face close to mine. Her blue irises with their random flecks of gray were the same as mine, and I gazed at them as if peering into a looking glass. Our hair was brown, the color of the dark honey that Mrs. Taggart poured into earthen jars. Our brows swept upward like wings. Mamma sometimes marveled at how alike we were, except for the purple mark that sometimes stained her cheekbone. She kissed my forehead and said, "Dear sweet lass. I ken you love your tea. Let's be away, then."

Her arms laden with flowers, cast-off shoes, stockings, and lap harp, she climbed the rise to the house. I followed happily, skipping and bouncing like a new lamb but never straying more than a few steps from her. We had spent the whole day together and had sought all our favorite places along the Tweed. Mamma had played the clarsach and we'd feasted on a picnic of bridies and shortbread and the luscious, sun-warmed strawberries. I believed she'd forgotten her stolen bairn, at least for a while, and I was thankful. The robbery of a brother or sister who would someday play games and provide company on long, dark days was disconcerting to me, but the loss of a child was devastating to Mamma. Every time it happened I was far more disturbed by her tears than my own fleeting disappointment.

"I cannot bear going inside, not on such a bonny day as this," Mamma said wistfully when we reached the garden. "Do you suppose we could persuade Mrs. Taggart to bring our tea outside?"

I wrinkled my nose. Mrs. Taggart, our housekeeper, never did anything inventive. A nippit woman with a sour temperament, she humored my father by serving tea as the English did, but it had to be done just so, with the dishes, milk, and tea pots placed carefully on china plates so none of the Bohea would stain the linen cloth, and all needed to be laid perfectly on the mahogany tea-table in the drawing room. How could she tolerate a wooden bench and a board set on trestles in the open air? The only advantage would be that any crumbs dropped from the Tantallon cakes or petticoat tails, or pieces of seed cake with their sprinklings of caraway seeds, could remain on the ground and be found by birds. What fun that would be!

It was portentous I was thinking of birds, for as soon as Mamma began arranging her burdens on a settle, I spied something shiny and black flopping on the lawn. I scampered closer and discovered it to be a rook. One wing rested crookedly on the grass. The bird tried to hop away from me a little, but I stooped to inspect it with care and it paused to measure me, in turn, from a liquid bead of black.

Mamma came to us and lifted the rook with her fingers, saying softly, "Wheesht, wheesht," in response to its quivering. It was panting with its thick ebony beak partly open. "The poor bird," she said. "His wing is broken. And he's dazed."

We searched the branches of the oak tree above through which beams of sunlight gently filtered, and surveyed the paths of beaten turf that crisscrossed the countryside. Auld James the gardener was nowhere to be seen, nor was Young James the groom, but my half-brother Malcolm crouched on the riverbank. He had been at the Public School in Melrose for most of the day. I watched him select a handful of rocks and throw each one into the water with all of his might to create sprays of diamonds. The backs of his stockings showed stripes of dried blood where Dominie had laid his cane.

I turned back to the appealing beastie in Mamma's hands. "Can you help him?" I asked, touching his glossy feathers. Pins poked my eyes and a swell of heat rose from my chest to my head. My love of animals was something else I had inherited from my mother. The rook was obviously suffering and I deemed it unjust that he had no words to use to ask for help, no language to describe where the pain was, and how deep.

"I'm not certain. I can bind the wing with linen, and we can keep him still."

"Will he get better, then?"

"We can hope so. He may never fly again though, Keeley. We must be prepared for that. But oh! His wee feet are so warm! Here, feel them. He seems to trust us, do you not think?" She cradled him against her breast, examining his wing with a light touch. "It must have been Malcolm."

I had no doubt this was his handiwork. He was seven years older than I and had a fondness for beleaguering feathered creatures, and me, with tossed stones. I wiped my nose on the hem of my blue duster and studied the bird's beak and eye. The glistening eye blinked.

"We'll care for him and give him water and food," Mamma soothed.

"I can make a nest for him."

Behind us came a low voice. "Kathleen."

Mamma and I turned. Neither of us had heard my father's approach.

He stood on the path silhouetted against a backdrop of apple trees and orange-red poppies, tall in his coat of black with the pewter buttons. I imagined he was just returning from one of his two sheep farms or his woolen mill. He removed his cocked hat and tossed it onto a settle as he walked toward us.

"Finlay," my mother said. Her hands stilled upon the rook.

Father's black hair, drawn into a queue, shone mahogany in the sunshine. Cheekbones and chin thrust themselves from the shadows on his face. When he was within a few paces from us, the arches of his brows drew close together. "What is this?"

"He has a broken wing."

He stopped at Mamma's side. He stared at the bird before his eyes crept up to Mamma's. "Have you gone mad?"

Her face became the color of parchment and I took a step backward, clutching a fold of her white chintz gown. Father's wrath was not to be taken lightly. At times I was the cause of it, especially when thunderstorms made me cry. He often forced me to suffer an hour or two in the dark cellar for my imprudence. Mamma seemed to have a similar fear of his anger, though I had never seen him lock her in the cellar.

"He'll die if I do not care for him," she said. "Last summer there was the robin, do you mind..."

Father plunged his hands between hers and tore the rook away. Mamma reached for the bird as her lips fell open. "You ken I care for all animals…" she began, but Father shouted, "You would do better to spend your time not wasting it on wild, broken creatures but giving me living, breathing sons!" He hefted the bird in one hand and flung him with great force into the air, and the flickering black rook disappeared behind the bank of hollyhocks.

I forgot to breathe. I was uncertain of where to look—at the verge of flowers and bushes where the stricken bird must now lie, or at my father who loomed above with a face as scarlet as the poppies.

Mamma said nothing. She gazed at the ground and I caught the glimmer of water in her eyes.

Father inhaled through his nose. "Look at you, Ket-*leen*. May God save your worthless soul. Your hair. Where have you been?"

She put up a trembling hand and pulled the white kertch from her head. Silken tresses fell to her waist all in a tangle.

"And your shoes. Where are they?"

She glanced at her feet and so did I. Bits of grass and earth were stuck to her toes and the hem of her gown was wet and muddied.

"This is not your Highlands, Ket-*leen*, where a gentlewoman walks with naked feet about the country like a heathen. Will you never do as I say? Is it the De'il that possesses you?" I wished he would stop saying "Ket-*leen*." Her name was indeed Caitlìn but he drew it out loudly and slowly as if it were an evil thing, even worse than the Anglicized "Kathleen."

She did not answer him but lifted her eyes to his. His were blazing, but he inhaled deeply and a look of regret began to come over him. He took another long breath and let it come out from him cautiously, quietly. He held his hand out to her. Mamma hesitated, but at last let his fingers swallow hers. Father took a pair of steps away and she followed; her other hand clasped mine and brought me with her.

He seemed to see me for the first time. "Leave the bairn."

Her grip tightened but she bent down to me, making her eyes come even with mine. "Run along and find Jennet. Mayhap

Malcolm will be there for his tea." In a whisper she urged, "First put on your stockings and shoes."

I bobbed my head in earnest. She joined my father beside the apple and cherry trees that edged the garden. Far away they went, separated by the length of an arm, he with his hands grasped together at his straight, dark back, she with her bare feet treading lightly on the grass and the pink ribbon at her waist floating in the breeze. When they were almost hidden by the interlaced branches of the fruit trees they came to a halt and faced each other. Father's hand went to her chin, lifted it. Slowly he kissed her.

I felt free all of a sudden to do as I was bidden, but I was not a dutiful child in the end. I dashed past the settle where our stockings and shoes and flowers lay and went in pursuit of the hurt bird. I searched and searched and finally found him. His head dangled when I picked up his little body, and I knew he was dead.

For days I thought about the rook. I had seen dead animals before—mice, of course, and the lambs and chickens intended for our suppers—but never had I seen a creature senselessly killed. Malcolm threw stones at birds, but he was a gloomy lad who did such things out of boredom, not anger. Learning that my own father, a grown man, held little regard for defenseless living things was a disquieting enlightenment.

He obviously cared for my mother. He was fond of taking her to the colorman's shop in Edinburgh where he bought her pigments so she could mix her watercolor paints. He was fascinated by her drawings and paintings, and had several of them framed and hung about the house. He loved watching her apply brush to paper as much as he enjoyed listening to her playing her clarsach. Father never sang or tapped his foot, but he often begged her to play in the evenings and kissed her fingers afterward and said, "What sweetness springs from these hands."

He did shout at her, however. He berated Mamma's Highland upbringing and criticized her management of the household. His anger leapt up from some unknown place whenever she did not behave as he thought she should.

I had become used to the power of his voice, but the threat of his hands was something new. Slender but strong, they handled his beloved horses with gentleness and examined the fine lengths of wool from his mill with reverence. I remembered peeking at him once during prayers and finding his sinewy hands gripping each other until their knuckles turned white. I had believed his bones were going to snap. That memory, almost forgotten, blended with the vision of him pitching the bird into the air and the result burnt itself into my mind's eye. It became clear to me that I must never let those hands near another of God's creatures. Father's horses were safe, I was sure, but nothing else. I was uncertain as to how I would save all of the world's animals from my dangerous parent, but knew I must be vigilant forthwith—and brave.

I knelt beside my bed before the week was out and made my vow, and begged Our Heavenly Father to keep the rook's soul safe with Him.

"And please tell the rook," I whispered against my folded hands, "that I am so sorry I could not save his life."

A fortnight later Jennet came to us in the sitting room. "There's a pedlar," she announced. "Mrs. Taggart's all for sending him off but I minded you wanted books for the lass, and asked him to wait. He says he's some for the wee one. Four in fact."

"We should go and see, should we not?" Mamma said to me brightly.

Father had long ago insisted that there be a tangible separation of our household and its affairs from our neighbors. Malcolm attended the school in the parish, but Mamma was forbidden to seek companions, visit the shops in the village, and attend the markets or the fairs. I imagined she was somewhat of a mystery to the folk of Melrose and beyond, as was I, but such isolation also meant there were few visitors at Gilchrist House. Each one was a novelty.

This one was a delight.

When Jennet, Mamma, and I reached the kitchen we found a jolly-looking man. Dirt lay in the grooves of his skin and a week's worth of whiskers speckled his face. He wore clothes of many different colors—brown trews, yellow tartan waistcoat, soiled green coat, scarlet wool knotted at his throat—and he was tapping his heels joyfully under Mrs. Taggart's affronted nose. Mamma asked him about his wares and he reached into his pack and produced chap-books of *Tom Thumb* and *Red Riding Hood*, a larger book titled *Toby Tickel's Collection of Riddles, Compiled by Peter Puzzlecap, Esq.*, and the second volume of *The World Displayed*, well worn.

"We'll take this one, I'm thinking," Mamma said after we examined them. I held up the copy of *Tom Thumb* for him to see. I wanted to plunk myself down right then and there and turn to the first page.

"A fine choice," he remarked. "For this wean?" He nodded his dust-coated head at me.

"She reads quite well, and has an appetite for it I can scarcely keep satisfied."

He bowed. "An accomplishment of which I cannot boast. But I do entertain myself in another manner." Without explanation he drew a bow and fiddle from a smaller bag. He plucked the strings one by one, listening intently. When he scraped the bowstring with a flourish up and down, mellow notes reverberated about us and I clapped at the merry sound. Tilting arm and chin, he threw himself into a jig. Mamma knew the song and began to hum along. Jennet tucked my rabbit under her arm and wheeled us about in a circle. Mrs. Taggart gathered a pile of washing, already laundered and dried, and fled the kitchen after giving each one of us a glance black with disgust.

The pedlar began to play "Lochaber No More," and Mamma sighed. The man raised an eyebrow and stilled his bow. "I hold that tune so dear," she said.

"She plays it on her clarsach," I added.

"Her clarsach!" The fiddle came down from his chin. "Have you a clarsach indeed, marm?"

"Oh aye," Jennet said. "Will I fetch it? How fine the two of you would sound together!"

The pedlar entreated Mamma with a look and she turned to us helplessly.

I cried, "Play it, Mamma, do." And Jennet was out of the kitchen and back with the harp before any of us had a chance to say anything.

The eyes of the man grew as round as teacups when Mamma sat on the wooden stool and balanced the clarsach. With care he brought his fiddle back up again and tuned his strings to hers. He positioned the bowstring and drew the first, wistful notes of "Lochaber No More." Mamma's fingers plucked chords, searching for the correct key, and when she found it she slid her finger backward for a few strings to produce an ascending glissando. The man played further measures and Mamma went along easily, matching her rhythm to his, finding the harmonies and adding chords. Jennet and I sat on the table to listen whilst Mamma and the grime-encrusted young man played song after song. The two gazed at each other, oblivious to the world about them and absorbed by the beauty of the music. Their faces showed love for the divine sound of their blended strings.

I noticed Father first. He had come to stand in the doorway. I jumped down to the floor when I saw the fury in his eyes. The pedlar's head came up and his arm fell. The abrupt ending of the music left a jagged hole in the room.

Mamma rose and put down her clarsach.

"Get out," my father said to the newcomer.

The pedlar reached for his bags. Unhurriedly he thrust his fiddle and the unsold books into them. All eyes were upon him as he stood, ready to go, a man dressed in gaudy colors and dusted with the dirt of the roads, but proud nevertheless, and refusing to be cowed by my father's murderous stare. The pedlar walked past me and I held out *Tom Thumb* with a shaking hand.

"Keep it, lass," he said in a soft voice.

My father stepped aside and allowed him to go. His creased eyes were no longer on the pedlar, but on Mamma.

"Finlay," she said. "You're angry. And there's no need..." She was within his reach and his arm flew out. The backside of his hand struck her cheek with such force she fell to the floor.

I ran to her, remembering the rook, but Father pinched my arm and tossed me toward the door. "Take her," he said to Jennet. We stumbled into the passageway and Jennet attempted to hold my head against her, covering my unobstructed ear with a palm when my father's voice raised itself in fiery wrath and let loose a wealth of words I did not comprehend. I was able to see Mamma attempting to rise from the floor. Father's fist swung through the air.

I could not bear it. I struggled out of the housemaid's grasp and ran away. My feet carried me to the garden where I hid under a gooseberry bush and hugged my rabbit until Mamma found me hours later. The flesh about her eyes was swollen and dark, and she gathered me to her without a word. I knew, in that moment, from whence came every inexplicable mark and bruise she had ever borne. The stains of purple upon her skin that I had taken for granted throughout my childhood were evidence of my father's betrayal.

Mamma said finally, "He did not hurt you?"

"No," I lied, thankful that my sleeve covered my arm. I was filled with shame because I had failed to protect her. Worse than that, I had brought today's misfortune upon her by urging her to play with the pedlar because I had believed it would bring her happiness.

When night fell, Jennet was dismissed from Gilchrist House. My father's voice bellowed throughout the rooms, and the maid's protestations of being sent away without the usual forty days of notice rang in counterpoint.

Jennet cried, "No wonder the others have left! Who would want to stay in this house with a master such as you!" Her voice was distorted with unshed tears.

She came into the upstairs sitting room, tying her belongings in a bundle and weeping at last. She embraced my mother and kissed my cheek with lingering tenderness. We waved farewell to her from the upstairs window until she disappeared amongst the trees just like the cook, scullery maid, laundresses, and other housemaids before her.

I looked at my mother's wounded face and felt the fires of dismay and anger burning hot in my chest. The death of the rook dimmed in significance. "Mamma," I said with passion. "We must run away. We can go with Jennet. We can hurry and follow her."

Tears filled her eyes. She shook her head. "No. No, dear heart, we cannot go. We must stay, for this is our home."

My mind whirred like the wings of a rising pigeon. She was one of God's creatures. The dearest of them all. I kept asking myself, "How can I save her?"

I failed, again and again. By the time I was ten years old Father no longer gave Mamma kisses amongst the apple and cherry trees, or asked her to walk in the garden with him. When I was thirteen he did not wait to take her behind a closed door to strike her. It did not matter if I put myself betwixt them, for then I felt the swiftness of his hand and Mamma begged me to leave them.

One February afternoon in 1782, when I was fifteen and Mamma was once again with child, she tidied Father's desk and accidentally knocked over the inkpot. Ebony liquid flooded onto the ledger that held the household accounts. Her tearful apology was not enough, nor was the subsequent clout from Father's hand. Father simmered all day and spent the night in her chamber. I suspected his presence was not welcome, but their intimacy was a matter of which Mamma never spoke. I relied solely upon her mood for determining Father's kindness toward her, or lack of it, and the next day her frame of mind was decidedly downcast.

Father left to visit the mill and Mamma and I occupied ourselves by sewing clothes for the coming bairn.

By this time I knew the truth about The Fairies. Mrs. Taggart had enjoyed filling my childhood with fear of the love-hungry, underground dwellers who had a penchant for bearing away wee bundles and raising them as Their own. "The Other People have stolen your mam's bairns, and They take them still," she had been fond of informing me. "You've been lucky, have you not? But be wary. They slink about on silent feet, and They listen. They follow the sound of the wee ones' voices. They would need only one moment, one quiet moment, to snatch you as well." It was a pity the miserable woman had chosen to repeat her advice most often when I'd lain in my bed waiting for sleep to come, with only a slice of her candlelit face showing in the crack betwixt post and door. Her words had inevitably sent me diving beneath my bedding. But not long after Jennet left us, Mamma explained why I had no siblings and why I did not need to fret about being abducted myself. Sometimes a wean grew within her, she said, a promise of a bairn to be, and then, for no reason, the promise went away.

Frozen rain pelted the windows, but in defiance of the winter murk Mamma exchanged her needle for her clarsach and filled the house with music. The years had changed her. She no longer laughed as she had when I was young. Her eyes no longer matched mine, for something inexplicable was missing from them. But her need, her love, for the sound of the harp had remained untouched. Her hands floated over the strings as if performing an ancient dance, her fingertips bringing forth chords both blissful and melancholy just as they had always done. Serenity flowed throughout the rooms but it was impossible for me to ignore yesterday's bruise beneath Mamma's eye.

When it was time for our supper she rose from her chair.

"Oh, the smell of that chicken roasting on the spit!" she said. "I am so ravenous…"

I looked at her in question because she did not speak or move further. My gaze followed hers. Blood was flowing down her ankles beneath her petticoat, forming a scarlet pool at her feet.

I could not endure the recollection of the remainder of that day. I hid the scenes deep in my heart, unwilling to remember the sight of her in her bed, unable to relive the moment Father told me of her death.

I buried the memories as if they were frightful things that must be put beneath heavy stones. Hidden and powerless—or so I believed—that is where they stayed.

The days after her passing were as blurred as a winter dusk obscured by a rimed window. A fierce wind came from the north, laden with snow. I lay motionless beneath my coverlet and listened to the screech and moan of it, but I was not fooled. It was not only the wind streaming past my window but the screams of banshees.

"'Twas your father who caused your mam to die," their voices shrieked. "'Twas you who failed to save her."

I believed them. Father had been cross because of the spilt ink. I could not know what had happened when he'd spent the night in her chamber, but surely, with her lying-in only three months away, she should have been left alone. Even if he had not used her badly that night he had for years prior to it, forcing her to try to produce another male heir when her body obviously could not sustain another pregnancy. And I had continually failed to persuade her to leave him. Aye, the banshees knew exactly who was responsible for Mamma's death.

From my window I watched Father and Malcolm ride to Melrose to see her buried. Father had ordered me to accompany them, but illness was so entrenched in my stomach, throat, and head that I was allowed to keep to my bed. With my teeth chattering from fever-induced chills, I stared out through the casement at the unending hills and snow-covered dykes. I watched the flying snow and listened to the impassioned wails. When Malcolm and Father returned, the wagon that had borne Mamma to the kirkyard was empty. The rectangular shape left on the wagon's bed by her coffin was already filled with snow and barely discernible.

I had no desire for the trays of food Mrs. Taggart brought upstairs. I remained in my bed for days until my fever broke, and then sought the unyielding confines of my wing chair. I wrapped myself in my coverlet and curled sideways, resting my head on the stuffed arm so I could look through my window and see the road leading to Melrose.

"I expect you'll come downstairs the night," Mrs. Taggart conjectured the afternoon she brought my tea and found me finally out of bed.

Suppertime came and went and I did not stir. A day passed, then another. It seemed that if I did not show myself, no one came to investigate. But one night the rattle of crockery and the aroma of cooking chicken permeated the haze around me. Confusion, smoldering in my slumber-deprived brain, caused me to leave my chair and open my door. Chicken for supper. Mamma was ravenous. Had I only imagined her death? Was she waiting for me downstairs? I listened with every sense heightened—and thought I heard her voice, low and sweet, addressing Father in the dining room below.

I forgot my fear of the dark. Blear-witted, I left my room and followed her voice, followed the warm and greasy smell of the chicken, followed the steps that descended in blackness. The glow of candles drew me to the room where Father sat in readiness for his meal.

I stopped, stricken. There was no sign of Mamma. The end of the table opposite Father's was bare. No dishes were set there, no one sat in her chair. Bewilderment deepened as I tried to remember what was real and what was a nightmare.

"Well," came Father's voice at last. "I wondered how long you'd choose to starve yourself." When I did not respond he gestured toward my chair. "Now that you're here, sit."

I found myself moving forward. I took my seat. Father stared at me.

"Mrs. Taggart," he called. "Can you not do aught to improve the child's appearance?"

Mrs. Taggart appeared and planted her crooked fingers on my face as she washed my skin with a coarse cloth dipped in icy water. She dragged a comb through my waist-long, knotted hair, causing tears to spring to my eyes, but I was not sure if they came because of the hair she pulled or because the wounds in my heart were being cut open afresh by Mamma's absence.

"Look at me," Father commanded when she was done.

I could not bring myself to turn my head.

"The De'il tak' your impertinence! You will do what I tell you."

A cuff on my ear forced me to meet his gaze. I studied his windburnt face, his painstakingly styled white peruke. I vaguely remembered speaking to him when Mamma was laid out in the parlor awaiting her funeral, and again when he'd come to my room to see if I was ready to ride to Melrose Abbey. All I could recall in any detail, however, was the night of her death when he had loomed over me with reddened eyes and told me she was gone. The memory peeked out from where I'd buried it and panic threatened.

He said, "How is it you've become ungodly and unkempt? You've been ill but certainly you are now well. Have you been continuing your studies?"

"No, sir."

"Your spinning?"

"No, sir."

"There's to be changes then. It seems you cannot be left unsupervised. Starting tomorrow you will come to me in the library prepared to resume your studies. And looking presentable, mind. With hair plaited and a clean frock."

"Aye, Father."

"Malcolm did not carry on so when his mother went to her grave, God rest her soul. It's damned annoying to have to look at you so. If you were a lad I'd send you off to university this very night." He rose and left me for a moment whilst Mrs. Taggart stirred the broth and began spooning it into broth-plates. He returned with a fat book and a ring of keys and placed them before me.

I recognized the volume as the housebook, and my eyes caught on the ragged, black shapes of dried ink spattered across the edges of the pages.

"They're your concern now," Father said. "As mistress of the house you are responsible. We'll see if you are any better at it than your mother was."

Mrs. Taggart's spoon halted in mid-air and drops of chicken broth fell to the table, becoming shiny, round jewels on the polished wood. She was clearly shocked, and eyed the items with her mouth ajar. The book held the household accounts: the quantities and prices for the linens, tea, brandies, china, and all the other plenishings of the house. The keys gave a person unequivocal power over Gilchrist House's doors, cupboards, and chests. Mistakes made with either were subject to the unpredictability of Father's temper.

Father reached in front of me and slid the ledger and keys farther down along the table to make room for our plates. The housekeeper's attention followed them, and slowly returned to me. Pure hatred shone out of her eyes.

The house became silent after Father led us in prayer. I could hear the distant ticking of the library clock.

Father looked up, holding a broth-soaked chunk of bread halfway to his mouth. "Eat," he said.

I dipped my spoon into my broth and lifted it to my lips. My stomach churned with nausea. My mouth ached with dryness. But I tilted the spoon and allowed broth to trickle past my tongue and go down my throat even though all I really wanted was to follow Mamma to wherever she had gone.

Every corrie, crag, and hollow,
Heathery brae and flowery dell,
Now awaken pangs of sorrow;
But my thoughts I dare not tell.
                    Soiridh! (Farewell) (Trad.)

Chapter Two

I brushed the library chairs of wine-colored velvet, swept the matching carpet, and in distaste turned to the book my father had thrust at me that morning: *The Education of the Human Race*, written by someone with the impossible name of Gotthold Ephraim Lessing.

Despite my resignation to comply with his wishes, the black letters started to run together and trickle across the pages. I lowered the volume to my knees with dwindling awareness, and unbidden, the image of Mamma was there before me: the silken hair, eloquent hands, and the sudden, unexpected rush of her blood. I turned away from it, closing the leather-bound cover of the book, closing my eyes.

The window rattled as gusts of wind blew sheets of water against the house. I swiveled to face the casement beside me and stared at the thick needles plummeting to earth. Leaves twisted and shook, and a stronger squall sheared off a handful and sent them to strike against the leaded panes. One great, green leaf remained plastered to the glass and peered in at me boldly before being whipped away.

I put the cumbersome *Education* back on its shelf. Father had instructed me to read its contents, absorb its truths, and report all that I had learnt on the next Sunday. Since Mamma's death only Father, Mrs. Taggart, and I, and sometimes Malcolm, attended Melrose Parish Kirk on Sabbath Days, sitting in the dim labyrinths whilst the uninspired Reverend Andrews labored on with his sermons. We spent Sunday afternoons and evenings at home, reading and praying in penitence and self-recrimination. That was when Father, an elder of the kirk, not only examined my knowledge of the Scriptures and the tenets of the Church of Scotland, but directed my scholarly education as well, which included a painstaking review of my record-keeping in the housebook.

I loved to read. I did not mind studying. And the household accounts were not as terror-provoking as I had imagined they would be. Father seemed to be proud of my aptitude for sums, though every mistake was met with stern disapproval. But since February I had difficulty concentrating on anything and wanted nothing more than to mindlessly wander the countryside. If I was gone for hours it seemed Mrs. Taggart did not care, and as long as the dusting was finished and the wool was spun, Father, despite his vow to keep me godly, sought my presence only on Sundays.

I haunted the carpets of green Mamma and I had explored, finding a fresh sorrow in the glades of bluebells and swaths of sweet violets she had loved so well. There was a new loneliness on the moorlands and the Eildon Hills. Every wild bird, every streaked cloud that drifted across the sky, reminded me of the times my mother and I had escaped to this peaceful world. When it rained I was fond of standing at the edge of the garden wrapped in a woolen shawl and looking out at the veils of water that could not obscure the misted velvet slopes and the redolence of earth and leaves. I listened to the ever-present, down-turning "huhs" of the rooks, and grieved because Mamma was not standing beside me.

I would be there now if my father had not tripped over me earlier and questioned my progress with Lessing.

The peat fire burning on the ingle, lit to take the chill from the wet morning, stroked the spines of the books with its glow and shone on gilt-stamped titles and decorative motifs. Some of my favorites were here, neglected, abandoned. I pried Robertson's *The History of Scotland* from its home between *Pilgrim's Progress* and *The Holy War* and smoothed the cover, discovering an old flicker of pleasure at the touch. From far away in the house came the crashing of doors, a deep, male voice demanding a pint of ale, and the shrillness of a happy, whistled tune. Malcolm was home.

Malcolm. I had almost forgotten he was staying with us at Gilchrist House for a week. He had rooms in Edinburgh now his years of studying law were over; he was pursuing a successful, burgeoning career with a knowledgeable advocate despite all the fierce arguments with Father. Malcolm had never been interested in the sheep or the woolen mill. In fact, his disdain for them had been present since his childhood. It was books for him, and philosophy and statesmanship and politics, and none of our father's threats or curses had deterred his study of them. They were too alike, Father and Malcolm. They shared the same temper, and the same resolve.

I opened Robertson's book and buried my nose amongst the crisp pages, determined to close my half-brother out of my mind as coldly as the other thoughts. I fingered the pages and wandered back to the window where rivulets of water streamed. "Oh aye, I remember this," I said out loud when I found a well-known passage.

"What are you remembering, our Keeley?"

Malcolm leant in the doorway, ale in hand. His likeness to our father never failed to surprise me. Every one of his twenty-one years had sharpened the resemblance further, whilst I possessed nothing of our mutual parent and never would. Malcolm's eyes questioned me as he lifted the wooden ale-caup to his lips. I resumed attendance to my book, thinking that if I were lucky he would tire of my unexciting company and saunter off. I would have fled the room but he was blocking the door and I knew better than to push past him.

"My God," he said. "I've forgotten how dreary Melrose is. How long have I been here? Three days? It feels a cursed year."

I turned a page. It was thunder in my ears.

"What are you doing?"

"Reading."

"Standing up and all? Is that what Father calls for now? We had to stand in the public school when we read aloud as lads, but isn't it ridiculous he forces you to do it all alone here in the library, with none to see you or hear you?"

I wanted to tell him he himself was ridiculous, but that was exactly what he wanted, and I clamped my jaws to keep from speaking. In my side vision I saw him lift the ale to his mouth, drink deeply, lick his lips.

"How I long to be back in Edinburgh town. Not fussing with the papers and the books. But visiting friends, and escorting women with their fans and silver shoes. Attending the dances at the Assembly Rooms on Thursday nights. Going to the plays and the suppers. The parties in the oyster cellars."

I said nothing.

"Will I tell you about them?" He waited, and fingered the lug of his cup. "Would you like to hear about what I do when I'm not closeted with my chin resting in a book like you?" He paused. "Do you not ken it's rude to be reading so, when someone is speaking to you?"

I inhaled a little.

"Do you ken," he said in a sleek voice as he pushed himself from the door-post and came forward, "how often you do not answer my questions?" Behind him the door slammed shut. He moved toward me, growing taller, filling my vision. He liked to dress well, as did Father, and his body, embellished with an embroidered sapphire waistcoat and a fashionable coat of indigo, reminded me of a glistening picture edged by a golden frame. Though damp from the rain, his black hair was smooth and held by a wide ribbon, and the stock at his throat showed not a single wrinkle. The pungency of his costly perfume reached me before he did, assaulting my nose.

"Even that question, I do not think you intend to answer," he said.

He drained his ale-caup and put it on the narrow walnut table. I watched him, knowing I should tear my eyes away. His face hovered above me. One of his perfect teeth was slightly crooked in its socket, a defect that sometimes conjured up a fantasy in which I reached up and twisted it a little so that it might match the angle of its mate.

"You've no intention of speaking to me today, do you?" He looked down at my fingers grasping the book and laughed deep in his throat. "Do you ken how dull it is to say things and get nought in return, to have to guess what you're thinking, all of the time?" He brought his hand up from underneath and knocked the book from me. The suddenness caused me to jump, and as the volume fluttered into the air Malcolm grasped me. He flung me about so my back was pressed up against the front of him, and his arms held me there.

"And so what are you thinking now, my sister?" he said at my ear. "Surely there's something you'd like to tell me." One of his palms traveled up from my waist, skimming over my woolen gown to rest with hot pressure upon one of my immature breasts.

Something acidic rose in my throat, choking me so that if I had wanted to answer him I would not have been capable of it.

He nuzzled my hair, inhaling the scent of it. "Such long, bonny brown hair," he murmured. "Such a flawless body, all unspoilt. Though it's young yet. I wonder if I can wait for it. One day you'll be a grown woman, Keeley, wed to a man who'll want you as much as I do. Tell me," he went on in a tuneless lilt. "Tell me, tell me, tell me, what it is you're thinking."

From somewhere came the strength to push at his arms. I discovered he was not holding me tightly, and at my first lunge of resistance he released me. I reeled away, but not before his dreadful hand clutched my breast in farewell.

He chortled as I fled from the library. I ran through the outside door and followed a track through the meadow, slippered feet skidding on the wet grass. I ran until the ache in my side drove me to my knees. I told myself that if Mamma were here he never would touch me so.

I scrubbed my arms and neck with rain, seeking to rub away Malcolm's lingering cologne and the memories of his touch. But the driving water soon evolved into a tireless assailant. I continued toward the town of Melrose, hesitating when I came to the thorny hedgerows. Thoughts of Malcolm and his laughter taunted me and I strode forward to a huddle of cottages, stopped in front of one certain thatched biggin of clay, and gave two light raps on the door. Regretting it instantly, I turned on my heel and poised to jump back over the bottomless puddle in front of the doorstep.

"Keeley Allanson!"

I spun to find the benevolent, white-capped visage of Mrs. Dundas, the lying-in-wife who had come to Mamma's side every time she had miscarried. I could think of nothing to say, for any explanation for this visit seemed to have vanished, and I stood looking at her foolishly with the rain battering my face.

She collected her wits and opened her humble door much wider. "Come in, come in, my bairn. You must think me to have a terrible lack of manners! To let you be standing there wi' the rain coming down on you like that. Come and dry yourself by the fire."

When I took a step inside, she clasped her hands together. "I'm so glad you've come," she said. "Poor lassie, full of woe. The greeting's not left you." At her words a great knot began to loosen in my chest and Mrs. Dundas caught me in her arms when I fell against her in a torrent of tears.

I made a great deal of noise and an occasional hiccup escaped me. I wept for Mamma and how much I missed her. I wept for my loneliness. I even wept for the anger I felt toward God who allowed unwarranted unfairness in the world. At last my tears seemed to wane and Mrs. Dundas held me away. Her reddened hands took my own and chafed them.

"My bairnie, your wee hands are too cold!" she declared. "And your toes, too, I'd be willing to wager. Well, there's nought for it. You need to be taking some things off, and toasting yourself." She steadied me, and crossed to the box bed to grab a length of woven wool hanging there. "It is summer, but the rain can be full of misery. Now. Off wi' your slippers, and put this over your shoulders, and I'll dry your hair for you."

I sank to a three-legged stool by the settle. She pried my shoes from my heels and rubbed my toes. Thick stockings were pulled up above my ankles and wool was tucked around me. She sat behind me on the bench so her hands could stroke my wet hair, pull locks apart, and dry them with a linen rag. Under her ministrations I had no will. Her fingers, gentle and methodical, almost lulled me to sleep. My hands rested on a hot bowl of porridge cradled betwixt my knees. I stretched my toes out to the fire.

This was the second time I had been inside one of the wee houses. The only light came from the open hearth in the center where a peat fire smoldered. Opaque ribbons of smoke rose to the ceiling where they found the hole in the roof of bundled heather, but not before they filled the air with their distinctive, choking odor.

"I miss Mamma," I said when I could speak. "Terribly, I do."

"How could it be otherwise?" she said and sighed. "The two of you so much together. Like sisters, I sometimes thought, more than mother and daughter. What have you been doing wi' yourself these past months? There's just you and your da. I saw your brother, though, the other day. He's home from Edinburgh then?"

I nodded. The memory of his embrace surfaced like a painful blow to my middle.

"Just a while yet, and he'll be an advocate all on his own. Your da dotes on him so, despite his lack of interest in the farms. But he brings you no amusement, does he? Is it mostly yourself, then, that keeps you company?" Mrs. Dundas drew another rope of my hair through her fingers, squeezing the rain from it. "Does he ken you're here?" she asked, and I knew she did not mean Malcolm.

"He's not at home."

"How could he mind? A lass without a mother. Morag Taggart's not likely to be looking after you as she ought, though I've nought against the woman, for she's a pious soul, but..."

"But her cooking is tasteless," I managed to say. She laughed and I turned to face her. "Her puddings are not like yours. And she does not make custard at all."

"There's few gudewives who know how to make a custard, even less a good one. 'Twas an art I learnt when I was gey young. I love cooking, you see, as much as I love bairns and the bringing of them into the world."

"Would you teach me?" I asked in quick excitement.

"To make custard? Why, of course I could, if you wanted to learn."

"Oh I would, very much!"

"Will we start today? Aye? Then it's lucky you are, for my milk plates are full, and haven't I an extra egg or two. Now we'll finish drying your hair, and I'll show you what to do first."

For the first time in months I felt a perceptible lightening of my despondency, and Malcolm momentarily forgotten, I smiled.

After I became accustomed to the size and dimness of the cottage that first day I could not imagine why I had thought it airless and dismal. It was filled with Mrs. Dundas's warmth and lively personality. My skill at concocting the rare custard grew and spread to other food preparations, all delightfully new. Mrs. Taggart was protective of our kitchen and had been ever since she'd had inherited it from Cook. She had rarely allowed Mamma or me to intrude upon it. But I longed to mix and stir and bake, and vividly minded the days when I had sat at Cook's knee and had been allowed to beat eggs and stone raisins.

By my fourth visit to the cottage I was completely at home amongst the midwife's potato and barley barrels, girdles, stoups, and brandering irons. I not only helped her cook for neighbors and new mothers and ailing folk, but swept the floor with a heather besom, carried in peats from the pile, and fetched new, tiny potatoes from the garden. I saved their thin peelings for her cow, a sweet animal Mrs. Dundas invited me to milk.

From the milk of sheep we made cheese, and from tallow and honey she had aged for a year we poured candles. A peace of sorts began to descend on me, fledged from the satisfaction of performing these fundamental chores with a good-hearted companion. For a while my mind could be freed from its endless circle of mourning Mamma, hating Father, and panicking about

Malcolm. My single worry was that Mrs. Taggart might question the amount of time I seemed to spend out of doors. She grudgingly accepted my walks and rides since Mamma and I had done that together, but I had to make certain I did not disappear for too long. I could not have her complaining of it to Father. Mrs. Dundas and I pledged solemn secrecy to each other about my visits and merely nodded when we met at kirk.

My new-found peace was laced with relief, for I was able to avoid Malcolm until his return to Edinburgh. When he visited again I shrank into a mouse, hiding myself so I would not become his prey, and often escaped to Mrs. Dundas's biggin where I could pretend he never existed.

One August afternoon I found myself pacing through Gilchrist House, wishing Mrs. Dundas had been home that morning when I had gone to see her. I suspected someone was giving birth and she had gone along to ply her special magic with her gentle and knowledgeable hands. Something pulled me toward our kitchen where Mrs. Taggart's gaunt meat pies and burnt bannocks sat cooling on the kitchen table. The thought of custard, Mrs. Dundas's wonderful yellow, creamy custard, made my mouth water. If I was quick, if I said nothing, surely there would be no raised eyebrows at my endeavor. I pinned on one of Mrs. Taggart's aprons and went to work.

I was checking the ashes in the oven when Mrs. Taggart returned. She stared at me with her narrow, black eyes. Much to my dismay I began to wilt under her glare.

"What are you doing?"

"I decided to make custard."

"How do you ken how to be making it?"

"I heard women talking at kirk." I dropped the rag I held.

"What women?"

"They sat on the bench behind us. They were rather loud. It was before the service started."

"Do you think me foolish enough to believe this? Someone has shown you."

I shook my head. My mind scrambled for words. "No—no. One of them shared the making of it with another. I heard it all. I mind it all."

"'Tis plain you're lying! I ken a liar when I see one." Her face was as hostile as Father's. I felt myself growing warmer as her eyes bore into mine. "Someone has shown you," she persisted. "You've been in someone's house."

The heat in my head loosened my tongue and I said, "And why should I not? Why is that such a terrible thing? There's no wrong I've done. Merely learnt to cook!" I stopped, taken aback at my own words.

Mrs. Taggart regarded me with a horror of her own. I might just as well have told her I no longer believed in God. "What evil have we amongst us now?" she cried.

"There is no evil. She's shown me how to make custard. And bannocks. And bread."

"She?"

The seconds ticked by and I sought for a path out of the quagmire I had created. Mrs. Dundas was not a bad woman. She was good, better than most, and had been called into our household numerous times when Mamma had suffered. She did not deserve to have her reputation attacked by Mrs. Taggart. I said, "I've been visiting Mrs. Dundas, the lying-in-wife. She's been very kind to me."

The information worked its way into Mrs. Taggart's brain. A new expression crept over her face, similar to the one she'd worn when she'd learnt she was not to be the recipient of the housebook and keys. "Away wi' you," she cried. She snatched the pins from my bodice and pulled away the tape of the apron. "You're not to come into this kitchen unless you're asked."

Freed of her soiled linen, I obeyed. For an hour I strode up and down the riverbank. I called Mrs. Taggart uncharitable names out loud and threw rocks into the water with more vehemence than I had ever seen Malcolm display. But underneath my tirade was a great fear she would mention the fact I had been visiting Mrs. Dundas to my father. I was caught, and it was my false bravado and lack of foresight that had caused it, after I had been so careful these past months to hide my secret. I did not understand what had compelled me to jeopardize something I held so dear. I threw an extra large stone into the river. "You are a half-wit," I said, and I was not speaking to Mrs. Taggart.

When it was time to join my parent for tea I did so with trepidation. I entered the drawing room to find that something was amiss, for Father was waiting and the tea tray was nowhere to be seen.

He watched me sit down. "Mrs. Taggart tells me you have been cooking."

"I wanted to make something for us. Something different." I paused, wondering how much to explain. "I was not allowed to finish it."

"Sit up. If you lean in your chair you must be ill and need your bed."

I straightened my back, clenched my hands in my lap.

"How often have you been visiting Mrs. Dundas?"

"Every—every so often."

"How often?"

"Every day." When I darted a glance at him I saw that his face was darkening.

"That is how you have been spending your time?"

"She was so good to Mamma. I thought I might repay her by helping her." Immediately I knew this was the wrong thing to have said.

"Oh? To do what, may I ask?"

I swallowed. "To scrape potatoes, and fetch peats and..." A tilt of my father's head encouraged me to go on. "And to milk her cow."

He took in a long breath and held it. I could sense the fury within him. He repeated, "To milk her cow." The expression in his eyes brought to mind other times when his disappointment had congealed into revulsion. "And have you repaid her kindness by filling her ears with every sort of gossip you could think of from this household?"

"I've told her nought," I protested.

His fist struck the tea-table and remained there. I stared at it, thinking of Mamma. I thought of the day she had died and needed to squeeze my eyes shut to stop the memory from hurtling through me.

"I'll not have my affairs or yours suffer the speculation of every man and woman in this village!" he said. "I've not raised you to be a companion, nor a lass working for a shilling wage! What must the folk think of my daughter milking the cow of the town's lying-in-wife? What must the folk think of me? Did you never think of it? Whose idea was it?"

I managed to shake my head. I said, "It was mine. I am sorry, Father."

"I'm disappointed in you. I thought you'd more intelligence than this. Perhaps I was wrong. But at least let us both be sure of this." He waited a long moment and then, enunciating each word precisely, said, "You are no longer to go to that woman." He folded his hands and stared at me for an added, intolerable moment. "Mrs. Taggart!" he bellowed.

The housekeeper joined us, bearing the rattling tea tray. There was a cruel tilt to her lips, a special grin that seemed to surface whenever she caught a mouse and gleefully killed it.

I poured the tea for us when we were alone. I held my cup and saucer in my hands, unable to drink or eat as I thought sorrowfully of Mrs. Dundas. Somehow I must escape to her house one more time and explain how I had spoilt everything.

Father, who usually took no notice of me, raised his voice again. "If you can do nought better than to sit here, ungrateful for this food, it would be wise if you left. Your behavior is not only an insult to Mrs. Taggart, and to me, but to our Lord who provides us with our sustenance." I needed no further prompting. I replaced my china on the tray, rose, and with quiet footsteps began to retreat. Father's voice halted me. "The more I think on it, I am better convinced you have suggested the appropriate action to be taken. For your slyness, for your lying ways, you may fast."

"Father?"

"And then, when you have fasted enough, you may apologize to me for your wickedness."

"Father. I apologize now."

"But you have not fasted."

Time, I found, often appears to creep forward sluggishly when there is a goal in one's sight or a yearned-for event. The minutes cannot tick away fast enough. But as the days passed I discovered the same observation can be made when there is nothing ahead but time itself, dividing itself endlessly into hours and days, and passing by out of habit and inertia. There were no changes to mark time's passage for me; no objectives to fix as milestones;

nothing with which to quicken its pace or divert my attention from it.

Boredom and fury led me to search my room for the unused drawing book my mother had given me as an encouragement to sketch. She had loved to create ink and colorwash drawings for me, and somewhere amongst her things was a tied packet of sketches with which she had delighted me when I was young. I had not inherited the urge to draw, but I imagined that writing might instill a measure of importance to my days. I found the book in a dresser drawer and sat at my table, quill and inkpot at hand. I dated the first page and wrote of my woes until my fingers were stiff. I wrote about Father and Mrs. Taggart and dear Mrs. Dundas. I wrote to assuage my loneliness and to find some hope for the future. Of Mamma I could not write much at all.

"*I think I must get away from Gilchrist House,*" I scribbled fearfully, testing the effect the written words had on me. "*I cannot live the rest of my life here. Mamma's spirit died long before her physical being, and I will not be able to bear it if that happens to me. I do not ken how much longer I can suffer to look at Father and mind the part he played in her death, however small. I have no delusions about the future. He gave me the housebook and keys because one day I will take Mrs. Taggart's place and be the only servant Gilchrist House employs.*"

I let the thoughts come as they may and with bitter resolve recorded them all. But when I hid the book underneath a box of handkerchiefs all I could remember writing was the pledge to someday leave my home.

I lay awake that night wondering how this might be accomplished. Was it even possible to recreate one's destiny? I knew it meant acquiring money. I had no idea how to begin doing so. I had no valuable skills, nothing to sell, and no freedom to seek work of any kind. And where would I go if, and when, I was ready? My experience and knowledge of the world were minimal. I thought of Jennet who had courageously stepped out into the night to find a new life. Where did one go when one was homeless? To kinsmen, perhaps—but I had none.

I was kept in my room for three days and given nothing but water. Father came to my door on the fourth. I kept my eyes downcast and dutifully asked for forgiveness for my waywardness. I was absolved, it seemed, for he threw open the door and left it that way.

Mrs. Dundas welcomed me at her door, surprise swallowed up by pleasure. I glanced in all directions before I tread over her threshold, dreading to see that I might have been noticed, but the path to her house was deserted.

Her cottage smelt of roasting lamb and sage, which reminded me how dearly I loved it. I knew at once that this was what I wanted: a home where I could feel safe, where caring for others mattered, and there was a reason for living. I told Mrs. Dundas of Father's displeasure and how I was now forbidden to visit her. Even as I spoke, my guilt was deep. If he discovered I had disobeyed him there was no telling what he would do. Whilst we talked I drank the tea she'd poured for me and nibbled on barley bannocks and looked furtively out her window, expecting to see Father glaring at me from atop his horse. Every second seemed to quicken my imagination. Father would ride by and call at Mrs. Dundas's house to see if I was there. He would see me leaving her door. He would lie in wait, hoping to catch me defying him.

Mrs. Dundas offered me another bannock and said thoughtfully, "My hope is that you'll not allow Mrs. Taggart to threaten you. If you enjoy cooking then you should cook. 'Tis shortsighted of her not to realize the two of you could help each other. One day you'll be a lady who has no need to do her own cooking, but for the present it could be a blessing. And you've a knack for it. Why, I gave the basket of the scones you made last week to Mr. Gunn, and he praised them over and over! He said there were none like them, not even in London's finest tea rooms. He came looking for more and I had to bake him a dozen, but I swear that they were not as tender as yours."

She was lying, of course, for her culinary gifts far surpassed mine, but her compliment made me smile and I was grateful for that.

We fell silent. I was bemused by her last words, picturing myself standing side by side with Mrs. Taggart, passing spoons and bowls back and forth whilst we created batches of sweet cakes together, and walking hand in hand to deliver them to a drooling Mr. Gunn.

I stopped smiling. "Mrs. Dundas," I said. "I wonder if I could make bannocks and scones and sell them."

"Sell them! Surely you've no need of money."

"I cannot stay with my father." I wiped my eyes impatiently, surprised at how quickly they filled. "I intend to leave when I am able. I have no money of my own."

"You're the daughter of a gentleman. Where will you go? How will you support yourself?"

I slid to the edge of my chair. "If I make sweets and cakes and breads, and am able to sell them, I could save enough to go. It would take years, but if I was patient…"

"To go where, my dear?"

"Do you think the innkeeper at The Black Horn would buy them?"

"Henry has been after me all these years to provide him wi' sweets. But you've not answered…"

"Would you help me?" I begged. "Everything, all of it, must be a secret."

I jumped when a knock came upon her door. I stood cringing whilst she went to open it. I was certain Father had come.

"Ah," cried a woman's voice. "You're at home! Fiona McNaught's pains have started. Will you come?"

In relief I helped Mrs. Dundas tuck linen-wrapped herbs into her basket as she prepared for her departure. She turned to me regretfully at last and we embraced each other.

I said, "I must think. I must plan. I cannot do it without your help. Will you ask the innkeeper? And pretend it's for yourself you're asking?"

"Oh lass, it makes no sense to me. I'll ask, but I cannot imagine how you'll be able to do this."

"There must be a way," I told her. "I'll try to slip away and come to you again."

I hurried home, torn by both hope and doubt. I wavered between confidence that I could thrust Mrs. Taggart aside and bake dozens of delicacies without being discovered, and fear that I would fail, just as I had foundered trying to protect Mamma. The only thing I was sure of was that every step away from Mrs. Dundas's house decreased the chance that Father would discover my disobedience, but also affirmed that my days of joy within its walls were finally over.

O father, a tod* has come oer your lamb,
A gentleman of high degree,
And ay when he spake he lifted his hat,
And bonny, bonny blinkit his ee.

*fox
The Broom of Cowdenknows (Trad.)

Chapter Three

The years passed. I left childhood behind and Nature changed me into a young woman. I thought of nothing but my future and how I might obtain my freedom.

Mrs. Dundas was kind enough to meet me in the copse at the end of the drive twice a week so I could fold into her apron the bannocks, scones, and currant buns I had made. In return she gave me coins, or a pound note if I had saved enough silver for her to exchange. She charged the keeper of The Black Horn every Monday on my behalf, never failing to tell me how guilty she felt at accepting his praise for sweets she had not made. She brought me flour, meal, and sugar for which I paid with my earnings so Mrs. Taggart would not notice the depletion of our stores, and I smuggled the sacks into the larder beneath my shawl. When Mrs. Dundas was needed for a lying-in, her loyal grandson took her place, filling his arms with my goods in exchange for the pence he dug out of his pocket.

I managed to bake every Tuesday when Mrs. Taggart was out of the house washing clothes and linens, and on Fridays when she went to the market in Melrose. She fiercely resented my forays into her territory but all harm from learning from Mrs. Dundas was entrenched in the past, and Father did not object to my effort to help with the household upkeep. Indeed, he seemed to enjoy the results of my toil, showing a keen appetite for the cakes I saved for us out of the secret batches destined for the inn. If I had been capable of feeling shame I would have thought it sad that his delight was a result of my endeavor to leave him.

With pride I often considered the growing purse of coins and notes hidden in my clothes press. I counted my earnings by candlelight and imagined how it would feel to press coins into the hands of hostlers to hire horses and innkeepers to rent rooms. I would have to rely on Mrs. Dundas's expertise to decide when I had an adequate sum to support myself. At times I was overcome by unexpected and tortuous self-doubt when I contemplated what my final step would be. My plan was to travel to Edinburgh or Glasgow where I could acquire rooms and look for employment, but beyond that I had no vision.

I could not thank Mrs. Dundas enough for her help with my day-to-day intrigue in which I sold things like a farmer's wife. My walks to the end of the drive with laden arms were a hazard. If either Father or Mrs. Taggart had occasion to question me or look beneath my shawl there would be appalling consequences, I was sure. I clung to Mrs. Dundas's promise of assistance with my eventual flight from Gilchrist House with blind tenacity.

When I turned seventeen she said, "I cannot say I'm not wary of this idea of yours. Leaving your home is rife with problems. For one, you'll be giving up some sort of inheritance, do you not think? For another, you've never known any other kind of life."

"But you do understand why I must go."

Empathy softened her smile and she put her hand over mine. "Your mother would understand, and aye, I suppose I do."

I said, "Mamma is still so much a part of the house. For that reason alone I sometimes consider staying and being the servant Father wants me to be. For I've no doubt of it. Who will care for him in his old age but me? I would not mind, I do not think, if I..." I did not finish, but I was certain Mrs. Dundas knew the nature of my confusion. A daughter should love her father and do her duty by him. But then a man should love his wife, and not be the cause of her despair.

After five years of saving I was impatient. Three or four stolen hours a week for baking no longer satisfied me, and patrons of The Black Horn were begging for more cakes and breads than I could provide. I had believed that by this time I would have enough money for my escape from Melrose but my purse was far too thin. There had to be a better way to increase my productivity.

Determined to find a solution, I leant against the ledge of the embrasure in Father's study one morning and dispassionately witnessed my parent's departure, my eyes following the pretentious gig as it struggled along the tree-edged drive. He was away to visit his farms, Whitestone and Clary. The mass of clouds hanging over the Eildons in the east was a distended black entity determined to spread itself over every sliver of spring sky, and dots of rain already stippled the window. I might have protested a jaunt into such weather had it been anyone else setting out, but I did not care what my father did as long as he left the house every day. I was alone now except for Mrs. Taggart, who continued to be the major hindrance in all my plans.

I abandoned the window, suddenly knowing what I must do, and went along the passage to the kitchen. I pressed my body against the wall to venture a look past the door-post. There was no missing Mrs. Taggart's spare figure. I knew she would be here, bent over her morning baking. How I loathed her, this woman who remained at Gilchrist House whilst all who were good and kind left it. Her only saving grace was her love for kittens. She was besotted by them, and routinely snatched them and their mothers from the stable in order to tend and nurture them in her own bedchamber until they were old enough to transport to new homes. It was not uncommon to find a wee head peeping out from her pocket, but in the company of others she acted as if she knew nothing about it. There were no telltale ears or paws jutting from her skirts this morning that I must pretend I did not see, and my step forward caused her to turn and study me with dark-circled eyes.

I hesitated long enough to absorb the welcome of the kitchen. The cavernous fireplace of chiseled stone held a perpetual fire that seemed to warm not only the cauldrons but my heart as well. Stoups and basins hung from the beams above like great, shining fruits amongst bunches of rosemary and rounds of cheese. With steady fingers I selected a likely bowl, and to Mrs. Taggart standing as rigidly as a stick at my elbow I said, "I'm going to cook today. You may go or you may stay, it makes no difference to me."

Her jutting jaw dropped. She let the mound of batter in her hands sink down onto the table.

I chose a cup and stepped into the larder to fill it with cream. There was temporary respite in the seclusion of the chilly room with its baskets of wrinkled potatoes from last autumn, the hanging haunches of venison, and the salmon lying on the stone floor. When at last I returned, Mrs. Taggart's tongue was flicking against her uneven teeth. She could not speak. She buried her wooden spoon handle-deep in the dough with the ferocity of a hunter slaying a wild boar in the forest and fled.

Relief was instant.

I began to make a milk pudding, and soon broke out into song as I mixed and measured and pushed to the back of my mind all thoughts of Mrs. Taggart. I boiled the rice in butter, eggs, sugar, and cream. I added lemon, spices, currants, and a splash of brandy before pouring the pudding into a pastry case. I placed it inside the shimmering oven and prepared to make my illicit scones.

When the plump triangles were cooled and hidden away, I eyed Mrs. Taggart's unfinished soup hanging from the lum-cheek-hook over the fire. She would be furious if I touched it. A cleaved head of a sheep, its trotters, a few collops of mutton, and dried peas roiled energetically in the black pot. My fingers caressed a carrot yet to be washed and scraped.

Never before had I touched her preparations, unless it was to rescue a scorching pot from the fire, but at the moment interference was difficult to resist. The bittersweet recollection of Mamma's particular sort of mischief concerning Mrs. Taggart materialized out of nowhere. How she had relished torturing the housekeeper by hiding things! A packet of thread Mrs. Taggart had been about to use, a candle she had put down for only a moment, even a basket of washing left temporarily in a bedchamber. My mother had loved a bit of devilry and sometimes took me into her confidence, allowing me to watch from a distance whilst the sparrow-woman searched for an item she was sure she had just handled. Sometimes she did not find it for days. Her discomfiture had Mamma and me holding our stomachs in silent laughter whilst the housekeeper shook her head in consternation, mumbled to herself, and searched and searched.

It was telling that Mamma's enjoyment for tormenting Mrs. Taggart had waned near the end. Mamma's enjoyment for most things had waned. Mrs. Taggart must have been puzzled when she'd realized that her memory was becoming better with age, not worse, as one would have supposed.

I let the past fall away and peeked at the vacant doorway. My hand slid along the table and grasped the knife. It was not mischief I was contemplating, I assured myself, but assistance.

Mrs. Taggart came in when the broth, thick with neeps, was gaily simmering, the pudding sat steaming on the table, warm and fragrant, and a few barley bannocks awaited the girdle. Shock contorted her face as she noticed her precious turnips heaving in the kettle.

"My broth. My secret broth. What have you done to it?" she mouthed, her voice a croak. She watched the rising bubbles as if each one carried poison within its glistening orb.

"I've added parsley and neeps and onions."

"You've ruint it! There are things I put in you know nought about. And my neeps. My lovely neeps!" Her skeletal hand hovered over the steam and I wondered if she would plunge in her fingers to scoop out the pale yellow chunks.

"I put them in as you'd have done, and the barley." I began to draw strength from her absurdity. I shook the basin I had been washing and turned to face her. "You were not here and I thought I would help."

"Thrown out of my own kitchen. My broth ruint. You think to take my place but I'll not have it. I belong here and you do not. Besides," she added as the adage must have struck her. "You've been singing in this kitchen and 'tis that what'll bring the Other People upon us!"

"Perhaps it's time, then, for a bit of excitement here in this house, Mrs. Taggart."

Her mouth opened and her eyes widened. But she forgot her horror as she discovered another indignity. "My bannocks," she cried. "What have you done to my barley bannocks?" She crossed to the table and tried to make her fingers touch them.

"I've made thin ones."

"They maun be thicker than that. You've ruint them as well!"

"When they're thick, like yours, they can barely be bitten. Have you never had them delicate, with butter spread over the top so they fold into crisp layers in your mouth?"

"There'll be no substance to them. You've wasted good barley."

"You were not here to tend to them. When I put them on the girdle..."

"When you. When you! Are you no' finished here? Must I be thrust from my kitchen all the day? What other havoc will you bring upon us? You've wasted good barley and good neeps and your father will hear of it."

A small stone thudded downward inside my stomach.

"Aye, your father will hear of it. You, interfering with my work. Wasting what the good Lord provided."

"I've more right to be in this kitchen than you."

The shards that were her eyes cut into mine. "You headstrong wench," she said and hissed something unintelligible.

A sound exploded throughout the house and both Mrs. Taggart and I jumped. "There is someone knocking at the door," I said unnecessarily.

Mrs. Taggart pulled her shawl about her sharp shoulders and

stamped through the hallway on her way to the front entrance. I listened intently. Mrs. Taggart's monosyllables echoed through the passage and were joined by the deeper tones of a man. She reappeared with her forehead creased and her lips turned down. "'Tis a man, fallen from his horse, and needing aid."

I forgot to be apprehensive and followed her, but as I approached the hall the stone in my stomach was joined by another.

The door was open, letting in some of the rain. A man, clad in a well-cut greatcoat and sodden with rain and streaks of mud, leant against the jamb, half in and half out. His head was bent, his face obscured. The thin hand gripping the post was muddied, as were the white ruffles of the cuff and a peeping edge of silver brocade. Beyond him, hazy in the curtain of rain, stood a seal-brown horse, its flanks all smeared with muck. It lifted first one hoof and then another in high-spirited restlessness and nearly trod its rein down into the soggy turf.

The man raised his head. Black-lashed eyes stared into mine. They were wide, the irises dark gray and unswerving. They were all I saw of him. Never had I been captured and transfixed by eyes that quested so, or found myself so explored, or been ultimately furnished with a wordless answer to a question I had not asked. I looked away. I discovered my palms had begun to perspire.

Mrs. Taggart unknowingly came to my aid by saying, "This is the mistress of the house."

He said something in an unknown language, and added in English with a northern inflection, "I only wondered if there were a place I might be resting for a bit."

Despite my resolution to avoid being seized by the enormous gray eyes, I ventured another peek at him, for I was arrested by his words. His voice was low, as though he spoke in pain, yet the intonation he used was the same as my mother's. One did not often hear the music of a Highland voice in Melrose. I suffered his scrutiny because I thought of Mamma all at once, and wished he would speak again.

Obviously he was waiting for a reply of some sort. My own voice came out scratchily, as if I had been trying to swallow dry, toasted bread. "You are hurt."

"'Tis my side, and I'd trouble you not, if I were unworried about it myself. My horse took fright at a bolting rabbit and threw me, and I landed down along the brae there, on the stones." He attempted to stand free of the doorway but his lids closed and he bent forward. I put out my hands as if I might catch him, but when he grasped the frame with his fingers and I became conscious of Mrs. Taggart staring at me, I withdrew them.

"Of course," I whispered. "Of course you must come in."

"Is there someone about who could be caring for my horse?" he asked, and with a hand swept the rain from his dark brown hair.

I turned to Mrs. Taggart. "If you'd go along to the stable and get Young James."

Miraculously, she complied. I stood looking at the man, wary of remaining alone with him. If he was aware of my discomfort he gave no notice of it. I cursed myself for my self-obsession. "Will you need help?" I asked of him, cringing when he cringed.

He attempted a smile and I was struck by the way it shone through the soil and rain on his face. "I walked from yon bank. I think I can be managing a bit more. But thank you. I'd be lying still out in the rain if I'd not spied your house, and been rewarded by your kindness."

Young James came to collect the horse, and I moved aside so the stranger might make his way past me. He came in, bent and stiff, holding an arm against his right side. Mrs. Taggart appeared a second later, wearing an air of disapproval so slight I was sure only I could notice it. "This way," she bid him, and he followed her into the drawing room. I shut the outside door and tailed behind, squeezing my thumbs in slippery fingers. She led him to a yellow damask-covered chair where he paused and shrugged off his greatcoat, revealing the dry coat of silver-gray brocade beneath. Mrs. Taggart took the dripping outer-garment betwixt her fingertips and, holding it at arm's length, crossed the room whilst the man lowered himself to his seat. He closed his eyes and furrows deepened in his forehead. Gingerly he leant back. I noticed for the first time his breathing was a little fast.

"You'll be wanting someone," I blurted. "Someone to see if aught is broken."

He opened his eyes and winced. "I do not believe that aught is. That my neck isn't is a mystery to me. McKay's usually a sure-footed brute, which is why I brought him on this journey to begin with. But not the least attention was I paying. I should have foreseen his frightened jig, or at least fallen properly."

I waited, repeating his words to myself and the way he said them, and became lost in nostalgia for Mamma's voice. When I realized how rude this was, I took a step closer to him. I must say something, I thought. I cast about in my mind for inspiration.

He solved the problem himself. "I've not done a thing well, it seems," he said, rising with difficulty. "I've not introduced myself. I'm Rab Fergusson, of Kirthgarran, Perthshire. And it is so very pleasant to meet you."

I bowed my head and curtseyed as I had been taught. I managed, "How do you do, Mr. Fergusson? I—my name is Keeley Allanson. My father is not at home at the moment. This—this is Mrs. Taggart."

He gave each of us a chivalrous but constrained bow. "'Tis kind of you, it is, to invite me in."

"Should I not send for someone?" I asked. "After Young James attends to your horse he could be sent to fetch Mr. Brander from the hostelry in Melrose. He knows how to—how to mend a great many injuries."

Mr. Fergusson placed a hand on his side and sank down once more. "To be honest, Miss Allanson, I'm only hoping a rib or two did not break in my fall. I'm not sure at all. Does this Mr. Brander live at a great distance?"

Mrs. Taggart was moving about the room, lighting candles in their china holders. She said, "I'll send the lad."

I chanced a look and found the stranger pressing fingers along his coat of embroidered silver, presumably in a search for pain amongst his ribs. Candlelight reflected from the buttons on his chest and the braid-trimmed cuffs.

He sensed me peering at him. "I hope I've not been uncouth. My boldness in coming to your door, and my sorry lack of manners! I'm sore ashamed of myself."

"Oh no. It's just that I know little about healing people. I've tended small animals before but..."

"You've done more for me than you realize."

My wits deserted me, and uncertainty, I said. "We have sheep's head broth. I could bring you some."

He raised his brows and smiled. "That would be a fine thing, Miss Allanson."

In the kitchen I took my time putting barley bannocks on the girdle to cook and finding a broth-plate. With the brass ladle I dipped hot soup, sending the intertwined aromas of savory mutton, onion, and turnip steaming up into my nostrils. Only when I heard Mrs. Taggart's return did I take in the tray.

The next hour was one of the most difficult I had ever endured. It was necessary to oversee the newcomer's meal and to entertain him whilst we waited for the arrival of Mr. Brander. I succumbed to my infuriating habit of becoming tongue-tackit, but somehow managed to murmur answers to his polite questions about the house, the countryside, and the weather.

He seemed to enjoy my barley bannocks. His face contorted in an expression of delight so intense that I thought his discomfort had suddenly increased. "These are exquisite!" he exclaimed. "Whoever made them has a magical touch." He glanced from me to Mrs. Taggart, and perceiving the older woman's sudden resentment, turned back to me. "You? I've never tasted a bannock such as this. How fortunate is your father to be treated to such fare! I haven't had aught so fine since I set out on my travels."

"You've been far?"

"Aye, in fact I'm just returning. I spent most of my time in northern England. Visiting farms. There's much to learn there that I can bring home for our folk to try."

"You're a farmer then," Mrs. Taggart stated.

"I sow oats and I raise cattle. I suppose that makes me one, aye."

My interest was piqued despite myself, but I had not the skill to reciprocate his amiable conversation and was forced to remain content with what he chose to tell. None too soon, Mr. Brander, known for his expertise in putting the bones of man and beast back together, arrived from The Black Horn to see what could be done for Mr. Fergusson.

"There's nought amiss," the hostler told us in his soothing horse-voice when Mrs. Taggart and I rejoined the men. "He's suffering great pain from the fall and though a rib or two have probably taken a severe strain, and possibly a crack, and I've tied a bandage tightly about him, nought seems to be broken on the gentleman." Mr. Fergusson was half-dressed in a knee-length waistcoat of cream silk and I looked away to concentrate on the burly, balding form of Mr. Brander.

"How fortunate," Mrs. Taggart said.

"But he's unfit for travel. He tells me he intends going north of Loch Rannoch and a man has a hard time crossing mountain and bog even when he's fit. I would think he needs a day or two of rest."

"Which I mean to be taking at the inn," Mr. Fergusson added. "I'll be away with Mr. Brander, for I've no desire to burden you further."

Mrs. Taggart glowered at me. I was unused to being looked to for guidance. I thought his idea of moving to The Black Horn a grand one, but surely, out of politeness, as mistress of the house, I was required to beg him to stay.

"That is nonsense," I said, turning to him. "There's no need for you to remove yourself. Especially if doing so will cause you more pain…"

He had already been watching me whilst he tied the stock at the back of his neck, and it took all of my courage to bear the probe of his unusual eyes. "Your compassion is deeply appreciated, Miss Allanson, but surely you'd not be wanting a virtual invalid invading your home, and a stranger in the bargain?"

Mrs. Taggart was still grimacing, but I cleared my throat and answered, "We have plenty of room, and it will be no trouble at all. I'm sure, in the circumstances, my father would wish you to stay." I wondered if that could possibly be true.

He smiled. "In that case I would be honored to remain. You make it difficult to refuse."

He was given Mamma's old room. Mrs. Taggart supplied him with one of my father's nightshirts and took his clothes to hang and dry; I sent up an infusion of herbs to ease his ailments. I told my father of our guest when he returned in the evening.

"Well," he grunted as Young James pulled off a mud-coated

boot for him. "A day or two of graciousness will do us no harm. I'll go up and welcome him myself."

"I hoped you'd not be angry. You've taught me it is honorable to aid those in need." As usual I had difficulty meeting his eyes.

Young James grasped the second boot and tugged. "It is our Christian duty," Father said.

Mrs. Taggart twisted her hands by his chair. "Is it also honorable for someone to squander our meat and meal?"

Father wiped rainwater from his chin with the back of a hand. "What are you talking about, Mrs. Taggart?"

"Your daughter invaded my kitchen, flung me out..."

I said, "I helped her prepare our supper. And I wasted nothing."

Father fixed the old woman with a wintry eye. "Is it *your* kitchen indeed, Mrs. Taggart?"

She knew better than to answer.

Mr. Fergusson appeared at our table for breakfast.

"How are you this day?" I inquired as I passed him a pot of gooseberry preserves.

He grinned. "The rest, and your herbs, and the generous supper on the tray last night seem to be restoring me." His fingers were warm against mine as he grasped the dish, and I felt the dreaded fire rush to my cheeks.

"Father?"

My father put down his coffee and reached for a barley-scone. I busied myself with butter and honey and bit my lip because Mr. Fergusson was intent upon everything I did. "Keeley tells me," Father said, "that you are returning from England. You've been to examine agriculture."

Our guest seemed to forget to butter his scone. "There's a great deal to discover."

"Have you any land under sheep?"

"Our sheep are worthless. Far different from the animals I've seen on my journey. I feel driven to learn all I can about the Lintons and Cheviots."

Father brightened. "You might be interested in seeing my farms before you take your leave. And my woolen mill."

Mr. Fergusson tilted his head and put down his knife. "You

own farms?"

From that point on it was clear I was no longer of paramount importance. They took their discussion from table to drawing room. My father found nothing more enjoyable than expounding on his monetary successes, and in Mr. Fergusson he found the perfect student. In the past year Father had allowed me to read the account books for the farms and increase my knowledge of Cheviot sheep, their costs, care, wool, and flesh, and—out of resignation for not having a son on hand to train—he had begun to share with me the daily tribulations of the woolen mill, citing the miseries and joys of wages, looms, competition, and qualities of fleece. Malcolm had listened with ill-concealed impatience when he had been at home, and I did my best out of resentful duty, but how Father must have reveled in his discourse with another farmer who seemed pinned by his every word. Mr. Fergusson settled in a chair and listened for hours, a hand pressed loosely across his lower chest. He moved about from time to time to ease his legs, and joined my father in a game of chess and a dram of brandy in the evening.

I prowled upstairs and lurked in the dining room, analyzing Mr. Fergusson unobserved. For once I wished I had acquired the art of conversation and the associated ease in the company of strangers.

Father was obliged to offer his apologies to Mr. Fergusson on the second day and ride to Melrose. When I emerged from my bedchamber I found the door to Mamma's sitting room open with the man resting inside, aware of my presence.

He called to me in his foreign tongue, which I was sure was Gaelic, and went on, "These are such comfortable rooms. I thought, with your father gone, I would enjoy them for a while."

"They are very pleasant."

"'Tis happy I'd be, if you'd join me."

Refusal would have been rude, and I did not want him to think I was disrespectful and ill-mannered. I took the chair across from him and stole glances here and there. The bedroom beyond appeared as it always had: neat, sparely furnished, and feminine with lace-edged linen and green checkered hangings on the bed. Delicate miniatures Mamma had painted ornamented the dressing table. Every inanimate object in both rooms, even the walls covered with the hand-painted paper from Edinburgh that my father had ordered for her, spoke acutely of my mother and emphasized her absence.

"This room," he said, "and the chamber beyond. They seem different from the rest of the house. Did you say they were your mother's?"

A moment passed before I could answer. "She spent much of her time upstairs, here."

"I'm sorry then, was she ill?"

"She enjoyed the solitude." He waited, and I said with a lower voice, "She and I also walked and rode a great deal. And collected things. Flowers, herbs, and that."

"You must have enjoyed it."

"We were good company for each other."

"And you miss her. Painfully."

I dared to look at him and met an expression of understanding on his face. He appeared much restored in health today and far better groomed than when he'd first come. His cropped dark hair, once muddied, was now clean and glossy, and he had shaved his face. Evidence of Mrs. Taggart's industry was plain as well, for his waistcoat and breeks were pressed, his hose laundered, and the black leather riding boots with their russet tops stood by the door, gleaming and unblemished.

"Is it difficult for you to speak of her?" he asked.

I swallowed past the hardness in my throat. "I've never spoken about her, to anyone. Hardly anyone."

"How long ago was it that you lost her?"

"Five years."

"How did it happen, if I might ask?"

"She bled to death, in childbed."

He widened his black-fringed eyes a little and said gently, "It was a shock for you."

I looked away and my thumbs became locked in my fingers. A shock. How could it be otherwise? A part of me wanted to look backward, to remember and to conjure up her image. Another part swelled within me and grew hot with bitterness. How would our lives have evolved had my father not hurt her during her last pregnancy? In hindsight I was sure that he had. If he had left her alone she might have given birth to a son, soothing Father's scorn and easing his desperation, and bringing her happiness at last.

Such introspection paved a treacherous path. There was no use in inventing tales of how things could have been, for daydreams led nowhere and did more damage to one's scars than leaving them untended. Memories were just as troublesome. Deep inside I had known that brooding on Mamma's death was a ruinous habit, but the ashes of my fourteenth, fifteenth, even sixteenth year had had to blow away before I could even begin to discipline myself. Even now I could only bring out recollections of my childhood if I was careful. They had to be handled one at a time. I could turn them over, examine them. Yet there were some that could not be quarried at all.

Mr. Fergusson's voice broke into my thoughts. I was reminded this was not the time to look too closely at anything.

"I'm sorry, Miss Allanson. To lose a parent, I ken how you must feel, for my mother is gone as well. Have you the comfort of grandparents?"

"Mamma was orphaned in Dundee, before she married my father. Nor are Father's parents still alive."

"Then there's just you and your da. You comfort each other."

I paused, thinking how strange that sounded. "He has a son by his first marriage. Malcolm lives in Edinburgh and is an advocate."

"I have a brother myself," he said, leaning back against the lavender bolster. "And three kinsmen I regard as brothers, though they're merely companions from the cradle."

I seized upon this change of topic. "Are you somewhat alike, you and your brother?"

He smiled and shook his head. "In some ways, aye, but Lachlan keeps to himself a great deal. He seems simple sometimes, but that's a false notion as a man soon learns. He's the wits to match anyone's, he's just less inclined to speak, and..." He hesitated, pressing his lips together. "He resembles a Celt perhaps, of ancient times." He laughed. "He and I do share a great fondness for hunting. That and finding fast horses to race."

"Do you race each other?"

"Now and then. Though the earl's stables are not what they once were."

He waited for me to speak and I managed, "And the others? Your kinsmen who are not your brothers but are regarded as such?"

"Lachlan and I are the sons of the steward, and Alistair, Coll, and Andrew are the sons of the housekeeper. We were raised together. Andrew is the eldest and lives nearby. He's a serious one, always thinking, always tending to the needs of others. Alistair, the youngest, is as wild as a lad could be. The De'il himself. Hardly ever at home now he's wed and living in Oban with his wife's family. He and Andrew, as you might imagine, often have their bluidy battles."

He waited so long to continue that I felt compelled to say, "And the other you mentioned?"

"Coll? He and I are steadfast companions. You'd like him, I think." He rested his head and shrugged deep into the cushion. "He was in North America until about four years ago."

"Why did he go?"

"He bought a commission in the army because the lass he loved promised to wed someone else."

"Oh."

"'Twas all quite a tragedy. The lass died before he left. She fell from her window, a tower window. Some folk wondered if Coll had, aye, flung her down, a conjecture he found impossible to bear. Since he's been back we've been able to piece together how it must have been for him, trying to forget, fighting in a far-off country for a cause that was lost. He did well with his soldiering and was promoted. But he was at Yorktown and taken prisoner, and held for two years. He speaks little of that, as he does of the other, but I can see the damage it all has caused him."

"He—he did not have aught to do with her death..."

"He says he's innocent. And I believe him."

"Are there some who do not?"

He hesitated. "The lass's father and mother, and brother especially, have never withdrawn their blame. And I suppose there will always be a few at Kirthgarran who wonder if he did not throw her to the ground in vengeance."

I was bewildered by my sudden inclination to defend the honor of someone I did not know nor ever would. In an effort to distance myself from this strange tale I said impassively, "Kirthgarran?"

"Kirthgarran," he replied. "And Kirthgarran Castle, long the stronghold of the Fergussons of Kirthgarran, north of Loch Rannoch, in the Grampians. Have you never heard of it?"

I shook my head.

"Graeme Fergusson, Earl of Kirthgarran, Laird of Strath Gruagach and Rathdale, is an auld and ailing man, but a foster father to all of us. Being Fergussons of the same blood, we were brought up at the castle and still consider it our home. The earl favors us especially now since his own sons were lost in war."

"That is terrible. That they were lost, I mean."

"It is. But speaking of comforts, I think we comfort him a great deal, and all is not as sad as it could be."

"I wish..." I began. To have a sister or a brother, not like Malcolm but like me, was a dream that had never come true.

He waited for me but when it was plain I would not continue, he straightened in the chair and said in a different tone, "Forgive me, but I'd never have thought you to be your father's daughter. Hardly any resemblance is there. I was struck by it when I met your father that first night."

"I've the look of my mother."

"She must have been a bonny woman."

I felt the annoying burning sensation in my cheeks but he did not seem to notice.

"The lads here must battle for your attentions."

"There is no one."

He whistled between his teeth. "'Tis these Lowland men. If you were in the Highlands, Miss Allanson, you'd not be left alone for a moment. In the Highlands beauty is appreciated with all the honor and gallantry a man is capable of giving."

I stood up and longingly regarded the door. He must have realized he was making me uncomfortable for his smile faded and he reached out an arm. "Do not go."

His hand came to rest on my forearm, and having never

been touched so by another man save Malcolm, I felt another blaze of fire sweep upward over my neck and face. The heat of it seemed to affect my voice as well. I said, "There are things I must do."

The pressing fingers slid away. His eyes crawled over the room as if seeking a new center of conversation, and then they seemed to find one. "The clarsach. It was your mother's?"

Reluctantly I focused on Mamma's harp. It had been sleeping upon the table, undisturbed, for all of these years. The morning sun dotted highlights amongst the carvings in the oak and shone on the strings.

As a bairn I had explored the engraved knots on its soundbox and post, running my fingers along the twisting crevices and tapping the pins that ran like teeth in a wide smile along the top. I had never been able to make up my mind about the animal carved at the bottom of the pillar. It could have been a dragon or a dog.

A magical sound flooded the air whenever the strings were plucked. Sweeping one's fingers downward or upward brought forth octaves of sweetness, and when the wind blew through the wires, notes streamed from the instrument like gentle threads. Mamma had said that when the wind caught them just so the strings became enchanted and played of their own will.

"Aye. It was hers," I said.

"Do you not play?"

"No. No. I did—before."

"I was admiring it earlier. I was hoping you could play. A bit of music is always enjoyable."

I took a backward step. The voice of the clarsach had been silent since the day of Mamma's death.

I should have welcomed this opportunity to practice the art of conversation with Mr. Fergusson, but his probing questions made me long to retreat. Shunning social discourse was to my detriment, I knew. One does not learn more of the world and its ways by escaping from them. But the sight of Mamma's things weakened me. I could maneuver between polite dialogue and troubled memories no longer.

I gave myself credit for remembering to curtsey, and said faintly, "I'm sorry, Mr. Fergusson. I am pleased to find that you are healing, and I have enjoyed our visit, but truly I must go."

I did not wait for his reply but fled like the frightened child I was.

Whaur has she sae late been roaming?
Ee Hoo, the Milking (Trad.)

Chapter Four

he following day Malcolm came to Gilchrist House
with the woman he was going to marry. He had
brought her to visit three times before. Elizabeth
Ramsay was a year younger than I, but whenever I was in her
company I stammered and twisted my hands and always said the
wrong thing. She was a woman given to dressing and preening
with perfection. She always knew the proper thing to say, even
if her voice was cold and devoid of feeling, and she never let an
expression cross her face unless it was absolutely necessary.

Mr. Fergusson was present when Elizabeth, Mrs. Ramsay,
and Malcolm arrived, and charmingly responded to my father's
introductions whilst Mrs. Taggart hurried to prepare a selection

of shortbread and currant buns to have with wine.

I remembered with remorse the exchanges that had taken place between the Ramsays and me in the past, for Father never allowed me the refuge of silence in those encounters, but expected me to play the part of the woman of the house. He pressed me to be gracious and articulate and to reflect upon him my gentle upbringing, with his humiliating displeasure to face if I failed.

I tried not to think ahead to the coming debacle whilst I searched the stillroom for a glass decanter to replace the cracked one in the kitchen. I found an etched pitcher and turned, but I could not move because Malcolm was in front of me.

"Wee sister," he said. He partially closed the door behind him with his boot.

Every instance of his depravity returned to mind. I retreated a step, bumping against the table at my back. He was elegant with his powdered wig and black, English broadcloth coat, but the man inside was not changed, had never changed.

"You're ever in a hurry." He lifted a hand and drew aside a strand of hair on my forehead. In the semi-darkness I could feel his breath on my face, smell his expensive scent. "How have you been? Are you enjoying yon Highlander as a houseguest? He seems pleasant enough."

"The others are waiting..."

"But there's time for greetings betwixt us. You ken how much I treasure seeing you."

I hugged the decanter to my chest. I had not heard his footsteps. I had let myself be cornered.

"You're looking well," he said.

"I want..."

He tilted his head. "Aye, you want?"

"I want to go. Please."

"Not yet. I've only just arrived. I have missed you."

"Please." His hands touched me: my chest, my hip. I feared I would crush the pitcher. "Please, Malcolm."

He came closer. His gaze followed his hands, his alarming, wandering hands. When one of them came between my thighs I stiffened. "God help me, you tempt me so, you dear woman. Are you the innocent you appear? You ken, Keeley, you could send a man into madness." His foot pushed the door shut and the click of the latch was loud. "But you like the feel of my hand. It excites you." I felt his lips brush my hair. "If you were honest, you would say so. In fact, if you were honest," he said as he pressed his body against mine, allowing me to sense the hardness of him against my hip, "you'd agree there is a natural conclusion to this."

He would assault me, his half-sister, here in this airless hole.

I pushed against him with as much force as I could muster. I caught him unaware and his hands slipped. I thrust the decanter into his breastbone. It crashed to the stone floor and shattered. In the next moment I tore open the door, and though bright light blinded me I did not pause. I ran away, unsure if he followed me. I heard his laughter; it was far behind me, and stayed there. I flew up the back stairs to my room and locked the door, intending to lean against it as well, but I fell to my knees and was sick.

Before Mrs. Taggart retired that night she conveyed the message that I was to go to my father in his study. I discovered him standing in front of a watercolor Mamma had painted, his favorite. He was running his finger down the glass that protected it. His head turned when he heard my footsteps, and the dying light from the yellow embers on the hearth lifted the planes of his face out of the darkness.

I dared not move. After many moments he began speaking softly, but with a familiar edge to his voice. "I cannot begin to understand your sudden impudence this afternoon. Mrs. Ramsay expressed great disappointment because you were not able to join us. I was forced to tell her you were not feeling well."

"I was not. I told Mrs. Taggart so when she came to find me."

"A sudden illness that befell you as soon as Malcolm and the Ramsays arrived?"

"I've no explanation for it."

"Was it not, rather, a decision to avoid your responsibilities?"

"I always try to do as you wish, Father."

Harshness crept into his voice. "I lied for you this afternoon. I will never do so again. Have you no more to say for yourself?"

"I am telling you the truth."

He took a step toward me, energy shooting visibly through him. His hand came out and knocked me so forcefully on the side of my head I lost my balance and fell. "Enough of this! Down on your knees, child, and pray to God for your salvation!"

I lifted myself up a little from the carpet at his feet. My head throbbed. I did not risk looking at him. My hands clasped together as I listened to my father's voice beseeching God in Heaven for forgiveness of my heinous sins, but his tone was far from humble. The rage in him seared us both.

The kirk taught us to honor our mothers and fathers, but did God ken that any regard I held for the man standing above me had been shattered years ago? The question remained unanswered but out of habit I knelt quietly whilst the prayers for my soul labored on. My throat felt raw from that afternoon's sickness and my eyes were swollen. I was unable to think much at all, or attend to my father's words. Eventually he ordered me away to bed and I obeyed, amazed that this was the end of the punishment.

I was soon to discover it was not.

I wrote in my diary, *"He could not have chosen a better sentence for me. As much as I do, indeed, enjoy the safety of my room, I am bitter about being kept from the outdoors. The upper storey of the house is warm and stale of air, and I yearn so for the scents of the garden and the fresh breezes that blow across the countryside. My feet ache to run through the yielding grass of the pastures, my hands to gather the new blossoms and to bring water to my lips from the spring.*

"For seven days I have been kept locked in my room, seeing no one but Mrs. Taggart, who brings me a dish of porridge once a day and rakes me with her sly eyes as if to say, 'See what a fool you are. You are insignificant.'

"For a whole week I have not been able to bake. Mrs. Dundas must have waited by the road and grown worried when I did not appear. Perhaps she had to give The Black Horn some of her own scones to avoid any questions. I am so hungry. Yet, if I think about what occurred I lose my appetite altogether, so perhaps that is a good thing to do. I am still not sorry for telling Father I was ill. I could not have borne to face our visitors. Being hungry, failing to fill my orders for the inn, feeling Mrs. Taggart's derision—they are worth it."

In small, careful script I added, *"But I must never, never find myself alone with Malcolm. The next time he will not let me go. I have protected him and his unnatural desire, and he will count on my timidity in the future. He looked up at my window when he and the Ramsays took their leave. He removed his hat and nodded at me with a conspiratorial smile. I shrank back, which no doubt only amused him. He thinks this is all a game, but one day he will not give up his prize. He will be grateful, and I will wish to die."*

On the morning of the eighth day Mrs. Taggart unlocked my door. I was free.

I tugged on my riding habit and asked Young James to saddle Benjamin, my chestnut gelding. I galloped far over the countryside, inhaling the soft air and reveling in the wind streaming past my ears. I rode through thick pools of wood anemones in the birk woods, and frightened roe deer that had come out into the open to eat the blossoms denied them during the winter. The birks were heavy with buds, and primroses sheltered in the niches at their roots. Curlews, oystercatchers, and swallows swept through the trees, sputtering happily.

"Come up," I said as I urged Benjamin over swelling hills spotted with ewes ready to give birth and new lambs skipping about on knock-kneed legs. I passed by shepherds who watched for foxes, rooks, and carrion crows whilst they searched for stillborn lambs and helpless, pregnant sheep lying upside down, unable to rise. The arable land was being ploughed and cottars were sowing grain. Cows had calved and were suckling their young or leaving them hidden in what they considered to be safe places.

"Benjamin," I called. "We'll go to the river."

We cantered to the Tweed where there lay a secluded meadow lush with young grass that rippled like the sheen on Benjamin's flanks. I dismounted, threw off shoes and stockings, and danced in wide circles. My horse watched me, and I thought he smiled.

I began a return to Gilchrist House by the cottages near the East Port of the town when I heard a man's voice calling me. I looked toward the road and saw Mr. Fergusson's horse, McKay, silhouetted against a hedge. Under a flowering wild plum tree sat his owner, a silver flask dangling from his hand.

Reluctantly I turned my mount and walked him along the stone-strewn track. Mr. Fergusson rose from the grass and put out a hand to help me dismount. I was not sure I wanted to take it but I did. His fingers steadied me as I slid from the saddle to the ground beside him. I had forgotten how tall he was.

"You've been unchained," he said.

I did not know how to reply. I finally said, "I was not certain you'd be here still."

He smiled. "Would I go without saying a farewell to you?"

"Have you been waiting?"

"I must be truthful and say aye, that is so. Perhaps I'd have been away sooner, but when I requested of your father a chance to speak to you, it was denied. So now, you've done your penance and I'm aggrieved because I must soon be on my way to Kirthgarran."

"You're quite recovered."

"There seems to be no lasting damage. Would you not agree 'tis time for me to be concerned about you? I was shocked when your father explained his treatment of you. It is not my place to be saying whether or not I agree with it, but I find this whole affair regrettable. Does he do this often? Lock you away, I mean? Why did you not wish to visit with the younger Mr. Allanson?"

I shrugged. The only sound between us was the mad hum of bees coming from the froth of white plum blossoms.

"May I walk with you, Miss Allanson?"

I nodded uncertainly.

He tightened the flask's cap and tucked it inside his silver-gray coat. Mr. Fergusson stayed by my side at a discreet distance, and after we passed a lass selling buttermilk from a goatskin, he said, "Your father seems to do quite well for himself, with his sheep and his looms."

"He likes to discover what is new, and what makes a profit."

"He showed me his mill. He produces quite a few stone of wool a year, he tells me, and he seems quite proud of it. I wonder he doesn't keep his son here to learn the management of it. After all, it will all be his one day, I'm told."

"They've had a routh of bitter quarrels. My half-brother

never showed any liking for it."

"Younger Mr. Allanson will find himself a burdened man the day he must see to his Edinburgh endeavors and his father's mill both."

Unless Father remarries, I thought, and continues his own endeavors to bring into this world the perfect replacement for himself.

"Your father would seem to be an ambitious man," Mr. Fergusson continued, "and yet I gather he blends little with the other weavers, for business or for pleasure. And sadly, he keeps you at home alone with him. He's a person of riddles. A devout man who strives to have a place in the Kingdom of God, but one who also seems to cherish the comforts and gratifications earthly wealth brings. A gentleman who earns a good living, I surmise, yet keeps less than a handful of servants."

"They've gone. He sees no need to hire others."

"Hm. Then there's you. You enjoy your home as well, but I think you're even fonder of your freedom from it." How he knew this I could not guess. He added, "'Tis natural to appreciate one's living space only as long as the possibility of leaving it exists. Otherwise it is a prison."

Somehow he could see what was in my mind. It rankled somewhat and I found myself defending my father. "He does not often deny me my walks."

"Where do you go, Miss Allanson, when you are out alone?"

I wondered how many places I could list without boring him. "I like to look at the ruins of the Abbey, and try to visualize it when it was first built, before it was destroyed and rebuilt and destroyed again."

"Show me." We had passed the mercat cross in the center of the town and the abbey itself lay at the end of the road ahead of us. He inclined his head, and with a questioning look suggested we walk toward it.

Feeling somewhat foolish I followed him, our horses coming alongside. "It was built by King David the First," I said. "He was eager for there to be many abbeys. It was he who ordered the others to be built as well. Dryburgh, Jedburgh, and Kelso."

"None of which were immune to attack and ruin."

"Alas, no. How sad it is. We can only guess where the monastery was. They were Cistercian monks, did you know?"

He grinned. "I've little knowledge of any kind of monk."

"Oh," I said, unsure of what he meant. "They had farms and bakeries and gardens, and orchards of apples and pears and plums across the river. They used stilts to cross at the ford. They had more flocks of sheep than any religious house in the country, and their wool was sold in the Low Countries and Italy."

"A rich target for centuries of invading armies, was it not?"

"It was demolished and burnt, so many times. Edward the Second, Richard the Second, Henry the Eighth. They could not bear to leave it alone. But in the 1500's it became a Protestant church."

"You seem to know a great deal about history." He smiled, encouraging me to continue.

We reached the abbey itself and stood looking at the remains of the once-lovely cathedral set amongst trees and hills. Pink walls made of smooth, rectangular stone rose from the daisy-studded grass. The presbytery, its gables, and the framing transepts were encrusted with carvings and statues of gargoyles, saints, martyrs, and angels.

"Our parish kirk is a vault built inside the nave," I told him. "There are some who are putting forth an outcry about the entire abbey, though. It's all tumbling down and becoming wretched. There are some who say it's deplorable to ignore such a treasure as this, the finest abbey in Scotland."

I stood for a moment longer, admiring the tall spires and arched windows, remembering the days when my mother and I had roamed the old kirkyard and the abbey lands as we'd tried to envision the events of the centuries that had come to pass, both peaceful and violent.

With a sigh I pulled Benjamin onward, giving the abbey a last look—and the kirkyard where Mamma now lay. We continued north, toward the Tweed.

His voice, gentle and soft, prodded me on. "Where else do you go, Miss Allanson?"

I took in the hills and peaks about us. "Bemersyde Hill," I said, nodding to the east. "If you climb it you can look down on the loop of the river where Old Melrose began." He was listening intently to me and I continued, "The Lammermuirs." I pointed an ink-stained finger. "And of course the Eildons, or Trimontium as they were anciently called, after the three peaks. My mother told me about King Arthur and his knights, who fought their last battle close by at Gala Water in the Vale of Woe and now sleep beneath the mounds, waiting to be awakened if the need arises."

"Let us hope that need never comes, for Scotland's sake."

"But it is comforting to know they are there."

"You've climbed these hills, I'm sure, a hundred times."

"From the top of North Hill there's such a view of the Lammermuirs and the Moorfoots, and the hills of Upper Tweeddale! And to the south, when the day is clear, the Cheviot Hills. The gorse is bonny in the spring and summer, and so is the heather later. I like to watch for kestrels and merlins as they fly and dive. Or to pretend I'm a Roman general, looking out over the fort and camps below and waiting for signals telling of approaching Picts."

I'd not noticed, in my enthusiasm, that we walked quite close to each other. I was brought back to the present. My strides stiffened when I realized I had shared my secrets with a stranger.

"Do not stop," Mr. Fergusson implored, and his brows curved upward. "It all interests me, as do you."

I shook my head.

"Tell me about the folk. The people in the village." He waited. "You've friends, certainly. Another lass you visit and laugh with."

I shook my head again, and we turned westward on the track that would lead us back to my father's lands.

We came to a spring-fed pool of water on which a half-dozen swans drifted. In a low voice he said, "I'll be gone, Miss Allanson, on the morrow."

I felt nothing but relief. I went to the lip of the pond where I had not been for over a week, and waited for him to continue. Black-headed gulls rose from the reeds on the opposite shore where they were busy at work nest-building. Tadpoles thronged in the shallows at the water's edge, lucky to have escaped the beaks of ducks and herons.

"I've stayed too long as it is. I've taken undue advantage of your father's generosity."

Unwilling to be disrespectful to him, I contended, "Have you not needed the time to heal?"

"Oh aye," he said, but he left the words hanging as if he had changed his mind. He was quiet after that, and I could conjure up nothing to say.

We continued our journey and I was aware of how firmly he placed his feet upon the ground, of how straight was his back. Yet he did not speak, and from my meager knowledge of him I thought that must be unusual. At last, when a flock of wood pigeons fluttered upward before us in an iridescent blur and settled down in a patch of young clover, Mr. Fergusson's feet slowed and soon stopped, and so did mine. His face appeared leaner than usual, if that was possible. We were close enough that I could sense the tang of whisky on his breath.

"Miss Allanson, I did wish to speak to you before I left. The waiting was miserable. I'd no idea how long you'd be imprisoned. Do you not ken why it is I wish to speak to you? I must be away yet I keep delaying it. Can you not realize why?"

I shook my head.

"I've discovered it is impossible to stop thinking of you. From the moment I crept to your doorstep a fortnight ago, I've been beguiled. Held captive. By you."

His declaration brought my thoughts to a standstill.

"It would be so easy," he said, "for me to fall in love with you."

I could say nothing. Inner fires scorched my cheeks. I turned away so I could hide them. I stroked Benjamin's nose and stared at one of the horse's huge, dark, liquid eyes. I tried to concentrate on the long eyelashes that grew from both top and bottom lids. The equine lashes wavered in the air.

"I wanted to tell you. I want to tell your father. I want to return here, and court you properly. To call on you and someday, perhaps..." He sighed. "There's fear in you, Miss Allanson, a fear deep inside I'm not understanding. You're bewildered, a bit afraid of me, perhaps. That's to be expected. But I'm thinking if you could take away the fear you'd find your heart ready to accept someone into it. Are you that surprised someone could care for you?"

A light touch of Mr. Fergusson's hand brought my gaze away from Benjamin and back to him. He was looking down into my face and I watched his eyes move to my mouth, linger there.

"Crivvens. How could anyone not care for you? I've been listening to your marvelous stories and have seen how you can be excited and full of imaginative wonder. That's the true Keeley Allanson, I suspect. A woman of gentleness and strength together. But I've alarmed you. Please, take time, time to think about what I've said. I want you to be happy."

I kept my face upturned toward him but my hands fumbled for my horse's bridle.

"Is it your father?" he asked, coming a step closer. "What has he done to you to cause you such fear? If I speak to him, when I speak to him, for I must, there'll be nought said to cause him any anger, I promise you. Miss Allanson, I..."

I could no longer look at him. I mounted my gelding. I nudged the horse's sides, whispering to Mr. Fergusson, "I'm sorry. I'm sorry," and I was gone.

How I dreaded the return to Gilchrist House. I stayed away all afternoon, haunting North Hill and riding through moors of harebell, blaeberry, and fern, glimpsing red grouse, roe deer, and droves of rabbits sitting near their burrows. When a woodcock flew in front of me emitting his hoarse call, it alerted me to the fact nightfall was threatening.

I arrived home, saw to the horse, and entered the hall. But there was Mrs. Taggart on sentry duty with her distaff and spindle, and as soon as I entered my room I heard Father's boots upon the stairs.

He came into my chamber. I was unkempt, my habit muddied, my hair fallen out of its snood and straggling unevenly to my waist. "I have been waiting for you since this afternoon," he said. "Where, may I ask, have you been?"

"Riding, Father." I stood still, despite a slight trembling, and waited.

"Mr. Fergusson and I had an interesting discussion. It has become evident to me, because of your absence in the past hours, that you know the nature of it, and even now without me having to tell you, you realize what he has on his mind."

There was no preamble, no explanation of my exile in my room, no acknowledgment of sins committed and forgiven. "I do not ken for certain."

"It seems the man wants to return and court you. Perhaps ask for your hand in marriage." He watched me. "Were you aware of this?"

"I suspected."

"Aye?"

I wondered if I should say, "Right or wrong, good or bad, if you dislike him, Father, it is somehow my fault, just as everything is."

His lip curved into a fleeting, humorless smile. "I take it he made no declarations to you."

"He told me he wanted to speak to you—about me."

"The man is quite taken with you. During his stay here he has seen a side of you that eludes me. I must say I was surprised by his intentions. I have been guilty of giving little notice to the years as they pass. You are, after all, a maiden of nineteen, as Mr. Fergusson reminded me. We spoke a good deal about you. There is no question in my mind he fancies himself in love with you."

"What was your answer?"

"I'm afraid I had to refuse him. He comes from a land of savages. The heathens of the Highlands are an ignorant, traitorous lot. Although his people were not outspoken Jacobites, the estates Mr. Fergusson speaks of seemed to have been narrowly spared by Government troops in '46 and after. The Kirthgarran Fergussons have since recovered grace with the King, but that hardly outweighs the centuries of treachery and savagery. I respect Mr. Fergusson. He seems a likeable enough man, not as feckless as many of his countrymen, and I'll not deny I've enjoyed his company. But I will not have a Highlander bargaining to wed my daughter."

I barely managed to reply, "Mamma was from the Highlands."

He did not answer at once. His expression changed little, but a muscle in his jaw flexed. For just a second his eyes met mine, and something in their cast reminded me of the day he had flung the wounded rook across the garden. He blinked, and the illusion was gone. "Your mother was," he agreed. "And I intend to keep you from making the same mistake that I did."

My lips parted, but there were no words there.

"We may consider this matter done. There is one other I wished to explore. You have brought to my attention that you spend a great deal of time walking about the countryside. You spent the entire day today riding. Is it fair to conclude that you wander about alone most of the time?"

I twisted my thumbs. "I have my household duties, but sometimes I..."

"I prefer you to discipline yourself and walk and ride only within sight of the house."

"The house..."

"I'll hear no argument about it, will I?"

"You never objected to Mamma enjoying the air, the countryside..."

"Your mother was a married woman. As Mr. Fergusson has reminded me, you are of a vulnerable age. Henceforth I do not want to hear of you going out alone. There is more spinning to do if you find yourself with an idle hand, and baking and brewing and washing, I would think. Mrs. Taggart's age is advancing and she could use the assistance. If you do take some air you are to have her accompany you."

"Mrs. Taggart. I cannot..."

"I've nothing more to say," came his voice as he turned away. "And neither do you."

Father went out to the stable and oversaw the saddling of Mr. Fergusson's horse the next morning. When it was done I stood beside my parent as duty commanded, waiting for our guest to pay his respects and continue on a journey Fate had interrupted, a journey I wished had never been.

Mr. Fergusson emerged from the house and came toward us. "I cannot tell you how I've enjoyed your hospitality and how grateful I am for the charity you've shown to a clumsy, hapless traveler," he said.

"You've a pleasant day on which to begin your journey, sir,"

Father remarked.

"That is true." He paused. "I cannot help but say I leave in grave disappointment. I had hoped my return journey to be taken with a much lighter heart and joyous spirit."

"It is a fact we do not often receive that for which we ask out of life."

"I suppose I'm not a firm believer in that, at least not yet."

I pondered the stony ground, though I knew Mr. Fergusson was looking pointedly at me.

At last Father said, "Good day to you, sir." The traveler responded with something in Gaelic. Father turned and started for the door and I followed him without hesitation. He had already gone into the house when Mr. Fergusson's voice came quietly.

"Keeley."

My feet stopped of their own will. I turned and faced him.

"Keeley, I'll not settle for his answer. I'll not accept there's no hope. I'll come back. That is something you can cling to, and believe."

We took a long measure of each other. He was coatless and hatless, and the little breeze fingered his dark brown hair. Behind him the impatient McKay nudged his arm with a downy nose but Mr. Fergusson seemed unaware. I turned and stepped into the hall, and closed the door behind me.

Where woodlands are green with trees well nourished,
  A scene of beauty to view,
I found with delight one stem that flourish'd,
  Of bright and beautiful hue.
That bough from above, desiring greatly
  With love unto me, I drew;
None else could have mov'd that tree so stately.
  'Twas only for me that it grew.

Fair Young Mary (Trad.)

Chapter Five

My diary was my sole friend.

"*28 April, 1787. My days are very different now. That for which I long is forever lost to me. I could disobey my father. I could entreat Mrs. Taggart to roam the countryside with me. But I cannot find it within me to do either thing, and so I haunt the garden and flee as far away from the house as I am able without losing sight of its chimney-sticks.*

"*20 May. How I long to find the early purple orchids and the rock roses. The cotton grass will be forming its soft, white heads. Nearer Melrose are rowan and hawthorn trees and the fragrance of their flowers now must be heavenly. The roe deer should have their new coats and be giving birth to their kids in the hayfields. And I must stay near the house and see none of these things. I blame Mr. Fergusson, who brought the little freedom I had to Father's attention. I hope he never returns to Melrose, for I will never be able to forgive him even though I know I am being unfair. It was my decision not to return home straight away that brought this all upon me, not his proposal.*

At nightfall on the sixth day of June my quill scrawled, *"I saw a man today,"* and my heartbeat quickened because the words made it seem all the more real.

"I wandered about the garden and went to the banks of the Tweed. It was a fragrant morning and I could not remain indoors. I followed the water and caught a glimpse of someone walking toward me. I was ready to run back home but he had seen me, and as soon as I turned he called out to me."

The voice that had hailed me was a young one, full of pleading. He'd seemed encouraged when I'd halted, and he had trotted closer. He was taller than I, of approximately my age, thin, yet solid of bone and muscle. Knee-length breeks of brown wool and an unbuttoned waistcoat were dusty, as though he had been walking for days and sleeping in his clothes. With some false starts he began to apologize.

"I was—I did not mean to scare you. I've not seen anyone since this morning. I was beginning to think everyone had been spirited away and only I was left here on earth!" He dropped coat, hat, and bundle at his bare feet. His eyes had difficulty meeting mine. "Can you tell me where I am? I've come from Galashiels."

Clearly he was not of the Lowlands. I replied, "If you go back to the road by—rather, beyond the house there, or follow the river, and go toward those hills, you'll come to the village of Melrose."

He nodded, examining the two visible peaks of the three Eildons. "And will I be reaching it by nightfall?"

"I'm thinking you'll reach it within an hour."

"What welcome news! I'd no idea I was so close." A smile touched his narrow-lipped mouth. "Could I—might I ask you something else, Miss? Is there any work, something at which I can earn a wage? I need a roof and food."

We made a fine pair, I thought, each stumbling over our tongues.

"There's little to be had," I answered. "The village folk here are farmers, or work at spinning and weaving, of wool mostly, though many—many still weave linen or work in the bleachfield on the west side of Weirhill, whitening the cloth."

He waited, tilting his head down, yet watching me closely with wide eyes of bluish gray.

"But the linen's not wanted so much anymore in the markets," I said, "and my father says Dutch flax is becoming too expensive, and the bleachfield is decaying. There's a cotton mill. In Galashiels, I've heard. They talk about starting one here, I'm told, but I'm unsure if they have."

"Galashiels had many woolen mills, with machinery, I mind."

"Oh aye, they compete with Melrose, drawing customers away, though we still have more looms. My father owns a woolen mill himself, but has no need for new apprentices."

"I've been trained as a blacksmith, but I would do aught," he said, and I noticed that his forearms, under their rolled sleeves of crude linen, showed evidence of heavy work. "Someone told me there was shoemaking."

"In Selkirk, aye, but that is farther southwest, along Ettrick Water. The folk here can barely sustain themselves. Some have emigrated for want of employment."

"The same is true where I come from. Aberfoyle. I'd hoped..." He did not finish but bent and retrieved his belongings. "Thank you for your help. I suppose I must go and see for myself."

A certain empathy rose in me, enhanced by the confirmation that, like Mamma, he was from the north. I blurted out, "I hope you do find something."

He nodded. "It has been a long while since I've had a kind word." He tipped his head. "Good day to you, Miss, then."

He slung his belongings over his right shoulder and settled into an earnest stride along the bank. He clapped on his cocked hat and jumped over a large stone, and the tail of his hair and his flimsy bundle bounced at his back.

Whilst I sat writing in my chamber that night a soft breeze wafted through the window and disturbed my candle flame. I could not stop thinking of the stranger. Because I saw so few travelers, each one made an indelible impression on me. I could picture him clearly in my mind: weary shoulders, unkempt, light brown hair, ragged breeks. I could hear his voice, tinged with the Highland nuances. For a man he was strangely unthreatening, and my concern for his welfare did not vanish.

I finished writing, *"I wonder if he did go along to Melrose. I wonder if he found work. Is he sleeping under the open sky at this very moment? More than once I have dreamt of how it would be to lie down under a star-filled sky on a summer's night and fall asleep, watching. It is, I suppose, folly to wonder about him. I will never know what became of him."*

The next evening, feeling restless, I walked down the bank toward the river. To my utter amazement the same man was sitting by the rushing water.

He was staring at the Tweed and the droop of his shoulders suggested fatigue, the angle of his head sadness. I took a step forward at last. The movement caught his eye and he pushed himself to his feet. "This isn't—am I in a place I should not be?"

"My father owns this land but he'd not mind you resting here, I do not think."

"But something tells me this is a favorite place of yours. There's a path through the trees and a worn spot here by the water, with moss to sit on. I'll take myself off to another place."

"No," I responded to my own surprise. "I do not mean to stay. But you are welcome."

"I've been wandering the countryside. Here, in some way, I'm reminded of home." His lackluster eyes seemed melancholy.

"You've not found a place to stay."

"'Tis just as you said. There's little enough for the folk here to do, and no shillings, certainly, to give to a stranger who would do the work they themselves can manage. I must go to Edinburgh, or Glasgow, I fear. Or list as a soldier in the end."

"Many have done that. Or emigrated."

"And yet it takes coin to travel to the East Indies, or the West Indies. Or America." He flattened his hand against the back of his neck. "Unless I sell myself to a landowner in one of those places and become a slave."

"I can think of other things," I ventured. "Sometimes

there's a need for someone in the candlemaking in Melrose. And sometimes folk find service at one of the big houses nearby. There's Traquair House for one, which you passed on the road from Peebles. But—well, they're Catholic at Traquair. Of course you'd not have to be, but, well, you are not—you are not—that is, it would be fine if you were as well, for it's of no matter to me, but, oh dear, I've no right to ask and nay, I'm not asking..."

"I'm not Catholic," he said, and smiled.

"Do please forgive me. I should not have mentioned it. One does not ask a stranger, I do not think." I needed to pause before I could speak once more. "Since you're a blacksmith by trade, you might try at the smiddy in Gattonside, which you can reach by the new stone bridge. But for that you'd have to pay a toll. You can still ford the river, though. There's a place near the abbey the monks once used, which costs nought."

"The best price one can ask for!"

"Mostly there are farms and holdings of all sizes here. There might be someone who needs his cows milked and fed and bedded, or his fields tended. Though it is betwixt planting and reaping."

"I asked at the inns if someone was needed to shoe horses, but had no luck."

"There are masons, wrights, and carpenters, and millers and brewers to ask if they need an extra hand. Is there nought for you at the home you left?"

His smile faded. "My home, as one thinks of a home, is no longer there." He must have regretted this for he added, "I'm sorry. I suppose I'm letting my self-pity show. This is disgraceful. I should leave after all."

"Please, no. Obviously I'm disturbing you and it's not the other way about."

"We could sit by the water together. I've had no one to talk to for days. You're the only person I've met who hasn't gawped at me, and it feels gey welcome." I sank to the ground. His face cleared a little as he settled on a stone beside me. "You must live nearby. Is that house yours? The one they call Gilchrist House?"

I considered the building amid its oaks and wild plum trees at the top of the bank. I studied its graywacke stone walls, steep roof of slates, and tiny-paned windows. It was a house of grand proportions compared to the others in our march of Roxburghshire. "Aye."

"You're lucky then, are you not? 'Tis a fine one and I've not seen many like it. You must be happy there."

I pulled at the grass and let the breeze catch the green scraps. They floated to the surface of the water.

"I do not come from such a splendid one," he went on. "We've always had little to call our own. My father's a smith. I helped him until about a month ago. There was not enough work for the two of us, but we were able to manage."

"Yet you left."

"Aye, I left." He sighed and shook his head, looking away. "I have to, at times, accept ale and porridge from gudewives as I make my way from one town to the next. It is a sore wound to my pride. I'm not a beggar. Yet some days I must be one. Which is worse, I do not ken. That, or the ache of hunger."

There were faint hollows under his eyes and I wondered if they had always been there. "Perhaps living in Edinburgh or Glasgow would not be as dreadful as you imagine it."

"Mayhap. But if I do not find work then there are only the two other choices left to me. Would I rather be an indentured servant, or serve the King in one of the new Scots regiments and fight for my living? Either one would give me food."

I could not help but compare him to a starving little animal, a kit perhaps, or a pup whose eyes say what his tongue cannot, and the instinct was aroused in me to come to his aid. I said, "I'll bring you something to eat."

He looked up sharply. "I've enough. If you think I'm looking for sympathy and hoping to gain something from it, I'm sorry. I'm not looking for aught."

"But—I'd like to help you."

"Sharing the waterside with you is more than enough. It feeds my spirit, which has been as hungry as my stomach."

More grass fluttered from my fingers to the mischievous current, and I said, "When will you be leaving?"

"The morrow? 'Tis foolish of me to stay. I'm starving and the nights are lonely but at least I'm free, and not within the walls of a city, nor at the beck and call of a sergeant or a master.

I'll search again, and be away the next."

"I'd be interested in hearing. If you find something. Even if you do not. I'd like to say farewell."

"And I'd like to see you again, Miss. I do not ken your name."

"Keeley."

"Can you come here in the early evening?"

"I'll come."

"I'd better be away. If I'm to be finding aught for my supper it will have to be afore nightfall."

The severity of his situation struck me anew. Perhaps someday I would find myself in similar difficulties.

He nodded his head in farewell. "Good night, Keeley."

"Good night..."

"Davy," he supplied.

I watched him walk away. I was impatient for the hours to pass.

"I've found nought," Davy told me when we found each other on the bank. "I did hear at the inn today that a man named Matt MacGivers injured his foot and needed help with his sheep and cows, but when I saw him he told me his son will have a go. I'm afraid it raised my hopes for a while."

I was sorry to hear this and murmured my sympathy. From a fold in my skirt I brought two barley scones and a slab of strong, golden cheese. Davy seemed upset by my generosity and at first would not take the food. "Go on," I urged. "I cannot bear to see anyone go hungry."

We sat by the water. He began to eat with deliberate slowness, but I could tell how deep was his hunger by the way he quickened his bites. I wished I had brought ten times more. When he finished I peered at him, and trying to keep my voice even, said, "Then tomorrow you'll go along to Edinburgh?"

He pulled at a brown thread at the knee of his breeks. "I've been thinking. I like it here. There's something here that makes me feel at home. Perhaps I've not enough patience. If I stay long enough, I'm thinking something will appear."

"Oh aye," I agreed.

"Tomorrow I'll go a bit farther but stay in this parish."

My happiness seemed suddenly fragile. "You will tell me what happens."

"Indeed I will. You've been a friend to me."

We said farewell and I rushed home, apprehensive about being discovered missing, but it was clear no one had given any thought to my whereabouts.

I saw him the next day and the next. The waiting betwixt times seemed endless, but whenever we were together I forgot about all the restive hours. I brought him scraps of lamb as well as oatcakes, scones, and cheese. After some indecision he always fell upon the food, which gave me a peculiar happiness. He did not seem eager to go on to Edinburgh and this added to my joy.

On the third day I said to him, "Then you're to remain another day."

Davy chewed the last of his bread and grinned. "I've yet to try a bit farther south. There are more farms there, I heard, and someone may want to hire a laborer. Even if it is only for a few days I might be given a place to sleep and a bowl of gruel. That is, I suppose, all one really needs out of life."

"You must miss your home."

The man's smile withered. He gazed first at the ground and then at me. His appearance had become familiar to me by now: the light brown hair, slightly wavy, caught in a hide thong at his neck, the thin cheeks, stubbled chin. I felt I had known him longer than for just a few days. I could see the sorrow in his face again and was filled with remorse because I had put it there. He said, "Thank you again for bringing the food. You ken I do not want you to, but I'm grateful all the same." In a different tone he declared, "I have something for you." He thrust a hand into his pocket, seemed to retrieve something, and hid his fist behind his back.

"Something for me?"

"I made it for you." Biting his lip, he brought the hand out toward me and unfolded his grimy fingers. In the callused palm lay an intricately carved figure of a lamb. I gasped. It was exquisite. At his encouragement I took the carving and turned it from side to side.

"What is it made from?"

"Heather root."

"Have you made a great many of these?"

"I used to spend my evenings shaping such things. My da showed me how when I was a laddie. I thought I might make you one. Do you like it, Keeley?"

"I do!" I cried. "It's so small, and yet so perfect. Are you certain you want me to have it?"

His fingers came over mine and enclosed the wee lamb in my own fist. "I made it for you," he repeated, and suddenly he let me go.

I smoothed the figure's surface with my fingertip, thinking of the warmth of his fingers. "How wonderful that your father passed this skill on to you."

The pure evening sunlight reflected from the river and made our spot glow with warmth. He squinted at the shallow water and inched a bare toe toward it before he continued.

"He's the reason I left Aberfoyle and began looking for a new life on my own. He was fond of beating my mother. One day last month he struck her and she fell against the hearthstones and died."

The muscles in my middle contracted.

"Many times I tried to protect her from him. But I was not always there. I should've been there the last time. I might've shielded her. 'Twas always when he drank. He was o'erfond of the whisky, and it made him bitter. When I came home and found her, he told me she'd fallen herself, but guessing the truth was simple. After she was buried I left. I could not bear to look at him. I could not bear to look at my own father."

"I'm so sorry," I said. There was a catch in my voice.

"I ne'er thought trying to forget would be one of the most difficult things a person could do. Hammering iron, struggling with an ox, laboring amongst rocks all day. They're easy compared with trying to forget something, or someone, half of you does not want to forget."

Without knowing how it happened, our hands joined. I did not quail from the strength I felt in his.

"You understand," he said in surprise.

I nodded. His hand tightened, and so did mine.

The days passed in a dream. I shared late-night suppers with my father but my mind was hardly ever at table. When I knitted my father's fine hose or spun wool I dreamt, and when I sat with a book in my lap in the library or counted my secret hoard of money I dreamt. I stopped marveling that a stranger had entered my life and became obsessed with plans for how I might see him again. Davy. He filled my mind. I clenched my hands every time I found myself wondering if he would leave Melrose.

One rainy day I dashed to the river, blinking away droplets that landed on my lashes. He was there, huddled in his thin gray coat, but he smiled broadly when he saw me.

"Good morning, Miss Keeley," he called as I reached him. He bowed like a gentleman, and I curtseyed in return. "A grand morning, is it not?"

"Is it?" I said, and laughed.

"It is indeed. For I've found employment. And I will be living in Melrose."

Happiness was so sudden I let my shawl fall from my hair. "That is wonderful!"

"I must return to a flock of sheep before long. Where might we find some shelter?"

Toward the house was a stand of ancient yews. "Come," I said. We ran together through the rain and up the hill to the trees. The bark on the twisted trunks and branches was black with moisture, but under the boughs the earth was dry and we crept underneath gratefully. I stood with my back to him, catching my breath, looking out at the bright, verdant pastures and hills. Very close to me Davy observed, "How good life sometimes feels. The smell of the earth and the rain! Today I'd not trade it for any amount of sun. I'm thinking all could be well again."

I turned. "What is the work you found?"

"Watching Matt MacGivers's sheep after all, and caring for his cows and that. 'Twas proving too difficult for his son who's beasts of his own. I've been given a place to sleep by the lumcheek, and food as my wage. 'Tis enough."

I inhaled the refreshing air. It was laden with the cool scent of grass and meadowsweet and the wet soil beneath. He was right. All could be well.

"Keeley," he said, lightly touching my hand. "I feel as if I've known you all my life."

My throat thickened and I did not know if I could swallow. But I was not afraid. With Mr. Fergusson I had been afraid. With Malcolm I had been sickened. I did not give either of them much thought now. I only said, "It is that way for me as well."

There seemed to be no reason why we should deny the direction in which our emotions carried us. He bent his head and placed his mouth on mine, a feather-light touch that destroyed the road back to simple friendship for all time.

Wi' a' that's mine I'd pairt...
Lassie o' the Witchin' E'e (Trad.)

Chapter Six

The color of my whole existence changed. I was euphoric knowing the person I thought about constantly was thinking about me in turn. Now that I no longer needed to worry about where Davy spent his nights, if he had enough to eat, and indeed if I would ever see him again, I was completely happy. Father didn't matter, Mrs. Taggart didn't matter. The only concern of any significance was when I might see Davy next.

He tended the sheep all day, and I, in blatant disobedience to Father's rules, threw my conscience away and spent countless hours with him in isolated pastures. My despair at my parent's edict that I no longer walk unaccompanied seemed foolish in retrospect. Obviously Father did not care what I did, for he ignored me as much as he ever had. I was able to complete my baking and meet Mrs. Dundas, tend to my duties late at night and early in the morning, and keep Mrs. Taggart so occupied with her own chores I'm sure she never knew whether I was in the house or out of it. I pretended to spend a great deal of time in my bedchamber and became quite adept at sneaking down the back stairs and escaping.

"You do not mind this?" Davy asked me once whilst we roamed the hillside for the second time that day. There had been a downpour the night before, a danger for heavy sheep that wriggled upside down in an effort to relieve the itch of hot, loosened wool. Several had become couped and we had overturned them together. I was covered with wet tufts of fleece.

"I sleep very well at the end of a day," I answered.

"After rolling sodden sheep, looking for sickness and rotting teeth?" he prodded.

"I'd rather be here with you than anywhere in the world."

He gazed at me. "So would I."

The solemnity of the moment was broken when a jackdaw lit upon the back of the nearest ewe. Back and forth the black bird went, keeping its balance on the oblivious animal, its bright eyes searching—and quick beak darting—for ticks and lice on head and rump alike. It was impossible not to laugh.

He was fond of gifting me with wee things he found or made: a brightly colored feather, a quartz stone polished by the Tweed to spherical perfection—a Fairy Stone, he called it—and a fanciful dragon's head he had etched into a piece of horn.

One day, after I watched him inspect the cleft foot of a lame Cheviot for scald and learnt it was nothing more than an injury caused by a sharp-edged stone, Davy trotted behind a tree, swooped to grab something, and presented me with a bristling bouquet of wild flowers so immense the leaves and tendrils swept the ground.

"This is to help you forget yesterday," he said.

The day before he had looked up at me from the underside of a sheep and pronounced the dreaded words, "Foot rot." He had turned the bulky ewe upside down, and I'd aided him in holding her firmly whilst he cut away the infected part as Matt MacGivers had taught him, being careful not to nick the healthy portion of the foot. The infection had exuded a foul smell, and my heart had gone out to the poor beast. Only minutes later Davy had treated two ewes that had been the victims of flystrike. It had been difficult to watch him clear away the infestations of maggots that had set in.

I took the flowers into my arms and buried my nose amongst the blooms. The mix of fragrances took away all memory of yesterday's trials. "They're grand," I said, and smiled at him. "You've found some of my favorites. Mallow." I aimed my nose toward the pink, dark-veined blossoms, and then at the handfuls of purple, red-violet, yellow, and white. "Milkwort, vetch, buttercups, and lady's smock. You've been everywhere to collect these."

"You ken the names of them all?" he asked in amazement.

"As well as my own."

"You must teach me! I ne'er noticed flowers much before. I look at the ground and I see weeds and sometimes bonny colors. Now look at that," he urged, pointing exuberantly beside my bare toes. "What is that? Do you ken?"

"It's yellow pimpernel."

"Yellow pimpernel," he echoed, staring at the starry flowers in an obvious effort to commit them to memory.

"My mother taught me their names," I said, remembering. We had often picked bouquets of flowers bigger than our hands could hold and I had memorized the names of all of them. Sometimes Mamma had painted watercolors of them, and I'd watched in amazement whenever her tiny brushstrokes of indigo and vermilion became blossoms trapped in paper. "Some grow only in bogs, and others only in hedges or meadows. There are some that bloom early, like primrose and wood sorrel. Many are used for healing, like colt's-foot. And some are braw but poisonous, like wood anemone, foxglove, and cow parsley."

Davy said, "Some that are pleasing to the eye and dangerous to the skin. Thistles, gorse."

I laughed with him. He reached down and plucked a slender stem of the pimpernel. With fingers barely touching me, he placed the flower behind my ear; I could feel him pull a lock of my hair over to secure it. There were no sounds but the rush of the water and the bleating of the sheep. And far away, the drumming of a snipe. "Someday I'll show you some very odd flowers," I said, scarcely above a whisper. "Sundews, that catch insects. Butterburs. Lords-and-ladies."

"I will learn aught you teach me."

"I've a book of flowers my mother had. I could lend it to you."

He ran a finger over the blooms I held between us. "Little good would it do. I do not read."

"Oh. My father was strict about my lessons. I was made to read a great deal." I made a sour face. "Some of the books were not very enjoyable."

"What did you read, Keeley, when you were growing?"

The titles floated in my brain. We sat on stones and I recited the words from the oft-thumbed volumes. "*Essays on the Original Genius of Homer. Sermons* by Laurence Sterne. *Moral and Political Dialogues. The History of the Decline and Fall of the Roman Empire.* And I must not forget one of my least favorites." I pretended to be a stiff politician and said pompously, "*A Historical Dissertation Concerning the Antiquity of the English Constitution.*"

"You've read these books, no doubt great big things bound in nowt-hide with gilt letters upon their covers. And I, I do not ken some of the words you just said."

"There's one you might like. *The History of Scotland.* I could read some of it to you."

A smile quivered at the corners of his lips. "Read to me. Will you do that?"

"I'll bring a book with me the next time, the next time we..."

"I cannot meet you for another two days or so, hinny. Mr. MacGivers is shedding the sheep and I must gather and bring them to the men with the shears." Shedding was a vital part of the year, quite dependent upon the weather, for wet or damp fleeces rotted in the sacks into which they were packed. My father was always on edge during shearing time and rode restlessly from Clary to Whitestone and back again, watching the shearers and the men who rolled the fleeces as they were lifted away, counting the tight sacks that were sewn shut and readied to be carried to his mill. I was sure Mr. MacGivers went through the same agony. "'Twill be the Thursday afore I can meet you again," Davy clarified.

I hid my face in the flowers and smiled. "I'll bring Robertson's *History*, and the flower book." I peered at him through the blossoms.

"And read to me," he repeated, as if he had been told he was about to inherit a thousand golden guineas.

The flock loved sweet patches of green grass, but it was Davy's responsibility to move the sheep from time to time so they would not graze too heavily in one spot or spread disease amongst themselves. On Thursday we took the animals to another pasture edged by geans. Together we examined udders and checked for injured or infected teats, and finally settled ourselves under one of the trees to watch for foxes that liked nothing better than a breakfast of young lamb.

I opened the book I had brought and read passages about Scotland's past. He seemed entranced by the sound of my voice and listened without a word. His arms, powerful yet gentle, rested round me; sometimes his fingers absently twisted strands of my hair.

When I came to the end of a passage he said into my ear, "There are times I find myself thinking, I wonder if she's going to tell me I can have a wish. One fine wish."

I laughed. "I have no power to grant wishes."

"Ah, but then you might. You remind me of the lass in the story about the piper of Windy Ha'."

"I've not heard that story."

"You do not know the tale? You remind me of the lass. She was a bonny stranger with a voice likened to silver bells. A farmer's son met her as he was coming home from cutting peats. He was completely enchanted by her. And before long, she offered him his greatest wish."

"And what was that?"

"He longed to be a piper," he went on after kissing my hair. "The best piper in the world. Suddenly she was handing him a set of bagpipes, all gold and velvet, and telling him his wish was granted. The lass made him pledge, though, to seek her again in the same place in a year's time so he might play for her."

"Did he agree, Davy?"

"Of course. He began to play and he was amazed at his skill. He could play tune after tune. He became famous the world over. He traveled and he played, and he could not have hoped for a better life. But the time came when he realized a year had passed. He went back to where he'd first met the sweet lass. And she was there. She was dressed all in silver. He played for her and she danced, and again he was enchanted. He followed her as she danced, playing his pipes, and drew ever closer to some caves at the seaside. She danced into a cave and he followed her, not even aware he was going in. And, so the tale goes, he was ne'er seen again."

"The lass. Who was she?" I gasped.

"A Queen. Queen of the Fairies. 'Tis said it was Midsummer Night he disappeared. And if you go to those caves at midnight on Midsummer you can hear the lad playing his pipes, still the bonniest music. But you must take care you do not go too close. You could also be led into the cave and be held there ever more."

"She does not sound like a good person."

"But she was, was she not? She came from nowhere and gave the lad happiness. She reminds me of you."

I turned to him, questioning him with a look. I lifted a finger and traced the side of his face, watching his eyes. I brought my mouth closer and he took my lips in his. When I shut my eyelids, my body pressed itself against him in an effort to ease an unfamiliar discomfort in tendon and muscle. One of his hands squeezed my leg, moved slightly across my thigh, and caused further, unforeseen twinges to ripple through me. He shifted his weight and pulled me against him.

He made a groan in his throat and thrust his fingers deep into my hair. His mouth was insistent, and when I responded with greater abandonment his arms and fingers held me tighter. His body pressed hard against me. His breathing quickened. "Ah lass," he said when he slid his mouth away and put his lips on my cheek and neck. Between kisses he whispered, "It could be wonderful. Betwixt us. God's Blood, if only..." He seemed to catch himself, and became still.

"What? If only what?" I asked dreamily, opening my eyes.

Slowly, warily, he pulled himself away and brought my head to his shoulder. "It's nothing. I was only blathering. But we must be careful, Keeley, oh so careful," he added, smoothing my hair. He sounded sad.

"Careful?" My twinges and stabbings remained. They vibrated within me, untended.

His answer was to gingerly rest his cheek against mine and give a shuddering sigh. For the rest of the day he did not kiss me again, though I wished he would.

We talked about everything. I was able to relate memories of my mother, describe my life to him, and trust him with thoughts that hitherto had only lain anxiously unspoken in my mind, including my plan to earn enough money to leave Melrose. He, too, was able to confide in me the recollections of his mother and the confusion about his father. He missed his mother just as I missed mine. He talked about his nightmares, tortured dreams in which his mother begged his protection. Sometimes, holding each other close, we aimlessly wandered the slopes and fields surrounded by clean and snowy ewes and their happy, two-month-old lambs. The leftover warmth of the day hung about our shoulders and the encroaching pools of cooler evening air encircled our feet. It was summertime, the fruits of the earth were ripening, and time, for the moment, was still.

With laughter in my throat one day I sang to him the verses from "Blow Away the Morning Dew."

> *He looked high, he looked low,*
> *He cast an under look;*
> *And there he saw a fair pretty maid*
> *Beside the wat'ry brook.*
> *Cast over me my mantle fair*
> *And pin it o'er my gown;*
> *And, if you will, take hold my hand,*
> *And I will be your own.*

"Are we folk living in a song?" he said.

"It seems we must be."

"There's no doubt you're a fair pretty maid. All that remains is for you to hold out your hand." He took my trembling hand in his. "And now," he said, "you are my own."

I believed I was.

I tried to join him every day. At times the weather made it impossible, and I was still careful about disappearing for too long a time. I spun wool like a maddened fiend late into the evenings. I rose early to brew our ale, to milk the cow, and to heat the smoothing-iron and press linen with the stone's flat surface. The most difficult part was behaving as if nothing were different in my life. Outwardly, I was the same quiet Keeley; inwardly, my heart soared. I had found a secret love, a disguised prince who had come to life out of one of my mother's tales. I did not know how I had lived without him in the past. Neither could I envision the future without him.

On Mondays I was always eager to find him, for Sundays were devoted to the kirk, reading the Scriptures, and reciting the Catechism for my father as usual.

The weather was fine one certain Monday and I was impatient to be out of the house and away. I fed corn to the hens, gathered their eggs, and ascertained that Father was gone for the day. I flung my shawl over my shoulders and grabbed up a basket, planning to return later with a fine harvest of Moncrieff Pippins as a tangible excuse for my absence.

Mrs. Taggart sauntered out of the kitchen and watched me. "So. You're off again to see your lad."

My hand halted an inch from the door latch. "What did you say?"

"You heard me, I'm sure."

"I know nought about what you speak."

"You've been seen together. Many times. Someone saw fit to tell the minister yesterday, though whoever it was feart your father's wrath, it seems, and took an indirect route. There was a letter, left on his sill. And likewise, Reverend Andrews told me, not your father."

The import of her words struck me with the force of a hurled stone. Across the room I could only stare at her, feeling the blood leaving my head. A kitten's black paw was reaching out of her pocket and batting at a loose thread.

"And I've not yet decided if I will tell your father. He certainly deserves to be told. A man should ken, do you not think, that his daughter has sinned and is in need of salvation?"

All I could think of was Davy and how this would affect him.

"I'll have to pray for strength, though," Mrs. Taggart said with lips beginning to curl, "if I dare to be the one telling him, him an elder in the kirk, what his child has become."

"How do you dare say this to me?"

"Time to have second thoughts, is it not? You'd have done better to have favored me these past years. Whatever happens to you now you'll no doubt deserve."

My hand grasped the latch at last and I burst outside. There was no need for any surreptitious wandering about the grounds before I slid away to the pastures. I dropped the basket and ran toward the low-lying fields with feet that hardly felt the earth. I continued running even when cramps in my side became almost too harsh to bear. I reached the summit of a hill. Below me was Davy's figure, leaning against a knotted stick amidst the grazing flock. I sailed down the slope calling his name. He looked up and smiled at first, but upon seeing my face he let go of his stick and began to trot toward me.

When he caught me in his arms I held onto him and smothered my breaths against his shoulder. He put a hand up to my hair and demanded, "What is it, my love? What's happened?"

I left the solace of his embrace and gazed up at his beloved face. "Mrs. Taggart has discovered I've been coming to see you."

His lips fell open.

"My father will never be convinced we've done nought wrong."

He did not seem able to speak.

"It is over," I went on. "I'll never see you again."

"Has she seen us together?"

Grateful that he said something at last, I answered "Someone else has. Someone has written a letter to the minister. He told our housekeeper about it because he is afraid of my father."

He lifted his eyes to sweep the horizon as if that very

someone was watching still.

"She'll tell him," I said. "Now that she's tasted her power over me she'll not wait long to tell him."

"She's not that brave, from what you tell me. You can ignore her sneck-drawing ways."

"She will tell Father."

He drew me close again and in the darkness of my mind I could see Father's contorted face. His fury had been barely kept in check when I had refused to entertain Malcolm and the Ramsays. What his reaction would be to the news that I had disobeyed his wishes, made an intimate friend of a stranger, and caused the neighboring people to talk about me was not difficult to envision. Every moral of his would be affronted. I had gone against every discipline with which I had been raised, and at the pinnacle of my disgrace would be the question of my chastity and the kirk's needling interest.

"Do not be afeart, lass. There's the two of us now, not just the one. Perhaps 'tis just as well this has come. You ken how I feel about you." I waited fretfully whilst he took my hands in his. "I love you, Keeley. I'll not be made to feel shame for something as right as that. Do you imagine this betwixt us is merely a flirtation? It is time your father was told. He'll have to be told if we're to be man and wife."

"Davy."

"You do not need to be explaining what his reaction will be. Perhaps 'twas foolish of us to spend this much time together, but we'd have been forbidden otherwise. I suppose 'tis no surprise we've been seen together. Your father will be furious, but I'm thinking he might be less so if he hears of this from you and me."

I twisted a pinch of his shirt between my fingers. "I did not think you'd want to marry me."

"Is it not what you, too, want?"

"Oh aye."

"I'll not be forced away. And I'll not allow you to be punished. We're going to be together. Always." He kissed me lightly and I fell under the spell of his determination. I had to think as coolly as Davy.

"I'll come to your house tonight and speak to him. He'll

not have heard about us yet from anyone else. But you must be ready. He'll no doubt throw me from the house and take his anger out on you."

"There'll be nought either of us can do then."

"Nonsense. I told you I'd not allow us to be separated. If your father will not have me, there's no choice but for you to leave. You'll hear when I come and ken what happens. Before I leave I'll signal you. You may have to come out by the window but we'll fly from Melrose to a place where your father will ne'er find us, and we'll be wedded."

"Leave Melrose," I echoed in a daze. I had always believed that I would be leaving Melrose alone.

"I found work before. I can do it again. I can do aught as long as I have you beside me."

We embraced again and I found the strength I needed. "'Twill be better if you go now," he said. "We do not want to put any strain on our luck. Go home and put together a few things, and wait. We'll meet tonight, whether we've your father's blessing or not." He smiled and his pupils grew. "Will the folk not have something to talk about tomorrow?"

We parted, our arms outstretched as our hands put off the final moment of release. Our fingers pulled apart and I turned and ran away.

I remained in my room all afternoon feeling ill, but there was nothing I could do but persevere. I could hardly sit still. I changed into a well-made gown of lavender wool for traveling. I crept to Mamma's room and gazed at the clarsach for a long while, knowing that after tonight I would never see this last link with Mamma again. I apologized to her as she looked down on me from Heaven. Surely she understood why I must abandon my home and possessions. I was certain in my place she would do the same, for the sacrifice of the clarsach was but a small price to pay for a lifetime of happiness. I was not unafraid of my mysterious future, I who had known nothing but a sheltered existence, but all my worries took second place to the wild and wonderful idea that Davy and I were always to be together. I sat by the window, the inside of me twisted into a thousand knots. I heard Father's return below and stiffened in my chair. I imagined the cause of every sound as it occurred. Tensely the moments passed by and the house settled back into solitude, but my heart was anything but calm.

The evening began to cool. The sky grew pale and rosy toward the horizon, and a star started to sparkle evenly in the clear heavens. Long, blue shadows stretched from the trees as rising wafts of warmth deserted the earth. At any moment Davy would be coming to introduce himself to my father and ask him if we might be betrothed. My fingers stroked the handkerchief in my lap that held all the things I could now call my own: my ivory comb, my savings, the gifts Davy had given me, one of the framed miniatures Mamma had painted of lambs on a hillside, and a lock of her hair folded in a square of linen.

The handkerchief was soft, made of Indian cotton, and I squeezed the heavy disks of the few coins that had settled to the bottom whilst I stared out into the late summer dusk, watching every minute, every hour, that crept by.

A creak came from the stairs. I sat up. The door to my room burst open and the panel struck the wall. I leapt to my feet, my bundle of belongings flying from my hands to the floor. Coins exploded from the handkerchief. Standing within the room was Father and his face was scarlet.

"May the De'il rieve you if what our housekeeper has just told me is true," he said. His tone was monotonous but strangled.

He came toward me and swept a book from the table by my bed. It spun to the floor and the crash caused me to jump again. I retreated a step, colliding with my chair. Father's attention was distracted by the last of the whirling pennies at his toe and he scooped one up, stared at it in his palm, and pinned me with his eyes.

"You lying, deceitful slut," he said. "So this is where your waywardness and disrespect have led you. At one time I thought I could trust you. At one time I thought you able to conduct yourself as a sensible adult rather than a headstrong child. Or perhaps it is not a matter of intelligence and maturity, but of cunning and slyness and compulsive dishonesty. Which is it? Do you yourself ken?" He came a step closer to me. "I rather believe it is the latter. A child with any intelligence would remember to do what it was told. You, on the other hand, have deliberately disobeyed me. I find this situation intolerable. Do you understand me? Intolerable!"

I cringed at his words. His face was inches from mine.

"There's no need to repeat to you what Mrs. Taggart told me, is there? You know every damned detail. You've been discovered meeting a man." The words threatened to choke him. "Someone left a letter for Reverend Andrews, telling him of this unsuitable behavior in one of his flock. Can you, even for a moment, imagine the shame, the humiliation, I feel? Not only to be the father of such a wanton sinner, but to have to be told by someone, someone outside our family, about your curcuddoch love-trysts! Can you imagine the loose talk that's been rampant amongst the folk here about you? It's unforgivable. As is your deplorable behavior and deceit. I curtailed your unsolicited wanderings away from the house but you flouted my request. And you've defiled yourself." He exhaled with lips that hardly moved, glanced at his hand with disgust, and hurled the penny across the room. "How many pence have you earned, then? And with how many? How much do you demand for a man to lift your skirts? I have been cursed by God! My daughter has become a whore!"

I attempted to shake my head. I had to try to make him understand. But he gave me no time to say anything. His anger quickened within him and began to burn out of control.

"I would ken who they are. I want their names. I want to know who this last one is!"

"Please, Father..."

"I wish to God I were not your father! Tell me who the lad is. I'll have it from you, Keeley. And now."

"You do not understand. He loves me..."

He struck a blow on the side of my face, causing my head to knock against the wall. A blow to my other cheek just missed my eye. I could not see, for a shimmer of blackness floated before me. I could hear his rasping voice say, "You're a harlot just like your mother afore you, and I'll not countenance such fornication from anyone in my house!"

Dimly I saw him move to my clothes press. "Is this what you wore when you went to him? When you lay wi' him?"

He grabbed a gown and ripped the fabric from neck to hem. He reached for more and lengths of violet, cream, and russet tumbled onto the floor. "And where was it? In the fields, they say. You lay in the field wi' him like a cur in heat!" He took a long, fierce look at me and shook his head, breathing through his nostrils. "Mrs. Taggart!"

She sidled into my room from the corridor.

"My razor!" he threw at her. "Fetch me my shaving razor, woman."

I realized I was on my hands and knees, and raised myself in time to see Father scraping together the pound notes that had fallen out of my handkerchief and throwing them in the fire. Mrs. Taggart returned, holding her hand outstretched, not wanting to look at me or Father.

"Losh!" she wailed as Father snatched the razor. "Losh!"

He grasped my hair with two hands, pulling it together. He twisted a waist-long hank of hair up beside my head and began hacking. Sheaves of brown hair spilt about me in ragged lengths. I dared not move as I screamed. His hand with the silver blade hovered inches from my throat, ears, and neck, and the razor rasped again and again until his hand was empty. My chin was locked in his fist. He held the steel inches from my face. He raised the blade to sweep it across my cheek.

"Losh!" Mrs. Taggart screamed. "May God help us, Master, you must not!"

Father's hand began to shake. His mouth trembled as well. He threw the razor out into the passage where it clattered away in a flashing spiral. "Will he want you still, I wonder?" he growled, but his voice was of a higher pitch than before, as if tears obstructed his throat. "Will any man want you?"

I heard his heavy steps and Mrs. Taggart's lighter, shuffling ones. The slam of my door sounded like a crack of thunder, and the metallic churn of the key in the outside lock was a dismal finish.

My hand found its way to my mouth, and a finger touched blood where a tooth must have cut my lip. I sank down to the floor again. My hand fell on my hair. Skeins of it slid along the carpet at my touch. Cold drops of blood appeared on my other arm and I discovered a slippery wound on my ear.

The tears that came eased my terror somewhat, but in the end held little comfort. I pulled myself up onto the chair by the window. "Where are you, Davy?" I called into the twilight. I would be leaving this house tonight. There was no need to ever see my father again.

I crawled to the fireplace and threw to the flames every leaf of my diary on which was written Davy's name. I watched as the pages curled and turned dark and disintegrated.

I waited by the open window, gripping the casement with white fingers and watching as a dozen more stars sprinkled themselves across the pale sky. The air grew cooler. The house was quiet.

I did not move from my chair as I waited and waited. Midnight approached. My lip swelled and my eye throbbed. But still Davy did not come. My foreboding increased in pitch with every hour that passed but there was no way to relieve it and no remedy for the pain beginning to grow in my heart and mind and body. Morning came, the birds sang nearby, and I looked out with dry, swollen eyes at a new day.

And still, Davy did not come.

A-down in the meadows the other day
A-gath'ring flow'rs both fine and gay
A-gath'ring flowers, both red and blue,
I little thought what love could do.

O Waly, Waly (Davis)

Chapter Seven

y fears proliferated as the days passed. I was shut up in my room. Isolated. Below my window a bored Young James paced, occasionally glancing at the horizon. There were no pebbles tossed at the casement, no whispers or whistles alerting me to Davy's presence. I cared little for myself; a prayer moved my lips, beseeching God to prevent Father from discovering Davy's identity and causing him injury. I did not believe such violence impossible. Doors slammed far away in the house. Father's voice reverberated, demanding food, drink, aid in removing his boots. He was seething. His wrath charged the atmosphere with lightning strokes that both crackled and ripped.

Mrs. Taggart took away my hair and spoilt gowns and brought a threadbare dress of her own. She draped it on my bed along with a message from my father. "This is what you are expected to wear from now on," she said.

She also hunted for every pound note that had missed destruction in the fire and every coin that had wheeled and spun across my floor. She kept them for herself, I knew—the assortment of silver pennies, sixpence, farthings, and pounds I had struggled for years to earn.

One morning I lifted my head from the cradle of my arms when the scrape of Mrs. Taggart's key was so loud I believed she had thrust the metal rod into my very ear. The door swung open and she stood to the side, allowing Young James to sidle into my bedchamber. Red-faced, unable to look at me, he hammered boards across my window shutters.

I feared my father had become a madman.

Mrs. Taggart came once a day to bring me porridge and water and to empty my chamber pot. Though she spoke hardly a word, she could not deprive herself of staring. At first I avoided her gawking, but as the mornings came and went my lassitude began to burn away. One day I reached for the little glass on my dressing table and turned the polished surface upward. In the dimness loomed a swollen mouth, a blackened eye, and purple mottling on cheeks. Ragged hair splayed out from behind my ears and hung at the sides of my neck.

The person in the glass was not Keeley Allanson. Whither she had gone, when she might return, were not matters I could bear to consider. But when Mrs. Taggart gaped at me the next time, I felt flames ignite in the muscles of my back and shoulders. They skimmed along my neck and burst through my eyes. She melted under their onslaught, placing the wooden cog of porridge before me and backing out of the room.

Sometimes I fell on a corner of my bed where I hovered in a state of exhaustion, sleeping an unrestful sleep poisoned by violent dreams, or collapsed at my writing table where I could just glimpse the ground below through a crack in the boards. Watching never brought Davy to me, but I watched nonetheless, unable to accept the futility of hope. I did not weep during my vigil at the crack until the day I witnessed the knacker man leading Benjamin away with a stout length of rope. My father had sold my horse for its meat and hide. I watched in disbelief and tears began to fill my eyes. I wept on my feet, I sobbed on my knees, I screamed through the slats for Benjamin to come back as if he could hear me, as if he had the power to decide his own fate, as if the man wearing blood-stained rags would take pity and let him go. I called to my horse and screamed for my father until I had no voice left.

Of course no one came near my door until silence laid cold and heavy for a day and a night. And when Mrs. Taggart opened it I climbed to my feet and bolted past her. Father was standing at the bottom of the staircase.

His lips were stiff when he spoke. "One more step and you'll be out of my house for good."

"You cannot send Benjamin to be slaughtered," I cried out, but only a whisper was expelled from my inflamed throat. "You must get him back! Do with me what you will but you cannot, cannot harm Benjamin!"

He began to climb up the steps, two at a time. "You dare tell me what to do! I say to you, return to your room or I'll help you down the stairs. And you'll not live to climb them again."

I retreated before his fist. His whitened knuckles were the last I saw of him as Mrs. Taggart shut my door in my face.

His voice bellowed, "Mrs. Taggart, can you not do your duty? Let her loose again and it's *your* neck I'll feel between my fingers!"

I sat in the chair by the window, sometimes dozing, sometimes jumping up with a hammering heart when Mrs. Taggart shuffled in to retrieve my congealed bowl and replace it with a new one.

In uneasy half-slumber I dreamt that Davy came for me and that he rode Benjamin. Upon awakening I could not remember if the dream were real or imagined, and tried to peer through the slats in the shutters to find the earth below my window. Davy was never there. And the memory of Benjamin's fate was a knife thrust into my breast.

I did not know how many days passed. The days and nights swam together in a haze unrelieved by sunlight or clock.

I pounded my door with my fists, calling for my father and

shouting for Mrs. Taggart until the edges of my hands turned purple. I tried tearing the boards from the window until my fingertips bled. I threw books and tables at the door and the window.

I visualized knocking Mrs. Taggart down in the doorway and running from the house. Father would not have to worry about my return.

One day there was commotion below.

I said out loud, "He's here!"

I strained to listen, pressing my ear at the crevice of the door and even lying on the floor where the gap between door and threshold was wider. Unrecognizable voices, footsteps, glassware clinking—the sounds were distorted by distance and the narrow crack. I waited for what seemed to be hours, stretched out on the floor with my head jammed against the bottom of the door. The daylight that pierced the shutter slats was fading into summer dusk when I perceived footsteps on the stairs. I leapt to my feet as the key rasped and the knob revolved. The panel was pushed open.

"Your father wishes to see you," Mrs. Taggart said flatly, dropping the key into her pocket.

I stared at her. I was allowed out and certainly, certainly, Davy was downstairs. I tread past her and inched down the stairs, afraid I might fall. How steep they seemed. My feet found the bottom step at last and led me into the drawing room. I squinted against the light coming in the tall windows. At the sight of my father something began to burn within me. It flared and shrank away, however, for standing beside him was not Davy but Rab Fergusson.

He was the first amongst us to move or speak. He bowed and came toward me with outstretched hands. "Crivvens," he whispered. "Miss Allanson." He stopped to examine my face.

I could imagine the picture I made. The bruises about my eye and cheekbones were no doubt yellow. I blinked in light I had not seen for days. Mrs. Taggart's gown fell ragged at my ankles. I pondered on the effect my shorn hair must have, and on the fact that I had not been given any water with which to wash, and found I did not care.

I did not take his hands and he let his drop. "Are you well?"

he asked.

"She is well able to care for herself," Father answered.

I freed my eyes from Mr. Fergusson's insistent ones. I would have given anything to be locked back in my bedchamber again. Of all the times for him to return to Gilchrist House he had chosen the worst.

Father moved to the fireplace. He sat in his chair and spoke with an air of detachment. "I've told him everything. Since the entire town of Melrose must know, it did not seem fair to deprive him of the knowledge."

Mr. Fergusson frowned.

"There is a purpose in having you brought downstairs," Father said. "It is to inform you of the solution that has been found for this God-forsaken situation. As you might guess, I have been at a loss wondering how to deal with this. I've been praying for an answer, any answer. I cannot keep you secure in your room for the rest of your life. That would be quite archaic. But neither are you to be trusted. You have brought the greatest shame upon this household that anyone could. Recovering from it will be one matter. Ensuring it does not happen again is another. Ultimately, I am responsible for you."

He sighed and drew his brows together in irritation. "I will not ask you for the name of your partner—or partners—in this folly again. Let us behave as if the whole nauseating situation is at an end. Let me put it as bluntly as I can. I no longer want you in this house. I no longer want to have to look at you."

I turned my head away.

"I have been considering sending you to Malcolm, yet now this possibility has presented itself. Despite what you have done, and what you have become, Mr. Fergusson has asked for your hand. I find no reason why I should refuse him. It will be the ideal solution for both of us. No respectable Christian in Melrose will have you now. I wish to avoid the investigation by the Kirk Session. And I do not fancy having the burden of a ruint woman on my hands, or on my son's, nor the risk of future humiliation. Do you understand what I'm saying? Mr. Fergusson wants to marry you. I regard him as somewhat of a fool for doing so, but he is the answer to my prayer. There will be no delay. I mean to speak to Mr. Andrews this evening and dispose of the matter by arranging a kirk wedding. Not a hand-fasting, nor a writ on paper with witnesses, nor one recognized by habit and repute, but a binding one in the eyes of God and the King."

As if seeking affirmation of this devastating news I whirled to Mr. Fergusson. It could not happen, it must not happen. I loved Davy, I was to marry him. Something had happened to prevent him from coming for me but it changed nothing. "I will not," I said but no sound emerged.

"You have no choice," Father returned. "That is, if you do not wish to find yourself begging for food along all the military roads in Scotland. I am giving us both an honorable solution to this problem."

"I will not marry him."

"Please," Mr. Fergusson appealed. To my father he said, "Perhaps, sir, she'd better understand if I spoke to her myself."

He considered the request and rose. "As you wish."

When we were alone Mr. Fergusson said, "He did tell me everything. But only his side of it. I want to help you. Confide in me, Miss Allanson, if it helps. Tell me. I want to save you from this. Can you not be seeing that? I'm your friend, not your enemy."

"You can do nought to help me," came my hoarse whisper.

"I can take you away from him. I can give you a chance for happiness. Did you hear what he said? He might send you to live with your half-brother. Your feelings toward him—I mind them well."

I drew an uneven breath.

"The man you've been meeting. You've surely no dream of a future with him? Your father would not permit it. He'd murder the lad if he knew who he was, and I'm thinking if you foster any hopes in that direction you'll be sadly disappointed. Turn instead to me, dear. Toward you nought has changed in my heart. I want to take you away from here and in many ways save you from yourself. Can you not see what I offer?"

"I do not want it."

"Perhaps not now, but in time you will. I'm sure of it."

I said nothing.

"If you fight it," he said, "you'll be making it worse for yourself. Your father's determined. If you force him, he'll lay waste the rest of your life. What a tragedy it would be. I ken something about you. I ken you live for your freedom, and I ken you need love. You'll find neither here, nor will you in the streets."

I turned away from him and crossed my arms at my chest, hooking my hands over my shoulders.

"Once you nursed me through an injury. Let me do the same for you," he said.

It did not matter if I assented or not. Father had made that plain. But I could not forsake Davy, and I refused to abandon my hope. I turned and met his gaze. "If you care for me, at all..."

"I've told you I do."

"Do one thing for me, I beg of you." Frustrated, I cleared my throat and tried to increase my volume but my effort was in vain. "Ask my father if we may take the gig tonight, for a short while. I do not know how many days I've been kept in my room. But—but I pine so for the fresh air."

He listened intently, watching my lips. Whatever he deduced from this request or however he felt, he did not show it. "I will ask."

"I'll be grateful to you."

"I do not ask for your gratefulness, Keeley."

I wanted to say more. Words came to my tongue and died.

He bowed his head and smiled, but it was a cheerless smile, and I could not bear it. I fled upstairs to wait.

"I ken not how I succeeded in persuading him," Mr. Fergusson told me later as he shook the reins of the carriage horse. "He's not inclined to grant you any favors the now. But I managed to have him agree to this by reminding him that soon you'll be my concern, not his."

I was hardly aware of him talking beside me. The pain in my heart from thoughts of Benjamin, and my impatience to learn what had become of Davy, were all-consuming. Mr. Fergusson drove us out from the house, skirted the village, and followed the lines of dykes across the pastures. I was not interested in the air or the landscape. As we traveled, the tension became palpable between us and the only sounds were my broken voice directing him to Matt MacGivers's farm and the rhythm of hooves upon turf.

We stopped when the buildings appeared in the distance. For several moments we sat and regarded the clay biggin roofed with thatch, the dung heaps and drying stacks of hard, black peats surrounding the stone barn, and the three cows chewing placidly near a byre waiting for their evening milking.

"'Tis where he lives," Mr. Fergusson said. It was not a question.

For the first time I was full of shame. "I had to come."

The horse threw its head and blew through its nostrils. Mr. Fergusson said, "I'll come with you."

"No."

He climbed down from the gig as if he'd not heard me and took my hand to help me. He looped the reins about a young plane tree. The walk toward the small, mean house seemed to last forever. Mr. Fergusson knocked on the door-post and stood several paces away. My blood thudded in my ears. An old woman came to the open doorway to peer at my face. Hers was brown and lined, and gray wisps of hair were tucked under a soiled cap.

"Are you Mrs. MacGivers?" I shouted so that my voice could be heard.

"Aye?"

So aware was I of her unchecked curiosity and Mr. Fergusson's presence at my back that I could barely open my mouth. "I'm looking for Davy." I had to say it three times before she could hear me.

"He's not here. Not any longer."

"He's gone?"

"He was the best helper me Matt ever had. He took fine care of the animals. He promised he'd be helping wi' the haying. We were lucky to have the lad at all, I suppose, but aye, aye, he's gone."

"I do not understand."

"Oh, aye. Gone for days. It was unco strange. He came, needing a place, as hungry as a man could be. And he left just as he came, wi' no warning at a'. Me Matt's got a bad foot. Now he maun tend the sheep and the cows himself. He was a canny lad, though, lass. I miss his company at the ingleside, when he sang and told his stories every night."

"But when did he go? Where did he go?"

She apparently understood and replied, "I do not ken. He seemed to be here to stay. And then home he came one afternoon, leaving the sheep and all, and said he was away."

"When—when?"

"It must have been oh, five days ago, I'm thinking. The day after the Sabbath. In the afternoon. He put together his few things and bade me and Matt a farewell and took the track to Galashiels, whistlin' a bricht, braw tune. And that was all. No reason, or aught, did he tell us, for a' that I thought we understood each other well. I still cannot figure it."

"My father," I whispered. "Finlay Allanson. Was he here? Did he come looking for Davy?"

"Nay, I've ne'er seen him here. Not him."

"Thank you, marm," Mr. Fergusson said. "You've been of help to us. Good night."

Her puzzlement could not be hidden as she returned the farewell.

Mr. Fergusson led me away. I think I would have forgotten how to walk if it had not been for him. I felt him looking at me intently, willing me to respond to him.

Neither of us said anything on the ride back home.

Father was waiting for us. He asked, "Did you enjoy your exercise?"

"Very much, thank you sir," Mr. Fergusson said.

"I have just returned myself. Mr. Andrews has agreed to post the banns. To save her soul he will perform the ceremony between you without delay, without informing the Kirk Session of her waywardness. It will be in three weeks."

It did not matter. Nothing mattered.

I was kept locked in my bedchamber. It was just as well. I had no desire to be under Father's constant supervision or to see Mr. Fergusson when he came from the inn. I avoided the chair by my boarded window, choosing instead to lie upon my bed looking at nothing. There the time passed slowly but it did pass, irrevocably.

One afternoon Mrs. Taggart brought me downstairs and left me with Mr. Fergusson, who directed me out into the empty garden. Auld James the gardener had been diligent in the past few weeks it seemed, with his pruning, clipping, and raking. The air was laden with moisture. I remembered other days like this, days when Davy and I had been together, and I turned away from the memories.

When we were near the apple trees Mr. Fergusson's feet slowed and his hand halted me. "I'd a visitor at The Black Horn today. A Mrs. Dundas."

I could not help myself. I lifted my face to his.

"Aye," he went on. "She wants to see you."

"My father forbade me. A long while ago." I was surprised to find that my throat had healed somewhat; that I could raise it above a whisper.

"She knows the truth behind all. I've arranged a meeting for you and she's waiting just beyond the garden. Come."

I walked with him in disbelief, but sure enough, near the cherry trees where the garden swept downhill toward the Tweed, I saw her plump figure in the black shawl. She came toward me. "My dearie," she said, and clasped my hands. "Both Reverend Andrews and I were at Peggy Kilpatrick's bedside this morning. He'd learnt she was ill wi' childbed fever, and I was there tending her. I heard, of course, about your marriage, but the things the Reverend told me in confidence caused me a great worry, and I could not rest 'til I saw you and gave you a fond farewell."

Mr. Fergusson had left us and was sitting on a settle far away, his feet apart and his forearms leaning on his thighs. Mrs. Dundas put her arm around me and began to take me away over the lawn, talking all the while.

"Oh, how I mind those long-ago days when you'd come visit me. We both found a great deal of pleasure in them, did we not? It has ne'er been the same, meeting you for a few moments to take the scones and bannocks you made."

"I should never have stopped coming to visit you. Father would not have found out."

"You did what you thought best."

"I have been a fool. I met a lad and came to love him. I wanted to tell you about him but I never dared. But now—he's deserted me and I'm being sent away, forever."

"You'll have your own home now. Perhaps not wi' the lad you hoped, but here's a chance to be a wife and a mother, and start anew. And yon gentleman seems to care for you, dear. It may seem a tragedy to you, but I can see the hope in it."

"To be wed to a stranger..."

"In time your heart will heal itself."

"Do such things happen in truth?"

"They do. That's what's carried me through the loss of a great many bairns, and a husband, and the other disappointments as lying-in-wife. There'll always be happenings in life we've no control over. Those are the times to be bending, and accepting. Somewhere, in and amongst all the dreadfulness, will be something hopeful to cling to. And time changes us, and our thoughts. We do mend, dearie. You do not believe it now. But 'tis aye true."

"For some, perhaps."

"Your own mother knew it. Her delight in life was you. I often think of her. You brought her happiness in the midst of all her troubles."

Thinking of Mamma made me forget my current misfortune and I said to her, "She wanted to live, Mrs. Dundas. She expected to live."

"Oh aye. She wanted to see you grown. She had such plans for you. She'd have seen you go to the ladies' school in Edinburgh, to learn dancing and lace-making. She'd have found you a suitor you both loved."

I remembered Mamma's stories and the predictions she'd made for my future. My favorite had been the one in which she prophesied, "You'll have silken gowns to wear of gold, with yards of silver galloon sewn upon them, and housemaids to serve you plates of confected ginger, and gardeners to bring you baskets of violets. You'll have a lovely loch to sail a boat in, and a burn beneath your window that lulls you to sleep every night with its tumbling." Longing for her was suddenly intense. "I miss her," I said. "I have never missed her more."

"She'd want you to be happy."

I wiped the mist from my cheeks. Despite what Mrs. Dundas said I was sure I would never know happiness again.

"Your mother hoped to have many children, but 'twas not to be. Every time I was called for the lying-in, or for giving her comfort when she lost the wean early, I saw the desolation in her. But never, never did she fail to give thanks for you and to talk of her love for you. Because of you she bore all else wi' great bravery."

"She had more than the losses of bairns to bear," I blurted.

Mrs. Dundas stroked my hair. "Your da?"

"Why was he so cruel to her? At times he acted as if he hated her."

She sighed. "I'm sure he loved her."

"The other day he called me a name and compared me to her as if she'd been a disgusting creature. There was no need of it. She was the dearest, most honorable person in the world."

"Your da knew that. But—there was something for which he could not forgive her."

I stood still. "What do you mean?"

Her nostrils constricted. "I've said too much. Oh dear, your da will have me drawn and quartered if he hears I've mentioned it." Her face turned white as she glanced about us.

Uneasiness gripped me as well, and I had to confirm that the garden was still ours alone save for the brooding figure of Mr. Fergusson far away. "Will you tell me?"

"May the Lord keep me, I should not. And I dare not stay wi' you much longer, for if your da returns and finds us together he'll cause even more anguish for you."

"There's little more he could do to me."

"Even so—well, perhaps I should tell you after all. Perhaps Caitlìn would have wanted you to know."

"Did she do something terrible?"

She hesitated and tapped her cheek with her fingertips. "If I tell you 'twill prove to you that hearts do heal. Your own mother's did." The arm about my shoulders hugged me closer. "Not a word to your da?"

I nodded.

"She told me something once," she said in a softer voice. "She'd been here for a year, and was giving birth to you. She was in such pain she thought she'd die, and there were moments when I did not believe she was in her right mind. She talked to me, between her bad times. She told me the story of your da's courtship." She began walking once more, and arm in arm we trampled the summer grass. "He'd lost his first wife to the consumption. He'd a bairn who was motherless. He was looking for a new wife and a stepmother for his son. Your mother was an orphan, and for want of a home and means to support herself had become a seamstress for a barrister's wife in Dundee. She soothed the woman wi' her music as well as her sewing, and affection grew betwixt them despite their difference in ages. Since the barrister's wife had kin in Galashiels, she visited there one summer and took your mother in tow as a companion. It was in Galashiels your da met her, being an acquaintance of the woman's brother. He noticed your dear mother during a visit to the household. Eventually he courted her. When they wed, months later, 'twas for love."

"She told me so. But that is where her story always ended."

"What she said during her pains I never forgot. She said she'd had high hopes for the marriage. She'd been lonely after her parents died. She was gey young, like you. And he was stable, well-settled wi' his inheritances and his farms and looms, and he promised a comfortable existence for her. And he was besotted by her. But on their wedding night..." She looked at the river and I followed her gaze. There was a mist that could not yet be called rain, and I was thankful for both the cool air and the familiar, soothing sight of the rippling water. "Your da discovered he was not her first lover. He became enraged. 'Twas an insult to the kirk as well as his pride. And though he demanded to hear of her past and why she'd kept it from him, she said nought. He decided she was a loose woman and a liar. I gathered that from the first night onward he treated her no better than a waiting woman or an errant child. He punished her..." She cleared her throat. "He punished her for deceiving him. I hope the Lord forgives me for telling you this. What goes on between a man and his wife is a private matter, and I've no right to repeat what your sweet mother told me in confidence, on the threshold of death, or so she thought."

I ignored her guilt and prodded, "Did she tell you? About her first lover, I mean?"

"She ne'er breathed a word of him. She kept it all locked

within her. Your da never forgave her for sinning or for keeping the explanation from him. I had the feeling she'd never told anyone, nor ever would."

"She would not have wanted to hurt him. Could he not understand that, and pardon her?"

"She bore it alone. She bore the loss of her first love, and later the loss of bairns. But she had you to love. She could overcome her disappointments because of you."

Father's behavior made sense at last. And I understood why Mamma had spent so many hours with a far-away look in her moist eyes. A lost love. She had suffered one as well.

Mrs. Dundas and I began weaving our way back to the garden paths. She said, "I said nought I meant to say today, and everything I did not. I've probably only added to your greeting."

I was lost in thought and found it difficult to respond. "You have not, Mrs. Dundas. I'm glad of what you told me."

"You must try to turn what grief you bear into happiness. You may have thought of running away. To Edinburgh. To Glasgow. To find a new life. But those places are not for you, dear. You'd finish up penniless, homeless, used by men. 'Twould be the end of you, you who are so sensitive and caring a lass. Even if you went to Melrose to throw yourself on the mercy of the Kirk Session, you'd suffer the harshness of its punishment and then mayhap the pity of the town, and henceforth scratch a living in a hovel, spinning wool for your bread. Take this chance for something better."

I sighed shakily.

"You will find happiness, I've no doubt of it. Think on what I've told you about your mother. And mind that you have my blessings, my dearest Keeley. And oh! I'd nearly forgotten! I wanted to tell you about the horse your father sold to the knacker."

"Benjamin!"

"I ken how you loved the beast. I wanted to spare you. The knacker man was offered a handsome sum for your horse by Mr. Ashford and he sold it to him. Henry Sinclair is a greedy yaup, and what man could not look at that horse and ken how well it was bred and how well it had been cared for! So he made himself a fine bargain, he did. You must worry no more about him, dear. Your horse is safe."

I closed my eyes. I imagined Benjamin galloping through a field, trotting down a road, nosing a handful of oats. Though it was not I who was his rider, nor was it my hand that offered the grain, joy flickered in my heart because he was alive. I could accept losing him knowing he was unhurt and in the care of an intelligent man.

"I dare not remain," my friend said, and her touch forced my eyes to reluctantly open. "So I'll be away. Take care wi' yourself, sweet lass. I shall think of you oh so often."

I hugged her hard and she kissed my cheek. The parting between us was more painful than I could have envisioned. The frizzed, graying hair peeking out from her kertch was frosted with a layer of fine droplets and I stared at her for a long while, trying to commit her soft face and smudged brown eyes to memory. I watched her figure grow small in the translucent drizzle until I could see it no more.

Mr. Fergusson had heard nothing of what we had said, and I was appreciative of his reluctance to question me when I returned to him. He allowed me to stay in the garden long after her leave-taking, and his escort back to the house was in silence.

The day of my wedding dawned. I found myself not caring how I appeared or what occurred, there being nothing of any consequence since I had discovered Davy's desertion of me. I thought a great deal about Mrs. Dundas's visit and what I'd learnt about Mamma—and I thanked God for Benjamin's good fortune—but nothing changed the present. Alone I donned the hodden gray gown and drew a comb through unwashed hair.

Mrs. Taggart came to fetch me at the appointed hour, but as we passed by my mother's old rooms I experienced an undreamt-of horror. I knew I would never see her bedchamber or sitting room again, but my farewell glance caused my feet to freeze upon the floor. Her rooms were bare. The curtains, the pillows, the chairs, the miniatures she had painted, the clarsach. All were gone.

"Mrs. Taggart. Mamma's rooms."

"Aye?" she responded, unconcerned.

"Her things. The pictures, the clarsach."

"Aye?"

"Where are they? Where is everything? What has been done with them?"

She looked through the doors, appraising the interiors. "Burnt."

"Burnt?"

"Your father's wishes. Burnt. All of it."

"But they were her things! They've been here since she's been gone!"

"If you ask me, it's high time to be cleaning out the rooms. He ordered it last week. Young James took everything out. Dusting will be easier. It was dreadful dusting in there. I imagine," she said, lifting an eyebrow at me, "he might order yours to the same end."

Mamma's delicate pictures. Her books. The clarsach, with its lovely golden wood and carved knotwork. All consumed by the fire of Father's torch.

I saw neither the stairs nor the gig waiting for me. I was aware of Malcolm sitting beside our father wearing elegant, dark clothes, an expensive wig, and a taunting smile. Father began the drive to Melrose. The gig jerked in and out of the ruts between the rows of oaks and sycamores. There was incessant movement of sun and shadow on the verdant hills beyond. The fretted, sapphire Tweed, meandering through its vale, sparkled. Soon the horse bore us over High Street, turned left at the mercat cross in the middle of the marketplace, and traveled The Bow, the road that led to Melrose Abbey. It might have been any Sabbath Day with the three of us going to worship at the kirk. I went where I was led, I stood where I was put; I was docile and obedient. I might not have even been alive for the hollowness inside of me.

The afternoon was warm, but inside the abbey where meager light fell, the cold air was permeated with dampness and the odor of mold. I pulled my cloak close about me.

The kirk was barrel-vaulted and filled with a maze of seat-lined lofts. The scaffolds rose in the darkness like a labyrinth, supported by walls and pillars no less irregularly placed than the warren of mismatched pews on the earthen floor. The gloom nearly obliterated the ribs of the high arches and the embellishments at their junctures, as well as the remnants of medieval carvings on the capitals of the pillars. I imagined the specters of kings and monks, stonemasons, lay laborers, and soldiers swimming through the cloying air around us.

Before long, the stout, gray-wigged form of Reverend Andrews materialized beside us, more ill-at-ease now than when the parish had found him guilty of adultery several months ago. Mr. Fergusson was at his elbow dressed in a buff velvet coat and breeches of buckskin. My betrothed stood out amongst the other men. He smiled at me, a bit awkwardly, I thought. His dark eyes seemed to disappear in the dimness.

The minister greeted us with polite utterances and an invitation to approach the altar in order to light a pair of candles.

The ceremony was quick and to the point. Mrs. Taggart had informed me that Father had given over quite a donation of silver that, in addition to the crying money required for our banns to be read, supposedly stretched the kirk's coffer and not the reverend's pocket in order to ensure a hasty, quiet wedding with no investigation by other elders of the kirk.

As soon as the vows were taken and the book was signed, Mr. Andrews hurriedly departed, leaving Mr. Fergusson and me standing alone. The reek of the fat from the snuffed candles drifted into my nostrils and I turned to escape it.

I came face to face with my father. He said to Mr. Fergusson behind me, "I realize we omitted a discussion about where you will spend the night. Have you a preference?"

"We'll be staying at The Black Horn."

"Very well. And you plan to leave for Kirthgarran tomorrow. I'll have her bag sent to the inn."

There was not a great deal he would be sending: an ill-kept riding habit of black with dark blue facings that I had never before seen, a man's shirt, a pair of riding boots, and the only mementos now left of my mother—her lock of hair and the miniature painting I had kept in my room. At the last moment I had thrust into the bag the scrap left of my diary and Rajjit, the flop-eared, stuffed rabbit from my childhood, rescued from the bottom of the clothes press where he had languished for a decade.

A weary Malcolm sauntered out the door. My father remained, observing me for a moment. Not until he was gone did I realize he had been saying goodbye. I was left alone with my husband within the echoing stone vault. My husband. The stranger to whom I now belonged.

Unmindful of the others I followed my parent out into the sunlight. I called out, "Father?"

I did not know what I expected, what I wanted, what I hoped to say. Father stopped and partially turned his head. His impeccably curled, white peruke, dark angling brows, and the long, fine line of his nose became incised in my mind. His voice came without any expression in it. "You no longer have the right to call me so. For as of this day you are disinherited, your mother never existed, and you are no longer my daughter." He looked up and added, "Malcolm has already seen to the legalities of it."

My half-brother, waiting in the gig, inclined his head toward me in a gesture of respect, but his mouth still wore its insolent grin.

To gang to the hielands wi' you sir,
I dinna ken how that may be;
For I ken nae the land that ye live in,
Nor ken I the lad I'm gaun wi'.
Leezie Lindsay (Trad.)

Chapter Eight

I was not hungry when Mr. Fergusson and I reached the inn, but I sat beside him on the bench whilst he dined on a light supper of roast rabbit and bread. Few words passed between us. I was not inclined to talk and Mr. Fergusson was subdued. There were few other patrons in the taproom, men I did not recognize who ogled us and whispered unabashedly to each other.

"Mag! Mag!" one of the men shouted to the woman drawing ale. He held up his empty ale-caup and shook it, but his eyes never left me.

As usual I was an object of curiosity for the local folk, but now, with word spread that the reclusive daughter of Finlay

Allanson was wed to a Highland stranger, one could not expect their tongues to be still or their eyes courteous.

I averted my own gaze from Mr. Fergusson but there were few places to put it if I also wished to avoid the gawking, bearded men at the other end of the room. I tugged the cap Mrs. Taggart had given me more fully over my head to ensure that none of my hair was visible, even though the linen was oily and smelt sickeningly of her.

I had hoped I would remain numb for days, even weeks, but the destruction of my mother's belongings had begun to awaken me. Contemplating the loss of her clarsach, sketches, and books was opening my heart to my other loss, though I had tried with all my might to prevent it.

How would I ever unravel the mystery of Davy's leave-taking? The questions were unending. Had Davy truly loved me? Had all his words been empty?

He had been gentle with me, caring. He had never forced us to become lovers, thus spoiling any theory that he might have been a licentious wanderer. He'd said he would risk everything for me. But he had gone. This action spoke the loudest of all. He had deserted me when I had needed him the most.

Mr. Fergusson finished his claret, and when he put down his cup he began to speak. "'Twill take six days. Perhaps seven if you need to rest more, or the weather's drauky. I'm hoping the Highland pony I bought for you proves worthy."

I thought of Benjamin and his rescue, and nodded.

He wiped his lips and went on, "He should, for he seems sure-footed enough, with a good deep chest. We'll follow the Tweed and reach Peebles tomorrow night, and the next day we'll begin our journey northwest through the Southern Uplands. We'll cross the Pentland Hills using the drove roads. After that you'll have your first sight of the Grampians, north of Stirling. There'll be bogs and burns and hills but at the end of it all will be Kirthgarran."

I nodded.

"I thought it better to surprise my family. They all ken I met you, of course. I could not keep quiet about you. But that I've wed you—they thought I'd not a chance of that."

I considered all the people I would have to meet. His brother and their father, the steward of the castle. The housekeeper and her sons. The servants. The earl. I would be expected to become part of their household. I must learn to survive in the wild lands of the north amongst people just as wild, although I was skeptical of my father's pronouncements about Highland folk. Mr. Fergusson did not seem untamed and uncultivated. Mamma had not been.

"I'm done with this. Will we go upstairs? I've been waiting to tell you this, but I've a grand surprise for you."

I got to my feet, blinking in the smoke, and followed him across the public room toward the narrow, uneven steps. The men tittered behind me. Mr. Fergusson bade me go first but when I reached the landing I stopped, unsure of where to turn. I glanced in confusion at the many ill-fitting doors and the meandering, tilted floor of the passage. My husband took my elbow and led me to the left, passing two or three doors in the murkiness before he paused, opened a latch, and stood holding a door open so I might enter.

"Your father was prompt," he said, indicating my bag thrown onto the center of the bed. "I left instructions for it to be brought upstairs when it arrived. And hot water for you. I see they've kept their promise and provided a stoupful as well as soap and linen. I thought you'd find it welcome."

My eyes slid from the dun-curtained bed to the empty chest. "This is not your room."

He closed the door behind him. Though I had been in his company for two hours I had not yet looked at him squarely. Alarm coiled around me but I knew it was unwarranted. He was well-groomed. Kind and honorable. He had saved me from Father and Malcolm. And Davy—Davy was gone.

He came close but did not touch me. "I ken what a strain today has been. You value your privacy, so I ordered a room made ready for you, gossip be damned. I'll not make demands of you, Keeley, not until you're ready. I heard what your father said to you this afternoon. It had to be a blow, no matter how disagreeable your home has been. I would be comforting you if I could, but I do not believe you'd accept it. I'll give you time instead, if you want it, time to spend by yourself to take in all that's happened. You do want it?"

A moment passed before I could understand what he meant. I murmured, "It is kind of you."

"Good." He untied the ribbon at my neck and lifted my scarlet cloak. He tossed it onto the bed beside my little bag and straightened his shoulders. "And now. I need to show you the surprise. 'Twill be a surprise, I guarantee! A splendid surprise!" He left the room, and I heard his footsteps go down the hall and immediately return. "Turn round," he prompted, just out of sight beyond the door.

I did as he asked, feeling foolish.

"Now, now, you may look."

I turned again, finding him in the chamber with me. I stared at him. In his arms was Mamma's clarsach. "Oh!" I cried and ran toward him. I touched the harp, stroked the wood, ran my fingertips down the strings. I clamped my eyes closed. "The clarsach," I whispered. "The clarsach."

"I told you you'd be surprised."

"It's Mamma's clarsach."

"Aye, that it is!"

I sought his eyes, ceasing, for a moment, to be afraid. "But how did you—where did you..."

"You were incarcerated, but I was not. I've spent the past three weeks in your father's company. I knew his intentions, and his rage. I was there when he bade Young James to empty your mother's auld rooms and build the fire. I knew the clarsach was something dear and I wanted to save it for you. I bribed the lad with more pounds than I care to remember!"

"How will I ever repay you?"

"Oh wheesht. Do you not understand 'tis a gift? Instead of tossing it in the pile he put it aside and I've kept it here, waiting for our wedding day when I planned on giving it back to you. You are pleased, Keeley? I'm sorry I could not save aught else. I'm still not sure about Young James's loyalty to your father but I must say he did delight in the notes he stuffed in his sark."

"I do not know how to thank you."

"I'll set it down here, will I?" With care he propped the clarsach against the chair. He unearthed the tuning key from his pocket and placed it in my hand. "You're not to be thanking me at all. I did it because it would make you happy. You can bring it with you, to your new home. Life will be happy for you there. This is the beginning."

My eyes kept straying to the clarsach.

His smile was a jubilant one. "Have a good sleep then, and we'll be up in the morning early and ready to start for Kirthgarran. I'm thinking the sooner we get there the better everything will be." He went to the door. Before he left he turned. "I promise you," he pledged, "you'll come to love Kirthgarran."

I wondered if he promised himself that one day I would love him.

There was a bolt on the door, a rare appointment in a place such as this, I believed, and after he had been gone for a few moments I pulled it home.

Men's laughing voices boomed in the taproom and uneven footsteps creaked in the corridor. I went to bed fully dressed and fought a losing battle with fleas. Dogs barked wildly in the yard. Women below began to argue about scorched pots and who should clean them. And thus, with my eyes stinging from the pipe smoke creeping upward through the floorboards, I watched the remaining hours of my wedding day ebb away.

The public room was disheveled and dirty in harsh morning daylight, and the women I heard arguing over the washing stirred themselves from a begrimed table long enough to serve us with bitter ale and bread smeared with butter at least a month old. The two lounged nearby, their hair jutting from their caps and their gowns reeking of grease and human odor. They watched me try to eat a scone, and I thought with curious nostalgia upon the many scones I had baked at home and sold to this very place through Mrs. Dundas. I was relieved when Mr. Fergusson finished his tankard of the inn's ale, settled our bill, and donned his greatcoat and tricorn.

Our horses were ready and waiting. Mr. Fergusson wrapped my mother's clarsach in a bit of gray drugget and managed to bind it on top of the saddlebag on McKay's rump. The groom held the reins of my pony whilst I stepped up on the mounting block, and my husband put his hands about my waist.

"I ken some ladies are fond of their sidesaddles," he said as he guided me upward. "But I've not seen you using one, and so did not think you'd mind riding astride. 'Tis better, in any case, for the mountains might have you falling off of them without a good hold on your seat."

I settled into saddle and stirrups, pulling the ill-fitting riding skirt into place and tightening on my head the matching cocked hat decorated with a limp, black feather. The new Highland pony was dappled gray with silken fetlocks and a mane and tail of white. I began acquainting myself with his movements whilst Mr. Fergusson levered himself onto McKay and controlled his horse's eager, sideways steps. The inn's yard was busy with folk coming and going, and I looked about myself trying to memorize the hostelry, the swinging board on which a head of a black ram was painted, and the cottages along the road.

Mr. Fergusson cut my muse short and said, smiling, "To Kirthgarran." He thrust his heels into McKay's sides and my garron dutifully followed his new companion.

We began our journey by taking the road to Galashiels. I said a goodbye to every landmark we passed, aware that I might never come back to the place of my birth again.

I watched as the points of the presbyteries, the transepts, and the ruined tower of the abbey lingered in the distance. A new poet named Mr. Burns—a young farmer who had recently published a book with great success and was now making a tour of the Borders—had come to visit Melrose Abbey in May. He had called it a magnificent ruin of widespread renown. I knew of the man and his visit from Father and I was in agreement with his words. I would miss my magnificent ruin.

I would miss my dear Eildons as well, my humped friends who settled comfortably amongst the Lowland heath with their familiar, gray-green shoulders and age-old scars: three mountains long ago sliced from one by the imps Prim, Prig, and Pricker at their master's bidding.

I would miss it all, and my heart cried, "This is all I know."

When the abbey could no longer be seen and the Eildon Hills melted away, I kept my eyes on Mr. Fergusson riding in front of me. Concentrating on the figure of man and horse as they tread through a fine, falling mist had a stupefying effect on me, as anything will when watched long enough. We passed through

Galashiels and continued west. Once we left the perimeters of Melrose nothing was familiar to me, and our surroundings held little interest. It seemed nothing could distract me from pondering upon Davy and my loss of him.

We had supper at a hostelry in Peebles and arranged for lodgings there, but instead of restoring me the food conjured up a vague sickness. They were short of rooms and we were forced to share one, but Mr. Fergusson was as considerate as he had been the night before and slept on top of the scratchy brown coverlet whilst I slept beneath it.

Despite the rigors of the day's journey and a swimming head, the unaccustomed presence of his body in my bed kept away the pressing need for sleep, though I heard him fall into an untroubled slumber.

I lay beside him, my body stiff, my senses alert. Fingers and wrists ached from clenching the coverlet. Mr. Fergusson's chest rose and fell. Emboldened after a time, I peered at his face and studied his straight nose, long lashes, and the edge of a cheek, finding it incredulous that the man beside me was my husband. His hair was rumpled over his brow, but in the dimness he appeared as finely-sculpted as a statue. I settled my head back down, fighting the old stirrings of panic in my middle, trying to mimic Mr. Fergusson's surrender to bodily needs. I let my eyelids close, but I was not easily swept away.

My second day of married life began much like the first, with an early breakfast and a timely departure. That morning, however, I was sore in every joint and dreaded anew the days of riding before us. Because of our enforced closeness the night before, I was unable to speak much at all.

We took the drove road north, passed the common grazing lands of Kingsmuir, paid a toll over the bridge, and crossed the hills to Romanno Bridge. Beyond West Linton we followed the Lyne Water and headed for Cauldstane Slap, the pass between the East and West Cairn Hills in the Pentlands. At noon I saw, for the first time, a drove of black cattle. The fold of about two hundred or so was attended by men and their dogs as it made its way south after having crossed the Water of Leith. Men and beasts had stopped for the night in the meadow beside the road,

Mr. Fergusson guessed, and now were on their way again.

"That pasture is a stance," he explained. "Free grazing land. The cows can only be driven for about ten or twelve miles in a day, or else they'll be ruint. The drovers sleep alongside their animals, wrapped in plaids, taking turns watching through the night with only ram horns of whisky to sustain them."

I observed the four drovers who walked with the longhaired, horned cattle and I admired their perseverance in caring for their charges in all kinds of terrain and weather. Their appearance fascinated me: they were unkempt, swathed in plaids that served as cloaks and sleeping blankets both, ever-watchful with dark, roving eyes. They were quick to whistle to a pair of scampering black-and-white collies.

"Where have they come from? And where are they going?"

Mr. Fergusson brought his horse closer beside me, out of their dusty path, and watched the cows lumber past us with switching tails. "They come from all over Scotland," he answered. "From Skye and Mull, and Sutherland, Inverness, and Aberdeen. We send our cattle south as well, with my brother Lachlan as topsman, every October. There are markets all through the glens, but the Falkirk tryst is the most important. These cattle are probably already sold and going to England, to the grazing lands of Norfolk or other English fens, to be fattened before they're slaughtered in Smithfield near London."

"I know nought about the cattle trade," I admitted.

"You'll learn a great deal living at Kirthgarran. Breeding and selling the kylies, the West Highland cattle, is how we make our living."

We watched the animals plod on, the dogs circling at their heels.

Deep into the Pentland Hills we went, following the cattle's track that threaded betwixt the slopes. By the time we approached Mid Calder I was exhausted and every one of my bones ached. Mr. Fergusson led us to the home of a family accustomed to lodging drovers and travelers, and for a shilling we were given a meal of porridge and a bed in a forkful of hay in an empty byre. I swallowed the oats and collapsed into the sweet, dried grass, vaguely aware of Mr. Fergusson tucking my cloak about me. I was asleep before he settled down at my side.

The names of the towns we passed began form a long list. The number of travelers we met upon the road increased, and there were more droves of cattle and sheep. Mr. Fergusson became visibly excited as we began making our way west toward the town of Falkirk.

"I'm guessing there've been more than thirty thousand black cattle changing hands at Falkirk in October when we've been there in the past," he told me when we stopped to water the horses and let them rest.

"I cannot imagine how it must be."

"You should see it, Keeley. I love going with Lachlan. Buyers and sellers haggle over prices. The grounds are a mass of men, cattle, sheep, dogs. You make your sale, finally, and celebrate with drink and food in one of the tents. There are booths for the Royal Bank of Scotland, The British Linen Company, the Commercial Bank—all to make it easy for you to deposit your money or to get notes. The crowds are full of sharpers and thimblers and gamblers, beggars, singers, and fiddlers."

"Are all the markets the same?" I asked in horror.

"Falkirk is the best, but 'tis the same wherever you decide to sell your fold. A man's year has come to a point. Have you made money? Lost money? Will the folk at home, who've entrusted their animals to you, be satisfied with the price you achieved? Or disappointed because the risk ended with loss, and their fortune is now gone? Jings, what a feeling to hold a year's investment in the palm of your hand!"

His eyes held a faraway look as he spoke, and I knew his excitement was genuine. He went on to say that if it were later in the summer we could stop at Falkirk and meet the buyers ahead of time to judge how prices were running this season. He would have welcomed the opportunity to be in the midst of shouting men and barking dogs, and I thanked God we were too early. "There are other fairs here and there. Smaller ones. Throughout the summer there's buying and selling. Drovers try to increase their herds for the larger markets. Others want to be done with it and go back home. If we're lucky we'll come across one."

I nodded, but could not feign anticipation.

Rain fell that afternoon, and instead of going on to Stirling we found shelter outside of Falkirk. Had he been alone he would have ventured onward no doubt, but he took pity on me and found us a room at a small inn. We spent hours drying our clothes over a smoky fire and tending to bowls of hot porridge balanced on our knees.

In the evening, when the rain dwindled and a freshening wind blew, he brought me outside to see the eastern sky brightened by an eerie, yellow light. I could not fathom what caused it.

"The new furnaces at Stenhousemuir," Mr. Fergusson said. "Years ago they began at Carron, smelting iron. They use coal now. They found it does better than the charcoal they once used in the West and Northwest Highlands, and of course one needn't cut down the last of the forests for it. They smelt iron for shot, and carronades, those short, wide-bored cannon, for the navy and the army."

"I mind hearing something about Carron, and coal."

"In Carron they use a steam engine for winding coal up out of the pit."

"Father told me about it," I remembered, and continued to gaze at the glow in the twilight.

"I thought you might like to see the sky. Even as we prepare for our night's rest, there are men ready to toil through the night, heaving mountains of coal and melting iron in perpetual fires. Cannon are being made, and British sailors and soldiers are arming themselves for war."

His observation caused me a great uneasiness. How little I knew of the world that spun about me.

The following days were indistinguishable from one another. I could not remember where we had been or how many days we had traveled, but I knew that each hour brought me closer to Kirthgarran and a new life for which I was unprepared. In Killin I was struck with astonishment by the Falls of Dochart, a wide, rushing onslaught of water that tumbled endlessly over rocks and boulders, but the torrent and my wonder faded as we progressed over roads that became narrow and rocky. Gorse and broom appeared in patches of bright yellow, and steep ledges above veiled themselves with ferns and foxgloves.

Often we passed through villages dotted with hovels and

goats, and begged for pallets for the night. Sipping goat's milk and nibbling oatcakes, I listened to Mr. Fergusson speak effortlessly with the folk in the musical, guttural sounds of Gaelic, and later, responding to the gestures and pointing of our hosts, I lay down upon heaps of bracken beside hearth fires and other bodies, and entreated God for dulling sleep.

Hills were covered with patches of dark green heather just beginning to bloom into a thick mat of red-violet. We followed the northern shore of Loch Tay and turned north once again toward Loch Rannoch, where my husband told me stories of the kelpies, the horses who lived within its waters. I was in awe of the perfect, peaked cone of Schiehallion that dominated the landscape for miles and miles. How beautiful it was, one day lying in sun with its sides sparkling as with emeralds and sapphires, the next soaked in rain, its top obscured in mist and its bottom painted in shades of aquamarine. Mr. Fergusson said its name meant "The Fairy Hill of the Caledonians" in Gaelic.

I lost count of the days I was able to see Schiehallion from the back of my pony. I lost count of the miles, the hours. We went farther north across Tummel Bridge and left the drove road altogether, entering mountain passes narrow and winding, and the hills that rose all around us were carpeted in a thousand shades of green as the clouds drifted and furled before the sun.

"Smell the air," Mr. Fergusson begged. "There's none like it anywhere."

I complied and found it cool and fragrant, a temporary palliative for my soul. Sweet bog myrtle cushioned our feet, filling the air with its tangy scent, as did the Scots pine forests that crept betwixt copses of trees and mossy ledges. Burns tore their way through rock-encrusted paths carved into the earth and the odor of wet soil was another layer in the perfume.

On the hills sometimes we saw the black dots of grazing cattle and heard their lowing. It was not uncommon for us to startle red deer and to send capercaillies scurrying through the bracken.

One day, during the ambiguous hour when afternoon bleeds into eventide, we rode by an estate crowned with a handsome, white castle. Mr. Fergusson told me it was Caiseal Àlainn, and explained that the sister of Kirthgarran's housekeeper was wed to the cook there. We viewed it from the crest of a neighboring hill.

"Do you mind," he asked, "what I told you about my friend Coll and the lass who threw herself to her death?"

I remembered. This was where she had lived. The western turret had been her chamber. Its narrow window glittered in the sun. Mr. Fergusson continued, "You may hear tales. Some say that Coll flung her to her death in a rage. There's few who speak of it, for the earl forbids it. But if you hear such nonsense, pay it no mind. 'Tis just a story with no truth in it at all."

"Do the two families ever meet?"

"The Hamiltons live abroad now, in France. They find it painful to bide where their Leslie died. Some say the tower is haunted by her."

"She does not haunt your friend, I hope."

His lips pressed together in a solemn line. "He allows himself to be haunted."

I was thankful when he kicked his horse's sides and led me away.

An hour or so later we came to a loch. "There's something I want you to see," Mr. Fergusson called. He gestured toward the bank overgrown with birk, rowan, and willow saplings. I had no choice but to surrender, finding my legs weak and my body more racked than any day before. He lifted me down from my seat and studied me, his eyes catching the late afternoon sunlight. "You could do with a bit of a walk," he said, pulling my hand. "You look half asleep and I'm thinking you've forgotten how to balance on your feet." He grinned, and pushing aside billows of jade-green leaves, led me downhill through the heather and bracken.

I came to stand beside him under the canopy of trees and gazed at burnished water. Thunder rumbled far away as I contemplated the little isle in the center of the loch and the fingers of sun that gilded its feathering of pine. My eyes skipped to the far shore and found, nestled in an expanse of luxuriant parkland sculpted at the foot of steep hills, a tall, rectangular tower and its many crow-stepped, gabled additions.

I took in a rapid breath. "Is it Kirthgarran?"

"That is Kirthgarran Castle," he said proudly. "Your home, and mine."

The walls were not lime-harled but of raw stone, a mixture of warm gray and sienna. Glazed windows with white-painted casements dotted the multitude of stories. Pepper-pot bartizans grew from each corner of the peaked roof, and wings attached at the front and back of the tower ended in chimneys embroidered with ivy.

"What do you think?" he pressed. "I always enjoy looking at it from here. The castle belongs there across Loch Seàrr, with the pines and the blue bens beyond. This is how I remember it when I'm away."

Together we considered the castle across the loch. Rowan trees grew by the walls and lined the grassy path leading to the front entrance. Closer to the edge of the water was a ruined stone wall with an arched opening.

I could not speak because I was overtaken by cold shivers that crept up my legs to the top of my head. The castle. The ruined arch. I had never been to Kirthgarran—but I had seen both of these things before.

Loud loud the wind did roar,
Stormy and eerie.

Lassie, Lie Near Me (Trad.)

followed my husband on the pebbled track that edged the lochside, trying to understand my reaction to the sight of the castle.

It was a relief that our travel was over, that I would not have to spend another day growing bruised in the saddle and smelling as seasoned as the warm horseflesh to which I clung, or another night bundled in a smoke-filled inn or byre, unable to eat, unable to sleep, with legs that cramped incessantly. I continued to wonder how I would ever survive the scrutiny of over half a dozen Fergussons, civilized or not. But the uneasy familiarity of the scene across the loch was a source of disquiet that kept erupting and displacing all else.

We slowed our horses to a walk when we reached the end of a path lined with the rowans and trimmed bushes. I looked up at the castle above me. A stone plaque built into the wall professed the date "1468" and featured a chipped thistle with a bee resting on it. All at once two dogs, lanky creatures with rough, gray fur, appeared beside us and sniffed at my boots. They showed their fangs. I shrank away from them as my pony backed up and rolled an eye.

Mr. Fergusson sent them darting away with an outstretched arm and a forceful "Off with you, you scurvy scoundrels!" and turned back to me. "How odd. I've never seen them before."

"They're frightful."

"I must ask where they've come from. Mayhap we've a visitor. Well, round the corner on the far side is the postern gate, and the stables are inside a small court. We can leave our horses there, but I want to come back to the main entrance. That is how you should enter Kirthgarran for the first time."

We passed the front of the castle and followed the curving path that led through a garden of gooseberries, currant bushes, and honeysuckles. The wild roses and hollyhocks were a disheartening reminder of home and Mamma.

Suddenly a man wielding pruning shears ran through the kitchen kail-yaird. His focus was the two gray dogs, for it seemed the brutes had abandoned us to stalk a dozen fat geese and the terrified young lad who herded them. The lad stood motionless, the front of his breeks wet, whilst the dogs ignored the approaching gardener and crept closer to him. The man's cries and the tossed shears caused the animals to break into a dead run up the hill and far away. I had been holding my breath, I realized. The gardener scooped up the lad and held him close; the geese began to emerge from their hiding places.

Mr. Fergusson shook his head. "The poor laddie."

We rode through an iron-hinged gate into a courtyard carpeted with grass. At the far end was a doocot alive with the cooing of pigeons, and to the side several peeled, wooden stumps rose from circles of sand. I did not notice the elderly man who came to take our horses until he was beside us and Mr. Fergusson began an enthusiastic greeting. The groom gawped at me as I dismounted, but my husband, unaware of his exorbitant curiosity, did not introduce us.

I turned away from my pony with reluctance. I had grown used to his personality and his wide, intelligent brown eyes. We had developed an unmistakable fondness for each other, and leaving Greyfriar, as I had named him, filled me with a sense of loss.

The strange feeling of recognition enveloped me yet again when we crossed the lawn and climbed the stone steps leading to Kirthgarran Castle's ironbound door. Everything was familiar: the tower roof above, the wooden door before me studded with black nail-heads and stained from centuries of rain, even the steps over which hundreds had trod. I rested my hand on the door, dark and smooth—but no insight about my sense of intimacy or knowledge came from this solid touch.

Mr. Fergusson heaved it open and turned to me. Taking my hand in his, he said, "Now I must be carrying you over the threshold. 'Tis good luck, is it not?" He gathered me in his arms.

I glanced about me as he put me to my feet in the entrance hall. We went through an arched doorway to the banqueting hall and passed a spacious fireplace, taller than a man, with logs laid in readiness for the torch. I looked up to see an iron chandelier hanging from a carved ceiling. For just a second I glanced at somber tapestry depicting a scene rife with wild boars and hunters.

I was flooded by the same, odd sensations of cognizance. My eyes told me I had been here before. My logical mind protested with alarm that I had not.

Our footsteps echoed in the double-storeyed room. Mr. Fergusson was too impatient to pause and explain anything. He went ahead of me, calling for anyone near, and sailed his tricorn to a long table. In several places there were stepped alcoves carved into the ten-foot-thick walls, allowing the placement of tall windows. Iron candleholders and crossed swords adorned the walls.

A man appeared in one of the arched doorways next to the gallery. His hair was streaked with gray and braided into a queue, though his brows were still dark and his face youthful. He turned toward Mr. Fergusson in surprise, slapping dusty hands against his thighs. "Rabbie," he began. "We knew little when to expect you. There was no word..."

"Da," Mr. Fergusson cried.

The man was about to speak when I must have caught his eye. He turned his head and his eyes widened. I looked in appeal to Mr. Fergusson, who came back to me and grasped my hand. "Da, this is Keeley. She is my wife."

There was no change of expression on the older man's face. The shock was already there. I gave a hurried curtsey. The man's expression did not change.

My husband seemed oblivious and continued, "Is she not as bonny as I told you? Keeley, this is my father, Sandy Fergusson, steward of the castle. Now your father as well."

At last the man reached out a hand and took mine, bowed and lowered his eyes, placed his lips upon my skin. When he straightened he said, "I welcome you to my family, Keeley Fergusson. Though I cannot say I—expected this."

My father-in-law was interrupted by his son's exuberance. "They'll all be surprised, by God," he said, giving my other hand a shake. "You never thought I could be so lucky and neither did the others." He watched me with a broad smile brightening his face, and glanced back at his father. "Is Lachlan at home, and Coll? Andrew would not be here, too, by chance?"

"Nay, he's away home. And Coll's been gone since this forenoon, flying the falcons with Gordon." I did not believe his mind was focused on his words.

"Will I send Kenneth along with a message for Andrew? I'll tell him it's urgent."

Sandy Fergusson's eyes pondered me still. "No doubt Keeley will welcome a moment to catch her breath."

"I did not see Kenneth in the stable. I'll leave you two to become acquainted whilst I look for him."

"No, no. Stay with your wife. She needs you at the moment, I'm sure. Make her comfortable and don't be forgetting your manners. Keeley, lass, I'll bring you some refreshment, you and Rabbie both." He nodded once and was gone.

Mr. Fergusson led me through the broad door at the right and up a pair of steps. I found myself in a far more restful room. The walls were stuccoed, the floor was padded with a tartan carpet dreary with age, and a bright fire beat on the ingle of flagstone.

I wandered to one of the mullioned windows where I could see Loch Seàrr. The sun was gone now, overcome by sweeping cloud. I was relieved to find that the view from this side of the loch brought no sensation of recognition. My strange feeling ebbed for the moment, but I was still shaken, and apprehension gripped me at the thought that anything at any moment could call it forth once more. A red-velvet bolstered settle was tucked into a corner. I longed to sit—to sit and disappear.

Before I could move, however, a heavy-set man with a wild beard strode into the drawing room. The hair that brushed his shoulders was lighter than my husband's, but the dark gray eyes that stared at me were the same. "MacNeil said you'd come," he rumbled, though I knew he was not speaking to me.

"Lachlan! No doubt you can guess this is Keeley."

The reaction from him was the same as it had been with their father. I wanted to shrink away to escape the look of wariness and astonishment. He gave no offering of congratulations or blessings, or even of welcome. As soon as the momentary shock was gone, he tried to avoid looking at me.

"You've wedded, then?"

"Eight days ago, in Melrose."

Lachlan eyed me once more, but seemed as unwilling to hold the gaze between us as I. I could not help but feel something was wrong, and it had nothing to do with my natural timidity or the surprise of the news. There were solid footsteps and Sandy came into the drawing room carrying a tray loaded with tumblers, a small pewter vessel, and a spherical, moss-green bottle of blown glass.

"We'll be having a celebration, I imagine," he said, far more composed than before. He poured amber spirit and a little water into four tumblers and handed them to us. "We'll have a toast. You two have had many a hard day, I'm thinking, and could make good use of a drop."

I was scarcely able to swallow the burning whisky. My husband proclaimed it was Kirthgarran's own, secretly made from the barley in the glen, and I remarked hoarsely on how potent it was. The peaty fire burnt a trail from throat to stomach where it lay like a smoldering coal.

The hour went by painfully for me, with Lachlan glowering, Sandy driving a reserved, polite conversation, and Mr. Fergusson pacing in impatience for the others to arrive.

A wave of acute homesickness washed over me. If only I were home, and could run upstairs to hide my head in my bed and escape. Here, I did not even know where my bed was. And I was afraid that anything I looked at would seem familiar although I knew, *knew*, I had never been to Kirthgarran before in my life.

I loosened my riding coat and took off my hat, but was loath to change into Mrs. Taggart's gray dress, and thus remained content to lower myself to one of the red chairs and wait just as I was.

At long last there was commotion and Mr. Fergusson sped through the door. I stood as I heard him exclaim, "Andrew, Anne, at last! And Mairi. I'm glad you came as well. You'll see why." They all appeared at once, and by the way their eyes sought me it was plain Sandy's message had conveyed something about the surprise. The dark-haired man who bowed to me was a few years older than my husband. He was introduced as Andrew, the eldest of the housekeeper's sons. Beside him curtseyed his wife Anne, a fair young woman, and Mairi, the housekeeper.

Andrew was the first to step forward. He put out a hand and I raised mine to meet it. He kissed it lightly. "*Fàilte air Cùirt Garan.* We all give you our welcome, Keeley. You're unexpected, but you are indeed welcome." The expression on his face did not match his sentiment. He, like Lachlan, alternated between staring at me and finding it difficult to look at me at all. None of them, save Anne who gave me a brilliant smile, appeared happy. Perhaps it was because I came from the Lowlands and was considered a foreigner. I could not prevent my hand from reaching up and touching my hair, and I wished I'd not removed my hat.

Mairi sought me next. She was of a willowy stature, slightly taller than I. Dark brown curls glazed with an occasional tendril of silver charmingly escaped her cap. She took both of my hands in her cool ones. "Welcome to Kirthgarran," she said softly. She must have been exquisite when younger, for clear blue eyes, full lips, and cheeks faintly dusted with blooms of color gave her the appearance of a gentlewoman. She looked deep into my eyes and gave me a kiss on a cheek. After squeezing my fingers, she let go.

Anne was touching my arm. "I did not think it would happen! Rab has done nought but talk of you! But we understood your father would not permit it. When did you marry?"

"The Tuesday last."

"You must tell us everything once you've settled in. It will be great fun to have you here. We are close neighbors."

My husband handed round more glasses and came to stand with his arm across my shoulders. He was smiling broadly. "To us! To Mr. and Mrs. Robert Fergusson. May the sun always shine upon us."

His family and kinsmen drank, their eyes on me. I discovered my hand was shaking when I raised my glass to my lips. If only they would stop staring at me in disbelief, I thought. If only they would not regard me as a creature they'd never before encountered.

The housekeeper said, "You must be tired, Keeley. I ken Rabbie's not easy to keep up with, and your journey could not have been peaceful."

"But you must be so excited," Anne burst in, shaking her golden head. "Traveling far beyond your home, seeing Kirthgarran for the first time. I hope you'll not miss your own home too much."

"I do not think I'll ever be able to find my way about."

My husband was no longer beside me. He and Andrew conversed by the sideboard. On the pretext of replacing my tumbler on the tray I went over to them. "He'll want to know you're home," Andrew was saying. "Could you not have sent a message and given us time to prepare him?"

"What would a few days have mattered? Keeley! We were just speaking of Lord Kirthgarran. He'll want to be meeting you, too, of course. You mind he's bedridden and cannot join us."

"I should go up and tell him you've come," Andrew said affably, but as he spoke his eyes probed my face. "Perhaps you should wait until tomorrow to see him."

"Ask him," Rab suggested. "He may not want to delay it."

A look passed betwixt them I could not understand. Feeling out of place even at Mr. Fergusson's side, I glanced away, but met with Lachlan's open observation of me. We both turned aside in consternation at having caught each other's eyes.

"You've met almost everyone," my husband said when Andrew left. "Coll's on the hills but should be back shortly. What do you think? Is it all gey confusing?"

"There are so many names."

He laughed and began to pour himself more whisky. "You'll sort them out before long."

Far-away echoes of thunder cracked across the skies. Deep rumbles rolled into the drawing room and prompted me to look out at the darkened loch. When I looked back, Mr. Fergusson was gone from the room, leaving me to fend for myself.

Supper was interminable. Being seated between my husband and Andrew at table in the dining room, searching for answers to the infrequent, stilted questions I received from everyone at one time or another, hearing the various odd words I could not decipher, trying to remember names—all served to exhaust me. I was unused to the number of people, the rise and fall of chatter, the amount of food. I ate almost none of the fresh trout served on queen's ware, nor the ripe bramble tarts for sweets, and the ale I was offered went untouched.

There was no escaping the questioning stares. I tried to forgive the families of Kirthgarran Castle their inquisitiveness. As the evening wore on, their increased attempts at hospitality seemed genuine and I convinced myself my weariness was responsible for my earlier, distorted perceptions. Yet my fortitude flagged at last when we visited Lord Kirthgarran.

Thunder echoed closer and a wild wind blew beyond the castle walls. We made our way through an arched doorway in the great hall and up a steeply pitched turnpike stair. My husband's candle threw flashing patterns of light and streamed long tendrils of smoke. I hurried to keep up with him as he led us to the storey above the hall. We reached a room where a massive door stood ajar.

The room was bathed in warm, yellow light and seemed spacious due to a pier glass mounted beside the marble fireplace.

Mr. Fergusson placed his candle on a table piled high with books and papers and went to the bed. Crimson damask curtains that matched those drawn at the windows were gathered against the posts, and the canopy above was ornamented with sprays of white ostrich feathers.

My husband reached out for the hand of the old gentleman who reclined against the bolsters. He was tucked in with rugs and coverlets, and the sleeves of an ivory nightshirt covered most of his wrinkled hands resting on top. His eyes were closed.

"My lord," said Mr. Fergusson with evident affection. "You're looking well this night."

The earl's wide face was bearded in gray and silver hair rippled down to his shoulders. Deep blue eyes opened and looked steadily at me.

"Sir," Mr. Fergusson continued. "This is Keeley."

I stood before him, my muscles tense.

"Andrew told you," he continued. "We were wed a week ago."

The man swallowed. It was audible in the quiet of the chamber. He began moving his head from side to side, eyes not straying the least from mine. In a low voice, and with a thick tongue, he uttered a phrase in Gaelic. Something about the words frightened me. I glanced at Mr. Fergusson, who had lost his smile. The earl shook his head again. He added more to his peculiar discourse, haltingly, painfully. I saw with shock that water filled his eyes.

I pressed my fingers together and looked again to Mr. Fergusson.

"Perhaps we should come back tomorrow," he said to Lord Kirthgarran. "You've not had enough time to absorb the news, it seems. I should have warned you, as Andrew foretold."

Lord Kirthgarran nodded, closing his wrinkled eyelids. The tears, forced out, crept down the grooves in his face. His hands grasped the bedclothes. He spoke again in his native tongue but switched to English, and his voice broke. "I beg forgiveness. My manners…"

Say something, I told myself. But I could summon no words.

Mr. Fergusson pressed the earl's hand, retrieved the candle, and brought me with him outside the room. Andrew was waiting for us, pacing. "He was too overcome," my husband said. "Perhaps after a night's sleep he'll feel the better."

Andrew seemed unwilling to speak. He glanced in my direction and replied in a flat voice, "I'll just go in and make sure he has what he needs."

All he needed, I thought, was to have me out of his sight.

My husband took my hand and led me into the darkness. We followed a passage that must have joined the tower to one of the wings. My feet misstepped in the dark corridor. I peeked at my husband's face but his eyes were narrow in the pulsing candlelight, his lips unsmiling, and I could not find it in me to question him about the interview with the earl. I followed him mutely as we turned an unexpected corner.

He pushed open an arched door on the left, halfway down the passage. Inside was a sizable bedchamber with a fireplace full of unlit branches. He bent over the tinder with the taper, causing a flame to burst forth.

"This is to be yours," he said as he placed the candleholder on the mantel. "The Green Room. I chose it because 'tis across from mine. Mairi promised she'd come tomorrow and help you put it to rights. For tonight I do not imagine you'll want to do aught other than sleep. There's a comfortable bed, with Spitalfields silk hangings," he added proudly, pointing. "And a clothes press. A commode full of big drawers for you. Down at the end of the passage is the garderobe."

I tried to thrust from my mind the unease Lord Kirthgarran had caused and Mr. Fergusson's unwillingness to explain it, and looked about me as the flames in the fireplace took hold and leapt high. The new light did little to add cheer to the cold chamber or dispel the medieval darkness clinging in the corners. The bed was imposing, crafted of heavy, wooden posts and canopied and curtained in forest green. Above us the beams of the ceiling were painted with curling vines, pointed leaves, and simple, cherry-colored flowers.

Mr. Fergusson continued, "I'm away downstairs, but I'll be back to check the fire and wish you a restful night."

I nodded and he was gone.

The window, set in a flagstone-floored alcove, housed

dozens of triangle-shaped pieces of glass and as I approached it and knelt on one of the window seats, a myriad of reflections of my hollow eyes and tangled, uneven hair was sent back to me. I opened the panel and was met with a brisk wind laced with moisture. Below, the landscape was dark, for the loch was slate-gray and whipped with angry white foam. The bent trees and grass were as black as the sky.

I pulled the window shut against the wind and crossed to the fire. I warmed my hands, looking about me. Beside the ingle was my bag as well as the clarsach, the only familiar things in a world far-removed from my little bedchamber in Gilchrist House.

Mr. Fergusson seemed to be gone a long time. I wedged some logs on the fire. I crouched on the wing chair facing the fireplace and watched the flames grow as they caressed the wood. My face grew hot and I began to relax in the heat, letting my body sag into the bolsters. I allowed my eyes to close. Dizziness came and then dissolved as I became accustomed to sitting still and being alone for the first time in over a week. I listened to the wind and the sputtering, crackling fire. When thoughts of Davy crept into my mind I was too tired to drive them away.

At last a tap came on my door warning of my husband's entry and he came inside, bringing with him the peaty scent of Kirthgarran whisky. The door shut without a sound. "They all would have liked to have seen you again," he said and smiled. "But they understood your weariness."

Roused from my semi-slumber, I murmured that his family and friends seemed kind.

He came close to me, not speaking. I had forsaken the chair, understanding this to be our final exchange of formalities for the evening, but soon realized just how close he had come.

His eyes sought my face. In the firelight they seemed enormous. Dark. As luminous as polished pewter. "I wish I could make you understand how I feel, having you here. Finally. A dream I ne'er dared hope for. How often in the past months I've said to myself, 'If only Keeley were here.' That you're standing in flesh before me here and now is the single thing I've ever wanted with both my heart and soul."

I nodded, so exhausted I thought I would topple over.

"I want you to ken that I'll not be saying aught to the others about why your father assented to our marriage. 'Twill be our secret. There's no need for them to know, is there? It, like all else, is in the past. We need no longer live in that."

He put his hands on my arms and drew his face close to mine, forcing me to look directly at him. "What matters is the present. This night, here at Kirthgarran, with you in my arms and the rain without, and my wanting of you. For I do want you, Keeley, my wife." His words broke apart as his lips fell on my hair and progressed down to my forehead.

My grogginess fell away as if I'd been picked up and shaken. I pushed at his shoulders but instead of letting me go he clutched me to him with insistence and his lips claimed mine. I was surprised by his strength and made an attempt to turn my head from his whisky-sharp mouth. His response was one of increased fervor rather than of understanding and compliance, for his kiss deepened and held me captive.

The embrace called back shattering remembrances of Davy's kisses, though his had never been this intense and intrusive. I slid my hands to Mr. Fergusson's chest and tried to push him away once more, but he moved his lips into the curve of my neck. He pulled me with him toward the bed. Lightning flashed through the room as he lifted me up the steps and onto the coverlet.

"Mr. Fergusson," I said, barely able to find my voice. "What you said. Before. Do you not remember?"

"My name is Rab. You must call me so, for I'm your husband. Say it, dear. You'll not find it difficult."

"Rab? Please listen."

He descended upon me, kissing my cheek, my ear; his hand disentangled itself from my fingers and traveled over my waist and hip. I pushed with my feet and tried to wriggle my way out from under him but the weight of his body immobilized me. His lips burnt the skin at my throat.

He let me go and knelt to remove his outer clothing but his eyes remained on me. I pulled my legs under me and crept backward on the feather bed-bolster until I reached the edge where I sat huddled unto myself.

When he began unfastening his breeks I closed my eyes.

Jock, I'm feart has left me fairly:
Should I live, or should I dee?

The Tocherless Lass (Trad.)

Chapter Ten

He sank into the feathers as he came to me and began to tackle the buttons of my riding coat and the blue waistcoat beneath. He pushed the circles of pewter through corded slits with impatient fingers. He pulled the coats from me with no great gentleness, and untied the shirtsleeves of linen at my wrists and the string at my collarbone. Buttons came free and garments were dragged away. I felt him take my boots, stockings and garters; with panic did I endure the untying of my stays and their removal.

My eyes came open of their own will when he at last struggled with my cuirtan chemise and its ascent over my head. I focused on his face as the chill air met my skin. His eyes were large but shadowed, his mouth open a little as he gazed at me. Round his head dark hair rose in tousled waves.

To be unclothed—with him—with any man—defied reality. I attempted to shield myself with my arms but his hands were stronger. He pulled them aside so his eyes could sweep over me. If the bed could have opened jaws and swallowed me whole into its maw I think I would have given thanks.

Yet in the dim light I saw my silver wedding ring flash, a grim reminder he was not unfair in his taking of what was legally and spiritually his. I was his wife, and he had been more than patient with his rights. There was no point in fighting his persistence. Mr. Fergusson would have what he wanted from the beginning. When he pulled me to him and brushed all of my clothing to the floor, I squeezed my eyes shut yet again. I lay paralyzed as Rab's body imprisoned mine and consummated the marriage he had so badly wanted.

But I never knew a man could hurt a woman so. I never knew this was how it might have been with Davy had he not left me. Surely it would have been different.

He rocked us back and forth with endless power. After the ultimate pain came, he pushed deeper, his fingers buried in my hair, his mouth searching for mine. I cried out, unable to stop myself, but his breathing only quickened and he groaned as he heaved, pressing his face against mine.

He seemed to reach a shuddering, wrenching pinnacle. His sweat fell cold on my skin when he pulled himself from me and rolled away. Though he was no longer inside me the rhythmic beating did not stop. I could feel him looking at me but I did not open my eyes.

Eventually his voice penetrated the darkness, the whisky on his breath still bitter. "You were a maid," he said, and I did not miss the taint of surprise in his words. His lips brushed mine.

He left the bed and shoved logs on the fire, muffling the snapping of the flames. Through a crack in my lids I saw him searching for his clothes and gathering them together. Next came the groan of hinges, the final click of the latch, and silence.

I was not aware when the rain started, but it splashed against the casement in heavy sprays, hurled by a fitful wind. For what might have been an hour I lay still, listening to the thunder, afraid to think, afraid to move.

I blinked when stark, blue-white light illuminated my chamber. The thunder rumbled overhead and I struggled to sit up, gripping the bedclothes. I stared out at the wild night beyond the window, feeling bruised in too many places to count.

Thunder and lightning occurred simultaneously, the boom so loud that my ears rang, the light so bright I could not see for a moment afterward. I jumped to the floor, bringing the coverlet with me. Through the window I thought I saw smoke hanging near the furthest edge of the castle with a faint glow behind it. I stepped up into the alcove, trying to trace the outline of the turret through the slanting rain.

Still bewildered, I opened the window, letting in gusts of wind studded with rain. The scent of smoke was unmistakable. As I watched, flames flickered from beneath the slate roof.

For a few seconds I stood still, unable to move. At last I grabbed my chemise from the floor and flung it on, covered myself with my shawl, and bolted out into the passage.

I tapped on Rab's door. There was no answer. I pushed it open and peered into the room. His bed was empty and neatly made, expecting an occupant that so far had not arrived. I backed out and began running down the passage.

I beheld a nightmarish maze. I could not remember the way Rab and I had come. Corridors looked much like one another, chambers behind tested doors were uninhabited, and all were enclosed in a blackness parted sporadically by lightning flashes cutting through narrow windows.

The thunder seemed to vibrate the very stone about me. I wanted to run, but fear of the dark stilled my feet to a hesitant creep. When I tried to call out, my voice was nothing but a mouse's cry beneath the outrage of the skies.

My foot hit against something cold and hard. It was a round stone. I slid it out of my path and went through a doorway I thought I remembered. The heavy door thudded shut behind me. At once I could smell fresh air and smoke. I was on a landing, and a small window in the outer wall became lit with lightning, revealing stairs leading both upward and downward.

I knew I was lost the moment I left my bedchamber, but

it was not until I discovered I could not open any doors in the stairwell that I felt my composure begin to desert me. I climbed steps to peer out of the embrasure. The burning tower was at the other end of the castle and I could see angry flames leaping from its roof despite the blowing rain. Acrid smoke drifted in through the cracks of my little casement.

I pounded on the ironbound door behind me crying, "Is anyone there?" I ran back to the little window. The wind howled. Lightning split the sky and thunder echoed through the mountains. In my watery vision faces streamed past, colored as vermilion as the flames. Mamma's, Father's, Davy's.

I had often thought in the past weeks I wanted to die, but I discovered just the opposite was true.

I sank to the cold, uneven stone steps as the fire leapt in the sky and called, "Rab!" His name was lost amongst the bursts of thunder and I called it again, this time unable to hold back the tears. They cascaded from me just like the currents of water falling from the top of the window. I dropped my head down upon my arms, and let myself weep at last.

Dimly, as if from afar, I became aware of a voice. There were hands on my shoulders. The voice called me once more. I raised my head, unable to see.

"*An-seo. An-seo,*" it said. The words were gentle. At last I was able to open my eyes and I gripped the arms in front of me.

"Rab?" My voice was gravelly.

"Nay, not Rab. Come now. It's a fright you've given me. Are you ill, Keeley? I assume you are Keeley?"

With the heels of my palms I pressed my eyes.

"Can you stand?" the man inquired, sliding one of his arms about me.

I rose with him. He held me against his chest. Traces of sweat and smoke clung to his body. I turned my face toward the window. "The fire…"

"The fire is out."

The glow in the sky was indeed gone. In its place a high crescent moon dodged in and out of layers of blowing, purple cloud.

"How long have you been here? Have you hurt yourself?"

I blinked at him as my tears began to return. "I was lost. And the door would not open. And the fire…"

"'Twas only the southwest turret roof. The fire-slaught struck directly and the fire was confined to the dry timbers beneath. There was no danger to you here."

I grew fearful at my loss of control. Someone had found me and I'd not died in the fire, yet I could not stop myself from sobbing.

The stranger pressed me to him and whispered, "Wheesht, now."

"I could not find the way downstairs. And the door would not open."

"'Tis over now, *leannan*. You're in no danger." There was no alternative but to let my tears quit of their own choosing and the man appeared patient enough to allow it. At length, however, he observed, "You're shaking."

I blotted my eyes again. I had as much control over my shivering as I had my tears.

"And damp, I'll warrant," he went on, holding me at arm's length. "And you seem quite weak. When did you last have aught to eat?"

"I could not eat. I have not eaten."

He frowned at me, took my hands in his, and said soothingly, "You've not been well taken care of, have you? Come away with me. I'll find you something to fill your stomach. Can you walk?" I nodded, but I was lightheaded and the floor seemed to tilt. The man's hands tightened on mine. "Will you change your clothing first?"

"I'd rather not." My shawl was on the floor, wet with rain that had blown in, but my chemise was unspoilt. That I was in the presence of an unknown man dressed in a single layer of fine wool did not seem to concern me at the moment.

"I needed a dry sark myself," he said, ignoring my state of undress. "Soaked through after helping put out the fire I was. I came down again and stopped to prop open that door. We usually keep it open. It is luck that I saw you. Otherwise you might have stayed here all the night." I took his words to heart and could not wait to leave. His hands let me go. For the first time I noticed there was a black-and-white collie beside us, stretching his nose toward me in interest and wagging his tail.

I said, "Oh, I'd not seen the dog."

"He's ne'er far from my side. This is MacDiarmid. *Suidh sios.* Now give us a paw, lad."

The dog lifted a white foot and his ears sprang in happiness. I took his paw and smoothed his head as he sniffed me. The man picked up a small lantern and my sodden, woolen shawl; with his arm he led me to the stuck door, now propped open by the stone I had unfortunately moved aside.

"It has a reputation for sticking, and so does the one at the bottom," he said.

He took me to a bedchamber, obviously a man's and probably his, and spread my shawl on a chair by the hearth. From the bed he grabbed up a length of woven lamb's wool. I hugged it to me, craving the warmth as he settled it about my shoulders. Though his face was difficult to see in the gloom I could tell his eyes were framed with dark lashes, and beneath the right one, along the cheekbone, I could discern a scar as long as my thumb. Though not deep, it was the result of a long-ago, serious wound.

As he arranged the folds of wool our eyes caught and held. His hands became still and left me. He asked me something in Gaelic and added in English, "Is that comfortable?"

"Aye, thank you." I'd not realized how chilled I had become in the stairwell.

His mouth curved in a smile, white teeth becoming a sudden contrast to smoke-streaked skin. "Come along. I'll show you the way down to the kitchen."

We went through a door I'd found in my frenzy but had abandoned because I had not been able to see anything in the passage beyond. The staircase we descended at the end of the corridor was recognizable to me as the mural stair near Lord Kirthgarran's bedchamber.

The great hall was deserted and invaded by the insidious scent of smoke. The staircase continued downward, bringing us to a kitchen with a vaulted ceiling. The flagstones beneath my feet were strewn with sand, and there was a fire burning in the arched fireplace. The man seemed to know where everything was kept. After seating me at the table next to the fire he collected golden oatcakes, soft cheese, the remains of a cooked game bird, and a bottle of claret. The dog padded beside me and sat, watching both his master's every movement and the growing collection of food. My host lit the wick in a double cruise lamp and lifted the lid of a pot hanging in the corner of the inglenook.

"I ken how to make tea if you'd be liking some," he said, peering in and dropping the cover. "Tea is rare, but we keep a hefty supply on hand for Lord Kirthgarran, who often asks for it. There's plenty of hot water here."

"No. No, I'm being too much trouble already."

"Nonsense. Tell me if you change your mind." He sat down at the table himself and poured dark red liquid into glasses. "This will help," he said, handing me one of them. "But be sure to take some nippocks of food with it." He broke a couple of oatcakes in half, put them on a wooden plate, and began scooping spoonfuls of cheese from the mound. With both hands I raised the claret to my mouth, and was astonished to hear my teeth chatter against the glass. He watched in concern as I took a swallow. "Will you have some of the goat cheese? Moor fowl?"

"Aye," I said, taking the plate. "Thank you."

He took a bite of oatcake himself and leant back in his chair. Though the fire beside me was low, it was beginning to warm me. I chewed little by little, as though I had forgotten how, and felt as fragile as a newborn babe. It seemed there was nothing left of the past and there was no future; time existed only at this moment, and all that I need do was chew my food and swallow it.

"You're looking better," the man said.

I was able to take another sip of claret without my teeth making such a noise. It began to warm me on the inside as the fire persisted on the outside.

"I do not doubt the fire frightened you. It could have done meikle damage. I was coming home, trying to reach the castle before the rain, but I misjudged. It was a bad storm. I saw the fire-slaught. The roof of the turret exploded and the flames shot up and spread to all the timbers that support it. By the time I came to help, all the others were there. The household was in an uproar. I was surprised to find Rab! I'd not known he—and you—had come."

"Are you Captain Fergusson?"

"Oh, aye. I beg your forgiveness. Should have told you. I suppose, since I guessed who you were, you would do the same."

He seemed unlike his brother Andrew, or his mother the housekeeper. I peered at him through swollen eyes. His hair, tied with a length of black ribbon, was ash-blond and caught glints from the fire, as did his eyes as they surveyed me.

He said, "You must be exhausted from your ride, and from your scare. Does the food help?" His voice was different as well. It had a deep, smooth timbre.

"I do feel better."

"I would have thought they'd feed you. And I'd have thought Rab would be concerned for your whereabouts. No one came to reassure you?"

I shook my head. Grease sputtered in the lamp. "Have they— has everyone else gone to bed?"

"Everyone but me and Sandy. We plan to keep watch on the turret roof, or what remains of it, to see there's not another outburst of fire. Soaked everything the rain has, but one cannot be too sure."

I put my hand down and stroked MacDiarmid's head. He smelt my palm and wagged his tail, and his bright eyes looked up at mine. He had been joined by a sleepy, striped orange cat.

I sensed Captain Fergusson watching me still. "You're warm enough?"

"Aye."

"And your chills are quite gone?"

"Oh aye."

"Will you have more claret?"

"I—I think not. I should finish this and go to bed."

"Sleep will do you a great deal of good, I'm thinking. Do you need something to help you? I learnt long ago the secrets of herbs and how to use them."

I smiled. "I think I'll have little trouble. And tomorrow it will be as if this never happened. Although the turret roof will still be in ashes..."

"It will be, of course. Did you see aught of the castle today?"

"I've seen little of anything."

"Then you've that to be looking forward to. It's a pity about the turret, though. We'll have to eye it in daylight and see if it can be salvaged. The roof was sagging anyway. Probably all four of the roofs should be replaced." He finished his oatcake and claret. "Will you have a look yourself? It might help ease your mind."

I hesitated but put my cup down and rose, surprised to find my dizziness had disappeared. Captain Fergusson took a few moments to put away the food and to dash the crumbs from the table into the fire. He picked up the lantern, extinguished the flame in the cruise lamp, and he and his dog led me back to the mural stair and upward to the topmost storey, the garret.

I could tell we were near the burnt turret when the smell of wet charcoal was carried into the castle on a breeze. He explained we were in a room known for its sunny exposure to the south and nicknamed the solar.

We climbed up a small stair into the turret. Above me stood the blackened rafters of a narrow, circular room with the night sky for its ceiling. Brittle beams stood at awkward angles against the walls, suspended from a broken framework of arches. Like a ruined ship, I thought, with spars half-burnt and fallen down. The damage to the roof had been extensive, but as he had said, it had been confined here. I turned carefully with my bare feet and surveyed the room about us. The damp, sooty walls glistened.

"We were fortunate," the Captain said as he came to stand beside me, his footsteps crunching on the littered floor. "With an isolated fire like this you always have a chance. And the rain did the most good. Without it I think we would have lost much more. You've heard of Kilchurn Castle? Lightning struck a tower there. Was it twenty years ago? They never repaired it as they should. The destruction spread and 'tis a ruin now."

Other footfalls grated behind us, and Sandy Fergusson appeared in a pool of moonlight striped with shadows from the charred beams above.

"No signs, are there, of any new sparks, eh?" Captain Fergusson asked my father-in-law, lifting his face upward and surveying the remaining supports.

"Nay. But I've been filling a gude few water-stoups in

caution. Keeley? Is all well with you?"

Captain Fergusson said, "She saw the fire and I thought I'd prove to her it was over and done."

Sandy's gaze probed mine. "No cause for worry. Not now."

"I'm sure I'll sleep easier, having seen for myself," I replied.

I pulled the wool closer about me as the chill wind lifted my hair. Gazing about at the destroyed turret room, I felt grateful for Captain Fergusson's insight and the opportunity to see that the fire that had so frightened me was indeed extinguished. The sight of the dripping timbers allayed the last of my fears, and I was comforted by the speculation I must have spent only an hour or two waiting in the stairwell.

"You do not need to come back with me," I said to Captain Fergusson. "I think I can find my own way now."

"No, no, no. I'd not want you to be taking any chances of losing yourself again. Once in one evening is enough. Are you ready, then?"

I said yes and bid Sandy a good night. He bowed his head and reiterated that we were, all of us, very safe.

Once more I followed Captain Fergusson through the castle. He led me unerringly through the passages, but hesitated when we reached Rab's chamber door, tightly closed.

"It's this one," I said, opening the door opposite. The room was just as I had left it, with coals in the fireplace glowing like rubies amongst lumps of white ash, the stained coverlet lying heaped on the floor, and the bed looming rumpled and disarrayed. Visions flooded back. I had almost forgotten. I turned, wanting to return to the timeless daze I had experienced in the kitchen. Captain Fergusson stood discreetly in the corridor.

"Aye?" he asked, watching my face as he handed me his lantern.

I remembered Rab's bedding of me and knew my cheeks must be flaming. Could he tell, I wondered? Could he surmise by looking at me I had lost my maidenhead this evening? "You'd have this back," I said. I held out the length of wool he'd given me.

"Keep it for now. You may need it more than I."

For one long moment neither of us spoke. He continued

to search my face as if looking for something, and I fancied he found it. He knows, I told myself. He can tell. I was mortified.

"Good night," he said, all at once dropping his eyes. He bowed his head. "Sleep well." He called to his dog and, without looking back, slowly disappeared into the darkness, leaving me to face the remainder of the night alone.

I ha'e nocht to offer ye
  Nae gowd* from mine, nae pearl from sea,
Nor am I come o' high degree,
  Lassie, but I lo'e ye.

*gold
Gin I Were a Baron's Heir (Trad.)

Chapter Eleven

I awoke thinking Mamma had only just died.

I believed it was February again, five years before, with sleet as sharp as needles crashing against the windows of Gilchrist House. Images floated before me. Mamma's hair, long and unbound, burnished by the sitting room fire. Her slender fingers, sweeping over the strings of the clarsach and releasing music both blissful and melancholy. The blood at her feet when she began to hemorrhage.

The illusions did not diminish even when I opened my eyes and found my hands clutching a knot of woven wool.

I sat up in the chair I had taken after Captain Fergusson's leave-taking, surprised I had slept the whole night there. A shape approached. My fingers pulled the wool up to my throat and I whispered, "Mamma?"

A moment or two ensued before the woman responded in a hushed voice. "Keeley, it is I, Mairi. Little did I mean to frighten you. But you seemed in great distress."

My vision cleared, and the housekeeper's kind face came into focus. "I thought you my mother's ghost," I managed to say to the figure before me.

"I'm sorry, my lambie. I was concerned for you, and did not mean for you to waken alone in an unfamiliar place. I've been sitting by the window, mending one of Lachlan's sarks. I meant just to have a keek in at you, to satisfy myself all was well, but there you were asleep in the chair, and in your dreams you appeared so aggrieved I thought to remain here until you woke. I did not want you to be thinking we'd forgotten you."

She was a figure of gentleness. Her hair was caught up in curls and covered with a snowy kertch; her dress was plain but becoming in a pale violet hue.

"I dreamt of my mother," I said.

Her forehead furrowed. "I wish I'd not frightened you. But this morning Coll did confide you'd seen the fire last night and had been caused some alarm. It seems no one wanted to disturb you when it happened, so no one came to you. How ridiculous! If I'd been in residence, lamb, I'd have come to you at once. But this is a household of men. A household of unthinking brutes. I'm sorry your first night in your new home was not one of peace."

"I should rise."

"'Tis near to noon." She came to me and touched my head. "Our Rab is worried about you, too, of course."

I looked away, remembering everything too keenly.

"Let me fetch you something to drink. It will help, I'm thinking. Then you can decide if you'll want to rise, or go to your bed."

She waited for no answer but tucked the wool round my feet and left. I found I could not ease my muscles enough to sink back into the chair's bolsters.

Mairi Fergusson was back in what seemed moments, bearing a tray. "Now you'll have a cup of tea," she said, and smiled at me.

"Two or three if need be. Will you have cinnamon, or whisky, or both?"

"Just cinnamon." I thanked her as she poured milk into a cup and followed it with hot, dark tea. She sprinkled in the grated spice and stirred it with a silver spoon. When I took it from her I welcomed the warmth of the china in my hands. In time I transferred some of the tea to the saucer and sipped, and the heat of the liquid spread within me.

"Everyone would understand if you chose to rest here in your chamber for the remainder of the day."

"Oh no. I will come downstairs."

Her hand touched my cheek, smoothed it, combed my hair back on the side with cool fingers. "I ken what would help you. A hot bath. Something to wash away the long days on horseback. Would you like that? I'll have the bath and a cauldron brought in, and Ròs and Kenneth can begin fetching stoups of water. You'll feel cozy then, with French soap and sweet herbs in the water, and no hurry for any of it, and more hot water when the other grows cold. 'Twould be heavenly, would it not?"

I was dumbstruck.

"Now. I'll gather the others and start it all, and you'll rest 'til it's aye ready. Have more tea and I'll fetch oatcakes fresh from Grizel's girdle. What about your gowns? Have you brought aught from Melrose we can shake out for you and air whilst you're bathing?"

"I brought nothing besides the riding habit and a gray dress."

"Dear Lord, this will not do!" she exclaimed, picking the frock out of my bag and eyeing it from top to bottom. "I brought some things with me this morning since Rab said you needed clothing. They're Anne's gowns and she said she'd gladly give them to you, and soon we can begin sewing for you. Thankfully you and Anne are quite similar in build. Are you fond of this?" she asked with an eyebrow up-tilted.

"It's all I have."

"We'll keep it in case you find yourself in a plight. A very dire plight! I'll bring it down to be washed, will I? You won't want to be sliding it over your head in this state. And we'll brush the habit and have it ready for another time. Coll dried your shawl and I've put it on the table there. Well, then. I think that's everything. A bath, new clothes, oatcakes, and tea. Is there aught else you need, lamb?"

Smiling tenderly, she left me once more, her mending and Mrs. Taggart's hodden gray dress in hand.

If I bent my legs and rested on my back in the copper bath, I was able to cover my body with hot, foamy water. At first the shock of the temperature and the sensation of immersion drew my emotions out of me in an unexpected wheeze, and I wept as I sank into the depths. I wept until my heart was eased, and I could at last press my face with a cloth.

The longer I lay the more I could sense the heat seeping into muscles, fingers, and toes, soothing aching eyes and head, but doing nothing to ease the pain Rab had left behind. I was left to myself, with extra water steaming and a young woman of the household named Airig tapping on the door at times to check on my progress. In a jar was honey water, a tincture of ambergris, musk, and spirits of wine, and I poured some over my head, lathered out the dust of the roads and the smoke of peat fires, and rinsed with clear water. Between my fingers I crushed a knit pouch filled with mysterious dried leaves and blossoms of pale green and amethyst, and was rewarded by a light, flowery aroma that I thought must include meadowsweet.

I could not bring myself to forsake the refuge of the bath for a long while. My chamber seemed more amenable than it had last night due to the homely accouterments of bath and towels, but the walls were still fashioned of plain, limewashed stone and the floor planked with dark timbers. The bareness of it all sent a current of piercing homesickness coursing through me.

I wondered when Rab would claim his marital rights again. I wondered if it would it hurt as much. I was unsure when the auras of fragmentation and unreality would leave me. I did not know when I would once more feel like myself, and when I would ever forget Davy.

Finally I found the energy to desert the fragrant water. From the chair I lifted gowns of dark rose silk and amber velvet. Beneath them lay hoops, kertches, a woolen petticoat, chemise, stays, slippers, stockings, and even a pair of riding gloves. There was also clothing for undress, day-to-day wear: a long vest of homespun and a petticoat of green-and-mauve tartan.

They were thoughtful gifts, but initially I was dismayed at accepting them. I told myself I did not care what I wore, but when I considered donning Mrs. Taggart's hodden gray that stank of perspiration, or the riding habit that reeked of horse and smoke, I realized there was no need to further suffer this detail of Father's punishment. I slipped on the tartan petticoat and sleeveless vest and ruffled my hair until most of the water was out of it.

I made the bed out of years of habit, my hands hesitating as I pulled up the bloodstained sheets. I considered scrubbing the spots with my bathwater, but decided that trying to explain sopping sheets to a housemaid would be more humiliating than suffering her silent conjectures about bloodied ones.

Airig was soon tapping and calling. She seemed to be an ingenuous woman, the same age as myself, with white skin, apple-red cheeks, and frizzy, russet locks. She fussed with the sleeves of my chemise and scurried about, looking over every inch of me. At last she stood gazing at my hair. "I beg your pardon, Mrs. Rab. Will you let me dress your hair for you? I've some pins and ribbon if you like, and if you sit by the fire you can dry your hair whilst I fetch them."

"I do not think..."

"I'll just run along and get them! I'll take the towels with me." She trotted away talking all the while.

She brought back a handful of items and combed my hair. At one point she paused, and tilting her head, asked, "Might I cut this piece? It does not well match the other side, but I could make it match."

I nodded uncertainly, thinking of my father with his razor. She went about her work with a pair of embroidery scissors, humming to herself.

"Aye," Airig sighed. "You're a bonny sight, Mrs. Rab! A bonny sight! Somewhere I'll have to be finding you a glass. It's so exciting you're here, that Rab has taken a wife and all. Nought has happened as fine as this in a long while. Not since Andrew wed sweet Annie. She's a canty lass, is she not? And yet no bairns in sight, though it's been almost two years, and she feels at fault, though I told her someone might have tied a knot in Andrew's handkerchief on the day of their wedding, unbeknownst to him, and so she must try everything she can think of to help. She's put a willow branch under their bed, and I hope you're not minding it, but I put one under yours, as well. There'll be fine, bonny bairns about the castle soon enough, I think. Will you not be pleased?"

There was no time to answer her, though I did not think she wanted a reply. About my head she placed a white kertch and fastened it to my hair with delicate pins of silver. In triumph she announced I was ready to meet the world.

Beams of afternoon sunshine flooded the great hall and brightened the aged tapestries. Not surprisingly, the feeling of familiarity stirred within me just as it had the night before. Airig suggested I wait in the drawing room and pointed at the wide doorway with its pair of carpeted steps.

As soon as I stepped into it, however, I stopped. Captain Fergusson was balancing one of his feet on the edge of a chair whilst tightening the hide lacings of a brogue.

My entrance caught his attention and he straightened. I was able to perceive him better than I had by firelight the night before. Leather knee breeks showed signs of wear, and coarse linen sleeves emerged from a stone-colored waistcoat. A smile grew on his face. "Good day to you."

MacDiarmid the collie came to my side and cocked his head, his tongue lolling out of his mouth. His eyes were bright and the color of chestnuts. I knelt to pat him and my fingers became lost in his black-and-white coat.

"Did you sleep well?" his owner asked.

"I slept too long."

"Like as not you needed the rest." Another smile curved his full-lipped mouth. "I envy you."

I minded the fire and the black, dripping beams of the tower room. "Did you stay awake all night?"

"Most of it. Sandy and I shared the watch. This morning I thought I'd fall over, but then I had a long swim in the loch, and it woke me fine."

I smoothed the dog's head and stroked the floss behind his ears.

"I told Rabbie we met," Captain Fergusson said as he took a leather coat from a chair. "He thought you safe in your chamber all the night. I said you'd been aware of the fire and had ventured out to make certain it was dead, and we'd walked into each other. He was pleased we had. Seemed he was disappointed when I was not here yesterday."

I had not expected him to be so tactful about my childish scare, but I was thankful. I sought for words, unable to forget my undressed state of last night and the warmth of his arms about me.

He reached for a glass with a swallow of ale left in it. "I believe my mother is looking for some food for you. To have someone to be fussing over is her joy."

"She's been very kind to me."

"I'm thinking she feels protective of you." There was something in his tone I could not identify. I looked up at him. The irises of his eyes were edged with a darker gray. Below the right one, on the cheekbone, was the long scar. I was relieved when I heard Mairi's voice behind me.

"Ah, there you are! And you look well. The garments are grand on you. And you must feel the better for the water and soap. As I promised, I've oatcakes as well as bannocks. The best in Perthshire." She came in and set a tray upon the gate-legged table. "And Grizel's butter and plum preserves from the stillroom. 'Twill keep you until supper, I'm hoping. Coll, you'll join us, surely."

He drained his glass and put it on the tray. "Nay, Mam, I cannot. Lachlan's waiting for me on the roof. I just came in to see Lord Kirthgarran. We've still more timbers to throw down."

"Is Rab there as well?"

"Gone to Rathdale for the new rafters, but he should be here soon." He shook on his coat and said to me, "The turret roof, or what's left of it, all has to come off. And may I tell you, 'tis quite a task to handle cabers fifty feet or so up in the air."

"You'll be careful," his mother admonished. "I'll not have any of you falling."

He grinned in obvious affection, tilting up his chin and crinkling his eyes at the corners. "There's nought to be feart. Like goats we are. Or corbies, atop our tall nest. Our claws hang on very well." He nodded to us both and left, the collie trotting merrily beside him.

At Mairi's urging I consented to eat, and settled myself in a chair with a plate upon my knees. I glanced at the shelves framing the fireplace. They were laden with porcelain figures of falcons and hawks, silver quaichs and candlesticks, and a ram's horn snuffbox ornamented with jewels.

He should be here soon, Captain Fergusson had said. I felt my face flare as memories of last night overpowered all.

"I do not mean to be over-bold," Mairi said, sitting beside the Dutch tallboy and spreading her fingers beneath the saucer in her hands. "But mayhap there are things I could be telling you about Kirthgarran. I'm sure that Rabbie has left great gaps in his accounts."

I swallowed a bite of the oatcake. "I'm afraid Rab—Rab has told me so little."

"I'm not surprised. He means well, always, but hasn't the patience to attend to details. I helped to raise him and still, I can ne'er hold him in one spot. He's ever going this way and that, and charming me out of my annoyance with him. He's become quite clever at that."

"There is one thing I've wondered about," I said. "He's never spoken about his mother except to say she is gone."

"Oh aye. Sandy took to wife a sweet lass named Gwen not long after he became the steward of the castle. Lachlan was born and Rab followed, but Gwen did not survive a third childbirth. Rabbie was a year in age then. He cannot remember her."

I thought of Mamma and this morning's dream flooded back.

"When Gwen died our families began to intertwine," she said pensively. "Poor Sandy was disconsolate when Gwen slipped away. She and I'd both been with child at the same time, so when my Coll was born a fortnight later I shared his care with Sandy to help ease his loss. I became a mother to them all—to Sandy's, and to the earl's." She sighed as she remembered. "Just so, that's how it all came about. The lads grew up together, as close as brothers."

"How terrible for Sandy." I put down the half-eaten oatcake. "And the earl. He lost his wife at the same time?"

"The countess died of lung congestion a few years after Gwen left us."

I heard a noise behind me and jumped, thinking it must be Rab. I turned to the doorway and watched a young man throw down an armful of firewood and stack the logs. I waited until he was gone and my heartbeat had slowed. "How many sons did the earl and the countess have?"

Mairi put down her saucer. "Two. They had two. Hugh and Walter. The earl doted on them. They were the world to him."

I sensed a deep grief within her. "They became soldiers, Rab said."

"Officers. They died at Gibraltar." She bowed her head. "The dear lads. Six years ago, and to us it sometimes seems like six days." Her fingers traced the rim of the saucer.

"Were you—were you the housekeeper, or their nurse? When they were young, I mean."

"Oh, neither." She smiled. "I was a housemaid here when the earl wed Agnes Raeburn of Rathdale. Rathdale is the name of the Raeburn lands that border Kirthgarran's. It was inevitable that the earl would wed her. They were childhood friends. Allies. And she brought a great deal of land with her to her marriage, though she was not the eldest daughter. We got on well together, did Agnes and I, and she decided I would be her maid, but as it was, I became more of a companion than a lady's maid. The bairns she gave the earl were a delight to us all, and I loved them from the start as well as my own. I would have become nurse to them, but Lady Kirthgarran would not part with me."

"But then she died."

Mairi looked up at me. "Aye, and Kirthgarran was left without a mistress. I began to assume more and more of the household duties, and at last replaced the auld housekeeper."

I ate the last of the oatcake and sipped some tea. I asked what I considered to be a courteous question. "And your husband? Coll and Alistair and Andrew's father? Is he employed at the castle as well?"

She shook her head ever so slightly. "I was never wed, lambie."

"Oh. I'm sorry. I did not mean to..."

"There's nought to apologize for. I've my own tale to tell, I suppose. Finish your tea, lass, and have a bannock. To live here, to ken us all, you must discover how things came to be. There's no shame in me at the telling of it."

I had made a social blunder. My father would have been incensed.

"Now, now," Mairi said, apparently understanding my silence. "Think no more on it. You mind that the Countess of Kirthgarran came from Rathdale? She'd an older sister. Eleanor. Eleanor was simple. By no means mad or out of her head, just simple. A sweet woman, in truth. She was heiress to Rathdale House and its lands when their father died. Lord Kirthgarran had a friend, Christopher MacLean, from the Isle of Coll. The two of them had been at university together. He visited Lord Kirthgarran now and then, and won, in the meantime, Eleanor Raeburn's heart. The two of them were wed, and Rathdale House, of course, became his home. But the union was not happy, as the years went by. She could beget no bairns, and, though it was long ago, I mind still the unhappiness on him." She had to shake her head and clear her voice. "It happened that we fell in love, Christopher MacLean, The Laird of Rathdale, and I. It was not planned. But we fell in love and we became lovers."

"Oh. I see..."

"We were happy. He was happy. I bore him a son. That was Andrew. Lord Kirthgarran was kind enough to keep me here. He needed me."

"You raised Andrew here at Kirthgarran?"

"Oh aye, the earl gave Andrew a home, and when Christopher and I had two more sons, Lord Kirthgarran treated them as his own. They were known as his foster sons. They were the natural sons of his brother-in-law, and although not related by blood to him, they were raised as gentlemen."

"Is Christopher MacLean still living at Rathdale?"

Mairi cast her eyes to the floor. "He missed his homeland, his isle. He was fond of the salt sea air, and the cries of the sea birds. So he told me many times. It was his idea to name our second son after the isle, and so Coll was named. What a surprise to see, as the years unfold, that he's the only one of the three to favor his father. Christopher had the dark gold hair, the gray eyes."

She touched a ribbon at her breast from which hung an oval locket of silver. She opened the clasp and revealed a curl of ash-blond hair. "This locket belonged to Christopher's mother. He gave it to me when Andrew was born. I put in a lock of Christopher's hair. So I could remember." She shook her head, realizing, perhaps, how far she was digressing. "When Alistair, our youngest, was of seven years, Christopher took his wife to the Isle of Coll to visit his kinsmen. It was April. Eleanor had long known of Christopher's betrayal and how I'd given him bairns when she could not. It was no secret. But she expected him to play the part of dutiful husband. He often took her to Perth, to Edinburgh, to the isles—to appease her."

Her voice broke. Her eyes closed as she snapped the locket shut, and her fingers caressed the silver. "In that part of the sea, storms can come up without warning. Christopher and Eleanor had already started out for the isle when the winds and the rain appeared. Their boat capsized, and they and the ferryman were drowned."

She blinked a number of times. "My sons felt his loss. Christopher had come to Kirthgarran often and had made much of the lads. I was grateful they had known him so. And grateful to Lord Kirthgarran for all he gave me. I was, after all, a sinner with love-bairns, a sinner in the eyes of God and the kirk who'd loved another woman's husband for years. Every time I bore a son, both Christopher and I were chastised in the kirk and ordered to pay fines into the box for the poor, and there were some who did not understand our sin, and slighted us, and criticized the earl for his determination in keeping me at the castle. And yet keep me he did, standing by me and warning all to leave the bairns and me in peace, and so it was done. The Kirk Session recommended that I marry. Anyone. But I'd no wish to. Never. Not—not even after Christopher died. And, until two years ago, when Andrew and Anne were wed, I'd no wish to leave the castle."

I nodded, trying to convey to her that I understood.

"My bairns and Sandy's are all the sons the earl has left now," she continued. "When Eleanor died, Lord Kirthgarran inherited Rathdale. She left it to him specifically, forestalling any possibilities that Christopher's sons could claim it. But the earl has honored Christopher after all. Lord Kirthgarran's own will promises ownership of Rathdale to Andrew. I'm still stunned by his generosity. And so is Andrew, who never dreamt he'd be blessed with such bounty. Andrew and his wife live at Rathdale now and care for it, and I've joined them. I continue to oversee the keeping of the castle here, but Airig carries the responsibility in my absence. Lord Kirthgarran should let me go and give the title of housekeeper to her. Eventually he will, I suppose. I think it is difficult for him to make any changes now, whatever they entail. And as for me, I do as he wishes, and yet I find a need to live at Rathdale. I feel close to Christopher there. There's much of him left at Rathdale," she said, her voice fading.

"Rab has told me none of this."

"He should have. But since he hasn't, then I'm glad I could be the one. I see by your face you understand how it all came about. Mine has not been a life I would have chosen had I the power to do so, but—there've been many gifts given me to offset the sorrow, and indeed, I'm grateful to God for all I have."

I considered her as she must have been: the young housekeeper of Kirthgarran Castle, in love with the Laird of Rathdale, loved in return. She did abide in his house now, but it was a terrible, lonely irony, for she would never be his wife; her sons would always bear her name of Fergusson, never his of MacLean. I felt a sudden empathy for her. There was something about her that reminded me of Mamma, something more than just the overlap of Mamma's face in my dream and hers in my chamber as she waited for me to awaken.

A song came to mind, one I had played on the clarsach years before. "Captain Digby's Farewell."

> *For my love sleeps now in a wat'ry grave,*
> *He hath nothing to shew for his tombe but a wave.*

All at once Rab strode into the drawing room. "Keeley!" He took my hand and kissed it. "I can see you've been well cared for. There's such a change in you! And you smell of flowers!"

I had forgotten about him. The rush of memory into my brain was as forceful as a surge of water through a dam. I squeezed my thumbs in my fingers. His skin had been so hot.

"Coll told me about you awakening to see the fire. I'm sorry you did, dear. It could not have helped your rest. At least you had this morning to sleep, a welcome change, aye?"

Memories of last night colored everything. I had seen him unclothed. He had seen me. He had touched me in ways I had not thought possible. We were the same people today, dressed in conventional fashion, but clothing was an illusion. Now that I knew what lay beneath I would never forget.

"Then you should be ready for tonight. We're having a celebration. Our infar. A feast in your honor as the new bride. The folk from the village are coming. We'll have Donald, Lord Kirthgarran's piper, who's played little in the past years but who, of course, minds most of the auld tunes. I've already told Grizel and she's wild. She wants every woman from here to Rathdale in the kitchen helping her. 'Twill be a fine evening, and all will forget their cares."

I found Mairi's gaze on me. I was sure she could decipher how I felt. "Is it not a bit soon?" she asked.

"Lord Kirthgarran suggested it. The folk want to meet her. And I'm proud of her. I cannot wait to show my wife to the Fergussons of Kirthgarran."

A look passed between Mairi and me. There was no need for words. She knew I was terrified.

My thochts are backward cast ...
Lassie o' the Witchin' E'e (Trad.)

Chapter Twelve

Before Rab and I joined the others for supper, he persuaded me to examine Kirthgarran Castle from the understorey to the roofwalk. Ignoring the cook and kitchen maids preparing our food, he showed me the kitchen with its vaulted stone ceiling and drinking well, and explained that it had originally been the guardroom with the turnpike stair leading to the living quarters above. Despite my discomfort in his presence I let my imagination carry me to a time when one's dwelling place was built with defense in mind, not contentment, and a man lived by arrow and sword. We ended our tour on the narrow walkway that edged the slate-covered roof with its window peaks and chimneys. The shell of the burnt turret was silhouetted against the blue hills beyond. Charred timbers had been removed but Rab did not seem interested in talking about it, for his topic of the moment was history and architecture.

His arm encircled my waist whilst he pointed out the additions that joined the 15th century keep, and I tried to focus on his words.

"The entrance in front, with its steps and the murder hole that juts out over them, was built later. So were the wings that changed the castle from a simple keep to a z-shape. From here 'tis easy to see the extensions that were added even later to create the drawing room and the library, and eventually the nursery, cellars, and stables. Those wings enclose the courtyard, the doocot for the pigeons, and the mews for the falcons. And there's the postern gate."

He turned us to face the loch and his warm hand moved from my waist to my shoulder. "From here you can see part of a curtain wall," he said, unaware of my discomfiture, "down there close to the loch. The arch for the gate still stands, but the rest is a ruin. Kirthgarran was built on the foundation of an older keep. According to legend, that castle was a court built within a thicket of trees, wild and unapproachable. In Gaelic it was called the court, or *cùirt*, in the thicket, or *garan*. It was Anglicized, corrupted through the ages, and became Kirthgarran. No sign of a thicket now, is there?"

"Is *seàrr* a word in Gaelic as well?"

"It means sickle. If you look up and down the loch you'll see it is rather crescent-shaped. And in the center lies the island, a natural one, not a man-made crannog. The burial ground for all the earls and their families. Beyond the loch, and behind us, lie the lands of the Fergussons and the village of Kirthgarran. Farther north is a glen called Strath Gruagach and that belongs to the earl as well. To the east is Rathdale, which was home of the Raeburns until Lord Kirthgarran's gude-sister died and it passed to him through her will."

I looked to the edges of the hills. The evening air was beginning to cool, though ripe summer nightfall would not come until midnight. The tops of the mountains and hills undulated in green, blue, and violet, depending on how far away they were. Somewhere robins sang their bedtime song, music I had once loved.

"So for centuries," Rab said, "this castle has protected the glen and all the folk who live in it. Our history is full of stories about clan wars and cattle reivers. And the English." He turned to me, his heel grating on the stone. Smiling half-heartedly he said, "These days there are other enemies. Our money, which is meaning less and less. Famines. The sweet promises of the emigration and shipping agents. The bondholders. The creditors." He sighed. "I think it must have been easier in the auld days." He shrugged and turned away. "If you look there, you can see the gardens. After supper we'll have a walk in them."

I followed his glance and saw benches placed amongst plantings of such things as red valerian and primroses. Beyond were old oaks with thick trunks. Apple, cherry, and pear trees formed a small orchard inside a stone wall. Of course there was the kail-yaird I had glimpsed yesterday with what seemed to be potatoes, turnips, kail, leeks, cabbage, and the like. There were a few rows of corn and a number of beehives, and what seemed to be a physic garden with lavender, rhubarb, and other herbs. I was smitten with homesickness.

When he pulled my hand to lead me away, I halted and with trepidation said, "Rab?"

He seemed to enjoy hearing me speak his name. "Aye, dear?"

"Ever since I've come, ever since I saw the castle and the ruin of the stone arch and even the hall, I've had such a queer feeling. As if I've seen them before. And we both ken I have not."

He considered this, and I was thankful he did not scoff at the confession. "A familiarity, then."

"It comes to me, now and then. How would one explain it? There's no sense in it, and I wonder if I'm dreaming whilst I'm awake. It—frightens me."

Gently he asked, "Do you have The Sight, dear?"

Though I knew I did not, I hesitated, watching his face and trying to think. I had never been able to foresee the future. Or witness the past. I shook my head.

His smile was sudden and curiously tender. "I ken what it

means. It means God intended you to be here."

Could He be that cruel, I wondered?

The families were already gathered in the dining room when we reentered the castle. I tried to visualize what a picture Rab and I made, arm in arm, wearing fine clothes, and wondered if we fit the image of a happy, newly-wedded couple.

Captain Fergusson and Andrew talked by the dining table but stopped when we appeared. I curtseyed, but the table was so extravagantly appointed that my eyes became trapped by the radiance of white linen as pure as swan's down and the competing shine of crystal glasses, silver candlesticks, and engraved pewter plates. Dishes of food lay spaced in an artistic array accompanied by salt, mustard and pepper boxes, a copper basket of knives with heather-wood handles, and a glass dish of golden pears and apples. I straightened, awed by the vision before me.

Lachlan rose whilst I gaped at the supper table, looking at me with the same closed and furtive expression as the evening before.

Anne came to me all aglow. "How well it fits you," she declared, touching the rose gown I'd chosen for the evening. "Though it should be taken in a bit. I'll help you with it soon."

Andrew said to Rab, "Lord Kirthgarran wanted to have a word with me just a few moments ago. It seems he plans to come downstairs."

"Downstairs! Is he well enough?"

"He seems very well. And he's asked for Donald to play, which he's not done for a year. I cannot understand it. After last night..."

They studied each other. Rab said, "Then he's to join us for supper, and for the celebration."

"He'll not tire himself," Mairi warned from the window seat. "He must not remain long after the meal."

Rab said to me, "He's not been out of his chamber for months."

I did not understand. My meeting with Lord Kirthgarran had seemed disastrous to me. Now he was about to leave his bed and face treacherous spiral stairs, draughts, and over-exertion in order to be present at my wedding supper. I glanced at the others. All attention was on me. Captain Fergusson and his mother did not seem happy.

My tongue could not respond to Rab's observation. I would never know the thoughts of those round me because I could not ask.

He was as tall as Andrew, not as frail as I had supposed, and he favored his right leg. As he limped into Kirthgarran's dining room supported on one side by Andrew and on the other by the bearded Lachlan, I could imagine him as he must have been in health.

Lord Kirthgarran was and always would be an arresting man. He had donned a great belted kilt and plaid of hunter green and hose of undyed wool. A short waistcoat and outer coat of black lent a youthful air to him. His eyes were on me the second he came in the doorway, yet there was no indication of tears this time.

"My lord," Rab said, rising.

"Rabbie," Lord Kirthgarran said and nodded. He considered the others. "Coll, Mairi, Anne." He bowed his head in greeting. I stood, and when I found his blue eyes on me I curtseyed. "You are welcome here at Kirthgarran, Keeley Fergusson. For now, and ever more."

I acknowledged this, curtseying again. Captain Fergusson had gone ahead and pulled out an armed chair at the head of the table, one tucked in with bolsters. The others helped Lord Kirthgarran to it and gratefully he sat down, his hands gnarled but at home on the linen cloth of his own table.

It was time for all of us to sit. Grace was said, and the meal began.

Donald stood in the great hall nearby and played slow but merry tunes on his bagpipes. I had never heard the instrument before. I watched the man's fingers fly over the chanter as his tight cheeks forced air into the mouthpiece and thus the turgid bag under his arm. The three tall drones over his shoulder added an extraordinary background hum to his melodies—melodies complicated and enhanced by countless gracenotes.

I discovered Andrew watching me. I became embarrassed by

my absorption with the piper and my disregard for the company at table. "Have you not heard the pipes before this?" he asked kindly.

"Never."

"An instrument of war, they are. Or so the English say. I'm sure Donald will show them to you if you'd like to inspect them close at hand. And he'll play tunes for hours if you ask him."

I replied I thought that would be greatly enjoyable. I picked up my fork. The two prongs of silver and the handle, engraved with a bee resting on a thistle blossom, gleamed in the candlelight. A tall lad placed a broth-plate of soup before me, however, and I hastily exchanged the fork for a similarly polished spoon. The soup was white, *potage à la reine*, and when I tasted it I found it to be substantial with cream and the flavor of chicken, egg yolks, and almonds.

Mairi, keeper of the household, apologized for what she considered the sad lack of crystal and silver. "'Twas soldiers first. The ones who came after the massacre at Culloden. They used Kirthgarran as a garrison for a week, easing their cares in the drawing and sitting rooms. They were not certain we were innocent of treason, of helping Prince Charlie regain his father's throne, or of hiding him afterward. Much of the glassware they shattered in their drunken quarrels. And after they left, many times it was necessary to sell the silver, the silver we hid whilst they were here, for food and provisions. There's little left now, a few quaichs, candlesticks, cups."

"There's little a man needs," Rab said happily, aiming for the platter of salmon and scooping up a slab of the fish with his knife. "A spoon to eat his porridge, a knife to cut his meat. And horn will do for one, and steel for the other."

Indulgently, Anne said, "Aye, that is how you would think."

The elegant glass at my hand was etched with two letters encircled by a crown, oak leaves, and thistles, and the stem was criss-crossed with lines.

"An Amen glass," Captain Fergusson said at my left, noticing my interest.

"Are those initials?"

He took up his own glass, holding it in front of a candle so that it reflected golden flames and the red of his velvet sleeve. "I and R. They stand for Jacobus, or Iacobus, Rex. Our own King James, who some believed should have been our sovereign. Or, if you look at the letters just so, they could also be read as GR, which, of course, would be the initials for Georgius Rex. With these glasses you could have toasted either one, the king over the water or the one sitting in London town, and ne'er be labeled a traitor. 'Twas customary to end a toast to either king with an 'Amen.' Lord Kirthgarran calls them his Amen glasses."

"They're so very delicate."

"They were buried in a box in the garden after the Battle of Culloden," Sandy explained. "Glasses like these were favorites for boasting secret symbols and words. It was too dangerous to speak names or to write them, so substitutes were found. Followers of James and his son Charles understood the emblems. Roses, for example. They stood for the House of Stuart. And a blackbird was for James, until Charlie came of age. Then *he* was the beloved blackbird."

My mother had taught me a song about a blackbird. I could hear her voice, telling me the story of James Stuart VII, King of Scotland and of England, a Catholic ruler with a Catholic son, a man who soon found himself out of favor in both countries. He was exiled to France so his daughter Mary and her husband William of Orange, both Protestants, could rule. When they left no heir to inherit the kingdoms after their deaths, another Protestant, a distant German relative, was chosen to receive the throne instead of James.

I remembered Mamma singing, *"I'll seek out my blackbird where'er he may be,"* when she described how the rebels who were loyal to the Stuarts sought to bring them back in 1715 and overthrow George I of the House of Hanover.

Mairi smiled, though a bit sadly. "Lord Kirthgarran will tell you a wealth of stories. His father was out with James in the '15."

I turned respectfully to the earl at my left. He had spoken little and eaten next to nothing. I was aware of his breathing, and of his keen interest in me. He now gave me a nod and said, "My father was arrested and taken to England for trial when I was but a bairn in my cradle, and he died in prison from wounds he received on the battlefield."

"Many of the other chieftains were hanged," Sandy added. "Some were attainted and their estates forfeited to the Crown. Kirthgarran was fortunate, though, and eventually earned a pardon."

The earl swallowed a spoonful of soup and said, "Aye, it was pardoned, but thirty years later. And when the second rising was put down, the Government did not at first believe I was innocent of treason. Those in power minded my father's loyalties, and assumed mine were the same."

"You did not join the Prince?" I asked.

He put down his spoon. "Word was sent that James's grandson had raised his standard at Glenfinnan, and the White Cockade appeared in the glens begging for clans to go to Prince Charlie's side, but no, neither the Laird of Rathdale nor I could find it within ourselves to join him. The Prince had brought no army with him. No money." He gave a sigh. "I saw nought but doom. And was ashamed of myself, for during my whole life I'd lived under the notion that James was not Pretender but rightful heir to the throne." He paused, clearing his throat. "I could think of nought but the love I held for my birthplace, my home, my people, and the need, the absolute need, to pass it on to my first-born son. And so I deserted my father's cause, and kept to my home in order to save it." His eyes drifted to his forsaken spoon and silence befell the table.

Captain Fergusson said, "When Cumberland's men came through the glens putting down the last of the rebels, the earl did not want to chance losing the Amen glasses, so he ordered them, along with some silver, a few swords, dirks, and a claymore or two, to be put beneath the soil for another day."

"And it's aye good to have them out of the ground," Mairi murmured, seeming eager to keep the conversation on this optimistic slant.

I nodded in sympathetic agreement. Lord Kirthgarran took his wineglass with a shaking hand. He admired it with a sad look, and took a sip.

"The weaponry is mounted on the walls in the great hall, since there's little need of it these days," Andrew said. "The last forty years have seen great changes in the glens. A man has a need to be a warrior no longer, unless he joins the King's army.

We try to be educated and cultured, and find our way in the union with England."

"The English ne'er saw Highlanders as warriors," Rab said. "We were traitors, heathens. An uneducated and mawkit people in need of being put down. In fact, they still treat us so. The laws and policies they write in London are cleverly worded so at first we think we're being treated as equals, but the truth comes out. We're not governed fairly, and then we are scoffed at because it seems we cannot manage our affairs properly."

"How can they think us uneducated and unintelligent?" Anne demanded. "One only need look at Kirthgarran. There are pictures here, books, Flemish tapestries, and other fine things. Why, consider this very room. How could one sit here and think us stupid, loutish folk?"

As she gestured to the wall friezes of leaves, blossoms, and buds painted in pastel shades, my eyes followed. The interwoven leaves and flowers created roundels that held Classical scenes of people draped in Grecian robes. Skillful artisans had decorated the high, rectangular ceiling as well, dividing it into curved triangular shapes. Rimmed in gilt plasterwork, each one was masterfully filled with vines and flowers. I had never seen anything so fine.

"Kirthgarran's embellishments are many, as money has allowed," Rab conceded. "As with any estate, there are times of wealth, and years of want. But the clan seats and the chieftains and the bonnet lairds are not looked upon as being typical of Scotland. The people of the glens typify the north. Poverty-stricken. Ignorant of English. Barefoot. Backward. And the Lowlanders—why, they try to be as English as the English." He grimaced at me from across the table. "I'm sorry, Keeley. But you've seen it. Your own father's a fine example."

I did not wish to think of my father.

"Change has come more slowly in the north," he said. "Here the landowners face famines and dying spirits. Where once every man was a soldier, ready to put his cattle into the hands of the aged and follow his chief to fight whenever trouble arose, there's now no honor in it, and hardly a sword or musket within a man's reach. Everything is lost but the need to spend money and the battle to find it in order to spend it. We're lucky if we can raise enough black cattle to..."

"Rabbie," Mairi said. "You've begun to warm to your favorite topic again. Surely there'll be time later for Keeley to be told of all our troubles. Can we not find a different path to follow whilst we eat our lovely supper? Something pleasant and less likely to cause one's blood to boil?"

Rab bent his head. "Aye, you're right, you're right. I apologize. Pay no mind to my sputtering, dear. A winter's fireside is the place for all this to be let loose. Alas, Mairi, it all began with your simple lament for the lost silver."

"A sentiment you did not share, if I mind correctly," Anne said, laughing.

"I shall hold forth no more. But I will complain about this. Da, you've not yet begun the toasting."

Sandy smiled, and raising his glass said, "To your good health, sir."

Rab replied, "And to yours."

It was only the beginning of the toasts. Every glass of wine must be dedicated to someone. When it was my turn I acknowledged Lord Kirthgarran, but the solemnity of the occasion caused my words to stumble.

Like the evening before, the meal seemed to go on forever. With bitter nostalgia I thought of the little table in Gilchrist House where my father and I ate our suppers in silence. I attended to my food. There was hot, broiled salmon. French beans. Pigeon pie. Friar's Chicken with parsley and cinnamon. Pickled walnuts. A second course was served by the young man I did not know and Airig's younger sister Ròs, a lass of perhaps seventeen with flawless skin, copper hair, and wide blue eyes that flitted here and there in excitement. The two offered fare from brimming salvers: tongue and peas, mushrooms, goose in sauce, boiled suet pudding filled with wild strawberry jam, lemon pudding with Naples biscuits, quinces in syrup, and glasses of syllabub with the frothed cream piled high on top of the wine. Already on the table was a Floating Island, the beaten egg whites and currant jelly floating on rosewater and cream.

I had never before seen so much food piled on a table all at once. Mrs. Taggart would have swooned.

The topaz candles of beeswax on the table lent a soft air and the room seemed overly warm. I could only taste a portion of my supper and listen to the cheerful talk, and occasionally glance at Lord Kirthgarran sitting propped up in his pillowed chair.

I had just taken a swallow of fruity wine when a clatter of footsteps approached and the lad who had carried water for my bath that afternoon skidded into the room. He stared at Lord Kirthgarran and reddened from chin to brow, yet breathlessly he kept still. He searched the faces about the table.

"Oh, Captain Fergusson, do come," he said in choked phrases. "'Tis fearful. Fearful."

The piper stopped playing and in consternation the Captain put down his fork and rose. "What is it about, Kenneth?"

"Your dog, sir. They're tearing it to pieces. Please. Come."

He did not hesitate and the rest of us followed, leaving Mairi with Lord Kirthgarran. We flooded out through the front entrance onto the grassy bank of Loch Seàrr. Down toward the water we went, from whence came the piteous crying of an animal. Rab was ahead of me and he turned, grabbing my hand and Anne's.

"Nay, go no farther," he said, but his words were lost in a rumble of growls. Two dogs, the wolf-like creatures I had met the day before, took turns at Coll's black-and-white collie caught between them. Sandy came running with wooden stoups that the men filled at the loch's edge and flung at the pair. Drenched and dripping, they backed off with their tails betwixt their legs. I tugged Rab's hand, trying to release myself.

"I've healed animals before," I told him as I pulled free.

Whilst Lachlan chased away the excited dogs with a stick, Captain Fergusson knelt beside MacDiarmid, whose coat was covered with blood.

I fell to the ground beside them. My napkin from the supper table was still clenched in my fist. I touched the top of the dog's head with my empty hand. "He's still alive," I said.

"But he suffers. He's been too good a friend I'd let him do that."

He stood, putting a hand out to help me to my feet. "It is kind of you." His brows were drawn together, and his concentration lingered on his dog. "But there's nought anyone can do."

Others, including folk from the kitchen, had come to stand

beside us. Captain Fergusson walked alone toward the castle. Sandy squatted beside MacDiarmid and laid a hand on the dog's side. Andrew took Anne away. A few moments later Captain Fergusson was back, holding a long silver pistol with brass fittings.

"Come," Rab urged, and we retraced our steps back up the bank. One last glimpse of Captain Fergusson revealed his outstretched arm with the white cuff of his sleeve falling down over his hand. The hand was extended by the muzzle of the flintlock. I turned, unable to look. Rab and I entered the castle through the oaken door. Just as we did so, the crack of the discharge came.

Except for Captain Fergusson, we all went back to the dining room. I did not know if the others felt like eating. I certainly did not. I took a spoonful of orange-flavored syllabub and could barely swallow it. I shook my head when I was offered some of the Floating Island.

"Those curs of Drummond's," Anne denounced, looking about her. "Coll loved that dog. They were together constantly. What's wrong with Ewen?"

"It is hardly Drummond's fault. He's just had them from his brother. For a fortnight now, is it?" Andrew said.

"They've made nuisances of themselves. Haven't they chased the sheep and the cattle and threatened to attack Margery? That is Ewen's own wife," Anne explained to me. "She and Ewen took the dogs and gave them a home after his brother decided he no longer wanted them. Now we can see why. All the bairns are frightened to the death of them, and it is only a matter of time before one of the wee ones gets bitten. They never let Coll's dog alone. Someone must tell Ewen to be rid of them."

"I hear he puts a great store by them," Rab said after emptying his wineglass.

Talk was thin after that, and of shallow subjects. I said nothing as the conversation went by me. I sat in my chair, my hands cold in my lap. There was little point in remaining at table as the gaiety was gone, and at some unspoken signal Rab and Andrew helped Lord Kirthgarran out of his seat.

"I would stay here with you," the earl said, "but I find I've need of my bed."

Mairi came to his side, her face drained of color. "I'll come upstairs with you and see you settled."

"Sandy can see to that."

"I'll see to that."

He acquiesced, apparently too fatigued to argue. I discovered he was looking at me. "Come to me. If not tomorrow, then soon."

"As you wish, sir," I said, and curtseyed.

Walking slowly, perhaps more slowly than when he had first come, he leant hard on Andrew and Rab.

Anne urged me to join her in the drawing room and until the others returned she talked a little of the evening that lay before us, although her enthusiasm was dampened by the death of Captain Fergusson's dog.

Rab kept his word and showed me how to reach the gardens outside. As we strolled through them, all I could think of was the form of the faithful black-and-white dog, its silky fur stained scarlet on the grass. I imagined I could still smell the acrid sulfuric odor of gunpowder hanging in the air.

I took little pleasure in the garden, and even less in the gathering that attempted to celebrate my wedding and my coming to Kirthgarran. Everyone had gone to much trouble to make it a success, and I was not unappreciative of the many candles and torches in the great hall, the music of the pipes as Donald played in the piper's gallery high above the floor, and the fiddling and the dancing—but it all seemed so meaningless.

Rab instructed me in the steps of the first dance, the shaimit reel, which was meant for bride, bridegroom, and attendants. As we had neither bride maidens nor best young men, Andrew, Anne, Airig, and one of Donald's sons named Geordie joined us, and I was pushed, pulled, and swung through the reel. It little resembled my solitary, impromptu dances by the Tweed. Our parched throats were later rewarded with rum punch and the further toasts that went along with it.

I heard much talk, some of it directed toward me informing me of Kirthgarran's history, the troubles since the Rebellion, and the problems the people now faced. I also heard whisperings behind my back, exchanges in Gaelic. My cheeks burnt when I realized that the farming and cattle men, haphazardly dressed in an assortment of breeks and old kilts, and the women with their plaids pulled over their heads, and even the children with their round, black eyes, spoke about me; it was plain from the way their glances fell on me and flicked away again. At times it seemed to be an unbearable scrutiny. There were some who stared at me as though I were a kelpie escaped from the deep waters of the loch.

I met Mr. Drummond the baillie, or factor, of the estates who owned the vicious dogs. I was introduced to the earl's falconer, Gordon, who along with his young apprentice cared for the earl's peregrines. I lost Rab several times when he spoke to others here and there or went in search of whisky. I saw Captain Fergusson not at all, though I found myself looking for him.

I was alarmed when a voice murmured something beside my left ear. I'd not realized someone was standing close to me beside the hearth. When I turned I found myself nose to nose with a pretty young woman who was about my age if not a bit older, with a heart-shaped face and abundant black hair that cascaded in waves over her shoulders. Her eyes were dark brown with a charming difference in their cast. I spent more than a few seconds staring first at one eye and then the other, attempting to determine if they were actually crossed or not.

Abashedly I said to her, "Pardon me, I beg you. I did not hear what you said."

She smiled but it was a knowing, condescending smile. "I said, you've the look of someone lost."

"I'm not. I'm not lost."

"I wonder what it is like to be brought to an unknown place. To ken nary a body, except for one." I must have appeared confused for she bent closer and whispered, "Your husband."

"Oh, oh aye. But I'm beginning to meet some of my new family, and the others who live here."

"There are some who'd find it overwhelming. So many new faces. But I think I'd find it a grand adventure. Meeting everyone. Learning names. Becoming friends. Learning secrets."

"Secrets..."

"There are always secrets. Every family has them. It takes time for them to be exposed. That's what makes life so appealing. Are you not curious?"

If at first I had thought her eager to be friendly, despite her haughty manner, my belief began to change. Her eyes probed, her lips came too close to my ear, and the slight smile with which she regarded me was anything but sincere. I did not want to appear kae-witted but I had difficulty understanding her. "Curious about what?"

She tilted her head as if to say she was enjoying our little game. "Each one of us has secrets, stories, things we'd rather not have known about us. Those of us who've always lived in Kirthgarran unfortunately ken a great deal about one another. You're the one who'll have the pleasure, learning about us all."

She expected an answer of some sort. "Aye, it should be a pleasure. Coming to know—all of you."

The woman peered both right and left and clasped her hands in front of her crimson petticoat. "Only a day you've been here, and I'll wager you've heard an abundance of things."

I thought fleetingly of Mairi and was ashamed because I had not been seeking any secrets from her this afternoon and yet had been told many.

"You have," she cried jubilantly. "I can see it. There are some I could tell you, to further you along. Or perhaps you already ken what I ken. I'm thinking one of the most interesting is how Rab nearly caused himself to be banned from the castle forever."

It was too late. I was ensnared.

"He's not told you? Well, I suppose 'tis not something he's proud of. Will I tell you?"

Weep not, weep not, my bonnie bonnie bride…
                    The Braes of Yarrow (Trad.)

Chapter Thirteen

My hesitation was enough of an invitation for her. She came even closer and confided in a low voice, "Five years ago or so. He was excited about a race-meeting, and planned to ride one of the earl's horses. But he discovered, after the race was over and he'd lost, miserably, that the groom here had fed and watered the horse in the morning as usual because he'd forgotten about the race. And he did not tell Rab when the beast was saddled and readied. The poor horse could not gallop as fast as Rab wanted, what with a belly full of oats and water. Rab took to the drink afterward when he guessed the truth, and later that night he set off a quarrel with the groom that ended in blows. The groom was gey hurt and nearly died, and left Kirthgarran when he was able. Rab was made to face his father and the earl. That was a stormy day. Sandy was disappointed and the earl was angry, and only with a great deal of humility did Rab manage to earn their forgiveness."

I did not want to know this. I watched her eyes, eyes that threatened to cross but never did, and I took a step away from them.

"He is fond of his whisky," she said, laughing. "But that I do not have to be telling you."

I looked away, knowing I had to get away from her.

"It causes his father great disappointment. Lachlan is a good son, but prefers his own company. 'Tis Coll who Sandy truly favors," she said, nodding her head at Captain Fergusson who had appeared on the other side of the hall. "I'd imagine that at times he wishes Coll were his son. They are that alike." She began to titter. "They are that alike. Now would it not be amusing to learn that in truth, Sandy *was* his father?"

"You must excuse me," I mumbled. I whirled and bumped into my father-in-law, whose ale spilt from his glass onto his waistcoat and turned a patch of the gray wool to glistening black.

Sandy brushed it with an effortless swipe of his hand and apologized for his clumsiness, whilst we both knew it was I who was graceless. I hoped that he had not heard the woman's musings, for I felt enough shame for both of us. I was relieved when I glanced at the hearth after the pleasantries between Sandy and me had been said and forgotten, and saw that the crimson petticoat was no longer there.

My melancholy grew deeper by the hour nonetheless. Toward the middle of the night I felt as I had the evening before: misplaced, dazed, disjointed. There were so many strangers round me that my hands grew damp and grasped each other, my throat tightened, and my stomach hatched creeping things inside. The merrymaking and the dancing would last forever, I thought, and I was flotsam, floating and dipping on the surface as a speck will do on the sea.

At last Rab, red-eyed and stumbling, his breath thick with the alcoholic sweetness of whisky, carried me off to my bed.

The raw recollection of the story that the bold, nameless woman had related to me was an unwanted adjunct.

Again my husband took what he wanted, a repeat of our first coupling. This time I knew what to expect but I had not healed from the night before.

I had thought I had no tears left to shed, but it seemed I was wrong. I was alone when I wept. Not for myself, but for the little dog who would never again look about with lively, chestnut eyes.

I did not venture far from my bedchamber during the next few days. I slept much of the time, giving in to a fatigue that drained my spirit. All round me the castle was silent, although if I listened I could hear distant pounding on the turret roof. Mairi had told everyone I needed a few days of rest, so no footsteps or voices arrived to disturb the relative solitude. I did not care. I wanted to be alone, and to sleep, and I wanted it to be like that always.

Other than Airig who brought me my meals, Rab was the one I saw consistently. When the late summer skies grew dim with dusk-light he would come, curious as to how I had spent my day, confused when he discovered it had been much like the one before it. Sometimes he stayed with me. Sometimes he did not. I no longer feared the unknown, for I knew now what a husband demanded of a wife.

"Anne was asking after you today," he said one night. "I rode over to Rathdale this afternoon, and she was hoping you were recovered. She made me promise to be bringing you there as soon as you feel like riding. She wants to become acquainted."

I nodded.

"Brooding here does you no good, Keeley."

I did not care if it did or not. I looked away.

"You must try to settle yourself. I'll not have you becoming ill, a recluse. You've a life to begin here. You've a husband. A husband, not a father. You're not locked in this room. It is time to come out."

I flushed, but his words meant little.

He tugged me by the hand to the poster bed, stripped my clothing from me, and lay with me. The excitement in him was instant; his hands were rough, his movements forceful and without any regard for me or the pain he caused. Not a word passed between us, but he smiled when he was satisfied, stretching his limbs out beside me and closing his eyes. He seemed to take no notice when I turned on my side. A few minutes later there was the kiss on my cheek, and he left, shutting the door behind him.

I remembered his promise to give me time to adjust to the changes in my life. How long had I expected him to delay his own needs? A month? A year? And what had ever led me to believe he would be gentle?

It mattered not at all. I was Mrs. Robert Fergusson, and it was plain what my duties were.

Mairi came one day. After surveying my chamber, she ordered Rab to carry in a Flemish tapestry she proudly described as being designed by a student of Rubens. Framed pastel drawings appeared and soon adorned the walls, and a colorful Turkish carpet was spread underfoot to soften the floor. She scrounged further for writing and dressing tables, books, candles, and various small articles such as combs, a looking glass, writing paper, an inkpot, and quills.

Grizel, the woman who did the cooking at Kirthgarran, sought me as well. From the first her response to me had been one of fear, and I was aware of her discomfort as she stood in my room. She avoided my eyes, twisted her sleeves. She wanted to be reassured, she said, that her cookery and the assistance of the kitchen maids were satisfactory. "You're daughter-in-law of the castle's steward. You might want to make changes," she said.

I lost no time in convincing her I did not mean to interfere at all. I was not mistress of Kirthgarran. Indeed, I was certain there would be tasks for me when I was strong enough.

I left my room only to go to the garderobe, a small vaulted chamber with a narrow window. The privy was built within the wall, and the vertical shaft below was full of cold draughts. It was not a place to tarry.

I could not stop thinking about Davy. I turned over the memories of our days together one by one, never once finding a clue as to why he had left me. Remembering our walks and our intimate conversations made me ache for his warmth and the touch of his lips. He had seemed genuine. I thought I had understood him completely. Trust had blossomed between us, and then he had abandoned me. No matter how hard I scrutinized his behavior in my quiet bedchamber with my new understanding of the needs of men, I could not comprehend what had happened. Perhaps he had been afraid of my father after all. Perhaps he had decided I would be happier remaining in Melrose than wandering, hungry and homeless, with him. Or he might have realized that the responsibility of my comfort was too much for him. But why had he not told me so? Why had he allowed me to wait for him whilst he went whistling cheerfully down the track to Galashiels?

When I had been at Kirthgarran a fortnight, a cold day dawned and Kenneth built up my little fire for me. I sat by the hearth in my chemise and shawl watching the logs burn, reflecting on the puzzle of Davy's conscience once again, but as the hours went by and I became lost in the leaping tongues of scarlet and gold, the memory of the lightning strike came back to me. It brought with it an unbidden sense of entrapment.

All at once the fire spat out a burning ember that landed amongst the folds at my feet. Whilst I searched for it, smoke curled upward, carrying the stench of burning wool. I leapt up, shaking the little coal free from my hem. I pounded the blackened hole in my chemise with a palm. The fright was enough to cause me to dress and flee from my refuge, down the passage, down the stairs, and through the front door. I halted only when I came to the edge of the loch.

The clear water of Loch Seàrr rippled toward the shore, catching shimmers of sunlight as it caressed the pebbles and stones beneath its surface in a soothing cadence. I sat on a stone and let my hand float in the coolness of it. Tiny fish came to investigate, hovering motionlessly one moment and darting away the next, followed by their miniature shadows.

I inhaled a clean, earthy fragrance in the air, a melding of greenery and water. Nearby, redstarts and willow warblers sang, and at times a cow leisurely bellowed.

I rose and took to a turf path. The track followed the burn

that came down from the hills and eventually crossed it by means of a curved bridge of stone. Beside the bridge was a kirk, and beyond that a heathered hill beckoning to be climbed. Mindlessly I clambered upward, disturbing bees and butterflies, but at the crest I stopped short. Far below me sat a lad watching a handful of grazing sheep. The animals were not Cheviots; they were thin, white-faced, and straight-horned with fleece more like hair than the rippled wool with which I was familiar. But the shock of the scene was absolute. It could have been a hill near Melrose with Davy's flock tearing at the grass.

The comparison brought the past back to overwhelm me. I sat down on the turf. If that were Davy before me, if I had a chance to talk to him, what would I say? What would he have to say?

I remained upon the hillside, flies and midges swarming about me betwixt bouts of wind, and continued to contemplate the solitary figure. I had to accept the fact that any man with a sense of right and wrong would not have done what Davy had done. Any person who cared for another would not allow her to suffer if he could help it.

I brooded until the afternoon was far gone and a long summer night took its place. The shepherd rose and started leading his flock homeward along a crooked path through the heather. When the top of his head disappeared behind an outgrowth of rock, I felt forsaken all over again, as if I'd just learnt that Davy had left Melrose without me.

Only when the wind began to blow fiercely and mind and body became completely drained did I think of returning to the castle. I stood, brushing bits of grass and heather from the skirt of my gown, and heard someone calling my name. I searched the slopes until I saw Sandy not far above, waving an arm.

He hastened toward me, his coat catching the wind. "Keeley," he called. "There's been a good wee bit of pitleurachie this day, with you being gone. Our Rab did not know what to think. He thought you unwell, I suppose. He bade us to join him and find you."

"I did not mean to stay this late," I said, fitting my feet back into their slippers and wondering when I would ever be able to forget the past.

"There's no need for apologies. Coll will be along shortly. Will we wait for him?"

His silver-threaded hair belied the fact he was fit, and I had difficulty keeping up as I followed him back toward the water. Hem and slippers caused me to struggle, but his feet were faultless amongst the crags of stone and profusion of heather and bracken. Soon I could hear the spate of the burn and see the arched stone bridge. Captain Fergusson was on the other side, leading a black horse toward us.

I had not seen him since the night of my infar. I thought of MacDiarmid, and if all had been well how he would be at his master's side now, panting and pricking up his ears. I wondered if Captain Fergusson thought of him still. Somehow I knew he must.

"So Sandy's found you," he said when he reached us.

"It seems I've caused a stir."

"You've come to no harm?" His eyes swept over me as if to content themselves I had sustained no bodily injury. "Rab discovered you gone," he said with a smile. "He was worried you might have wandered and lost your way, or fallen."

"I should have told someone."

"Nonsense. But you're away now? Will you ride Dominie?"

"I do not mind walking."

The three of us turned up the path toward the castle. The horse, a proud beast with black feathering at the fetlocks and a tail that threatened to sweep the ground, was obviously well-bred and needed no encouragement to follow us.

"He's grand," I said, touching the luxurious mane and admiring the arched neck and small, neat head. "I've never seen such a breed."

"He's a Friesian. The earl hoped to breed him, but then lost interest. He's a bit long in the tooth now, but a hardy fellow nonetheless. Still striking to look at, is he not?"

I agreed and ran my hand down his neck. He responded by tossing his head. Unfortunately, I could think of nothing further to say. My mind was still caught up with thoughts of Davy and my loss of him.

"There'll be a reeving-wind this night," Captain Fergusson

pronounced, lifting his face as we walked into the strengthening breeze. "And rain. I'm hoping no harm will come to the grain."

I could sense the subtle sharpness in the gust, the promise of moisture. "I saw black cattle, and oat fields in the glen, or I thought they were oats. And barley."

"Aye, oats and bere and corn, all grown on a score of small farms. All will be ready by October, if too much rain does not fall and cause it to rot in the fields. We're all wary. We've had our share of famine in the past and I do not think we could survive it again."

"Lord Kirthgarran is dependent on the people and their welfare, then."

"It has always been so. The folk and their ancestors, mostly Fergussons, were the earl's providers. His army when he needed one."

"A laird and his vassals, of medieval times."

"Much the same," Sandy agreed.

"But the Rising in 1745 changed a great many things," I said.

"True," the Captain said. "We've had to reinvent a great deal. The clans fell apart in the reprisals. Even the chiefs who'd not sided with the Prince lost their jurisdiction over their clansmen."

"Yet the Fergussons here have remained."

"Most of them. They had to accept separate farms, fixed leases, regulations. Lord Kirthgarran is no longer benefactor and protector, but landlord. Luckily, now that the Highlands are no longer a threat to the throne, we've won back a few things. The Highland Society of Scotland encourages clanship as well as agriculture. Some mind the auld ways. Others, like my brothers and Sandy's sons, ken them from what we've been told. But there are new problems."

I looked ahead at the castle with its rebuilt bartizan roof. "Rab mentioned them," I said, remembering. "Creditors, emigration."

"We battle them every day. Lord Kirthgarran hasn't the strength to fight. Andrew made a pact with Rab and Lachlan to save Kirthgarran from bankruptcy, and I joined them when I returned from the war. We had to pledge ourselves to the folk and assure them we meant to be helping them."

"Why do they emigrate, then?"

His voice deepened when he answered. "Because shippers babble enticing tales of wealth in America. The agents are bent on growing rich from transporting human beings, since there's no money in sheep and cattle any longer with the colonies raising their own. Unsuspecting families who hope for a new, bright land are gathered and packed into filthy ships that kill many of them before they even cross the sea. The discontent amongst the folk here is sometimes bred by the emigration agents themselves. They lure them away, and leave the farms empty or severely short-handed. Leave the land and the landowners to suffer."

"If there's not enough grain or cattle raised and sold, rents cannot be paid, and Lord Kirthgarran cannot satisfy his own debts," I said, remembering Father's account books.

"That's the way of it. It's all come to a matter of money. The folk must use coin to pay rent for the land allotted to them. They must pay to remain in the homes their fathers took for granted! No longer can they give over a share of their grain and cows, because Kirthgarran's debts must, in turn, be paid in coin. And to add to the misery, our Scots pounds have not stopped depreciating. The rents are not enough, though they've been raised, and raised again. And when a family leaves for America, more land lies fallow, and less cattle are sold, and fewer coins go into the coffer."

"Have you made a difference, you and the others?"

He considered, and said, "I think so. We learn all we can about coaxing oats from the soil and that, and then show the cottars, and stand by them to prove the earl still cares for their well-being."

"It's different where I come from. There's not been all this upheaval."

"The Lowlands are prospering. Too well, I sometimes believe."

"What do you mean?"

"Have you not heard the plans for developing the Highlands that the businessmen and politicians spout? Plans already put into practice in many a place?"

I could think of none and said so.

"There are a number of bond-ridden chiefs," Captain Fergusson said, rubbing the neck of the horse, "who've been offered large sums for their lands. Rent, in other words, for their holdings to be used as sheep runs by Lowlanders who've more ambition than they've land. Unfortunately, it means clearing all the hills and glens and forcing everyone away. The financiers become rich whilst the people become homeless with nought to call their own."

"Does Lord Kirthgarran intend to follow this plan?"

"He's no wish to," Sandy answered. "And neither do the lads. But many families are leaving. They not only emigrate to North America but to the Lowlands where a man can be earning a wage for a day's work. The cotton mills beckon to them, and the cities, though they scorn them. Edinburgh. Glasgow. Dundee. We've too few folk to properly tend the land, and too many to be raising sheep."

"What can you do, then?"

"Stay together, I'm thinking," Captain Fergusson said. "Feel the auld clan ties. Tend the land together. There's much of the loyalty left. Lord Kirthgarran was always respected as chieftain. I hope the folk in the glen care for him enough that they'll keep trust in us. I believe, aye, I do believe Kirthgarran can be kept whole and if not wealthy, at least able to support itself."

"And if you are successful or not," I said, "what will happen when..."

He glanced at me. "When Lord Kirthgarran is gone?"

At my nod his whole manner changed. He looked far away, and his hand fell from the horse. "Kirthgarran passes—because there are no living children to inherit—back to the Crown."

I was confused. "But there must be other kin..."

"The law is plain." He spoke without expression. "Kirthgarran and the lands attached to it in Strath Gruagach are entailed, you see, and he has no choice. The tailzie stipulates that upon his death, the castle and the estate, farms and all, must go to a direct, blood descendant. A son if he lives. A daughter if there is no son. But because there is neither all will become the property of the King and Parliament. They'll do what they will with it."

"And you? And the others? Rab and me?"

"Most likely the estate will be given or sold to a favorite.

And if that man thinks kindly of us there may be homes for us here. If not, we'll have to find others."

"But the care of Kirthgarran, the farming and the cattle and everything you've all been doing..."

"Will be done by the Court of Exchequer, or by someone Parliament appoints or gifts the estate to."

I discovered my feet had stopped. It took a moment for me to grasp his words. Kirthgarran and all its possessions were to be lost. The men had halted as well. Captain Fergusson's hand stilled the horse.

Sandy watched me warily. "Rab's not told you this."

It was an echo of Mairi's words. I shook my head dazedly.

Captain Fergusson said, "Perhaps you should ask him to explain it to you. I can see I've upset you. Little did I mean to."

"There are many things I've not been told, it seems."

I could sense his embarrassment. He glanced at Sandy and gave Dominie's shoulder a long stroke. I was thankful when we began walking again and reached the end of the footpath. The castle lay before us. Kenneth came to take the horse into the stable as soon as we passed through the postern gate.

"All is not as bleak as I've portrayed it," Captain Fergusson said as we crossed the grass of the courtyard. "For one thing, Lord Kirthgarran has remained here. Many of his fellow landowners have given in to the temptation of living in the South, trying to be Englishmen as the English Government hopes they will. But he's not broken ties with his kinsmen, nor turned his back on them, nor incurred debts they do not understand yet must strive to pay for him. The folk seem to trust us, as his agents. And King George and Parliament may prove to be merciful and wise, and give Kirthgarran to the earl's closest kinsmen, the Fergussons of Lund. Andrew will inherit the small estate of Rathdale in any case, for that's a recent acquisition not subject to the tailzie, and the earl has promised it to him."

"Yet none of these things changes the truth. Kirthgarran is destined to pass out of his family if it prospers or not."

"That's the truth of it," he agreed unwillingly. "It would have gone to Bàtair, or Uisdean, who was younger, if one of them had lived. Nay, do not be puzzled. I'm sorry. In English it's Walter and Hugh."

"Lord Kirthgarran's sons?"

"They both joined the 73rd, the Highland Light Infantry. MacLeod's Highlanders. Lord Kirthgarran was against it but they were headstrong. He especially wanted Walter to stay, for he was his heir, but he would not listen and despite bitter quarrels, I'm told, he went along with his brother. Their battalion was sent to Gibraltar the next year and there was the siege by the French and the Spanish." His voice changed again, softening in volume, though I thought he strove within himself to keep it from doing so. "I heard none of it myself 'til I returned four years ago. They died within a week of each other, in '81. Walter from an exploding shell. Hugh from the bluidy flux."

"I'm sorry," I whispered, my breath catching.

"It was more than Lord Kirthgarran could bear. Learning the news caused an attack of some sort. He became so weak they thought he'd not recover. His greeting has caused a decline ever since. He has, at times, been bewildered, forgetful—and his speech slurs." He paused, and Sandy nodded grimly.

"Last year," the steward added, "he suffered another, milder attack, and it affected his right side. His arm and leg mostly. It's put him off balance and he's forced to keep to his bed a good part of every day."

"I wish..." Captain Fergusson began, but he stopped abruptly. He went on in words I did not believe he had first intended. "I wish you could have known him before. He was robust, full of fight. I mind how he was when I left. The change in him is unsettling. A part of him has lost the will to live." After a few seconds he gestured to the castle door. "They'll be waiting for us."

There was too much to think about, too much to examine and sort and put together. And still, there was one thing that felt unfinished. "Before we join the others I wish to speak of something to you," I said to him.

Sandy took his leave of us. Captain Fergusson seemed to force away his somber mood, and for the moment I struggled to put behind me all he had said.

"Captain Fergusson..."

"Coll," he corrected me.

My confidence wavered. "I've not seen you since it happened.

I wanted to tell you. I was upset about your dog. I wanted to tell you I've felt wretched about him." In light of everything he had told me this seemed insignificant. I felt foolish as I waited for his response, but for my benefit, I supposed, he accepted my sentiments in the same solemnity with which they'd been given.

"There's no need. I knew."

"Do you think, someday, you'll find yourself another dog?"

"It is possible, I suppose."

"I looked for you, during our wedding ceilidh."

"I was there for a time."

"And the past fortnight..."

"Rabbie told us you needed rest," he finished. "I hoped you were not ill."

His eyes seemed translucent, bottomless. I shook myself, aware I had been staring into them. "I think I've recovered a little," I said.

"Have you been eating well?"

"You always think of food."

He grinned with one corner of his mouth, letting some amusement touch his eyes. "For that you must blame the army."

"After today," I said, drawing my woolen shawl about me, "I think I could eat a supper meant for two people."

"Then you must," he urged. "You must eat whilst there's food to be had. You may be finding someday there'll be nought but slug jelly and you'll rue the day you passed by haggis, neeps, and tatties."

"Slug jelly?"

He lifted his chin and laughed. "I'm afraid that's what we called it when we were young. I had it just the once, and ne'er forgot."

"But what is it?"

"In times of great want, the sole source of meat is the lowly black slug, who glides upon the ground as if he's not a care in the world. Grizel collected them one year and put them into jars with enough salt to melt them. They became jelly after a time, which she sliced and fried like collops, and served to us in the winter to take the hunger from our bellies. But ach!" He wrinkled his nose and shook his head. "They were gruesome. A nightmare. I'd eat grass afore I'd taste them again."

"Does she often make this—slug jelly?"

"Not ever since, to my knowledge, due to the uproar we made. But she saved our lives, for which we owe her a great deal, I'm thinking. In any case I do not suppose there'll be any of it on the table tonight, so you need not worry. And I'll warrant our suppers are already set out. Do you wish to put it off any longer?"

I shook my head. Together we went inside.

Rab was relieved to see me. He had ridden, he told me, round Loch Seàrr. Perhaps he had been struck by a fear that I had left him. "I found your chamber empty, the fire cold. No one had seen you," he scolded as he caressed my shoulder.

"I needed the air," I said, feeling a flutter of alarm. He is not my father, I told myself.

"When the afternoon was gone it occurred to me you might become lost. I grew fearful then. What made you go out alone? Someone should've gone with you."

"I wanted to be alone. I did not become lost. I've spent the most enjoyable part of my life out of doors. I found myself longing for it."

He sighed. "You need offer no excuses, dear. I mind what you once told me about your walks and rides. From now on I'll expect your wanderings." He gave me a look of gentle affection.

I could not forget, however, that he had not told me about Kirthgarran's fate, or how all of our lives would someday be changed by the whim of a king.

"I'm away to Rathdale," Rab said one morning, pushing himself from the table.

In a small voice I asked, "Will I go with you?"

He halted, stunned, I supposed, but with a grin he bowed effusively and took my hand. "That would be a fine thing, Mrs. Fergusson!"

It was not because I wanted to call upon our neighbors that I volunteered to accompany my husband. I had not ridden Greyfriar since our arrival, and my fingers ached to touch his head and smooth the thick hair on his body, to gallop him into the wind and feel his joy. Somehow it would unite me with Benjamin—at least in spirit.

With Rab's encouragement echoing in my ears I hurried to change into my riding habit.

When I crossed the courtyard to meet him, ready to ride, my attention was diverted by the sight of three falcons perched on the short, wooden blocks. It was the first I had seen them. The birds paused in their preening and followed my progress across the lawn with large dark eyes, sometimes bobbing their heads.

From the stable door Rab said, "The earl's peregrines."

I had difficulty taking my eyes from them.

"He used to hunt with them. There've always been peregrines at Kirthgarran. He's a few left. Four, I'm thinking."

"He must miss the hunting, as he misses so many things."

"The earl wants nought to do with them anymore. Gordon and his lad Magnus see to them. They take quite a bit of exercise and require constant care. But Coll likes to hunt with them. He and Sandy often fly them."

"But you do not?"

He laughed. "I've not the patience. 'Tis a musket I reach for when I've a taste for flesh, not the talons of a bird."

One of them jingled a bell tied with a jess to its striped, feathered leg. They were all tethered to their blocks. I turned to look squarely at Rab. "How ill is Lord Kirthgarran?"

He sighed and inspected the fastenings on the well-worn bridle in his hand. "Last spring we thought he was going to die."

"Coll told me he's been bedridden for a year."

"He had a shock six years ago when he heard that Walter and Hugh were both dead. Mairi and my father nursed him. He survived, but he was weak, and every year since then has found him weaker, and last year, for no reason, he suffered another attack. This one has forced him to stay in his bed. If there's another..."

I let the words remain unspoken. "There must be a physician who attends him?"

"In Pitlochry. We send for him when he's needed. He says there's nought that can be done. Herbs do not help, nor does bleeding. Lord Kirthgarran's grief, as much as the attacks, causes him to be an invalid."

"And yet—the other night. He came downstairs."

"It was you…" he said.

"What about me?"

He hesitated. "You make him want to go on."

I forced myself to lay my thoughts before him. "I do not understand. What was it he said the first time I saw him? He seemed sad. The words were not in English."

"I do not mind them."

"He wept when he saw me. He spoke some words, and repeated them again and again. Can you not mind what he said?"

"Not exactly," he insisted. "He wished he was as he used to be, that he could welcome you to Kirthgarran properly, as earl, standing in his hall."

"But to shed tears."

"Think how it must be for him, dear, forced to keep to his bed. He thinks of us as his family. He was aye touched by you. He was disturbed because he could not welcome you as the man he used to be."

I was unconvinced, though I was no expert in the study of human nature with my frail experience of people.

With relief I greeted Greyfriar when MacNeil brought him to me. I decided, as I petted the garron's warm nose and ears, that I would not procrastinate. I would keep my word and visit the earl. Lord Kirthgarran's health really was of no concern to me, but for my residence here at the castle and his generosity to Rab, I owed him the courtesy.

Time and chance are but a tide…
Duncan Gray (Burns)

Chapter Fourteen

stood at the half-closed door of the keep's bedchamber for a long while, my stomach knotted whilst I tried to build the courage to tap. Perhaps he would be asleep. Perhaps I would annoy him. I thought of a thousand excuses that would allow me to walk away. Finally I made my knuckles rap twice, lightly, upon the door-post.

For a second there was no answer. A low voice said, "Come."

The room seemed larger in daylight. The Earl of Kirthgarran was sitting up in his curtained bed just as he had before, and he lifted his head when he heard no one speak. The transformation from apathy to joy in his eyes was so immediate and honest that my guilt at postponing this interview deepened three-fold. I curtseyed, wondering if my gesture conveyed more shame than respect.

He said in his halting speech, "It is good of you to come! I've thought much about you and how you must be finding life here. Sit, my lass. There's a chair here, waiting for you." He pointed with his left hand.

"I've waited too long to come and see you," I said as I sat stiffly beside him.

"The passage of the days does not mean to me what it once did. I used to count them, and fret and worry over them, but they're of little consequence after all." He was speaking in such a rough, deep voice I guessed he must have just awakened. "If either of us needs to apologize, it must be me for the way I took your coming."

I was unsure as to how to respond. "I'm relieved to find you have English as well as Gaelic."

"Rab has told me you do not speak the ancient tongue. But, being young as you are, there's still time for you to learn."

Perhaps, I thought. Someday.

"You're finding your way about the castle, the glen."

"Gradually. I've been lost, but just once."

"And now you mind your way the better because of it. That is the way of things. You're settling in, and soon will no longer be a newcomer. I hope our Rabbie has shown you all there is to see."

"I've not seen much of the countryside. There was—that is—I am afraid I haven't been able to explore much. I did not feel well when I first came."

"Were you ill, lass?"

"Weary, I think. But I've rested and feel better. And yesterday Rab took me to Rathdale," I added, remembering the laird's dwelling-house with its mullioned windows and crow-stepped gables, the surrounding meadows, fertile corn fields, and woods of oak and ash. "But I've not yet seen the glen of Kirthgarran, nor Strath Gruagach."

Lord Kirthgarran seemed pleased nonetheless. He breathed deeply as he gazed at me. "Rab's a good lad, they're good lads, all of them. They are what are left of my family. I consider them kinsmen, and you as well. You must be happy here, lass. I'll stand for nought less."

"You are kind, my lord."

He became silent at that, and I thought his eyes dimmed. At last he pronounced, "Kirthgarran is your home now. You must always think of it so."

I fumbled, "Aye, it is my home."

He lay back upon his pillows. I observed him, hoping he would not mind. He had kind eyes, eyes that were the blue of an evening sky when the sun is disappearing below the horizon and violet begins to blend into the deepness of it, just when stars first begin to appear. His other features were bold, his jaw square beneath the beard, and I could imagine him leading men on a march into battle with assurance and experience.

There were dark depressions beneath his eyes, though, and grooves beside his mouth not hidden by his moustache. To his shoulders fell the silver hair, once jauntily tied behind, no doubt, as he rode about his lands and saw to the needs of his people. He was the chieftain; he would have ridden out with a henchman and a dozen men at his tail, all bearing arms and ready to serve. His eyes sought mine at last, and I was lured away from my musings.

"Rab has told me how you came to meet, and how at first your father was eager to shield you from all suitors. But then he had a change of heart. Unfortunately Rabbie is not much of a storyteller. He tells me a few details and expects me to be filling in the rest. I'll not trouble you for a recounting of your courtship. I'm simply happy all went well in the end. I'm afraid I *am* a relentless storyteller. It's all I have, the memory of the auld days. I hope, sometimes, that you'll indulge me. I can think of nought better than to impart to you the history of Kirthgarran."

"I am fond of stories."

He smiled. "We will get along, I'm thinking. Are you fond of reading?"

"Oh aye."

"You'll enjoy our library then."

I was sure I would. I looked out through the window that faced the loch and watched as Lachlan and Coll practiced swordsmanship on the lawn. I had seen them before on several mornings. All the foster sons seemed to delight in crossing broadswords and discovering who could disarm the other in the least amount of time.

They created blood-chilling spectacles and though I knew they were in exercise, I was frightened because the sparring appeared to be so much in earnest. Coll had been trained well and was aggressive with his movements, but on previous occasions both he and Lachlan had caused my head to spin as they had lunged and crashed together. They seemed to embody warrior spirits from the Dark Ages. Even from this distance today I could perceive the narrowed eyes and the grim mouths that often emitted growls and heaving bellows. If I were an opponent I would quail because of the expression that came over each face.

Lord Kirthgarran was observing the play also, and when I glanced at him in apprehension, ashamed of my manners, I saw that he was smiling. His eyes turned to me. I was ill-prepared for what he said next. "Rabbie has told me you play the clarsach."

"It was my mother's."

"I've a fondness for music. Both me and my wife, my dear Agnes, we loved it well. She would sing sometimes, and I thought it fine to listen to. There's not been..." His voice halted and his blue eyes wandered. "There's not been much music amongst these stones lately. I've forgotten, nay, not forgotten, pushed away, the memory of it. But the stones yearn for it. As my heart does. The past cannot be captured," he said as his gaze came back to me. "Yet one has some control over the present. Donald comes at times to ask if I'd care to hear his fiddle, or the small-pipes, but I always tell him no. I'm thinking it's a mistake. I found his playing the other night as lifting as a wind from the hills."

I agreed.

"But for bringing peace to my soul I've always favored the sound of a harp."

I remained silent.

"I'd be grateful if you would play your clarsach for me."

I struggled to force my voice above the volume of a whisper. "I've not played. I have not touched it. It has been too long."

"You no longer play?" he asked, with a note of disappointment.

"I've not played it for several years. Since my mother died, I..."

"I was hoping you would bring it with you sometimes, and ply the strings a bit, only to pass the time. But if you do not play it, then it's a silly question I'm asking."

I had begun squeezing my thumbs in my fingers. "I think I'd make so many mistakes my music would be quite unpleasant to hear."

"Then you would consider it?"

"Nay, I could not. I cannot." I looked at him, afraid.

"I'll make a bargain with you. I will ask nought more than to hear the clarsach once, and then I will lie here happy." He did not smile but I could sense his patience. "It's difficult for you, my dear lassie. I can see that. But if ever the time comes when you change your mind, you'll find me a simple and appreciative audience, and realize there was nought to worry over."

His eyes looked a little tired. I had stayed too long. "I must let you rest."

"But you'll be back soon. Just yourself, with no clarsach."

I rose and went across to the door, finding him watching me. I went through the opening, baffled at the pleasure my visit had brought him.

Ewen Drummond the baillie arrived one rain-swept evening. I knew now his position went back to those years before 1745 when he had been Lord Kirthgarran's most trusted man. The two were of an age, and I suspected they had enjoyed each other's friendship all these years.

He came into the drawing room dressed in his usual dark breeks and coat, his thin figure bent, his lined face punctuated with bristling eyebrows. He laid his wet cocked hat on the mantle. The queue of gray hair at his back was dripping.

"Ewen," acknowledged Andrew. "This is a dreich night for you to be about."

"The rain's not so bad the now," he replied. "And I had need of speaking to you."

Coll handed him a glass and they all settled down to talk. I listened for a time whilst Ewen related what he had heard about a cottar planning to emigrate with his family. Their voices became quieter and I heard occasional phrases such as "North America" and "two other families."

I sat at the Saxony spinning wheel in the corner. As a new wife I was expected to spin flax and sew deid-claes, dead-clothes, from the woven linen, first for Rab and then for myself. They would be the shirts and stockings in which we would one day be buried, and they must be made, stored away, and occasionally aired. Mairi had given me ample flax so I could begin. I was glad to have something with which to occupy myself.

The evening was typical of those I had spent so far at Kirthgarran. Though Rab and the other men were occupied during the day with the overseeing and care of Kirthgarran and Rathdale, after supper was done and night approached they usually sprawled about the big drawing room.

Sometimes the cook, maids, and other servants were drawn to the fireside as well, and all would collect in the hall where larger gatherings of folk were more easily accommodated. But the drawing room offered the most comfort, and Rab, Lachlan, and Coll often settled there in the evening, sometimes joined by Sandy, Donald the piper, the baillie, groom, falconer, and visiting friends, and—more often than not—by Andrew, who spent more time at Kirthgarran than he did at Rathdale. They sang and told old stories or recited ancient poetry, tapped their feet to the music from Donald's fiddle or small-pipes, shared accounts of the farming folk, drank abundantly of ale and whisky, and smoked tobacco in long-stemmed, clay pipes.

I wondered which state caused me the more anxiety, being alone with my husband or sitting forgotten in a room full of men. When Donald drew his bow over his strings or squeezed the bellows under his arm and piped sweet tunes, I listened and forgot myself. But more often than not I cowered in my chair by the hearth, out of notice.

I wished Rab would let me leave. It was a desire of his I accompany him in the evenings, but it afforded me a great deal of puzzlement since it was obviously not my sole company he craved. "You are my lady-wife," he often said. "The new bride of Kirthgarran." He urged me to sit with him and then turned to the others for his entertainment.

Ewen rose and retrieved his hat when the clock chimed

eleven. "I'll have a look in at Lord Kirthgarran, and then I must be away. Margery will be wondering what's become of me."

"She'll be relieved, no doubt, to see you've not been washed away into the loch," Sandy said.

The gentleman stopped several paces from the door. "I'd nearly forgotten," he muttered, turning. "Have any of you seen my dogs?"

"Your dogs, sir? You mean those de'ils your kin thrust upon you?" Rab asked.

"My dogs," he insisted. "They've not taken their food for two days now. I've not seen a tail of them. Have they been about, do you ken?"

Coll, standing before the fire, studied Ewen. I could not help but think of poor MacDiarmid.

"They're on a frolic," Andrew suggested kindly. "No doubt begging a meal from someone in the glen."

Ewen shook his head. "They never miss their food. They mind where their scraps are put. They come every night, and sleep by the lum-cheek."

"We'll keep watch for them," Rab promised.

Still shaking his head, the baillie went on his way upstairs to see his old friend. In time Andrew left for home, and it was not long before Rab and I were alone. I gathered flaxen thread from the spindle with weary fingers. Only the frequent hiss of the fire and the splash of whisky into a glass broke the silence. Rab turned his back to the gate-legged table and swallowed a thimbleful of the drink, peering downward.

"It seems a long day," he said.

"Have you been haying?"

"Aye. We're desperate to be cutting because of the weather. At this time of year there's always worry, because if cut the grass wet it will rot, and turning it over a number of times to dry it causes it to fall apart and lose its goodness." He paused. "I've been neglectful these days. I've not asked how you've been spending your time."

"I've been to visit Lord Kirthgarran."

He tilted his head, eyes wide. "It meant much to him, I would guess."

"He did seem glad to see me."

He put down his glass and reached for the whisky. The spirits were in a ceramic jar and he dipped himself a drink with the ladle, spilling some on the hand holding the tumbler. "And did you enjoy your visit?"

"I did not find it unpleasant."

"You'll see him again."

"He expects me to."

He gave a grunt of pleasure. "I'm thinking you'll find a companionship together, you and Graeme Fergusson. 'Twill be good for him." He paused. "And good for you."

I gave him a questioning look.

"There's only half of you here with us, Keeley. I'm not sure where the rest of you has gone but I'm hoping, someday, to see her again."

I thought briefly of the hour we had walked our horses by Melrose Abbey, when I had forgotten myself and shared confidences with him. She exists no longer, I wanted to say. Instead I rose, intending to go upstairs.

Rab took a quick swallow. "Bide a bittie. I'll go with you."

I wandered about the room as he finished his whisky; touched an etched gunpowder horn stoppered with silver; ran my hands along the bindings of books on the table. At last I stopped in front of the shelf that held the remaining collection of family silver and studied a plate engraved with ornate scrolls.

"You've improved the earl's spirits," Rab said behind me. "To him you're the sun, shining through the mist, brightening his world. Kirthgarran suits you, Keeley. Did I not tell you so before? And you suit it. I can sense these things. How rightly you belong here." Though he meant to be charming, his poetry caused me to feel conscious of the actual picture of gloom I must be. His footsteps came behind me. He settled a shoulder against the wall and seemed to content himself with watching me.

"The silver is so handsome," I said faintly.

He turned his attention to the shelf. "There's not much left, as Mairi told you. But at least the finer pieces have been saved."

"This cup is lovely." Like the plate, it was elegantly chased. The bell-like top was meant to resemble a thistle blossom and the handles were serpentine. My father had not owned such costly items. I could not resist the lure of the handle, and I stroked the warm metal.

"A wine cup," he said. "A king might have had such a one at his table."

I lifted it from its resting place. It was a pleasant shape, the shine of its surface deep. The engraving incorporated thistles and vines. I tipped it to look inside, and all at once Rab's hand came over mine and held it fast. I glanced up to find him staring at the cup. "What is it?" I gasped.

His hand tightened but he would not answer. He laid his tumbler on the shelf and with two hands forced me to replace the cup in its original spot. He brought my hands to his chest. "I'm done with my drink," he said huskily. "Time we went upstairs." I let him draw my hands up to his lips where he kissed my palms with deliberate ardor. His eyes questioned, beguiled. "Come with me."

"But you were telling me about the cup."

"Have we not seen enough of it? Let's be away upstairs. I'm weary of everything, but you."

"But something is wrong."

"Nay. Nought, nought is wrong. Come with me. Come," he said, pulling me away. I had no choice but to allow myself be led.

He blew out all the candles on the mantel but one, and the room slid into semi-darkness. How black a night it was. The heavy sky without obliterated all light, and I could hear the soft trickle of rain. Rab grabbed the candleholder. With a sure hand he began to take me toward the doorway leading to the great hall.

I turned at the last possible moment. I fancied I could see the plate and the thistle cup shining faithfully on their shelf, glowing in the flickering light from the hearth. But Rab's hand was insistent and I was soon forced to forget them, as his will intended.

I had not sought the garden as much as I'd imagined I would, but whenever I followed its paths I found a vestige of peace. One morning I decided to walk there and scatter a pocketful of crumbs I had saved.

Whilst the birds pecked and fought over the assortment of morsels, my attention drifted to the arched remnant of the curtain wall by the loch, and I wandered to the loch's edge. Ivy-leaved toadflax and red valerian battled for space with herb robert amongst the fallen stones at the base. The fragrance of damp earth beneath my bare feet rose to meet me, and when I touched the stones, the moss that clung to their surfaces sprang under my fingertips.

This was all that remained of an ancient castle far, far older than Kirthgarran, built on the shore of Loch Seàrr as a sentinel at the mouth of the glen. The wall fragment rose and turned at a corner, creating a delta of protected grass. One lichen-encrusted wall was perforated by the open arch, and a bit of vaulted roof remained above.

The sensation of familiarity came over me again. I had not felt it since I had first come to Kirthgarran, but it was just as strong, just as exasperating as it had been then.

I peered through the arch at the mountains that lay in the south, trying to understand from whence came this eerie feeling. There was nothing in my memory that included it, no pile of stone quite like it that should cause this pang, this echo of recognition that lingered somewhere in my mind.

I turned and gazed at the castle. Its walls were weather-beaten, patterned with stones of brown and gray. Black studs stood out starkly against the oak planks of the ironbound door. The door, too, had brought this creeping sense of cognition, and still did.

The chattering of ducks from the lapping water and the bleating sheep behind me were all at once joined by the rhythmic beat of horse's hooves. The black horse with the feathered fetlocks cantered out from behind the castle with Coll astride. I was in the shadow of the arch and he did not notice me, but I could see his face clearly. It was solemn, preoccupied.

I contemplated stepping out to hail him, but just as I was about to do so, a woman called out from the path. I recognized her at once as being the cross-eyed woman at my infar, and I shrank deeper into the shadow of the vault.

Coll slowed his horse; the Friesian's long black legs strode gracefully over the turf toward her. The two were so near I could distinguish their features, hear their words in the clear air.

"Captain Fergusson," she said laughing and dipping a flippant curtsey. "My own true love."

He'll tell ye o' the wild McPhates wha focht at Prestonpans,
Or the night he focht at Bridgton Cross wi' a razor in each hand.
Baron James McPhate (Hunter)

Chapter Fifteen

Coll remained seated and looked down on her with an expression that would have chilled my blood had it been directed at me.

Her voice was high and lyrical despite her bitter reception. "How braw you look this day, sir. I do not think I'll e'er recover from the wanting of you—and the spurning you gave me in return."

"What is it you want?"

"You ken *who* I want."

He allowed the horse to circle her and to toss its head. "Have you no soul, Isabel?"

"I've a reason for coming." She took something out of her

pocket and held it toward him. "He left his knife. He'd not want to be long without it."

"He's not here."

Her lips twisted in disappointment but she did not take her eyes from Coll. "Perhaps, since you seem to resent me being here, you'd be giving it to him yourself?" She moved closer to him and held it out. He grasped the clasp knife and she slid the back of her hand against his in a sensuous gesture. "Kirstie's been speaking of you," she said in a sultry tone. "You've not been courting her as you ought. She misses you."

His look toward her was one of loathing. He jerked the horse's head about, causing Dominie to prance in surprise. Coll dug in his heels and the horse's powerful hind legs contracted. Man and beast bolted away as if one.

"You've no intention of offering to take me home?" she called after him. "I thought you better mannered, sir!" She watched him gallop away toward the hump-backed bridge. Her laughter was high and malevolent. With her shoulders still shaking she lifted her faded crimson skirts and traipsed back down the path.

I watched her shrinking figure. I wished I'd not remained concealed, for I felt I had peered into something private. I left the stones and returned to the garden, my spirit as ponderous as my feet. After all this time it seemed I knew little about the people with whom I lived. It was clear I merely lived on the surface of Kirthgarran.

"It was Coinneach Fergusson, Laird of Strath Gruagach," the earl told me the next time I called upon him. "Cousin of James the First. He was given the title of earl and the lands of Kirthgarran for repayment of loyalty. And James gave them by letters patent. Royal charter, lass. Sheepskin. That is what kept them secure. There were others who wanted the land and the castle he built for himself. Others who thought the sword stronger. But he held them. Firmly. His son was the second earl. And I, I am the seventh."

I could not help myself. I listened to all he had to tell me, seduced by the intrigues of history.

"Coinneach chose the bank of Loch Seàrr on which to

build," he said. "From every angle one can see if an enemy approaches."

"Was there much fighting then, to keep Kirthgarran from being taken?"

"Long ago there were families hungry for land, or revenge for some wrongdoing. Murrays. MacNabs. But the feuds did not last."

"Were the Raeburns of Rathdale ever an enemy, my lord?"

"Nay. Allies from the first. The lands of the Fergussons and the Raeburns were joined by loyalty."

"Now they are joined by law."

"Rightly, I should have wed the eldest Raeburn daughter, Eleanor. But it was her sister Agnes for me, even when I was a lad holding onto my mother's skirts. She was fair, so fair."

"It must have been a happy time."

"We were merry, for a while. My friend Christopher wedded Eleanor, but the love match was not what he'd envisioned. Eleanor failed him in many ways. And Christopher fell hopelessly in love with Mairi. And then my dear Agnes was laid to rest. Nought seemed right after that. The years pass swiftly in hindsight, do you not find that so? And then..."

I waited patiently but distress overcame him. He did not wish to continue. He blinked at his coverlet several times.

At last he said, "Christopher said to me many a time, 'How can I thank you enough for the home you give my sons, a home I cannot?' His grief was deep, lass, and yet he would not leave Eleanor, though he might have been happier if he had. He should have taken Mairi away. To France, Italy. America perhaps. They could have had their sons, pretended they were a family. Eleanor would have greeted, but she would have let him go." He sighed. "But he stayed, and in the staying made no decision at all. He wanted both of them. In the end—there was the great tragedy. It was to his grave he went, with Eleanor, as soon as they left Sonna Bay. He would have approved of that. It was the sea he loved, not the hills and the cattle."

"He and Eleanor left everything to you, I've been told."

"Aye, but what consolation were the lands and the house at Rathdale to me? Mairi was tormented more than I. Life gives us wounds we tell ourselves we can live with, but the scars never lose their tenderness."

I could say nothing, thinking about this.

"Coll, for one, is not the same lad who left us nearly a dozen years ago. We could all see the change in him when he came back. But, my thanks to God, he did come back. My own Walter, and Hugh, my braw sons, they were not so fortunate." I feared more tears but he was holding himself in firm control. He said stubbornly, "Walter was born during the '45. He was our first-born, was our Walter. Hugh came two years later. When the French and the cursed Spaniards besieged Gibraltar—eight years ago, that was—they hastened to join the battle. I fought with Walter before he left. I did not want him to go. Yet he defied me, and took up his sword and joined his brother."

"And that is the last memory you have of him? Your quarrel?"

He nodded. "Then came the last year of the fighting, the third siege. I've heard tales, from those who've returned. I often imagine how it must have been. The French and the Spanish ships crowding in the bay. The burning of the floating batteries. The endless sound of the guns. The men, unrelieved, hungry, in the fortress ashore. The sick, waiting." Gruffly he cleared his throat. "I received the letters. And that part of my life was over. That, that is a scar that will never heal."

I turned my head away and pretended to study the picture on the wall. There was a voice inside my head. "You are not to care," it instructed. "These people mean nought to you. Opening your heart to them will only put it in jeopardy—again. And that you will never do."

One of Lord Kirthgarran's foster sons always came in the afternoon and helped him walk a short distance, up and down the passages or about his bedchamber. It did him no good to lie abed all of the time, I was told. He must stretch his limbs and keep his muscles from wasting away. He always sat in his chair for a while afterward, and this was when he hoped I would visit him.

Every day he had a new story to tell. His eyes came alight whenever I settled on the foot-cushion beside his chair to spend an hour or two in his company. I was wary of becoming caught up in his excitement, but I admitted he had many treasures to share.

Sometimes he spoke about The Rising.

"For years after the battle at Culloden, every man in the Highlands was suspected of treason," he said one day.

"That seems incredibly unfair."

He regarded me benevolently. "Fairness was irrelevant. It became so the day The Butcher, Duke of Cumberland and brother of King George, slaughtered nearly every man on Drummossie Moor."

"My mamma used to tell me of it."

"The stories of the massacre, and the pillages wrought by the King's armies after, preceded the arrival of the soldiers here. We heard that it had not been enough that the order of no quarter had been given on the field, or that the Duke had urged his soldiers to kill all of Prince Charlie's soldiers where they lay, wounded, on the ground, or to throw them, still alive, into a great, burning pit of a grave—or to collect the survivors of the battle and shoot them, one after the other. The cleansing must take place."

"My mother called it the great harrying of the glens."

"That it was. The Duke went on his rampage throughout the Highlands, and men, women, and bairns were viewed as nought better than vermin. They were hunted as such. Troops came here, ready to murder us all and burn the castle down about our ears. I was arrested and taken to the Tolbooth for questioning. What I saw there, lass, I cannot convey to you. The men lying in their own filth, their limbs raw from their chains, the unconcerned executions." His eyes closed. "But by a miracle I was freed. The Campbells gave evidence I'd not taken part. Their word saved me, and my family."

How well I remembered Mamma's account of the '45, told to me as part of what she called my education. My father had recounted it to me also over the years, but with none of Mamma's sympathy or understanding.

"The Crown decided we were naughty children," Lord Kirthgarran said, leaning his head back against his bolster. "So the Black Act was passed, and we were punished. They forced laws upon us. Forbade us our kilts and our pipes and our ancient tongue. The clans were scattered, and the chiefs were without power. Those who rebelled further were imprisoned or transported to America or the West Indies as little more than slaves. Our mountains and glens were filled with sorrow. We wore the damned Lowland breeks, we raised our kine up again, we watched families separated and deported as indentured servants, and we lived unprotected, with no right to arms or weapons."

"But all that is over."

"It's better now some years have passed, aye, and George the Second is dead and gone. Five years ago the Act was repealed, though it had not been enforced for years before that. And many ancestral lands and estates that had been forfeited to the Crown and administered by the Court of Exchequer have been restored, by the grace of Parliament, to the auld chiefs or their kin." He became quiet and finished, "We're no longer a threat to peace, it seems. Charles Edward Stuart is drinking himself insensible in Italy. We're encouraged to foster pride in our clans, and in the bravery of the men we give to Britain as soldiers."

"The lives of my parents were not as bloodstained as yours."

He seemed to try throwing off his melancholy and with eyes wide open said, "Tell me about your family."

I fought the urge to unburden myself. It would be a relief to let my words flow as the earl's had, to let them tumble from me, a deluge of loathing, sorrow, resentment, and loneliness. He would understand. He would listen and nod, and his eyes would fill when mine did. Perhaps his hand would reach out and take my fingers in his.

But I could not let that happen. I gathered my words together with the utmost care. "My mother came from Dundee. Her parents, James and Margaret MacKerras, gently raised her on the Firth of Tay. They lived far from clan intrigues, and were somewhat untouched by war. My father inherited Gilchrist House and its farmlands from his father and several Allansons before him. We lived there in solitude, he, my mother, my half-brother, and I."

"Then you ken little of our strife," he said softly. "I'm glad of it."

The moment passed. And somewhere deep inside, I was disappointed because it had.

I would not allow myself to be drawn into the emotional tides in which Lord Kirthgarran sometimes drifted, but I often found myself gazing at the portraits of his family.

Hanging in the short passageway between the great hall and the dining room was a double portrait of Graeme Fergusson and his new bride Agnes, painted forty-four years earlier. Whenever I gazed at it I let it pull me backward in time to the days before the '45 Rising, before the Highland ways began to change. The painter, Fletcher Buchanan, whose signature appeared in elegant script at the bottom right-hand corner, had captured the proud young earl with skill.

There was no mistaking it was Lord Kirthgarran. The evening-blue eyes were wide, full of compassion, intelligence. His hair was dark brown, unpowdered, drawn back with a ribbon. His clothing was the kilt and plaid of his people, with coat and waistcoat of maroon. He was holding the hand of Lady Kirthgarran and I searched her face with curiosity, wondering about this woman who had taken his heart. She, too, had hair of brown, curled and frizzed and framing a face that seemed very young. The delicacy of the brushstrokes suggested a woman of sincerity and warmth. She was smiling and clasping the arm of her husband. In the background was a filigree of trees and shrubbery, and the castle of Kirthgarran.

I looked at the picture often and liked to visualize Lord Kirthgarran as he had been before the deaths of his wife and sons had taken his vitality from him.

One afternoon he said to me between careful sips of tea, "Have you learnt any Gaelic, lass?"

"I have not, no."

He lifted up a morsel of bread from the tray at his elbow. *"Crioman arain,"* he said. "A piece of bread."

I copied his pronunciation as best I could. "Kree-mun arran."

"Copan," he went on, touching a chipped cup.

"Ko-pan."

He smiled. *"Tha mi cho sona ris an righ."*

"Ha me…"

"I am as happy as the King."

I believed he was telling me the truth, but I could not understand why.

The remainder of hours in each day was troublesome to me. Lethargy persisted, and beyond spinning flax for table linen and sheets, and sewing dead-clothes for Rab and myself, I felt a lack of purpose. Idleness allowed me to think and I did not want to think.

Rab was not often at home. He came sometimes for his tea or to talk for a few minutes with Lord Kirthgarran, but he was extraordinarily involved with the goings-on in village and glen and did not appear until supper at nine o'clock.

I did not see Mairi for several days. I found that I missed her.

"Sandy," I said to my father-in-law one morning. "Will Mairi be coming today, do you think?"

His eyes regarded me kindly. "She's gone to visit her sister."

"Oh, the one who lives at Caiseal Àlainn," I replied, remembering. "Where the young woman…"

I was shocked by my own words. No one ever mentioned Leslie Hamilton. I hoped Sandy would not realize what I'd been about to say, but the quick surprise in his expression told me he had. "Rab—told me how she died," I said clumsily.

He turned away. I could not think how to salvage our exchange.

"Mairi will return the morrow." Sandy pushed a settle closer to the wall. He did not wait for a reply before he retrieved a cluster of keys from the mantel and left me.

I regretted having told the cook I wanted nothing to do with Kirthgarran's kitchen. After all, I was merely the wife of one of its tenants with no special privileges. Surely there were tasks I could perform to aid in the daily life of the castle and its folk and to help fill my days. There was cheese to make, fruit to preserve, floors to wash, ale to brew.

I wandered through the passages of the castle with their hanging claymores and axes and peered into the chambers above, remembering the histories Lord Kirthgarran was feeding to me bit by bit. All the while I mulled, and when I recovered from my disastrous mistake with Sandy, I stole down to the kitchen.

The cavernous room was nothing like the kitchen in Gilchrist House but I still felt its welcome. Grizel was hunched, scrubbing the table with a pale blue rag, her back toward me. She was short and plump, quite the opposite of Mrs. Taggart. None of the kitchen lasses seemed to be at hand.

I said quietly, "Grizel?"

She turned as if I had shouted. Her eyes fastened on me and her features contorted. When she took a step backward and clapped a hand upon her lips, she bumped an earthenware crock of oats on the table. It fell to the floor and burst upon the stone, sending the grains everywhere. Kit, the orange cat that must have been lurking behind her skirts, streaked by me in a panic to escape.

The cook had always seemed afraid in my presence. She was petrified now. She stared at me as if she had never seen me before, but gradually recognition returned to her.

"I'm sorry," she muttered dryly. "Oh marm, I'm sorry." She pulled her gaze from me and gaped with alarm at the shards of crockery at her feet. "Foul-tak-me! Look what I've done!" She moved aside and grasped a heather besom. She began to sweep away the evidence of her clumsiness.

"You must let me help you," I said, reaching for the largest of the jagged pieces on the floor.

"It is my fault. I'll do it."

I put two pieces on the table beside the scrubbing rag and she swept furiously, digging at the slippery oats in the cracks betwixt the flagstones. The currents of heat from the fire lifted gray wisps of hair from her neck, and she bent to use the corner of her apron in mopping beads of sweat from her brow.

"I did not mean to startle you," I said.

There was no answer. She did not dare look at me. When she plucked the pottery from the oats her hands shook.

I lost all plan of what I had meant to ask her. I retreated as soon as I could, and she made no attempt to ask me why I had sought her.

After supper I asked Rab, "Is Grizel a skittish woman, do you think?"

"Stalwart Grizel? I would not think so. She's the bravery of a lion."

"I startled her in the kitchen today and she seemed more frightened of me than usual."

"I've never known her to be frightened of aught." He fell into a chair. "One night a rat dropped from the rafters to her feet and without a thought she threw a pudding at it. Perhaps today she was minding a story someone told her earlier, about ghosts or nightmares, and when you surprised her she was already primed."

He dismissed it so lightly. He made me feel foolish for pursuing the matter. Perhaps I had exaggerated what had happened.

There was one thing I did not embellish or imagine, however. The silver wine cup with the thistle engravings no longer sat upon its shelf in the drawing room. I kept watch for it, glancing at the shelf every morning when I came downstairs, but there was no doubt. It had, quite suddenly and unquestionably, disappeared.

Oh cam you by yon water-side?
Pu'd you the rose or lily?
Willy's Drown'd in Yarrow (Trad.)

Chapter Sixteen

The weather was temperate one afternoon, allowing me to sit under one of the lofty oaks in the garden. Wild roses bloomed about the stone benches, and delicate honeysuckle edged the grassy paths and served as resting places for wrens and goldcrests when they dropped to earth to look about with quick, bright eyes.

Since the gardener was done for the day I felt I was alone in the world. Without thought I began to sing. I had not done so since Davy had deserted me. The ballad that came to my lips was about Hardyknute, and as I meandered through the verses I realized I could have been relating the tale of Lord Kirthgarran.

> *Stately stepp'd he east the wall,*
> *And stately stepp'd he west.*
> *Full seventy years he now had seen,*
> *With scarce seven years of rest.*

At the end of the verse a deeper voice joined mine.

> *The tidings to our gude Scots king.*

I looked up to find Coll standing beside my bench, his leather breeks brushed clean, his shirt unsoiled beneath the stone-colored waistcoat. The sun had burnt the tops of his cheekbones and nose. "Keep on," he appealed to me. He sang,

> *Came, as he sat at dine.*

At first I could not respond, yet when Coll began to sing I became daring, and accompanied him with a low voice.

> *With noble chiefs, in brave array,*
> *Drinking the bluid-red wine.*

I pressed my hands together, seeking further courage.

"I could not resist joining you," he said.

"You know 'Hardyknute.'"

"One of my favorites." He smiled.

Thinking I was to be alone for hours, I had not pinned my hair up under my kertch nor attended to my dress, and was dismayed when he tossed his brown coat onto the settle and sat beside me. He leant forward with his elbows upon his knees. His thigh touched mine.

"Do you mind the rest of it?" he asked. "A hundred verses, there must be. Does it not then go on,

> *"To horse! To horse! My royal liege!*
> *Your faes stand on the strand;*
> *Full twenty thousand glitt'ring spears*
> *The king of Norse commands."*

He watched my face as he recalled the words. Hesitantly I joined him and when his voice fell away I let my own dwindle. "You're faring better than I," he encouraged.

"I fear there are only pieces left in my memory. Phrases, a measure or two..."

"Aye, but the ending, the *ending*, remains with me. How he returns home after the battle of Largs victorious, and yet finds his castle dark, with no evidence of his beloved wife."

I pondered the difference between Hardyknute's unflagging

courage in battle and the loss of his love. It was the latter that felled him to his knees.

"Here's another," Coll said after a moment. "A song that's more hopeful." He began singing a song in Gaelic.

His voice was profound, melodic. My pulse slowed and I became filled with reverence as I listened. I watched his lips and was taken in by the unknown sounds as they were drawn out and fitted to the tune. Rising and falling notes came unhurriedly from his throat, nurturing the measures. I wanted the song to never end.

I whispered when at last it did, "It is beautiful."

"Try the melody with me." He began the first verse. I was able to grasp the tune and by the third time through I was able to copy him.

"Of what does it tell?" I asked

"The man finds himself in battle. He's cut down by the enemy and left for dead, but in a dream his love comes to him and begs him to live, and he does."

"There are sounds in Gaelic that do not occur in English! Lord Kirthgarran has been teaching me." I said, *"Crioman arain."*

He laughed. "A piece of bread, aye."

"It's only a beginning."

"But that is the best place to start."

He pulled a rose from the stem beside him. With a finger he smoothed the petals, becoming absorbed in it as the seconds passed by. I reached into my mind and sorted through a dozen things I might say, but one by one discarded them. I said, "There was a song my mother knew. She promised she'd tell me the words one day. I cannot mind any of it except the tune but, I wonder, if I hummed a little of it, perhaps you'd recognize it."

He hesitated. "Try and see."

For a second or two the tune was nonexistent. Gradually a fragment presented itself, dredged from the old memories, and I offered it. Another fragment came. I was able to string the notes together and produce part of the melody.

"Oh aye," he said.

"You do recognize it. The words as well?"

"It is a song of lament. Mmm. I think I mind some of the verses.

"'S tric mi sealltuinn o'n chnoc a's àirde,
Dh'fheuch am faic mi fear a'bhàta."

How extraordinary it was to hear the slow air reincarnated in Coll's voice. He reflected the sorrow and wistfulness inherent in the music and sent forth the notes, both sure and tremulous, in flawless tempo. But for the difference in pitch it might have been Mamma singing. The words with their unique cadence and unknown weavings stirred recollections of her and how she had sung on a log carpeted with moss beside the Tweed, and blinked tears from her eyes.

He stopped when he caught sight of my face. "Is that how she sang it?"

I nodded, too overcome to speak.

"There's more. I'm sure if I sat down with paper I could remember all the verses and write them out for you."

"What do they mean?"

"*Fear a' bhàta?* The boatman. The lass who tells the story is greeting for the lad who left her. He sailed upon the sea and never returned, though he promised he would. Her friends tell her to forget him but she cannot let go of her pain. In English, oh, it would be:

> *"I climb the mountain and scan the ocean*
> *For thee, my boatman, with fond devotion.*
> *When shall I see thee? Today? Tomorrow?*
> *Oh, do not leave me in lonely sorrow.*
> *Oh my boatman, Na hóro éile."*

His eyes became bold and yet disturbed as they regarded me. I did not think of Davy who had never returned for me, but of Mrs. Dundas's explanation for Mamma's broken heart. Perhaps there had been a boatman in my mother's past. Perhaps it had been a sailor who had loved and then left her.

"Will I stop, then?" Coll asked. "It hurts you to hear it."

"She never sang it in English. I never understood what brought such greeting upon her. But please, if you can remember more of it..."

He watched me still, his face expressionless despite the troubled eyes. He went on, singing of the boatman who promised to bring a silken gown, a tartan plaid, and a golden ring on his return. Mamma, too, might have waited for a silken gown and a ring of gold that never came. She must have given up hope. And then wed my father.

> *'My heart is weary with ceaseless wailing,*
> *Like wounded swan when her strength is failing.'*

I was adrift in memories of her. An old wound opened within me and I longed for her with the intensity of the young lass who still lived inside me.

Coll said no more but waited, eyes unwavering. At last I raised my gaze to him. He said, "From what you've told me, I fear your mother was a wounded swan herself. And you'd give aught for her to be with you still."

I nodded.

"A parent's love is an impossible thing to replace, and yet—we do not have to let go of the people we love. Even in death." A pause. "Did your father not share your grief when your mother died? Surely he loved her as well."

"My father did not honor her, not as he ought to have. He shouted at her when she misplaced something, or if she did not perform a task in a timely manner, or if she forgot to do it altogether."

"Criticism of that sort can become very painful."

"Whenever he discovered she made a mistake in the household accounts, or if he thought she did not oversee my half-brother well enough, his voice would fill the house. He would pray for her soul. Sometimes he made her copy passages from the Bible. He gave me the same punishment, at times. Or else he locked me in the cellar. Sometimes he cuffed my ear, which was better. But Mamma—Mamma often felt his hand—or his fist. I hated it when he struck her."

"He did not often do that," he said as if he hoped I would agree.

"I've tried to forget. There's much I've taught myself to put aside. I mind only that however he showed his displeasure, he harmed her."

"It was constant? This punishment he felt he owed her?"

I could not stem the rush of emotion that poured through me. "He used her brutally. I will never forgive him."

"Perhaps he does not forgive himself."

"He is a man without conscience."

He was thoughtful. "What must it be like, to have none? I have often wondered."

"I do not think it would be something desirable. Without morals a man is capable of anything."

"But at the end of a day, he'd not have his mistakes coursing through his head like bolting horses, ruining his sleep."

I did not want to ask him if this was how he suffered, but the desire to know was too strong. "What could you have ever done to cause yourself such regret?"

He failed to answer for so long that I wished I had not spoken. He grunted and said, "I'm afraid there are too many occasions to be listing. One does not live through a war without some remorse. For the innocent women and children he harmed. For the blood he spilt in a cold temper. For the disregard of prisoners pleading for their lives. And—there are other things. I'm not the untainted, benevolent man you seem to think I am."

"I'll never believe that you and my father are aught alike."

There was sorrow in his eyes.

I continued, "I wish I'd been brave enough to tell Father how I felt. I keep the contempt within me still, and I think it festers there." I could feel it even now, the unyielding mass that clung hot and immovable behind my eyes. "If I could but lash out at him, and make him see how I resented his treatment of her." I surprised myself. I had not meant to say so much.

An arm came round to pull me to one of his shoulders. My face fell against his neck and I could not help but draw in the scent of him. Leather. A faint whisper of soap. Sweet brandy on his breath. "What heartbreak she suffered," Coll said. "What despair you endure, still."

With difficulty I confided, "As much as I miss my home, and feel as if the earth has fallen out from beneath my feet, I have discovered that there is relief in living under my father's roof no longer."

He squeezed my shoulders before his arm slid away, but his other hand covered mine and remained. Thus we sat, looking out at the loch over the plantings of shrubs and creepers, the late delphiniums, columbines, and lavender.

Spatters of shade from the leaves of the oak stirred in

the breeze, bringing to my mind other shadows thrown by the boughs of the wych elm beside the River Tweed and the countless sunny afternoons Mamma and I had sat amongst them. I had loved kneeling before her with my hands on her knees, watching her lips as verses poured forth. The language had always been a mystery to me, perhaps deepening my inability to decide what part of my mother had fascinated me more: her beautiful mouth forming the words, the source of the angel's voice, or her hands, slender and pale, effortlessly stroking the strings. Her tapered nails were tinged with the healthy pink of apple blossoms. Her wrists were discolored by bruises.

My head turned swiftly, an old response that ended the progression of a memory.

Coll was contemplating the languid waves swelling onto the stones at the shore. He was lost in rumination much as I had been, but his eyes had become heavily lidded and his lips had curved downward. I looked back at the water, mindful of each one of his fingers closed over mine.

"Ah well," he said. "The song. I'll help you learn the words. Perhaps there's one or two tunes you can be teaching me."

"Perhaps."

"I must be away," he went on, giving me all of his attention. He patted my hand. "Kirstie has invited me to sup with her. The piper's daughter," he added. "They live just over there." He pointed beyond the garden. "Donald, and Kirstie, and her four brothers."

"I've not met her, I do not think."

"I'm sure you must have. But no matter. She comes to the castle now and then. You might become good friends." He pushed himself to his feet and retrieved his coat. "Keeley," he said, pausing. "Your singing. It is beguiling."

I should have returned the compliment but I was struck dumb, and his shoulders disappeared behind the honeysuckles long before I could mutter a response.

The settle seemed empty without him. The pink rose he had tossed unmindfully to the ground caught my eye, and I reached down to retrieve it.

He had crushed it mercilessly in his fingers. The fragile petals were limp, creased, curled into nothingness. Yet I cradled it in my hands for a long while as I watched the shimmering waters of the loch.

I said to Mairi when she came to the castle that night, "When I first came to Kirthgarran, you told me about the silver. You said some of it had been sold."

"I felt the loss of those braw things deeply, as if they were my own," she said, shaking out a freshly laundered bedsheet.

"I've been noticing some of the silver. The pieces on the drawing room shelf. The thistle cup has disappeared."

"I ken it well," she said, wrinkling her forehead. "Where do you think it has gone?"

"I've not seen it for a fortnight."

"How odd. 'Twas not taken down to be cleaned, or polished? Airig or one of the others might have forgotten to put it back."

"That is what Rab believes." I could not add that my husband had behaved strangely toward the cup on the night I had first noticed it, and also when I had questioned him about it later.

"But you do not think so," she said.

I had no theories except that Rab knew more than he admitted, and I would not tell her this.

"Have you questioned anyone?" she asked, tilting her head.

"I hate to cause a stir. I did ask Airig and her sister, but they have not touched it."

"It is difficult to believe it might be lost. Do you think it's been—stolen?"

"Oh no! I cannot imagine anyone at Kirthgarran doing such a thing."

"Neither can I. Someone must have moved it. Perhaps the earl requested it, and it was never put back. I'll ask the women in the kitchen. You'll tell me if you find it? And I'll do the same."

I agreed. I felt better having confided in her, and caught two corners of a sheet and brought them to her waiting hands.

"The silver," Mairi moaned. "What a shame it was to sell it through the years. If only Kirthgarran could have shown profits sooner. Now the lads work so hard. There's ne'er enough time to do all they must do." She ran her fingers over creases as she folded, and I grasped another sheet from the pile.

"Do they ever rest from their duties as tacksmen?" I asked.

She shook her head. "In the spring they inspect the black cattle, all of which have grown weak from winter, and they decide which ones are to be sold and which are to be bred. They attend the newborn lambs and the goats, and prepare for planting. They even aid with the ploughing and the sowing. In summer, they strip peats at the moss, cutting and stacking the blocks to dry, and collect firewood from the forests. Many times they repair thatch on the roofs of the huts and cut bracken to stuff into bed-bolsters. It is then they join the tenants as they ponder the barley and the oats and corn, and hope for enough good weather to coax bounty from the meager soil."

"And then there is the harvest, and the selling of the kylies," I said. "No one can predict what prices the cattle or the grain will bring, Rab says. A poor summer yielding next to nought, and little success at the cattle fairs as well, will mean a winter of want with no escape."

She inspected a tear in a sheet and added it to a stack of mending. "They tell me the yield of oats and bere this year seems adequate, but whether there will be enough to make a profit and pay debts remain to be seen."

I found myself saying, "Coll seems preoccupied. Do you think it's because of that?"

The merriment in her dark eyes faded. She pressed linen to her breast. "Have you noticed it, too, then?"

"Sometimes I think it's my imagination," I told her. "And after all, I've known him just a short while. Perhaps his disquiet is not new."

"But you are perceptive. I've seen it as well, Keeley. Sensed a discontent. Oh, how I greatly fear..."

She let her words dwindle away but I was gripped by them. "What do you fear?"

"That he will leave us again. He has soldiering in his blood, and the King is ordering new regiments to be raised all the time. I pray he'll not find the life too quiet here, the situation of his life too oppressing, that he will buy another commission."

"Has he led you to believe he might?" I asked, struck by an odd dismay of my own.

"He's ne'er mentioned it. But sometimes I do fear it."

"I do not think he has happy remembrances of the army.

He speaks of it very little."

"Coll has a sense of duty that all but destroys his own feelings. He's like all men. Duty is all that matters." She was talking about Walter and Hugh, and Coll's father, too, I knew, and she went on fervently, "If foreign wars ever stir that feeling of duty in him I've no doubt he'll go again. I wept for days when he left for America. I thought I would never see him again, and I did not think I could bear it. I'd just lost his father, you mind." She gazed at the stacks of linen and touched the locket at her breast. "Sometimes when I look at my dear sons I think on Christopher, and my heart is eased because it is brought home to me that I've not lost Christopher at all."

"They cannot replace him, but something of their father must live on in them."

Mairi nodded, smiling, but joy did not reach her eyes. "When Coll came back unharmed four years ago I could imagine no greater happiness. Ever since the death of Lord Kirthgarran's sons I'd felt a premonition that Coll, too, would not return. But he was safe. I hoped he would feel at home here again and marry and be happy at last. Perhaps it will take more time. I know he's been unhappy, but he is a man, and a man will not tell his mother the dark secrets in his mind."

"Then you do not know what troubles him?"

"It could be a blend of things. Or it could be one thing. But he would not tell me even if I asked."

I understood.

But I did not understand why the thought of Coll leaving Kirthgarran caused a stone to plummet in my stomach. It was something I had not felt for a long time.

I picked several boughs of the deep pink roses in the garden and placed them in an earthenware jar for Lord Kirthgarran's bedchamber. There he could look at them and breathe in the fragrance of nature. He told me he loved them well, and day by day as the buds opened and the petals flared, I trimmed leaves and stems and added new blossoms when the others faded.

It occurred to me that like a rose itself, Kirthgarran was unfolding before me. I was beginning to know the folk, the pathways through the garden, the parkland, and hills. Loch

Seàrr changed daily as water will, sometimes becoming glass-like and sparkling with the kisses of insects and rings made by fish, sometimes sulking in a mood of dark blue-gray or blending with the sky, soft and wreathed with mist.

As for the castle itself, I fancied it had personalities of its own. On bright days it seemed familiar, trustworthy; on days of dark rain or fog-enclosed nights its walls seemed to spring upward from the earth, transcending time, bringing to life the ancestral memories of men who had built and loved and fought long ago.

At Lord Kirthgarran's invitation I explored its chambers and passageways. My apprehension about finding strange and dreadful things was fading, and on those occasions when the moon cowered behind cloud and shadows lengthened into the mist curling about its feet, Kirthgarran did not unnerve me as it once had. I accepted it as a brooding friend who is overcome by oppressive moods.

The earl's stories came to even greater life with the location of the landmarks he described. In the garret I found old armor: a cuirass from the 1600's and a pot, a round, steel helmet with a pointed ridge at the top. On a wall in one of the empty bedchambers hung a fascinating picture featuring lions and birds and Fergusson knights on Crusade. In every unoccupied room I checked cupboards and drawers, wishing I could discover the silver thistle cup. Although some were locked, many were not, and I clung to my hope that I would find it and learn why it had been removed from its shelf.

One day I came upon a place that threatened to soften my distrustful heart. I discovered the old nursery.

I wandered into this large room one early evening, followed by the orange cat that appeared to enjoy my company whilst she hunted for mice. The floorboards in the chamber creaked, the fireplace gaped, the air hung stale and musty. I remembered the earl reminiscing about a day during his boyhood when a family of rooks had flown down from a nest in the nursery chimney. The birds had caused an uproar as they had swooped through the castle here and there, chased by men, women, and gleeful children for hours.

Against one wall was a linen press filled with table linen and napkins woven in lavender-knot and birds-eye patterns. A wee bed kept company with child-sized stools and chairs. Hung near the hearth were abandoned collop tongs, milk stoups, wooden cups, pewter bowls, brandering irons, and other things once used to cook the nursery meals. And by the window, a carved wooden cradle and chest.

The cradle rocked back and forth at my gentle push, rumbling on the floorboards. It was devoid of blankets and linens, and thus difficult to imagine holding the delicacy of a swathed child. I crossed to the chest and after pondering for a moment, heaved it open to find it filled with infant-sized clothes.

Minute gowns of lawn, daintily stitched, soft woolen garments that felt like down against my cheek, and exquisitely woven linen shirts embroidered in blue, lavender, and white were all folded and laid in rows. I caressed the handiwork with my fingers. What care, what love, had gone into them.

I lost touch with time as I stared out at the mist-bathed slopes through the streaked window.

"How would it be to have a child?" I said aloud. "A child to sew for during the months of waiting, a child to rock in this great cradle, a child to hold in my arms and love?"

I did not need to wonder. There was a hollow place inside of me, a place no one could fill. My mother had found happiness with a bairn; I could, whilst touching the infant garments, understand why. If I had a wean to sing to and to hold, surely this aching emptiness would go. What I needed most were not household duties or mindless tasks, but the bearing and care of a child.

I knelt and put the wee gowns and sarks away, folding them as precisely as they had been, and regarded them as my hand stroked Kit beside me. I was young, as was my husband, and there was no reason not to believe I would be blessed with many children.

As I touched the empty cradle an old saying came back to me. I said, "Push an empty cradle, and soon it will be filled."

I dropped the heavy lid down on the kist amid a cloud of dust motes. The cat and I left the nursery. It was a conscious hope now. I could endure lying with Rab if I thought it might lead to a bairn.

I said to Kit, "Mayhap this room will be used again soon. Perhaps I am already with child."

I went back to my bedchamber and took the stuffed rabbit out of the drawer where I had placed him after my arrival at Kirthgarran. The sight of my childhood playmate and the softness of the drugget in my hands brought a rush of nostalgia, but the wistfulness was tainted. I turned Rajjit's head upward and examined the gaping hole that had once been his mouth. Malcolm had shredded the cloth with a finger a long time ago, warning me to keep still when I'd caught him kissing the scullery lass behind the kitchen door. I could still hear his words. "Look what happens," he'd said slyly, "when you do not keep secrets to yourself." I'd felt sick when he'd ravaged my dear rabbit and I had hidden him in the bottom of my clothes press thereafter, unable to look at his ruined face.

Even now it was difficult, but in sudden inspiration I pulled rose-colored thread through my needle, sat in the middle of my bed, and went about mending the hole of his mouth. My stitches provided him with an overly large smile but at least he would be able to speak again. I fingered the bracken inside the limp body. It was crumbling, but that, too, could easily be replaced.

Satisfied, I laid him back in the drawer, nestled on a kertch, to wait. We would both wait. It was the first time since my marriage that I allowed myself to feel anything akin to optimism.

I did not tell Rab I found the nursery, nor did I confide in him my dreams for the future. It was as if he had nothing to do with them. I was his wife and if there were a bairn he would certainly be its father, but beyond that I sensed an attitude of uncaring in him. He seemed distracted much of the time. I blamed myself, for I did not love him and could not turn to him as a wife should. I did not expect him to devote himself to someone cold and withdrawn.

For the hundredth time I told myself I must forget Finlay Allanson and all the wretchedness he had caused. I must learn to allow unqualified love to seep, unchecked, through the raw crevices in my heart that Father had hewn. I must forget Davy as well, and the pain his betrayal had rendered.

Because Mairi had supplied my bedchamber with the French

marquetry table, and paper and ink were easily at hand, it seemed natural to resume the keeping of a diary.

The desk was a fine one, with a front drawer lined invitingly with scarlet velvet for writing and a side drawer designed for holding pounce and ink. As the weeks crept by I felt myself increasingly drawn to it. Writing had once been a means for me to sift the grain from the chaff of my life, to understand and record what occurred, and at times to comfort myself, but I was not convinced it could help me now. My heart—my spirit, perhaps—had become hardened within me. I was alarmed by the awareness that I had chosen this state for myself, but I remained unwilling to alter it. It was due to the curse of idleness that I felt driven to write. I did not have enough to do. I must write, or be overpowered by my own irritability.

I began by listing the activities dotting my days.

"I visit Lord Kirthgarran frequently," I wrote carefully on a clean sheet of paper. *"He has asked me to read to him from* Humphrey Clinker.

"The minister, Mr. Cameron, arrived the other day, since he comes every three weeks to hold services at the wee kirk and to see the earl. He seems to be a friendly, jovial man. I have shared prayers with him and the rest of the family on the Sundays he is in residence in the castle. He is nought like Reverend Andrews.

"I often embroider for hours alone in the solar, for I have started a satin-piece, and the sun always seems warm through the windows there. I have spun enough flax for Rab's dead-clothes, and have given it to Ewen Drummond's wife, Margery, to weave and full so that I can begin sewing the linen sark, and I have started knitting the stockings out of wool.

"The other morning Airig asked me if I would like to gather mushrooms, for I rather think she believes I am lonely. Together with her sister Ròs we filled a basket with white field mushrooms. She told me they have to be picked early in the day, for tiny maggots will infest them as the hours pass. We also found some chanterelles, all yellow and frilly, growing in a wood of birks, firs, and beeches. We had them for supper, delectable with butter.

"I sit at the lochside at times, listening to the quiet sounds the waves make as they stir the stones at the edge. Sometimes on warm days I walk in the water, or sit with my feet in it. Mamma would have loved it here. The water mirrors the sky and clouds above, providing one with an ever-changing

display of colors. When the weather is not so fine the loch is like liquid glass, or alive with raindrops, all gray-green and silver. For some reason the water helps me to forget much of what has happened.

"But often the days drag by painfully. And I feel useless. I do not want to sit by the loch hour after hour like an idle bairn. I roam the gardens, watching the gardener as he trims bushes, spades earth, or pulls leeks, and I listen to the music the birds make, and nod at the women with reddened hands and legs who come every week to boil water in a cauldron at the lochside, hitch up their skirts, and with their feet pound our linens clean in a tub. Sometimes I speak with them a little as they drape our clothes and sheets on the bushes to dry, or converse with the wee laddie who watches the geese all the day and wants to practice his English. I have discovered he is Kenneth's cousin, another grandson of MacNeil's. His mother is the henwife and his father is one of those who tend the earl's cows.

"The other day I was able to remember some phrases in Gaelic that Lord Kirthgarran taught me. I asked the lad, 'What is your name?' He said it was Iain. I asked him then, 'How are you?' and he said 'Fine', and gave me a wide smile with his two front teeth missing.

"But of what use are the passive things I do? I spin a great deal and knit, and sometimes feed corn to the pigeons in the doocot, but I must ask Mairi and Airig for tasks that are of more help than the feek-fike with which I fill my days. I would aid Grizel in the making of candles and soap, the salting of venison and beef, the preserving and pickling of fruit, but I cannot. She is afraid of me and does not want me near her. Every time she sees me she watches me fearfully and drops things."

She was, of course, not the only one who grew troubled whenever I approached. I was soon to learn how prevalent a feeling the fear was, and did not need the knowledge of any spoken language to translate it.

Grouse frae the muirlan' and trout frae the fountain.
Hush Ye My Bairnie (Trad.)

Chapter Seventeen

A remarkable sight met me when I went to Lord
Kirthgarran's door one morning. He was not alone.
Sandy was leaning against the windowsill, and
Gordon the falconer was standing beside the earl's chair, his
left fist thrust into a leather gauntlet on which clung one of the
peregrines.

"Come in, come in!" Lord Kirthgarran entreated me from
his seat. "Look who has come to visit me."

I was intrigued by the falcons but had not yet approached
any of them in the courtyard, uncertain of their habits and
training. As I moved forward, the bird swiveled its head to fasten
a calm but watchful eye upon me and then bobbed its head up

and down. "I do not wish to frighten it," I said.

"Fenalla has been handled these thirteen years," the earl countered. "She'll not be frightened if you come close. I'd not touch her, though, or wave your arms about."

She was a striking, slate-gray raptor. Her eyes were immense for her size and outlined in yellow; her curved beak was sharp and darkened at the hooked tip. Under the white throat her breast tapered down between powerful legs feathered in rows of slate and white.

"Did you once hunt with her?" I asked.

"Years ago. She was always my favorite, brought to me from Holland when she was but a young lass. She's forgotten me now, though."

"She'll be remembering you soon enough," Gordon said. Belled jesses on the bird's legs secured her to the leathern leash in his hand, and deadly, black talons clutched his hide glove.

Sandy nodded in agreement. "They've long memories. Before long she'll mind you again, sir, and go to you as she used to."

Gordon turned to me. "You've not yet come to see the birds, marm."

"I thought I might disturb them."

"Only the tiercel, the male, is overly temperamental. The others are undaunted by newcomers. You should be introduced to them. They've been watching you, and waiting for an introduction." He grinned.

"Come down now," Sandy said, pushing himself from the ledge and unfolding his arms. "Coll plans to take Athdara hunting but you can meet them all before he's away."

I glanced at Lord Kirthgarran who leant forward and nodded his head. "Let him show you. You'll find it a pleasure."

I followed my father-in-law down the mural stair. Maids in the kitchen were all astir, for it seemed one of the earl's herdsmen had just come down from the shielings with a garron laden with cheese, butter, and milk. He was explaining he needed a stone of meal to take back to the women on the hills as well as more flax for them to spin, but Grizel was embarked upon a tirade. Someone had taken a succulent joint of venison from the larder, a treat she had been saving for the earl.

"You'll get your meal and your flax," Grizel threw at the man as she latched the larder door and leant against it, glaring at the maids. "As soon as someone here admits to thievery!"

"It was not any of us," one of the women retorted. "Have you counted how many hungry men live in this household?"

"Are you saying I do not feed my men well?" Grizel shrieked. She continued with a stubborn rant that had the herdsman rolling his eyes and the maids retreating into a frightened huddle.

Sandy and I stepped round the flurry and sought the door. I felt emboldened to say to him, "It is strange to see a falcon indoors."

"Only a week ago Lord Kirthgarran decided he wanted to reacquaint himself with them. He's not touched one since his sons were lost."

"Why is his interest renewed?"

He held the door open for me and stood aside. "Perhaps his mourning is lessened enough."

I hesitated upon the step and studied his face. "Are you surprised?"

"I am. But glad of his change of heart. He loved hunting with his peregrines. When he recovered from the deaths of his sons he avoided them, and it grieved me. No one can be gladder than I to see he wants to remember himself to them. If they must be carried up to his chamber, then so be it. They'll go to his fist in no time, and make him happy again."

We went out and crossed to the blocks. Dominie, the Friesian, was waiting nearby and one of Gordon's brown-and-white dogs came prancing to us.

Two falcons clung to the tops of the wooden posts. The blocks were about a foot tall. They rose from pools of sand dotted with the birds' castings, the egg-shaped balls of feathers and bones they had been unable to digest and had regurgitated. Round dark eyes pierced mine as I went as close to the perches as I dared.

The apprentice Magnus was just coming out of the mews with a smaller bird on his wrist.

"The tiercel, Lailoken," Sandy said. "Not as fine a hunter as the falcons. But he's still a good footer. Here's Ailsa and Athdara. They fly in cast, meaning they hunt well together and do not fight over their quarry." The falcons fluttered in the air at our approach. They had some freedom though their thongs kept them tied to their blocks. "They bate to fly to the glove, for they recognize me and pair the sight of me with food."

"Are they hungry?"

"Athdara is. She's not been fed, for Coll needs her hunger if she's to be hunting for him this morning. Ailsa's not yet put over her crop, digested her meal that is, but the peregrines feel an attachment to Coll, Magnus, and me, and will not find contentment 'til they're put on the glove or we leave their presence."

"Rab mentioned you and Coll often hunt together," I said, unable to take my eyes from the handsome birds.

"I took Coll first when he was a laddie and seemed intrigued by hawking. A great many days we've spent on the hills with the falcons since then. Walter and Hugh had a passion for them as well, and why, I suppose, Lord Kirthgarran found it difficult to handle them afterward."

Lailoken, now tethered loosely to his perch, ruffled his feathers, clicked his talons, and watched us warily.

Magnus handed Sandy a gauntlet and said, "I need to fetch a pigeon, for when Fenalla returns." He bowed his head to me and strode toward the doocot.

"I'm thinking," Sandy said, "you'd enjoy coming along one day, to see the falcons fly and stoop. Rab cares little for it, but Coll could show you, or so could we both. There's grouse aplenty, and we can take one of Gordon's dogs or beat the bushes ourselves. Or if you'd rather, we can be flying them to the lure."

I was astounded and struggled to find an answer. Athdara's attention left us and her head turned. She stretched out one wing and a leg and held them suspended as she bobbed her head. I looked behind me to find Coll coming toward us, pulling on a gauntlet.

"So you've come to meet the longwings," he said, and smiled.

"I should have—long before this."

He bent down to Athdara who had forsaken her posturing and bated wildly to reach him. He put his gloved hand close to her and she leapt onto it. "Gordon has manned and cared for them well," he said, kneeling on the ground and stroking her feathers. "They'll ne'er be tame, wild birds ne'er are, but they've been handled and trained for years, and find us inoffensive enough."

"She seems to have great affection for you."

"She might. Or," he said, laughing up at me, "she's impatient to be after her breakfast."

Sandy patted Coll's shoulder. "I was asking Keeley if she'd care to go along with you someday and watch."

"You should," he said to me in excitement. "You cannot know the true grace of the peregrines 'til you see them fly. Nor appreciate the trust they have in us when they hover and wait on us, hundreds of feet in the sky, watching for when we spring their quarry. The trust continues when they bring down their prey and allow us to take it from them, willingly."

"One day I will come."

"Let's make plans for the morrow, aye? And, if you think you'd like to fly a falcon yourself in the future that could be arranged as well." He smoothed the falcon's feathers again. "Will you hold her?"

"Now?"

"You must be talking to her softly, and not petting her, but I'm thinking in a few minutes she might go to your fist. Have you a glove, Sandy?"

A gauntlet was pushed onto my left hand and my fingers swam in oversized casings of thick hide. Coll grasped the falcon's jesses and released her from the block, straightened beside me, and allowed the bird to become comfortable on his fist.

With his encouragement I spoke to Athdara, praising her and whispering lofty endearments. Her yellow-rimmed eye targeted mine and stared. In time her nervous fluttering decreased. Coll brought me inside his arms, pressing my back close to his chest, and held my left arm against his, glove to glove. He talked to Athdara again and she became quite calm. When he whistled and Sandy pushed his finger against the back of one of her feathered legs, she hopped from Coll's fist to mine.

I held my breath, feeling the slight weight of her. I trembled with the thrill of it. She found a secure footing and her toes curved about the folds of leather. As she ruffled her feathers and settled herself, looking from me to Coll and back again, I had to hold back bubbling laughter.

"There," Coll said at my ear, "there, she's done it. Hold still now, and talk to her. I've got her jesses. She'll not fly at you. You'd still better not touch her, though, for she'd give you a bluidy clawing if you startled her."

I held my arm rigidly, admiring the beauty of her eyes and twin streaks of slate pointing down beneath them, contrasts to her creamy throat. The feathers of her back and wings were edged with light gray, giving her a lustrous sheen in the morning sun.

Coll's arms remained about me, a steadying force for which I was grateful. The longer Athdara remained on my gauntlet the more serene she became.

It became necessary, though, to surrender her at last so she might have her morning meal. Coll liberated me and the falcon crossed to Sandy's wrist. She went willingly to Coll's glove once more when he was mounted. A soft leather hood sporting a topknot of red feathers was dropped over the bird's head and Coll pulled the braces with his teeth to tighten them.

"Be there rain or not," he said down to me, "you'll come with us?"

"Rain or not."

He nodded and grinned, whistled to Gordon's hunting dog, and they were off. Athdara rode comfortably on her master's fist, temporarily quite blind but contentedly so. I watched until Kenneth unlatched the postern gate and they disappeared along the path.

I said to Sandy, "I'll ask Rab if he wants to come tomorrow as well."

"You must be prepared to be disappointed in that, I'm thinking. Although if I'm wrong, I swear to catch a pigeon of my own and eat it for breakfast." He added, "Alive."

There was no need for Sandy to refuse his usual morning cog of porridge in favor of fresh bird.

Alone, I joined the men at the mews the next day and followed them on foot to the hill above the castle. Gordon and Coll carried wooden cadges on their backs and the peregrines rode within them, hooded and at ease.

Though the day cleared and became warm after a fine rain, I did not care what the skies provided. I was fascinated by the ritual of the hunt. One by one the raptors were flown until Ailsa and Athdara were simultaneously cast off Coll's and Sandy's wrists. They circled about us, pumping their wings in the wind and ringing—rising in spirals—until we could hardly see them. They waited on their men, looping high in the air, patiently watching whilst Gordon beat a flapping grouse from the heather.

The birds stooped, plummeting earthward at a speed difficult to fathom. Had I not been told the outcome I would have believed they sped to a certain death at our feet. One of the falcons reached the flying grouse first and leveled along the ground in a blur, making a tearing, sizzling sound in the air. She crashed with a great thud into her quarry. Her companion took over, binding the fowl to her with her talons amidst a swirl of the prey's feathers, and biting it behind the head as they fell to the heather. The grouse was bagged and the falcons returned to the men's fists at the prompt of a whistle. They were given portions of their catch to enjoy, a just reward for their work.

"The peregrines are flown every day," Gordon told me, "whether it's to the lure or a live quarry. They need the exercise, the conditioning. Sometimes as I watch them fly I ken they do it joyously, and are in love with the wind and the sky."

He told me about each of the birds—how they came from Holland, either trapped in passage or taken from the eyry, and how they were manned, kept fit, and tested daily by a fingering of their keel so their weight could be monitored.

"And how do you find it all?" Coll asked me at midday. He handed me an oatcake from his bag and we sat on flat stones to enjoy them. I squashed down the guilt I felt at finding pleasure in something away from my husband's side, for surely that must be wrong in a new marriage. I was surprised I found pleasure at all, for I had thought my heart would never feel it again.

"I am enchanted," I said, and discovered I was laughing. "They make me want to fly."

He took a bite of cake and grinned. "If only we could."

Lord Kirthgarran was feeling exceptionally well, and in the

afternoon insisted on being helped out of the castle so he might sit by the loch. In an armed chair padded with the inevitable bolsters and tucked in with a quilt over his knees, he leant back to enjoy the soft grass underfoot and the glass-like water beyond. I could think of nothing but the peregrines and what I had seen, and I sat on the wide rug at his feet, sharing my stories of the hunt and the birds and their antics in the air with an exuberance of my own that astonished me. Tea was brought out and served along with a tall pile of Grizel's gingerbread, sweet with treacle. Donald discovered our little party and fetched his fiddle, and for an hour or two he played a repertoire of cheery songs. Kenneth and one of Donald's sons took the boat out onto the loch and fished, whooping with pleasure whenever a pike was brought dripping from the water, whilst Ròs and one of the kitchen maids filled bowls with shiny black brambles they picked from wild canes nearby.

Donald's daughter, the woman named Kirstie, joined us and knelt on the rug. She was introduced to me although I vaguely remembered her engaging, unguarded face and the lustrous ringlets that framed it.

Her smile for me was not as bright as the one she flashed at Coll when he made his appearance carrying wee Iain on his shoulders and trotting as if he were a horse. He breathlessly spoke to her in Gaelic and reached for her hand as he lowered the lad to the ground, but Iain was soon betwixt them, offering Kirstie a half-melted sweetie from his pocket.

The songs Donald played were too inviting for the others to simply listen. Choruses and verses sprang from their lips, and in the spirit of camaraderie I found myself singing amongst them. Iain preferred to run in circles on the grass, chasing his geese and clapping in time to the music.

When Donald began playing "Lochaber No More" and the voices rose round me, I tried to sing but found I could not.

Coll abandoned his duet with Kirstie and glanced at me. Donald ceased playing and tilted his head in puzzlement, his bow hovering in the air. Lord Kirthgarran's forehead furrowed. Nothing would come from my throat. I tried to think of an excuse for my odd behavior, knowing they expected me to say something. I could see Mamma playing her clarsach with the pedlar. I remembered how Father looked as he came in the door.

"Something else," Coll suggested. "Something lively we could dance to."

"Are you wanting to dance?" Kirstie asked him, pulling his sleeve.

"Well, perhaps not. Too much tea and gingerbread inside of me."

Every pair of eyes was staring at me and I tried to smile. "They're coming back in the boat," I said shakily. "I can help clean the fish if you'd like some for supper, my lord."

"There's kitchen maids aplenty for that," Rab scolded.

"You cannot mean you do not know 'Lochaber No More,'" Donald said.

I shook my head. The music was gone from my heart.

"Calum!" Coll shouted to one of the lads in the boat.

A head popped up.

"Bring in your catch and run along home. Quick now. We're wanting your da's pipes. And Kenneth. Take the fish to Grizel and fetch us the heather ale she's been hoarding all this week. You lads will have some of it as well."

The young men increased their fervor with the oars, pulling close to the shore within seconds. They jumped into the water and splashed us as they dragged the boat onto the pebbles.

"So 'tis the pipes you're after now, is it?" Donald said, laughing. "And if I'm of no mind to play them?"

Coll tucked Kirstie's hand under his arm. "Then I will."

Iain stopped spinning in a circle. "You do not play the pipes, Captain!" he exclaimed.

"I'll learn today, will I not?"

"Calum," Donald called to his son. "Fetch the pipes, but under no circumstances will you be giving them to the Captain here. Unless," he added, winking at us, "you wish your poor ears to be broken."

Moments later I sat with a cup of honey-sweet ale in my hand. Donald sucked the reed in his chanter to moisten it, screwed the pieces back together, and inflated the leather bag of his pipes, producing squawks of air that leaked from chanter and drones.

Whilst he twisted the drones up and down, tuning them, I began to recover. The piper played lively tunes as he strode up and down the shoreline, and I began to forget the sight of my father's uplifted fist.

Coll gave me an apprehensive smile, and so did the earl.

The day would have ended happily had Lachlan not arrived home at twilight and brought his ale-caup to the table with news to relate.

Our supper was of the freshly caught pike and brambles with thick cream. Lord Kirthgarran remained with us in the dining room, as did Donald with his son and daughter.

Lachlan took one of the chairs and said, "Douglas Hamilton is home."

Voices stilled and spoons remained poised in midair. Kirstie drew in her breath, and when she turned to look at Coll many eyes followed hers.

"Douglas," Sandy repeated.

"Aye," Lachlan said, staring at his ale. "I met his factor an hour ago. He was on his way here, to talk about cattle."

"What is on his mind?" the earl asked with a hint of suspicion.

"The Master's home," Lachlan replied, "and intends to stay. He's thinking to buy some of our cows, to start a new fold."

I turned to Rab and asked for an explanation for the sudden downturn of everyone's mood.

Rab said at my ear, "Douglas is Leslie Hamilton's brother. From Caiseal Àlainn."

I knew then. He was the one who had accused Coll of throwing his sister to her death.

"Home from France, then, and for good?" Sandy inquired.

"Aye. He sent his man to buy thirty cows. Douglas is tired of France and wanting his own home again. He sent no message but that he'd pay in gold—and his man chose the cows and said he'd send their herdsmen for them in the morning." He opened a purse and stacked a few coins on the tablecloth. Everyone considered the twinkling column. It was a welcome focus, for Coll's face had become stone and it was far too difficult to keep looking at him.

When Rab and I later strolled on the banks of the loch waiting for the first stars to appear, I noticed Coll sitting on a boulder by the ruins of the curtain wall. He was staring out at the water, lost within his own mind.

Kirstie saw him as well. She went halfway to him but hesitated beside us. Rab nodded in Coll's direction. "Go on, lass. He'll welcome you."

"No," she said sadly. "I saw it coming on him. It's not my company he wants tonight."

"The news of Douglas's return is a blow to him."

"It is to us all."

Rab sighed, turning his head to ponder his friend. "If you're there beside him, he'll speak to you. And then he'll forget he wanted to be alone, and be cheerful again. Heed me, Kirstie. His moods do not last long."

"But I'm thinking I intrude too often. He'll come to me when he wants. He always does." She raised her face to Rab. "Tell him I said good night." She backed away, turned, and hurried to join her father and Calum.

We followed the edge of the water, away from the ruins. Stars emerged in the summer sky. I glanced back before we went inside and discovered Coll walking away from the castle and the cottages. Into the night he vanished. It seemed he wanted no one's company at all.

With longing did I think on our morning together when he had been happy. I watched him as he followed the path along the loch, but finally, wordlessly, I ascended the steps to the castle entrance and accompanied my husband inside.

On an overcast day Rab rode to Rathdale, and I joined him. Anne was the perfect hostess and produced wine and plum cake for me when Rab and Andrew disappeared into the study to talk of financial matters. We were joined by Mairi and spent a pleasant hour.

"Will you have something?" Anne inquired of Rab when the two finally emerged.

"I'd love to, Annie lass, but have you peered outside in the last half hour? I've an errand waiting to be done in the glen before we're away home, and I hardly think the rain will oblige us."

Indeed, none of us had noticed, but the sky through the window appeared black with cloud and the air was already vaporous. Anne brought out my cloak and Rab's greatcoat, and we were soon on our way again.

We galloped over land unfamiliar to me. A mist rose amongst the heathery hills and fragmented into veils of white as it moved across the tops of the slopes. We glimpsed a roebuck chasing a doe, for it was the season for their mating, and I caught sight of swallows flying low over the moorlands before us. It all put me in mind of my rides about Melrose and how readily I had once sought such simple, quiet pleasures.

I surmised we were going north, perhaps the long way round Loch Seàrr. We began climbing hills when the rain started. I pulled my cloak close about me but the rain was insistent, and before I could cover my cocked hat with the hood, water was trickling down my neck. Rab walked his horse ahead of me, but when the water came down harder he paused and I came beside him.

"It seems we've been caught," he said.

"How much farther is it?"

"Only beyond the next rise. I must talk to one of the men about the kylies. We'll be out of the rain then."

We pressed on. I grew alarmed when Greyfriar's hooves slipped on the slick ground, but at last the cottages of the village were visible through the sheets of rain. A rough track led down the slope to the bottom of the glen, and I was surprised to find, emerging in front of us, a young ox pulling an unwieldy sledge fashioned out of timbers. The platform was raised at the front behind the ox's rump, dragged in the mud at the back, and laden with sheaves of grain clumsily covered with flattened sacks.

One man was walking beside the crude sled. Another was leading the ox forcefully along and one other figure, carrying sickles, was descending the hill. Ahead was an aged horse fitted with panniers woven from willow twigs, followed by a group of women and bairns who must have been reaping. Stubble over most of the shallow slope pointed to the fact that the folk had been trying to cut oats here before the onslaught of rain, but they had not been able to get the sledge to the granary in time.

"Randall," Rab hailed. He raised a hand in greeting to the reaper walking homeward with the sickles. The ox pulling the sledge raised its head in alarm when the man leading him bellowed, *"Hup! Hup!"*

Randall trotted over to us. He spoke to Rab and gestured at the cut field. We sat our horses for a moment, surrounded by the soft, endless patter of rain upon the heath, our clothes, our animals. I wondered how oats could grow on such a stony hillside as this.

All at once there was a burst of *"Haud!"* and a stream of angry sputtering followed when the ox attempted to descend a pitted length of track over the crags.

It arched its head upward, eyes rolling in fright whilst the man pulling its harness cried, "De'il swarbit on ye! *Haud! Haud, brùid!*" The forefeet slipped upon the wet stone and the ox scrabbled to regain its footing, yet in doing so it jerked the sledge sideways into a groove of rock. The man shook the leather straps and shouted *"Hup aff, marbhphaisg ort!"* but the ox panicked. It darted forward so quickly the worn ribbon of leather hooking it to the sledge snapped and threw the loaded boards off balance. The edge caught the man walking alongside at the knees, knocked him down against the rock, and slid over him as the terrified ox struggled.

The man holding the animal attempted to pull it back but was kicked in the chest by a flailing rear hoof, felling him to the ground as well.

Rab slid earthward and ran with Randall toward the wounded men.

Tears of despair from the weeping sky,
  Falling to the earth beneath,
And o'er the gloomy heat
  Hangs a misty pall of death, of death!
          Heavy the Beat of the Weary Waves (Trad.)

Chapter Eighteen

scooped up Rab's forsaken rein and guided my pony and McKay down the track to the sledge, where the men began unhitching the frenzied ox so it would not drag the boards. Rab trampled spilt sheaves heedlessly as he circled the load.

The beast, freed of its burden, was sent away with a *"Hisk!"* It cantered past me and the men turned their attention to lifting the sledge up from the body of the farmer. I dismounted and knelt beside the one who had been kicked. He was face-up in the rain, his head lodged against the sharp boulder it had struck, and his eyes were closed. Dark blood welled alarmingly beneath his skull and trickled into diluted streams of pink. I felt the pulse in his neck but it was weak. I removed my cloak and covered him with it, wiped the rain from his swarthy face, and pulled his black hair away from eyes and mouth.

Voices and bodies emerged from the gloom as men, women, and children hurried toward us, Lachlan and Coll amongst them.

The men arranged themselves about the sledge with Lachlan taking the most crucial position, and in unison they chanted, *"Aon, dà, trì,"* and heaved. The load rose, balanced precariously, and fell away with a great, creaking shudder, allowing others to drop to the injured man's side. They felt his limbs and inspected those of the man under my cloak.

I stood shivering as the unconscious men were lifted and transported down the hill. Some of the people seemed familiar to me. Two or three greeted me cordially, yet others gave me anxious glances and whispered amongst themselves. All at once I discovered the woman in the crimson petticoat standing beside me.

She caught me looking at her and turned to stare back at me. I was struck by a beauty that even rain could not diminish. Framed by a black knitted shawl was her heart-shaped face. Her cheeks were shiny, rosy. I wanted to turn and run. She cocked her head, said something in Gaelic, but when I did not respond she said in English, "You're Rabbie Fergusson's bride. I mind speaking with you at the castle when you first came."

"Aye."

Her eyes swept over my face, my dripping hat, and hair. "Did you see the mishap?"

"Rab and I were just riding past when it happened."

She peeked back at the men bustling about the sledge, and smiled a little.

Another young woman joined us, breathless from running. Kirstie nodded to me and in Gaelic asked something of the woman beside me.

"Yon sledge caught on the stones and the ox was frightened," she replied in English. "Seumas was knocked down, but Simon was caught underneath the grain."

"Isabell! Are they—is Simon..."

"They're both alive. They're taking them down now, to be

looked after." She added, with teasing in her voice, "Did you see who is here?"

The newcomer searched the group. In a few seconds her cheeks turned red.

Her friend went on mischievously, "Aye, he's here. They're all away home now. You should go to him. He'll no doubt be pleased to walk with you."

The men prepared to leave the hillside, shouldering the sledge over the rough track, bringing the ox back to hitch it up again with rope, and carrying the injured men down over the hill. The women and bairns dispersed, too. It was a somber procession down to the clachan.

I collected Rab's horse and mine but did not ride even though I shook with cold. Isabel coaxed Kirstie until she left us and crossed over to Coll's side. The sledge had been hitched and was being dragged down the hill beside them.

Isabel said, "Dear Kirstie. She's loved him since he came back from the war in America. The years toddle along and still she waits." She was watching the two of them, but gave me a quick, sidelong glance.

If I could have managed it I would have leapt to Greyfriar's back and led McKay home, but the rain was suffocating, leather was slick and uncooperative, and McKay began showing an irritable unruliness that demanded all of my strength. The discomfort I felt in Isabel's presence was the same as when I had first met her, and again there did not seem to be a way to escape. She took Greyfriar from me so that I could better tend to McKay, and though I resented her intrusion I discovered I needed the assistance.

"She's convinced," Isabel said, "that Coll will ask her father for her hand."

McKay tossed his head with annoyance. I said, "I do not think anyone would be surprised at that."

"Some believe he's waiting to judge her loyalty. If she does not tire of him and turn away, then she'll have proven herself." She stepped round a protruding stone. "And will not find herself dead at the bottom of a tower."

I sucked in my breath and stared at her tilted eyes and curving lips. "How can you say that!"

"Losh. I'm not the one to blame for the sentiment. It's what's being said. Or have you not listened? You seem to have heard what became of the Hamilton lass."

"She killed herself—out of remorse."

Isabel gave a hearty laugh. "Leslie Hamilton was in love with one person only, and that was herself. She'd no more take her own life than she'd part with one of her bonny French gowns."

"Then you think..."

"'Tis not just me who thinks. Give ear to what will be said now Master Douglas Hamilton's returned."

"I'm sure people have forgotten. I'm sure it's a tragedy best forgotten..."

"Do you suppose Douglas Hamilton will ever forget what befell his sister?"

"Perhaps he no longer blames Coll."

She blew air between her lips. "Why would his thoughts change?"

McKay must have sensed my sudden lack of attention to his behavior, for he pulled away and gained his freedom. I reached for his rein and missed as the horse shied and stepped sideways.

All at once Lachlan appeared beside me. "I'll take him," he grunted. He planted himself in front of McKay and with a deft hand grabbed his bridle. The animal lowered his head and snorted, but became the perfect horse and began walking calmly beside his new master. Isabel was silent as well, and I dared not look at her. I ached to snatch Greyfriar's rein from her hand.

The two unconscious men were carried into a hut and many followed them inside. Rab was one of them. I made my way there as well. Since Lachlan seemed willing to care for both our horses, I deserted him and Isabel and went through the open doorway.

The two-roomed dwelling would have seemed close merely because of the pouring rain outside, but filled with anxiety-ridden folk it was suffocating. Dampness and aimless smoke from the peat fire enshrouded us. I surveyed all of the faces round me. I saw no one I knew. The two men had been taken beyond the partition.

Soft, muffled voices filled the low-raftered hut but soon an elderly voice rose above the rest. A man was gabbling in fear. I discovered him crouching near the fire in the center of the room, and to my horror, realized he was looking straight at me. Voices dwindled. I sensed people moving away from me.

He spoke, again in Gaelic. Rab emerged from the other room. He went to the old man and listened and tried to quiet him, but before long my husband pulled me into a dim corner. His dark hair dripped water down his forehead, and his eyes seemed black. He rubbed his nose with a glistening hand and muttered, "Damn the man."

I glanced at the bent Fergusson by the fire. He was still eyeing me with fright. Of Rab I pled, "What is it?"

"This is his home. It would not do to offend him."

"What do you mean?"

"What's happened is unfortunate. But he's afeart of having you here."

"Me?"

"I suppose I should have told you before this. You ken that superstitions abound amongst the folk. Some of them believe the fire in the turret on the night we arrived was an omen, a foretoken."

I am sure I must have appeared stupid. I repeated, "An omen?"

"The fire-slaught setting the roof afire. They think it was because I wed you and brought you to Kirthgarran. And now they believe you caused the ox to bolt."

I stared at him with mouth agape.

"The coincidences are unfortunate," he said. "But there they lie."

They thought I would bring no good to Kirthgarran. It was why they whispered about me and did not come near. I said finally, "But why do they think so badly of a newcomer?"

"'Tis how they think, Keeley. There's no reasoning with them. I try, and it comes to nought."

"How long have you known? Why did you not tell me? I've wondered why they seem wary of me. It must be why Grizel— and some of the others—I wish you had told me!"

"I wanted to save you from it. To avoid bringing you heartache."

"Is it because I'm from the Lowlands? I would seem to be an enemy simply because of that." I turned my eyes to the man by the fire and asked Rab, "Do *you* think the fire was an omen? Do *you* believe my presence caused the sledge to catch?"

"Crivvens! Look at you now, making no sense at all. You belong at Kirthgarran. The De'il stick them all if they contradict me. Hear me well, Keeley. That night a simple fire-slaught struck the tower roof and caused it to burn. 'Twas no more than an accidental act of nature. Today the beast was harried at his head and slipped in the cursed rain and was not the victim of a glance of your evil eye."

I put a hand to the wall to steady myself. "Then what should we do now?"

"He'll not have you stay here."

"I might cause the men to die?"

He did not answer.

"I might cause this house to crumble, to crumble and fall down upon us?"

"Keeley. I cannot help what these folk think. I would denounce that auld man's ravings to refute, to prove, that this fear of theirs is irrational..."

"And why do you not?"

"Because of those two lying injured within. If you stay and one of them does succumb, think of the talk then. It will be doubly difficult to lay it to rest."

"By leaving I'll be admitting I am a source of harm, of evil."

"But by staying you'll be taking unnecessary risk. It is better to be away. 'Twill silence the auld man. Then the people will forget."

I did not think they would. "Let us be away this instant," I demanded with sudden impatience. "The longer we prolong it the worse it will be."

"I'm not coming with you, dear." I was unable to comprehend and sought his dark eyes. "Do not look so shocked," he said. "My place is here. I must make sure the men recover. The folk have to see that I care."

"Do you not think," I struggled, "it would be best if you came with me? It would show them you trust me, that we belong together."

"What is best is that I remain here."

I walked away from him toward the gaping doorway. A man was urgently hammering a horseshoe into the lintel above the door and did not look at me. Iron was always used to ward off evil.

Rab placed my cloak about my shoulders. As I tied the ribbon at my throat, Coll and Lachlan splashed through the mud toward us and took shelter in the doorway.

"How are they?" Coll asked, nodding at the interior of the hovel.

"Simon is coming awake," Rab said.

For the first time Coll looked at me, watching as I pulled the hood over my hat. "Are you leaving?"

"I'm away home."

"Now? In this rain? Are you not going to..."

"I'm away home."

I walked past them to the side of the house where Lachlan had tied the horses. I stepped round a dung heap and fumbled with wet leather, attempting to untwist my pony's reins from the branch of a tall and gangling beech. Whilst my fingers slipped and pulled, Coll appeared beside me.

"I told Rab I'd see you home," he said, reaching for McKay's bridle.

"I mind the way."

"I'll not let you travel alone."

"Are you not needed here?" I asked, still cross, but I was immediately sorry I'd spoken so.

McKay was freed and so was the pony. I levered myself upward and sat. My saddle was wet, my clothes were soaked, everything was drenched. I tightened my hands on the reins as Coll sprang onto McKay's restless back and brought him under control.

I touched the pony's side with my heel. "Come up!" I urged to the animal, and we were off.

As we rode homeward my ire began to dissipate into disappointment as if the water falling from the skies cooled and washed it into charred lumps. Coll was quiet as he rode beside me, and I was preoccupied, thinking remorsefully over everything that had happened. The village folk distrusted me. I wondered if the lightning striking the castle was the only fodder for their superstitions, or if there were something else, something at which I could not even guess, a sentiment stronger than mere dislike for a foreigner.

I thought of Grizel, startled in the kitchen. I thought of the man by his own fireside, staring at me in terror.

I thought of Rab, sending me home in the rain without a word of regret.

We were not yet within sight of the stone bridge when I realized the rain was coming down harder. Coll motioned for me to follow him and I did so, careering away through sheets of water that threatened to choke off my air.

We came upon a ruined hut. Grass carpeted the floor and a great many stones had fallen from the walls, but a fair amount of thatch overhead provided a dry space, and Coll dismounted to lead McKay inside. I followed, pulling Greyfriar through the gap in the wall. The sudden relief from water flooding head and face and body was anticlimactic. Above us were dry, cobweb-strewn rafters. On all sides, through the door and through the edge of torn-away roof, the rain cascaded relentlessly down, but we were inside, out of it at last.

"We'll stay until it lessens again," Coll said.

The horses seemed content enough and I turned to peer out at the water-washed landscape. The muffled thrum against the roof of heath became a rhythmic background. The scent of wet soil and heather filled my nose. I removed my hat and glanced at Coll who seemed oblivious to his soaked greatcoat.

I managed to say, "I was unforgivably rude to you before. I mean to apologize."

His eyes were the color of rain, I decided, when he turned them on me. He gave a half-hearted smile. "You've a right to be wild about such frivolous superstition. I do not think you need to apologize."

"Rab told you, then."

"It was an unlucky happenstance you were riding near the sledge when the ox bolted."

"It will not help dispel the fright some of the folk feel when I'm in their presence. Now I suppose it will be worse." I wondered why it mattered to me.

"They'll be seeing the folly of their thinking in time, I'm sure."

"They almost make me believe I am cursed in some way."

He shook his head and said, "But you must not. You'll fight this and you'll win."

"Am I at war with these people?"

"I'd treat it as a war, if I were the one they feart for no apparent reason."

"But you are a soldier. You're used to thinking in those terms."

"Everyone must battle in his life. Only when a person faces his foe does he learn its true nature and thus how to defeat it." He was right, of course. One did have to fight. For happiness. For sanity. I had not done so for some time.

Coll looked away and focused beyond the jagged doorway. Perhaps we were both absorbed by memories.

Unbidden came Isabel's insinuation that Coll had done murder—and that Kirstie's life was in danger as well. The idea was so implausible and dreadful that I clenched my teeth to make it go away.

I wanted to ask him about Douglas Hamilton and how he felt about his return to Scotland, but I lacked the courage. The silence between us was strained and I did not know how to break it. McKay tossed his head and Coll lifted a hand to smooth the horse's nose.

He said, "I've written out the verses to the boatman song for you. I'll give it to you when we're home."

"That is very thoughtful of you. Thank you. And—I've been thinking—I feel the better for speaking of my mother the other day. Perhaps it was hearing that song again. Or perhaps it was realizing you understood how I felt."

"I was glad to listen."

"I do not often talk of her."

"I suppose I do not often talk of my father."

"It does not mean we do not think of them."

"No. It does not." He glanced at me, expecting me to speak further of my mother, I thought, but when I did not he ventured, "Someone has told you, certainly, about my father."

Again I was relieved to be shown a safe course for conversation. "Your mother told me."

"My father lived at Rathdale with his wife."

"But he often came to Kirthgarran to see you."

"Mam's face would alight with joy. And I'm sure ours did as well. We would clamber over him and he would laugh and smile, but I do not think the joy of those moments ever lessened his sorrow." He let more of his reserve fall away. "He watched us grow. He taught us to ride." He smiled. "He even showed us how to prime and shoot a pistol. But he did not live with us, we could not live with him. Because of that he meant all the more to us."

"He must have cared for you all."

"Oh aye, he made it plain. And we worshipped him. Yet a mystery he was to us, a man who disappeared for days, sometimes weeks at a time, but one who made a great fuss over us when he returned. When I finally understood the nature of our situation I was surprised." He was thoughtful. "I believe my father intended to leave Eleanor at one time. In fact, it was just before I was born. Mam told me she'd been content then. He'd promised her he would take her and their bairns far away. He asked her to name me, their coming child, after his home isle. But time went by. He grew sadder and sadder. He could not leave his wife."

"He broke his pledge to your mother."

"He loved her just as much, but he could not leave Eleanor. I gather Mam was ne'er as hopeful after that. She knew our father could not openly acknowledge Andrew or me, or Alistair who came after. She says she greeted for Sandy because he lost his wife and a bairn, but I think she appeased her guilt at her inability to provide us with a father by encouraging us, especially me, to regard Sandy as a replacement. She could not depend on Christopher's daily presence, but Sandy was close at hand, with sons of his own, and it seemed natural enough for the families to meld. I suppose I did have two fathers when I was young. The steward who was always there, and the distant, revered caller."

"I've seen that you and Sandy enjoy each other's company. Now I better understand why."

"'Tis a tangled household we live in. I've not even mentioned

Lord Kirthgarran, who was a foster father to us all. You must have been confused at first."

We looked at each other steadily. I had forgotten the rain, Rab, everything. I thought it was the same for him.

"I think—if our father had lived he would have made provision for us. He died too young, unexpectedly, without the foresight to legally name us as his heirs. Mam wrote to his family on Coll after his death, asking if there was any place we could take amongst them, as natural sons of Christopher MacLean."

"What was the answer?" I asked, though I could guess.

"A warning never to contact them again. A religious lot, they were. In their view, Christopher's indiscretions were unforgivable. Such a sin as adultery, and fathering three bastards besides, had no doubt earned him a place in eternal hellfire and they wanted nought to do with any of us."

"And yet he had loved going home. He must have been received by them when he and Eleanor visited."

"They apparently tolerated his transgressions whilst he was alive. When he was dead it was different. There was no need to be generous. Or noble."

"But to be kind to three fatherless lads of their own blood would have been a Christian gesture."

"How many people have been killed in wars fought in the name of Christianity, or tortured because they would not convert? Folk do not often see the hypocrisy."

I gazed at his face, at the long scar under his eye. "I suppose they do not."

He said, so quietly that had I been any great distance from him I would not have heard him, "It is effortless to talk to you."

I could not seem to respond. There was no reply on my tongue and my mind was not seeking words. I did not dare to move. His eyes held mine.

McKay's nose intruded between us. Coll grasped the bridle. "The rain lessens. We should go before we miss our chance."

How I dreaded going back out into the world of water, but it seemed preferable to the broken-walled hovel that all at once seemed too confining.

We led our horses outside and headed back toward the

twisting turf path. We soon clattered over the slippery stone bridge. The rain merged with the burn and swirled over the rocks below. We rushed on, as fast as the water, until the towers of Kirthgarran speared the clouds. Twinkling lights in some of the windows promised warmth and dryness within.

There was a man on the path. He must have seen us approaching, for he stopped walking and seemed to wait. I could not tell at first who he was, but I soon recognized the black cocked hat. He was huddling under a plaid. He was obviously on his way home to the wee house he and his wife shared nearby. Both Coll and I reined in our horses.

Ewen Drummond's face was pale but his eyes were red with controlled fury. I had never seen him look so. His attention was all on Coll and his usual politeness had vanished. He behaved as though I was not there at all.

"I've been looking for you, Captain," Ewen shouted through the rain. Streams coursed down the brim of his hat and splashed to the ground. His lips were bloodless.

"What's amiss?" Coll replied, holding the bridle firmly as McKay tossed his head. "Is Lord Kirthgarran not well?"

"His Lordship is at ease. You've no worry there. It is with me you need to contend. You may think me auld, and aye, perhaps blind, but I can see still with these eyes. My dogs have been found."

I stared at the choler in the old man's face.

"Aye," he continued. "Did you not think they would be? A farmer's lad discovered one and his father the other. Both dead, both poisoned, there is no doubt."

I glanced at Coll, who said, "Aye, I'd heard they were found. You're thinking I was the one who did it."

I had not known this had happened and I glanced from face to face. "Where were they found?" I asked Ewen.

"Beyond the kirk, near the burn. Only a few yards from each other. And many, many days dead."

"It was not an accident then?"

"There was a naked bone nearby. As if they'd been given a morsel and then crumpled to the earth to die when the poison within did its work. And buried nearby, dug up by an animal, was a scrap of the blue cloth that was once used to cover the earl's table. The many-times-mended cloth that Grizel tore into rags. It must have held the meat that killed them."

Coll said nothing. His eyes were no longer the color of rain but of cold steel.

Ewen snorted through his nostrils and said passionately, "Who'd more reason to do away with my brave dogs than you? They wounded your animal, and I was sorry. If I'd thought you harbored them such hatred I'd have given them back to my brother, out of harm's way. You'd only to tell me. I would have given them back."

The muscles in Coll's jaw tensed. "When Lachlan told me yesterday they'd been found, I was certain you'd think it was me who put them down."

"I do not care to believe it was you."

I studied Coll's face. His brows were drawn down, and his lips were narrow. Rain gleamed on his skin.

"Well," Ewen said, apparently impatient to get away out of the weather now his anger was spent. He screwed his hat upon his head. "Perhaps I was too hasty. But you were all I could think of. You, and the vengeance you might have had inside you. It was someone from the castle. And I believed it was you." He glanced away and then back at Coll, a bit doubtfully still. He turned to tread through the grass.

My companion did not urge McKay forward at once. He was silent, forgetful of my presence. Before my eyes was the vision of him holding out the silver and brass pistol, readying himself to put an end to MacDiarmid's suffering. I thought of wee Iain trembling in the kail-yaird when I had first arrived at Kirthgarran, and could not deny that even I had often wished death upon the gray dogs.

There were many plants that could bring about the desired result. I remembered my mother pointing them out to me: monkshood, deadly nightshade or belladonna, marsh marigold, thorn apple, castor oil plant, henbane, poke weed, rue. Even the foxglove could be dangerous, and was worthy of its nickname, "deid man's bells." There were mushrooms, too: the elegant white death angel, and the ugly, puckered, black lorchel. All of them, soaked into a bone or scrap of meat, caused death; some were instant, some caused days of sickness before their work was done.

Coll kicked his horse into a canter and I followed.

MacNeil took our mounts in the courtyard. We hastened into the castle where Sandy greeted us, and I thanked Coll formally for his escort. He helped me peel my cloak from my shoulders, but it was Sandy to whom he spoke.

"There's been a mishap in the fields," he began. My father-in-law listened to the story. I had no wish to visualize the whole event again and retreated, unnoticed, toward the stair.

I wanted only two things. To wallow in a hot, strong cup of Lord Kirthgarran's Bohea, and to see the end of this wretched day.

I waited as the hour grew late. Grizel had prepared a supper of cockie-leekie with fowls in it, and it grew cold on the table whilst I despaired of having any company in the eating of it. I took a broth-plate upstairs and joined Lord Kirthgarran who was enjoying his supper from a tray.

"My lord," I said, stirring my soup, "do you ken that Ewen's dogs have been found dead?"

"It was only a matter of time before someone put an end to them."

"They were horrible. But do you think it was Coll?"

"Hm. Could have been. I suppose I'd not find it a surprise. He does take matters into his own hands, does our Coll. And it's not a bad thing, is it? Solving problems. Taking action. It was why he was promoted in the army, I'm sure."

"The dogs *were* dangerous," I said, filling my spoon with broth. I did not like to think that Coll had poisoned the animals, but I had to admit I was thankful the bairns of Kirthgarran— and I—would no longer be afraid. I must put it out of my mind, I thought.

Night came and still no one returned home. In the morning I accomplished a few simple enterprises. I looked in on the earl. I cut new nibs on a handful of quills in the library. The rain stopped and sunlight flirted amongst the clouds, sparkling elusively on the dark waters of the loch and painting purple streaks onto the mist-covered hills. Yet no one appeared on the track. I found I could not wait and left for the stable.

"Will you help me saddle Greyfriar?" I begged MacNeil when he came upon me leading the garron into the stable from the paddock.

The groom began to open his mouth to respond when a voice called behind us, "Good morning to you."

Greyfriar lifted his nose in alarm because I turned so suddenly. A gray-haired gentleman astride a dun horse was advancing toward the stable from the postern gate where Kenneth had admitted him. He was a traveler. Leather saddlebags bulged behind him and a wrinkled, dark green greatcoat hung from his shoulders.

He came within ten paces of us and dismounted, exposing us to an unidentifiable odor with seasoned perspiration as its main ingredient. Small eyes that spoke of worldly experience peered out from behind heavy lids, seeking first me and then MacNeil. It was upon me that they rested at last. He traced my figure from head to toe, offered a bow, and stretched his lips in a closed smile. "Are you the lady of the castle, my dear?" he asked.

I was relieved when Kenneth came to stand beside me. "I suppose you could say I am," I answered, curtseying. "Though I am not of Lord Kirthgarran's true family."

"It is the Earl of Kirthgarran on whom I wish to call."

"He is not expecting visitors."

"Nay, he'd not be expecting me. I am here to introduce myself, to make myself known to him."

"He is not well."

"Let me begin by introducing myself to you, my dear lady. My name is Henry Baird. It is the wool trade I wish to discuss with Lord Kirthgarran. Will you give me the honor of learning your lovely name, so I may address you most proper?" He wiped a palm on his expansive stomach and reached out plump, brown fingers to take mine.

"Mrs. Robert Fergusson," I said. He kissed the back of my hand. I withdrew it and rubbed away the moisture his thick lips had left behind.

"Mrs. Robert Fergusson. I suppose 'twould be too great a fortune to find you a widow? I thought as much. Well, it is my loss." He smiled again, this time exposing large, tobacco-stained teeth that reminded me of those of a horse.

I turned away and encouraged MacNeil to throw a saddle over Greyfriar's back.

"A pleasant day for a ride," Mr. Baird said with sarcasm.

I gave him a quick glance. "By your appearance I'd surmise you've had a long journey and would welcome a rest and something to restore you. I'll take you inside, where you'll be given refreshment. No doubt our steward will attend to you and advise you if indeed you may see the earl." To MacNeil I said, "Will you care for his horse?"

I did not know where I found the words or the nerve to say them, but there was no time for wonder. I led the way back into the castle and found Sandy at once, who agreed that the stranger must speak to him first.

"I'll accept a dram," the newcomer said ungraciously, taking a glass from Sandy with four fingers and delicately thrusting his littlest one into the air. "And then I will wait, for however long I must, to be shown to His Lordship."

One of Sandy's brows lifted.

I left them to their battle. Nothing could force me to stay and play the part of hostess.

Love, sweetest love—let it soften thine heart.
Fairest and Dearest (Trad.)

Chapter Nineteen

hilst I walked Greyfriar toward the cluster of cottages huddled in the glen I tried to imagine what I would find. Women who had been talking to one another with their arms full of weans and pails and baskets ceased their chatter and stared at me as I approached. Would I be stoned as a witch or a wicked enchantress if Fate had been so unkind as to claim even one of the men's lives? I forced myself to the door of the cottage I had vacated the day before.

I compelled myself to call into the opening. At first my voice was nothing but a murmur. I tried again.

A face appeared. It belonged to the man who had been besotted by fear the day before.

I said, "Good day. I have been—I have come to—I was wondering about the men. The men. Simon? And Seumus?" I could feel my heart pounding in my throat and in my ears. I thought he must be able to hear it as well.

Cloudy eyes showed alarm. He was missing several teeth and mouthed words silently.

"Mayhap Rab is here? Or Coll?"

He hobbled away. I stroked Greyfriar's hairy muzzle for comfort, knowing the women at my back still watched. A few seconds later the tall frame of Andrew filled the entrance.

"Oh Andrew! How glad I am to see you!"

He stepped over the deepest part of the mud at the doorstep, and put an arm about my shoulders to bring me a few paces away from the cottage. "You look frightened to the death."

"I need to discover how Seumus and Simon are. I need to find Rab."

"Rab's not yet home? He left hours ago."

"He's not come home at all and I've not heard the fates of the men. Are they…"

"No, no! Simon, the one knocked down by the sledge and pinned against the rock, has a gastrous bump upon his skull and a headache to match, but he'll be up and about today, no doubt. Seumus, the other, is not as fortunate. His head seems to have swollen, and he's not come out of his faint. But you're not to worry. Rab did not come and tell you?"

My fingers twisted themselves whilst I sought to understand. "He's come not at all."

"Well. But, well, he must have been waylaid. I'd have sent someone to you if I'd thought he'd be so slow."

"You do not think Seumus will die?"

"We all must say our prayers for him. I had hoped he'd come round before this."

"And there's nought that can be done—other than pray?"

"The bleeding's been stopped. But still he does not move. I'll be sure to come and tell you if aught comes to pass." There was pity in his look.

"A visitor has come for Lord Kirthgarran. I think Sandy means to fill him with whisky and turn him out the door. He seems intent on discussing the wool trade with the earl. His name is Henry Baird."

Annoyance curved the corners of Andrew's mouth. He nodded as if he understood something I had not said. "I'll ride back with you."

The aged man of the hut had grown valiant enough to scrutinize me through his doorway. I gave him a weak smile. He took a step backward but I was sure his eyes were fixed upon me until Andrew and I disappeared.

I was in the garden when Rab came home. His bloodshot eyes had shadows under them, and his face was dark with stubble. We measured each other. I waited for him to speak, but when he did not I said, "There's a caller for Lord Kirthgarran. He's been here for quite a while with Andrew and your father."

"I see." He began strolling toward the courtyard and I fell into step beside him.

I said, "I could not wait for the news. I went to the cottage to see how the men fared."

"You ken Simon is well, then. And Seumus—he lies stricken, but alive. I waited with them all night."

"Andrew told me."

He raked his tousled hair with a hand and appraised me dolefully. "You're indignant still. Because I sent you away."

I was torn between wanting to argue and pretending none of it had happened. "I'm troubled about Seumus."

He kissed my cheek. "Where is our visitor?"

I envisioned myself demanding to know why he thought it best I leave the cottage without him. I imagined shrieking like a harridan and asking where he had been this morning. But no words came. I followed him into the castle and upstairs to the drawing room.

He threw his coat onto a chair, and rolling up the sleeves of his shirt, asked "Is he in the library?"

I nodded.

He tilted his head. "You wanted me with you last night."

It seemed one way to express it.

"I'll be making it up to you, dear. I was tormented being away from you."

I lowered my head, unable to tell if he jested.

He smiled nobly, and after ladling a glass full of whisky from the sideboard, left me to seek out our guest.

At nine o'clock Rab came to the supper table with Mr. Baird at his side. Still crimson-eyed, he explained to me, "Our guest will be staying the night. Will you see to having a room prepared?"

Coll, Lachlan, and Ewen Drummond were introduced. Sandy seemed reluctant to elaborate on any part of Mr. Baird's affairs, saying merely, "We've important affairs to consider tonight."

Ewen's anger of the day before had vanished, and yet there was a stiffness between him and Coll. No one spoke of the gray dogs; it was as if they never existed. I had accepted the possibility that Coll had ended their lives, but Isabel's malicious gossip about Leslie Hamilton's death did not warrant a second thought.

"He is not a murderer," I reminded myself.

At the end of the meal the men disappeared outside and I sought the remoteness of the earl's bedchamber. Although I knew the earl had been told about the wool merchant, he did not mention him. Airig's sister was in the room, straightening the bed linens whilst the earl sat in his chair.

On the previous day we had been reading *The Expedition of Humphry Clinker* by Tobias Smollett, but we neared the end. "What will be next?" I murmured as I fingered the disorderly pile of books on his bedside table.

"I've read them all, lass. It will be for you to choose."

"Are there any in the library you'd like me to read to you?"

"Perhaps. There are a great many there."

I had explored the shelves several times. They were populated by such wealth as Capell's edition of *Shakespeare*, Walpole's *The Castle of Otranto*, Dalrymple's *Ancient Scottish Poems*.

"There are interesting-looking books there, with intriguing titles," I complimented him.

"A friend of mine in Perth is a bookseller. He saves books for me throughout the year, ones he thinks I'd be liking. Andrew and Anne usually go every fall to buy them, as well as to purchase the stores we need for the winter."

Ròs exclaimed from the bedside, "I cannot wait! Grizel

shrieks about sewing needles and salt. She'll finally stop her complaining—for a bit." Lord Kirthgarran and I smiled at her. She blew her fluffy red hair above her brows and bid us both good night.

"It occurs to me, of a sudden," Lord Kirthgarran continued, "perhaps you and Rab would care to be going along with them to Perth this year. They're thinking of leaving soon after Samhain. Have you ever been?"

"No."

"It's not such a city as they have in the Lowlands, but the things we need can be had easily enough. It might be a pleasant change of scene for you, afore the wind and snow set in. You could find books for us. I've a few coins put aside to spend on that."

Buying books for Lord Kirthgarran seemed an enjoyable task, indeed, I thought, refusing to ponder the fearful challenges that travel and new places would present.

I opened *Humphry Clinker* and found the place where we had stopped. Matthew Bramble, Lydia, Tabitha, and the dull-witted Humphry all came alive in the letters Matthew wrote home to his doctor throughout his search for good health in England and Scotland. We had just finished the passage in which we discovered Lydia's lover was a wealthy man's son and not a pauper when Sandy came upon us and asked if Lord Kirthgarran wished to take to his bed for the night.

It was late when I joined the men in the drawing room, but it appeared they felt obligated to entertain our odoriferous visitor. Ewen Drummond had gone home but Mr. Baird was caught up in a discussion with Rab and Andrew about Calvinism, and I, balanced on the edge of the settle and idly fondling the ears of the orange cat, soon decided I would defy Rab's wishes, excuse myself, and go to bed.

I raised my head just in time to see Coll coming toward me. He sat down at my side and for a moment listened to the talk surrounding us.

"I fear I'm not one for discussing religion," he whispered to me. "It's been too long a day, with overseeing the spreading of lime and convincing the cottars of its benefits, and showing them how to sow rye grass and clover and assuring them of their needfulness as well."

"Do you not wish to argue about Moderates and Evangelicals?" I asked, putting from my mind the confidences we'd shared in the broken cottage the day before, and all that Isabel had said about him earlier. "Surely you have views about Calvinism that are just as particular as your opinions about lime and clover."

"My views would lead to blows. I've not the patience to be bandying words about tonight." He sent Mr. Baird, who was profoundly engaged in the pith of his conversation, a hostile look. "You did hear that Simon is not gravely hurt?"

"But Seumus shows no sign of waking."

He gazed at me for a moment longer. "It may mean nought. I once saw a man lie as still as a corpse for a fortnight, and then awaken as if only one night had passed."

I had not heard Rab come toward us. He reached down, startling me, and took my hand in his. "My sweet wife," he said, smiling. He pulled me to my feet. "I'm thinking we need some amusement. Why do you not fetch your harp? Music would be a fine diversion for our guest."

I turned from the scent of whisky on his breath. Mr. Baird was beaming at me as he sucked on a clay pipe.

"Come now. I'm sure we'd all love to hear you play," Rab prodded. "I'll even fetch it for you…"

"The hour's rather far gone," Coll interrupted. "We're all weary."

"'Tis ne'er too late for music. I'm surprised you're not agreeing with me, Keeley." He was unsteady on his feet.

"I cannot."

"Come, come."

"Do not press her," Coll said.

Rab dropped my hand, his eyes on Coll. "Do not answer for my wife." More calmly, he said, "We've a duty to amuse our guest."

"But not at Keeley's expense. God's Wounds, man, she's said no."

"It is no concern of yours what I ask of my wife."

"It is when you're so fou that you embarrass us all."

Rab turned and strode from the room, scaring the cat and

sending her under the chair. I remained standing, staring first at the door through which Rab had gone and then at the floor so I would not have to see the faces of the others. Andrew poured a bit of claret into a glass. He brought it to me and pressed my fingers about the curve of the vessel whilst he gestured for me to sink down again beside Coll.

"Have a sip, Keeley. It will help."

I did as he suggested, aware of everyone's eyes upon me. The liquid went down like molten lead. I forsook my glass and laid my hand against my temple.

"Take no mind of him," Andrew went on. "He was up all the night and into the whisky half the day."

Mr. Baird chuckled.

I rose and said, "I will take my leave of you, gentlemen. You must—you must excuse me."

"Of course," Andrew began, but just as I curtseyed, footsteps echoed through the hall. Rab appeared in the doorway and in his arms was my clarsach.

"Sit down, my dear. I've fetched it for you. And now there's no excuse for you not to indulge us."

"Rab," I said in disbelief.

He held it out and I had no choice but to take it. He pressed my shoulders downward, and if I had not found the cushion I surely would have fallen. As I met Mr. Baird's lustful stare through spirals of tobacco smoke, the urge to run welled up in me like blood from a wound and the claret hardened in my stomach.

"A merry tune," Rab suggested, lounging in a chair.

Mr. Baird licked his wet lips. I put down the clarsach and left the room.

Behind me Rab's voice rose in an accusing cry. "Keeley!"

I grabbed up my hem in one hand and took to the circular staircase. It was not long before I heard his footfalls behind me and I quickened my steps. I faltered in the darkness. He overtook me in the corridor near our rooms and the lantern he had been carrying dropped to the floor. He seized my wrists and brought them to his chest. I peered up at him in the semi-darkness and when his voice came, it seemed too loud. "Why do you run from me?"

I attempted to pull away but his fingers tightened.

"I never ask you to play. Why do you deny me?"

His breath was sharp. Fervently I wished for more light than the lantern's glow at our feet, light that would allow me to see some remnant of the man I knew as my husband. The tale that Isabel had imparted to me at my infar about the injured groom who had fed Rab's horse before the race-meeting leapt about in my mind.

He said, "I should have let Young James throw the damned thing on the fire after all."

He held me for a long moment. I looked at his eyes, wordlessly beseeching him for patience, but the expression in them was cold. He pulled me farther along the passage. He released one of my wrists when he opened the door to his bedchamber and brought me inside. He pressed it shut with his shoulder. Dying embers on the ingle sent a flimsy glow throughout the room. His lips found my neck and his fingers slid round my back to hold me against him.

He began to murmur, "My sweet, sweet Keeley. I missed you last night so. Have I hurt you? I have, have I not? Crivvens. You ken 'tis not what I'm meaning to do at all. Not at all, at all." He brought me crookedly to his bed. "I embarrassed you. Little did I mean to. Do you forgive me, dear wife? Forgive a man who wants only to love you?"

At the edge of the amber bed curtains, on the top of the bed-steps, he stopped. I did not know what he meant or wanted, but he was too impatient to wait. He propelled me about, pushed me down against the high edge of the feather bolster, and came behind me.

He fumbled with his breeks whilst his other hand swept aside my chemise. I attempted to pull away but it was useless, for he was hard against the back of me, disinterested in everything save his own desire. My surprise was short-lived as humiliation and disgrace plucked at me, bit into my flesh. He did not appear concerned that my feet slipped on the platform in an attempt to escape him.

My shame was a stone in my throat I could not swallow. I was pinned against the bed. There was something inhuman about him behind me. I could not see him. I could not touch him. He satisfied himself, caring nothing for me, and then he stood unsteadily, pushed me fully onto the bed, and collapsed beside me. We lay in the dark, he a captor, I a prisoner, until his hold loosened from me and his breaths lengthened. He had fallen asleep.

Dry-eyed, willing the physical pain to subside, I stared at the shape of the dark head lying close to my shoulder.

I thought about my father. I thought about my mother. And I pictured the track leading away from Kirthgarran Castle, wondering if I had the courage to take it.

...how sad the waking.
The Islay Maiden (Trad.)

Chapter Twenty

He woke when the sun sent a crimson blush creeping through the arched window and the open curtains of the bed.

Once, not long after Rab had dozed, I had attempted to crawl out of the bed but he had bestirred himself and asked me to stay. He'd groped at my clothes, pulling them from me, throwing his and mine far away to the floor where they still lay in dark huddles. He had tucked me under his arm and pulled coverlets over the both of us. It was the first night we had spent together at Kirthgarran.

He rolled onto his back, bringing his face into the sun's light, and he rubbed his forehead as if it throbbed. At length he regarded me beside him. A warm hand tenderly clasped my arm. "The De'il stick me," he mumbled against my hair. "What must you think?"

I did not know. After a night of thinking I could no longer think at all.

"I was not very caring of you, was I? I've a vague memory of it."

Lying against him in daylight with nothing between us was something new. I could sense the long length of him, naked and warm, curved behind me. I knew not what to do. I studied the bedposts that reached to the ceiling and ended in carved, pointed knobs. My eyes traced the designs stitched into the amber bed curtains.

"Forgive me." I felt him take one of my arms and study the bruises he had put there. His thumb stroked the mottled skin. Eventually he stretched and sighed, sat up, and threw the covers from him. His back was toward me and a ray of the low sun fell across his flawless shoulders as he swept his hair from side to side. "Will you rise with me?" he asked. "We'll have a cup of ale together."

I sat up, covering myself with the bedsheet.

"The drink. Crivvens. I should have left you alone."

He appeared mollified by his own words and moved from the bed, lifted pieces of clothing from the floor, studied them groggily until he determined whose they were. He laid my gown beside me. He pulled on his breeks. Sitting on the bedding beside me, he asked, "What think you of our visitor from Dumbarton?"

I cleared my throat, searching for a return of dignity. "I do not care for him very much."

"Well, that's a pity. We may be doing trade with him."

"What do you mean?"

"Do you not ken what he's come for?"

"No."

"He's a mill owner. He raises sheep. He processes wool. And his damn pockets are so filled with gold their seams are nearly split."

"I do not understand. Kirthgarran has no wool to sell."

"No, but Kirthgarran has the land to raise the sheep."

Something stirred in my mind. "The glen, the farmland..."

"Baird's friends have begun a thriving industry, you see. He himself already rents lands south of here, but they're not enough. He made inquiries before he came. The land here is just what he wants."

I sat up straighter, keeping the linen tight about me. "But it is farmland, and pasture for cattle."

"That it is, but if put under sheep Kirthgarran will no longer be wasting away, crumbling with the weight of countless debts that've been heaped upon it."

I remembered then. Coll had told me with disgust of the cold-blooded schemes of the wool mill owners. "If the land is turned into a sheep walk it means the people must leave to make room."

"Aye, it means that exactly."

"You're not going to force the folk away."

"This is not an easy decision. Do not think we make it lightly."

"It's not your decision to make."

His dark gray eyes chilled. "You've no need to remind me of that."

"Someone must remind you. You've no right to decide this behind Lord Kirthgarran's back."

The iciness remained as he regarded me, but it melted away when he reached out a hand and touched me. "We intend to put the matter before him today. Of course it is his decision. We merely saved him some trouble by considering the good points, and the bad."

"Do you all agree with this plan? Are you as one?"

"No." He stroked my shoulder once and let his hand drop. "Coll and my father are against it. Lachlan and Andrew waver. But, as you say, it is not up to us, is it?"

"Lord Kirthgarran is ill. You would not badger him with this. He cares for the folk..."

"The folk! What bluidy loyalty do they deserve after they emigrate one by one? 'Tis time he thought of himself for once, do you not think? You ken how far sunken Kirthgarran is. There'll be nought left in a few years. Lord Kirthgarran must be made to see that this is a chance to be salvaging everything."

"Perhaps it's only a chance for you to put your hands on a bit of coin." I thought of the missing silver cup and wondered again what had happened to it.

He inhaled, surprised at my tongue. His head tilted. "There's many who are supporters of the wool trade. There's no doubt in my mind that whatever happens to Kirthgarran after the earl is gone, sheep will be part of its future. If we make the change before then, and it is known we are responsible for the upturn of its fortunes, then King George, or Parliament, or the Exchequer or the Fergussons of Lund, or whoever is going to make decisions, might think kindly enough of us to keep us here. You want to stay, do you not?" His lip turned downward and cynicism frosted his eyes once more. "That's one way of looking at it, is it not? Either the folk in the glen go, or as soon as the earl dies, we do. I ken which I would prefer, even if you do not." We had never before discussed Kirthgarran's future and its lack of heirs. He seemed to assume I knew of our precarious positions. When I could think of no answer he rose and shook out his shirt. Barefoot, he trod to the door and turned. "Are you coming?"

There were unexpected pinpricks behind my eyes. "I'll be along."

He plunged arms into sleeves and left me.

Mr. Baird took his leave of us after presenting his land-rent proposition to Lord Kirthgarran.

"Nought can be decided immediately, you understand," Sandy said to the mill owner as he escorted him to the great door of Kirthgarran Castle.

"And I've pressing matters to which I must return," Mr. Baird replied. "But I look forward to Lord Kirthgarran's reply. Let us hope he sees reason soon."

No one was happier than I to see him riding away in much the same manner as he had come, with his saddlebags wadded full of belongings to the point of overflow, and his coat wrinkled and thrown about his shoulders.

I told Airig I wanted no dinner and clumsily reassured Andrew, Coll, Lachlan, and Sandy that I'd suffered no harm the night before when Rab had followed me upstairs. They were anxious for me, it seemed, and I was touched by their concern. In relief I sought the silence of my room.

Clouds lingered in the sky. I watched them through the alcove window from one of the seats carved out of the castle wall. A heavy mist fell, soaking the earth, and before long the sun peered bashfully down.

I wanted to leave Kirthgarran.

Mrs. Dundas had assured me I would find peace and fulfillment in my new life. She did not know that my husband would ignore me for days on end and then inflict damage when the drink overtook him. I wished I could ask her, "Is this what I am supposed to be thankful for? Is this indeed what God intended for me?" I hardly thought she would answer yes.

None of this—my marriage, my banishment to Kirthgarran, my estrangement from my father—was of my choosing. I had been given choices, I supposed, and I remembered them all: living like a beggar on the roads, casting myself on the pity of the Kirk Session, struggling to survive alone in a strange city. The blow of Davy's rejection had impaired me so deeply I had not resisted the easiest path presented to me. I had not cared, then. But these days I thought less and less of Davy, and remembered what I had once wanted more than anything, before I had even met him. My own wee house, with a garden and a cow, and sewing or cooking to do for the neighboring folk. And peace.

I could leave Rab by declaring I was too unhappy to endure my life at Kirthgarran any longer, and simply walk away. A grass widow I would be called, forever wedded but otherwise free. Or a deed of separation might be drawn up between us and signed, legally ending the marriage. Where the papers might be written, or how, were monstrous thoughts so overwhelming I could barely contemplate them.

"Rab would have to agree," I said out loud.

I knew that if I were with child, I must stay. I could not subject an innocent bairn to the uncertainties of the world. Having to leave Kirthgarran after the earl's death was a less chilling notion than providing for a bairn alone.

But alone—where would I go? I thought I might be able to remember the route we had taken from Melrose and follow it backward, pleading for food and bedding in the same places we had stopped before. But my destination was an unknown, and I could not exist for long without money. I thought with longing of the small mountain of pounds I had spent five years earning, and then lost.

My pride would keep me from returning to Gilchrist House, or Melrose for that matter. I must settle wherever I had a chance to support myself. What I would do for my living and how I would fend for myself until I found it were bewildering questions just as they had been years before. To buy my own cottage would require money. I had seen the squalor of my father's woolen mill and I could not picture myself working in such a place, or toiling in a cotton mill, or picking kelp on stony beaches for the kilns in the soap and glass manufactories. No doubt one of those fates would have been mine had I innocently left Melrose with my baking money.

People always needed nursemaids and dairymaids, but I would have to travel to find such positions, just as Davy had done. I could become a cook or a kitchen maid and save my earnings so that one day I could take a wee house, but there was only one way to find such a position: by walking from town to town. It was not until I watched the peat smoke rising from a far-away cottage that I thought of another solution.

Emigration.

The word filled me with terror and relief at the same time. My eyes followed the trail of smoke as it rose above the farm-toun. How many such traces had there been of the families who lived there? How many were gone?

They had gone somewhere. They had had help. *The shipping agents,* Coll had said.

I stood up and pressed my hands against the panes of the window. It did not matter how far away a man went, Ewen Drummond had once lamented, because once he made a decision to leave his home he might as well leave Scotland for the anguish that beset him.

How I wished that the farming folk who had been born amongst these hills and glens did not fear me. I could ask them how their kinsmen had emigrated. No doubt many of them now held their own wee cottages on the other side of the Atlantic.

The green of the hills suddenly became precious to me. If I

were to leave the country, if I were to join a group of men and women bound for a new beginning in a far-off land, sustained by a plan forged by a knowledgeable agent, where would I go? Would I have a choice? Would it be North America for me? North Carolina or Canada? Or Jamaica, where I might find work in the sugar cane fields?

I pressed my forehead to the cool glass. The memory of Rab and his violence the night before surged within me. "I will not live like Mamma lived," I said.

Emigration. It was a possibility. I needed to discover more.

The pigeonholed desk that crouched in the middle of the library was an oaken brute of a secretary that made even the lacquered Chinese cabinet in the corner seem small. Ewen Drummond, seated in front of it, seemed dwarfed by it as well.

"Do the accounts interest you?" he inquired.

I sat beside him in a manner that I hoped seemed free of care and replied, "You do not mind that I see them? Lord Kirthgarran invited me to look."

"I'm delighted you find them appealing."

"I kept the housebook at home. And Father used to show me his ledgers for the mill and explain the entries."

"You've experience in these matters."

"Only simple ones. I am good with sums."

"Perhaps, Mrs. Fergusson, you'd care to aid me at times in the keeping of these records?"

He could not have shocked me more. "Would I not be taking over a duty that Sandy or one of the earl's foster sons attends to?"

"My eyesight. It grows poorer every year. I could use someone to read figures. To write letters for me."

I was not averse to the idea. Spending time with him, in point of fact, was just what I wanted. I watched him turn a page of one of the great books. He glanced at me in expectation and the long hairs of his feathery eyebrows lifted. "I would be honored to help you, sir," I said.

"Very well, then!" He urged me closer and I moved my chair to the desk. I had to admit I felt very much at home in the library where walnut bookcases displayed a range of literary work and framed colorwash studies embellished the stuccoed walls.

Ewen slid three books toward me. The figures in the estate ledger ranged from sums of old debts to expenditures for current necessary items. There were years of records relating the income gained from selling the kylies. I noticed that the last entry recorded the sale of thirty cows to one Douglas Hamilton for one hundred and fifty pounds Scots.

In the household accounts that Sandy kept were sums for provisions in the kitchen's larders, payments given to the extra women who came from time to time to give the castle a good cleaning, and lists of monies provided for laundresses, privy rakers, and the joiners who occasionally replaced beams riddled with woodworm. Listed also were the annual wages for the servants, gardener, stableman, and others: four pounds annually for the henwife and each of the chamber, kitchen, and dairy maids; eight pounds for the cook. The third volume was a Cellar Book professing the money spent for the earl's supply of sack, claret, red and white wines, brandies, and syrups. Some were expensive; others were smuggled and cheap.

I examined them all and said, "I see there is a great deal I do not know about the estate."

Ewen's wrinkled features softened as a smile spread on his lips. "The twenty farms found at Kirthgarran, Rathdale, and Strath Gruagach, some large, some very small, depend on the raising of the black cattle. Together the cottars can keep a fold of about four hundred, and depending on prices, a little over a hundred a year can be sold. The earl has his own and sells about the same number. The animals are not as hardy as one could wish. They cannot feed in snow if it is over five inches deep, and the hay we manage to grow for them is poor and tasteless."

"I was told they must be coddled in England because they are so lean." Clearly Ewen Drummond enjoyed talking and all I must do is listen.

"Aye, that is so, so it is. In summer the cows are taken to the hills where they recover from their winter starvation, but for the English markets they must be fattened, and it is only on English pastures that they find their fill. The soil here is thin, you see, and so is the grass."

"There's straw to be had from the oats. Could not the cattle have that?"

"Ah no, that is because we parch the oats in the straw to render the grain. It makes the straw unusable as fodder." He stacked the books in front of him and put the silver cap on the inkpot. With blackened fingers that matched mine he smoothed a sheaf of papers and attempted to line up their edges. "Perhaps we need to make more changes in the way we do things. The lads have spoken about spending time amongst farmers in Hampshire in England to learn if there are better methods."

"You've made a great many improvements already, I think."

"It has been difficult. Letting the tacksmen go was a decision not easily come by. Before the Rising, the tacksmen, close kin to Lord Kirthgarran, held the land of him and tended to their tacks as if they were their own. They received rent from the farmers, and all the profits from the land were split amongst them and the earl."

I sat back in my red velvet chair, thinking I would soon learn what I wanted to know, but I was not unaffected by his story.

"We wondered what would happen if the earl became the sole landlord and another man, or men, were hired to oversee the holdings. The only problem," he explained as he laid his hands flat on the books, "was that such men would not have the centuries of knowledge that the tacksmen possessed by right of birth, nor perhaps the same loyalty, since there was no immediate profit for themselves."

"When did the tacksmen leave?"

"It was, eh, perhaps six years ago. Two left willingly, overcome by stories from the colonies. Because of the rise of the rents, which was needed if Kirthgarran and the rest were to survive, the tacksmen and their tenants felt the clan was dying. They were dispirited, as well as hungry."

Agriculture was much different in the Lowlands, I mused, where landowners did not have to contend with the overabundance of laborers or the lack of them. Rents were expected and paid and tenants who could not meet their obligations were removed.

"Here at Kirthgarran," he continued, "some folk emigrated to America because they could not ignore the beckon of a happier place. What man would not want land of his own and the fruits of his own labors? When the tacksmen here wanted to go, others wanted to follow, to remain together, to work together in a new land. America promised full bellies. Land for their children. The right to bear arms again." He stopped and pondered, staring at his hands. "When the tacksmen left, Sandy's and Mairi's sons volunteered to take their places. They put the rents toward maintaining the estates and freeing them from debt. Their own pockets go empty but it is the bond with the earl and the love of the land that keeps them. But, though the effort is admirable, the fact remains. Each tenant does the work of two men. Some have a good piece of land, and others have nought but a hut and some grass for a cow. Some pay the rent with the selling of the cattle and the grain. Others depend only on the strength of their backs and how many hours of labor they can supply. The fact that we stumble along year after year and somehow survive is not a feat of magic. It is the result of the time the lads put toward the lands and the little they take out of them."

"The families that emigrate. Where do they go? How do they know where to go?"

"There are agents who fill manifests and for a fee will arrange the particulars."

I tried not to appear too curious. "Where do the folk find these agents?"

"The names are well-known. They are passed about the country. I've a list here, in fact. At times they send letters to the earl, urging him to send his poor farmers to North America or the island plantations. Sometimes, infrequently, they journey through the glens themselves, gathering innocent folk with their lies of how simple it is to cross the sea and become wealthy."

He flicked the edge of a loose paper sticking out of the estate account book.

"Hm," I murmured, opening the book and glancing at the fine script on the paper. There were names and addresses. "They are dishonest men, then?"

"One must ne'er believe tales of ceaseless bounty and effortless lives. The shippers are after money, and will say aught. They have their purpose, though. Certainly there are colonies of our kinsmen in America and Canada that prosper. We've had letters that prove that. But a man hoping to escape poverty must take care to believe what only sounds sensible, to hear the truth beneath the cunning talk."

"That would seem to make sense," I said.

In my bedchamber I wrote the letter. I had memorized the name of the man who headed the baillie's list: Samuel Hume, of Oliphant Road, Glasgow. I asked Mr. Hume the questions that plagued me. How did one find a place to go? Could one woman alone manage such an undertaking? What if I had no money? If I decided to leave Kirthgarran where should I go first?

When Reverend Cameron came to Kirthgarran I handed him the letter, sealed with cherry-red wax. "Will you see this on its way?" I asked. He agreed, but there was puzzlement in his eyes when I added, "And please, tell no one here I have written this?"

He assented again and fortunately chose not to question me. Instead, he patted my arm with compassion and thrust the folded paper into his pocket.

The first step had been taken.

I was not sure how fervently I wanted to leave Kirthgarran. Rab was not the only person here. There were others of whom I could become fond. Would that not be enough compensation for my husband's intermittent harshness?

I did not know. I could not make a decision until I knew better about my choices. I must be patient and wait for a reply to the letter.

The eagerness for the information tumbled away sometimes, replaced by a terror when I contemplated my actions.

I could not avoid Rab or the others forever. In the evenings I attempted to make myself as invisible as possible at the spinning wheel by the chimneypiece. I was thankful Airig had put my clarsach back into my room, for it made it easier to pretend the events of the other night had never occurred, a deception everyone, even Rab, seemed to accept.

I watched and I listened as my husband presented every possible argument in favor of putting Kirthgarran land under sheep. The sound of his voice caused the recollection of our recent night together to haunt me.

"Kirthgarran may soon be forty thousand pounds in debt and the annuities do not stop growing," he said one night.

Coll, usually unconcerned by his friend's ramblings, broke a twig into pieces and shot the fragments into the fire one by one. "Kirthgarran is beginning to show a profit. After Culloden it suffered because no one knew how to increase production. And aye, thirteen years ago during that terrible winter a third of the cattle was lost. But since then the income has grown. Have you not looked at the account book?"

Andrew sighed and added, "Lord Kirthgarran has done little these past years but wrestle with his conscience. How much to be given to the creditors? How much to be kept for the folk who mind still the affection for their chief, and toil though their spirits are broken? I agree with Coll, Rab. Despite the juggling of the income, the debts are being satisfied."

"But at what pace?" Rab countered. "In one year the land-rent could bring the earl as much as *we* do in three."

"He's right," Lachlan said. "But..."

"But whole families will wander homeless," Coll finished. "Impoverished, with no hope." He tossed the remaining sticks into the flames. "You cannot measure profits against human suffering."

Rab leant back in his chair. "But that's exactly what Lord Kirthgarran is doing. He's not refused the offer, has he?"

"He'll not turn his Fergussons out of the glens."

"His Fergussons cannot support Kirthgarran well enough."

"Will you be the one to throw a family from its house and set fire to the thatch?"

"If need be."

Coll leapt to his feet. "They do not deserve it, Rabbie! And the earl does not deserve to be torn in two by us."

"He'll make his own decision."

"Will he?" Coll demanded, his eyes hard as he searched Rab's. He strode away, startling me when he banged the door behind him.

As the week passed I began to see that the tempest into which we had been plunged was not going to end by way of a quick pronouncement. The intensity changed, the pace of the arguments lessened, but still the Great Question hung in the air and caused short, heated debates to flare at odd times throughout the days.

If the Fergussons of Kirthgarran were forced to leave, would I go with them? Would that be my answer? I had a notion that they would not want me amongst them.

During one of my visits to Lord Kirthgarran I discovered he was uncommonly pale and looking much older than I had ever seen him. Rab had been there before me under the guise of a caring kinsman, but it took little imagination to discern that his true motive in coming to the earl's chamber had been to talk about the sheep. Overnight Rab seemed to have become driven by this idea of letting the land. He was obsessed with the promise of freedom from debt it entailed.

"Will you not talk to me about the sheep?" I asked the earl.

He stroked my hand with his good one. "Not today, my lass." He smiled sadly.

"Rab is too strong in his convictions. I've heard them arguing. He does not argue with you, does he?" Coll could hold forth admirably, but a man weary of argument, weary, indeed, of life itself, would find himself battered by Rab's persistence.

"Rab hopes I will rent the land. It is not an unsound proposition."

"But it is a painful one."

"It is that."

When I left him I was not satisfied with his state of mind. Emboldened, I approached Grizel and received only a wild-eyed look and no recurrence of her frightened screaming. I begged a bowl and spoon, and reminiscent of my days in Gilchrist House's kitchen, went to work. To my surprise Grizel was sympathetic to my cause and after a time became not just hospitable but cheerful.

That afternoon I placed a large cog of warm custard before the earl.

"Lassie," he rumbled deep in his throat. "Have you made this for me?"

"I learnt how many years ago. I've never forgotten. It is a remedy for everything, my lord, and so you must take every spoonful."

I watched him as he ate. Some of the suffering Rab had induced began to drop away. He pronounced the taste of the custard was much to his liking and in time the bowl lay empty.

"You must not care so deeply," warned the irate voice in my head when I helped the earl lean back upon his pillows.

I ignored the unwanted advice. Rab's insensitivity to me was one thing, but I could not abide it when it affected Lord Kirthgarran.

I could not abide the injustice that was done to Coll either. News of Douglas Hamilton's return to Scotland brought forth the stories of his sister's death once more, tales that had subsided over the past twelve years, it seemed, but were ready again to serve as an irresistible source of entertainment. The babble was fueled by the disclosures by Caiseal Àlainn's servants, including Mairi's sister, that Leslie Hamilton's ghost had been seen running up and down the corridors and that weeping had been heard in the cold hours of the night.

"Now her brother's at home," I heard one of our kitchen maids say to another, "she means to be remembered."

The earl's edict that Leslie Hamilton's death must never be discussed was adhered to in his presence, but in the corners of the kitchen, at the lochside where the women washed their clothes, and, I was sure, behind many a cottage door, the lass who took her life because she regretted scorning Coll Fergusson was a favorite topic.

Airig sometimes mentioned to me the essence of the whispers she heard amongst the tenants, and it was always with indignation and ire that she cursed those who even hinted that Leslie had gone to her death not out of choice, but with the aid of her rejected lover.

"Coll must hear those lies," I said to her one night in my chamber. "He must. Why does he not defend himself? He remains quiet and yet I would expect him to storm through the glens daring anyone to say to his face what they conjecture in private."

Airig shrugged her shoulders. "If it were you or I in need of such defense, there's no doubt he'd come to our aid. But for himself he does nought."

I bent forward. "Do you mind the night it happened? I've no interest in the gossip, but no one has told me how it all occurred. You ken I'd not repeat it, Airig."

She could not prevent herself from looking once at my closed door. I thought she must be feeling as guilty as I at ignoring Lord Kirthgarran's decree. "I was gey young. But my mother told me years later. Leslie Hamilton was going to wed a baron from Caithness. She'd once promised herself to Coll, you understand. What a fool she was to desert him for the other! Coll was truly in love with her. When Leslie told him he took her scorn hard. He hoped to buy a commission in the army so he'd not have to stay in Scotland and be reminded, but he did not have enough money until Lord Kirthgarran gave him what he needed. And then when the betrothal to the baron was to be announced, Coll went to see her, but she laughed at him and sent him away. Later, when all her guests were in bed, she went upstairs, and so they say, pinned to her breast the Luckenbooth brooch Coll had given her the year before as a pledge for marriage, and jumped from the ledge of the window. Her body was found in the early hours by one of the kitchen maids who screamed and screamed and brought the whole household awake."

"And then?" I urged, horrified.

"Leslie's parents were desolate. They could not believe she'd thrown herself down. She'd been happy at the dancing and the announcement of her marriage. They minded Coll being in their midst only hours before, and how angry he'd been when he'd ridden away. 'Twould have been simple for him to come back, slip up to her chamber, and lie in wait for her. He would've frightened her into retrieving the discarded brooch and pinning it to her gown. And then he would have pushed her from the window, as final punishment for having rejected him."

"He would never do such a thing!"

"Of course he would not! Not our Coll. But Master Douglas came riding to Kirthgarran with fury in his face, my mam said, and struck Coll with his fist. Men had to tear the two of them apart. 'Twas sad and a', being that Coll and Douglas had been braw friends before."

"And Coll told him surely that he'd not been back to see Leslie."

"Oh aye. He said he'd been riding for hours, all through the night, thinking and trying to put the past behind him, saying goodbye to the hills he'd soon leave. He'd returned to Kirthgarran at dawn."

"Douglas did not believe him?"

"No, he thrust the Luckenbooth into Coll's palm and took himself away, and after Leslie was laid to rest on the moor instead of the kirkyard, because no one could prove it was not a suicide, the whole family fled to the Continent." She shook her head. "And now Douglas is returned, and 'tis as if a dozen years have not passed, and Coll says nought."

"He must not feel the need because of his innocence," I concluded. "Even though you and I would have him refute Douglas's accusation with all the breath in his body. He is troubled by it, though. He cannot hide it. The talk reminds him of Leslie Hamilton, and how much he loved her."

She thought about this, and she agreed. "And loves her still," she added.

Rab did not come to me for several nights after Henry Baird's departure. I dreaded being alone with him again.

The harvest was just beginning. Although some of the grain was already cut, October was the month in which most of it was reaped, and the men gathered in the evenings and conjectured about yields. They spoke about the corn and its quality. It was a respite from the inevitable talk of sheep. Sometimes Andrew came, at times Rab arrived home late, and for a few nights only Coll and I sat by the fire.

Coll produced a whistle he had forgotten he had, an instrument a sailor had given him and taught him to play on the voyage home from North America. In my honor, he told me, he intended to remind himself how to play. The flute gave forth a pure, sweet tone that, whilst of a high pitch, was delightful to the ears. The dark wood gleamed in the firelight as his fingers flew over the holes and produced notes and gracenotes that at times sounded soft and low, and at others sharp and shrill and rollicking.

I would have been quite content to sit and listen to him play for hours, but he urged me to accompany him whenever

I recognized an air or a simple song. I found I was able to sing at his side, and he often played different harmonics to my voice that betrayed a love and understanding of music as deep as my own.

On one such night Coll showed me how to hold the whistle and place my fingers upon the holes. I put it to my lips and found that squeals often burst forth from it, which interrupted my scales. I also tended to drool into it, which he regarded with high mirth. In the end I was relieved to hand the whistle back to him.

He tilted his chin and laughed as he tapped the instrument in his palm, shaking out my saliva. "'Tis fortunate, it is," he teased me, "that you do not play the pipes. You'd have a bag full of water under your arm at night's end."

I ducked my head, laughing, too. How I wished that laughter would fill the castle instead of the constant drone of quarreling over the sheep.

Sandy came into the drawing room and lowered himself to the settle by the hearth, a stricken look engraved on his features. He and Coll exchanged glances.

"It is Seumus," my father-in-law told us. "I've just heard. There were convulsions. He ne'er awakened. The vigil is over."

How durst I go down in
The dead of the night?
Where there's no fire a-kindled
No candle to light.

False Lamkin (Trad.)

Chapter Twenty-One

T he change in the air at Kirthgarran was subtle, but I was acutely aware of it. When in the company of the farmers and their wives, I was followed by eyes knife-edged with alarm. Mothers pulled their bairns closer to their skirts. Sometimes men turned the heads of their oxen to prevent the beasts from seeing me.

Grizel, who had recently received me in her kitchen with some favor, now found it difficult to pour ale into my tumbler without shaking, and I noticed that rowan ashes had been strewn on the kitchen windowsills. When I asked her why this had been done she mumbled, "To keep us all safe."

"Damnable bad luck," Rab said on the eve of the man's

funeral. "Let's hope they find something else to worry them so they forget about you, Keeley."

Coll seemed determined to keep me from brooding. When his day's work was done he invited me to the fireside in the drawing room and strove to discover how many tunes we both knew. He sang laments and lullabies and strathspeys; songs about silkies, the seals who came upon land and turned into humans; songs extolling love with its joys, partings, infidelities, and trysts by watersides with men who would not marry; lusty ditties, patriotic tunes, and historical ballads. Each one was delivered with the question, "Do you ken this one?" and he expected me to join him when I did.

The familiar and beloved titles, "The Four Marys," "Bonnie George Campbell," and "My Brown Maid" flowed from our tongues. We sang bits and pieces of them all.

I was grateful for Coll's perseverance. If not for his single-mindedness I would have, indeed, been obsessed by the perceptions the folk of Kirthgarran held of me. It forced me to remember the solace music could bring.

One night I sang "Flowers of the Forest" for Coll despite the memories of Mamma it carried.

"I ken it well," he said. "Was it about 1514? The battle at Flowdenhill? The best of the men killed. It puts me in mind of Walter and Hugh."

"I wish I'd known them."

"They were honorable lads. I'd no way of knowing they fought in Europe whilst I myself was in North America. Nor that they died."

"You never speak at all of your time in the army."

"I have the good memories," he replied in a low voice as he polished his wooden whistle with his shirt. "When I first went I was still a lad, and thought the army a fine thing."

"Did you go straight to the colonies?" I asked with hesitation.

"We gathered in Stirling first, and marched to Glasgow. There we joined the 42nd, the Black Watch, who were destined for America with us. There must have been six thousand soldiers in Glasgow, billeted in taverns, alehouses, and even tents. Yet we were a handsome, disciplined assemblage, and received a meikle lot of praise from the city folk."

"It was a shock, I imagine. Such a change from your life here."

A rueful smile touched his mouth. "I rushed to join the 71st when the Master of Lovat raised his troops. So did a great many. Some were tempted by the idea of owning land in America afterward. Some even became stowaways on the transports so they'd not be left behind because the muster was oversubscribed." He paused. "There were grumblings later in the war, of course, when reinforcements were almost impossible to find." He blew a few notes through the whistle and put it on the table beside us. His eyes caught mine and he settled into his chair, folding his hands behind his head. "Finding myself a British officer in the King's army," he continued, copying Lord Kirthgarran's comfortable manner of storytelling, "although I wanted it very badly, *was* a shock, aye. Yet I was taught to love the regiment as a wife. To love her as dearly as my own honor. We had review parades with full regimental dress and our hair powdered. And there were the drills, or exercises as we called them. I learnt to command the sergeant so he might order the troops to march or load and fire their muskets. 'Seize your firelocks! Cock your firelocks!' I can still hear the words in my sleep."

I edged forward on my seat and asked more eagerly, "How long was it before the men were deemed ready?"

"Only a few weeks after our arrival in Glasgow. The orders came and we sailed down the Clyde and then from Greenock with a full naval escort. 'Twas a frightening time. The ships were noisy things, all groaning timbers, haphazardly tossed about on the seas. Below decks it sounded like gigantic rocks were hurled against the wood of the hull. We suffered storms, and biscuits full of weevils, and a despair, for all our bravery, at leaving Scotland. For seven weeks we were trapped on those hellish vessels, not knowing what on earth we'd find at the end."

"And what did you find?"

"The harbor at New York, in the midst of a summer so hot it made us all sick. We joined the army of General Howe, and in only a month saw our first battle. We were put in the front lines. We'd no experience, but Fraser's Highlanders had earned the reputation in the Seven Years' War of being brave—and it was thought bravery was a fine exchange for rawness."

His smile disappeared and I wondered how much I should pry. "I think that must be one of your unhappy memories."

"I was an officer, but it did not pardon me from the cruelty of the battlefield. I learnt it is one thing for a man to fire a musket at a line of enemies fifty yards away, and quite another for him to look into the eyes of a man who intends to kill him with his bayonet if he does not kill him first with his. Sometimes during a battle bayonets were turned into corkscrews after so many thrustings."

I held my breath, the picture clear in my imagination. "From a distance war is seen to be gallant, and a source of pride."

His hands came down and he rested his wrists on the chair's arms. "You do not hear of the details. The loss of limbs. The ravages of the pox. Meals of nought but hard, wormy biscuits and salted beef. Bodies strewn on a battlefield awaiting burial. How many here at home knew, for instance, that there were scouts who went out from our ranks and returned with bluidy scalps as we made our way across the country? They hung the dripping pelts about our camps like prizes."

I hoped I hid my horror, but I was sure I did not.

"It was a different kind of war," he explained. "The rebels did not stay in formation, content to push forward in a line, but came at our men out of the trees or from behind stone dykes. My troops, on the other hand, could only shoot when so ordered, and in volleys. We had to assess the country as we traveled. Scrounge for hay for the men's beds. Wait for the Government to issue new coats when the ones we wore turned to rags."

"It was not quick to care for its men?"

"We seemed to always lack supplies, and later recruits. My lads marched uncountable miles. Forded rivers and streams. Every day it seemed. And toward the end there were no changes of clothes or tents for them to sleep in."

He was far removed from it all, but I could see something in his eyes that suggested he would be able to relive every moment of the war with little trouble. I attempted to draw back a little, to make my questions less probing. "It seems you did not spend all of your time in New York, then."

"Sir Archibald led us to the Southern colonies where it was

easier to fight. Winters were impossible in the North, for the cold and the snow forced everything to a halt. Marching the men through snow was a mistake. Their kilts froze with ice and the edges cut their legs to ribbons."

I allowed his words to fade between us. His gaze left me and fell upon the swirling flames in the fireplace. "I did not mean to appease my curiosity at your expense," I said.

His quick smile brought me some relief, and I was glad when he shifted in his chair and leant closer to me. "It all happened a great many years ago," he said. "I've grown used to living with these memories, and please, do not feel regretful for being inquisitive. I'd not care to think you had to be watchful when in conversation with me."

"And I would hope that you'd tell me if I grew too meddlesome."

"I could never imagine you so."

I thought I had already pried too much, but let his words lie.

He seemed to be thinking whilst the fire snapped and sizzled at our side. The warmth of the hearth offered contentment, and words between us did not seem necessary. I found myself relaxing. We were so close that our knees almost touched.

"We were remembering songs," Coll reminded me. "I mind an Irish one about a man called Edmund Ryan, killed in 1724." His eyes held mine. He inhaled a little, and started to sing.

> *Thine eye is like the moon's soft ray,*
> *Tinted with the evening's faded blue.*
> *Its first glance stole my heart away,*
> *And gave its every wish to you.*

He seemed closer than before. His eyes looked at my lips. There was something tangible between us and the air became vibrant. My body was pierced by a sharp aching. I shut my eyes as dizziness overtook me.

Time stopped. I sat thus, listening to my heart—and waiting for the lightheadedness to end. I could feel him near me. A hand, lifted from my lap, could touch him. There was the scent of him: the outdoors, fresh wind, and earth. The heat. Was it just from the fire?

I jumped when voices carried through the great hall beyond.

Rab and Lachlan. My lids opened, the vertigo drifting away like ripples in a tarn when I once more met Coll's eyes.

Lachlan was grumbling about the harvest. He wanted to go hunting. He had seen stags on the hill at dusk and was impressed with the size of one of them in particular. I drew an uneven breath and Coll looked away. By the time the two men entered the drawing room the heat seemed to have settled in my face. My cheeks were seared, and I lifted them away from the fire to welcome the newcomers.

"I'll stalk the stags on the morrow and have Kenneth wait with a pony," Lachlan was saying, and Rab responded that his stomach was already growling in readiness for some fresh venison.

My list of things to avoid seemed to be growing longer. I wrote them in my diary.

"Avoid the farmers in the glen.

"Avoid Grizel.

"Avoid the joy that is beginning to manifest itself whenever I sing with Coll."

A blind panic was threatening to burst within me, a pod on the verge of cracking and scattering seeds to the winds. I could not examine it. To do so would cause it to swell further.

"Avoid the misery that grows somewhere inside of me and cannot be touched."

The decrees pounded their way through my mind every night as I lay, trying to fall asleep. How simple it would be to demand of myself, "Avoid everyone." To never see the anxious faces of the farmers again, to never hear the crimson-petticoated Isabel's tactless opinions, to never suffer the touch of Rab's rough hands. These things would be welcome.

With wry surprise I realized the only people I would not care to shut out of my life were the earl—and Coll.

I awoke in the middle of one uneasy night with a cry ready to escape my throat. I had been dreaming, so trapped by sleep I had to claw my way to consciousness. I remembered being a bird circling above the castle with people shooting at me from the slit windows. Arrows filled the air and embedded their razor-sharp heads in my arm. The archers attempted to drive me away because of the threat I posed to their kin, their crops, and their homes.

I sat up in bed. My arm had fallen asleep and I rubbed it to ease phantom pinpricks. I reached for the candlestick by my bedside. The candle was a stub and the last coal in my grate had gone black.

I opened my tinder box and struck the fleerish against the flint. Sparks fell to the flax tow I had placed beneath and twinkled hopefully. One became a flame, which I transferred to the candlewick using a wooden splinter.

The passageway was dark and I cupped my free hand about the flame. A second glow of light emanated from Lord Kirthgarran's chamber. It surprised me that he would still be awake; I believed he always retired early and required much sleep. I felt my way down the corridor and stopped at his cracked door.

"My lord?" I called.

He was indeed asleep. The candleholder with its twin tapers still burnt beside him and a book had fallen across his chest. I put my candlestick down on the table and gathered up the volume, but when I touched one of his hands I found it to be cold. He was breathing, but slowly and imperceptibly. I called, more loudly than I had before, "My lord?"

His face remained vacant, his eyes solidly shut. I put my hands upon his chest and patted him, calling his name once more. The result was the same. I ran all the way back to Rab's chamber. I knocked once upon his door and hearing no reply, lifted the latch and pushed it open.

His bed was empty. The curtains about it were drawn back and the coverlet was pulled up neatly.

I flew down the passages, wending my way to the northern wing. I stopped at a door at my left and called Coll's name.

Out of the darkness, muffled by the door, came his voice. "Keeley?"

"There may be something wrong with Lord Kirthgarran. Can you come?"

His door flew open. He put a hand on my shoulder and brought me back the way I had come.

Coll rushed to Lord Kirthgarran's bedside and examined him as I had done, feeling his hands, placing his ear on his chest. "Sir," he called, taking the wrinkled hands in his. "My lord, waken for a moment."

He did not cease until the earl stirred and with difficulty opened his eyes to slits. The little firelight in the room glinted in the sleep-filled eyes.

Coll watched him for a moment. "Do you feel well, sir?"

"Aye," came the answer, as meek as a whimper from a child.

"Go back to your dreams," Coll urged. "All is well."

Lord Kirthgarran nodded. His eyes slid closed.

I tried to catch my breath. Coll's gaze lingered on the earl. "He slept so deeply," I said. "His hands were so cold."

"He takes a sleeping draught at times. Grizel makes it for him, and on occasion, so do I." He searched the little table with his gaze, put out a hand, and lifted an empty tumbler. "I imagine he took one tonight."

"Why does he need it?"

"He worries." He replaced the glass and examined Lord Kirthgarran one last time before asking me, "What brought you to his chamber?"

"I saw his candlelight on my way downstairs."

"He should be looked after with more care, even in the night. Sometimes I think we do not watch over him nearly as much as we ought. He had a valet, but last year, after the man died, the earl refused to have another."

I thought Coll too critical of himself and the others. Sandy and the foster sons all took their turns in caring for the earl. I knew Lord Kirthgarran well enough by now to imagine the loathing with which he would receive the suggestion for a new manservant.

"You did well," he said. "We cannot presume he is always sound." He blew out the earl's two tapers and the room was swept into blackness.

I realized with annoyance my candle had burnt itself out and was no more than a puddle.

"My candle's gone. I forgot to get a new one."

"I'll find you another."

We left Lord Kirthgarran's room together. I was not eager for Coll to realize how uneasy I became in complete darkness—a remnant from my childhood when Father deemed that spending a few hours alone in the black, airless cellar was good for my soul—and I followed him as close as I dared.

Coll lit a candle from a coal in the grate of his own chamber and handed it to me. I looked about with more care than on my first night at the castle, and saw that his room was much the same as my own. Arched windows looked out into the night, and a canopied bed with drapery and coverlet of mulberry brocade stood opposite a small grate.

My attention caught at once on the dressing table. A woman's silver Luckenbooth brooch of two hearts and a crown lay beside a miniature in a gilt frame. The painting showed a young lass on the verge of womanhood. Her beauty was breathtaking.

I could not look away from it. Her hair was dark auburn, curling about her in ringlets; her eyes were blue and far apart in her delicate face. Faint pools of rose highlighted her cheekbones. The artist had depicted a certain haughtiness, however. I did not miss the up-tilted chin, the coldness of the eyes.

I sensed Coll beside me. He lit another candle from the one I held in my hand. The new one flared, brightening the little face in its hammered frame. I had been staring at it too obviously to pretend otherwise and he glanced at it as well.

Awareness of where and how I found myself enveloped me. I had only thrown my shawl over my chemise. Coll stood near me, his hair flowing haphazardly beyond his shoulders. The skin of his throat seemed warm in the candlelight.

"You're wondering who she is," he said.

I thought I knew already.

He brought his flame closer to the miniature. His arm brushed mine and I was quite unable to control a tremor that ran through me. I put my candle down and folded my arms, hugging myself to ward off the trembling.

"Her name was Leslie Hamilton. That was painted when she was sixteen. A bairn still."

He was purposefully keeping all expression from his voice, I believed. I whispered, "How bonny she was."

"She was bonny. We were to have been wed, the two of us.

I believed, in my very soul, we would be."

"Do not feel you must tell me about her."

"It does not matter. Like as not you've heard the tale already. She was the daughter of a family who live about an hour away."

"You had known her from childhood..."

"Mam's sister is the wife of the cook at the castle. Aunt Molly. We would visit her and Uncle William when I was young, all of us together. I never took much notice of the son of the household, nor of his younger sister. Then, the summer I was done with St. Andrews University, I turned into a lad of sixteen. It was as if my eyes were opened."

"And it was the same for her?"

"Apparently it was. I had considered her too proud, too sure of herself. But there we were, fast in love and making fools of ourselves. We talked of marriage. They were golden days, days of innocence. It all appeared so simple. She would defy her mother and father. She would disinherit herself."

The darkness, the candlelight, the two of us being alone in such an odd way, created a timeless aura. I watched his face. The shadows softened his cheekbones.

"And then I went to see her one day and she behaved as though she could not wait for me to leave. The next time she'd not see me at all. She refused to tell me what was amiss but it was not difficult to discover. She'd begun to believe, like her parents, that no good would come of a marriage to a bastard son of a housekeeper. I learnt she'd promised to marry a laird from Caithness." His voice was still flat, devoid of all feeling. He waited, and added, "In the end, she did not know what she believed. But by then it was too late. For both of us."

I forced myself look at her picture again, fancying I could see her as she must have been. Young. Impetuous. Half in love, and then shrewd. Her coldness had turned to despair. Perhaps Davy had been like her—in love one minute and perplexed the next. Perhaps even now, wherever he was, he was regretting the choice he had made.

Taking one final look at the portrait, I said, hoping to console him, "There are people like her the world over. They do not ken their own minds, or are swayed too easily."

"I wonder if it would be better to be like that. To be able

to change your mind, or tell yourself one thing whilst believing another. There's no sorrier a fate for a man than to want something, absolutely and without waver, and to ken with just as much certainty that it can never be his."

I wanted to reach out to him but I resisted, tightening my arms. "That was why you decided to become a soldier?"

He took a long time to answer. "Everything reminded me of her. My father was gone. I suppose I wanted to escape. I thought it would be the easiest thing to do."

"I heard what happened."

"'Twas foolish of me to visit her. I think I wanted to believe she would change her mind if she saw me one more time. Perhaps there was a vengeful streak in me. I wanted to say to her, 'This is what your fickleness has caused.' I was going to America to fight and I wanted her to understand she'd likely ne'er see me again. And yet, there was that wild thought, too, that she'd be realizing she'd made a mistake and would come with me if I asked her."

I did not want him to go on but he seemed withdrawn from his own words.

"I thought the entire interview was a failure. She allowed me to see her. But it was obvious she was determined to marry her laird. She seemed little disturbed by the news of my commission. Her family was giving a ball so the betrothal could be announced. I'd gone that day because it was her last chance, I believed, to change her mind. But no. She laughed and even invited me to the gathering that night, and in return I cursed her. The next morning Leslie's brother was here, demanding to see me, overcome with sorrow and anger. He said after the ball was done, after she'd gone up to her chamber, she'd fallen from her window and had died on the stones below."

I closed my eyes involuntarily, visualizing it.

"He accused me of going back, entering the castle by stealth, and murdering her. But I told him she must have thought things over and had a change of heart, must have decided the man was not the answer to her dreams, and realized she was going to lose me when I marched away in a few days' time. They found that brooch pinned to her gown. The Luckenbooth I'd given her long before, when we'd pledged ourselves to each other. She'd not been wearing it for months, but she must have been thinking of me after the gathering." Silence prodded me to look up at him once again and he finished, "In truth I've never been able to convince myself I did not kill her."

I could not bear to hear him speak of such guilt. "She chose to do what she did. You are not to blame."

He shrugged. "I should never have gone to see her. If I'd not said to her the things I did, she might have remained content and wedded her laird."

"But you did not imagine she'd take her life."

"She'd be alive to this day if I'd let her alone."

"Her death was not your fault."

"I certainly believed it then."

"Did no one comfort you? Tell you it was not so?"

"Some tried. But I was bewildered. I was eager to leave for Glasgow, for America. But I did not realize then that a man carries his cares with him. They cannot be left behind like a bundle of rags."

"Some say it takes time to heal."

"In time I did. It is easier now, I find, to allow myself as few cares as possible."

He sounded like me. "Has that become more difficult," I asked, "now that Leslie's brother has returned?"

"Douglas will remain forever convinced that I threw her to her death." Coll placed his candle on the dresser beside the miniature. "I apologize for keeping you. I'm as long winded as the earl with his endless stories." He flashed me a smile. "No doubt you're wanting your bed."

I lowered my gaze, afraid to speak.

He said politely, "Keep the candle. Will I help light you back?"

I shook my head. I retrieved the candlestick and went out into the corridor, and he did not follow me.

I lay in my bed, unable to forget Coll's words and the sentiments behind them. My desire to comfort him was an urgent thing, a longing of immeasurable proportions, and as I stroked with mindless fingers the lamb's wool he had once given me, I was obliged to see before me a truth of my own, one that I had long been denying.

Though hurricanes rise, though rise ev'ry wind,
No tempest can equal the storm in my mind.

Lochaber No More (Ramsay)

Chapter Twenty-Two

"I have something for you," Rab said the next evening as he followed me from the table where we had just supped. "And 'tis something you're not expecting at all."

He had been gone all the day long. I was distracted and had not bothered to discover his whereabouts, assuming he was bundling grain or storing it in the granary. I could not forget arising in the night and finding his bed empty. In any event he was home now, stimulated from his day it appeared, and inclined to be gentle.

"Come to the sitting room," he begged. He took my hand in his and I followed in his wake, although the heat of his hand conjured up his fury of the last night we'd been together. It was all I could do not to flinch.

The sitting room was next to the drawing room, smaller and more private, with a tiny window. When we entered it my feet sank into a patterned, dark brown carpet. Rab's saddlebag lay on top of an octagonal table of inlaid oak.

"I've been near Kinloch Rannoch. I've long known a man there," he said as he pried open a buckle, "who was ne'er of much use to me. Until now. You'll see why in a moment."

"Why did you go?"

"There's a race-meeting every year on this day, and I raced McKay. He and I won a purse full of money. Now. You must close your eyes."

He took my hand again and drew my fingertips back and forth over cloth that spilt out of the old bag. It was slippery, soft, smooth. I opened my eyes. I was touching the top fold of what appeared to be leagues of dark turquoise silk. The color was a delight to look upon and my fingers slid over the silvery, lustrous surface. Beneath the folds peeped handsome linen stamped with tiny flowerets of shaded violet.

"You're to make yourself a pair of frocks. There's Brussels lace, smuggled, I'm certain, and ribbon and buttons I'm assured will please even the most discerning eye. Do you like my choices? I'm determined you'll not be clothed in drugget like a landless laborer's gudewife. 'Twill be silks for you, and brocades, and fine linen and Indian cotton."

"You bought these for me?"

"Of course for you. Who else? I'd look fine dressed in coat and trews of purple blossoms, would I not?"

My fingers lingered on the soft silk and delicate linen, and I sought to drown the guilt that had sprung up within me. "I do not need any new gowns."

"Look at what you wear now. A dress that's mended and ill-fitting, discarded by Anne, beginning to fray. Your father raised you to expect better and I'll not fail you. You are the only mistress Kirthgarran has and 'tis gowns of these that you'll wear."

His tenderness was unexpected, and his pride in me had not been mentioned in a long while. I had never asked for aught and I hardly thought he noticed such things as clothes, but apparently he did. "Should you have spent the money on me?" I asked.

"Half was for Lord Kirthgarran. Half was for me to do with as I liked. And yet, you've not said you like these."

"How could I not? They are what any woman would love."

"I thought perhaps you might wear the silk at the Feast of Samhain. We're to have folks come to sup with us, and more will follow for the dancing afterward. Airig's a clever seamstress if you feel inclined to use her, and so is Mairi."

"You're mistaken if you think I'm accustomed to such weavings as these. My father was not a wealthy man, and my gowns were always modest."

"At least be aware you deserve better."

I had no way of knowing if he was apologizing, in his own way, for his insensitive treatment of me or if the thought had never entered his mind at all. I allowed myself the barest wish that there could be contentment found in our marriage. With all of my will I raised my eyes to Rab and presented to him what I hoped was a believable expression of affection, whilst keeping concealed in my heart all thoughts of his fair-haired kinsman.

I did as Rab suggested and asked Airig for help in cutting and sewing a gown from the dark turquoise and a day dress from the stamped linen. Mairi had some patterns from which to choose, designs she had used for Anne, and for the time being sewing helped to occupy my mind.

I blamed myself for allowing my returning emotions to focus on Coll. I should have tried harder to trust Rab as I felt I must, and turn away from Coll's natural kindness.

My prayer was that it was not too late to shift my misplaced feelings to where they belonged. I could care for Rab if I tried, and thus divert myself away from the thoughts and desires that plagued me. If I conveyed affection for Rab he might not treat me so brutishly. Salvation, I was convinced, would be found in an abandonment of myself in him, and I had been shamefully laggard in this. I had to increase my efforts to please him. I had to pretend I enjoyed our marriage bed. A child might draw us together further and I beseeched God each night that I might soon carry a bairn within me.

The alternative was to admit I loved Coll and could love

no other. I would have no choice but to leave Kirthgarran then, for I could not bear to spend my life feeling the way I did now.

"Tell me about the farming and the cattle," I begged Rab. "Take me to the tops of the hills where the folk watch the kylies grazing."

We climbed the slopes and I met the women who churned butter and made cheese from the milk. With their children they slept in the open shielings. It seemed a simple, happy way of life, and their wariness regarding me was not as pronounced as the mistrust their sisters held in the glen.

Another day I asked him about the isle in the center of the loch. "Show me the graves," I pled. He rowed me in a wee boat to the pine-shaded island and we walked amongst the stones, some of which were so weatherworn I could not read the names.

When I did not seek Rab's attention I threw myself into other activities. I picked gooseberries by the basketful. I used the spinning wheel and helped Airig turn fine, Kirthgarran wool into yarn. I gathered clusters of round, crimson jewels from the rowan trees beside the castle and braved Grizel's once-again fearful looks whilst I made jelly for us to enjoy with our venison.

But the gratification of helping, and the sight of clear, red jelly made with my own hands, could not keep me from longing through each minute of every day for a glimpse of Coll, for a word to exchange with him, or for the sound of his voice even if he spoke to someone else. I was constantly aware of him—when he left the castle and when he returned, what he wore, what he ate, what he said—and I was aware of all these things even as I pretended I was not, lowering my eyes and attempting to seem occupied whilst my heart thundered inside of me and my usually collected mind scattered itself far and wide. The happiness I gleaned from a moment of his attention warred bitterly with my self-reproach.

I visited the falcons and delighted in them, but I could not indulge myself in learning to hunt, not when the hours I would spend with the raptors would also include Coll. I accepted Gordon's compliments about my ease with the birds, but did not pursue his proposed lessons in handling.

"I'll teach you the art of falconry myself," Coll offered.

He seemed disappointed when I declined. I told myself I would be content with holding Fenalla when she was brought to Lord Kirthgarran's bedchamber.

I turned to the Bible. I had thought there might be a family Bible in the library but all I could find was a small one, much worn and bent. As I flipped through its pages looking for answers, I could hear my father's voice in my head. Where was the comfort I sought? Instead, a verse from Matthew shouted out at me from the printed page: *"But I say unto you, That whosoever looketh at a woman to lust after her hath committed adultery with her already in his heart."* Man, woman, it didn't matter. I was guilty.

And in Ephesians: *"For this ye know, that no whoremonger, nor unclean person, nor covetous man, who is an idolater, hath any inheritance in the kingdom of Christ and of God."*

It was a promise echoed in Revelation: *"But the fearful, and unbelieving, and the abominable, and murderers, and whoremongers, and sorcerers, and idolaters, and all liars, shall have their part in the lake which burneth with fire and brimstone: which is the second death."*

I closed the book. It was a unique sensation: I was frightened of myself. But nothing I did prevented me from conjuring up sinful daydreams. One of the worst involved holding in my arms not a bairn with dark hair, but one with ash-blond locks and translucent gray eyes.

I often sought the earl in his chamber, for that was the only place it seemed I could forget myself. I was with him the day Lachlan led three men, two collies, a garron bundled with supplies, and a fold of two hundred shaggy cattle south to the market at Falkirk. From the earl's window we watched the stream of black cattle leaving the grounds through a soft mist.

"The beasts," Lord Kirthgarran said at my elbow, "require gentle treatment since they're a mixture of heifers and bullocks and come from different grazings. They're fairly wild from their freedom on the hillsides. If they're startled or hurried, they'll be apt to stampede or run away in different directions."

Half of the fold had been given to the earl for rent money; the other half was of his own breeding. All were destined to travel the roads Rab and I had taken—liable to bridge tolls of as much as two pence a beast, customs dues, and possible stance fees—and to be sold at the end for a sum that depended on the yearly demand.

"Until thirty years ago cattle raiding was still common," he said as we watched the hooves trampling the silver dew coating the grass. "It was dangerous to take them through Lochaber, Badenoch, and Rannoch because there were men who hid in the passes eager to lift whole herds. Stolen cattle were driven at night and hidden on mountaintops or in the forest during the day, until they could be sold."

"Lachlan faces no such danger now, surely?"

"The cattle reivers are gone for good, but what remains, of course, are the dangers of nature. In wet weather the rivers are impossible to ford, and though the kylies are strong swimmers, the weakest animals can be swept away or drowned. In dry weather the hill passes do not provide enough feed. And the beasts cannot be hurried, or their feet will be spoilt, and they'll lose the little weight they gained in the summer months. Even die."

"I never knew they were so fragile."

"Oh aye. They must be divided into smaller herds along the way so they'll not hurt each other in the narrow passes or over the few bridges that do exist, which they detest. The sound of their own feet on the timbers terrifies them. Lachlan and his men will be watchful when they stop every midday to rest, and even more so during the nights when the cattle graze freely in the pastures. They'll be too hungry and tired to stray far, but if the moon rises late they might be tempted to wander, and for the first few days they have a homing instinct that must be thwarted."

"Rab says the price this year seems to be three pounds a head, though he was hoping for more."

"Three pounds is not bad at all," the earl pronounced. "The demand for Scots cattle is still steady. They supply better meat, certainly, than big Irish bullocks! The English like to salt beef, and fat beasts are the best for that. The Navy Victualling Board is a big buyer. Britain's soldiers and sailors need to be fed." He smiled at me indulgently, though I thought he must have been thinking of his sons.

"Ewen assures me Kirthgarran's debts seem to be growing

less due to the sales of the black cattle," I ventured, meaning to pay him a compliment, but I wished I had held my tongue. Lord Kirthgarran's brows drew together.

"The English demand for mutton and wool is increasing as well. Sheep farming is becoming a big, profitable trade. You ken that, Keeley. Your own father makes his living by them."

"The grass is better in the Lowlands," I said warily. "And most of the sheep are Cheviots, not the small kind you have here with fine-textured wool that weighs no more than a few ounces when shorn."

"Farmers are starting to grow better grass. They close it in with dry-stone dykes or turf walls, which leave less land for common grazing for cattle and choke off the drove roads. Already the cattle are decreasing in Breadalbane and round Loch Tay, and it may come to pass that the call for Scottish wool will overtake the need for beef." He drew a deep breath and would not look at me, choosing to peer out the window instead. "The lads tell me our sheep's lack of wool is a result of us keeping them inside all winter. We always believed the winters would be fatal to them if they were kept in the open. But it's not so, apparently. They not only survive but prosper. The Linton breed, with black faces, is filling the lands about Loch Earn, Glen Dochart, Glen Falloch, and Cowal."

"I know of the Lintons."

"They're larger and hardier, are they not, than what we have here? They thrive on winter hillsides. I must ask myself, is it not more profitable to use the hill grazings all year long, rather than just the summer months when the cattle are let free?"

"Sheep do better on low ground."

"That is so," he concurred. What neither of us said was that the low ground was where the folk lived, and grew their oats, corn, and bere. "If one were to compare the amount of the rent from tenants who raise cattle, and the amount of rent that is given by Lowland sheep owners for use of the same land, the difference is significant. The rent for sheep runs is three times more."

How did one argue against such logic?

He had thought much the same, it seemed, and he gave a deep sigh. "Kirthgarran's debts are the result of inherited liabilities.

Poor investments. Income from the estates that never seems to be enough. When I was a lad, a man's worth was figured from how many men he could call to come to his side, and how many black cattle stood grazing on his lands. But it is all different now. The solitary power in this world is money."

"You've made your decision, have you not, my lord," I asked softly.

"Not yet."

He turned to look at the cows as they moved past the castle and headed for the western curve of the loch framed by golden autumn leaves. Our eyes followed the men striding beside and behind the kylies, hardy men who walked easily on this first day of the ten allotted for the journey. They whistled skillfully to their happy dogs trotting alongside.

Reverend Cameron came to Kirthgarran Castle for the Sabbath, having been gone the usual three weeks. I felt hot blood flush my face when he handed me a folded paper.

"Were you expecting a reply to your correspondence?" he inquired.

I could not find any fitting words. I shook my head, then nodded, and the minister's eyes were soft with sympathy.

I carried the paper in my gown until I could think of an excuse to go to my room. There I split the seal and opened it.

"My Dear Mrs. Fergusson," the writer began, and what followed was a sincere discourse on the aspects and procedures of leaving Scotland. The hand was tiny and well-formed and covered the page. I raced through the lines, finding answers, problems, solutions. I would need to consider them and read each sentence a hundred times.

But my overall conclusion was that I would only need a small amount of money, a loan from Mr. Hume if need be, in order to join families bound for the New World. There would be a place for me to wait in Glasgow whilst a ship was made ready and the lists of passengers grew. I would become part of a community across the sea, work for a living, save enough to pay back Mr. Hume, and perhaps even prosper enough to buy land of my own. The man signed the letter, *"Samuel Hume, Esquire,"* and included instructions on how to reach his office.

He extended a welcome with no timely boundaries, and added a word of solace because he understood how difficult a decision this might be.

"Difficult" could not begin to describe what I contemplated.

I folded the letter into as small a square as possible and stuffed it into my writing desk. I closed the drawer but I could sense its presence there. Like a hand it was, reaching for mine from across the mountains. I could have my cottage after all. I could sow vegetables and herbs, and milk my own cow, and be a well-known seamstress or a cook. I could even take in an orphaned child, someone like the lad that Young James had been, with no home and no one to love him. The more successful I was with my endeavors, the more bairns I could save and call my own. I could have a house full of them if I wished.

And to do it all meant leaving Scotland. The thought both comforted and revolted me. Telling Rab I could no longer remain his wife and offering him the choice of abandonment or a legal separation would mean freedom. So would my escape from the frightened stares of Kirthgarran's people. But leaving Coll, and the earl, would mean heartbreak.

For some reason Coll no longer sought the ingle in the drawing room in the evenings. Perhaps he felt he had fulfilled his mission to distract me from the blow of Seumus's death. I sat alone until the other men arrived and was often drawn forcibly into the great hall. I missed the exclusive, musical duets with Coll but it was just as well they ceased, for I had looked forward to his company far too much.

I was overly sensitive to the renewed story of Leslie Hamilton's death. My agitation about being labeled as a herald of death and destruction paled in comparison to the concern I felt for Coll whenever Leslie's or Douglas's name was mentioned. The trepidation was well-justified, I discovered, when Douglas Hamilton came to see the earl.

Lord Kirthgarran sent word to our newly-returned neighbor that he hoped Master Douglas would honor us with a call since he himself could not travel to Caiseal Àlainn to welcome him home again. The invitation was an obvious attempt to begin mending the injuries of the past, and the earl counted on Douglas Hamilton's sense of civility and courtesy to further it along. He wanted the sightings of Leslie's ghost to end; he wanted the whispers about Coll to be snuffed out once and for all. When a note from the Master of Caiseal Àlainn arrived, accepting the solicitation, it seemed these things might eventually happen.

We gathered in Kirthgarran's hall. Sandy met Douglas Hamilton at the castle entrance and bid him to enter, and when I saw him I was reminded of the miniature of his sister on Coll's dresser. He approached the earl with self-assurance but his deep-set, blue eyes roamed everywhere, quickly, and with a purpose. He took off his French cocked hat, revealing meticulously barbered hair of the same dark auburn shade as Leslie's, and abandoning his quiet search, gave his full attention to Lord Kirthgarran in his chair.

"My lord," he said in a low voice as he bowed. "How kind of you to send your regards. My regret is that you find yourself unable to come to Caiseal Àlainn."

"Then you do not think me too presumptuous to invite you here," the earl said and smiled.

"Of course not, sir. In fact, I've brought you a gift. A fine bottle of Bordeaux wine. My favorite, in fact. If I could have brought a barrelful back with me I would have."

Lord Kirthgarran accepted the elegant bottle with grace and Douglas went on, "Will you accept my condolences? About Walter and Hugh. I heard—after I returned."

"Thank you," Lord Kirthgarran replied solemnly, and nodded to the rest of us so that we might be introduced. "You mind Sandy our steward, and his sons Lachlan and Rab. This is Rab's bride, Keeley."

I curtseyed whilst the earl continued, allowing myself a moment to examine Douglas's visage. It was an intelligent face but there was tension there, and his rather cold eyes soon left me and narrowed. To my right, Coll bowed.

Although Lord Kirthgarran did his best to keep the conversation continuing in a light spirit, Douglas and Coll became locked in observation of each other. Their features betrayed little but I could imagine the inner thoughts of each.

"This is the man I accused of flinging Leslie to her death,"

Douglas would be thinking.

"Does he blame me still?" Coll would be wondering.

Douglas's head turned when the earl invited him to be seated and partake of some of the Bordeaux. Sandy brought out the Amen glasses, and we sat at the long table under the chandelier where a dozen candles burnt. The men sipped and talked of black cattle.

The dialogue was pleasant enough, but there was no escaping the undertow of uneasy wariness. Coll said nothing at all and Douglas did not address any questions or remarks in his direction. The strain of it grew as the minutes passed. Lord Kirthgarran asked Douglas about France and the social turbulence that was turning it on its head.

"The French seem to be taking heed of what the Americans have been saying about equality, and the injustices between rich and poor, titled and nontitled," the earl said. "Does Louis fear for his throne, do you think?"

"King and country are both on the precipice of financial ruin," Douglas predicted. "The First Assembly of Notables has been dissolved. De Colonne, the minister of finance, has been replaced by a corrupt man who still plans to go forward with the land tax. France's mood is ominous, sir, and I know not, truly, what is going to happen next."

"Do your parents intend to remain there?"

Douglas began to answer, but he appeared to forget his words. Two seconds passed. Three. Four. He looked up at Lord Kirthgarran. "If there's trouble, they'll no doubt come home."

Lord Kirthgarran was slow to respond. "Hopefully they'll not be caught up in any turmoil..."

"They prefer to remain for now. It is much easier. Myself, I longed for home."

"I cannot blame them," the earl said.

Douglas attempted to say something and failed. He shifted in his seat. Lord Kirthgarran's hand went to the bottle on the table, but Douglas declined the offer and pushed back his chair. "No, no, I thank you but I don't wish for any more. I think— well, I..." A muscle grew hard at his jaw line. "I think I must be away, my lord. Yes, I must be away."

He rose, and one by one the rest of us stood. Douglas took

a step but must have realized he was closer to Coll than anyone else and the men exchanged glances. Douglas walked past him.

Sandy fetched the visitor's hat, but Coll strode after him. "Douglas. For the sake of God."

The man's face stiffened. "I should not have come."

"It cannot go on like this. This, betwixt you and me."

"I'm sorry. I thought I could forget—for at least an hour. But it cannot be done."

Coll's voice deepened. "Do you realize how I regret..."

"Regret! Regret killing her?"

The question froze the air about us. Lord Kirthgarran said, "Coll has sworn to all that he was here when your sister died."

"You did not know her. None of you knew her, not as I did. She would never take her own life. She did *not* take her own life." He moved toward the arched doorway and as he walked he became more inflamed. He spun on his heel and the silver buttons on his coat flashed. "I apologize to you sir, dear Lord Kirthgarran. You invited me to your home in good will and I told myself I could manage this but lo and behold it seems it is beyond me to do so. I am so sorry. So very sorry. I cannot forget what happened. There's been a great injustice done, and I'll not rest until my sister's bones can be dug from the shameful moor and placed in the family grave, properly, where they belong. I do not know yet how to prove that man guilty, but prove it I will." Douglas stopped himself, shuddered, cleared his throat. He turned his eyes to Coll and the contempt he had tried to hitherto hide now swept over him. He curtly bowed to Lord Kirthgarran. "By your leave, sir."

The scene he left behind was like one of those *tableaux vivants* I had read about, when players strike poses and do not move or speak in order to portray a moment in history.

Lord Kirthgarran was the first to move. He lowered his head in defeat.

Oft her music cheered me.
O, I Love the Maiden Fair (Trad.)

Chapter Twenty-Three

A utumn had never been a favorite season of mine. Daylight ended early, creating long, cold evenings that curtailed walks on the hills and in the garden. The birks, apples, and rowans lost their leaves as insistent winds whisked them from their branches and sent them skirling away. The tree skeletons reached through heavy mists, seeking an elusive sun that rose ever lower in the sky. The ash trees kept their leaves longer, but at last even their pale green shapes fluttered to earth. Sometimes when I went outdoors in the morning the grass was outlined with a delicate tracery of frost, and I knew it was a matter of time before the tops of the hills became mist-wreathed and powdered with white.

The animals knew it was the ending of summer as well. Hedgehogs scurried about, seeking to eat enough to sustain themselves through a winter's hibernation. Birds feasted on ripe berries and gathered into flocks, ready to fly to warmer places. At dusk we heard red deer stags roaring at one another as they competed for hinds in this season of rutting.

"Lachlan's returned!" cried Kenneth one dreary October night, disturbing my somber watch of the dying world through a drawing room window.

A figure of a man had indeed appeared out of the mist to stand on the entrance steps. Sandy took a brace of candles across the room, but it was not Lachlan who stood in the doorway. He was a stranger to me and apparently everyone else, a tall gentleman exhausted to the point of collapse. He asked for Coll Fergusson.

"Damn my eyes, 'tis Murray Campbell!" Coll exclaimed at the sight of the man. They embraced heartily, each clearly overcome with good cheer at the sight of the other. "A braw friend," Coll explained to us gathered near. "We were together in Fraser's. You look ill-used, man. Come, have a dram and rest yourself."

Murray Campbell grinned and swept aside red hair with a freckled hand. "If it's Kirthgarran's illegal *uisge beatha* you're offering, I'll not be refusing that."

"You've ridden from Argyll, aye? It's a mean journey. I'll give you more than a dram."

The newcomer's smile faded, even as he patted Coll's back in agreement. "It will be welcome."

Coll led the man to the fireside and introduced him to all of us, one by one.

An hour later Lachlan returned to Kirthgarran, lending truth at last to Kenneth's excited cry.

Andrew and Ewen were summoned, and the others gathered round the weary and dirt-stained Lachlan ready to hear his news. I had difficulty determining if Lachlan was pleased or not, but he spread money on the table in the great hall and delivered a short description of the tryst, the sale, and the haggling that had gone on. As the silver coin glittered beneath the candle flames and the men pondered the bank notes and receipts, it became evident to me that the transaction had been a failure. Some debts had been paid, it appeared, but others still lingered and would linger for a long time.

Still, it was a homecoming worthy of celebration and poor Lachlan, muddied from head to foot and smelling worse than a stagnant bog, was regaled and commended and prodded to furnish further details. He went up to Lord Kirthgarran first, however, to show him the results of his labor.

We all felt disappointed when Murray Campbell took his leave several days later. His stories of life in Glasgow were entertaining, and being a blithesome man full of quick smiles, he spread an air of conviviality about the castle. He left as quietly as he had come, with handclasps all round.

"Mr. Campbell enjoyed his stay, I hope," I said to Coll as we watched him ride away on his restored horse. "Was it something important he came to tell you?"

Coll tossed me a small apple from a basket the kitchen maids had left in the hall. He took one for himself and bit into it hungrily. "Oh no. Just news of friends. Men we both knew in the 71st." He chewed and winked at me.

Near the end of October the women came down from the hills and took to reaping. They sang as they worked, either cutting the oats and corn or pulling the barley, and beside them the men tied the sheaves and stalks.

Rab brought me with him to watch the last field being cut. I had to steel myself against their apprehensive peeks at me.

"Cottars in fields everywhere," Rab said, unaware of my disquiet, "are placing their bonnets upon the ground and cutting small handfuls of grain with their sickles as they face the sun. The sheaves are spun about their heads three times, sunwise, whilst the rest chant a blessing on the harvest."

When the last sheaf was cut, all tossed their sickles at it, for it was unlucky to know the identity of the final shearer.

"The last sheaf, the *cailleach*," Rab pronounced. It was ceremoniously tied with ribbons and would become the focus of a great many toasts; it would be placed prominently in Kirthgarran's hall for the Feast of Samhain, and a portion of it would be saved for next spring and buried in the field to ensure continuing fertility.

Despite the threshing and winnowing of the grain that followed in subsequent days, my husband and the other men of the castle were able to find time for themselves. It was a season of plenty and leisure, and preparations for celebration began with a certain lightness of heart. Rab and Lachlan went off with muskets for stags and grouse, and Coll sought the hills alone with Athdara. Sometimes he and Sandy went together. Every morning I watched him follow the burn on Dominie's back, his arm held out with the hooded falcon perched on the leather gauntlet.

I immersed myself in the planning along with the rest of the household. Airig and I sewed relentlessly upon my silk gown so it would be completed in time, and I tread carefully about Rab, trying to sense his every mood, seeking to cause him pleasure so that I might bring us closer together. For a time this seemed so possible I was convinced my love for Coll was only an infatuation, an unlucky fascination that surely must pass in time.

I must be grateful, I told myself, that my feelings were coming back to life, that I was not the dead person I thought I was. But the rationalization brought me little comfort.

A week before the feast it rained heavily, and Rab, unusually moody and restless, gave himself up to the whisky. Our coupling that night was not as compassionate as it had been the last time, but he spent the night in my chamber.

When cold daylight drifted through the window I rose with him and wrapped my shawl about my chemise. Rab seemed indolent on this gray morn. He took his time getting dressed. He picked up the cream silk waistcoat he had worn the night before. It was richly embroidered and studded with horsehair-stuffed buttons.

I began straightening the bedding when something clattered to the floor at Rab's feet and rolled to mine. I bent to pick it up. "You've dropped your knife," I said.

"The pocket under the arm is coming apart. I keep forgetting about it." He took the wee, flat-handled clasp knife from my outstretched hand. "What a wonder I've not lost this before now. It falls out with a will of its own. It was my grandfather's, did you ken?"

I forgot to take back my hand. An image was floating before me. In place of my hand was another's, holding an object out toward Coll. *He lost his knife,* echoed the words in my mind, and, *I did not think he'd want to be long without it.*

I heard myself say, "I did not think you a forgetful man."

"Alas, 'tis often true. How good it is of you to see only my best side! I wonder if you'd care to sew this for me. I'm never thinking to ask anyone to mend it. It would be my own foolish fault if I did lose the knife."

I took the waistcoat from him. He appeared unaware of me as he fastened his sark; he was unchanged, unconcerned. But I did not regard him in the same manner as I had a moment before. It took all of my determination to prevent the carefully placed sheaves of hope to which I clung from tumbling down. They teetered, ready to fall like bunches of straw from a top-heavy rick.

It could not be true, I thought, but the threat of ruin was relentless.

He kissed me on the cheek, heedless of my silence, and left. A knife falling upon the floor was no real proof a man was unfaithful, nor was a woman returning a knife to the castle. Even if the two knives were one and the same, the fact that a woman returned it did not mean she was his lover. There could be a score of other explanations.

I could hear Isabel's clear voice and see her slight figure in the crimson petticoat.

"It is not true," I said aloud—twice—so that the utterance and sound together would surely make it so.

I found a needle and sank to my lime-green chair to mend the torn pocket, but my hands lay still upon the silk.

I sat for a long while in my chamber. My little clarsach lay upon a table just as it had for years in Gilchrist House. I thought of my mother as I studied it, and wished I could bury my face between her neck and slim shoulder as I had done so often in my childhood.

Spots of light from the surface of the loch danced on the

ceiling. They flickered on the harp and its engraved designs. I picked up the instrument, sat myself down, and settled its weight onto my lap. My fingertips touched the strings. Five years of disuse had caused the brass wires to relax from their pins and the notes were discordant. I went through the ritual of tuning all twenty-three strings, fearful with each creaking turn of the wooden-handled key that one would break after its lapse into slackness. I rested the soundbox back against my left shoulder so that the music, as believed by harpists of old, would come from my heart. My right hand, my masculine hand, touched the lower strings. Plucking them with my nails and dampening them, as my mother had taught me, rewarded my ears with a plaintive and poignant chord that made all time and place diminish. I moved my fingers tentatively, but found that after years of abstinence they still minded their places.

Most of my early days were tumbled together and resembled little more than a field of rubble, but some were as discernible and solitary as the Brothers' Stones in St. Boswells, pillars standing bold and upright amongst moss-grown cobbles. One of those days flooded back to me now. The one I had tried my hardest to forget and could not.

It was February. A winter's afternoon in my father's house with sleet rattling at the window in the sitting room. My father had ridden away earlier, leaving Mamma and me to pursue our sewing for the coming bairn, but it was not long before Mamma picked up the clarsach and filled Gilchrist House with music.

Mamma sang "Flowers of the Forest." Her hands swept over the wires of the harp as if they performed an ancient dance and her voice followed, sweet and mournful. She passed the instrument to me and rested her head against the chair whilst she listened to a melody I had composed. A wistful look softened her face. As I played on, she closed her eyes. The lines about her eyes and mouth relaxed.

I put the clarsach on the table. "Mrs. Taggart will have supper laid," I said, looking at the clock. "Will we start without Father?"

She rose. "I think so. I've been so hungry of late," she said and laughed. "Oh, the smell of that chicken roasting on the spit! I am so ravenous..."

Her abrupt stop caused me to glance at her. She stood still with a strange expression on her face. She shook her head and her hands covered the unborn child. "Oh Keeley, something is wrong."

I froze as well, studying her face. She looked down and my eyes followed hers to her ankles where blood trickled down. Already there was a pool of blood upon the floor.

"Mamma," I whispered, wondering from whence it came, this mysterious dark essence that lay staining the wood. Our eyes met. I held her as we went to her bedchamber. She lay down on her bed and she said the dreaded words. "Keeley, dear, go and find Mrs. Dundas. Ask her to come."

For a few heartbeats my feet would not move. Finally I ran across the fields slippery with freezing rain, seeing only the pathway to the lying-in-wife's door, hearing only my jagged breathing and the crunch of my flying feet. I reached her hut but she was not there. A neighbor told me she had gone to Effie Menzies's cottage and I went in pursuit of her. When I found her I was so breathless I could not speak, but she determined the crisis and together we made our way back to Gilchrist House.

Mrs. Dundas had the ability to bring everything under control, or to at least make it appear that way. With confidence she tended to my mother and sent me away with the apologetic yet firm judgment it was not a fit place for a lass of my years. I cared not for what I might see or what gruesome mysteries I might discover. I cared only that I might be beside my mother to offer what comfort I could, for surely she needed me. But I was prevented, and the wall separating us might have been made of seamless stone several miles thick for all the access I was allowed her.

I was left no choice but to pace in the little sitting room, forgetful of my hunger, unaware of my slippers that were soaked through. No amount of Mrs. Dundas's optimism could force me to forget that Mamma's time of confinement was three months early. My eyes kept straying to the floor where Mrs. Taggart had wiped away Mamma's blood.

Finally the lying-in-wife emerged from the chamber, her usual smile absent. "Send Young James for your father, lass," she commanded. "Be quick now."

Father appeared an hour later, lines of worry etched between his brows. He desperately wanted another child, and he wanted a son. I reflected, cruelly, that it would be ironic if his temper was the cause of her miscarriages. I suspected there was something amiss with Mamma that kept her from conceiving easily and something mysteriously delicate about her that prevented her from carrying bairns for nine months. I had been the exception, it seemed. I wondered if Father affected her ability to produce another child. Perhaps he did nothing more than increase her anxiety, which in turn caused her difficulties. The pressure he put on her to give him a son was unyielding.

The rasp of hinges met my ears again well past midnight. Mrs. Dundas's face was ravaged by exhaustion and worry. She said not a word to me but descended the stairs to fetch my father from the library where she had forced him to go earlier. I stood, disgorging myself from the cocoon of my coverlet, but I did not move quickly enough. They entered my mother's chamber and the door closed firmly behind them.

I put my hand up against the wood, willing my fear to evaporate so I might push it open. But a part of me did not want to see, did not want to know. I withdrew. Father's murmuring voice came to my ears. I waited in the isle of candlelight, and the darkness about me was a cold, black sea. The door opened and closed.

"Keeley," Father said. "Your mother had a difficult time."

I could do nothing but stand before him, letting him say the words, allowing my ears to hear them.

"There was nought that could be done for her."

The light fluttered on his face. There seemed to be nothing familiar about him. He was a tall, well-made man who was a stranger to me. His nose and eyes were red from weeping. Behind him, Mrs. Dundas's self-possession dissolved in the face of grief and she sobbed soundlessly.

"She only needed to rest," I began.

"She has gone to her eternal rest."

But she could not leave me, I thought. She would not. How often she had told me I was all in the world she had, all she cared about. And her pain. I was horrified to think of her suffering. I took a step forward and wordlessly begged for the truth from my father's swollen eyes, but his expression did not change.

I strode away from him calling, "Mamma?" and burst into her room. I stopped at her bedside, shocked into silence at the sight of her face on the unwrinkled pillow. There was no suffering in her features, but neither was there recognition nor love, nor even the quiet breathing of one deeply asleep. She seemed younger than I ever remembered seeing her, and her bountiful hair was spread sweetly under her cheek. Her hands lay thin and still. There were other things I did not want to see: the bowl on the chair full of water stained scarlet, the torn sheets in a bundle at the foot of the bed, sodden with blood. The scent of blood and death teemed in the close, candlelit air and sickness spread through me.

My father's hands gripped my shoulders. "It is too distressing. You should have waited." I was unable to resist the hands pulling me out of the room and propelling me to my own bedchamber. Father said something to Mrs. Dundas. I was aware of the lying-in-wife coming to me and attempting some solace, but I could not hear her, nor could I speak. The candlelight flickered in the darkness.

I was in my little bedchamber at Gilchrist House no longer, but watching the light bounce on the ceiling from the water-reflections below. Kirthgarran. Mamma had died five years ago. Time had passed. I was no longer the little daughter huddling under the counterpane. Everything was gone, changed, misted. Everything was gone except the clarsach.

My hands tightened upon the soundbox. I blinked my eyes at the quivering patches of sunlight. When I was able, I played two notes, then three. A fragment of a melody called to me through time and my fingers knew where to go. Musical phrases appeared out of nowhere and wove themselves together. I hugged the clarsach to me and played, and played.

At last the strings remained still. My hands rested flat against the pillar as I listened, tense, breath withheld. I wanted to go back in time so I would not be without a mother, and not have a husband who was an adulterer. Not live in a place surrounded by people who feared me. Not love a man who could never be mine.

"Mamma," I whispered. "Mamma, I miss you so."

I waited, and the answer came, as clear as a tone from a string. "I am with you, my dear heart," she said. "Always."

To see thee and to hear thee...
My Brown-Haired Maiden (Trad.)

Chapter Twenty-Four

When the last day of October dawned I slipped up to Lord Kirthgarran's chamber. "I brought you your breakfast," I explained, putting a small tray on the table beside him.

He smiled when he eyed the contents—brose, scones with fresh butter and marmalade, a chunk of strong yellow cheese, and his *sgailc*, his dram of whisky—as if all of it was a surprise. He straightened in his bed. "Thank you, lass."

"Mairi and Anne are here. And the hall and the kitchen are filled with servants and folk from the glen, ready to cook and dust and polish."

"I thought the food already prepared, and the silver

sparkling," the earl replied mischievously as I passed him his brose.

Indeed, Grizel and her enlistees had already outdone themselves. A vast collection of puddings, cakes, and bannocks baked with egg, butter, and sugar coatings stood in rows upon the wide table; fowls and vegetables were in readiness for the stew pots; venison was roasting on the spit over the fire.

"There's still much to do," I said, buttering a scone for him. "Everyone has a task. Even wee Iain. He's been snatched from his flock and put to work carrying water. But he's having a terrible time of it. There's a young man with powerful arms, someone I've never seen before, who's turning the spit on its raxes. Betwixt pailfuls Iain is keeping his hands pressed to his ears because of the groan and screech of them, and he cannot hear the women scolding him to dip more water."

The earl grinned. As he ate I described to him how the game room, usually filled with hanging pheasants, partridge, grouse, ducks, and rabbits, now seemed incredibly empty. The ever-present stock pot hanging over the fire with its simmering contents of fried bones, leftover skins, and vegetables was devoid of its broth, and the fat on top had long ago gone into the pastries. The dairy's cool, stone shelves were bereft of eggs, milk, and pans of thick cream.

The earl beckoned me closer and whispered, "Has Grizel made a Nun's Cake?"

The queen of all the dishes was presently sitting in honor upon the kitchen dresser. Grizel's triumph stood tall on its plate, a creamy, yellow tower speckled with caraway seeds. I had followed its progress the day before, even bravely taking a turn, under Grizel's watchful eye, at the thirty-five eggs that needed two hours of beating. I had savored the lick of batter from my finger. It had been delightful with butter, sugar, and brandy. After three hours in the oven last evening it was finished.

"It awaits destruction," I said, and the gleam in his eyes increased.

I felt so warm toward him that I opened my mouth to say, "There's something I must tell you, my lord. I have found the daring to play the clarsach again." But I caught myself just in time.

For a week now I had been remembering more and more. Planxties composed by the blind Irish harpist Turlough O'Carolan such as "Miss MacDermott" and "Hewlett." Old Scots ballads that had no names. My mother had taught me all of them, but it would take some practice to arrive at the point where notes flowed like water from a spring. I had resolved to perfect my cross-overs, cross-unders, harmonics, and glisses. Already I believed I played better.

But the playing had not been painless. Each time I picked up the harp I suffered as much as I had on the first occasion, for memories of Mamma skirmished with the need for solace that only the strings could bring. I played at night by the light of a candle, alone and quiet. I doubted I was ready to share my endeavor with anyone, though I knew the earl would find pleasure in the knowledge of it.

I turned to the tray so the earl could not see my face and rearranged the butter and marmalade dishes. I was relieved when he began telling me about other cakes he had enjoyed, and why. I gave him his *sgailc* and forced myself to smile.

I was appalled at how quickly the day flew by. I swept and dusted and put beeswax tapers into the iron candleholders on the walls and the triple candlesticks of pewter on the tables. I stirred soups, cut barley cakes, and filled wooden bowls with puddings, sauces, leeks, and potatoes.

I found Mairi polishing the Chippendale chairs in the drawing room and began asking her questions about the napery, but she cradled the sides of my face with her hands. "You've done enough," she declared. "It is time you saw to yourself. Look at you! Your nose is black and your petticoat could be used to dust the shelves."

"What is the hour?" I asked, aghast.

"Late enough for you to be disappearing. Airig will help you dress."

"Already..."

"Off with you," she ordered. She swiveled me about and pushed my shoulders.

I filled a dish with water and brought it to my room where I flooded away the grime of the day's work. Airig appeared, bearing a small gallipot covered with leather.

"'Tis some cream," she said. "Made of the oil of sweet almonds." She moistened it with rosewater and rubbed it on my arms, neck, and hands. When she dropped the silk gown over my head and spread the skirt evenly over my oval panniers, I began to feel the first prickles of uneasiness. I flattened the silk and lace sleeves to the middle of my arms. Airig knotted ribbons and straightened the panel of silk that flowed down in back from my shoulders to the floor.

"Oh," she said, pressing her hands together and standing back. "How bonny you are."

I smoothed the bodice with its flounces of Brussels lace and ribbon and slid my damp fingers to the point at my waist. My hair had grown a little and Airig pulled it up high in the back with ribbons that curled to my shoulders. She produced a perfume she had made from a blend of Apothecary roses and rubbed droplets into my wrists. As a last touch she pinned a length of black velvet ribbon about my throat. I was not accustomed to fuss about my appearance or my scent, but it was the least of my worries. Fergussons from near and far would be in the hall tonight, and I must face, once again, many terrified glances.

I'd not realized that my industry during the day had been a blessing. Idleness prompted all sorts of nervous ills to attack me. My insides cramped, my feet went cold, my fingers grabbed my right thumb and squeezed without mercy. I waited with Airig, hoping Rab would come and collect me soon. When he did not, I asked if she would inquire across the passage as to when he would be ready.

She came back, biting her red lips. "He's not there, Mrs."

I went downstairs alone.

Lord Kirthgarran was already seated in the hall, bolstered as comfortably as possible in his carved chair. At times like these, when he strove to seem his best, I could catch a glimpse of the man he used to be. Tonight he was the laird in his hall again, the earl in his castle, dressed in black velvet and dark tartan with a cairngorm brooch holding the plaid at his shoulder, his hair drawn behind and powdered; I could see him again as the stern yet compassionate man who had protected his home and family and kept a bloodthirsty government at bay. I did not dwell on the threadbare edges of his coat or the lined face and wrinkled hands, the right one held in his lap. His dignity and pride were what he hoped to project, not the ills of an old man.

Coll said behind me, "Keeley! How grand you look."

I revolved and swept my eyes over him. He wore a claret-colored coat, black and sepia waistcoat, and great kilt. "As grand as you?"

"I'm sure there's no comparison." He smiled, the skin beside his eyes crinkling, and he put out his hands to cover my own. "You're shivering."

How odd it was that he did not know how I felt whenever he touched me, did not realize how I yearned for his warm hands to bring me toward him, did not guess how I dreamt of resting my palms against his chest to feel his beating heart beneath.

I was not certain that I could walk away from Kirthgarran. I did not want to live my life without Coll. But loving him silently in a stunted, brother-sister manner, watching him wed Kirstie and father children, suffering my own marriage: these were not the ways in which I wanted to spend all the days of my life.

Perhaps in the spring when I would not have to travel in snow I would leave Rab. By then I might be able to convince myself that I had the strength to choose my own future. Whether it took more strength to run away or to stay and face one's trials I did not know, but to make changes within myself, to cease passivity and demand equality, would be as challenging to me as seeking another life in another country.

"Have any of our guests arrived?" I managed to ask him.

"One or two. More any moment."

Rab was at my elbow and Coll released me. "The gown does you justice," my husband told me, holding me at arm's length. Like the others he was wearing fine clothes, his wedding clothes. He offered me his arm. "Now, Mrs. Fergusson, let me escort you to table, where all is in readiness for the first guests to arrive, and we can pay our respects to the earl."

The thought of leaving Kirthgarran brought such a sudden stab of distress to my heart that I vowed I must shut it out of my mind, for tonight at least.

A trestle-table had been set up in the hall to accommodate

the extra twenty-four others who had been invited to dine with us to celebrate the year's harvest. The hundred beeswax candles I had placed earlier now lent the warm fragrance of honey throughout. Airig, her parents, and a multitude of brothers, sisters, cousins, and fellow Fergussons stood waiting for the word to begin serving food. The fine crystal and silver were out, winking in the candlelight, and a rotund, earthenware bowl by the merry fire held stalks and fronds of herbs and grasses. Beside it, in a place of tribute, was the *cailleach*, the last sheaf cut.

Rab presented me to Lord Kirthgarran and the earl responded by saying, "Ewen and his wife Margery have come. I asked them to bring something." He reached toward the chair beside him and grasped a parcel of dark wool. He offered it to me with his good hand. "It is for you, lass."

I took the bundle and let the folds fall downward. They cascaded in a pattern of deep green squares divided by crimson lines.

"I asked Margery to weave you a plaid. Her father was a weaver and she learnt the trade long ago. She still has his loom and follows his ways. She tried to copy the auld tartan, as much as she could, studying a piece I gave her. It's been years since it's been made, my father's favorite pattern. But I'm thinking she did a fine job of it."

I gathered the square of wool into my arms and buried my nose in it, smelling peat fire in the folds, and sheep, and the fresh air of the mountains. "I will treasure it always, my lord." He knew I would. I covered my shoulders with it, hugging it to my chest.

Rab smiled at me. He was exuberant in his praise as he fingered the fine, woven wool until a burst of voices at the other end of the hall announced the arrival of our guests.

I was content to wear the plaid whilst we stood beside the earl's chair and welcomed them. How fine I felt in my new gown and the tartan shawl. I greeted both strangers and acquaintances alike, trying to remember all my social graces.

"Ah, here is Kirstie," Rab said, "and Calum, Douglas, Fergus, and Geordie." At their tail Donald bristled with the drones of his pipes. Kirstie and I curtseyed; the men bowed. Others entered the hall and my attention was drawn away. Rab introduced me to those who had come from Rathdale.

All at once I was face to face with someone I did not think to see at all. She was not wearing her petticoat of crimson but a gown of sea-green camlet. Her rippling hair fell thick and dark at her back with twin braids on her breast.

"Isabel." Rab took her hand and his eyes caught the flames of the candles as they met hers. "You mind Keeley, my wife."

Her restless dark brown eyes turned to me, and I fancied both she and Rab considered me with amusement.

I lowered my head. "We've spoken before."

"And 'tis always such a delight," she said.

She was to dine with us. The realization cost me the use of my tongue. Gratefully did I turn to Gordon, the master falconer, and the woman at his side. They addressed me warmly and expressed their pleasure at having been invited to join Lord Kirthgarran's table for the Feast of Samhain.

Others arrived whilst Donald played the pipes, and when all were present Rab led me to the seat reserved for the mistress of the household at the earl's left. Fretfully I observed Isabel taking a place nearby at the trestle-table.

The earl ordered his best wine to flow freely. I was expected to make the first toast, and I raised my glass to him, said something I could not remember afterward, and sipped.

I was urged to begin serving the soup of the first course, *potage à la reine*. When I tasted a spoonful myself, I eyed with dread the dishes of woodcock, wild duck, smoked salmon, and Salmagundi that seemed to mock my sudden loss of appetite. Later there would be venison, haggis, Minsht pies—heavy with meat, fruit, and spices—plum pudding, Ratafia cream, and of course, Nun's Cake. I watched Ròs and the others waiting upon us, and listened to the lively talk being launched about me.

I caught Coll watching me and I turned industriously to my soup, dipping my spoon into the thick, fragrant liquid. I ventured glances at Rab, who laughed during the meal and emptied glass after glass of deep red wine between prolific toasts, and at Sandy, who sent his son scathing looks. Lord Kirthgarran was feeling well this early in the evening and more than once patted my icy hand as if to say all was well with him. He did not seem to notice how little I consumed.

When the first, second, and third courses were eaten to the company's full, we lingered over cheese, wine, sweetmeats of sugared almonds, barley-sugar, and gingerbread tangy with brandy. The candles flared about the hall and were replaced as needed; autumn dusk sank into darkness beyond the tall windows. Kenneth laid more logs in the fireplace, and soon the conversation about the table grew desultory and relaxed.

One of the men from the glen rose and produced a fiddle, and Coll could not refrain from joining him with the whistle he drew from his pocket. With such joyous music it was difficult for some to remain at table, so the dishes were cleared away and the trestles and boards taken down to provide room for dancing.

More folk began flooding into the hall. I searched the new faces, sometimes meeting panic-stricken ones just as I had predicted. Some of the men and women touched colored threads tied at their wrists or fingered objects within their pockets—talismen against evil.

I was still seated beside Lord Kirthgarran and realized I had not seen my husband for quite a while. I said, "Have you seen Rab?"

He wrinkled his brow and glanced about. "It seems he helped remove the tables."

The fiddler's brisk notes and Coll's circling harmonies faded as I went in search. The drawing room, sitting room, dining room, and ante-rooms were all deserted.

"Anne," I called when I came back to the hall where a reel was in progress. "Have you any idea where Rab has gone?"

"I think I saw him go downstairs."

I picked up my turquoise skirts and made my way down the steps. The kitchen was hectic, piled full of plates and cups to be washed and trays of sweets waiting to be sent up to the hall. "Is Rab here?" I asked one of the maids, thinking it unlikely.

"He went out," she replied, pointing to the door.

I slipped into the courtyard. The sky was dark, but the fir-candles, the dried splinters of fir roots driven into the sconces on the castle walls, flared and imbued the air with the subtle fragrance of turpentine.

There was no one in the courtyard so I passed through the postern gate. My senses became adjusted to the dim landscape and I stood by a wall in the garden to take in the beauty of Loch Seàrr. Mist rose in patches from the water's surface. On the hills and beside the ruined arch burnt the bonfires of Samhain. Silhouetted figures danced about the flames at the lochside, shrieking and laughing, and I wondered if Rab was one of them. I inhaled the sweet air but a voice quite near forced me to check myself and stand still.

"You've been ignoring me."

It was a woman's voice, soft in a whisper, laden with gentle roguishness. It came from the other side of the bushes. I stood as still as stone. It came again, just as soft, just as mischievous. "Have you forgotten I'm still alive?"

"Crivvens. Not for an instant." His own whisper was husky with emotion.

"Why've you not come to me? It's been days."

"I've felt every day as you have."

"You mock me," she said petulantly. "You've your bonny wife to keep you warm. And I wait for you. Endlessly."

"I'd be with you if I could."

"Lover's talk! Full of sweet words that mean nought."

"We did not come here to talk, did we?"

I exhaled with caution, forcing my eyes to remain on the loch. The shrubbery kept me from their view, but I could not continue to stand like a statue. I heard the woman sigh and my fingers curled into fists.

"Why do you torture me so," she murmured. "You tell me to meet you, and you make me lust after you, and I've been gey angry with you."

"Isabel. Why?"

"Have I not just told you? It's been days. Days I've spent picturing you and her together."

"She is my wife, after all."

"Your wife! When 'tis me you love."

He grunted. "You think so?"

"To blazes wi' you!"

"Why are we quarreling, my sweeting, when 'tis in a more pleasurable way we could be spending this night?"

"Because," she said, her voice growing more tender, "I'm jealous."

"You've nought to be jealous of."

"There's your marriage bed."

"With none o' the warmth of yours, dear. Hers is as cold as the sea from which she sprang."

"I want you. Tonight."

"You're making that rather obvious."

"It will happen. I ken you want me."

"That, too, is obvious."

"Come away with me. Tonight. Will you promise? Will you stay with me again? She'll not notice, will she? You told me she'd not care."

"A dangerous game, this."

"But you're reckless. As reckless as I."

I took a silent step backward, and then another.

"I hardly think," Rab said to her, "I'm wanting to wait until later."

When she moaned I turned and ran.

Shall I expect thee to-night to cheer me?
Or close the door, sighing, sad and weary?

Fear A' Bhata (Trad.)

Chapter Twenty-five

onald continued to play his pipes in the piper's gallery, and in the light of the candle flames and glowing wood fire men danced amongst sword blades crossed on the floor. Roars and war-like cries escaped many a throat. Andrew refilled the bowl of meal and ale, a heady punch with coins and tokens settled at the bottom. If a person spooned a ring into his cup, not a button, he would be assured of finding a lover, and there had been great glee all the evening as folk peered eagerly into their drink.

I wandered, lost, through the cheerful company. When a farmer's wife drew her daughter to her side, touching a small stone suspended from a string at her throat, I smiled and pretended I did not know I was the one from whom she needed protection.

The fire in the hall was snuffed out and ceremoniously relit with a torch that had been brought down from the mountains. This meant that the cattle had been driven round mountaintop fires to ensure harm would be kept away in the coming year, and that they would soon be brought down to the low-lying lands for the winter. I watched the fire until my eyes caught on Coll dancing a minuet with Kirstie. She was grinning at him with unmistakable adoration. Later I glimpsed her enclosed in Coll's arms in one of the alcoves where they obviously wished to be alone. The ache inside of me threatened to grow when he kissed her, and I rejoined Lord Kirthgarran, hoping to become engaged in conversation. He raised a whisky cordial in salute and began telling me about the origins of Kirthgarran's *uisge beatha* whilst I clamped my mind closed against the ruthless, unwanted thoughts that clawed to get in.

When revelers began leaving for home, the earl called for Lachlan and Sandy. He raised himself to stand between them and said, "Join me in the drawing room. Tell Coll, Andrew, and Anne. And Rab. There is something I must be telling my foster sons." The men were puzzled. "And you, Keeley," the earl added. "And Mairi and Ewen."

Sandy replied, "You are grave, my lord. It is something of great magnitude, then?"

"For too long have I suffered the indecision. But tonight I have settled it once and for all. My mind is clear, and before I take to my bed I feel the need to voice it."

His announcement could be nothing but a judgment about Mr. Baird's offer.

Solemnly we gathered in the drawing room. At the sight of Rab the mayhem of emotions I had been trying to avoid threatened to shatter my fortitude, and I moved closer to the window so others blocked my view of him. Sandy shut the door, causing silence to descend upon the ten of us.

Lord Kirthgarran looked round, his eyes lingering on each face. "I am going to clear my lands, and put them under sheep," he said. The lines in his face seemed deeper than when I had first met him, and for all his talk of being a happy man who felt well, he looked ravaged.

Ewen said, "Is this what you honestly wish to do?"

The earl shook his head as if his thoughts could not be put into words. "The folk will not understand. I hardly expect them to. But I've come to see this is something that must be done. In a few years it will be a new century. One hundred years gone. My life, more than half that. Change has to come. Change must, or there'll be a Kirthgarran no more."

"You've spent your life keeping Kirthgarran together," Sandy said. "I mean not the fields and the hills and the burns, but the people. The people your father left you. They've fought just as you have."

Lord Kirthgarran dropped his eyes. "It is not the same as it used to be. A man can no longer measure his wealth by how many fighting men he has, or how many kylies. It is coin. Coin. The last forty-two years have changed everything. If a man does not think of money first, he cannot survive."

"You're allowing yourself to believe you're beaten," Ewen pronounced.

"Only a foolish man will stand in the middle of his boat until it sinks to the bottom of the loch. There is a time when a man realizes he is going to drown unless he tries to save himself. Then he must leave the boat. He must leave those he cannot save."

I glanced at the others. I could have predicted what I found. Coll was seething though he tried to hide it. Many appeared resigned and somewhat blank. I could not look at Rab at all.

"Your Fergussons," Coll said.

"A man must do aught to survive," the earl said, "to save himself and those dearest to him. Sometimes it is necessary to sacrifice many, for the few dearest ones."

"You mean to send them all away?" asked Andrew. "Have you planned where they will go?"

"It will rend me in pieces to tell my Fergussons to leave their land. Even those who emigrate of their own free will do not do it without sorrow." The moisture in his eyes glittered. I pictured the letter from Samuel Hume in my writing table.

"We do not doubt you've given this careful thought," Ewen said, "but I cannot pretend to find it to my liking."

"It must be," the earl countered.

"You'll leave the announcement until at least tomorrow," Mairi said.

"I needed to tell you this night, as soon as I myself knew. But aye, aye, the folk should not be told until later. I'm thinking, Ewen, you'll draft a letter to Mr. Baird. Discover his wishes and how they best suit us. When we have the whys and wherefores of the agreement we can better call the clansmen together and tell them when they must leave, and how. And we must find buyers for all of our cattle. There will be no room for them either."

I saw the question on most of their faces. How does one tell a family it will be evicted from the land it has tilled for four centuries?

"We're going to be rich, my wife," Rab said close to my ear as we stepped into the hall. "'Twill be a new beginning for Kirthgarran."

I watched the earl make his unsteady way toward the stair, Lachlan and Sandy supporting his arms. The rest of his kinsmen came from the drawing room and moved past us, grim and white-faced. I turned with a sick heart toward my husband and was able to say, "It will be an ending for some."

"Jings! Are you still not convinced? You'll see. You'll see when you've a dozen satin gowns and slippers to match. When you do not have to sweep the bluidy hall but can watch servants do it. When you wish to winter in London, and can."

I looked at him and pictured Isabel in his eager arms. I said, "I've no wish to spend a winter in London."

"But to be able to. That is the point. And when the sheep come and Baird pays his rents, you'll be able to do all of those things and more. There'll be golf, and race-meetings, and new horses in the stable that will win hefty prizes. Hunting and whist with friends from London. Concerts and dances in Edinburgh where we'll arrive at the Assembly Rooms in sedan chairs, or better yet, a carriage."

I held my tongue, for there was no use in trying to dissuade him from the delusion that now Lord Kirthgarran saw his way of it, the estate would be instantaneously free of all debt and collect nought but profits. He was soaring whilst visions of tall columns of gold danced before him. He was ecstatic. He had won. I did not know how I would be able to suffer his gloating voice or the avaricious flash in his eye.

"Come dance with me," he exclaimed. "My wife I've not yet swung about! 'Tis long overdue." He spread out his hands.

The music of the great Highland pipes, the clamor of voices—even the heat of the fire—overwhelmed me. I stepped backward but he followed me, catching me with his hands. I would have resisted further had it not been for the company surrounding us.

A reel was just beginning. I minded the steps vaguely from my infar when I had first come to Kirthgarran, and reluctantly allowed my hand to remain in his. We queued up along with the others and traced the hall in a dizzy confusion of loops. People round us clapped in unison and cheerfully shrieked.

He had been with her. The heat of the hand clutching my waist went through my gown to my skin.

When it was over he kissed me heartily on the mouth and I turned from the blend of whisky and perspiration he exuded. "'Tis a fine night, is it not?" he said.

My eyes slid beyond him. Isabel was watching us, flushed and sensuous as she pretended to listen to a man talking into her ear. She turned away and put her arm through his, but I was not deceived. I would never be so again.

"Just think," Rab went on. "When we have money this could be our way of life. No expense too much. Balls in London. French wines. Fine horses. I tell you, dear, our dreams are going to come true, all of them!"

I pulled away at last. "They are your dreams. Not mine. You've no idea what it is I want."

"Your dreams cannot be that different from those of other women."

"My dreams..." I began, but I realized this was not the place to let my feelings come back to life. Rab lost interest when I did not speak further. His attention was garnered by Ròs who was gazing longingly at partners lining up for a reel. She was holding a tray of tumblers and he took it from her. He deposited it on the table and escorted her to the line, kissing her when the fiddler drew his bow over the strings. The reel began and happily

Ròs reached for Rab's hand.

Several times throughout the night I was forced to dance, to talk, to smile, when all I wanted was to succumb to the blackness inside of me. Andrew, Anne, and Mairi left somberly for their journey back to Rathdale. I said farewell to Ewen and Margery Drummond, thanking the woman again for the woven shawl. I did not notice when Isabel left. I was not surprised to find Rab missing as well. I climbed the three-stepped stair to one of the windows and peered out into the night, but the stars lit an empty path down into the glen where my husband had no doubt seen his lover home. Soon there were just a few men left beside the ingle, men who, like Lachlan, appeared ready to drink and smoke until morning, tell stories about their ancestors, and sing songs. I excused myself and escaped outside.

I wrapped my plaid about me and tread over the turf to the ruin by the water. The bonfire had been abandoned by the young revelers who only a short while ago had spun in circles about its sparking flames. They left behind a calm, welcome quiet. There was a mound of untouched sticks and logs at the ready, but it seemed the couples had gone off into the night with other things on their minds. "They're off to tend fires of a very different nature," someone had announced in the hall after observing their dispersal, thus launching a spate of ribald songs about love amongst the corn rigs.

It was possible now to hear the little waves at the loch's edge tumbling stones on the beach. I sat on a stone from the ruin and put out a hand to touch the ancient wall. How strange that even after all of this time it did not fail to call forth an irksome echo of familiarity. Perhaps Rab was right in that God had always intended I should live here at Kirthgarran. I was only feeling the assertion of His will. What sin would I be committing if I defied Him and left it?

A deep, eerie call of an owl cut through the night. A prediction of death, some would say. Far away on the hilltops bonfires still burnt. The Celts had believed this was the start of the time of darkness, the end of one year and the beginning of another. On this eve one could divine the future and see the dead who were able to return to earth.

The whispered passion I'd heard between Rab and Isabel in

the garden, and their callous remarks, loomed over me no matter in what direction I faced. Rab had gone to her instead of me. I had forced him away by my coldness. From now on whenever I was with him I would think of Isabel and her possessive, mischievous smile. I did not greet for my husband but I did feel a sense of betrayal and loss: the loss of hope, of happiness, of a dream. I had to reiterate to myself that there was no reason my desire to have a bairn should shrivel and die in the face of Rab's unfaithfulness. Many marriages were not fashioned out of love, and Rab seemed willing to bed us both.

The hour grew late whilst I pondered. If I went to my bed I would not sleep. At least here I had the company of the flickering stars and a curve of moon, and the eternity of the night from the black loch to the invisible, flame-dotted hills.

I froze when footsteps crunched on the path and the figure of a man emerged from the darkness.

"Gu sealladh sealbh ort!" Coll exclaimed, his voice loud in the hushed night. He came toward the bonfire, the flames revealing his claret coat. "I thought you a ghost," he said. "Not a welcome vision, on this night of all nights."

"I did not think I could sleep."

His footfalls became muffled by the dewy grass. He pitched a couple of logs onto the coals and sat beside me. The sticks became outlined by flames. He said in a voice that must have been only inches from my ear, "Did you notice how drawn the earl seemed?"

"How could I not?"

"Coming to a decision about the sheep has been difficult enough without all of us nipping at his every side, wringing our hands, and holding forth without end. He's seen the only family he has left split in half."

"It has been trying," I agreed. "But now that it's over and his resolution has been made, the discord will be less."

"I'm not sure. The months ahead are not going to be easy ones, for anyone."

The emptying of the glens was to be nought but devastation. Families were to be forced to leave their homes and their last backward glances would settle on me. I could already hear them denouncing me as the cause of their woes.

He said, "There is a difference between wanting to leave your home and being told you must."

"You're more apprehensive about Lord Kirthgarran than you are about the folk who must leave."

"He has aged before our very eyes in the last weeks."

I sighed. "How I wish Mr. Baird had never come."

The brightening fire lit the contours of Coll's face. He looked down for a moment before he spoke. "The earl needs you, Keeley."

"He needs all of us."

"Rab seems oblivious to it. Oh aye, he's aware of the earl's physical ailments, but he troubles himself little with his spiritual ones. If he did, he'd never have chipped away at him over this sheep matter. He tends to view him as he was when we were lads. Strong, self-sufficient, certain. But Lord Kirthgarran no longer possesses those qualities. The losses of Walter and Hugh were cruel blows that sapped the heart and strength from him."

I did not wish to talk of Rab, yet I knew what he meant. I studied the ribbons of mist curling about the isle in the center of the loch. I said, "You'd not say any of this if you did not already believe my feelings are the same as yours."

"I only wanted to be reassured you can see behind Lord Kirthgarran's stalwart front."

"Of course I can. We must try to outweigh the damage Rab's eagerness for change has wrought, and prevent it from happening again."

"The earl thinks so much of you, Keeley. You have it in your power to make him happy."

"I am no one. You are part of his past, his home, his family. A stronger ally than I." When he did not reply I continued, "You are here. You will always be here, will you not? One would think, from the way you speak, you are planning to leave."

At the look on his face a phantom gripped my throat.

"I've made it too obvious," Coll answered regretfully.

"You—you are leaving."

"At Christmas. Perhaps sooner."

The invisible hand squeezed my throat.

"The East India Company," he said. "It's asked the King for military aid in India. One of the new regiments being raised is to have Sir Archibald Campbell as its Colonel. 'Twas him I served in Fraser's. His kin will be making up a good part of the regiment, but it seems there are a few commissions left to be filled."

I could not speak. He went on, "When Murray Campbell came to see me a few weeks ago he'd already become a lieutenant. He brought me a message from the Lieutenant-Colonel who's raising the regiment. I was offered a commission for a captaincy."

I moved my head from side to side, trying to say, "No."

"I'm not sure what you know of Indian affairs," he said. "There's a son of Hyder Ali called the Sultan Tipu, who seems to be on the verge of throwing the British out of India. He's allied himself with the French, who in turn want the possessions held by the Dutch. From what I've been told, the East India Company is becoming terrified. If it loses its holdings it loses money and trade and, well, its whole reason for being, and it's not likely to give up all it's gained in the past hundred years or more. The Government agrees apparently. There are to be four new regiments raised just for the company's protection. Two of them from the Highlands."

I managed to say, "Wasn't there a treaty of some kind?"

"You're thinking of the Treaty of 1784. It's true. Lord Cornwallis cannot declare war. But it does not prevent Tipu from attacking first. Whilst he was signing the treaty he was telling his subjects, and the French, that he need only wait for a better moment to rise against the British in India again. Tipu has sent ambassadors to Paris and they've been heartily welcomed. And he still holds British prisoners, men who should have been released in '84. Mahrattas are begging for protection. There are those who believe so firmly war is in the offing that these regiments are being raised. Murray told me the condition of the company's own troops is shameful."

"You want to leave Kirthgarran so badly you would face death in a foreign land? Again?"

Coll seemed taken aback and answered, "I'm a soldier."

"And feel a duty to go?"

"The years have not bled it away. The American war, my service. Aye, remnants of duty remain."

"You hardly ever speak of the American war. And now, to

go halfway round the world, to India, and perhaps die there..." I shuddered. "Do not tell me you go because of duty."

An uncomfortable silence grew between us. Finally he said, "I'm thinking ahead to the day when Lord Kirthgarran is gone and the castle and all the lands belong to the Crown. Will there be a place for me here? Will any of us be assured of a place? 'Tis time I got on with the planning of my life and stopped letting chance have its say in it. This is a good opportunity for me. Be happy that I can do what I've been trained for. To be an officer in the King's army is an honor, and if I decide to leave it there'll be land and trade to take up in India. A means to earn a good living."

He planned never to return. I said, "Surely your love and concern for Kirthgarran and the earl tell you that you should stay."

"But there'll be no torment, will there, with one duty to perform. I'll be serving the King. That will be all that matters." I thought he sounded angry.

"And it will not matter if you're killed?"

"If it is in the line of duty. Was it Horace who said, '*Dulce et decorum est pro patria mori*?' It is sweet and proper to die for one's country."

"Please do not say you would welcome death."

"The possibility exists but it is not my intention to die."

"Are you certain? Could it be that your going has little to do with duty or concern for your future, but much to do with Leslie Hamilton?"

"Leslie?"

"Do you not ken I see you greeting for her still? Memories of her surround you here. You cannot let go of her." I could sense him tightening, seeking to control himself. "You're running from her, again. You, who once told me never to run from aught."

"You have it all quite wrong."

"I do not believe you've ever lied to me. It's what I've always revered between us. The honesty. It is possible, I suppose, you do not understand it yourself. You wish to escape from the memory of Miss Hamilton. The loss. The guilt you feel, wrongly. You escaped so once before, and in this same way."

"My life here long ago stopped having aught to do with her."

"Am I so wrong, then? You love her. Still."

"For the life of me I cannot understand why you believe that."

"Even if I am wrong, have you given no thought to what this will mean to your mother? And Lord Kirthgarran? Do you think he can face losing a foster son?"

Clipping his words he said, "He'll have others to comfort him. He'll have you."

"He's already lost two sons." Lashing out at him was the last thing I wanted to do, especially since I had also thought of leaving, but I could not seem to stop. "You would do this," I said. "Something that would hurt the earl more than anything anyone could do."

"He will understand."

"I do not understand. You say one thing and do another. You say he needs us. He needs you more than he needs me. You are heartless."

"Keeley," he gritted through his teeth. His hands fell upon my shoulders. I could feel tears beginning to spill onto my cheeks.

"You'd leave us," I went on as I tasted salt in my mouth. "You'd leave your mother, who loves you so..."

"Keeley," he warned again, his voice impatient.

"And Lord Kirthgarran..."

"*Leannan...*"

"And me. You'd leave me."

"May God save both our souls," he exclaimed. "Can you not understand it is because of you I must go?" His fingers clenched my shoulders. I thought my bones would break. "It is because I've come to love you—that I must go."

I stared at him. His hands left my shoulders and gathered me desperately to him. His head turned and my lips were there against his.

What sweet relief it was. To press my body close to him, to feel his mouth upon mine, warm, questing, asking, and answering. A sensation I had never before experienced streamed through me as our mouths opened and sought each other, something that reckoned with the person I was, something that harked back to me as a child, me as a woman. The kiss was a fulfillment, a coming home, and I met him with an abandonment I had not known I possessed.

There was too much of him to touch and to feel. The velvet of his coat on his shoulders. The tautness of his warm neck beneath the fine linen stock. The smoothness of his hair. One of his hands buried itself in my hair as it held my head and brought me tight against his lips. His other was iron, binding me to him.

I felt his heart pounding beneath his waistcoat when his mouth released me. His breathing was quick, and so was mine.

He grasped my fingers and held them against his chest. His eyes sought mine but then he stiffened. Something changed. "Keeley," he said. "Keeley."

He was going to stop this between us. I could feel the resolve creeping under his skin. I kissed his hands enclosing my own.

"We cannot do this. We cannot," he said.

I shook my head. I did not want to listen. I rested my forehead against his hands. I felt him looking up at the sky. He was struggling to catch his breath. He was squeezing my hands but he was leaving me, leaving me.

When he removed his hands I knew it was over. I could not look at him. I hungered, and yet reason had returned.

I stood. He did not attempt to touch me. The loch and the sky seemed to revolve as I walked in a crooked line toward the castle lights. Sandy was standing by the entrance and nodded to me, but I could not speak. I entered the hall, took to the stair, and soon I was in my room.

I leant for a long time against my door. Eventually I removed my gown. For long lapses I found myself staring into the air oblivious to my surroundings.

I knew I must put myself to bed. I slid the pins from my hair and pulled the wrinkled ribbons free. Like a sleepwalker I crossed the floor, stepped up into the alcove, and opened the window. The dark mass of the loch slept below and beside it was the persistent flicker of Samhain flames.

I lay down on my bed. I had been given a taste of something

that would haunt me for the rest of my life. Something inside of me had been kindled as with flint and tinder and was burning slowly and terribly and of its own accord.

How much time passed? I was unaware.

I rose and dressed. On soundless bare feet I went to my door. The darkness was absolute but I gave not a thought to it as I drifted along the passage. I passed the doors. I skimmed down the wedge-shaped steps and across the wet grass.

I saw the shape of him where I had left him, by the ruins, by the fire. He was leaning against the wall. When he sensed my presence he turned.

"Please," I said. "Hold me. For only a moment. It is all I will ever ask for."

Coll groaned and reached for me, and the warmth of his body shut out all the rest of the world.

There's no music in my harp
My fingers knew naught but pain
Then your kiss, that wondrous barb,
Brought song to my life again.

Eriskay Love Lilt (Trad.)

Chapter Twenty-Six

ently he brought me into the shadow of the ruins. I held my cheek against his chest, striving to calm myself. His lips pressed against my hair.

Presently, with hardly an indrawn breath, he murmured, "Rab?"

"Gone to be with Isabel."

"The damned fool." His fingers touched my face and slid down to my shoulders.

To be close to him and alone with him, to have all of his attention on me, to possess the freedom to touch him: these were heady things in which I wanted to bask. He enclosed my hands in his, his fingers feeling for mine. When we held each other I told myself my longing was answered and my wish was fulfilled.

For only a moment, I'd promised him, and now that moment was well over. The time had come for me to return to the person I was, and to be content with a memory that must sustain me.

I began to tell him but his mouth took mine. Our arms tightened and I returned his kiss. Everything was exaggerated. Taste. Smell. Touch. A hand stroked my back, traveled to find my breast. I gasped, unaware my body had been crying out for him so. The firm touch caused a terrible, wonderful ache within me. As a wife who had been bedded I knew to what the ache must lead. I yearned for it. And yet I was afraid, too, fearful of sin, unsure of the man whose breathing was coming faster in my ear, and even more distrustful of myself who did not seem to care about anything but these driving new feelings.

He pulled me with him, deep under the arch. Together we sank to the ground in the corner. He struggled with his coat and let it fall beside us. His deliberate movements spoke of his own wanting, and we fell from our half-sitting stance to lie tangled on the sweet grass.

His work-worn fingers delved beneath my chemise and struck fire as they moved. His mouth possessed mine whilst he rolled on top of me. The dark, gentle night about us was a shield; the stones that enclosed us were layers of armor protecting us from eyes that might glance innocently from a window. I was lulled into a deceptive sense of safety with just enough wisdom to know that we must remain absolutely silent. And thus, we became one.

Our hands drifted apart and I lifted mine up to touch his hair. The thick, unbraided queue fell through my fingers like molten gold. I plied my hands through the opening of his shirt and slid them across his shoulders, discovering the deep groove of a scar above one shoulder blade.

The force of his movements brought something alive in me, an ache all at once urgent, demanding. It grew until it was almost too much to bear, and then it burst forth in an agonizing flare of sweetness, a sweetness that rolled through me on waves.

His mouth swallowed my cries, his fingers gripped my shoulders. He found his own joy, which brought me to another culmination of sweet pain and relief I had not ever felt before this.

Afterward, holding me close, he began singing in Gaelic, a long discourse of which I had no understanding except that in his low, musical voice he told me wondrous things as ancient as the words themselves.

We watched the throbbing coals of the fire through narrowed, sluggish lids, half asleep, half awake, floating in a timeless haze of warmth and love.

Coll did not move, and his breathing came slow and deep. I inhaled the masculine smell of him and put out a finger to trace his brows and his cheek, finding the side of his face to be rough with new beard. Beyond the wall I could hear the indolent waves tumbling over stones. I listened for a few minutes but nature's lullaby was not strong enough to prevent awareness of the approaching morning. The sky was still dark despite a slight glow above the eastern horizon, and the air had become cooler and damper, precursors to the arrival of a new day. I squeezed my eyes shut and buried my face underneath Coll's chin, seeking more of his warmth. Unexpectedly his hand cradled me to him.

The small movement brought forth a thud in my stomach. There was a memory now, a mindfulness of how it had been with him, and my body had learnt commendably. A stab of shyness assailed me, but the rising awareness of my form lying tucked in alongside his, affording me the feel of his legs and torso and chest, overcame my apprehension and replaced it with unchaste craving. He must have experienced a similar reaction for the flame burst forth between us again.

We came together, more slowly this time, more tenderly. With hands and mouth he brought forth an anticipation that pushed away everything except the need to bring him close, to draw him into me. I was unused to such attention, and inhaled abruptly at times in response to his intuitive hands. When he finally brought me under him I was too close to the edge and rose immediately to the peak, astounded I found myself in the same place as before: the center of a blaze of rapture. He found the pinnacle also, and lay spent at my side, holding me.

I felt time passing. Small convulsions began blossoming deep in my abdomen. The future began to loom before me. I tried to force it to recede but the panic would not vanish, and when Coll kissed me and turned his eyes to the east to judge the hour it was all too severe.

In my head whirled the thoughts that had been forming for hours. I needed to speak them before I left him, and from some unknown source I had to find the courage to begin. I sat up.

My mouth was dry but I forced myself to say, "You do not have to go to India."

He gave me a regretful half-smile. "For your sake, and mine, it is the kindest thing I can do."

"No, no, you do not understand. You must stay here. It is I who should go."

"That's impossible."

"I've been considering it for weeks. I wrote to someone. An emigration agent. He's written back to me. All I need is a little money..."

He raised himself on an elbow. "What are you saying?"

"I've been so unhappy. I do not think I can continue to live here as Rab's wife."

For a moment he could not seem to speak. "It will get better," he said at last, somewhat hoarsely. "I assure you it will."

"If you knew everything you'd not say that. I have thought about it and I'm certain it is better I go. Get word to your friend that you do not want the commission after all."

"Keeley, you cannot possibly leave. And to consider emigrating! When I'm gone..."

"It will be the worse for me. I do not think I can live here without you."

Coll scrutinized me, choosing his words carefully. "Tell me what it is I do not ken." His eyes compelled but I could not find a way to describe Rab's bouts of cruelty. When I failed to answer he sat up and pulled me toward him. His arms came round me as he said, "Tell me about the agent."

"It—it is a while ago I wrote to him. He wrote back to me, telling me I could wait in Glasgow, board a ship, sail to North America. I only need a few pounds, not much. I could ask the earl for it. I've yet to decide if I will go to the Carolinas. Or

Nova Scotia. Or perhaps I'll have no choice at all."

"My God. What did you plan to tell Rab?"

"That I do not want a marriage with him. I never did. It was arranged by him and my father. I thought I would ask for a deed of separation."

"He'll never sign it."

"He might, if he realizes how distraught I am. If he does not, I'll go anyway. I'll leave and he will never find me. It's what I want. To be free of him. Forever. So then, do you not see? If I am gone from Kirthgarran, you do not need to be. You are the one who should stay."

"I've already decided. And I have a commitment to that decision."

"There must be a way to reverse it."

He shook his head as if he did not want to believe anything I had told him.

I said, "Do you not realize that if you leave in December I'll go myself as soon as the snow melts? Perhaps I'll go tomorrow! What will your gallantry have accomplished? Neither of us will be here to care for the earl."

"You've no idea what it is you're suggesting. The hardships. The dangers the agent forgot to tell you about. Lachlan and Andrew and I will force Rabbie to give up Isabel. We'll enlist Sandy's influence. Isabel's power over his son is something he resents bitterly. Perhaps she should be driven away, something Ewen could easily do. We spoke to Rab once about her, and for a while he seemed to abandon her. But now he's apparently gone back to his auld ways. I do not ken how you discovered his—attachment to her. You should have asked for our help. But no. We should have seen you needed it, and pressed him harder. We've failed you."

"There's no one to blame. And there's no unraveling the past. You must understand that I will not stay at Kirthgarran."

"How determined you are to convince me of that."

"I am determined but I cannot bear you to be angry with me."

"Oh *leannan*," he said, using his thumb to smooth my cheek. "I'm not angry at you. Not at all. You're in pain, and not understanding the cruelties of the world. When Murray arrived and offered me the commission I thought joining the 74th was the best solution. For me because it is misery to have you so close, to care for you and not be able to show it. For you because I was becoming aware of your growing fondness for me, and I thought if I were not here, distracting you, you'd turn to Rab at last. But it seems I've misjudged your feelings for him. Until now I was confident you could forget me and be content. Now I'm not sure. So it is not anger I feel, but fear. Fear for you, and your future."

In spite of all my brave words before, I was full of fear as well. He sat thinking. The lapping of the waves had been joined by the low tones of cows bellowing for their milking and the intense morning-song of birds. When Coll looked down at our hands his manner changed. "Well," he said. "I'll not argue with you further. If you've made up your mind to leave then I cannot dissuade you, can I? Just as you cannot dissuade me. But there is a promise I ask of you. Tell the earl first."

"The earl?"

"Tell him today. Tell him you find your life here a sorrowful one, enough so that you mean to leave Kirthgarran. Tell him about your plans to leave the country and show him the agent's letter so he'll believe you."

"He'll not want me to go."

"Of course he will not."

"He'll try to persuade me to stay."

"Perhaps not. The last thing he wants is your unhappiness. 'Tis the last thing I want."

"There is no happiness for any of us, it seems."

He was silent.

"I will promise," I said. I watched his gray eyes, his solemn mouth. "I do promise."

He nodded, smiling a little.

"But I must tell him today?"

"I'm bound by duty to begin recruiting soldiers for my regiment, and should wait no longer. I need to tell Lord Kirthgarran about my commission at once, but I want to do it after he's recovered from the shock of your news."

"Does it matter who tells him first? Your announcement will be the worst."

"It is part of the promise. I would be here when you tell him. I can help comfort him. If you wait until I'm gone I cannot."

"He's going to be wretched."

"As you said, there is no one who'll be left happy." He seemed to regret this and held me hard against him. "'Tis difficult to surmise when Rab will return."

"I should go."

I reached for my plaid and stood stiffly, allowing the folds of my skirts to fall to my feet whilst I brushed away fragments of grass. He rose as well and retrieved his coat from the moist earth.

Misery darkened his face when he wrapped my plaid about me. He watched my face and his eyes pondered my own. "We are glaikit, you and I. Fools like no other. But Keeley—oh Christ. If you only knew how I felt."

"I feel the same."

"Will this be enough? Do you ken..."

I stopped him with a tender kiss. Before we parted he crushed me to him.

I stood on my own at last, legs feeling as if they could not support me. Tottering on cold feet I crept out from the protective ancient walls. The sky was no longer black but a heavy, foggy gray, and a wisp of rose outlined the farthest edge of hills.

Even as I dashed across the lawn I grieved at our parting. I ached for Coll's arms, for the touch of his hand, his lips.

I climbed the back stairs, avoiding the hall where I imagined the storytellers from last night must now be stirring. How could I bear to live like this? Perhaps I should leave Kirthgarran now. Two months of living beside Coll with this forbidden love festering within would be intolerable. The roads were still passable; I could leave for Glasgow within the week.

Dressed and groomed, and wondering how I accomplished either task, I found myself in the kitchen, a victim of habit. Without a word I lifted the earl's tray and mounted the turnpike stair. "I brought you your breakfast," I said to the earl in his bed.

As always he smiled at the brose, the scones with butter and marmalade, the chunk of strong cheese, and his *sgailc*, as if they were all a surprise. The whites of his eyes were pink, and his hand trembled as he reached for the porridge, yet his smile did not waver. "Thank you, lass. I must have been an hour, lying here, thinking of this. Why is it, do you suppose," he said, digging in with his spoon, "that the more you eat the night before, the hungrier you are come morning?"

I sat and spread a dollop of butter on a scone.

"It was a merry night, was it not?" he went on. "Grizel's food, the company of friends, the cows down from the hills, and the oats and bere safely stowed."

"Although your decision, sir, to bring the sheep to Kirthgarran was unexpected."

He swallowed and looked up, and I wished I'd not said that. He cleared his throat. "A decision, cleft in two. The benefit. The harm. I pray to God I have chosen wisely."

With alarm I said, "I have no way of knowing, nor does anyone. But no one can say you did not weigh the matter and come to a judgment you believe in your heart to be the right one. That is what matters most, I'm thinking."

There was a sorrow in his eyes that was not there a moment earlier. He stirred his brose and seemed to decide he wanted no more. "Come, come," he urged, handing me the dish. "I want to think on other things. Something pleasant. Tell me what you suppose you'd like to buy in Perth."

I offered him the scone but he did not want it. I replaced it and the brose on the tray. On impulse I took his weak, right hand and massaged the muscles.

"Perhaps," I said thoughtfully, trying to ignore the dread that twisted my stomach, "I'll buy a pure white horse with a bridle fitted with ostrich feathers."

A crack of laughter broke from him. "Be sure and examine its teeth," he said.

"And a cage full of birds to sing to us. A cage made of gold."

"Solid, of course. Not painted on."

"Of course. And speaking of gold, I think I want napery of gold galloon. And then a new dining room table made of mahogany on which to spread it."

He laughed and shut his eyes as if seeing something inside

the wrinkled lids. "And a chandelier of crystals, four layers, fitted to hold one thousand tapers," he suggested.

"Twin chandeliers," I said, feeling worse. I could not continue with this. He was expecting me to accompany Andrew, Anne, and Rab on an expedition to Perth when it was very likely I would be on my solitary way to Glasgow. I could not fool him any longer. I was false and the guilt of it was crushing me from within. I patted his hand and stood, unsure of what I meant to say or do. His smile faded.

No good would come from postponing the declaration of my intentions. I could not continue to face him knowing that soon his contentment with the world would be spoilt. "My lord," I began. "There is something I must tell you."

"What is it, my dear?"

"I—I cannot think how to say this. You are the first to know."

He gazed up at me affectionately, intensifying my anxiety.

I said, "I must go to my bedchamber and fetch something." If I had Samuel Hume's letter in hand it might be easier to explain. He nodded and somehow I withdrew and made my way through the passage.

I stood in my room and was assaulted by all manner of things. Wretched apprehension at what I was about to tell the earl. A realization of the depth of my feelings for Coll, and despair because our union had deepened them. Dismay at committing adultery. A yearning to return to Coll's side and anger at the world because decorum and God's law dictated I could not.

I felt for the square of paper in my writing table drawer and took it out. *Show him the agent's letter,* Coll had begged of me, *so he'll believe you.* The easiest way to tell the earl would be to simply hand him the letter and let him read it. I could then answer his questions. Already my voice seemed strangled. Perhaps the less said the better.

How would he respond? How long would it be before Coll told him he was leaving as well?

In less than two months Coll would be gone. I would go before that. I must. Perhaps I would not tell Rab. I would just go, and he would never discover where.

"The earl is waiting!" I chastised myself out loud. "He's

waiting for you and you're drifting here in the midst of all your miserable thoughts!" I looked down at the paper in my hands and willed my feet to move.

How grateful I was when I returned to Lord Kirthgarran's chamber and discovered he was still alone. His breakfast, largely uneaten, stood cooling on the tray at his bedside. Pine logs steamed defiantly on the hearth and threw little warmth. The morning sun was obscured by thick clouds that layered themselves forebodingly in the sky.

I crossed the doorsill and stopped. The earl's eyes settled upon me, and grew wide with confusion. "I've wanted to tell you," I said uncertainly.

He stared at what I carried. Even though the day was gray, the strings of the clarsach shimmered like silken threads. I cradled the instrument as if it were a living thing. Somehow I propelled myself to the chair and dropped to its cushion.

His eyes shone. The sight of his tears brought forth my own, and I balanced the clarsach on my lap, brought the soundbox to rest against my left shoulder, and touched my nails to the taut wires. I blinked to clear my vision but I only made it worse.

I began to play "Colin's Cattle" and the notes filled the room as if they were drops from a waterfall. They sprinkled about us and pooled at our feet like a tarn on a hillside where the black kylies graze. I could visualize such a hill. I could almost smell the heather. I imagined Mamma walking in her white dress carrying an armful of the sprays, and somewhere—just out of sight, holding Athdara on his gloved hand—Coll. He was riding Dominie. He was smiling, thinking of me. He was safe.

With a start I noticed Coll standing in the earl's doorway. Memories of this morning when we had been inseparable, warm and wrapped together under the ancient arch whilst the fire snapped beyond, pierced my heart. The moments of loving him, and of being loved by him, should have been the last moments we knew. Time should have stopped, for there was nothing worth unfolding now. He watched me play and the concern in his beloved features softened. His head bowed and a tender, understanding smile touched his mouth.

He had known I would not be able to tell the earl. He knew

me better than I knew myself.

I drew some solace from my daydream and the music. Because he shut his burdened eyes and tilted his head, I was certain Lord Kirthgarran was finding consolation in an old dream as well.

A fingernail, wet from dashing away one of my tears, slipped on a string, but I pressed on and hoped the earl had not noticed. It was such a relief to weep, even if it must be in silence.

I glanced at the figure in the doorframe once again. And thus the bargain was sealed between Captain Coll Fergusson and me, with no further need for deliberation or review, for regret or explanation. It was I who would be staying at Kirthgarran, and he who would be leaving.

And frae danger keep him free...
My Heart is Sair for Somebody (Burns)

Chapter Twenty-Seven

My husband opened a jar of whisky in honor of Coll's commission after his foster brother announced his news.

Lord Kirthgarran suffered Coll's declaration that he intended to take his place in the newly forming 74th, Highland Regiment of Foot, as badly as I had feared. The announcement was a repeat of history, and I imagined the earl relived those moments when his sons had declared they were going to Gibraltar. Sandy's face became silent, as stiff and hard as a mask, and although Mairi tried to remain calm and question Coll logically, it was obvious she would soon lose her control. White-faced, she withdrew from the rest of the family. Anne started after her but

Coll put out a hand.

"Let her be," he said. "I'll go in a bit and talk to her."

Lachlan, Andrew, and Rab accepted his decision with respect and bid him luck and good fortune, but I knew they would feel his absence deeply. They had worked together over the last few years to keep Kirthgarran from foundering, and the common cause had perhaps bound them more closely together than they might have been. Rab suggested the whisky and we all drank to Coll, except Lord Kirthgarran whose hand shook too badly to lift his glass.

I had a difficult time facing Rab. I wondered if he saw a difference in me. I would be astounded if he could not, because the whole world had changed.

He had spent the night with Isabel but I was no less shameful, no less wicked than he, and I was overcome alternately by self-reproach, elation, and despair. My practical side told me that everything must be hidden from Rab at all costs and I behaved as normally as I could. As the morning progressed and we began our preparations for the journey to Perth, I did not believe Rab found anything amiss. He was his usual self: preoccupied, cheerful, disinterested in me. When he tossed down a glass before getting the horses ready, I visualized the days and nights ahead of me. Nothing, after all, was changed. Rab was still my husband and would always be. Coll was preparing to leave for a war halfway across the world.

I could not resist peering at Coll across the room before our leave-taking. He was listening to Sandy, but I knew his concentration was lost when our gazes caught on each other and a fleeting smile crossed his face. How I longed for him, even now. How I loved him, more than before. What a mistake it had been to taste his love. There would be no forgetting. There would be no joy in anything else. There was no joy.

Three days of travel through a bare, November landscape brought Andrew, Anne, Rab, and me to the Bearded Stag, an inn just west of the town of Perth, that ancient capital of Scotland before Edinburgh took away the honor. The journey was uneventful, a slow walk by horse south of Loch Rannoch. I saw Schiehallion again, this time dusted with light snow at its peak. We went east along the River Tay, past Dunkeld with its own ruined cathedral, and south. The nights were spent at the cottages of family acquaintances. Reaching Perth at last was welcome, for there was frost in the mornings and the hills were exceedingly cold. It was not unheard of to have a heavy snowfall in November, and we all hoped for a speedy return with continuing dry weather.

The miles were filled with my thoughts of Coll. I relived the hours we had spent under the ruined arch. The images aroused me, causing me to yearn for him, but at the same time I marveled at what a sinner I was. Visions of hellfire danced before me. My shame was deep whenever I stole a look at Rab and considered how I deceived him. I had driven him into the arms of another woman and had given myself to a man he himself loved.

Even so, I fell asleep every night clutching the memory of Coll to me like a sailor hugging a spar, floating in the sea after a shipwreck. Words repeated themselves endlessly in my mind: "Coll is leaving Kirthgarran in six weeks and I will never see him again."

Since we all lodged in the same room at the inn, with Anne and I sharing a bed and the men happy on mounds of fresh hay, there was little reason for me to be alone with Rab or even speak to him. He had not been looking forward to our trip, but he'd become resigned to it as the days had gone by, and soon even seemed to enjoy it. The highlight for him would be a visit to a sheep farm outside the city, and he talked incessantly about what he had heard about Meadow Farm.

My hope was that we would go to the shops and quickly find what we wanted, but Andrew was of a mind to treat me to some sightseeing and planned a few short ventures for us all. He brought us to the top of Kinnoull Hill from which we could see the town, the River Tay, and the Lomond Hills in the distance. He urged us to explore the ruins of Huntingtower where James VI had been imprisoned for a year, and we visited St. John's Kirk where John Knox had denounced monasteries in the sixteenth century and thus had instigated their destruction.

We visited the parklands of the refurbished Scone Palace, home of William Murray, Earl of Mansfield, and gazed at Moot Hill nearby, the site where many a Scots king had been crowned whilst sitting on the Stone of Destiny. The Abbey that once stood next to it was gone. A mob spurred on by John Knox had burnt it and damaged the Palace in 1559. And the Stone itself was gone, imprisoned in London, or at least hidden by monks and lost forever, for some said it was a replica the English soldiers had stolen away. I looked at the empty lawn and wondered just how many beautiful things were lost to mankind because of passions that drove men to destruct what had once been revered. Abbeys. Cathedrals. Vows. Nothing was safe.

We explored the historical places and haunted the shops, thus filling the three days we spent in Perth. The shops were intricate troves of all variety of riches, far better than any wandering pedlar's pack, and Anne's delight in choosing items for the coming winter was infectious. Together we eyed the shelves of cooking pots, needles, fishhooks, thread, paper, and ink blocks, and watched eagerly as the proprietors took down and wrapped our purchases. Whilst the men laid in a supply of flints, powder, and shot, Anne and I inspected the perishable goods and ordered salt—casks of sea salt for preserving and fine, elegant salt from Cheshire for our tables. We selected sugar cones wrapped in blue paper, flour, tobacco, Jamaican pepper, imported Seville oranges, lemons, raisins, almonds, coffee, and tea leaves and bricks. We even had money enough for some chocolate, which, Anne assured me, the earl favored as a hot drink on chilly winter mornings.

The bookseller's was all I envisioned it would be. There were cases of books: old and new; red, green, black, and brown. Large and small, they were delightfully stacked and spilt and stuffed about the shop, filling the air with their dusty, musty, leathery odors. Mr. Shaw, a heavy-set man with tiny black-framed spectacles and a gray wig, took my hand when we were introduced by Andrew and gave it a warm press.

"How wonderful," the shop owner hummed like a purring cat. "Lord Kirthgarran must set a great store by you reading to him. I've saved him a few precious beauties this year, I have. Wait 'til you see!"

I would have been content to stay all afternoon, but as soon as we removed our coats, Anne stopped and covered her mouth with a clenched fist. She said, "Andrew? That fish I had at the inn. Oh—I hope I'm not going to..." Andrew covered her shoulders with her coat and guided her toward the door.

I began to follow, but Anne gasped, "No, no."

"Why don't you stay?" Andrew suggested to me. "I'll take her back to our rooms, and then come and collect you. Rab will not have his curiosity about Meadow Farm's sheep slaked until nightfall, I'm thinking. Will you be comfortable on your own?"

Alone. Here. A strange shop with folk who stared at me already. Old anxieties ran rampant.

I hesitated too long and Andrew took it for agreement. "I'll be back as soon as I can," he said, and they were gone.

Mr. Shaw presented me with an armload of volumes to inspect and sat me down in an upholstered chair. He drew up a low table upon which I could range the books whilst he talked about tea and scones and marmalade, and promised he would have his wife bring some and share it with me.

I felt the eyes of the other customers boring into mine as they contemplated my special treatment, and I knew my face was as scarlet as the leather binding of the book I gripped in my fingers. Mrs. Shaw restacked books on the table to make room for trays and cups. I made small remarks amidst her flowing stream of congenial talk as we had our tea, but thankfully I was allowed time to read, to examine, and to think by myself.

My choices included two books by William Blake, a novel by Frances Burney, and an interesting journal by James Boswell who had accompanied Samuel Johnson to the Hebrides. I remembered seeing Johnson's own *Journey to the Western Isles of Scotland* in our library, and decided Boswell's point of view on the enterprise might be of interest. *An Arabian Tale* and *A Hymn to Na'ra'yena* rounded out my selections.

At one point I discovered an auburn-haired man in a dark blue waistcoat at the side of my chair. Mr. Shaw, keeping a watchful eye on my progress, appeared with another book and introduced us. He was Mr. Grant, his apprentice. The young man endeavored to engage me in conversation, but some perverse whim of the gods had stolen away everything I had learnt about social grace.

"This, this, is a prize, Mrs. Fergusson," Mr. Shaw interrupted at last. "I've been anxiously waiting to give it to Lord Kirthgarran.

For it's a gift, one I've been saving for months. He'll find it a breath of fresh air, so he will. It's called *Poems, Chiefly in the Scottish Dialect*, by a young ploughman from Ayrshire who's already a success. Robert Burns. This was printed in Kilmarnock and difficult to find, but I managed it. Have a look, my dear. You'll be enraptured."

I had heard the man's name before. I took the book and leafed through the poems, most of which were concerned with unhappy love affairs. The language was unique however. It was my own, the soft lilt of the Scottish Lowlands.

There was one poem that caught my eye and I read the musical verses out loud.

Wee sleekit, cow'rin, tim'rous beastie,
O, what a panic's in thy breastie!

I lifted my eyes from the page and met with those of Mr. Grant, the apprentice.

"I've read them," he said. "But how much better it is to hear the words spoken."

"They're aye grand," I said unevenly. "Lord Kirthgarran will love these poems." I looked down again at "To a Mouse, On turning her up in her Nest, with the Plough" and thought, so will I. The men smiled and Mr. Shaw rocked on his heels, his hands folded across the ample middle of his brown waistcoat. He sniffed once, as though close to tears.

He produced other things for me to take to Kirthgarran. "I've saved for him the last three issues of the *Aberdeen Journal*, almost in tatters as you can see, but still legible, and a copy of *The Scots Magazine*."

Young Mr. Grant said, "Is there aught we can be providing for you, yourself?"

I was by now used to the apprentice's glowing attention, and answered, "Do you have any song sheets, or music books?"

His eyes caught light and he grinned. "That we do!" he exclaimed, lifting a finger, and he was away to rummage about the shelves. Mr. Shaw and I followed. The apprentice soon handed me a new volume. "Here's *Scots Musical Museum*, newly printed. A fine collection. Contains three songs by Burns himself. And, let us see, there are older, used books. Where are they? Ah yes, here's one. *Ancient and Modern Scots Songs*, put together by a fellow named Herd. You'd enjoy that, I'm thinking. And we have a volume of Oswald's *Caledonian Pocket Companion*, which is mostly music notation. Why they call it a pocket companion I have no idea. Who has pockets as big as this?"

I looked over all of the books, knowing I could not afford the newer one. "I might take Herd's," I said, skimming through the songs and recognizing one or two. "It seems to have a great many I do not know." I pictured myself sharing this with Coll.

"Have you not finished your business, Mrs. Fergusson?"

I spun about. Rab stood at the entrance, impatiently counting out coins in his palm.

"I've found some books. Anne was feeling ill..."

He looked up. "I saw Andrew. I've come for you myself. We've been invited for tea at Meadow Farm, and I've come to collect you. Mr. Shaw," he said, giving a little bow to the bookseller. His eyes came to Mr. Grant and whilst Mr. Shaw returned his greeting Rab stared at the apprentice. "Have we met, sir," Rab inquired, "or is it only my wife you wish to know?"

The poor man blinked. He was dumbstruck. Mr. Shaw pulled his spectacles down from his eyes to look closely at Rab.

"Take what you have," Rab said to me, stepping between me and Mr. Grant. It was a blessing that the apprentice was a civilized man; anyone with a temper would have invited my uncouth husband to settle his insult in the street outside.

"May I take the liberty," Mr. Shaw interjected, "of keeping you for just a few more minutes? There's something else I wanted you to take to Lord Kirthgarran."

Mr. Grant bowed and backed away, giving me a look awash with sympathy. In misery I stood beside Rab whilst the bookseller presented us with a tall, homespun-wrapped object.

"It's called an Argand Burner," Mr. Shaw said, unveiling it. A hollow tube of glass was bracketed by a brass holder and attached with a side arm to another brass stand. It resembled an ornate candlestick with a rounded base, and the top was capped with a filigreed point. "Invented by a Swiss chemist," he explained. "The wick is hollow, and I'm told, because more air reaches the flame, it burns brighter than seven candles! Graeme will enjoy it I'm sure, at his bedside, reading his books. I'm sending along some oil to use with it."

But Rab was already steering me toward the desk. Mr. Grant kept his head lowered as he wrapped the books in paper and string and secured the lamp and oil with extra lengths of hairy twine. Rab threw down his coins, wordlessly pressed me toward the door with its little bell, and the kind, warm voice of Mr. Shaw reminding us to give his regards to the earl was lost in the bustling noise of the street as we joined the traffic of foot, hoof, and wheel.

The journey home through the mountains entailed careful packing of our items and dividing them amongst the ponies. I was fearful of breaking the Argand Burner with all of its pretty glass, but there was nothing to be done but bundle it tightly and take care with it, as well as the jar of oil, bottles of wine, and blown-glass flasks of smuggled French brandy that Andrew had ingeniously secured.

I was impatient to return to Kirthgarran. The inconvenience of travel with its soreness and cramps, the tiresome watchfulness for bogs of black peat, and the coaxing of our horses to take the hated cattle bridges over roaring water were more easily tolerated because home was the end point. The nature of our little company warranted a close proximity to Rab, and I fretted over the way he had behaved at the bookseller's. My humiliation even colored my pleasure in the books I had bought.

Our homecoming was met with gaiety, and our supplies were unpacked and fussed over. My senses were intensified with the anticipation of meeting Coll, but he was conspicuously absent and my disappointment grew as steadily as the white mist gathering on the hilltops.

I hastened to Lord Kirthgarran's room where I displayed the splendid books. He was as taken with the Burns volume as I, and I read several poems aloud to him, unmindful of the late hour.

When it was to my bed I went, I went alone, for Rab had disappeared. There was no mystery as to where.

The usual group was gathered at the kitchen table for breakfast the next morning and I was given a hearty greeting. Rab stood up and procured a chair for me whilst Grizel scooped porridge into a wooden cog and set it at my place with cream, a horn spoon, and a small glass of whisky.

Coll nodded to me and murmured something about a welcome back from our sojourn. His eyes widened with affection for just a moment, but when they had a difficult time meeting mine I did not want to attract undue attention and turned away.

Swallowing past the lump in my throat was no easy task. Eventually Coll and Lachlan rose, tossing the remainder of oatmeal from their cogs into their mouths. They were off to stalk the red deer, they told us, and were glad of the new flints and powder we had brought. Kenneth leapt up to join them, high spirited and joyful at the prospect of guiding a garron for bringing home the stags.

I watched the men grab up muskets and powder horns and disappear into the courtyard. My throat closed even further. I put down my spoon and stared at the swirls of amber and white in the handle whilst Grizel praised the quality of the tea and chocolate we had bought, and extolled the unquestionable virtues of West Indian sugar.

I stood on the steps of the castle's entrance beside Ewen, Sandy, and the earl's foster sons and watched the farming folk of Kirthgarran gather on the lawn. When Andrew spoke to them in English and Gaelic, horror darkened every pair of eyes. They realized that their own Graeme Fergusson meant to turn them out of the homes they had been struggling these forty years to keep.

Andrew was pale. He must have stood in this same spot years before, begging Kirthgarran's kinsmen to throw their lots in with his and develop the land into a prosperous patchwork of farmland. Now he was telling them the opposite. From Kirthgarran and Rathdale and Strath Gruagach they must go forth and build new lives, apart from one another.

"How is it to be done?" someone cried. "What skills have we, to find new work? What money to buy homes, even food for our families?"

"Lord Kirthgarran will give you every assistance he can," Andrew said.

"But what does that mean? We're not fools to believe he's

even a pound to spare. If he's nought for himself, what can he give us?"

There was an outpouring in Gaelic. I could not blame any of them for fearing the future. The women held their bairns in their arms and wept. The men clenched their fists, looked at one another, and cried as well. Their greeting circled the castle's chimneys, borne on a strong wind.

Terrified eyes stole looks at me. One woman in a green shawl pointed her finger at me and muttered something into a neighboring ear.

The reaction was later related to Lord Kirthgarran who listened with abject pessimism. He had known what to expect and his prophecy was fulfilled. I sat beside him as Andrew described the folk and their reception of the edict.

"They are in shock," the earl said when he was done. "Overcome with alarm and betrayal. I will never be able to comfort them."

Andrew moved to the window, crossed his arms, and stared out. A muscle contracted in his jaw and his eyes narrowed; I wondered if he was reliving the delivery of his speech.

Lord Kirthgarran said, "They will lose their homes, and I will lose my family. My blood sons are gone, and my foster sons are going to follow."

"Coll will not be lost to you," I corrected him. "He will be safe, and sooner than we ken he will come home again." What a lie it was. There would be nothing changed in a year, or two, or three.

He replied, "It is just like Walter and Hugh, going off with their blood stirred by valor."

"Coll came home safe once before. There's no reason not to believe he'll do so again."

"None of us can foresee when his time will come to leave this earth."

My hands gripped each other, my thumbs painfully squeezed inside my fists. "In any case, my lord," I managed, "you've your other foster sons. And you have me. I'm not likely to become a soldier in His Majesty's army."

This seemed to be the comfort he needed and a hint of happiness touched his eyes. I thought I heard him mutter a phrase in Gaelic that sounded like "mo lon du" but I had no idea what it meant.

And every night in my dream I see thee,
And still at dawn will the vision flee me.

Fear A' Bhata (Trad.)

Chapter Twenty-Eight

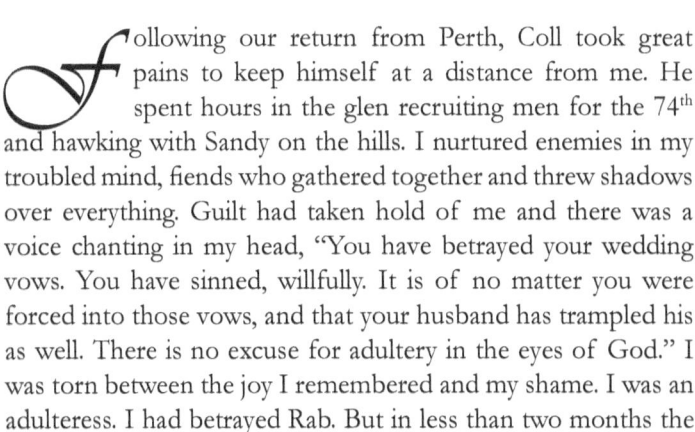

ollowing our return from Perth, Coll took great pains to keep himself at a distance from me. He spent hours in the glen recruiting men for the 74th and hawking with Sandy on the hills. I nurtured enemies in my troubled mind, fiends who gathered together and threw shadows over everything. Guilt had taken hold of me and there was a voice chanting in my head, "You have betrayed your wedding vows. You have sinned, willfully. It is of no matter you were forced into those vows, and that your husband has trampled his as well. There is no excuse for adultery in the eyes of God." I was torn between the joy I remembered and my shame. I was an adulteress. I had betrayed Rab. But in less than two months the man I loved would be gone forever.

We came face to face in the drawing room one morning.

"How are you?" I whispered.

Coll's eyes were grave. A hand reached out and took my fingers. "Well enough. And you?"

"I've missed you so."

He nodded, tightening his grip. "There've not been many chances for us to speak. How often I think on that night and wish it back again! And to hear you play the clarsach for the earl—do you play for him still?"

"Every day."

"I'm sorry if I seem cool to you. It's not what I mean. We must be so careful. My last intent is to hurt you..."

He would have said more but voices came louder from the hall. Airig and Ròs laughed and provoked each other with comments about prospective sweethearts. Coll released my hand and I took a step back as the sisters came in with a foxtail for dusting and brick-dust for polishing brass.

"You've been looking for soldiers to join you?" I asked him.

"I'll lose the commission if I do not recruit some rank-and-file for my company."

I wanted to ask him if that would that be such a terrible thing.

He continued, "The panic appears to be running high in the War Office. The proposed date for reviewing the regiment is the 25th of December. It sounds like madness to me. I cannot see how it can be accomplished."

"How many men do you need to gather?"

"Not counting any of the officers, commissioned or non-commissioned, or drummers, the raising order calls for eight hundred and twenty men to make up eight battalion companies, plus a Grenadier, Light Infantry, and recruiting company. Eight hundred and twenty men! God's Wounds, I do not ken if there are that many suitable men in all the Highlands!"

"Were not the mountains and glens always considered good recruiting ground for the army?" I asked when Airig and her sister paused to listen.

"At first. There's not a better or more eager fighter than a clansman. But see what emigration has done, and the coming of the sheep. I need to bring in as many men as I can from those who are left. They must be fit and honest, willing to be molded into good soldiers, and not tempted to be taking their bounty money and deserting as soon as they can. 'Twill be hard enough with a man's memory being long and the American war not yet forgotten. That ended sadly, and I doubt a man who's seen the returning soldiers, sick and tattered four years ago, will jump forward to join the army now."

"You were one of those who returned so," Ròs said.

"I mind the day," Airig said. "We did not recognize you."

Coll smiled at her. "I might as well have been a beggar."

"And so hungry, and yet so ill you could keep no food inside you," Ròs recalled.

The image was ghastly. But at least he had been alive. I thought of the scars on his cheek and shoulder. Musket ball, cannon shot, swords, arrows—what did the men of India use in their battles?

"Then pack me off with sacks of Grizel's oatcakes when I go," Coll teased the lasses. "Enough to last for a long, long while. They'll be good, I'm thinking, even if they're as hard as stones."

They laughed, poking each other, and I smiled, too, visualizing Coll lugging oatcakes from post to post. I discovered his eyes on me, and the laughter in my heart threatened too easily to turn to tears.

"We'd better start making them now!" Airig said and laughed. "Just how many bags do you want?"

The clock ticked away at Kirthgarran with alarming speed.

One afternoon Airig told me her mother was ill with fever and she was going to visit her. "Will I come along?" I asked, feeling so dispirited I would do anything to keep myself occupied. We set out together for the farm-toun on foot, taking turns carrying a basket heavy with a posset, apples, and fresh butter. We spoke of many things, and I was grateful for Airig's company. Her mother and father lived in a wee house near the largest cluster of homes in the glen. I was invited inside and spent an hour there, sitting by her mother's bedside and talking with the older couple who knew some English. Her father dropped a heated stone into the posset to warm it, and the ill woman weakly drank of it. By the time I left she was in a natural sleep.

I was to travel home alone since Airig wished to stay the night, and as much as I had enjoyed the afternoon, I looked forward to my peaceful return to the castle. The day was cool and I lifted my face to the breeze from the northeast as I began walking past the cottages, but all at once I was not alone.

"What an unanticipated pleasure," Rab said with amusement in his voice. His dark eyes were lively. "Thought I'd have to walk with no one's company but my own."

"So you're away home, too."

He matched his step to mine. After a moment he said, "Do you ken, dear, I'll be leaving for Strath Gruagach with Lachlan in the morning? The day after is the 11th. Martinmas, when the rents are due. Coll and Ewen collect money here at Kirthgarran, Andrew is responsible for Rathdale, and Lachlan and I sit with the books in Strath Gruagach. There'll be meikle weeping going on, I'm sure. But numbers are numbers, and down into the book they must go, and into the chest the coin must go. 'Twill be the last time we collect the rents. That is quite a thought."

I was dismayed by his coldness but I should not have been surprised by it. Rab chattered on, turning his mind toward the vitality of the wool trade, his favorite topic, and seemed not to notice that I did not respond to his monologue.

My brooding was interrupted when a figure came toward us on the path. It was the old man into whose dwelling the injured men had been taken. He was hobbling along, coat flying, short white hair bristling in the wind. He stopped still when he saw us.

Rab greeted him unconcernedly, prepared to walk past him, but the gaunt man did not move and thus blocked our way. He muttered something in Gaelic. The wrinkled features contorted with emotion and the pale eyes threw forth fire. He uttered something again, exposing long but sparse, discolored teeth on his bottom jaw, and his malevolence made me want to shrink backward.

Rab was not unaffected. His cheerfulness turned to impatience. He replied something in Gaelic and added coldly, "It's too late, man," in English. There was another sputter. Rab listened, frowning, and when the tirade was over he said in disgust, "Go home, auld one, go home whilst you still have one to go to."

This silenced him, for whether he understood the words or not, the meaning was clear. He brushed past us, ambling on stiff joints. I tugged at Rab's arm.

"What was it? Why did he look like that?"

"The fool," he remarked, throwing him one last look.

"But what did he say?"

"The folk realize I was the one who influenced Lord Kirthgarran's decision to empty the glens. Airig and the others heard us continually arguing, they have families, and the gossip seeps everywhere. So I'm being charged for the misfortune that's befallen them. They're not blaming Lord Kirthgarran half as much as they're blaming me."

"Is that what he just told you?"

"Oh, I've been aware of the folk's feelings. This was just another useless attack on me, to show what he thinks of my interference. He prattled on about his son and daughter having to leave their homes, about how he's going to be dying in the desolate world beyond. It's enough to sour one's stomach."

"Rab! Can you not understand his fears? To be homeless at his age—to worry for his bairns and their families…"

"Sweet wife," he said, stopping me. "Do not have compassion for the man and do not defend him. He blames you just as much."

"But I…"

"He called you the Harbinger of Death, De'il stick him. He said you've brought this upon them, and I'm accused because I brought you here. You've influenced me, changed my heart to stone, and likewise has Lord Kirthgarran been affected. So do not feel kindly toward him. We'll be well rid of him, will we not. Nay, we'll not mourn the likes of him."

I was silent as Rab took my arm and led me forward, but the relative peace of the afternoon was shattered. The anger in the man's weathered features filled me with trepidation. I had a nickname. I was a herald of death. The folk believed I could summon fire-slaughts that shattered castle towers, enchant oxen and cause them to stampede and kill, and magically enslave men to do my bidding. I wished to send all the clansmen away and knock down their houses.

My husband seemed unconcerned by the incident and resumed his optimistic ramblings, but I was subdued all the way home, and the sight of the aged Fergusson hobbling away down the track stayed with me for many days to come.

I wrote long passages in my diary. I dared not mention Coll, so I soothed myself by writing about anything and everything else.

"I am the Harbinger of Death. I am feared by many of the folk of Kirthgarran, it seems. And why is that? I am sure they do not wish me physical harm but their fear will always keep me separate, distant, a cursed human being who might not be human after all.

"How does one live within such a community? It was different when I lived in my father's house. We were not allowed to associate with others. But now, when I can have a normal life, I am ostracized. Something dreadful stands in the way of me being considered one of the Fergussons who people the earl's lands and home. I have no family except for Rab and his father and brother when I could have the comfort of scores of clansmen just as they do. I never thought belonging would be something that I would want—but I find that I crave it now that I see what it can be like.

"Sometimes I think about the missing silver cup and if I will ever see it again. Occasionally I explore a room with the imaginative expectation of finding it tucked away in an ancient cupboard. Some of them are locked but a great many are not. I'm convinced that if I can find it I will discover why it has been hidden. Where can it be? In the dungeon, that deep pit Rab once showed me? A secret hole or passage? Rab must know more than he claims. Has he taken it and sold it? I am as mystified as ever, and have little hope of learning its whereabouts.

"I despise riddles. And there is not one to frustrate me, but many. Why does the view of the castle across the loch, as well as that of the arched gate and the great hall, call forth feelings of familiarity in me? And who was it who poisoned Ewen's dogs? Ewen blames Coll still, I believe, though to my knowledge the baillie has not accused him of it more than the once."

I asked myself, "What will Kirthgarran be like when Coll is gone?" I could do without the physical coupling, but his company, the sound of his voice, the recognition of our special bond in his eyes—they had become the matter of life to me.

I sat alone in the solar one day thinking of such things

as I half-heartedly sewed lace onto the dress Airig and I had fashioned out of the stamped linen. A fine picture I made, sluggishly picking a knot out of tangled white thread, as lovesick as Robert Burns in his poetry. I felt no desire for anything. The days of November were no longer new. Soon it would be only forty days until Coll left for India with his regiment. I gazed at the wee flowerets of mauve and violet on the linen and did not hear the footsteps. A voice cleared, and I looked up. It was Sandy.

"Lord Kirthgarran is awake and asking for you," he said. "He wants to know, will you be taking tea with him?"

"Of course." I rose, forsaking my unfinished gown, and found Sandy observing me. My father-in-law filled many roles at Kirthgarran: ghillie to the earl, manservant, footman, and steward of the castle. He was ever-willing to put his hands to a chore begging to be done. Today, however, his blue eyes seemed dull and shadows dwelt beneath them. I began to feel my old self-consciousness return. "Lord Kirthgarran is well?" I asked.

"As well as can be expected."

"You mean—you mean because of the glens being cleared, and because of Coll's going."

He nodded.

I said, "These are a great many changes for Kirthgarran."

"Changes," he repeated, "that need not be. We both ken the true reason why Coll will no longer stay."

"Do you suspect something, then, the rest of us do not?"

"I know, as I've seen, as I've felt. It's been enough. I know him like a father knows his son."

There was no doubt the expression on my face betrayed me. Somehow I said, "Coll's decision was as much a surprise to me as it was to everyone else."

"What's done is done. I only want his happiness, for that is all that matters. But who is happy now? Not him. He could have been."

"Do you think I wish him to go?"

He contemplated me still, grief obscuring his usual calm gaze. He said at last, "He makes his own decisions, does our Coll."

"I would do aught," I said brokenly, "to convince him to

stay."

"But he'd not listen. He listens to no one when he's made up his mind. It was just so, the last time."

I inhaled, seeking control of myself. "You missed him greatly, I suspect."

"Almost a dozen years ago. He was the first to leave. And then there was Walter and Hugh. But Coll was like my own and had been from the day of his birth, even more than the others. My wife died," he added.

"In the same manner as my own mother."

"In childbed," he acknowledged. "As it often happens. I never thought she'd be one of those to succumb. A hale lass she was, and full of health, but all was not well with the bairn and in the course of two days I watched her wither in front of my eyes and finally go, taking the child with her. But Mairi was there beside me with her own newborn sleeping in her arms, and lacking the lad's father, she put Coll, swaddled, in my hands, and embraced us both. We wept together. For the loss of my Gwen and our bairn. For the lack of a proper father for hers."

"You never wed again."

"There came a day when I asked Mairi to be my wife. Our families could have become one. We could have found contentment together, I believed. But she said no."

"I did not know."

"I asked her again, after Christopher and Eleanor drowned. But she'd not have it. Her loyalty to the other was too strong. Perhaps it was just as well, for my days were full, tending the affairs of the castle, keeping the household fit whilst Lord Kirthgarran saw to politics in Edinburgh. I did what I could to help raise the lads. It seemed Coll was always at my elbow, interested in all that I did, especially when I went hawking with Gordon. He had his own falcon and flew her well, even as a laddie. It was my shoulder he sought when he wanted a ride up the hillside, and my smile he craved when he could read his first words. Something happened, you see, when Mairi put him in my hands all those years ago."

"You have needed each other, I think."

"It is a bond without words. Something each of us knows, without telling ourselves or each other. If you asked him he would tell you the same."

"He has told me."

"He left us for America when his heart was broken. If I could have prevented it I would have. But I could do nought then, and can do nought now, for all that I would give everything I have to keep him content. He must go his own way and find his own healing. You cannot blame me though, for wanting it to be otherwise, for thinking if only you and he had not wrought this between you. I suffer for his heart once more, and wonder if this time he will be so lucky when he faces a godless enemy."

"You blame me," I said, trying to remain calm, "when you know I fear for him just as you do."

"Perhaps it is idiocy. To wish for things to have happened differently, that is. Certainly I've no right to pass judgment on anyone, him or you. I struggle with it, if I must be honest. Certainly I do not want Rabbie wronged. But I see the heart being ripped out of you as well. There's no comfort for any of us, least of all Coll, who feels he must seek honor for the three of you. Honor may ease his pain, but it will not free him of it. Understanding may ease mine, but it chills me to the core. I am helpless because I cannot wish Rab ill, or you, or soothe Coll, who I hold as close as a son."

I did not know how to respond to Rab's father who was discussing my waywardness so matter-of-factly. Were he to ask if I was guilty of adultery I did not know how I would answer. It was possible he did not ask because he already knew. I said, "Are you sure Coll will not listen to you?"

"I've said all I could. And still it makes no difference. He's decided to go, and go he will, and all I can do is pray for him. And you?" he asked. "Will *you* pray for him?"

"Must you even ask?"

"I suppose not. But your prayers will not be any more fervent than mine." He gazed at me a moment longer before he turned and walked away.

Most nights I lay sleepless in my bed and this particular one was no exception. I conjured up a dream with which I tended to torment myself. Coll would come to my room and we would be as blissful as we'd been before. Sometimes this placated me but at others the dream caused nothing but wretchedness.

I lay in my bed and heard the latch lift. The seconds seemed to creep by. The door opened. I was frozen, daring not to move. I could see through the open bed curtains that a tall figure had entered my room. I sat up with Coll's name on my lips. He was beside my bed and the curtains opened wider as he called, "Keeley?"

It was Rab, who I had not seen for three days. He fell into my bed beside me.

"I've need of comfort," he said. "What a homecoming I've received. My feelings have been sorely wounded. I need my wife who knows how to soothe the hurts of others."

Trying to force some life into my voice, I asked, "What is wrong?"

"I've quarreled with Coll, and he was quite fierce, I tell you. Rarely have I seen him so wild. I must have provoked him more than I meant." He kissed me amid the fumes of liquor.

"What you are talking about?"

"Coll! We were having a dram downstairs, just the two of us, and I told him I ken why he's accepted that commission. You ken, too, do you not? Or you should. He's furious about the glens being cleared. He feels I won and he lost and he cannot abide it. So off he's going, keeping his pride intact."

"Is that what you told him?"

"Aye and rightly so, and he told me to mind my own damned affairs. We argued about the sheep all over again, as if the decision had not even been made. It's obvious to me his misplaced loyalty to the farming folk is causing him to do this honorable thing. Ah well, if he wants no part of the sheep then let him leave. We'll miss him, for a while, but we'll get o'er that. We got along without him once before. We can certainly do it again."

"I hate to think of you quarreling, especially since he'll be away so soon."

"It was good for him. He's been too morose lately, worse than Lachlan. I hope he appreciates my help in venting his feelings. God's Blood, how he flew at me! That's why I've come to you, for I ken there's one person who appreciates me."

As he took hold of me I persisted, "I wish you'd leave him

alone, Rab. He's feeling a great conflict. In many ways he does not want to go at all."

"And has he told you what these are?"

I hesitated. "Are they not obvious? He dislikes leaving Lord Kirthgarran."

"No one is forcing him to."

"But he is troubled by it."

"So he has you as champion. I meant to stir your sympathy for me, not him."

"Sometimes you take your enjoyment at the expense of others."

"I did not come to your bed for criticism. Nor for hearing you think you understand Coll better than I. Your loyalty is admirable, but alarming." He gave me a quick kiss. "Let's abandon this distasteful subject afore I become a jealous husband."

I took his warning and stilled my tongue. I had come close to betraying myself. In time he would go back to his own bed and I would be able to experience my frustration in private. Now I must concentrate on making my mind a blank. This was something becoming easier with practice—but I misjudged the thrust of the memory of lying with Coll.

For the first time since before the harvest celebration, Rab claimed his marital rights. I did not want to compare him with Coll, but his lack of gentleness was a difficult trait to endure. When Rab kissed me there was no answering fervor in me, no delight at all. Indeed, there never had been. I missed Coll and his tenderness. I missed my own passion. And worse, I felt I tarnished the beauty of the night Coll and I had spent together. It was a bitter irony, I thought as Rab did what he liked with me, that I felt unfaithful to a lover who could not ask for faithfulness.

Rab was away with Lachlan one afternoon looking at horses for sale, and I decided to ride alone to Rathdale. I had not seen Mairi since Coll announced his intention to buy his commission. I needed to get away. The castle was stifling, my longing for Coll too intense.

Kenneth saddled Greyfriar for me. "There, Mrs. Rab," he pronounced, leading the garron out into the courtyard. He helped me onto the mounting block and into the saddle though I did not need it; it seemed to give him pleasure to wait upon me. I took the reins from him and with the squeak of leather I was off.

I felt freer than I had for a long time. I knew the way to Rathdale well by now, for I had ridden either alone or with Rab several times since my first visit. It was an unusually fair autumn day and I rode easily, lulled by the motion of my pony. Before long I saw the house in the distance, and Mairi welcomed me inside.

"Such a lovely surprise, lambie," she said as we settled ourselves in the drawing room. "Anne and Andrew have gone to Dunalastair to visit her brother and so it is nice to have company."

She sounded well but did not appear so. Her eyelids seemed heavy and her hair was somewhat unkempt. "Are you ill, Mairi?" I asked.

"Oh no, just dreading Coll's departure. I'm minding those days when he was in the colonies. But I want to stay busy this time. I've been to see one of the cottars, helping to tend one of their sick bairns. I was there most of the night. I think if I make myself useful I'll not brood on my own trouble."

In spite of her unease she made me feel at home. I hoped that when my bairns were grown and I had much of my life to look over, I would be as content and serene as she. It would be something to look forward to, though I knew she had known much insecurity and nonfulfillment in her earlier years. I wondered what she would say if she knew we had something in common: the love of a man we could never call our own.

We were discussing Lord Kirthgarran when something outside the window caught her eye and she leant forward. "Why, I believe we have another visitor," she cried. She rose and went to the glass.

Feeling curious, I joined her. The window looked out over the moor and I glimpsed Coll galloping toward the house.

In a moment he came in, bringing the tang of fresh air with him. His hair was askew and his cheeks were bronzed, and as he kissed his mother who clung to him, his eyes were all for me.

"Come sit!" she urged, so delighted her voice was highly

pitched. "'Tis braw to see you! You do not come often enough. But I'll not scold you. I do not want you leaving in disgust."

He took a chair as he threw his black greatcoat onto the settle. "As if I ever would," he said indulgently.

"I was hoping you'd come soon. December—December seems to be creeping upon us." She was attempting to be unemotional and seemed well in control, much more so than when Coll had first told her about the regiment. "Andrew and Anne are not at home, but Keeley and I were having a fine visit. How grand it is for you to join us!"

He looked upward through his lashes at me. "Our minds must be in tune. Both choosing this afternoon to call upon you, I'm meaning."

"Aye," she said, laughing. "Now will you have some ale, or perhaps some whisky?"

During the next hour or two I thought I was dreaming. Mairi was overjoyed to have us both with her, and she kept the conversation lively and interesting as she directed it amongst us. I could hardly believe I was seated tranquilly, at least outwardly so, only a few paces from Coll who was making a great effort to be sociable in his mother's company. In appearance he seemed quite comfortable talking to her, yet whenever I spoke I could feel his eyes on me, gazing at me with great intensity.

There were a few moments when Coll and I were left alone in the room. Cook had made extra scones, Mairi said, and as she knew Lord Kirthgarran was particularly fond of them, she wished to send some back to Kirthgarran with us. She went to the kitchen and Coll and I watched each other. We said nothing, but his eyes held mine and I felt they were trying to tell me something.

Mairi came back and placed a linen-wrapped package on the table between us. "'Tis the wee things that make him happy," she said thoughtfully.

When the afternoon was nearly at its end I said I had better start for home. The days were shorter now and dusk came early.

"Are you leaving as well, my son?" she asked regretfully of Coll.

"If Keeley does not object we could accompany each other

home."

"Who will I entrust with these scones?" she asked. "You, lambie. Coll might be inclined to have them for himself on the ride back."

Together we took our leave of her and I stood by whilst Mairi placed her hands on either side of Coll's face. I think she was envisioning the day when she would have to bid him farewell for a much longer time.

We found our horses in the stable. In front of the groom Coll was polite, reserved. The animals were soon readied, and without a word passing betwixt us we mounted and began our journey. The sun was low in the sky, dyeing the horizon pink. We rode out of sight of the house. There was not another person within miles, I believed. Without warning, Coll's hand reached over and grasped Greyfriar's rein so both of our horses stopped together. I looked up at him.

"It was not by accident we both came to Rathdale," he said.

"You knew I was there?"

"I caught sight of you leaving Kirthgarran. I asked Kenneth where you were going."

"Did you want to speak to me?"

"I cannot endure this any longer, Keeley."

I could not speak for the lump in my throat.

"I remember that night," he said. "And I see you before me every day. And I'm discovering I cannot do without you. I cannot seem to shut out my feelings any longer. I have tried, for there's no future for us. But you haunt me. Day and night it is the same. There's no help for me. No help save to give in to it, knowing there'll only be more pain in the end. That is, if you are of a like mind."

The lump seemed larger. I nodded and waited for him to continue.

"There's a cottage farther on. The family who lived in it has emigrated. We could speak there, alone. I need to talk to you, *leannan*. I think we both need to talk." He let go of my rein. For a moment he searched my face, and then he was away, with me cantering beside him.

The lime-harled house was on Rathdale lands, sheltered

from the winds in a little hollow with yews and honeysuckles softening its rounded corners. It reminded me of the broken hut where we had once sought shelter from the rain because it was made of the same piled stone and thatch, yet it was in good repair, apparently having only just been vacated.

Half of it was a byre and we led our animals there. Whilst Coll removed the bits from their mouths and hung their bridles on pegs, I went through the partition and surveyed the living quarters. It was a simple home and much of the handcrafted furniture had been left. The heath covering the roof was fresh and weighed down with stones tied with ropes of braided heather. The shelves were bare and the hearth in the center of the floor swept clean, but it was almost possible to believe the family would be coming home again at any moment.

A hand came to lightly lie on my shoulder and I could not control the excitement that sprang through me. I turned and Coll and I held each other fast in a hungry embrace.

What happened next was inevitable. There was a feeling of safety within the house, an aura of time having stopped and nothing else mattering but that we were together. Coll's kiss blazed with the fiery ardor of a man who has too long denied his feelings and needs, and I exulted because my needs were the same. The doubt, the guilt, the vision of hellfire—how quickly they evaporated when he touched me.

The fern-stuffed bolster in the crude box bed was a far cry from the feather beds we had at Kirthgarran, but I gave it not a thought as Coll sat on its edge and held me on his knees. I clasped him to me and kissed the top of his head, and my bones turned to water.

Perhaps he only meant to keep me cradled close to him, but the wants of our bodies intruded. How were we to keep lips from seeking, or hands from delighting in the warmth and smoothness they found beneath their palms?

He said, "My mother spent most of her life wanting someone she could not have. When I was young I watched her face come alive whenever my father came to Kirthgarran, and die again when he left. I vowed I'd never live like that. And I never believed I could betray Rabbie's trust, in aught. But now it seems I'm caught. And so are you. It is a choice, in the end, is it not, for each of us, but it seems as if our hearts have chosen for us. Somehow the pain we will face if we are discovered, and when we part in December, seems a lesser hurt than what we endure now, denying ourselves."

"It is a terrible choice," I said. "But if I may spend even a day with you before you go, my soul will bear the joy of it forever."

"Keeley." He sighed and held me closer. "It is enough to be here with you, to hold you. I would lie with you, but there's more to the tie between us than the blood running hot in our veins. To hold you, to touch you, to feel your breath and hear your voice, it's all I need, in truth."

"I feel that way as well," I told him. "And yet, I do not feel ill-used by you. I never have."

"I would hope you've not..." he began, but his words faltered, and when he moved a little we looked at each other. His mouth came toward mine and I met it eagerly. The passion flashed between us, took hold, drew us into a myopic cosmos that excluded all the world about us. There was nothing for us but each other, and we were lovers once more.

Nestled in peace in the crook of his arm with his greatcoat heaped over us for warmth, gazing at the interior of the cottage painted a deep rose from the sinking, glowing sun, I realized I would not have exchanged the bracken beneath us for a gilt and satin bed in a palace.

In the tranquil aftermath of the storm we shared, I could delude myself. We were a poor farming man and his wife. This was our cottage where I swept the earthen floor and put peats on the fire to cook our humble meals. This was the home to which he came at night and where we raised our bairns. I could picture the kail and gooseberries plucked from the garden, the mended clothing piled on the stool waiting to be mended again. And yet there was happiness in me, indeed, even ecstasy.

I brought my face close to Coll's. My fingers touched his cheek. I said, "I know we must be cautious. And I never thought myself a greedy person. But will we come here again?"

He enclosed my fingers and briefly touched his lips to mine. "Every moment, every hour we can manage it, we must be together, whether 'tis here or some other place. If the De'il is willing, our sins will remain our secret." He closed his eyes and our foreheads came together as he added, "But what price we'll pay for his silence—I have no way of knowing."

Where the stream loups owre the linn,
Below the ben that tow'rs abune,
Where deers and roes in freedom rin,
'Twas there I vow'd to lo'e ye.
Lassie Wi' the Gowden Hair (Trad.)

Chapter Twenty-Nine

A lthough autumn was far-gone and our days marched steadily into the jaws of winter, I became enchanted with a poem I found in William Blake's *Poetical Sketches* that began,

O Autumn, laden with fruit, and stained
With the blood of the grape,

And finished with,

And all the daughters of the year shall dance!
Sing now the lusty song of fruits and flowers.

The images reminded me of our hairst kirn. The next lines from "To Autumn," however, seemed to describe what was happening to me.

> *The narrow bud opens her beauties to*
> *The sun, and love runs in her thrilling veins.*

Love. It was running through me just so. Airig told me I looked different.

"You seem so bonny, Mrs.," she said one day whilst she helped me card washed, Highland wool and fluff the thin fibers in preparation for spinning. I continued to be taken aback by the quality of it, still unused to the flaxen hair of the mountain sheep that did not at all resemble the coats of the Lowland Cheviots. The wool was plucked from the animals rather than shorn.

She contemplated me with curiosity. "Yet it's not that you've done much different with yourself," she went on. A thought seemed to strike her and she leant forward to squeak, "It cannot be, can it? Is it a bairn?"

"No, no," I replied quickly.

"How much fun it would be to have bairns about," she said and moaned. "I truly must attend to my own self, and find a husband."

She began to speak about this man and that, comparing the qualities of all those who had expressed an interest in her. The list was lengthy, for she was a capable and handsome young woman who showed, despite a tendency to chatter on and on, a nature of unmistakable compassion. Her sister Ròs had admirers as well, but the attraction in her case was due more to youth and beauty, for she did not share Airig's maturity. They often teased each other about certain suitors who found them both appealing and could not decide between them.

Her question hung on in my mind. As I pretended to listen to her comparisons, I started counting days. How long had it been since my courses had come upon me? It must have been mid-October, before Samhain. They were a week or two belated by now, but that was not remarkable. Twenty days, thirty, even forty, could pass between them, making them somewhat capricious. I had been experiencing the customary discomforts of their approach for quite a while now—the tightness, the pains—but they had not yet come.

Coll strode into the sitting room. Nonchalantly he handed me a sheaf of papers. "Ewen will be coming later this morning," he said. "Here's a letter Lord Kirthgarran would like copied, and some figures to subtract from the accounts. Did you plan on helping Ewen today?"

"For a while, aye," I answered, putting aside my carders. I ran my eyes over the top page. The paper underneath was folded, with my name scrawled upon it. I pulled it open, shielding it from Airig to read with delight the words Coll had written there.

"The day is oddly warm—for all it is November. Will you come up into the hills with me this afternoon? If so, walk to the bridge, at about half past twelve o'clock."

I lifted my eyes to him. He was watching me mischievously, waiting for a response. "I'll give this to Ewen this morning."

"Good. Then I'm away. Don't be looking for me until later tonight for I'll be helping tar the sheep."

The tarring was an outdated custom, I thought. The cottars here coated their nearly naked sheep with a mixture of tar and butter to help them survive the cold of winter. The tups had already been turned in with the ewes since it was the annual mating time if one wished to have lambs in March. Next year at this time things would be different. The tupping would be on a grand scale, and I doubted there would be any tarring of the Lintons.

After Coll left, copper-haired Airig resumed her extensive discussion about her suitors and I continued my carding, tapping my feet and humming a little song only I could hear.

The appointed time drew near and I slipped away to the burn. Coll was mounted on Dominie's bare back, hidden in a dip of the land between alders. He was watching for me through the leaves and gave a low, down-turning whistle. I ran to the enclosure and he held out a hand.

"Come up. We'll have our steed take us far, far away."

I leapt to a stone and pulled myself onto the horse's rump, afraid of tearing Coll's arm out of its socket whilst he levered me upward. I let my skirts fall where they may, aware of Dominie's heat beneath me as I gripped Coll's waist. He kicked his brogues into the Friesian's sides and the animal lunged out of the wooded depression to begin a gallop up the slope.

We traveled up and down hills, through pasture, trees, and heather. What bliss it was to press my body close to the man before me with no encumbrance of a saddle, to feel the horse's powerful muscles rock us back and forth with every spring. I laid my cheek against Coll's warm back as we flew over the countryside, clothing and hair streaming behind us.

At the top of one hill Coll gave a tug on Dominie's bridle, bringing him to a canter and then a walk. When at last we halted, Coll slid to the frost-bleached grass and reached up to help me glide to earth beside him. Dominie snorted when the bit was taken from his mouth. He inspected the hills beyond, flaring his nostrils when he caught unseen breezes and fragrances, and moved his feathered, ebony fetlocks through the grass and sweet bog-myrtle.

We were on the top of the world, I was sure. The loch below seemed small, a crescent of frosted aquamarine, and Kirthgarran Castle was a toy with which a bairn might play.

The sensation of the horse's hot coat underneath our thighs and the prolonged contact of our bodies as we'd thundered over the hills had not dissipated. I discovered I had my back to a red, flaking trunk of a pine. Coll's lips fell upon mine.

"It was too long of a morning," he said against my mouth. "All I wanted was to be here with you, *leannan*." His hands were on my hips, bunching the amber velvet of my gown and underlying chemise into clusters.

"'*Leannan*.' What does that mean?" I murmured, and inhaled the leather scent of him.

"'Sweetheart.' It means 'sweetheart.' *An toir thu dhomh pòg?*"

"And that?" I asked, motionless as a hand discovered my bare upper leg.

His mouth, lingering beside mine, said quietly, "It's how to ask, 'will you give me a kiss?'"

"I would like to learn that."

"*Tha gaol agam ort.*" His questing fingers traveled upward, smoothed, found their objective. I was more than ready for him. My eyes closed as I lost my breath.

"Tell me," I said at last.

"It means 'I love you.'"

"Hah geul ah-kum orsht," I imitated. He lifted me effortlessly, supporting my thighs. My arms were about his neck, and my legs wrapped round his hips, warm beneath his kilt.

"*Tha gaol agam ort-fhèin*," he went on. "Which is, 'I love you, too.'"

My eyes opened. Before me were his own lucent gray ones. Clear. Sincere. His lips captured mine and he pressed me into the tree without mercy. His voice, when it came once more, was husky, and all hint of banter was gone. "God above, Keeley. Tell me to stop."

"I cannot. I do not want you to stop."

"I am depraved."

"Then so am I."

He lowered me to him and I met him gladly; soon the gentleness between us turned to desperation. I kissed him as greedily as a wolf takes its food. His mouth, the warmth of his shoulders beneath my hands, the feeling of his face against mine—my attention stirred and shifted from each of these sensations and back again. There was the unbearable rising heat between us, the unremitting necessity of movement, the upsurge of the hurt that was not a pain at all but an elation. I craved the taste of him. I existed for the power of his passion, and mine.

Regrettably, when I felt him shudder as well, his arms gripping me fiercely, sadness swept through me. He knew at once that something was amiss and his gaze was full of concern.

I could not bring myself to ruin this day by putting into words my dread of his leaving for India. His commission was not something we often mentioned. I clamped my eyelids down, forcing the pain to leave my breast. I wiped my nose with my petticoat. He held me tightly, pulled us away from the tree, and revolved in a slow, counterclockwise circle.

I kissed his cheek and drew back to look at him, more in control of myself. "It's unlucky to go widdershins." He pressed his face between my neck and shoulder and reversed our direction. "You're making me dizzy," I said into his ear.

"You make me so, all the time."

He put me to my feet and pulled me about in a wide circle until we were both unsteady. We tumbled to a patch of moss beside a pool of water where froth created by a waterfall drifted over brown, spotted stones.

"Are we safe here?" I asked, looking about us, forgetting what we had just foolishly done in the open.

"We can see if anyone approaches," Coll said. "And we've

the perfect hiding place." He gestured toward the ledge behind the waterfall. It seemed to be a wall of bracken and vine standing undisturbed amongst tangles of wild juniper. "One of Kirthgarran's stills is hidden inside a shallow cave there. Not an easy target for a gauger searching these hills. Behind the curtain of leaves is a bin where the barley is malted, and the tub where all begins to ferment. There are racks of wooden casks ready to be filled and a dozen ceramic jars in baskets. They use the water from this tarn and bring barley up from the glen. I often come to check the folk minding the still, and see how the distilling progresses."

"I promise I'll not tell any excisemen."

"I think they gave up looking for all our stills long ago," he returned, smiling.

He went on to tell me about still seizures, the Wash Act, the Scotch Distillery Act, taxes, and duties on whisky, and with a surge of energy pulled me to my feet and brought me behind the falling water into the cave. He pointed out the different parts of the still with its odd, copper sphere bristling with coils and explained how it turned peaty water into alcohol with the help of sprouted barley and a peat fire. The smoke, always a problem for illegal distillers, was cleverly diverted to a hole in the cave wall where it could join the mist from the linn and remain virtually undetected.

The cave was black without torch or lantern and I was gripped by my old fears as I considered the eerie shapes of the coils and the bulbous vessel half-eaten by the darkness.

"There are many who're willing to pay for our whisky," he said proudly. "We make a slight profit from smuggling a few jars here and there. If we could afford the duties, I've often thought that making it would be the way to bring Kirthgarran back from the brink of bankruptcy."

Satisfied with his lesson, Coll was content to forsake the secret distillery and recline against a sun-warmed boulder in the bog myrtle, with me settled between his knees. He tucked my plaid over my shoulders and brought his arms round me, placing his cheek against my hair.

His hand stroked my arm and we became lost in the wonder of each other, the fermenting of whisky—illegal or otherwise—

soon forgotten.

At length he said, with a voice as soft as the rush of the waterfall, "I wonder if you ken that Rabbie will be away from Kirthgarran for a week or so. Since the rents have been taken in, it's time for Lord Kirthgarran to pay debts to some of his own creditors. Usually Rab and I go together, as couriers, making a circle. Lachlan will take my place this time because of the recruiting I must finish."

"When do they leave?"

"In a day or two."

"He's not yet told me."

"He is kind to you, is he not?" Coll asked. "I cannot forget the night Henry Baird was with us, and Rab asked you to play for him."

I could not forget, either, and I tried not to alter my expression. "He does not wish me ill."

"I wanted to run after him when he followed you up the stair. I wanted to knock his head against the wall and take you away. But little could I be doing that. All of us had to pretend it was none of our affair, what Rab did. But Andrew talked to him later. Warned him to take care with you."

I was touched that others had been concerned.

"There's sometimes an expression in your eyes that makes me long to ask you how it is with you and him. Or how it was with you in the past. Sometimes there is anger in your eyes. And sometimes there is sorrow."

I began telling him of my childhood. I painted for him a picture of my mother, Father, dear Jennet the housemaid, sour Mrs. Taggart, and Malcolm. I told him how life had been for me in Gilchrist House before my mother's death and after. I told him of Davy and how my father had given me to Rab to be rid of me.

He listened without a word as I told him all. I felt it all tumbling from me, for once the words started they would not stop. When I began speaking of Davy's desertion and Rab's return to Gilchrist House, Coll's embrace tightened and his face turned toward my ear.

"When I wed Rab, without even a cow for a tocher, my father disowned me," I said flatly. "Though it was he himself who arranged the marriage. And thus, he neatly closed the chapter in his life that had aught to do with my mother. I suppose for him—now—it's as if neither of us ever existed."

Coll said nothing. His thumb stroked my arm, but I wondered if he was aware of it.

"I came here as Rab's wife but it was not what I wished. Those first few days were the most difficult. I could not stop wondering why Davy had betrayed me."

"And now?"

"I think of him not at all. What I felt for him was nought like this."

He was silent again, and his fingers stilled.

"I was a child for too long," I continued. "I knew little of life. I was lonely, and Davy was so unlike any man I knew that he did not frighten me. And then he was gone, and I was married to Rab. My life was turned upside down but..." I found the words to say, "But even then, even in those first days, there was you."

"I felt it, just as you."

"If you'd been the one to pass by Gilchrist House that day and fall from your horse..." He touched my lips, stopping me. I could not guess what he was thinking. I said, "How much of our lives is governed by Fate, do you think?"

"Perhaps there's no such thing as Fate. What we regard as such is only the behavior of others which, known or unknown, affects our lives."

"You've affected mine. I will never be the same."

"I do not deserve the happiness you've given me," he said suddenly. "It's selfish I've been. I've broken God's law. Cuckolded my friend and turned you into a disloyal wife."

"We've both been selfish," I replied. "The guilt I feel sometimes is overwhelming, and I ken you feel it, too. But mind that Rab is not without sin himself."

"It does me little good to know I'll bring you pain, in the end." Taking a different tack, he continued, "You must be honest with me about Rab. He certainly does not mean to be cruel. When I leave, when this, between you and me, is over, I need to believe he's going to be a good, loving husband to you." He paused. "He does care for you."

"Is Isabel for sport, then?"

He made a sound deep in his throat. "Isabel. He seduced her years ago. Or perhaps it was the other way round."

I sought his eyes, startled. "Years ago?"

"Their involvement is by no means a new one."

"Then he..."

"Isabel has been Rab's mistress now and again since I came back from the colonies. I think they became lovers whilst I was there."

Rab had known her, had loved her, before that day he had come into Gilchrist House as an invalid. Astonishment washed over me. "I thought he turned to her because I could not please him."

"Is that what you told yourself?"

"I believed it was my fault."

"No," he assured me. "Do not torture yourself so. They've been lovers for years."

I felt myself go cold all over. Rab had lied to me. He could not have loved me as he'd claimed, not at first, and not now. And I had punished myself with self-hatred, assuming I had been the cause of the distance between us. My lips began to move, and from somewhere came my voice. "Why did he marry me? Is it because she's not suitable for marriage? Did he fall in love with me as he claimed?"

"He wants you both, it seems."

"Perhaps it was not me he wanted at all. Perhaps it was the connection to my father. My father and his sheep, and the mill, and the money it all represented. That was what he wanted. It was not me, after all. It was never me." My gaze swept over the waterfall...the stones...the tarn...whilst I tried to put fragments of sudden insight into words. He could not have foreseen my father disowning me. My disinheritance must have been as much a shock for him as it had been for me. To be accepted as my husband, and then to have his schemes for raising sheep—and perhaps his hopes for renting Kirthgarran lands to my father— thrown to the winds at the door of the abbey, must have crushed him. "My father wants nought to do with either of us."

"Rab did not suspect?"

"I've been so blind."

"You cannot fault yourself for believing what you were told.

Lachlan and Andrew and I will force Rabbie to give up Isabel."

Toward what end? I wanted to ask. I would stay with Rab as long as Lord Kirthgarran lived, but I did not care if my husband kept a mistress or not. When the earl was buried on the island in the middle of the loch I would be taking my leave of Rab, and Isabel could have him every night if she wished.

"You and I tend to use Rab's infidelity as an excuse," Coll went on. "And the meetings between the two of them as opportunities for our own. But it's not the way to live one's life. I'm determined for it all to come right. When I'm gone and your life must return to decency, the others will remind him of his responsibilities toward you and watch he does not mistreat you. As much as I love Rab, if I thought he was adding to your misery—I swear, Christ defend me—I'd have his head on the end of a pike."

He meant what he said. I could see it in his eyes.

He fell quiet and raised his head to gaze about us. "There's a chill in the air, despite the warmth of the day. And sitting still like this is something best done on a July afternoon."

I was chilled to my marrow, but not because of the weather. He whistled to Dominie and we both caught sight of his black head and pricked ears. Our ride back down to the bottom of the hills was a solemn affair, and our parting left us both with heavy hearts.

Thou'rt the music of my heart
Harp of joy, oh cruit mo chridh.

Eriskay Love Lilt (Trad.)

Chapter Thirty

Rab and Lachlan prepared to carry payments of debts to Lord Kirthgarran's peers at Blair Atholl and other estates. "It will be our turn to weep," Rab said, giving me a bitter grin. I regarded him with a mixture of emotions I dared not examine closely, knowing now the origin and depth of his dalliance with Isabel.

The weather turned colder than it had been, causing the freakish warmth to fade into the past. Swathed in coats and plaids, the two men mounted garrons and I watched them canter along the lochside until their forms were no longer visible. I was ashamed of my relief.

Mairi came to Kirthgarran that morning to assess the

condition of the stores in the kitchen's larders, to confer with Airig about the amount of linen in the aumrie, and to decide how much spinning needed to be done. She did not look well. Her eyes were dark with lack of sleep and it was not easy for her to smile.

Airig confided in me her concern. "She's counting the days until Coll must go to his regiment. But she's spending a great deal of time amongst the folk, bringing them food and remedies, wearing herself thin with the toil of it. All in an attempt to forget."

I wanted to comfort Mairi, just as she had soothed me so often in the past months, but I could find no words to use. I had no such comfort even for myself.

Coll tended to his obligation to seek enlistees for his battalion by visiting desperate farmers, raw lads, and ex-soldiers in the glen who might welcome the three-guinea bounty, and I, in a fever to stay occupied, braved the nervous glances Grizel and her maids threw at me and cooked. Cauldrons of Grizel's barley ale simmered in the background whilst I baked Naples biscuits and stirred almond pudding. I filled puff pastry cases with a cream rich with sack, butter, sugar, and nutmeg.

All at once a wild shrieking from a chorus of voices erupted. MacNeil's wee grandson, Iain, stood in the middle of the kitchen. The women screamed at him, and Grizel flapped her apron and brandished a heavy spoon. I crossed to the lad, cutting through the maelstrom about us, and in English asked, "What is it, Iain? What is wrong?"

"'Tis a puddock," he answered in the same language. He glanced at his hands. Sure enough, cradled in his fingers was a huge, still frog.

"Is it alive?" I asked, stooping beside him.

"I think it is dead."

"It's such a big one," I observed, reaching out a finger and touching the animal's bumpy back. It was as stiff and cold as ice. A whisper of grief touched me. "Where did you find it?"

"Away with that thing now!" Grizel screeched.

"By the loch," the lad said. "I thought it was a stone, so still and so hard was it. I wanted to show you."

I glanced at the distraught women surrounding us. I knew

well why they shouted at Iain. "It is an oddity. How thoughtful of you to think of showing me! But now, should we bury it, do you think?"

He nodded solemnly, and we carried it outside to the lee of a large rock near the water where there was soft sand. I scooped out a hollow with a sharp stone. He laid the puddock into it; both of us covered it with sand.

"Will it grow?" he asked in wonder.

I had to struggle not to smile, and reminded him it was the custom to bury the dead, and we must mark the site with a stone so we would not forget the fine animal and the important life it had once led. Unfortunately there seemed to be no difference between our makeshift grave marker and the other stones on the shore. I told Iain a twig placed on the spot might be more noticeable. The lad ran to one of the rowan trees and came back bearing a small stick. He inserted it into the sandy mound.

"Rowan is magical," he told me. "'Twill keep evil away."

I could picture my father sneering at the marker, for an imaginative mind might perceive it as a cross. In his view it would be an unbefitting, superstitious mixture of pagan and black papist symbolism. "Heresy. And all for a beast," he would have scoffed. My mother and I had often buried wee animals, unbeknownst to him, sometimes using a stick for a marker and sometimes a stone. I minded the day we buried the rook Father had thrown across the garden. A great sigh escaped me and Iain peered at me in confusion.

"I was just thinking about something else," I said. "But it is true. The rowan will keep all sorts of evils away. You're quite clever in choosing it. Iain, do you ken why the women were screaming in the kitchen?"

"They do not like puddocks."

"Nay, it is more than that. People say that if a puddock comes into your house, it means someone will soon die."

He was struck dumb.

"None of the women wanted that to happen, so they were all after you to take it back out."

"Is someone going to die?" he asked with barely a voice.

"I do not think so. The puddock was not alive, was it? I think that makes a difference."

He was thoughtful. "We should put a stick on MacDiarmid's grave." He pointed toward the ancient arch of stone on the bank. "Captain Fergusson buried him by the loch. MacDiarmid loved to play by the water. He put him there so he could be near it always."

The ruin stood tall and dark against the sky, and in my mind's eye I could picture the collie prancing in the grass about the stones and splashing in the loch. "Aye, we must get another twig of rowan," I said.

He dashed back to the trees. By the ragged wall he showed me where he remembered Coll's dog had been interred, and I encouraged him to place the stick. Iain said solemnly, "Mam stitched a piece of rowan into the edge of my sark."

"Into your *sark*? But why?"

He was abashed for a second, but answered, "My mam thinks you're a wraith."

"Whatever do you mean?"

"She says you're either a specter, or a wraith, but she thinks you're probably a wraith." His face grew grim. "And that means you're going to die. I do not want you to die, Mrs. Rab. I hope you do not. I hope 'twill not be I who causes you to die because I brought the puddock into the castle."

I was so startled I did not know how to respond. Were the folk seeing my wraith? If one's second spirit was seen, it indeed meant that death would find that person—within a year.

"Iain," I said, taking his wee hands in mine. "Who else believes I am a wraith? Am I seen as a wraith always, or only sometimes?"

"Mam, and Da, and my auntie, and my grandda, and my kinsmen. The lot of them. They say you're a wraith whene'er they see you."

I was a vision of death about to occur.

"*Are* you one?" he asked. "I've ne'er seen one afore you. I've ne'er seen a specter either."

"I am not a specter or a wraith," I told him. "I'm very much alive. And I'm not going to die. At least not until I'm a very auld woman sitting in my chair with a cat and a length of knitting so long that it curls about my feet!" I squeezed his hands but was afraid of frightening him. "Does your family say I'm someone to be feart? That I bring danger to Kirthgarran?"

He shrugged. "They think you're a wraith and Mam put twigs in my clothes, but they ken I talk to you and they say 'tis fine since they trust the rowan to do its work." He regarded me sadly, knowing he was upsetting me. "If you're a wraith, Mrs., you're a very friendly one. I do not fear you."

I told myself I was not a ghost. I was not a wraith, a spiritual twin of myself, teetering on the edge of non-existence. I must not take the words of a bairn to heart.

But he was repeating what his elders said, and even though Rab had often warned me to ignore the mystical and irrational beliefs of the folk, I had grown up believing the very same tales and legends myself. Where and when did one separate truth from fiction? Did I believe there were Harbingers of Death? Could I be one of them—destined for an early death myself?

Iain had lost interest in the subject and was twitching at my side. He said, "I'm going to look for more puddocks. Lest there be more in need."

"Hopefully they'll be well-sheltered," I said absently.

He smiled and ran along the edge of the water, the geese waddling after him in a noisy gaggle.

After supper it started to snow. The flakes drifted to earth, small and insignificant at first, but soon the ground was coated and the air was filled with silent, falling clusters. I waited in my chamber until midnight and slipped stealthily to Coll's as we had prearranged. Whilst the bitter winds blew without, we lay in front of the fire on sheepskins and sipped mulled wine, marveling at the intricate ferns and stars painted in frost upon his windowpanes.

Although I attempted to be carefree, Iain's words from that morning still ran through my mind and it was not long before Coll noticed my distraction. I told him what the lad had said and finished, "What does it mean, Coll? Have you heard them calling me those things?"

He leveled a look at me and did not respond for many seconds. "I've heard it, aye."

"Do they say why they believe I am dead—or about to be?"

He shook his head and pulled me closer.

I said, "The talk of death and wraiths appearing, when they only have to do with me, makes me wonder if they see something I cannot see, if they ken something I do not ken."

"They may blame you for the fire in the castle, and the ox trampling the men. But it is in the nature of folk to look for supernatural goings-on. They mean nought by it. We're all convinced of that now. It will pass. You're not worried about your safety, are you?"

"No, but it is disconcerting. More than that. I feel I do not belong here. That I never will."

"'Tis difficult now, but you must not listen to the talk," he cautioned. "I've no doubt it will all simply wear away, like stones tumbled to pebbles in the burn."

I thought briefly of his unwillingness to address the rumors that persisted about Leslie Hamilton and realized his advice must be based on his own outlook. "It is not only that," I went on. "There are so many mysterious things. One of the silver cups is missing. I've asked about it but no one seems to ken where it's gone. Nor do they seem worried."

He sipped his wine. "There's no mystery. The earl decided to sell it. Lachlan took it with him when he drove the kylies to the tryst."

I watched his eyes. For just a second they left me and I wondered, stunned, if he was lying to me. "Does Mairi know?"

"I do not think so, and we should not tell her. Not yet. The earl wanted it done in secret. He's embarrassed because of the lack of ready money to pay his debtors."

"I thought he was done selling the silver…"

"Apparently he felt the need."

I wanted to believe him. Selling another silver item was not implausible. If Rab had not taken it away from me whilst I'd been examining it I would have accepted Coll's explanation without question. But Coll's demeanor was odd, constrained. I sat watching him, thinking, attempting to find the right words to use.

"Do not let it trouble you," he urged. He put down his glass and removed my slippers. "With the sheep coming, such a thing will surely not happen again, as much as I hate to admit it." He rubbed my feet between his hands. "I heard you playing your clarsach for the earl tonight."

I let it go, unwilling to tamper with the closeness between us. I had been overly imaginative. He had no reason to lie to me, about anything.

I told him about a song I was in the process of composing. The music was meant to convey our afternoon by the waterfall, the fragrance of the pines that had surrounded us, and the blue hills that had risen on all sides. I promised I would play my clarsach for him when it was finished.

"I will memorize this song," he prophesied. "And when I'm far away on the subcontinent its recollection will bring me back to that day."

My arms went round him in dismay and he picked me up, carried me to the bed. He drew my gown away. The fine, Indian cotton sheets felt cold after sitting so close to the flames, and I shivered as I dove underneath and pulled up a coverlet. Coll unbuttoned his breeks and shed them and his sark. When we had grasped each other for a few moments in an attempt to regain our warmth, his fingers resumed their quest for things to remove and my chemise was the next victim.

I ran my hands over his skin and accidentally touched the wide groove on his back. Visualizing the scar, I said, "You were wounded. In the colonies?"

"The Siege of Charleston. I was unhorsed and met with a bayonet, but I was fortunate, and the chirurgeon was very good."

I felt the blood leave my head. "And this," I went on, my finger hovering under his eye.

"Near Guildford Courthouse. Musket fire that only grazed me."

"It's lucky you were not blinded."

His hands smoothed my body and ran down to my legs. With his touch came the tingle, the surge of excitement, the beginning of the pleasures to which I was addicted. Evidently the same was happening to him. "I did have some luck, did I not?" he said.

"You must have been overjoyed to come home to Scotland." I paused. "Or were you? I ken very little of what it was like for you. Were you simply told one day that it was over, and that you were being sent home?"

He kissed my cheeks, my lips, my ears. "There was a siege at Yorktown. We were outnumbered and it became clear as the days passed that no relief was coming." His lips moved to my throat. "We had little food and the stores of artillery ammunition were running out. Cornwallis surrendered and we were taken prisoner. The Articles of Capitulation were signed. We marched to the field where we were expected, marched between the lines of American and French troops, our colors encased, with the band playing. Each regiment in turn marched forth and threw down its arms."

"It must have been humiliating."

He pulled hair away from my eyes and said pensively, "It did not end there. We were sent to prisoner-of-war camps whilst we waited for the war to end. Another two years. My battalion was sent to Pennsylvania. A great many men died from fevers or the pox. I'd a fever myself for a while. Nearly died, I did, but I mind little of it."

It might happen again, I knew. There was no telling where his soldiering in India would take him.

"In the stockade I was allowed to visit my men, and lived within the pickets in a wee house with a servant, but 'twas not freedom. It was never freedom. Not until King George signed the provisional articles of peace were we free. We were sent to Charleston and sailed to Scotland, and Perth, and the 71st was disbanded."

A long touch of my hand brought him back to the present. I held his hands in mine and marveled at their thinness; they were the hands of my lover, hands that had caressed me with gentle care, but they were also the hands of a soldier who had killed when necessary despite a battalion of troops at his disposal. Too clearly I could envision those hands gripping a sword and a musket once more. They would do so in a matter of weeks.

I rolled on top of him. I would keep him here, trapped, and never let him leave. It was a fantasy in which I indulged myself as we fiercely came together. I flattened my palms on his chest. His hands seized my hips. Before long we were overcome by our needs and soared to the heights, struck mute and helpless and filled with the indisputable conviction that we were one.

Holding back the tears that threatened to surface after these emotional, physical unions was becoming more difficult these days, and at that moment, in his rumpled bed with the fire blazing and the snow falling quietly without, it seemed impossible. As he held me, our passion depleted, I pressed my knuckles hard into my eye sockets and willed the vile water to stay where it was. Happily, I seemed to be successful and Coll did not notice my struggle. His dark mood had melted away with our coupling and a hand stroked my shoulder, tangled itself in my hair. A crack from the fire announced the presence of a bead of sap in the burning log, and a stray draught carried the scent of wood smoke leisurely across the room.

"Let me show you something," he said. He crept out from the covers and rummaged about in a dresser drawer. He lit a candle from the fire, tossed more logs onto the coals, and climbed back into bed with me. He handed me a pistol. "This is one of a pair, made in Doune. They were given to me by Lord Kirthgarran before I left last time."

"So they were his?" I asked, knowing this was the pistol, or its twin, that he had used to end MacDiarmid's suffering. I slid my fingers along the smooth, cold muzzle.

"Aye. He should have given them to Walter or Hugh, but the earl did not suspect his sons would soon be joining the army themselves. He treasured these and I was touched he offered them to me. I vowed someday I'd bring them back, together and unharmed. And I did." Into my hand he placed a piece of folded leather so worn it was as soft as butter. I looked at him in question, but he urged me to take it. "It's all I have left of those days. That, and the pistols."

I unfolded it cautiously. Inside was a tarnished circle of brass that filled the palm of my hand. It appeared to have been cast, since there were molded words and designs upon it, and I turned it so I might better read it in the candlelight. A thistle occupied the center and was surrounded by the Latin motto *"Nemo me Impune Lacesset,"* meaning, I knew, "Touch me not without impunity." The cross of St. Andrew went from one edge of the circle to the other, with a crown at the top and the number "71" in a circle at the bottom. All round the circumference were words in Latin and I said them to myself: *"Quicquid Aut Facere Aut Pati."*

"My bonnet badge," he explained. "We each had one, with a black cockade. I saved it because of those words. They translate, 'Whatever is to be performed or endured.' It's what was expected of us. It was what I came to expect of myself. We do what we must. It is not just a matter of honor. It is how we stay alive."

I was moved by his belief in these words. I traced the edge of the badge and wondered how many skirmishes, how many battles, it had seen; how many days Coll must have worn it and forced those words to soothe him. "You did not stop believing in those words when the war was over, did you," I asked.

He took the badge from me. "They've been carrying me ever since I first read them. When we were released after the imprisonment and the regiment was brought home, I thought I could go on with my life as if it had not been changed. For a time I had odd dreams. I did not have to think of fighting anymore, of obtaining supplies, caring for my men, carrying out battle plans. I wanted to indulge myself. I wanted to make the past disappear. I've always been fascinated by painting and music and books. I'd faced death and beat it and I wanted to celebrate by learning more about them and about science and architecture. I heard about Frenchmen sailing high in the air in baskets suspended from huge bags filled with hot air from smoking fires just beneath, and thought, 'Would it not be aye grand to invent things such as that, or discover new scientific explanations for things, or to design buildings that would cause folk to stand in awe?' I was dispirited, for we'd lost a war and the shame went deep, but I was glad to be home, glad to be alive. I wanted to go off in all sorts of wild directions."

He turned the badge from side to side, letting the firelight catch on the embossed design. "I came home to Kirthgarran, an ex-soldier on half-pay, with a dozen plans in my head. I was ill, and a sight to look at with even my own mother not knowing me. But I had ideas. I soon discovered, though, that Walter and Hugh had died in Gibraltar, and Lord Kirthgarran was an invalid, and there was a famine all over the countryside. And being here brought back the loss of Leslie all over again. 'Twas then I saw my dreams were just that. Dreams. There was work to be done, a past to forget. And Kirthgarran had to be saved. My brothers and Sandy's sons had pledged themselves to it and to one another, and I joined them. I'd been taught how to survive. The words showed me how. And so, I kept on, surviving."

"But you were not happy."

He wrapped the bonnet badge in its leather scrap and put it beside the candle. He turned to me and contemplated me intently. "You have reminded me how it is to be so."

I said, "I think that one appreciates happiness more, having known despair in his or her life."

"And one appreciates it more, knowing it cannot last."

His eyes, holding mine, saw what his words had done. He cringed. "And by speaking of its ending I've started to rip it away. Come." He pinched the candle flame and gathered me close. "It's a fool I am, reminding us. Do you not think that happiness is the brightest when one closes the mind to the past and the future, and tends only to the present?"

I agreed of course. But the damage was already done, and even his tender ministrations could not obliterate my realization: if it were true that joy was more profound when judged against a measure of life's sorrows, then the opposite must also be true. The currents of despair would be very deep for one who had soared blissfully at the top of the sun-filled sky.

My thoughts they deceive me,
Reflection it grieves me…

                              The Blackbird (Trad.)

Chapter Thirty-One

A survey of the countryside from the main entrance the next morning provided me with a vision of a world containing only a few colors. Snow coated the ground and every twig of the leafless trees. The dark green featherings of the evergreens were frosted and in the distance the treetops were trapped by a haze of frozen mist. The pale sky, purged of its burden, was mirrored in the blue-green loch.

"It is the Otherworld," I murmured. "Untouched. Perfect."

I was surprised that, imbued with the tranquility of the fallen snow, I should have trouble swallowing my breakfast. Grace was recited, and the others spooned porridge, cut slabs of Cheshire cheese, and balanced cogs on their knees. I found I could eat little for the squeezing sensation in my stomach.

Coll's eyes caught mine across the table. "Not hungry?"

I shrugged, stirring my oats and cream.

"Take care, Keeley. Respect the porridge and mind the slug jelly."

Sandy cried out in dismay, remembering the dreadful fare, and Grizel's voice rose in protest as she defended her decision to stave off hunger at the castle. The others were too young to recall that particularly lean year, and Grizel and Coll took turns describing the inventive cuisine. Their memories heralded the end of any breakfast for me.

Jewels glistened in the snow when the sun peered out. The trees wore their coverlets of white for a time, but the vulnerable counterpanes melted and sloughed to the ground in clumps as the air grew warmer. I watched from a window as Coll sought the unbroken path beside the burn. His mission was to curry favor with a man who had previously shown a mind to list in the regiment, and to consult with a farmer who claimed one of his cows had tail-ill. This last matter reminded me that in the spring all of the earl's cattle would be sold. There would be a final drove to the trysts before the sheep came.

We talked about it later that afternoon when we sat in the drawing room and Coll warmed his wet feet by the fireside. I intended to give stockings to Iain to wear during the winter and had just started knitting the first one. Coll grumbled about his soaked, drookit brogues, but I thought he was glad of the excuse to sit cozily for a while and put his responsibilities aside. Neither of us said the words, but we both knew Rab and Lachlan would be gone for only one or two more days.

"How dowie it will be," he declared, "when the kylies are taken away and smoke rises no more from the cottages in the glens."

"It must seem that all the years of planning, and breeding the cattle, and working alongside the cottars have come to a meaningless end."

"'Twas not an end like this I expected."

"I wonder if there could not be some compromise made. Part of the land given over to sheep, and the rest left to stay as it is, farmed and used as pasture for the cows."

"It could probably be done, with some forethought. But Lord Kirthgarran has not the enthusiasm for such a plan or even the desire to leave it to us to devise. Quickly and thoroughly he wants it done, with finality."

We spoke in a desultory manner for a time whilst my knitting wires clicked and the logs hissed. Life could be like this always, I mused, with the two of us speaking of estate affairs, the light beginning to fade outside as the day drew to an early close, and a fire burning brightly before us, warming our toes.

Sandy disturbed the quiet scene when he came into the drawing room but he was not alone. At his side was the red-haired Murray Campbell.

"The De'il take it all, sir," Coll cried, rising from his chair. He shook the hand of the newcomer.

Murray nodded, smiling widely. "Captain."

"What brings you to Kirthgarran? I was not expecting the pleasure!"

Lieutenant Campbell was dressed in his uniform and I stood, disturbed by the sight of it. When he removed his greatcoat he revealed a coatee of scarlet with white facings. A belted kilt and plaid secured at his shoulder was of a dark, almost black, tartan. Impressions of gold lace, red-and-white diamond-patterned hose, and crossed belts on his chest struck me all at once.

"I'm a galloper," the man said amiably. "Things are wild in Argyll and Edinburgh. Wait 'til you hear! There's no time for travel back and forth for officers raising their companies, so I'm one of those who carry messages and try to do, in a matter of weeks, what should take months. I have news, Coll, and orders for you, as well as your uniform. To the tailor in Glasgow you may have to pay a visit, but we followed my measurements, which are similar to yours, and I'm thinking you'll have enough wool to cover your backside."

Coll laughed and put an arm across Murray Campbell's shoulders. "You do remember Keeley Fergusson."

"Aye," said the soldier, bowing. He reached for my hand and kissed it with wind-whipped lips as crimson as his cheeks. "I mind you well." His eyes, a deep, dark blue, were warm and friendly and I attempted to overcome my awe at his appearance.

I curtseyed and said, "It is pleasant to see you once more."

Coll invited him to relax and he collapsed into a chair, tugging at the high neck of his coat. At the sideboard Coll splashed water and whisky into tumblers for us all. Sandy laid the newcomer's greatcoat and bonnet aside and sat with us in order to hear the news.

Murray groaned in pure delight as the drink went down his throat, and he leant back in his chair, closing his eyes. "I've been living on a horse for weeks," he told us. "How, on God's earth, a regiment is to be brought together in three months is a bluidy mystery to me, pardon me, marm."

"Before you begin your tales, will you have some victuals? You must be famished as well as thirsty," Coll said.

"I cannot mind when last I ate."

I took the opportunity to escape and rose. "Let me get you something," I said. I was not eager to hear the details of raising the regiment. The sight of the uniform alone was turning me cold. I retreated to the kitchen where I made no haste in putting together a tray of greasy goose meat and barley bread. The flesh of the bird caused my throat to constrict, a reminder of this morning's discomforts. I wondered if I was becoming ill. Grizel poured hot broth into a glazed dish and added it to the tray as well as a serving of crokain I had made. Even the spun sugar concoction drizzled on top of cream and preserved apples made my stomach turn.

"Feeling oorit, are you?" she asked, handing me a spoon.

"It might be a cold coming. A fever, perhaps."

She put the back of her hand to my forehead and shook her head. "I'll make you a hot toddy."

I declined, not wanting even that. Grasping the tray, I returned upstairs to present the lieutenant with his meal. There was no excuse then. Murray Campbell had begun his stories of the 74th and I had to listen.

"Word's been sent to Sir Archibald," Murray said, "but Inverneill does not yet know he's been given a colonelcy. It's rare that one is given so, and I expect he'll be much pleased. But as Governor and Commander-in-Chief at Madras, he'll not know of it until shortly before we ourselves arrive in India. It takes five to six months, they say, to make the trip round the Cape and on up to the subcontinent, whether it's a ship carrying letters, or troops."

"Seven weeks was hell," Coll mused. "What will half a year of it be like?"

The other shook his head as he chewed a sliver of meat. "I do not dwell on the thought. There's too much in my mind to thrash over. The King appointed the Lieutenant-Colonel, Gordon Forbes, from Aberdeenshire, as you ken. I came to you as quickly as I could at the end of last month because he began directly selecting officers, and you were one of those he hoped for. Apparently he was told to meet Inverneill's brothers, James and Duncan, in Edinburgh." He shifted in his seat. "But when he arrived he discovered from the Campbells' man they were making appointments to commissions as well! Some commissions were offered when they'd already been filled! It was, of course, James and Duncan who received the warrant for the raising of the 74th, if you mind, for after all, they are Sir Archibald's agents in this country. Your commission is safe, I must assure you, but there's been meikle confusion and everyone involved is in turmoil. When Sir Archibald's brothers arrived in Edinburgh they were able to mend matters somewhat but not after strong words were exchanged."

"Who was in the right and who was in the wrong?" asked Sandy.

"It's troublesome. Gordon Forbes sought the consent of the Lord Advocate, Islay Campbell of Succoth, for his commission appointments. Succoth represents the Duke of Argyll and 'tis necessary to have his consent, surely, for any appointments made in Campbell territory. And yet the order for the raising was endorsed to Sir Archibald, and received by James and Duncan Campbell, as agents for Inverneill. The wording of it implied that in the absence of the Colonel the appointment of officers should include a captain, two lieutenants, and two ensigns. The remainder would be appointed by the Lieutenant-Colonel in agreement with the War Office." He took a sip of whisky. "It would seem, on the surface then, that the brothers were right in appointing officers. But they became over-eager. The result is that the Lord Advocate is fuming, and the War Office has sent non-committal replies to any appeals that have been made. In any case, all the commissions have been filled and Forbes is on his way back to Argyll, barely speaking to the Campbell brothers. He wants the regiment moved to Glasgow as soon as possible. James and Duncan remain in Edinburgh still, writing letters of apology to those who cannot have the commissions promised them. And letters of complaint, I imagine, to the Duke and others."

As Murray talked on and on I found myself seizing my thumbs hard in my fingers. Coll and his recruits would be marching to Argyll and joining the soldiers billeted there; all would be reviewed on Christmas Day. Shortly afterward, the armed and uniformed regiment would move south to Glasgow, possibly taking in more recruits along the way, but the final destination was England where the transports would be boarded and readied for the voyage to India.

I realized, as I listened to the plans, that I had been gravely mistaken in my figuring. Coll needed to bring in his recruits by the 25th after walking with them from here to Argyll. He would be leaving a week before Christmas. My fingers, clamped into fists as they were, still allowed me to count, and I stared at them in my lap as I subtracted days. There were twenty-three until Coll would go. How could I have been stupid enough to disregard the days of travel? My enlightenment was painful and I found I could not join in any of the polite banter ensuing amongst the men round me.

Suppertime arrived and our guest was treated to a fine table. I managed potatoes and cabbage and little else. The men and I joined Lord Kirthgarran in his bedchamber afterward, where we sat round the fire as we had on previous evenings, but on this night we had Murray to divert us. He had removed his coat much earlier and sat in his waistcoat and kilt, his stock loose about his neck, a tumbler clasped in his hand. His stories turned from informational discourses about the regiment to gleanings about India and conjectures about the life he and Coll would find on the post there. He shared what he had heard from other soldiers who had returned from the hot, strange country.

"Hindus begin spring in February or March," he said, "and have a fertility festival called Holi, when there's dancing and colorful processions of all kinds. For a while the air is as cool as it is here, and every tree bears flowers, flowers of every hue. But in May and June the heat builds like fire in an oven. Brain-fever birds and ones called barbets screech from trees without end. Dust covers everything, and the earth becomes parched, and all growing things wilt. Fierce, hot winds scour the land. Folk wait impatiently for the monsoon to start. And when it comes it's aye welcome, for the earth steams like a black pudding, and the birds sing and the insects buzz, and people dance in the water as it pours down."

He shook his head as he imagined it with the rest of us. "The only drawback, I'm told, is that the rains are unending and continue for three months. Mosquitoes, moths, and green flies drive people mad. In October, when the rain does dwindle away, the Hindus celebrate something called the Durga Puja. They have a Mother Goddess, named Kali, or Durga. They tell me she's a fearsome creature, for the carved figures of her are black, with necklaces of skulls and tongues that stick out."

He listed the illnesses that abounded, diseases for which there were few known causes or cures. Typhoid, cholera, consumption, smallpox, and scurvy were common in the British Isles as well, but Murray had learnt there were additional ailments that took the lives of many, including dysentery—the bluidy flux—and an assortment of fevers, some deadly from a single strike, and others intermittent, recurring from time to time until the victim finally surrendered. There were animals, too: man-eating tigers, and snakes.

I listened, unable to move.

Murray's topic soon changed to politics, and the reason the 74th was being raised at all. In the state of Mysore, a powerful part of India, a Muslim soldier named Hyder Ali had overthrown the Hindu dynasty many years ago. He and his son, Tipu Sultan, were both greedy and energetic rulers who continually sought to enlarge their holdings. There had already been two Mysore wars. The French were deeply involved, and whenever the French had interests in trade and commerce in an area so must the British, no matter in what part of globe it occurred.

"The troubles bubbling at the moment now include the Dutch, for France and Holland have just agreed to a treaty whereby the French are going to garrison the Dutch holdings in India," he said. "It means an increase in their power there. Tipu

Sahib intends to use this development and has sent emissaries to King Louis to invite the French into an alliance. In the past, any mischief from Tipu, along with his French partners, has caused critical interruptions in trade. It seems the French in Mysore are going to increase. And their renewed kinship with the fanatic Muslim bodes ill." He took a long drink. "As soon as the East India Company realized what was happening it jumped to protect its interests, as well as its very presence in the country, and called for reinforcements for His Majesty's troops at Madras. But there were very few available. 'Tis why new regiments of the line are being raised."

I became the first to offer regrets and say good night. I kissed Lord Kirthgarran's white and solemn cheek and left, but Coll called after me and thrust his head out through the door.

"I think Murray is ready to collapse," he whispered. "It's safe, I think, for you to wait in my bed if you want. Rab and Lachlan do not travel in darkness, so it's not tonight they'll be home."

I agreed and he disappeared.

Twenty-three days, my mind recited.

I locked myself in Coll's room and lay in his bed, unable to sleep. Twenty-three days. How would we ever say goodbye? How would it be, with him gone and life resumed with Rab? Prickles began spreading from the top of my head to my stomach and then to my feet. Twenty-three days and I would no longer see Coll nor hear his voice; never feel again the solidity of his body nor his arms crushing me to him. I turned my face into his white sheets, pulling them over my head. Had I been a lunatic, I wondered, to let myself care for him so deeply that the thought of losing him threatened to stifle the very breath from my body?

I fell into a distressed sleep at last and dreamt incoherent fragments. A man was lashed to halberds and flogged, whilst tigers and strange birds screamed from the trees surrounding him. I could not tell if the splotches of red were flowers or sprays of the man's blood or scalps hung in the branches. Men, coughing and dying in a barracks hospital, were attended by black goddesses with necklaces of skulls hung about their necks. Coll stood on a rock, waving to me, and was bayoneted from behind.

I awoke, damp with perspiration. I turned over on my side and bundled the bedclothes into my arms, hugging them.

And what if I were with child? Many days had gone by. The elation I had once felt at the prospect seemed to dim. If I had indeed conceived a child, when would I know for certain? The ultimate question was, of course, who was its father?

Sleep came again, but it was hard won. This time I was awakened by the sound of Coll's key in the lock. He was soon hovering over me, rubbing my nose with his and calling, "Keeley. Keeley, my own." My arms came up and encircled his neck. He laughed and fell on top of me, and had to steady himself with his elbows. "Oh, you're so sleepy and so warm."

"Come in with me," I muttered, pulling on his shoulders and finding he was wearing his coat. I slipped my hands inside to seek the smooth skin beneath the muslin of his shirt, but could not find it.

"I would, dear, but I'm going to ask you to come out."

"No," I mumbled defiantly, attempting to hold on to the blankets and him both.

"I ken 'tis difficult to get up. But you should, you truly should. Later, I'll coorie doon with you in your nest. I promise."

I buried my head in his shirt. He smelt of fresh air.

"Come," he cajoled. He regained his balance and slid an arm under my shoulders. The other found the back of my knees. Despite my protests he pulled me from the bed and since I clung still to the coverings, they came as well.

"Why?" I asked when he deposited me on the floor. He discovered my gown nearby and held it out for me.

"I want to take you outside. To the roof."

"In the middle of the night?"

"I'm afraid so. It's something unexpected. Something you'll quite enjoy."

"But I must go to the roof?"

"Oh aye," he nodded, smiling. He gave my gown an inviting shake.

With unsteady hands I removed the bedding from my shoulders and slipped into the gown. I turned and Coll tugged the laces into place and tied them. When he folded a retrieved blanket about me I was reminded of the night we had met. I revolved to face him.

"I think you'll be warm enough," he judged. "Now dress your feet and come with me."

I stabbed my feet into my shoes and took his hand. He scooped up a lantern by the door and brought me through the corridor, past Lord Kirthgarran's bedchamber and up the turnpike stair to the garret above. A set of steps led to a narrow wooden door and Coll led us thence, lifted the latch, and gave it a shove. Another step and we were outside on the roofwalk rimming the top of the castle.

The air was frigid. I drew the blanket more closely about me. There were two inches or so of snow left from the day and it crunched under our heels.

I did not need to ask why we had come. We faced north as we came onto the walkway, and the black, starry sky was filled with ribbons and veils of magnificent colors. Pinks, whites, and greens swelled and heaved above the mountains. The transparent curtains rippled, disappeared for a second, then reappeared with renewed intensity, never staying the same.

For a few moments I merely watched, unable to say anything. Coll placed the lantern behind us at our feet. Owls hooted from somewhere to our right. My arm went round Coll as I felt his come round me, and we stood together, watching the spectacle.

"The northern lights?" I asked foolishly, for certainly they could be nothing else.

"Are they not splendid?"

There was no predicting them; they moved like plumes of smoke in the heavens, flickering here and then there. The colors changed without plan.

"How did you happen to notice them?" I asked.

"Murray left his saddlebags in the stable and we went down to get them. We watched for a while, and then he went to his bed. But I knew you must see the aurora. Have you ever seen the lights?"

"Once, when I was young. My mother brought me outside. But I do not recall the colors."

"They're dazzling," he said. "I've seen them a few times, but tonight is especially good. Do you ken, long ago in Norway, folk thought they were auld women dancing and beckoning with gloved hands?"

"What a wonderful story."

"No one knows where they come from, or why, but there's many who like to conjecture."

The colors shifted. Flashing beams shot up and a rosy hue furled across the black expanse in front of us. A bite of wind, leaping out of the night, somehow found its way between my arm and body and I leant closer against Coll. The veils of rose were taken over by similar ones of green.

"The hoolets are noisy tonight," he remarked, listening to the owls. "I wonder if they see the lights, and ponder, just as we do, from whence they come."

I gazed up at him, smiling at the thought, and at the same moment he looked down at me. His lips brushed my own.

I said in such a low voice I could hardly hear myself, "You've enjoyed Murray's visit. He's full of fascinating stories. But his presence has reminded me so utterly of the time that is passing."

"I know," he replied, equally subdued.

"I think, though you do not say it, you will never come back to Scotland."

He did not answer, and I knew I had spoken the truth. I would never see him again. The familiar pins pricked my eyes. "Coll," I said, with a tongue gone dry, "what would you say if I asked to join you—when the earl is gone?"

An icy stillness settled between us. Not even an owl called. Coll's muscles seemed to have frozen, too, as he held me. Finally, out of the darkness came his answer. "You are another man's wife."

"The legal ties bind us." The words came from some hidden wellspring within me. "But he has not my heart. I would go to you knowing it would mean living in sin. There is nought for me here, or anywhere else, without you."

"Do you ken what you're saying?"

"I do not have Rab's heart."

"He would never let you leave him."

"But I will leave, when I am no longer needed at Kirthgarran. It might be years. But when I go I'll not ask Rab's permission. If you wanted me with you…"

"'Tis not a question of me wanting you," he interjected. "I have fair driven myself mad thinking about it. For I have thought of it, Keeley, more than you know. If I believed for one moment it was possible for us to be together—but it is not. For one matter, Rab would come after us, prepared to kill us both. Somehow he would learn where you'd gone." He rested his forehead against mine. "You cannot leave Kirthgarran. We've spoken of this before."

"I am staying for one reason only."

"You belong here, no matter what happens. I can never be the reason you leave it."

"Rab would just turn to Isabel. I could leave Kirthgarran behind."

"Which you must not do."

"Because you have a feeling I belong here? What of my feelings?"

He said softly, "I am thinking about you most of all."

I could hardly make my lips move. "How can I let you go, knowing I will never see you again? How can I say goodbye to you?"

He seemed to search for words. "I would never ask you to share the life of a soldier. To have no money and to live in married quarters, pretending to be man and wife. To suffer the heat, and the other things Murray told us about. To be in the midst of war, and to face the reality of being left alone there if I fell in battle."

"I would bear it all if it meant being with you."

"I love you too much to ask you to live that sort of life."

"You're not asking. I am willing."

"I'll not do it. I am weak, and selfish, but I must do the honorable thing at some point."

"You are neither of those things."

"I've my own thoughts on that."

"I cannot help but wonder if you are condemning us both to misery all of our lives."

"You'll not always feel this way."

"Just as you will not?"

He drew away and looked at me. His face was difficult to see in the darkness, but his voice, when he spoke, conveyed his grief. "'Tis not easy to battle wills with you. You'll not accept what I tell you."

"I cannot, because your soul says something different."

"I've often been convinced you can see into it. A place even I cannot always fathom."

I was desperate to understand him. I said, "Tell me what it is you want."

"I want you, *leannan*, as much as I want my very life."

"If we both want the same thing then the answer is clear."

"It should be. I would send for you when the earl's end came. I would keep you forever with me."

"I told you I'm willing to take the risk that Rab would follow me."

"But there is something else."

"What is it?" I pled.

He drew breath heavily and said, "We are mad to even talk of this."

"There's something I'm not aware of. Please tell me what it is."

He stood for a long while, absorbed by his thoughts. He stared at the trails of color undulating in the sky.

After what seemed like hours he looked down at me. A hand came up under my chin. "There's something I must do, something I thought was out of my hands, but mayhap it is not. I must do it before we talk of this further. Will you trust me?"

I hated mystery and wished he could be plain with me. "I do trust you."

"It makes no sense to you now, but if you could only give me time."

"You may have all the time you need. But there is so little of it."

"I must see I make the best use of it."

"I wish you would not speak in riddles."

"Wait, Keeley. Can you?"

"If it means there will be hope for us, I can."

"I cannot tell you what it is you want to hear," he said. "I ken what you want. And dear God, I want the same thing. As the time grows closer for me to leave I become more filled with despair." He sighed. "No one can foresee the future. Sometimes it does not take the shape we expect. At the very least, understand that I can make our parting easier for you to bear."

How that could be I did not know. My mind spun but I had given my word.

For that night and for the few days that followed I held onto my dreams as tenaciously as the last of the frozen snow clung to the castle's stones.

"Oh, what lassie, what, does your Highland laddie wear?"
"A scarlet coat and bonnet wi' bonnie yellow hair..."
The Blue Bells of Scotland (Trad.)

Chapter Thirty-Two

When the cock crowed the next morning I crept to Coll's bedchamber and witnessed him donning his uniform for the first time. It was not easy for me to watch him collect the items and lay them out as a servant would later do for him in India. The twelve ells of tartan he had been given were drawn out on the floor on top of his belt and tucked into pleats. It was a great kilt, a *breacan fheile*, the kilt and plaid formed from one piece of wool. Wearing a shirt, a stock about his neck, red diamond-patterned hose, and hard-soled shoes, he reclined on the tartan and buckled the belt about his waist so the edge of the kilt would be just above his knees. I helped him arrange the pleats better when he stood, and after he shrugged on his white waistcoat and red coat, he lifted the tail end of the tartan to his left shoulder. There was a loop at the corner and I slipped it over the button sewn to his coat.

The weave of the coat stretched across his shoulders, swept down his chest, and ended in facings of white. He wore a gorget at his throat, a glossy, half-moon of brass suspended by ribbons, a vestige of the armor that soldiers of old once wore and a testament to his rank. From his belt hung his sporran, a pouch fashioned from badger pelts and ornamented with tassels of white fur. As Coll adjusted collar and sleeves I twisted the buttons protruding from gold, lace-trimmed buttonholes, turning the embossed seventy-fours so they were all upright. Belts, baldric, and scabbards, the white leather bands that would carry dirk, pistol, and sword when he was on parade, lay waiting on his dressing table.

Whilst I bound his tail of hair with black ribbon, I glanced at him in the looking glass and could not help but be struck by the change in him. He was every bit the army officer, a commander of skill and experience who would call orders to the lieutenant and sergeant beneath him, and critically eye the enemy across a foreign field.

My fingers faltered and I felt myself retreating into my reserved self. I took a step backward and after a moment of straightening a cuff, Coll became aware of my contemplation. He turned and reached for me, held me against the stiff wool and brass at his chest. "It is difficult to be patient. But we must both be forbearing."

"I've made my promise and I will keep it."

He smiled. "For now, will you come with me to see what Murray thinks of my new attire?"

"He did well guessing your measurements."

"We are somewhat similar," he agreed. "Even the shoes fit."

"And the bonnet?" I asked, eyeing the table where lay the hat of black, lustrous feathers and diced band of red and white.

"Later."

My attention moved to the square of leather we had left on the little table by his bed. I retrieved it and tucked it into his hand. "You should take this with you, when you go. So you remember."

"My auld bonnet badge? Well, aye, perhaps I should." He rubbed the soft leather and dropped it inside his sporran.

It would take time to become used to seeing him thus. I found it increasingly difficult to keep a blind eye to the future, when the uniform and what it represented brandished themselves so blatantly before me.

I slipped from his bedchamber to my own where I attempted to make myself presentable for the day. I met Coll downstairs perhaps thirty minutes later, where he and Murray were making plans to visit the clachan together. The sight of two uniformed soldiers, they felt, might cause the men who wavered in their decision to list to make up their minds and become foot soldiers in the Highland Light Infantry.

During their absence Rab and Lachlan returned.

I suffered the kiss Rab placed on my cheek, the embrace in which he exuberantly gripped me. "My God, how lovely you are!" he cried. "Yet how pale. Are you ill?"

I tried to smile. "Tell me of your journey."

He and his brother shed saddlebags, coats, and bonnets as Ròs came running with Grizel behind her, eager to welcome back the travelers. The cook supplied food and drink as the two settled down in the dining room and related the high points of their venture to those of us gathered round.

I barely heard a word they said. Rab's return meant that there would be no more stolen time spent in Coll's company. Memories from the past week flashed through my mind. Cooking and delighting Coll and the earl with sweets. Playing songs on my clarsach, including the one I had written about the waterfall, whilst Coll accompanied me with his whistle. Meeting in the paddock and riding horses onto the hills. Walking in the wood where the grass was outlined with miniature, glittering diamonds until the sun melted them. Crunching the narrow white ribbons of ice that formed at the loch's edge, and Coll laughing at my childish amusement.

When Coll and Murray returned they greeted the brothers cordially. I sat at the side, knitting Iain's stocking, forgotten and ignored as news and pleasantries were exchanged. Lieutenant Campbell took his leave of us not long after. Coll disappeared.

Rab and Lachlan went to visit with Lord Kirthgarran.

I was left alone to sit by the chimney-side and pull out all the stitches I had made that afternoon, for my mistakes were both foolish and plentiful.

There was upheaval in the castle. Ròs discovered that a lad for whom she pined was going to list in Coll's regiment.

Airig confided that her flirtatious sister had not decided she was in love with the man until he'd told her he was leaving, yet the tears she shed were noisy and copious. For a whole day we listened to her sobs and sniffles, and watched the beauty of the young lass become marred by reddened eyes and nose. Airig had little sympathy for her sibling, for Ròs was known for her fickleness and cravings for attention. She was an innocent, child-like maiden, however, and had long endeared herself to the earl's household, and if she missed any compassion from her sister it was well compensated by empathy from others.

Unlike Ròs, I did not have the luxury of expressing my feelings. Even as I wrote in my diary I felt constrained, for little did I dare to pen anything incriminating should inquisitive eyes find my papers. There was some relief, though, as there had always been, in putting down thoughts, however vague.

"It is raining. The snow has all been washed away. It, like other things, is only a memory. I wait, wondering what weather will come next. Four more days and it will be December.

"Rab is home. Although he was cheerful at first, he now seems temperamental and often strays into melancholy or a simmering irritation. There is no outward explanation other than the dreary rain, and I cannot ken for sure what is causing his moods. He stays much at home since his return, as does Lachlan. I have not been sleeping well. And my appetite is hampered by queasiness. I must seek a tea of chamomile, or some hartshorn jelly."

I did not write I thought I might be with child. I did not know if it was so, but I suspected, and was torn between excitement and fright.

I asked myself when I might tell Rab—and Coll—of the possibility. There was no way to discern which of the two might be the father. Rab would be thrilled by the news. And Coll? If I should someday choose to leave Rab, would Coll still welcome me if I had a child? Five or six months on a ship, an arrival in a country either torn by searing heat, monsoon, or war, married quarters in the barracks, the prospect of a childhood spent on a military post amid disease and clouds of biting flies—were these things he would allow a bairn to suffer? A far more pertinent issue was whether or not Rab would allow me to leave Kirthgarran if he believed he was the child's father. He might give me a choice: Coll or the bairn. I could not contemplate abandoning a son or daughter.

There was nothing Coll could do to make our separation less painful. I pictured him riding away on Dominie, his scarlet coat bright against the new snow on the hillsides, his eyes holding mine for as long as possible until he turned forward and led the handful of men who marched with him. Everything we had shared would be gone. What seemed real and fulfilling now would become nothing more than a tale whispered and swept into the mists of history.

Unable to spend any time with Coll, I fell into a withdrawn, self-recriminating state. Rab did not seem eager to leave the castle and spent his nights in either his bed or mine. The ease between us was crumbling. He drank overmuch and said little, wanting intercourse but obviously, and understandably, finding himself dissatisfied with it. I had nothing to give, and turned my head whenever he lay with me. He avoided remarking upon it, but I was convinced his present moodiness was caused by the glimmers of revulsion that shone through my compliance. I was confused, for he had Isabel to comfort him. Isabel, whose bed offered the warmth that mine did not.

I sought Lord Kirthgarran's company a great deal and tried to hide my turbulent emotions. Sometimes I took his right hand, weak and bent, and massaged the palm and stiff fingers whilst he shared the stories of his youth with me. His wasting muscles were thin but I liked to think that if I manipulated them and brought warmth to them with my rubbing, his hand might someday regain a little of its use.

"Make the most of every moment," my inner voice hurled at me now and then. Graeme Fergusson and the love I held for him would one day be swept into history as well.

Rab had been home three days when something unsettling occurred after tea. Rain poured from the sky and flooded the windowpanes. Ewen had left a letter for me to copy that morning and I went to the library to find it. It was laid out on the big desk. Whilst I wrote I listened to the rain. My quill dipped into the ink again and again. The small, slanted lines of my handwriting began to fill the paper.

The letter was nearly finished when I became aware of floorboards creaking. I looked up. I expected to see someone standing in the room.

The light from the candle at my elbow was not strong, but it was daylight after all, and if anyone had come in I would have had no trouble seeing him. The library was as empty as when I had entered it. I bent once more to my work. Within moments, however, the creak came again: the unmistakable groan of the wooden floor. This time I was not so sure the sound came from within the chamber. It was possible it originated from behind the half-open door.

I called out, "Hello? Is someone there?" The rain beat at the windows and I believed I heard the sound once more.

Uneasily I rose and tiptoed to the door. Holding my breath, I pushed it open. The passage beyond was clear. There was no one.

I would have thought I had imagined the noise, or merely heard boards swelling on this damp day, if I had not spied the water on the floor as I turned to shut the door. A puddle with a wide, dry center lay near the threshold of the library door and drops of water in the passage traced a path that disappeared into the dimness.

I stared at the puddle. Someone had been standing here and watching me write at the desk. Whoever it was had been soaked from the rain and had stood by the door, hoping to remain hidden from me.

I could not envision who might act so strangely. Perhaps I had witnessed the appearance of a specter, a long-dead Fergusson who had once lived within these walls. I went back to the letter, knowing I must finish it, but I started at every little noise. The squeak of my own chair...the wind hurling the rain...

With relief did I seek the companionship of Airig, who

acted so normally I was soon able to regain my composure. Why I did not mention the odd occurrence to her I did not know. Being spied upon was not the first disconcerting event to have happened since I had come to Kirthgarran. Perhaps I feared discovering the truth behind the puzzles more than I suffered their annoyance.

I contented myself that afternoon by helping the women dust and polish. I found a heather besom and took it into the great hall where I began sweeping the floor. There was a release of tension as I attacked the dust and collected it into piles.

Not long after I started, Rab happened to walk through. I caught sight of him as he halted and began to come toward me. "What are you doing?" he asked incredulously.

I thought it was plain, but I answered, "I am sweeping."

He reached my side and grasped the stick. "You're not to sweep. Do you hear me? You're not a servant. Let Ròs do it."

"I do not mind helping," I replied, baffled. "There's much to do, and so few hands."

His voice grew louder. "You're not to sweep."

"What does it matter? I do many things. I spin, and I cook a bit. You did not mind when I swept this hall before."

He threw the besom from him, sending it bouncing and sliding far across the floor. "There was a difference then. We all took our part before Samhain to ready the hall. This is bluidy drudgery. I'll not have you doing it. There are others who receive pay for what they do. Do you understand?"

I nodded, sufficiently reprimanded, but I did not understand.

"Spin, if you must," he said. "But leave the dirt of our feet for others to take care of." He left me and grabbed the besom when he reached it. Whither he took it, I did not know, but it seemed he did not intend for there to be any chance I might make use of it again.

I paid little attention to where my footsteps led me. I felt I belonged nowhere. Lord Kirthgarran was sleeping, trying to rid himself of a headache. I had no desire to rejoin the other women. I went at last to the drawing room where dark prevailed except for the ever-present fire on the ingle. Coll had left his weapons here. The sword, pistols, powder horn, and dirk he would carry with him to India were spread on the sideboard. The sight of them caused my throat to tighten. I turned away. The rain had not let up at all and it washed down over the glazed windows, blurring the landscape beyond to a dull gray.

I stood at a casement and watched the downpour. There were nineteen days left.

"A dour day it is," said a voice behind me. "A good day for drinking the earl's whisky and reading books."

I turned to find Coll leaning against the sideboard, his arms folded, a smile lighting his face. He was not wearing his uniform. His muslin sark, linen waistcoat, and leather breeks were familiar and reassuring. How long it had been since we had been alone.

"You're looking sad," he said. "And we cannot have that."

"Have you a remedy?"

His eyes, tinted as gray as the rain, captured mine. "You want to be sewing. Your embroidery frame is in the solar where you left it, but it's been days since anyone built a fire there and it's as cold as a tomb. What you'd like," he continued playfully, straightening, "is for someone, like me, to help you bring the thing downstairs where you can work on your picture in warmth and comfort."

"Will we go together to get it?"

"I cannot be carrying the wooden stand and the basket of silks both, so aye, you have to come and do your part." He glanced at the door and his voice fell. "We can vanish briefly, but should not press our luck. We must come downstairs and be good for the rest of the day. But I have nought to do in all this rain, and intend to stay inside and enjoy the fireside. You can sit here and sew, or knit if you prefer, and I'll read to you. How would that be? Find me a book, Keeley, and I'll entertain us for a change."

The prospect seemed so wonderful I felt all my troubles drain away.

"We may be joined by the others, but hopefully I'll not bore you as I'm certain to bore them." He paused, seemed to remember something, and pulled a folded paper out of his pocket. "And here, you should take this lest we get waylaid. I wrote it, just in case."

I took the paper from him and giving him a curious glance,

unfolded it. Written on it was the single sentence, *"Remember that I love you."* I put it in my own pocket. I said in a low voice, *"Tha gaol agam ort-fhèin."*

He seemed pleased that I remembered the words.

Up the turnpike stair we went, to the topmost storey. The solar was chilly and gloomy, but as soon as the door swung shut he seized me and spun me round. I pressed my nose into the hollow between his neck and shoulder, breathing in deeply of the scent of mountain air, horse, and sweat. When my feet were returned to the floor he enveloped me, making a low sound in his throat that told of immense pleasure.

"Oh, how I have missed you," he murmured.

"Rab has been keeping house. He's never far from me."

"I've not dared come close. It's been the De'il's own work, with the rain making it difficult to tell someone I'm going for a walk, or a ride, for all I'd be considered an idiot, and then you'd be subjected to the same scrutiny. It took me forever to think of this idea."

Days of forced separation after a week of intimate indulgence created an urgency that was not gratified by a mere embrace. Our lips sought each other with uncontrollable intensity. Our bodies knew each other and pressed for responses. If time had allowed, or if the room were not so cold, there was no doubt what we would have done, but it was vital to keep our wits about us and avoid what our senses demanded. With effort Coll pulled his mouth away from mine and held my hands against his chest. What I would have preferred was for him to lower me to the settle with his weight on top of me, his lips and hands heavy and insistent, and for us to sink into a shameless abandonment in each other. But I was conscious of the minutes as they staggered by as keenly as he, and knew this was not the time.

He said, "I have to ask you for more patience."

"Patience?"

"I've not been able to accomplish what I wanted. I think it may take another day or two."

I buried my face at his chest. "Of course. Of course. Whatever it is you need, you may have."

"'Tis not fair to you. But there's nought I can do to hasten this."

Disappointment fluttered but I thrust it away, determined to live in the present moment.

His fingers stroked my neck, my back. The delight of it was enough for the time being. I looked ahead to the coming hours and was content thinking we would be together. We would have to be virtuous, and pretend innocence for the sake of others, but it could be done. We had done it before.

When it seemed we had been missing for too long, Coll and I ruefully withdrew from each other and collected the items for which we had come. I took up the basket of silken thread and he grasped the floor stand with its oval embroidery hoop. Together we returned downstairs. At the last moment, in the hidden curve of the stair, he gave me one final kiss. I almost spilt all the thread out of the basket.

Coll was accurate in his prophecy that we would be joined by others and that they would be bored by his reading. The days of rain seemed to be having an adverse effect on everyone. Lachlan paced restlessly from drawing room to great hall and back again, and finally, with a tumbler of spirit in his fist, threw himself down at the table in the sitting room to play cards with Rab. Rab had obviously been warming himself with the *uisge beatha* for quite some time, and judging from the arguments that sprang sporadically from the next room, and the steadily increasing volume of the voices that spawned them, neither brother was finding solace in the drink.

Even Coll was not immune. As I plunged my needle through the linen stretched over the frame, forcing silken threads of emerald and violet to become evenly-spaced stitches, he sipped from his own glass. The quarreling voices beyond created an anxious backdrop and after an hour of listening to it he closed the covers of *An Arabian Tale*. He became quieter in his demeanor, and his smile did not often surface.

Andrew, Anne, and Mairi arrived, a surprise to us all. Soaked as they were, they seemed strangely jubilant. They joined us in our evening meal and remained afterward in the dining room.

Andrew addressed us all and said there was something he wished to announce. "We wanted to wait until it was certain," he said, glancing round at his family. He seemed unable to go on and in uncharacteristic helplessness looked at Anne.

Anne blurted out, "Andrew and I are to have a bairn."

There was much noise in response to this news. Everyone wanted to have a chance to embrace her and she began to cry. I was happy for her, and yet could not avoid thinking of my own situation. As I hugged her I wished I could ask her questions. I wanted to know: How do you feel? How do you know it's true? Do we share any of the same discomforts?

Rab did not leave the whisky alone, and the announcement provided a reason for a fresh glass. Ròs and Airig cleared plates away and brought Grizel and Sandy to join us in our excitement. Airig's face was alive with anticipation, and I knew she was already making plans to sew infant clothes. I noticed that Rab was especially attentive to Ròs, filling her tumbler, laughing with her when she giggled. She whispered something to him and he agreed, smiling, and put a hand on her wrist.

Mairi said, "When I went up earlier, Lord Kirthgarran was suffering from a headache and wanted to retire early, but he'll still be awake, I'm sure. He'd welcome such good news as this." Everyone concurred and she went with the expectant parents to tell him.

The rest of us sat at table, waiting for their return. There were pieces of cheese to nibble, and crumbly cakes to taste.

"It seems you've found a few Fergussons to go with you to the soldiering," Rab said to Coll as he draped an arm over the back of his chair. "So the regiment will not be filled with Campbell Whigs."

"I've found a few, aye."

"For a handful of men, at least, there's no worry about what to do come spring."

Coll agreed warily, wondering, I supposed, what the point of this observation would be.

It was dark without, and the rain continued to stream noisily down the panes. I eyed Rab circumspectly for he seemed on the verge of becoming quarrelsome. He said, "I wonder if 'tis not a mistake Lord Kirthgarran is letting the folk stay on his lands until the spring."

"A mistake?" Coll responded. "What would you have him do, turn the folk out in the cold of winter with no money, no place to go?"

"His compassion may prove to be the ruin of him. Just wait and see if they do not convince him o'er the winter months he is unjust and cruel, and by their persistence force him to change his mind."

"You'd condemn them for something you yourself were more than guilty of? Your persistence in persuading the earl was a remarkable feat of doggedness."

"You were not without a certain perseverance yourself."

"Is there any point in going over this again? What's done is done."

Rab selected a morsel of yellow cheese and bit into it. "Aye, that is so. But I'd have them all leave tomorrow if that were possible."

Coll shook his head and took a drink from his tumbler. "And what would they do at this time of year? What will they do in the spring? Become fishermen, with no boats, no nets, no homes on the shore to return to at night with their catches? Become weavers? With no knowledge of looms or the ability to buy them? Or would you have them live in huts at the seaside and pick kelp to burn for the glass factories, as many of the homeless folk from other glens do? That would be the best, I think, for they see cities as mass graves and know a man's labor there is hardly worth a pence, and the slums they would live in worth less than that."

Rab seemed unperturbed and chewed thoughtfully. "There's land for them if they wish to keep to their farming."

"Is there? It is barren."

"There's always America."

"You say that as if it's an answer for everything."

"It was an answer for you once."

Coll's jaw clenched and his fingers tightened upon his glass. I wished I could think of something to stop this repeat of the row they had indulged in more than once. Sandy, reclining in a chair by the fire, was scowling at the two men. I looked at Lachlan in supplication, but he, too, seemed at a loss.

"In any case," Rab continued, "as you said, 'tis already settled, is it not?"

"Will it ever really be? This whole matter might never have been necessary."

"You're a fool, Coll. We live in a state of poverty! This is a business proposition, suggested by the most shrewd of financiers. You're living in the past when a man could give his rent in grain or cattle and a landowner had no need of notes. What good will a sheaf of grain or a cow do now when what we need is money? Harsh times these are, and they demand harsh measures. If the money values and the produce prices were constant—but they're not. We face bankruptcy. We cannot afford to be sentimental."

"Caring for one's family is not sentimentality."

"Is that why so many of our so-called family have emigrated? Because of their undying loyalty?"

Coll rose, tipping his chair precariously. "The land cannot support everyone." He stalked to the sideboard and leant against it. "At first there were too many folk in the glens. The land was split amongst sons until there was hardly enough to stand a steer upon, much less to grow food to support a family and the earl as well. Some saw their neighbors leave for America and they followed."

"And you feel responsible for them?"

"I feel responsible for those we begged to stay."

Rab snorted amiably and shook his head but Coll went on stubbornly, "Despite the famine four years ago we were doing better. We learnt new farming methods. We were struggling together. The future looked promising."

"'Twas not promising enough."

"Have you seen what's happened elsewhere where the sheep have dispossessed the cottars? The chiefs are ruint. The tacksmen and clansmen are ruint. Who's making a fortune? The financiers who use and then abuse them."

"Then that's something we'll avoid. We have our heads. We'll learn from the others." He paused. "The debts are greater than the risks."

"The debts," Coll said. "There are others who've worse debts and they do not resort to these drastic schemes. We'd several strengths in our favor. Lord Kirthgarran did not choose to live in England and send his children to English schools and lavishly entertain his peers. He remained here and avoided spending money he did not have. And by doing so he showed he cared for his tenants. He does care for them, Rabbie. We all do. Or did. I cannot speak for you. You forced him into this decision. He'd never have turned his people out had you not painted such a picture of Kirthgarran's debts. His mind you clouded with guilt so he had no choice but to decide as you wanted him to."

"'Twas the only decision to make."

"That is your opinion. In mine, Kirthgarran was on the way to healing itself and succeeding."

Rab began to lose his amused look and a flush crept over his cheeks. "Well," he pronounced, riveting Coll's eye. "It matters little now. Your opinion, I'm meaning. You've chosen to leave, too. Leave Kirthgarran and fair Caledonia together. Your opinion is as important as a dead horse rotting by the wayside."

I stood up from my chair. I was aware of Airig, Ròs, and Grizel melting away through the door and Lachlan stirring uncomfortably. Sandy turned his eyes toward the fire in exasperation, clearly livid.

Rab slid his blurred eyes from Coll to me and back again, and straightened in his seat as a new idea seemed to strike him. "Let's speak of your leaving. What are your plans? What of that sweet lass you swive at arm's length? What does Kirstie think of you going off like this?"

Coll's jaw was stiff. He glared across the table.

"I take it she's not going with you?" Rab asked.

"'Tis no concern of yours, is it."

"I'm thinking your social affairs have ne'er been my concern. Perhaps I've been amiss. Perhaps I should have paid more attention. Whenever you and Lachlan went seeking whores in Edinburgh or Glasgow I never cared. But I find myself thinking on poor Kirstie and what she must be feeling. You're not going to desert the sweet lass? You, with all your sentimentality, your affection for others, would not do that to the one woman who loves you?"

Coll's face took on a deadly cast.

My husband tossed down a swallow of his drink and surveyed him. "What would she think of you then? What would any woman think?" He turned his eyes on me. "What did you think, Keeley, when you were deserted so?"

I felt the blood leave my head.

Coll strode round the table and grasped the neck of Rab's shirt with two hands and lifted him from his seat. Holding his face inches from Rab's, he said in a dangerously low voice, "It is time you kept your tongue. If you cannot do it, then God's Nails, suffer the consequence at my hand."

Their eyes locked and though I could not see what passed between them, the fury was evident in both their stances. Rab unhurriedly brought his hands up and placed them over Coll's. He grasped the fingers and removed them from his shirt. A second later he picked up his tumbler from the table and left the room.

Coll watched him go, a pulse beating in his neck. He finally sought my eyes but there was little he could say. We were not alone.

Lachlan muttered, "What he wanted to gain from that, I do not ken."

Coll could not seem to think of a response. He appeared to have a difficult time recovering, and took more of the whisky from the bottle on the table. He sat, planted his elbows, and scraped a hand through his hair. He took another look at me. His eyes were affected still, full of a blazing rage. "I apologize for him, Keeley," he said. "He should never have said that to you."

All at once it was necessary to pretend all was well, for his mother, Andrew, and Anne returned from the earl's chamber and were still in their bright state. Sandy remained silently by the fire but the rest of us attempted to share their joy by asking polite questions and nodding agreeably at the answers. Rab's malicious frame of mind rankled and yet I could not allow myself the extravagance of pondering it. This was an enchanted time for Andrew and Anne that must not be spoilt by family quarrels, and surely Mairi did not need to know of the poisonous words Rab and her son had uttered.

There were beds enough at Kirthgarran and no reason for the three to return to Rathdale in the rain. Mairi retired to the room she had long ago used as her own, and soon Andrew and Anne went off to one near Coll's. I longed for my own bed. I craved the void of sleep.

Coll gave me a candle from the table. He came with me to

the stair. He cleared his throat. "Do you think—will he leave you alone tonight, do you think?"

It must have been agonizing for him to ask, he who could not prevent my husband from taking what was his right both in the eyes of the law and God. It was a painful matter for both of us. I paused before I answered him, for I had wondered what lay in store for me upstairs as well. I could not bear a repeat of the night when Mr. Baird had stayed at the castle. "I'm sure of it. Wherever he's gone, he's most likely asleep by now."

"It was unforgivable, what he said to you." He gathered me to him for a moment, bringing me peace.

"You were his prey," I clarified.

"He must suspect, somewhere deep in his mind, that you and I are closer than kinsmen."

"I suppose I have thought that, too."

"We must take care. 'Tis not me I worry over. Let Lachlan go with you upstairs, or Sandy. I should not."

"He will not harm me, Coll."

He released me and shook his head as if he were not sure. I could not judge his eyes in the dim light. I hugged myself, aware of an uncomfortable tingling in my spine, and added, "I should go upstairs."

"Sleep well, *leannan*."

"You'll bide for a while?"

"I plan to get blind drunk, and have Lachlan drag me to my bed."

I made my way upward.

Rab's door was partly open and a streak of firelight spilt out into the passage. I tread to my own door opposite with the intention of slipping inside and bolting it, but my hand stilled upon the latch. A young, female voice drifted out from the other room, a young voice rising in laughter and squealing.

I could not help myself. I turned and crossed to Rab's doorsill.

For a few moments the scene before me was so peculiar I needed to pause and absorb it. Rab stood by his hearth with Ròs in his arms. The longer I stared the more I realized the gesture was not one of comfort, but of lust. She struggled as he held her from behind, though clearly she enjoyed his hands running down her body and lingering on her breasts. His hair had fallen over his brow, and his shirt was open to his waist as he pressed against her, burying his lips in her shining, red tresses. He said "Hush, hush" to stem her little outcries, and she bent her head when she lifted her shoulders.

"I'm sorry. It's just that—it tickles and no one's ever touched me like that—and you shouldn't—because you're wed to Mrs. Rab and all..." Her words were slurred.

"But you're a comely lass, Ròs, and lonely. I'm lonely, too. And there's none such as you. Here. Here." He kissed her throat and she giggled again. Though she attempted to say no, she turned to him and let his lips fall upon hers.

How long I would have stayed there at his cracked door and watched him seduce Airig's sister I could not have predicted if she had not begun to abandon her mischievous flirting. She must have sensed Rab's handling becoming more serious. A few innocent, stolen kisses and an admiring grope from a hand of one of the reigning men of the earl's household, even if he was married, was one thing. But he was pulling the chemise ribbon free from the gathers below her throat, ignoring her interfering fingers. When she tried to back away from him he would not let her, and he clutched her hands with impatience.

"Nay, Rabbie," she cried in a voice slightly louder than a whisper.

He hushed her again, although he smiled. "Wheesht, Ròs. You cannot be so loud."

I found the voice to say, "Ròs."

Steady! Courage take ye
Though a tempest should blow.

A Boat Song (Trad.)

Chapter Thirty-Three

oth of their heads lifted; both sets of eyes fastened on me.

Sudden comprehension caused the lass to close her lids and moan. Rab dropped her hands and she covered her face with them. The moan grew to a wail. "Oh Mrs.," she wept. "Oh Mrs! I'm so sorry. I'm so sorry! Have pity on me, oh do." And the tears gushed from her.

Rab took a deep breath and let it out. He watched me through eyes that seemed to have difficulty focusing.

I said, "Ròs, you must go."

She nodded her head violently, her hands fixed to her face. She attempted to take a step away from Rab, but he put an arm about her shoulders and prevented her. Her fingertips slid below her eyes as she peered at him.

"Let her go," I said to Rab.

I was disconcerted because he would not speak. Ròs moved again, but Rab held her fast. She looked at me in horror, wanting desperately to please me, I thought, and yet finding herself unable to do so.

"Why will you not let her?" I asked.

His gaze narrowed, and he seemed to be thinking. "Because she is warm, and up until a second ago, willing."

"How dare you do this," I threw at him. "She's frightened. You're frightening her. And you stand there, insulting me in this way."

"If I let her go, will you take her place?" He turned his eyes to Ròs and swept them over her streaming face. "Will you let me kiss you and not turn away as if you loathed me? See then, this is how it is with a woman who's warm and willing." He brought his mouth to hers and pressed his lips there. She moved not a muscle, overcome with terror, I believed, if one could read the look in her eyes.

"You not only taunt me but her. Let her go."

"Not until you reassure me," he warned me, gazing at Ròs still. "'Tis true, I think, after all, that it's you I'd rather have. But I need to ken, will you let me kiss you? Will you let me touch you, and not find a way to shrink away?" His free hand traced her breast. Ròs stood much like a rabbit caught by a wolf's stare, one who dares not to flinch or run but looks back at her captor with unseeing eyes.

"What must I say to you!" I cried. "If your quarrel is with me then send her away and face me as you would any adversary."

He waited long enough, as this thought pushed its way into his mind, for me to garner courage and step toward Ròs. I took her hot hand and pulled her away. Rab released her slowly, causing her to convulse in great, shaking sobs. She stood sniffling and gulping for a moment and then she was gone.

My husband and I stood a little apart, observing each other. Although unstable on his feet, his gaze was unwavering. The dark eyes, shining in the light from the fire, held mine until I said unevenly, "Isabel is not enough?"

He blinked, glanced once at the floor, searched my eyes again. "You ken about Isabel."

"How could I not?"

The eyes narrowed in concurrence. He said, "Isabel is a shrew."

"What has happened betwixt you? Is she no longer welcoming you to her bed?"

"We had a disagreement. It happens now and then."

"And so you must take Ròs, who is an innocent and knows nought of such things?"

"She was here," he replied, shrugging. "And you were not."

The guilt crept through me as he meant it to do. I thought I had done quite well, surmounting my timidity by allowing anger to swell forth, but the ironies of everything filled my mind. Despite the artlessness of Ròs and my need to protect her, it was unfair to accuse Rab of debauchery when only a few moments earlier I had reflected upon the depth of my love for Coll. I could not berate him for his adultery. I was as damned as he.

"She must have had a wee bit whisky to make her forget herself so," I said, hearing weakness enter my voice. "She is a sweet lass. Surely you do not mean to ruin her."

"I did not plan it. She came up to bring me spirit, as I asked her. And then..." He shook his head, as if the whole affair was too complicated.

I could think of nothing else to say either, and began to walk away.

His hand grasped my wrist. "Where are you going?"

"To bed."

"Oh no. Not yet. I let her go, as you asked. But you and I are not finished."

"What do you want to speak about? Ròs? Isabel? I know you love Isabel, Rab. I know you far better than I did when you first brought me here. You did not love me then. Your heart belonged to her, and still does."

This must not have been the reply he expected, for he needed to think and it seemed to prove difficult for him. "I love you, Keeley."

It was the first time he had ever said the words to me. "You do not," I said. "You love whatever it is I seem to represent. A person who loves does not try to hurt the other as you've tried to hurt me."

"I love you, Keeley. You must not doubt it." He reached forward, took the candlestick from me, and put it on the mantelpiece. I tried to step away as Ròs had done earlier but again, his hand was stronger. He went on, "I understand you better than when you first came, as well. You're not the meek lass I wed. You've fire in you, though you keep it too hard under control."

"There are some things that make me angry," I agreed brokenly.

He came closer. An arm went about my waist, securing me to him and sending quivers of apprehension running through me. His breath was strong with whisky. "I suppose it's to be expected. A man and his wife must come to understand each other whilst they spend their lives together."

"Will you let me go, Rab?"

"I think that's what excites me the most about you, wondering when the fire is going to appear and how brightly it's going to burn." His hand began stroking my side and slid upward. "What are we to do now we ken some truths about each other?" he inquired as his other hand pulled my pelvis against his, letting me know how aroused he was. "You ken I have a physical hunger you cannot satisfy. I ken you have a hidden temper." His lips grazed my ear. "And a lust to match, for Coll."

Shivers shot up and down my limbs. He kissed the side of my neck.

"That," he continued, "you do not hide so well. But the problem will solve itself, for he'll be gone in less than three weeks. There's still hope for us, do you not think? All you need do is turn that lust to me and perhaps both our dilemmas will be obliterated."

"Let me go," I said, the words barely audible.

Instead of complying, his arms brought me closer. "'Tis a fine time for a new beginning. Now that we understand each other better. Isabel has nought that you do not have. And your dreams about Coll might not be true. He might not be the lover you imagine. You'll never ken, will you?"

I was thankful he did not guess how far my lust had taken

me. I tried to turn and could not.

"I'm going to have you," he murmured. "Now. And you'll be thinking on no one but me."

He moved his hands, intending to lift me up from the floor, but I thrust myself away at the same moment. I was free except for my left hand which he somehow caught and held tightly. "Do you think there'll be any love in me for you?" I forced myself to say, pulling my hand, refusing to wince at the pain he caused.

"I do not suppose there ever was, but your ire will more than compensate for your lack of passion."

"This is not the way to bring us closer."

"Let us say I look forward to a lifetime of trying." His hand bent mine at the wrist and I had no choice but to come closer to him as he desired. I stifled a cry, and his lips kissed my squeezed, red fingers. "Mayhap I was wrong," he said, his eyes bright. "Would it be better if you pretended? Do it, Keeley, if it makes it easier. Pretend I'm Coll. And I'll make things even better by pretending you're Isabel. Ah! What an interesting tumble it will be! Coll, sheathing his weapon in Isabel!"

I struck him on the cheek with all the force I could collect. I had never struck a living thing, and it was plain it was the last response he had foreseen. Yet not more than a second passed before he returned it, stinging the side of my face with his palm.

He found his voice and said in a different tone, "So. Are we to take to sculting each other, then?"

The marks of my fingers remained on his left cheek. There was an unusual look in his eyes, and without a word he tripped my foot with his own, causing us both to fall to the floor. His body was heavy. One hand seemed to have trapped both of mine and the other was unbuttoning his breeks.

I thought, this was what my mother had endured. There was no doubt that my father had sometimes taken her in this same way, forcing his will upon her until the day the blood poured from her and the bairn who wanted to be born could not find its way into the world. I thought, if there were a bairn within me I would not have the same thing happen.

I fought him. Had he been sober he might have managed

better for he was the stronger of the two of us, but his reactions were slow, and at one point I was able to slide a little away from him. His fingers closed about my left ankle. I kicked with my right foot and my wooden heel caught him in the face. The release of my leg was instant. I waited not a second but scrambled to my feet and went out through his door.

Through the darkness I fled, heedless of my fears. Months spent in the castle had taught me how long the passage was, where the mural steps were to be found. I slowed to a creep as I felt my way down the turning, twisting, stone wedges. When I reached the bottom, enough light came from the fire in the great hall to suggest their shapes in the darkness.

The light was brighter in the drawing room. I lurched up the few steps to its door. I could not surmise what impression I made on Coll and Lachlan who lounged before the fireplace with bottles and glasses and clay pipes between them. Both men rose at once.

Behind me I heard Rab's footfalls and his breathing. I turned. He stopped a few paces away, his face distorted with rage, and the cut on his cheekbone was bleeding. The flesh about his eye was beginning to swell and grow purple.

He hurled himself forward, reaching for my arm, but Coll was there between us.

"What is it, man?" Coll demanded, none too sober himself. "Christ, is it murder you're after?"

"'Tis nought to do with you. 'Tis Keeley I want."

Coll raised an arm, thrust it against it Rab's chest. "You're not likely to have at her in this state."

"God's Blood!" Rab shouted. He struggled a moment, gave up, and retreated a pace. At his left was the sideboard where Coll had left his weapons. In a smooth arc, Rab extracted the silver sword from its sheath and hefted the ornate basket hilt in his hand. The point came to Coll's throat.

"Rab!" I whispered.

A smile lit Rab's face. His hand, balancing the blade, shook when the steel tip touched Coll's skin. Coll himself was still, but his eyes were not. They burnt like twin fires.

"What is it you're about?" Coll asked coolly.

"Take it. Take it." Rab turned it so the pommel was near

Coll's hand. "'Tis what you've wanted for a long while, just as I have. Take it, for I plan to get myself another." He tossed it and Coll caught it. With determination Rab strode away into the hall. Coll followed after him. I ran behind them both, only to find that Rab had taken a broadsword down from the wall. He held it in front of him, kissed the blade, and faced the other man with malice. "Will we see who can draw the most blood, sir?" Rab suggested. "The gallant soldier or his unprofessional kinsman?"

The wrath boiled over in Coll and he raised his arm. He swung the sword at Rab's taunting face. I called to him and leapt forward but Lachlan seized me.

"You'll be killed," he growled at me.

"They will kill each other," I cried, but he would not loosen his grip.

The two men lunged at each other. I was convinced they were bent upon murder. They circled about the table, causing a chair to crash to the floor. Their swords rang and flashed fire from the flames beside them. Rab was at a disadvantage without the military training Coll possessed, but neither of them was clear-headed at present, making their inaccurate attacks all the more deadly. Rab slashed out at Coll's middle but had to fall backward when Coll, incensed, advanced upon him. Their blades crossed again. The rasp and scrape of steel upon steel was unnerving to me. I writhed in Lachlan's arms.

"Stop them, please, Lachlan. Do not let them do this."

Coll continued his forceful attack. Back and forth his sword went in a pattern of cuts and thrusts, meeting Rab's each time. He could not keep up this spurt of strength, however, and he slashed downward, missing Rab's arm by inches. Rab took the advantage and threw his body forward against Coll's. Blood appeared on Rab's forearm when they separated.

Rab swore and pursued Coll again. They crossed in front of the fire with their breaths coming in grunts.

I spurned Lachlan's hold on me and did not cease my struggle to free myself. Combined with the smell of perspiration and spirit-laced breath, his hard grip was my own nemesis, and I believed that if I could only escape him I would be able to run between Coll and Rab and stop this encounter that was no game.

Coll's sword struck Rab's again and again and Rab retreated in earnest. He was forced against the wall. Coll pressed Rab's sword arm against the stone and held his own blade aloft as if he meant to behead him with it.

A wineglass soared across the hall and shattered against the wall beside Rab. Pieces of crystal sprayed to the floor.

"Throw down," a voice demanded. Coll remained poised, his arm trembling, his eyes boring into Rab's unfrightened ones.

"I said, throw down." Sandy came closer. "For the love of God, what would the earl say were he to see the two of you at each other's throats? Whilst he himself is upstairs in his bed and trusting you to be honorable men as his own sons were? If he could see you now it would be breaking his heart. As it is breaking mine." His face seemed bloodless. His voice came again, filled with wrath, as neither man moved. "The two of you, who I held on my knee at the same time. Bairns together. Kinsmen. You disgrace the name of MacFhearghuis. You disgrace me and all the men who came before you."

Coll seemed to hear him at last and his arm lowered. He blinked the sweat from his eyes. Rab, enraged and pinned to the wall, heaved his breaths.

Lachlan's arms relaxed about me and his bristling beard touched my cheek.

Coll took a step backward, his boot crunching on broken glass.

I did not know if they touched each other accidentally, or if only Coll moved, but Rab suddenly cried out. His sword flashed and sank into Coll's left arm.

Blood spread, staining Coll's sleeve. Coll watched the glistening tide of blood and seemed puzzled. I wriggled out of Lachlan's grasp and ran to him. Rab's broadsword fell clattering to the floor beside us. My fingers found the cut edges of Coll's sleeve and pulled them apart to reveal the source of gushing red beneath. The edges of my vision turned black when I saw the wound. Coll seemed unaffected by his arm although the vexation in him was evident as he turned away. Rab was unable to look at anything but the floor, and tears ran down his cheeks.

Coll flung his sword onto the long table and lowered himself to a chair. Lachlan grabbed candles and lit them from the fire.

"I'll fetch water," I offered, surprised I could speak.

When I returned with a bowl and a handful of rags, I discovered Coll had removed his shirt. Candlelight shone on his skin, bringing into relief the long, old scar on his back and the new wound on his upper arm. Sandy poured whisky liberally onto a square of linen, splashing the spirit to table and floor, and held it to the gash to staunch the flow of blood. He packed the wound with lint. The edges of the skin were held a little apart to prevent matter from being kept inside and causing the wound to fester. Sandy was careful not to stuff the lint in too firmly, and covered it with a cloth dipped in linseed oil before he wrapped linen strips about the arm and tied them.

I touched Coll's cheek, finding it cool. The scents of metallic blood and spilt whisky surrounded us.

Sandy regarded me flatly when his task was done. "'Tis a deep wound, but the healing will begin now it's been tended. In a few days I'll remove the dressing and put in new lint, and change it twice a day after that. If it's kept clean and soft and bandaged so, he should have little trouble with it." He stood and left us.

Coll gazed blearily at his arm. I took the opportunity to take the seat Sandy vacated and immersed a clean rag into the water. I wiped the blood from his lower arm and patted the skin dry with another piece.

"Where is Rabbie?" Coll asked.

I searched the hall. "He's gone. I know not where."

He grunted.

"How is it?" I asked. "Is the pain very bad?"

"Nought to be fussing over. I'm not used to having someone fuss over such things."

"Will it affect your joining the regiment, do you think?"

"No," he said, contemplating the question. "And then there's half a year to pass before we face an enemy. If Sandy says it will cause me no difficulty, I believe him."

Sandy returned, bringing a new sark and a lantern. "Is it to bed with you?" he asked Coll. "Or will you sit up until the whisky pulls you into a stupor?"

"Wherever I go, whether it's to my bed or the floor here, Keeley should not be left alone."

My father-in-law nodded. He had not asked for the reason behind the bloodshed this night but I feared he did not need to. "Well?" he asked, gazing at Coll, Lachlan, and then at me. "What is it to be?"

I was uncertain where Rab had gone, and though I suspected his mood was one of remorse I did not want to take the risk of being found by him.

Sounding weary, Coll said, "Lachlan, will you stay with Keeley?" and levered himself upward. Sandy helped Coll manipulate his arms into the clean shirt. The two men were of a height, and a look passed between them. I supposed that Sandy said, without words, how relieved he was that the wound was not deadly, whilst Coll gave his thanks for his help, and a sheepish apology for having lifted a sword against Rab.

Self-consciously I waited whilst Sandy smoothed the open fronts of the shirt against Coll's chest. He said, "I'll clean up here and see if I can find Rab. He'll want to know it's not a mortal injury." He took a rag and began to wipe the floor.

Lachlan led the way upstairs but I insisted we see Coll to his chamber. Coll took to his bed with a groan of relief, fully clothed and all, and rolled on his right side. I pried off his brogues and pulled the coverlet over him.

"I'll wait in this chair until he sleeps," I said bravely, sitting on the edge of the cushion.

Lachlan nodded. "I'll see you to your chamber then, and sleep outside your door." He flung himself down on the sheepskins before the fire where Coll and I had often lain. Despite his effort to be watchful his head soon slid from his hand. He rolled to his back with an arm hooked over his eyes. A deep snore emanated from his throat and I watched him descend into a deep, untroubled sleep. Just so he must have slept wrapped in his plaid on the hard ground when he took the cattle over the hills to Falkirk.

Coll called to me. I abandoned the chair and went to his side. "Lie here beside me."

"Lachlan is here..."

"He's asleep. He sleeps like death. Lie here with me, just for a while."

Against my better judgment I climbed between the mulberry

curtains onto the bed. How foolish we were, with Lachlan at our feet, Andrew and Anne close by, and Rab's whereabouts unknown. Coll's injured arm came over me as I lay beside him, facing him, the coverlet loose over me.

I could visualize his duel with Rab too clearly. There was no doubt he was an experienced swordsman, that he knew what to do on a battlefield, that all else would fade in his mind as he single-mindedly pursued his foe. He had killed in America and he would kill again. The ability to take another's life was a facet of him I must accept.

His arm was heavy and yet his fingers caressed my shoulder. The vision slid away. He was the Coll who loved me, and in the darkness I touched his chest and was filled with relief.

"Tell me," he said in a low voice. "What was it Rab did to you?"

"Tomorrow. I'll tell you then."

"Tell me now."

I pieced the words together. "I was on my way to my room, and discovered Rab seducing Ròs. He'd not shut his door properly. I was able to persuade him to let her go. But he wanted me, instead, and..." I paused, but went on, "I was not of a mind to have it happen. I told him I knew about Isabel. He said they'd had a disagreement. It must be why he's been in such a foul mood of late."

I could feel his virulence rising, much like the fur on Grizel's cat whenever she spied one of Gordon's hunting dogs. The tension in his arm was infectious. I dreaded saying the next bit, but knew I must. "He told me he knew I had feelings for you. But he thinks that is the sum of it, and does not know we've been lovers."

He drew a careful breath and let it escape him in a long, drawn out trail.

"We quarreled, and when he tried to force me to lie with him, I could not suffer it."

His hand squeezed my upper arm as he attempted to control his reaction and comfort me instead. "It made him furious," he concluded.

"I had difficulty getting away. I kicked him. Oh Coll, I kicked him in the eye. How could I do such a thing? I did not want to hurt him. I only wanted to get away."

His hand brought me closer to him and I felt his chin on the top of my head. Eventually he said, "I did not want to hurt him, either, and yet look what I did. I tried to kill him."

"I was so frightened, watching you. If either of you had killed the other, there would be the gallows, waiting for the neck of the survivor. How could I bear it?"

He had no answer. I thought the remorse must be wretched for him and yet it did not obliterate his rage.

"And now," I murmured, "I know not what to do. How will it be for all of us tomorrow? How will any of us look one another in the eye?"

"I do not ken," he replied. "My mind is so thick I cannot think."

"You are still angry."

"It may never leave me." He held me, but as the moments passed his arm began to loosen, and his breathing began to slow.

I said, "This thing you feel you must do, what you spoke to me about before. Will it make a difference still?"

He had to ponder it. "Aye."

There was no use in asking questions about it. I remained as silent as he, and felt him relax as the minutes went by.

I had to tell him. I must. There would never be a good time to do it. "Coll?"

He muttered a little noise.

"There is something else. Are you awake? I must tell you something."

He made the noise again, though this time it was a little longer in coming.

I took a deep breath. "It may make a difference. I have long put off telling you, because I have not known for sure. I still do not know. There are signs, but it could be just that—my courses are coming upon me and are taking their time. I wish I could know for sure. But I think—I could be with child."

Nothing. He uttered not a sound. I held my breath. He did not move. I dared not move. I said, "Coll?"

There was no answer. He had fallen asleep.

I forced myself to rest beside him whilst I listened to my

racing heart and willed it to slow its reckless pace. The sound of it in my ears became drowned by the rain pattering on the glass of the window and the rushing burn tumbling in spate below the castle walls.

Why should thy cheek be pale,
Shaded with sorrow's veil?
Why should'st thou grieve me?
I will never, never leave thee.

I'll Never Leave Thee (Trad.)

Chapter Thirty-Four

aybreak arrived. I rose from my bed and threw on clothing. Lachlan was asleep on the other side of my door, curled on the floor in the passage where I had left him the night before. He awoke and accompanied me to Coll's chamber.

Coll smiled groggily and reached for my hand when we entered, keeping his bloodshot eyes shielded from the light from the window. The rain had stopped, finally, and the absence of its gurgling created a welcome silence. He said, "A drink. Of aught. I'm getting up."

"I'll fetch you a cup of water," I suggested, pulling up his loose sleeve to examine the bandage. No red streaks traveled his arm—the crimson stripes that were a sure sign of poisoning—but they would have to be watched for, as well as any other sign of infection. His fingers pinched my skirts, slowing me from my retreat, but soon fell away.

Lachlan offered to go for water but in bright daylight I felt relatively safe. In the great hall I paused, and crossed to the entryway to open the door facing the loch. The world was rust-colored and wet, with the sky stained pink at the horizon and growing into a light blue higher in the heavens. I floated down the steps, breathing in the cold air and finding my exhalations misting in front of me. My head ached and I suffered a lack of sleep that made my eyes hurt.

I wondered, as I squinted at half of a white, mottled moon, where Rab might be and in what state his mind would be this day. I never wanted Rab to touch me again but he would never permit me to keep my door locked against him. I visualized myself standing as I did now, on the banks of the loch, but with a babe in my arms. "I will stay with the earl until the end of his days," I said to a heron who solemnly watched me from the water's edge. "And if I have a child I will stay until the end of mine. But how will I bear my life with Rab?" My bravery, so proudly buckled round me last night, began to come undone.

I washed my face with the cold water of the loch and dried it on my skirt. I tread past the front of the castle and followed the path to the gardens. The rowan trees had been stripped of their berries and the orange skins littered the ground beneath their branches, evidence of the birds that had harvested them. The gardens were well washed; the benches sparkled in the morning sun. Chaffinches flitted through the shrubs as they looked for food but the sight brought me none of its usual cheer. I swung aside the postern gate and crossed the soggy courtyard. I pushed open the kitchen door. The heavy door crashed behind me.

Grizel was by the fireside, stirring a pot with her spurtle, and the sweet, nutty aroma of porridge filled the huge room. My shoes crunched on the sanded flagstone floor. Without looking round, she called, "So you're here already! I thought you would be. I even put your food on the table. If you hurry..." She put the wooden stick down and straightened, beginning to smile.

"I've not come for breakfast," I told her, finding it a challenge to exist in the present and forget my troubles.

She drew a quick breath. I was sure she was going to scream. "Oh!" she gasped, catching herself. "It's you! *A chiall.*"

"You thought I was someone else."

She nodded, wiping her hands on her apron. My eyes fell on the table beside her where a cog sat filled to the top with steaming porridge. There were piles of oatcakes and barley bannocks, a glass of whisky, plates of eggs and boiled fish, yellow cheese, butter, honey, and currant jelly. A breakfast fit for a king.

"Someone will have a fine breakfast." I stated the obvious but I was mystified because she would not speak.

"Aye," she said too quickly. "'Tis—for Sandy."

"I only came for water."

"Oh, aye, aye." She crossed to the dresser where she slid a pewter mutchkin from the shelf. I took it from her, noticing her hand was trembling. I dipped the vessel in the pail of fresh water by the hearth.

She watched me as I left, wringing her hands. Her nervousness bred a similar condition in me. I made my way up the spiral stairs to the great hall. Sandy was there, tending the fire in the huge fireplace. He turned as soon as he heard my steps and his brows came down. His face seemed dismal, but his eyes smoldered.

I wondered yet again to what degree he suspected my infidelity to his son, and how deeply he blamed me for last night's folly. I was able to say, "Good morning."

He nodded gravely.

"Did you find Rab last night? How was he?"

"Aye, I found him. He was with Lord Kirthgarran. The earl was asleep, but Rabbie was sitting in his chamber, in the dark. Waiting, I suppose, for word, if there was aught to come. I convinced him all was well with Coll and that their stupidity had no ill consequences, for which he was grateful and wept more. I put him to bed and he seemed calm enough."

I discovered I could not meet his gaze. I knew I would never be able to explain what had occurred between Rab and me. I turned, eager to take my leave of him. Then I remembered. "Grizel has your breakfast ready."

"My breakfast?"

"She has it waiting on the kitchen table."

"I had my meal an hour ago."

I stared at him. All at once I knew Grizel had lied to me. The food had been for someone else, someone about whom she did not want me to know.

Dreading what I might find, I went back to the kitchen and stood looking at the table. The food was gone. The plates, glass, and cutlery were nowhere to be seen and Grizel herself was missing. I was reminded of the day before when I had heard the floor groan outside the library door.

I turned away, incapable of considering what it meant.

Coll had decided he did not want to lie abed any longer and was sitting up when I arrived. His arm was stiff, he said, but no worse. Even so, I suspected a drop of whisky would go into the cup of water as soon as he could get some. Lachlan was going to help him shave and Airig was off after hot water. There were noises coming from the bedchamber next door. We parted, but not without a tender glance between us and a wish that we could be alone.

"Be wary of Rab," he whispered.

I was lost. I could not eat. I fretted about meeting Rab. In my chamber I changed into the newly-finished, flowered linen gown, for the sleeves were long and covered my wrists. Airig soon found me. We talked of the events of the night before. She had been horrified when she'd learnt from Sandy that blood had been spilt between Rab and the Captain. It was a drunken quarrel, Sandy had told her, and the wounding had been an accident. There was no mention of me or any part I might have taken in it.

Airig was incensed at Ròs, who had slipped into bed beside her the night before and wept and wept. The story of me coming upon her and Rab had finally emerged, and Airig had not blamed Rab at all. The fault was on Ròs' shoulders, for she was a flirt, a seductress, a witch who enchanted men. Airig had no sympathy for her, just a great desire for forgiveness from me though it was her sister, she said, who should ask for it.

I told her she must worry no further and added, "Where is Ròs'?

"She's at home, with our father and mother. In shame, I

might add."

"It was not all her fault, Airig."

She scowled at me, unwilling to hear anything unpleasant about Rab. I said no more, for I was not in the mood to create a rift between us.

When Mairi, Andrew, and Anne took their leave, Rab was there in the hall, tight-lipped and silent. I cringed when I saw his blackened eye with the cut beneath. He avoided looking at me and at Coll who stood nearby clad in army kilt and white waistcoat. How matters stood between the two of them was impossible to tell, for their faces were like stone. Andrew watched them both, preoccupied, and Mairi held back tears.

Anne embraced me. "It will all fade away," she reassured me buoyantly. "As lads they often had their clashes. Never quite like this," she admitted, stealing a quick look at Coll. "But they're so close. It cannot last."

"I hope you are right, Anne."

"Mairi takes everything so deeply to heart. It's unfortunate this had to happen before Coll left. I'll be glad when my bairn arrives, if only to cheer her! She'll love having a grandchild. It will ease the pain of Coll being away. She spends so much time now, alone, by herself, locked in her chamber and not even wanting me near. Or wearing herself away tending sick folk in their cottages. But with a wean about, she'll learn to laugh again, do you not think?"

I agreed with her. I would have responded with more spirit, I believed, if I were not so conscious of Sandy's eyes upon me. There was no doubt he blamed me for last night's disaster. I could not remain under his gaze after the three returned to Rathdale, and I retreated upstairs.

Lord Kirthgarran must have been told of the row between his foster sons, for nothing else could explain his dismal appearance. His blue eyes were shadowed and his color was that of linen paper. The drapes were drawn at the windows and he wanted them to remain so. He did not speak of Coll or Rab, and I did not dare refer to them, but I was eager to somehow restore him to his usual self. He asked me to play the clarsach and I was only too glad to fetch it.

"What is it you'd like to hear, my lord?"

"Something sweet and long, something to fall asleep by."

"Does your head still pain you? Will Grizel make you a draught? Or an infusion of chamomile?"

"The music is what I need, lass. You choose what it is to be."

I settled myself by his bed, alarmed by his weakness. I plucked chords randomly until I could think of a quiet lullaby, and then I began to play, thumbs up, fingers caressing the strings.

His eyes closed and his breaths deepened. Airig came in and sat on the stool at my feet, her hands clasped in her apron as she listened. When I ended the tune and found that Lord Kirthgarran was overcome by slumber, Airig tilted her head and smiled.

"How soothing it is, indeed. It makes one forget all the drumlie things."

"It soothes me to play, as well."

"How I wish my mother could hear you," she said wistfully. "She's not recovered. Not as she should. The fever has left her but she remains frail and uncaring. It's more than all that, though. It's the clearing, I think." She added after some thought, "I've not seen her this day, but I know she'll be feeling worse, for if Ròs leaves service here at the castle because of last night she'll not be sending home the wages."

"I wish no one had to leave the glens, Airig. And hopefully Ròs will not leave service."

"Would you play for our mother?" she asked. "She loves music dearly. If that does not lift her spirits, nought can."

I liked Airig's parents, for they were warm-hearted folk who did not stare at me or shy away from me as if I were evil. Their wee house reminded me of Mrs. Dundas's dwelling in Melrose where I had spent so many happy hours, and sometimes I wished I had been raised in a wee but-and-ben like theirs with simple chores to occupy myself and down-to-earth expectations of life to which to cling. I was still hesitant to play my clarsach in front of others, but I was not as self-conscious as I had once been.

"Perhaps it is a good idea," I told her. "And if Ròs is there, I can talk to her and tell her I forgive her. Then she can come back to the castle and everything will be as it was."

I wonder if she heard the deceit in my words. Nothing would ever be the same again.

Beside her parents' glowing peat fire we spoke of the winter's fickle weather, Coll's going away, and the springtime when great change would take place. When I played my clarsach Airig's mother's face lit with joy. At times the family sang in Gaelic to my tunes, and it was a peaceful hour we spent.

Ròs lurked in the shadows until Airig dragged her out. Her eyes were red and swollen, and she kept biting her lips. Stray tears threatened to jump out from betwixt her lids.

I said to her out of the hearing of her family, "It's quite all right, Ròs. I do not blame you for what happened. Rab—Rab did not truly think about what he was doing."

"I do not ken, Mrs. I do not ken if I can ever come back."

"You're the one who must decide. But I hope you do. You are needed. The earl and I would miss you terribly."

She was doubtful. She puffed copper hair out of her eyes and smeared her tears away. "How can I ever see Rabbie again?"

"I think he'll be on his best behavior," I confided. "And if we must speak of this to Lord Kirthgarran, we will. We must all try to muddle through. None of us knows what to do, but we must take each day as it comes."

She nodded her head over and over, eager to agree. At last she said, "I am so very sorry. I never meant for any of it to happen."

"I understand."

She was obviously much relieved until she caught Airig scowling at her. She gave my hand a squeeze and disappeared into the byre.

I wanted to take my leave after that. Airig's mother invited me to have ale and bannocks with them, but I was too restless. Airig thought she would stay. I yearned to be off for home.

The sun was neither bright nor warm, but such a treat to see after all the days of rain. It was the time of year when birds gathered in flocks and flew about searching for seeds and insects in their restive journey from cold lands to warmer ones. A veil of thrushes shifted through the air before me and settled in unison to peck at the ground, but before I could reach them they lifted upward again and sailed through the sky. I wandered into the garden and rested my clarsach on one of the stone benches. The loch was still calm, and a handful of wild ducks waddled on the shore.

The jingle of harness broke into my reverie. Approaching from the track to the clachan was Coll.

I met him by the garden wall. His eyes were tired but he seemed better on the whole, although there was a grimness about him that did not disappear when he smiled. "Are you away?" he asked.

"I've just come back. I've been to see Airig's mother who is ill."

"How is Ròs?" The grimness was displaced by a flare of rage. I saw it kindle in his eyes and remain. I sought to find an answer that would not breathe further life into it.

"She's tearful and wanting forgiveness from me. She wants to come back. I told her I thought Rab would be remorseful as well. Is he? Have you talked to him?"

"There've been no words between us."

There was no resolution, then. "Did your mother ask many questions before she left?"

"She tried. Neither Rab nor I offered much. We've disappointed her. Luckily Sandy has made it seem as though it was a foolish row with both of us fou and out of our heads. The earl, too, accepted it as such." He began walking toward the courtyard and I followed. He was wearing his scarlet coat, and I knew he must have been making himself visible in the glen, seeking recruits. He asked, when we came to the gate, "Have *you* spoken to Rab?"

"I've been avoiding him, and he's been doing the same."

He found my hand and held it. His temper seemed to cool. "Will you meet me at the Rathdale cottage?"

I was filled with longing. "When?"

"You could go now. I'll follow."

I changed my clothes and returned to the courtyard ready to ride. Coll and Dominie were no longer there. In the stable Greyfriar was in his box, nuzzling an empty oat bag.

"Ah, Mrs. Rab," MacNeil mumbled happily. "Have you come to take the lad for a bit of exercise? He needs it sorely."

"I have," I answered, fondling the garron's silky white mane. "I need it, as well."

"Ach, the rain, the rain," he sighed, reaching for a bridle. "It puts aches in a man's bones and a chill in his blood. Let's hope for a day or two without it, or the laithfu' snow."

He brought Greyfriar out and saddled him, poking him in the stomach to remind him to exhale. The pony's hair was growing thick for the winter and he looked much different than when Rab had first bought him for me in July.

Moments later I rode fast for Rathdale.

The freedom was intoxicating. The wind rushed past my ears. Amber and amethyst hills, grass, still green, a sky of delicate blue—the colors were exhilarating after days of gray.

I made my way to the abandoned cottage in the hollow of yews and honeysuckles. Greyfriar seemed to remember it. After I led him into the byre I petted him and he blinked his wide eyes at me and tossed his head in pleasure.

From the window I saw Coll coming. The black shape of him on the horizon metamorphosed into horse and soldier, though the dark tartan was difficult to distinguish from the beast. Soon Dominie joined Greyfriar as a stable mate once again.

Our arms came round each other. Dominie snorted through his nose and Coll laughed as he considered the horses. "I imagine if they could talk they would say, 'What have we done to be penned like cows?'"

We came away into the main apartment. The air was cold and I would have loved to light a fire on the hearth. I put my cocked hat and cloak on the wooden table, and Coll began removing the slings from his chest into which dirk and pistols had been thrust. He released his plaid from his shoulders and unbuttoned his coat. With care he began to pull his arms from the sleeves and I helped him, gingerly sliding the coat from first his good arm, then his injured one. Only the slightest bulge within the volume of his left sleeve served as a reminder of the blood, the fiery whisky, the packing of the lint.

I averted the memory and Coll's mouth was there against mine, carrying my spirit on its usual journey. Though I knew not how we reached it, we fell upon the bracken-filled bolster in the box bed, his body on top of mine. In desperate need I aided him in his hunt for bare flesh and sought ways to bunch clothing out of the way.

There was an odd mixture of temperatures: his fingers were cold and intensified the exquisite pleasure of their touch. His mouth was warm and melting. The feverish chaos between us blazed into abandonment. I dropped into a hazy world of flaming gratification. Every sense was consumed by him. I gave myself up to the ecstasy.

Where did the hours go? We stole time from the world, the universe, God's scheme of things. Yet it was never enough.

Our coupling had a tranquilizing effect upon us, but for me the devastating threat of our eventual separation could not be obscured.

Perhaps it chafed him as well, for I could tell he was troubled. His resentment and antagonism toward Rab still burnt, especially when he saw my purple-dappled wrists anew and took them into his hands for study. He said nothing, but his eyes became smoke-gray.

We did not speak of his leaving for Argyll to join the regiment, except once when he referred to the secret task he hoped to complete. "It will be soon, my dear heart," he promised, his voice low. "Tonight, perhaps. Or tomorrow. I am sure of it."

I did not ask him how I would know, or what would happen, and he would not elaborate. He drew me close against his body, ran a loving hand through my hair, and brought forth fire between us again for which there was only one remedy.

Time trickled by, unheeded.

Coll pulled himself from the box bed at last and towed me to my feet beside him. "You should go back first," he suggested.

I held his coat as he inserted his arms and settled it cautiously on his shoulders. "Grizel had venison roasting over the fire when I left," I said, trying to find something neutral to say.

"I would rather sit at table and look at you."

"You make it difficult sometimes. It is all I can do to ignore you." I thought of Rab and his knowledge of my hidden affections. Apparently I had not hidden them as well as I had believed. I said, "Let me help you with your buttons."

He watched my face as I fumbled with them. He was not

smiling. When I was finished his cool hands took mine. "I plan to call upon Kirstie tonight, Keeley, for a few minutes. I'll not be long."

"I've often thought about her."

"Rabbie may have purposefully provoked me last night but I've not been able to forget his words. She did take the news badly—of my joining the regiment."

I ducked my head so he could not see my face. "She loves you."

"She does not understand why I'm leaving her. I've hurt her and I never meant to."

"You've never told me how it was between you."

"There were never any promises. I never brought her to my bed."

"What will you say to her?"

"I do not ken. I'm deserting her, but I'm afraid that began to happen months ago. I must try to convince her that although she means a great deal to me, I cannot feel we belong together. Perhaps, one day, if you'd not come, she and I..." He would not finish the thought.

"You're being too hard on yourself."

"She had dreams. I never tried to dissuade her from them. Like it or not, I am responsible for her greeting."

"If you can find words of comfort for her, then she'll be grateful, I think."

His hands left mine and one touched my cheek, forcing me to look at him. "After last night I cannot imagine how I can leave you to spend the rest of your life with Rab."

I dared not feel joy—or hope.

"I should not have told you that," he said. His eyes narrowed. "What I mean to do is to give you a choice. To come to me—after the earl is gone—or not."

"A choice? I thought you meant only to make our parting less painful. I do not need to be given a choice. I already know what I would choose."

"The time is not right. But it will be. I promise." His good arm enfolded me, crushed me, before he let me go.

I put on my hat and cloak and led Greyfriar out between the yews. I lingered on the sight of Coll's frame outlined by the rough door-cheeks, sought his eyes, and mouthed a farewell. My heels kicked the garron's sides and we bolted over the moor back to Kirthgarran.

The song, the dance are all in vain…
O, Tell Me Where She Rests To-night (Trad.)

Chapter Thirty-Five

We were a small party at supper, Sandy, Lachlan, Coll, and I. Grizel's platter of hot venison steamed on the dining room table along with earthenware bowls of colcannon and sausage-coated eggs. The queen's ware at Rab's place remained empty, proclaiming his absence only too loudly.

Ròs had returned. She fluttered about the table in her pretty yellow gown, pouring ale from a jug, obviously shaken but nonetheless content and bravely ignoring her swollen eyes.

There was very little talk. Outside it became dark, for a mist began to rise and the stars and moon were hidden by blankets of cloud. When our quiet meal was finished, Coll made his excuses and left for the home of the piper's daughter. Unsettled, I went up to see Lord Kirthgarran who had eaten his supper and drunk a small glass of wine. His color was better but he seemed subdued. His eyes fastened upon me whilst I sat back into the soft chair beside his bed.

"You were asleep when I left you this morning," I said, trying to throw off my agitated mood, for he was watchful this evening.

"My dreams were all of music, my lass."

I was aghast. I'd been so preoccupied by my plans to meet Coll that afternoon I had hastened inside the castle and left my clarsach on the stone settle.

I explained I must retrieve the harp and flew down the stair. The land was unearthly outside of the castle walls, for fog wreathed the grass and shrubs. I stumbled to the postern gate despite the light of the lantern I carried. I started when I heard a voice and reeled to see my husband coming out of the stable.

"Keeley," he said, not unkindly.

I took in a breath to steady myself. He had a lantern of his own and the light created a glowing, white sphere about him. Lit from below, his face seemed demonic, the cut on his cheek angry. His brown hair was uncombed, wavy and damp about his face. I wondered if he had been dreading this meeting all the day as I had been.

We gazed intently at each other and I said, "I am sorry, Rab, that I hurt your eye."

"I'm sure I deserved it."

"Do you not remember?"

"Do I remember?" He shook his head a little. "What do I remember? I mind finding Ròs in my chamber. I mind thinking I wanted to bed her, and trying to. And then you were there. And I made a fool of myself."

"You were not altogether yourself."

"I said things to you I never should have said, and threw you to the floor like a whore not worth tuppence, and tried to kill the kinsman I love like no other." There was anguish in his voice.

"Then you remember everything."

"I wish I did not. It would be easier to live in the light of day. You and I—Keeley, we need to settle this between us."

"I do not know what to do."

"I should start being honest with you."

I screwed my shawl tighter against my throat. "What have you to tell me?"

"Things to bear out what you yourself said last night. Mayhap this is not the time nor place to do it. But certainly, before we leave this conversation, there are a pair of things I must tell you." He glanced down, finding it difficult, I expected, to begin. His eyes searched the ground and a muscle in his jaw pulsed before his gaze came back to me. "One is that you're indeed right. It is Isabel for me. It always has been. She and I fell in love years ago, and though we've had our disagreements and at times the words fly thick and unseemly between us, there is no one like her. I tell you that because I think you believe you've failed me. You should not, because I never expected aught from you."

"If you loved her," I faltered, "why did you come back to Melrose? Why did you ask my father for me?"

"I wanted to save you. I wanted to have you here."

"And what of Isabel?"

"I thought I could have you both. But I've become confused. It is Isabel I want, and then 'tis you I want. If it is love I feel for you, I do not know. In my heart I never expected it, but of late, without reason, I've been jealous of Coll because I think the two of you could have made each other happy. It makes no sense at all to me. I do not love you but no one else must. I do not require your love but want it anyway. I cannot fathom it. It's what sends me into madness."

"And it was not this way at first?" I asked, astounded.

"You are a gentlewoman, born to live in a place such as Kirthgarran. You belong here, as Isabel does not. How could she live in the ancestral castle, the daughter of a landless laborer? So at first it was fine, aye. But now, things have gone very wrong betwixt you and me. I close my eyes and picture bonny bairns climbing over our knees, and the tower in the background, and sheep grazing on the hills. So here's the second thing to tell. I'll keep the vows of our marriage. I'll give up the woman I love. I'll send her away and be faithful to you. And you must become the wife I find I need."

"What kind of a wife is that?" I could not make my words more than a trembling murmur.

"You must be mine alone. Your clothes and books and clarsach and that, all moved into my chamber so it becomes yours as well. Every night you must spend in my bed, and lie with me as I've discovered I need it. Give me sons. And never think of leaving me. For if you do, I will come after you, Keeley, and bring you home again. It is, after all, what the vows of marriage mean, do they not? Commitments to each other. We should have kept them from the start."

"You make it sound as if I'm to be a prisoner."

"Your father kept you as a prisoner. You were locked in your room at times, with nought but water and porridge. Do you think that is what I offer you?"

"You told me a long time ago that a home, even if loved, would be a prison when the freedom to leave it no longer existed."

His voice softened a little. "Kirthgarran is not a gaol, dear. Anyway, I do not think you realize you cannot make the decision, to go or to stay."

I strove to ignore the illusion of evil that the lantern light cast, but there was no relief from the creeping unease his words caused. "There's something that frightens me," I said. "There is a threat behind what you say."

He was contemplative. "I give up much, making Isabel go. I suppose I want to be reassured it's for the better."

"And what will happen if I cannot satisfy you? If I cannot love you, or pretend to love you as you think I ought, or give you sons, or if I become so unhappy I long to live anywhere but here at Kirthgarran?"

"Even as you say those things, something boils within me. How have I reacted in the past? What did I do last night? Will I do it again? Crivvens, Keeley, I do not ken. You know, you must know, I am sorry for everything. I never mean to hurt you."

"But you do."

"If Isabel is gone and you turn away from me, will I do things I regret? I hope I will not. You do not know how deeply I pray for that. I give you the best pledge of which I am capable. I told you I would try. I cannot be more honest, more sincere than that. Would it please you better if I lied?"

"What you're expecting me to do is to forget everything, forgive us both, and be grateful you're to give up a lover. You'll have your dream, it seems. And what will I have?"

"A happy life, I hope. A husband who will give you aught you ask for. What did you want when you befriended the shepherd lad in Melrose?"

I straightened and at last was not afraid to look him in the eye. "Trust, I think. Will I have it with you? Will you be able to trust me? What if you imagine me spending too much time with Lachlan? What if I, feeling starved for real love, turn to someone else? What if there is another woman in the glen who catches your eye, because I cannot be who you want me to be?"

Impatience creased his brow. "What guarantees are any two people able to make? Do you ken how many bluidy marriages there are without love? The world cannot all be falling apart because of it."

"Mayhap you should just keep Isabel. Keep her, if she is the one who makes you happy."

"But she does not. She has not. It's what I'm telling you. It's you I've decided I want. You and no one else."

"But you love her, Rab. I ask for nought but to be left alone. Whilst Lord Kirthgarran is with us, at least, I will know contentment."

His impatience dissolved into ire. "You've turned this into a fine argument. What do you suggest we do to repair the damage between us?"

"I do not know."

"Is it more to your liking to have things remain as they are?"

"It's not what I envisioned when I married you."

"You had to be forced into that."

"We are back at the beginning," I said, "because I do not understand why you ever wanted it."

"It matters not what I wanted then. You know what it is I want now." He began to put out a hand and I retreated.

"Can you not see? Even now I am afraid of you."

"Jings, you've heard nought I've said! I want you to care for me. Why would I hurt you?"

"You may not want to, but perhaps you will, if not today, then another day, and that is the possibility I cannot live with."

He said, less heatedly, "You're forgetting again, you do not have such a choice." He attempted to reach for me again, but I whirled away and headed for the door across the courtyard. He was there beside me at the door. His hand fell upon mine as it curved over the handle.

"Please don't," I said with passion. In surprise his fingers dropped away.

I heaved on the door. I stepped into the kitchen. Grizel was there, engrossed in her knitting as she sat beside the fire, with the orange cat putting out a sleepy paw to pat the dangling skein of yarn. She looked up as we came in but I did not speak to her. I started up the mural stair to the great hall above. Before I took a second step, however, I halted.

"I've forgotten my clarsach." My voice sounded quite lifeless.

Rab, beside me, stopped as well. I glanced at him anxiously, but now that the lights of the lanterns were aided by the kitchen fire and the cruise lamp he seemed normal. His eyes were round and luminous. His lips were turned down in a face covered with the shadow of unshaven beard.

I did not know what kind of a woman I was. I did not understand how I could reject the apologetic embrace of a man who genuinely meant to mend the wounds between us and become a loving husband. Conflicting emotions cut and dashed wildly inside me.

"Where is it?" he asked softly.

"I left it in the garden this afternoon. On a settle."

"Is that why you came out?"

"I have to fetch it."

"I'll get it. I ken you're not fond of the dark. Go upstairs and after I curry McKay I'll bring it up to you." He turned and went back the way we had come.

I was too distraught to play for the earl as it was. After some consideration I went back down to the kitchen and put my lantern on the table.

"Grizel, at times you give Lord Kirthgarran a draught that makes him sleepy. Could you make it for me? I—I've not been sleeping well lately, and I do not think I can bear another night without sleep."

"I make it from the *lus a bhalgair*, the foxglove," she told me, nodding and folding up her knitting. She went into the larder after buttermilk. A targe, a leather-covered shield ornamented with brass nails and once worn proudly on the arm of a warrior, served as the cover of the milk cask. Whilst she lifted it and prepared to dip in a tumbler I discovered I could not keep still and began wandering about the kitchen.

Grizel gripped a hot stone from the hearth with her tongs and dropped it into the glass. She began measuring flakes into a mortar. I crossed to the door and opened it. Kit was by my feet and I picked her up and held her soft, warm body at my breast as I peered out through the mist. The cat began to purr and I stroked her throat, feeling the vibration there.

A sharp crack caused me to jump. The cat's ears twitched and she leapt from my arms. My hand went to the door-post. There was no doubt in mind that the noise had come from a discharging firearm. I called out the door, "Rab?" The silence was as pervasive as the mist.

I waited, listening intently, but when no answer came I grabbed my lantern and ran across the courtyard and through the postern gate. The shape of the settle in the garden was enveloped by the glow from Rab's lantern. My clarsach was lying on the ground beside the bench, and so was Rab.

I fell to my knees beside him. My hands felt for his shoulders. I brought my face close to his and touched his cheek. He was breathing.

"Keeley," came his voice.

"Oh Rab! Aye it is me. Do not speak." I tried to glance about me, to see if anyone else was near.

"Help me—help me up." To my horror he struggled to rise.

A form grew out of the fog, and then another. Grizel and Sandy knelt beside us. MacNeil brought another lantern and Sandy pulled Rab's coat aside.

Rab lay back, gasping. My arm was underneath him and I could feel the wetness there, the warmth, the stickiness. The flames showed a sheen of sweat on Rab's face. His eyes were closed and there was blood at the corner of his mouth. Blood covered his chest. As I looked he began slipping farther down to the ground. Together we crumpled to the grass. My gown, white with printed, violet flowers, became sodden with his blood.

"Rab."

He was weak. His eyes were open, and he whispered between hard-won breaths, "Keeley?"

"I'm here. I'm holding you." My tears fell on his colorless face. I smoothed his hair. I wanted to scream, "Who has done this?"

"I cannot see you," he uttered. "Nor can I feel you."

"I'm here. Oh, I'm here. Feel me holding you. I'll not let go." I wept, hearing the irony in my broken voice, remembering our argument about promises.

There was blood everywhere. The extent of it seemed worse than before. His breaths came shallowly. One. Another. And then there were none at all.

I called his name. I looked at Sandy in panic. Rab's body lay limp against me. My arms bound him to me but it was a body without life.

Lachlan fell beside us. He lowered his ear to Rab's mouth and I watched the realization of his brother's death take hold of him. For many moments he did not speak and when he did I could hear the tears in his throat. "What happened? What was he doing?"

My lips could barely move. "He was here in the garden."

"Was he alone?" Lachlan demanded. "Were you here? Did you see anyone else?"

Sandy's head was bowed so I could no longer see his face, but his hands shook as he touched his son's face. Grizel was sobbing.

With difficulty I made myself think. "He came out alone. For just a moment. I heard..." I squeezed my eyes shut hoping it would help me think. "I heard the shot and I came. But I only saw Rab."

Lachlan got to his feet and as he did so, Coll appeared beside us. I looked up at him. The picture we made must have been a horrible one. Disbelief flooded his face as he took in the sight of me, soaked in crimson and holding Rab's lifeless form whilst

Sandy stroked his son's cheek.

"My God," Coll choked out. He sank beside me and felt for a pulse in Rab's neck.

Nothing was very clear to me after that. I was aware of being coaxed up from the ground. I tried to resist. Eventually I was lifted and taken to the kitchen.

Sandy and Coll carried Rab inside and started to lay him on the hearth, but Sandy's legs crumpled. He sat crookedly where he landed on the flagstones and buried his face in Rab's coat, unable to move further.

With rags they blotted Rab's blood from my gown. Others came: Ròs, who screamed until she had to be removed; Airig, who fell to her knees to caress Rab's still hand; MacNeil, who wielded a horse rug to cover Rab's chest; Kenneth, Gordon, and Magnus, who stood in the doorway with Grizel.

Coll sat on a settle beside me. My head was pressed to his chest and I could hear his voice reverberating from within. I was not sure to whom he was speaking, or even what he was saying. Buttermilk had spilt on the floor and no one cared. The cat was cringing on the windowsill with ears laid flat until MacNeil tossed her out the door.

I was aware of being taken away. A sobbing Airig helped me remove my dress and chemise and wash my arms. But I was frightened by being away from the others. I begged to rejoin them and they gave me whisky that burnt my throat.

They asked me to tell what happened and I repeated it again and again. I discovered Lachlan had already searched the garden and surrounding parkland but had found no one. MacNeil and Coll went out as well, but came back with no answers—just my clarsach, which they placed on the table.

Coll said, "I heard the shot. I was walking with Kirstie. If only I'd paid attention when I came back. I might have seen someone."

The only likelihood was that a Fergusson who bitterly blamed Rab for the impending clearance of the earl's lands had sought revenge. Perhaps the man had been in a rage and had not intended to murder him, but the fact remained he was probably a madman. To shoot anyone in the back was the height of dishonor. To kill someone coldly as he stood was an atrocity.

The slayer would be found. Everyone vowed it.

Lachlan said, "We have to tell the earl."

"And my mother," Coll added. "And Andrew and Anne. Someone must go to Rathdale."

Coll and Lachlan went to tell Lord Kirthgarran together. I should have gone but I was not sure I was in control of myself. I stayed with the others in the kitchen, unable to tear my eyes from the sight of Sandy cradling his son's body in his arms, and told myself that in a few moments I would go and sit with the earl. But the thought of what was going on in Lord Kirthgarran's chamber filled me with dread. How would he respond to the news he had lost another member of his family? Could any of us provide solace to a man who had already lost his share of loved ones?

Footsteps scraped on the stone stairs. Lord Kirthgarran appeared with Coll and Lachlan on either side of him. The earl was wearing his nightshirt and his feet were bare. He lumbered forward with his foster sons holding his arms. His face was contorted with rage.

"My lord," I cried. "Why are you out of your bed? You should not have come. Coll, why have you brought him?"

"We had no choice," Coll replied. "He wanted to see Rabbie, and said he'd crawl on the floor if he must."

The earl stared down at his foster son. His breathing accelerated, his face became crimson. I went to him, afraid, wanting to plead with him to come away. His lips parted and he slurred, "There is no end to it!" His distress grew. His face became splotched with red. He was trembling and Coll and Lachlan attempted to draw him away, but it was too late.

He gave a great shudder. He convulsed once and his legs gave way. The men attempted to hold him but it was useless, and all went on their knees as they gradually lowered him to the floor.

He lay at our feet, Earl of Kirthgarran no more.

I was in bed. Awake. Sleep could be a refuge, or it could be Purgatory, depending on whether I dreamt or not. The last two days had been a combination of both—first one, then the other.

Sometimes it was Purgatory to be awake. Memories would

not go away. They were persistent, and I was forced to believe in them.

I was aware enough during my haze of sleep and dreams and memories to sit with the bodies in the great hall during the lyke wake, keeping watch as custom demanded, taking turns night and day amongst the circle of candles. The men were stretched upon their strykit boards, dressed in their deid-claes of fine linen shirts and knitted stockings, and covered with linen shrouds. Agnes had long ago made the clothes for Lord Kirthgarran. Remembering that I had finished Rab's clothes only a few weeks before tore my heart afresh.

I cried and then did not cry, repeating the rhythm of it over and over. I recognized all of the folk who came from the glen to pay their respects to Lord Kirthgarran and Rab and to touch the bodies. I felt the anguish in Isabel's breast as she threw herself on Rab and had to be carried away.

It was said that if a person touched a body and then it bled, that person was responsible for the death. Therefore it was with intense concentration that all visitors were regarded. But no new blood came from Rab's wound when he was stroked or patted, and no one came forward to confess murder.

There were covert glances thrown in my direction. I was the Harbinger of Death. There were those who believed it was my presence at Kirthgarran that had brought about the deaths of the earl and his foster son. But little did they know of the guilt I suffered. If I had not forgotten my clarsach in the garden none of this might have happened. If I was not terrified of the dark I would have rescued it myself. My guilt grew, rather than diminished, with time.

I was aware of the questioning that went on, the search that began in order to find evidence leading to the identity of Rab's cowardly and dishonorable murderer. He was not only his murderer, I told myself. He was Lord Kirthgarran's as well.

The passing-bell rang as a man carried it through the glen, crying the death of the two men. Andrew and Anne came, accompanied by Mairi. She fainted at the sight of Rab lying lifeless and bloodstained. Sandy was inconsolable, and though I embraced him, and his words in turn to me were kind, it was clear he meant to grieve alone. I could not forget the sound of his keening voice when he wept over the dead son he held.

Kirthgarran was a house of mourning, a land of mourning. Shock ran deep in all directions. In my daze I realized the Crown now owned Kirthgarran and not too far in the future there would be the complexities of that problem to face, with the solicitors at hand to lend their aid. The loss of the estate had been dreaded for years and I could not imagine how the others bore it, although the trauma of the deaths, for the moment, surely overshadowed all else.

I did not know what we would have done without Andrew who arranged the funeral, sent for Reverend Cameron, and wrote to the solicitors. He notified the crowner of Rab's murder and then questioned folk himself. The effort was fruitless. Someone was hiding the truth and only God knew when it would be revealed. Everyone was uneasy walking about the castle grounds in darkness. I was told many reported seeing corpse-lights, or deid-lights, in the birk wood and hearing odd, dull knocking noises in their houses that predicted more deaths.

"Death comes in threes," the cottars recited as they paid tearful homage to the men laid out in the hall.

Lachlan found the misshapen lump of lead in the garden. The ball had gone through Rab's body and ripped into the grass. He was not sure, but by testing the heft of it in his hand he thought the amount of lead did not warrant it being a ball from a musket.

"Nay," he said. "It must be from a pistol." Water swelled unchecked in his eyes when he told me. "A ball for a Brown Bess weighs about 500 grains. But one for a pistol, like a Light Dragoon, 'tis usually half as heavy. Like this." The difference was remarkable enough to be of use in the search for the weapon and its owner.

Coll said to me once, "You said that you and Rab were both outside earlier, near the stable. Do you know how close you came to being injured as well? What would I have done if I'd lost you, too?"

We held each other and contemplated the import of his words. Whoever had wanted Rab dead might have desired— might still desire—my death as well.

On the day before the double funeral I doubted my head

would ever clear. My mind was filled with visions of Lord Kirthgarran: how he had smiled when I'd played my clarsach, how he had taken me back hundreds of years on travels through history with him, how he had held me in his weakened arms and conveyed his affection for me.

I could see Rab as well, the Rab who'd fallen from his horse and limped to the door of Gilchrist House, listened with interest to my stories of Melrose Abbey and the Eildons, and come anxiously to my side in the summer when my father had ordered me to appear downstairs.

I rose from my bed. Airig had put me there a half-hour before, telling me I must sleep. The thoughts, however, pressed themselves less mercilessly upon me when I was up and about. I shook the wrinkles out of my skirt and absently pulled down my sleeves. I was worried about Coll's arm, too, an unwelcome adjunct to my visions. Sandy had stirred himself and removed the bandage and lint yesterday morning, revealing the beginnings of infection at the edges of the wound. He had applied a poultice of bread and milk softened with a little fresh butter, and had repeated it in the afternoon and again this morning. Though Coll said he felt well, Sandy talked about watching for a fever and wondered aloud if he should not bleed him, a procedure at which the steward was adept. These were bleak ponderings, and I tried to banish from my mind horrific thoughts of gangrene.

When I lay in my bed I felt helpless. Thinking I could prevent infection by staying close to Coll was irrational, but being at his side, feeling his aliveness, fooled me into believing nothing could possibly happen to him.

The funeral was planned for tomorrow afternoon. The last thing I wanted was to be alone on this almost-final day. People had started arriving for the burials, responding to the word passed through the glens by men riding Kirthgarran's fleetest horses, and although I did not desire to sit amongst strangers I did feel a need for Rab's kinsmen. I drifted from my room and was faced with Rab's chamber. Inside, his bed awaited him as if it would ease his bones this night. His dressing table kept safe his razor, his watch, and clasp knife. Everything of his was all at once precious to me.

I went farther along the passage and came to the earl's

open door, where only two days before I had stopped to see Lord Kirthgarran. The pier glass and pictures had been draped with white linen to prevent his spirit from going in the wrong direction when it sought Heaven. Books we would never read and the Argand Burner lay abandoned on his bedside table. I thought about his hand I had been massaging. I believed it had been gaining strength. I remembered Fenalla, his beloved falcon, who had learnt to recognize her master once more. Never again would she fly to his fist.

In the great hall I found Airig amongst the others, keeping watch beside Lord Kirthgarran and Rab, guarding the spirits hovering overhead and keeping them from the De'il and his minions until they joined God at the time of burial. I was soothed knowing they were assured of places in Heaven. Yesterday Mairi had joined me and the other women of Kirthgarran to wash and dress the men, preparing them for their final rest. We had rearranged the candles about the bodies on their deid-deals and trestles, and placed dishes of salt upon their breasts to prevent swelling and to further keep the De'il away. Gold coins had been placed on their lids to keep their eyes closed. The coffins would come tomorrow.

I retreated from the hall, leaving the folk to their vigil, and wandered through the drawing room where the clock had been stopped at the time of Lord Kirthgarran's death. The sitting room was empty, as was the dining room. Upstairs I met Andrew just leaving the library. "Oh Andrew, I was looking for you, and the others."

He regarded me with sudden consternation. His face showed the agony of the past days, a visage common to all of us. "Keeley. I thought you were resting."

"I cannot sleep. I do not want to sleep. Where is everyone? In the library?"

His eyes flew to the closed door and back again. "Aye," he said hesitantly, "but…"

"May I join you? Is Anne here, too? I know Mairi is keeping to her bed at Rathdale, but…"

He stepped beside me. "Perhaps later…" I did not understand. I already had my hand on the latch. He reached out. Too quickly I opened the door.

What I saw in front of me stopped me cold. My breathing ceased, and if my heart had been less strong it might have halted as well.

The checkered drapes were drawn closed at the windows, as curtains were all over the castle. There was a low fire. In the glow Coll and Lachlan lounged in chairs, their stockinged legs stretched out in front of them whilst they conversed with a man sitting in a similar position between them. As soon as they saw me, Coll and Lachlan stood. But the man in the center did not move.

We stared at each other. Eventually the man did rise from his seat, slowly. When he took a step toward me Coll warned, "Alistair," and put out a hand to hinder him.

The man pretended not to hear him. He was watching me in fascination. "Keeley," he said in the voice I remembered.

It was Davy.

Oft ha'e I roved by bonnie Doon,
  To see the rose and woodbine twine;
And ilka bird sang o' it's luve,
  And fondly sae did I o' mine.
Wi' lightsome heart I stretch'd my hand,
  And pu'd a rosebud from the tree;
But my fause lover stole the rose,
  And left, and left the thorn wi' me.
    Ye Banks and Braes o' Bonnie Doon (Burns)

Chapter Thirty-Six

ow long was it before anyone moved? Was it a decade later when Andrew spoke behind me? "'Tis my fault," he said. "I was not quick enough."

I might have been cast out of lead. I could not stir my eyes. All they perceived was Davy's face floating disembodied before me. He returned the observation and I felt time spin backward to the day I had told him about Mrs. Taggart's discovery and we had stood in the midst of the sheep with our fingers pulling apart for the last time.

Something was wrong, though; something was altered. There was a presumptuousness, a polished confidence, shining out of his face, and I was not the same person I had been.

There was admiration in his eyes. With those familiar yet unknown lips he grinned. "How dear you are. How dreadfully I have missed you."

"Alistair." It was Coll's voice, ominous.

I attempted to speak. "Who are you?"

I felt Andrew's hand on my back. "This is a blow. Sit, Keeley, please."

"You never suspected?" said Davy. "Never once?"

"Alistair." This time Coll's voice was savage. "Perhaps it's better you go."

"But we've just been reunited. It's unfair of you, Coll."

I gripped the hand Andrew offered me with both of mine. He appealed to the young man, "It would be better if you left us. Now that it's come to this. Mind, lad, what she's been through. 'Tis a shock for her."

Davy was reluctant. He appeared intrigued with the sight of me and unwilling to end this unexpected meeting. My head felt as light as thistledown and the floor seemed far away. Andrew led me to a chair. I sat and closed my eyes, thinking this was one of my dreams, but when I opened them again there was Davy gazing at me with a curious expression.

"Someone," I said, "must tell me what this means."

Davy was ushered brusquely out the door.

"None of us wanted it to be this way," Coll said. "We wanted to break it to you gently. Not like this."

I could not make sense of his words. "It's Davy."

He shook his head. "Oh my dear heart, I'd give anything not to have this happen this way."

Andrew said, "We'll explain everything to you."

Lachlan stared at his feet and sank to a chair.

"It's Davy," I repeated. "And—Alistair?"

Andrew took in a long breath and nodded. "Coll's and my younger brother Alistair, aye."

Coll dragged a chair in front of mine and took my hands as he sat on the edge. "There's a gey lot to explain. You've had questions, I ken, ever since you came to Kirthgarran. We'll answer them now. It's all been too long in coming, but not one of us could foresee it would go on like this. Or end like this. Can you listen now? Do you feel well enough? We'll bide for a bit if you want to recover from the shock."

I glanced upward at the door through which Alistair had exited. "No. Now. I must hear. Everything is so muddled." I squeezed Coll's fingers and implored, "You must tell me what all of this means."

For a moment my eyes clung to his. I was afraid of what I was about to discover. Nothing must be as it had appeared during all of these months, and Coll was as deep in the conspiracy as anyone. His eyes bid trust and offered strength. I let my gaze drop to our hands enfolded together. I sensed him turning to Andrew.

"I'm uncertain how to tell you except to begin when it started for us," Andrew said. "I do not ken if you'll forgive us. What we did was unforgivable. But perhaps you can understand why we did it and know we regret it. Heavily."

I looked up. His blue-gray eyes had difficulty meeting mine and he paused, searching for words. He took the seat beside me, the one Alistair had vacated. "Very nearly six years ago it was. Coll had not yet returned from the war. Lord Kirthgarran was failing. He'd been ill and bedridden ever since the deaths of Walter and Hugh. He was a man without hope. He had us, of course, but not his own sons, true sons to whom he could pass Kirthgarran and Strath Gruagach, sons who lived with his own blood in them, bairns he'd sired with his countess and loved. He felt the end coming near and so did we. He spent whole days poring over his past, regretting this and regretting that, dropping into silent trances in which none could reach him. He talked to us sometimes, remembering Walter and Hugh, and asked us, as if we were God Himself, why they'd been taken from him. And he talked of another thing, something he'd done that he lamented." Andrew's discomfort increased. He leant forward and rested his elbows on his knees, dropped his hands together in a knot. "You see, Lord Kirthgarran had three children. There was a younger daughter. He regretted the past bitterly because if he'd acted differently he'd still have that daughter beside him, or so he believed."

I was very still.

"When he was young this was a lively household. Walter and Hugh were boisterous sons with many friends, and the earl himself counted several men as such. Life was difficult after Culloden but Lord Kirthgarran spared not his friendships, even though the estates could not boast of a fine table or a well-stocked wine cellar, and there was always a welcome guest here for the hunting, or a supper, or a ceilidh. After Lady Kirthgarran died he was solemn, but he'd always been a robust man, a canny man sought out by his friends and neighbors. As a member of the peerage he had political connections in Edinburgh, and there were always interesting folk coming from the city to visit. We were part of this exuberant household. Growing up here was exciting for Sandy's sons and my brothers and me. We were raised as foster sons. This much you know."

I nodded.

"Lord Kirthgarran doted on his sons," Andrew continued, "and he doted on his daughter. Her name was Lady Nóra. She became more special to him after Lady Kirthgarran's death because even though she was still a lass she was the woman of the home, the woman in his life. Can you see how it was? The energetic man, bereaved, but consoled by his growing bairns, life going on as usual, Kirthgarran being held together. Then the tragedy happened, ten years or so after the countess died. I mind it myself though I was a young lad. It was one late summer day. The castle was filled with friends and family and there was hunting, for Kirthgarran could, at least, offer plentiful venison. The men hunted the stags and at night there was revelry, and the ale and whisky flowed free. The harvest that year promised to be good, and the cattle were healthy, awaiting the drive to market. One of Lord Kirthgarran's greatest friends from Edinburgh was here, enjoying the hunt, the food, the spirit. Apparently he drank to excess that night and stumbled about the castle. And stumbled upon Lady Nóra."

Andrew found it impossible to meet my eyes, and studied his hands instead. "He raped her. It was the worst thing that could have befallen her. She was an innocent, quieter than most, with no knowledge of the vices of men. And he was a big lout, perhaps thirty years older than she, rough and not known for his fastidiousness. She went to her father sobbing, wearing her torn clothing, and told of the attack by his friend. And the earl was astonished and distressed beyond words until his friend, too, went to him and in desperation, and sudden sobriety, I fear, claimed Lady Nóra had taken advantage of him and seduced him in his drunken state, and then torn her own gown to make it appear the opposite.

"The earl was rent in half. Who was to be believed? His oldest friend or his beloved daughter? Perhaps if she'd begged for justice or spoken out more vehemently he might have believed her. But she accused the man once and only once, and withdrew into herself and said nought. Lord Kirthgarran was perplexed and outraged. He took his friend's word and not hers, sparing the man from a magistrate's inquiry and subsequent exile. But she was degraded in his eyes, soiled, and, Lord Kirthgarran thought, a liar. He could not bear to look at her. And she in turn was so baffled at his behavior and the man's attack that she lapsed into a great pit of despair. She was suddenly bereft of her father's affections and whilst not an outcast, she felt unworthy to be his daughter. In time it all might have dissipated, and if not forgotten at least accepted, and certainly Lord Kirthgarran would have come round and believed her. But a bairn came of it. I think that was the final blow."

He stopped and pondered the floor to gather his thoughts, and after a moment continued on sadly, "She was not well. I mind the change in her. Mam took care of her, but no one can make another eat when she does not want food, no one can make another want to live. The bairn was born too soon, small and weak. Lord Kirthgarran was beside himself with shame and regret. He visited her chamber one night. It was the night the bairn died, only eight days auld. He said to her, 'Perhaps it's just as well,' and she told him he was wrong. In those eight days she'd come to love her infant son and believed he was all she had in the world. The earl left her, unable to hide his frustration and pain, and the next morning she was gone."

Andrew rose, forsaking his chair, needing to walk, it seemed, as he went on with the tale.

"She left Kirthgarran frail and ill, a lass used and scorned. Lord Kirthgarran was heartbroken. Yet—he had his pride. He made no effort to search for her, and forbade everyone to do so. He did not disown her but he did not attempt to find her. He believed she would come back. But the surprise of her leaving wounded him deeply, and years later in his bed he was full of misgivings. He realized at last he might never see her again. He admitted he should have believed her. That, after all, he did believe her. He could see his friend for what he'd been, a dishonest lecher who'd eventually drunk himself to death in England. He'd lost Walter and Hugh and he would give his soul to see his dear daughter and tell her he was sorry. Because he'd been so stubborn and full of pride he had most likely ruint her life. He wanted to make it up to her. He wanted to see her, to tell her he'd never stopped thinking about her, and loving her. But she was gone, irretrievably, and the years would not turn themselves inside out just to please him. He was a lonely, aged man who'd made a mistake."

He sighed. I fancied the story was becoming even more difficult for him. He stopped at the fireside and pushed at a hearthstone with his toe. My eyes did not waver from him although they had begun to burn.

"So," Andrew said, and exhaled forcefully. "There we were. The ailing earl surrounded by his foster sons who could do nought but listen helplessly to his longings. We thought him on his deathbed, as I said. He was wasting away and at the center of his deterioration was his regretful memory of Lady Nóra, wondering if she were still alive, wondering if she'd suffered further because of him. He wondered if his estate and the earldom would come to an end, for without her there was no heir, and everything—the lands, the title—would be dissolved if she could not be found. Rathdale would be safe with me because of his will and the absence of a tailzie, but Kirthgarran was another matter. I had an idea, and put it to the earl. What if we began a search for her even though years had gone by? We could place advertisements in the newspapers, spread the word she was being sought. Perhaps she'd not gone far away from these hills at all. Perhaps it was not too late to find her. It seemed to breathe new life into him. With our help, he thought, perhaps his blackbird could be returned to him."

"His blackbird?"

"Aye, 'tis how he thought of her. His dear blackbird who'd flown away. She'd been flown from Kirthgarran for sixteen years, but he became filled with hope she could be found."

Andrew moved away from the fireplace, went to the massive desk in the center of the library, and opened a drawer. Whilst he looked through the contents, I gazed back at Coll who was watching me with concern.

Andrew returned with a locked book and inserted a miniature key in the mechanism. Inside, between two pages, was a torn, yellow sheet of a newspaper. He plucked it out, shook it open carefully, and held it toward me. I took it unwillingly.

"This is the kind of thing we did," he explained. "As I said, we began about six years ago. We wrote to newspapers such as this, the *Aberdeen Journal*, and placed advertisements. We traveled to inns and homes of acquaintances, waiting for word to come or pieces of information we could string together. When Coll came back he joined us, traveling here and there, asking questions. On occasion someone told us something only to earn a coin, and the facts did not match."

The paper in my hand rustled in the silence. It was a page of advertisements, and near the bottom, circled in faded brown ink, was one in particular.

"*15 June, 1783*

"*Loving Father seeks to be reunited with His Blackbird: daughter Lady Nóra Caitlìn Fergusson, who left Home on 23 March, 1765. Birth date is 17 July, 1748. Brown hair. Blue eyes. She plays the Clarsach and sings. Compensation provided for true and verifiable information. Ask for A. Fergusson at the Silver Gate Inn, Inverness, or R. Fergusson at Ralyside, Nairn.*"

The tears that had been burning my eyes spilt down over my cheeks. I read the gray print a second time, a third time. A sob broke from my throat. I looked at Coll before me. His face swam in my tears. From his expression I realized he knew. Of course he knew. He had known all along. So had they all.

I could say nothing. I stared at Coll, unable to wipe my eyes.

Andrew was pacing, and came back to retrieve the paper from my lax fingertips. "She took it with her. The clarsach, that is. We thought it might be something to spur someone's memory, so we put it in the advertisement. It had belonged to Lady Kirthgarran, her mother, and her mother, Keeley Raeburn, before that. She left Kirthgarran in the cold of a March night and took the harp with her. But you have brought it home again."

"Mamma," I said, my lips trembling.

Coll nodded, fearfully.

Andrew sat back down in his chair, on the edge.

Beside us Lachlan exhaled.

"Lady Nóra was aye your mother," Andrew said cautiously. "It was for her we searched. She was the blackbird of Kirthgarran."

Chills spread over my legs as another flood of tears fell from my eyes.

Andrew said, "And Lord Kirthgarran was your grandsire."

I had to keep control of myself. I could not let the upheaval within me have its way. There must be time to absorb what he was saying. I struggled with it, turning my face away from them all, seeking to convince myself they must not witness the emotion on my face. The phrase echoed in my muddled mind. *Your grandsire.* Coll's hands clenched mine.

At last I thought I could speak, but I was wrong. After another attempt I was able to articulate, "There is more."

Andrew stood, paced again. He hesitated. Coll used a thumb to wipe my cheek, first one, then the other. I raised my face, knowing I was unprepared for whatever was to come next.

Andrew cleared his throat as he pulled a hand through his short, dark hair. For a moment his fingers lay still on his skull. "Lord Kirthgarran beseeched us to find Lady Nóra. He wanted to see her if he could. Ask her to come home. If she could be found she would be the one to inherit Kirthgarran and the other estates, not the Crown. You know the lands and castle are entailed in such a way that only a blood descendent can inherit them. Walter was gone, and so was Hugh, but Nóra, hopefully, was still alive, and it was written a daughter could receive them. Last winter, a year ago now, we had word that someone had read one of our advertisements and remembered her. The daughter of a solicitor from Dundee. She wrote me a letter and met with me at her own home in Perth. Her mother had once employed a seamstress, a young lass who'd played the clarsach. The lass had been something of a mystery, coming out of nowhere and asking for employment. The date she supplied was 1765, just what we'd been looking for. She called the lass

Caitlìn MacKerras. The solicitor and his wife, the Sinclairs, were still living, and I went along to Dundee where I met them and heard the story firsthand. The seamstress who'd come to their door had claimed she was from Dundee and recently orphaned. When she'd first inquired at the household she had very little to say about herself other than she'd spent weeks looking for work, but her sweet nature and bonny face won her service, and in the course of the two years she lived with them, her songs and music became as indispensable to Mrs. Sinclair as her sewing. The woman brought Caitlìn with her everywhere, and to Galashiels whenever she visited her brother. In Galashiels the lass met an acquaintance of this brother. He was an older man of means, a widower from Melrose with a young son. He wooed her, and wed her. After that they never saw her again. She was nineteen when she married the landowner. All the details fit together. Mrs. Sinclair was able to describe her and the clarsach exactly. In 1767 Lady Nóra would have been nineteen. There was no doubt. We'd found our blackbird."

"Last winter," I repeated.

"Aye, last winter. I rode to Melrose and asked the folk there about her. I discovered she'd died five years earlier, soon after we'd started looking for her. It was a cruel disappointment. I cannot tell you how saddened I was, how I dreaded telling Lord Kirthgarran our search had been for nought. But I was told there was a daughter. I was also told that the widower, Finlay Allanson, was a man who protected his privacy and would not tolerate a probe into his family or affairs. I saw you, whilst I was in Melrose parish. You were riding a chestnut horse and you stopped to pick flowers. I knew at once you were Lady Nóra's daughter even from a distance. There could be no mistake at all. And when you arrived here at Kirthgarran and I saw you close at hand, I was taken aback by the similarities. We all were. You've the same color hair, the same blue eyes, the same chin. Well. Last winter, after I saw you in Melrose, I came back home, not quite sure what to do."

I stiffened. I searched Andrew's face, looking for answers, and found only awkwardness.

"Are you wanting me to go on?" he asked. "This is a great deal for you to hear all at once. If you need time to think, to reflect upon it all, then you only need say so."

"You must tell me now. I have to know. All of it."

"This is not easy to tell, Keeley. Putting it in words makes it sound as cold-hearted as it really was." He drew a breath. "I've no pride at all in what we did. None of us do. We have thrown our honor away, and it cannot be retrieved."

My eyes would not leave his, and he continued. "I came home," he said, "and told the others what I'd found. The five of us—Lachlan, Rab, Coll, Alistair and me—looked at one another and thought the same thought. If you were to come to Kirthgarran and take your mother's place, the lands, the title, would be yours. You were a peeress in your own right. There was no question of it being so. But the next thought we had was that if one of us wed you, the lands, the castle, and the houses would be ours to enjoy worry-free for our lifetimes. If one of us lived at Kirthgarran through marriage to you, the rest of us could also. That is how closely we hold one another. Of course there was Lord Kirthgarran to consider. We wanted only what was the best for him. Finding a granddaughter, Lady Nóra's progeny, was going to restore him to the man he once was. He knew everything would pass to her on his death. But he would be further contented if one of us—who'd been reared here and knew how to look after the land—was her lawful mate. Aye, we told ourselves, we'd do what was best for everyone."

I willed Andrew to go on, to finish it all. He rubbed his nose and mouth with a hand, blinking at the fire, and resolutely turned back to me. "We told Lord Kirthgarran about you. He was beside himself with grief, learning about Lady Nóra, but his spirits renewed themselves because of your existence. He wanted to see you. He wanted you brought here. But amongst ourselves we were concerned. Your father's character was a problem. It was likely Finlay knew nought of your mother's past. If he discovered his wife had been a member of the peerage and an heiress to an estate, and that she had passed the title and lands on to you, he might decide to accompany you here and advise you on matters that would benefit only himself, or force you to make changes that would jeopardize our circumstances. There was your half-brother also, a shrewd man of the law who would be someone else to contend with, someone who might question our livelihoods and convince you to do the same. There were many probabilities. Our home was at stake. What we wanted..." Andrew paused and said reluctantly, "What we wanted was Kirthgarran for ourselves. One of us to legally share it and the others to benefit. Rathdale—wasn't enough." He shook his head ruefully. "Hence, we told Lord Kirthgarran we'd fetch you to him, but amongst ourselves made a more complex strategy. Several things were clear. Your father, and you, must not know the true nature of the situation. And time was of great value. Lord Kirthgarran seemed better, but we could not depend on his health lasting. If one of us was to marry you it must be done quickly. I—I was already wed to Anne."

He appeared to become even more embarrassed than he had been, and I, foreseeing what he was going to say, turned my head away so I would not have to look at him. I stared at the fire. The transparent flames of orange played at the logs. Vaporous streams lifted sparks into the hungry chimney and golden stars flashed against the charcoal-black stone.

"It was decided that Rabbie would go along to Melrose," he said. "He waited for a good opportunity and feigned falling from his horse as an excuse to go to your door. But it did not go well betwixt the two of you. Rab asked your father for your hand but was refused. And you—it was not—what I'm meaning is, you did not seem overly drawn to Rab, enough to want to elope with him. Rab came back to Kirthgarran, told us what he'd observed, and what you and your father's reactions had been. We'd no time to examine your feelings toward different suitors. And short of telling you the truth we did not know how to bring you here. If you were told about Lord Kirthgarran, your mother, and the inheritance, we could not trust you to keep it from your father. And how could a man say to you, 'We are strangers but marry me anyway, quickly, with no questions?' It was then we resorted to this horrible scheme. It occurred to us that if you were disgraced, your father might let you go. More than let you go. Send you away and thus weaken any interest he might have in your future. So we devised the plan. Alistair, who's a year older than you, played the part of a lad who, we thought, might be appealing. He was—successful. It might all have come to a satisfactory conclusion but for the fact that he—you see, he already had a wife. He's always been a wild sort. He'd carried off a lass at eighteen and had wed her. Therefore he could not marry you."

My hands lay dead in Coll's. I watched the tongues of fire leap and subside. Sparks burnt themselves out and vanished in the draughts.

"It was Alistair himself who left the letter for the minister, which led to your father's discovery of your meetings. It's partly Alistair's fault you were disconsolate. We'd told him not to tarry, not to touch your emotions, for all we needed was a small measure of your time spent in his company, just enough to alarm your father. But Alistair seemed to enjoy the ruse, and Rab, waiting impatiently in Galashiels, finally persuaded him to do what he was supposed to do. Rab went to your home several days later, and his offer for your hand was not refused by Finlay a second time. It surprised us all, in truth. The whole idea had been so farfetched we never thought it would come to pass. Any deviant factor could have sent the whole thing crashing. But everything took place just as we'd mapped it. It was Alistair's turn to wait for news, and he was told by Rab there was to be a marriage. He came home then, to relay the message to us all, giving us time to prepare, giving him time to take himself and his wife away to Oban."

Coll finally spoke. He tried to capture my attention as his voice soothed, lulled. "It was wrong of us," he admitted. "We realized it the day you arrived here. Until then you'd been a faceless stranger, a woman who could make the future bright for us. But all of a sudden there you were and we realized our mistake. You'd become too fond of Alistair, we discovered, and were wounded by his leaving. Even Rabbie was overwhelmed by what he'd done, taken you to wife under false pretences. And he told us how your father had behaved toward you, beating you, keeping you locked away. We were horrified. It had all been so vague for us—a trick that involved an unknown young woman with no flesh and blood to her. The fact that you were Lord Kirthgarran's granddaughter was all we could consider. But as soon as we saw you here at Kirthgarran, as soon as Rab told us what had happened—when the weight of what we'd done became fully felt by us—we were sickened and wanted to tell you." He shifted in his seat. "The earl learnt you were married to Rab and did not know of your heritage, and suddenly he fastened upon the idea of keeping you ignorant. He was ashamed of how he'd treated your mother. He thought if you knew the truth you'd despise him. He wanted you to come to know him and perhaps care for him first, so when he did tell you, you'd be able to forgive him. He was overjoyed his granddaughter had married one of us. He thought, you were coming, you'd learn to love Kirthgarran, you'd accept everything, even the black past, once you, too, were a part of it all. He knew nought of our plan. He thought it a coincidence one of us had wed you after we'd found you. You were now his blackbird, Keeley. *Mo lon-dubh*, he called you. He'd sought a blackbird, and one came home."

He would have said more, I believed, but I did not respond. I could sense his frustration in his fingers.

Andrew went on instead. "Lord Kirthgarran saw the resemblance right away. It brought him to tears. But he was adamant. You were not to be told who you were. So we cleared the castle of all that might point to Lady Nóra. The family Bible, with the names and dates written in. Watercolor sketches she'd done. We hid them all away. But there were troubles nonetheless. Older folk who remembered the daughter of the castle saw you and regarded you as Nóra's specter returning to the land of her birth. Others who had not known Nóra regarded you as a wraith, thinking no, you were not a ghost, but a flesh-and-blood person no matter what their elders told them. They whispered amongst themselves and became more afraid of you after the tower burnt and the ox bolted in your presence. Grizel was sure you were Lady Nóra returned from the grave to haunt us all, and we had to convince her you were Nóra's daughter who did not yet know of the connection with the earl, and that it was to be a surprise when Lord Kirthgarran decided to tell you. Our mother, and Sandy, even Gordon, MacNeil, Ewen, and Donald, knew who you were the moment they put their eyes on you, and guessed at what had been done—though they did not know Alistair's part in it. They still do not know. My wife Anne, Airig, and Ròs never knew Lady Nóra, only that she was Lord Kirthgarran's lost daughter, but we had to tell them a little so they'd never mention her to you. Because of Lord Kirthgarran's wishes, we had to make them all pledge to say nought to you at all until the earl himself confessed.

"There was one time you became interested in the silver and Rab was showing you the thistle cup, until he realized it had been given to Lady Nóra on her birth and bore her name engraved on the back, as well as the date. It had been overlooked. He took it away and put it with the other things, in a locked cupboard. You must have been puzzled by that, but there was little any of us could do or say. It was all deferred to Lord Kirthgarran. He told us to tell you the cup had been sold so you'd not be disconcerted by its absence. He did not want you told who you were. Not yet. And we felt obliged to honor his desires. That it all came about, that no one here at the castle ever erred and mentioned aught vital, that folk from the glen did not offer welcomes or oaths in English that you could understand, that you did not find trinkets or books or other objects we might have neglected—it's surprising it all lasted this long. None of us expected it to. It was due to respect and love for Lord Kirthgarran that no one ever broke the truth to you.

"But he *should* have told you," Andrew continued. "It went past the time when it should have been done. He felt assured of your affection. He thought you'd probably forgive him. But he kept delaying. As soon as he did tell you, we meant to confess to you what we'd done. There would have been no secrets." He waited, but as I still said nothing, he added, "A few days ago Alistair nearly forced it all out. He'd been staying with his wife and her parents. Alistair, unfortunately, falls into boredom easily and has not been content since his necessary—banishment. He's been gambling and accumulating debts. He came home for money. He almost crossed your path when you were here in the library. Rab told him there was a purse in the desk drawer, and he went to get it, all but walking in on you as you worked. Another time Grizel had a breakfast ready for him, and you chanced to come into the kitchen when she was waiting for him. She did not understand why the two of you could not meet, but she did as we asked and helped keep him from your sight. He slept in the stable one night, with MacNeil keeping that a secret as well. We wanted him gone, and sent him away to Rathdale. We had to ask Mam and Anne not to say aught about him to you, and promised that shortly we would explain why."

He was thoughtful but soon said firmly, "We realized when Lord Kirthgarran died you'd have to be told everything, and quickly. I've written to the solicitors and they'll want to see you as soon as they arrive. The Fergussons of Lund are coming tomorrow. They've all been told of your existence. In fact, Lord Kirthgarran wrote letters and settled it all as soon as you came, months ago. It's entirely lawful, Keeley, and I ken there's too much for you to take in now, but there is one important fact of which you must be aware. By the letters patent you are Lord Kirthgarran's heir, a peer of the realm. You are Lady Kirthgarran, Countess of Kirthgarran. The lands, the title, the castle—Kirthgarran and Strath Gruachan—they are all yours."

I did not reflect on what I should have. I did not consider my good fortune, or my relief at having all the secrets revealed, or even the pain I had been caused by the plans of five avaricious men. I pondered on Graeme Fergusson, the man who had been my grandsire. He had taken my heart and opened it, and I had never known we were of the same blood, that the history he had often related to me was my own, and that I had every right to love him. I had lost him before I knew he was mine. I would never be able to say I did love him despite what he had done to Lady Nóra, his daughter, my mother.

I considered Mamma, and how it had not been a lover responsible for her lost chastity. My father had punished her after their marriage for having given herself to someone out of wedlock, but she had never told him the truth. She had never told him about Kirthgarran. Or her father. Or the earl's false friend.

Whenever she sat with the clarsach in her lap and wept, or sang the song about the boatman, she was not mourning an unfaithful lover but the home of her childhood, and her father's love.

I pulled my hands away from Coll's and stood. I was calm when I should have been anything but that. I looked straight at Andrew and said, "Is that everything? Everything?"

"The only matter left is to give you your mother's possessions and the objects we put away. And to tell you again how sorry we all are. If Rabbie were here," he said sorrowfully, "if we were all here, together, we would all tell you so. Rab would tell you, forbye, that he did care about you. It may have been a bargain we all made together, to and for one another, but his affection for you was genuine. He confided to me on the day he died that he meant to devote himself to you. It was all his own idea, nought we had to force him to do. The deception Lord Kirthgarran continued would soon have been at an end, and Rab would have been here for you, in all honesty a devoted husband."

I turned toward the curtained window.

Andrew must have risen from his seat, for when his voice came again it was quite close behind me. "You cannot know how I wish Rab were here, to add his sentiments. I'm convinced he would reassure you that although you were used at first, he came to love you."

I said, "I think I am done listening, Andrew. It is too much."

"Certainly it is. Certainly it is." A moment passed, and he asked, "What can we do for you? Is there aught you need, or want? How can we best see you through this?"

"I think I just need to be alone."

He patted my shoulder with affection and slid his hand away. I heard their footsteps and the creak of the floor. But I knew I was not alone.

Coll's voice rose behind me, so low I could barely hear it. "You'll think all that has happened to you is based upon lies. But there's one thing that is not."

I was silent.

"Will you let me assure you my love for you is true?"

"Please. Say nought more."

"But this is just as important as anything said here today. You have to know it. I live in agony, knowing what we did to you. But I love you more than my life and my honor, and fear you'll not remember or believe it, and that is more than agony, more than I can endure."

"Please. Just go. Just leave me."

He remained still, but after a moment I sensed him turning on his heel, and he, too, was gone. I was left alone with nothing but the echo of his footsteps in that vast, empty room.

I sank to the window seat and brought my feet up on the

bolster. I knew I must try to remember everything they had told me. I realized I could go back in my mind and think of days, individual days, and hours—*minutes*—that could be interpreted differently now I knew what had occurred to bring them about. There was nothing in my life not tainted by the deception. From the moment Rab had knocked upon the door of Gilchrist House to this very day, I had believed life to be a certain way only to discover it was not that way at all. Even my own mother had deceived me. I had never known who she actually was.

And Coll...

I hugged my knees and pressed my head down upon them.

Now that my life had all raveled apart, I did not know who I was—who anyone was—nor did I know how to fit any of it back together again.

I found the track of the swan on the lake...
An Cóineachan *(A Fairy Lullaby) (Trad.)*

Chapter Thirty-Seven

When the skies beyond the crack in the curtains grew black with nightfall, Airig came to me. They must have told her the truth had been revealed, for she asked no questions of me when she appeared in the library. She merely put her arms about me in sympathy and made me drink the hot barley water she had brought. I accepted her embrace, even hugged her in return, but something was broken inside of me. Tears had come and gone and there was nothing left. No hurt. No sadness. Just a dark, flat blankness. If there was any emotion to spark and fizzle behind it, it was fury. It peeked out now and then.

Whilst Airig sat with me I retreated deeper into myself. She said to me, "Will you have supper with the rest?"

"No."

"Will you go to your chamber, then? I'll warm your bed, and bring you a sleeping draught, and rub your forehead with sweet almond oil."

"It does not matter," I replied listlessly. I rose with difficulty, went to the door with her, and found Coll and Andrew leaning against the wall of the passage beyond, talking as they waited in the light of a candle. They straightened when I appeared. Drained and dry, I had no reaction, no sensation of anything.

Andrew was the first to speak. "As you can see, we could not leave you."

I nodded.

"We sent Airig in to you. We thought she would be the most gentle."

I stopped, nodding again.

"When you're ready we can give you your mother's belongings," Coll said. "Will you have them tonight? Or would tomorrow be better?"

Determining a preference seemed to be an unmanageable task. Yet seeing her possessions and touching the last remaining evidence of her existence might satisfy some unknown need. "Where are they?"

Andrew said, "In her auld room. We can show you. The cupboard is locked but we can open it for you, and give you the keys."

Before I could even think of doing such a thing, however, I needed to stop in the great hall.

I halted beside Rab, but it was Lord Kirthgarran upon whom I felt compelled to gaze, a man I had known well but who had been dishonest with me. There were many questions I would later utter, looking up at Heaven—a multitude of thoughts I would send him in the days to come—but for now it was enough to lay my hand on his arm, to whisper his name, and know we had been of the same blood.

The others stood discreetly outside the circle of leaping candle flames, but at last I turned to Andrew. I had no idea which bedchamber had been Mamma's and followed him as he lit the way up the mural stair. We went to the wing where my own chamber was located. Close to Lord Kirthgarran's room Andrew pushed in an arched door and went inside. I entered also, watching him light the tapers in a pair of double candlesticks. I was surprised to find a fire already burning in the fireplace, warming the chamber. They had expected me to come, it appeared. Coll was behind us, with Airig.

"This was her room," Andrew explained, glancing about. I had explored this bedchamber before, finding nothing remarkable about it, but that was what they had intended. The poster bed was draped in dark green silk. There was a writing desk and a clothes press. Nothing within the room proclaimed it had once been the home of a seventeen-year-old lass who had suffered physical attack, childbirth, and the untimely loss of the bairn. A walnut tallboy stood at one side, and Andrew took a key from his pocket and inserted it into the brass lock in one of the top, hinged doors. A small click announced it was free to unlatch. "Her things are in here," he said. "Some jewelry, books, paints, and that." Behind him the doors of the cupboard gaped, exposing boxes and papers. "Will we stay with you, as you look at them?"

"No. I would rather be alone."

"Do you wish Airig to stay with you?"

"No."

"There's a portrait," Andrew told me.

My eyes left the tallboy, found him instead. "Of—of Mamma?"

He nodded. "Aye, and of her brothers. It's in Lord Kirthgarran's dressing room, stored behind furniture. We can fetch it for you."

Blankness and fury shifted somewhat, made room for apprehension. I could not answer, but he must have sensed something in my alertness. He glanced at Coll and the two left the room.

I waited with Airig. She made herself industrious, straightening the forest green folds of the curtains drawn at the window, squaring the fringed edges of an Indian carpet woven in reds and greens. When the men came back carrying the gilt-framed canvas between them, I held my breath. They placed it on the floor, leaning it against the bed frame so the light from the fire could illuminate it. It must have been three feet tall and five feet long. I perceived an impression of colors, of rich oil paint carefully placed, of faces and velvety folds of clothing and the texture of leaves. I felt as if I were about to look at a light too bright to be borne, and my eyes slid sideways, squinting at it a little as if the vision would hurt. Courage won out, however, and unaware, I sank to my knees on the carpet, my gaze transfixed on the expanse of framed linen.

"Fletcher Buchanan was the painter," Coll said. "He was known for his double portraits. He later went to London to pursue his career. But he finished this when Lady Nòra was sixteen, before the—tragedy. Beside her is Walter. And standing next to the oak is Hugh."

Nòra, Bàtair, and Uisdean MacFhearghuis, children of Lord and Lady Kirthgarran. The three were in the garden of the castle and there were roses in the hand of the lass. I remembered the name of the artist, for Lord Kirthgarran's portrait had been painted by him perhaps twenty years earlier. The man's skill had improved over the years. He had expertly caught the fine overlap of dark, medium, and light green leaves overhead, the tangle of wild roses, the shape of the castle in the background. The range from light to dark throughout the scene was wide and yet subtle, and the shade under the oak tree with its deep greens and browns was dappled with light. Soft, summer sunlight played upon the young lass's white gown and the delicate blue of the sky above.

The lads were dressed alike in kilts of dark green, waistcoats of ivory, jabots and lace cuffs of dazzling white, and coats of velvet brown. They were painted during the existence of the Disarming Act, surely, but a painter could add anything he wanted to his work, including kilt and plaid. The hair of the lads was brown like their sister's, drawn into jaunty queues, and their eyes were blue like Lord Kirthgarran's. They smiled, happy with life. Hugh, leaning against the broad tree, might have been seventeen or eighteen. His brother, the Honorable Walter Fergusson, standing at ease in the center, was perhaps two years older and would have become Lord Kirthgarran, the eighth earl, had he survived.

The lass, though, trapped my eyes and did not let go. She

could have been me a few years ago. She sat on a settle holding the roses in a relaxed, sloping hand, a slight figure in her white dress with the blue ribbon at her bosom. Her head was bent somewhat, as though shyness prevented her from watching the artist at work with the boldness of her brothers. The blue of her eye sparkled and the bloom on her smooth cheek was translucent. The snowy cap on her head crowned tresses that fell to her waist. She smiled, too, just a little, finding amusement in something that added a glint of life to her serenity.

The painter had been meticulous with his details, for the roses appeared real enough to be gathered, and the lace of the layered leaves overhead nearly stirred with a desultory breeze. The brothers and their sister were caught in a moment of peace on the banks of Loch Seàrr, in their father's garden. They were caught in linseed oil, pigment, and turpentine and seemed as fresh as when the paint had been applied. The brushstrokes were sensitive, meticulous, sealed under a glistening coat of varnish. So vital had the subjects been. I felt Lord Kirthgarran's pain as I drank in Buchanan's portrait. Not one of them was still alive.

I had not noticed that Coll, Andrew, and Airig had left. The door was open but they were gone. I swept my gaze about the room, from the merry fire to the polished furniture and closed, damask curtains. The picture caught me again, and I went within once more, searching for and finding the person who had become my mother.

When I went to the tallboy I felt much calmer. I reached inside and brought out boxes with hands that barely trembled. During the next few hours I examined everything that had been placed there.

There was a velvet-lined box of jewelry. It contained a pennanular brooch of hammered silver, its surface chased with leaf and vine designs, and a necklace set with perfectly-cut rubies and silken, white pearls. It would form a low collar when worn, with loops of rubies suspended on each side of a larger, central stone. It was not meant for a young lass, and I wondered if she had ever worn it.

A pair of silver hairbrushes with soft boar bristles nestled beside a chatelaine hung with various keys. I guessed the latter might have been her mother's, a treasure bestowing responsibility and status to the woman who pinned it at her waist.

As Andrew had promised, I found the Bible, an immense, nowt-hide volume that seemed centuries old. Inside were written names and dates. I leafed through the pages, the light from the flaring candles behind my shoulder allowing me to see the flourishes and curls of scripts. There, at the end, I found them in a combination of English and Gaelic: 1743, the marriage of Graeme to Agnes Raeburn. 1745, born, a son, Bàtair Seumas MacFhearghuis. 1747, born, a son, Uisdean Niall MacFhearghuis. 1748, born, a daughter, Nóra Caitlìn MacFhearghuis. And the death dates: 1755, Agnes. 1774, Christopher and Eleanor MacLean. 1781, Bàtair and Uisdean.

If someone could be found with an elegant hand, I thought, he or she would have to add the rest: 1767, marriage of Lady Nóra to Finlay Allanson. 1768, birth of Keeley Allanson. 1782, death of Lady Nóra. 1787, death of Lord Kirthgarran and his granddaughter's husband, Robert Fergusson, who had been wed that same year.

In addition to the Bible there were other books, ones my mother had most likely cherished: *Mother Goose Tales*, *Aesop's Fables*, and one titled, *Tom Thumb's Song-Book For All Little Masters and Misses, To Be Sung To Them By Their Nurses Till They Can Sing Them Themselves*.

Hidden behind them on the shelf, where Rab must have put it, was the silver thistle cup. Overlooked it had been, Andrew explained. I turned the mellowed, tarnished vessel so the back of it faced me, and read the scrolled engraving cut deep into the metal.

"Given on this day of her birth, 17 July, 1748, to Lady Nora Kathleen Fergusson, by her Loving Father, Graeme Fergusson, Seventh Earl of Kirthgarran."

Rab's alarm, when he had glimpsed the engraving on the cup in my hands, must have been intense.

"Crivvens,"he had probably thought. "We've forgotten this."

He had forced me to place it back on the shelf and taken me away. I would have recognized the birth date. I would have known the name Kathleen, English for Caitlìn.

A shallow, stained box contained charcoal, amber pieces of gum arabic from some far-away, exotic place, and pigments.

She had always painted, it seemed. The chunks of minerals and lumps of earth were stored in separate compartments with squares of parchment wrapped round them. The squares were labels, written in faded, sepia ink. They brandished names that I had heard long ago when Mamma had made her paints in Gilchrist House from apothecary treasures such as these.

The foreign words were old friends. I had loved to hear them recited by my mother's lips as her hands had ground them into powders with a brass mortar and pestle. Green earth or terre verte. Greenish-blue azurite. Blue cobalt. Transparent Prussian blue made from salt, potash, and a compound derived from blood. Vibrant green verdigris. Naples yellow ground from lead antimonite. Orpiment, which provided a bright yellow. Vermilion produced from cinnabar. The ancient, red-orange of realgar. Red ochre. And the earthy browns of burnt sienna, umbra, and terra di Colonia.

I remembered her adding the different powders to wet gum arabic and smearing the mixtures on a scrap of glass with a heavy glass object she called a muller. There was a muller here, beside the box of pigments, much like the one she'd had at Gilchrist House. I had watched her grip the smooth, bulbous top and grind gum arabic, honey, and ox gall into the pigments with the flat bottom. Sometimes she had let me do it, guiding my hand with hers, going round and round in small circles until the mixture resembled smooth warm treacle an hour later. These were her watercolors, the paints she had used to record flowers, the Eildon Hills, and the Tweed upon thick paper made from linen. The paintings and sketches created in Melrose no longer existed, except for the one miniature I had brought with me, but I found their predecessors in the cabinet here, pressed together in an uneven pile.

Warily I separated paper leaves, feasting my eyes on the world presented on their surfaces. The paintings were the work of a young lass, but they were beautiful. Here was the castle, its warm stones reflected in the waters of the loch; the hills about Kirthgarran depicted in gentle swathes of blues and greens; an interior view of the great hall with its fireplace and mounted broadswords; detailed studies of purple heather; the ancient arch by the shore.

Surrounded by the pool of pictures I understood at last why the sight of the castle across the water, the weather-ravaged, main door to the tower, and the gateway of stone at the loch's edge brought forth a sense of familiarity in me. She had painted them here and she must have reproduced them again in Melrose to comfort herself. She must have shown the scenes to me as a bairn. Perhaps I had even watched her paint them. Somewhere, in the haze of my childhood, I knew she had shown me her heritage and mine and then hidden the images away when I was old enough to ask questions. Only when I beheld her real-life subjects with my own eyes had a door in my memory become unlocked. It was only now that the door fully opened.

The pictures were not the entire legacy. She had told me stories of ladies and lairds, and ruins by lochsides, and clansmen who paid fealty to their chief. There had been tapestries in her tales, and family trees, and towers viewed across water. Thinly disguised, her memories had been woven into stories of her own invention but they had possessed the landmarks from her childhood. The stories, like the paintings, were dim to me now, forgotten except for generalities. But the details must have lodged somewhere deep inside my childish memory, causing me the odd twinge whenever I encountered the actual images before me.

Saddest of all was a roll of blank paper in the cupboard and the beginnings of a sketch of a lamb with its mother. She had never finished it.

Instead, she had been deserted by her father's love and had borne a wee son. On the night of the bairn's death she had taken the clarsach and slipped out of the castle. She must have followed the same track we had taken when we had gone to Perth, said goodbye to Schiehallion, traced the River Tay, and made her way past the mountains to Perth and farther east to Dundee. Having made most of the journey myself I could visualize the terrain and my heart went out to Mamma, who in all probability had been cold, sick, and desperate.

The last things I found were her clothes. They were folded in the drawers beneath the cupboard, the locks of which were easily opened with the keys Andrew left on the bed. Gingerly I ran my hands over the wool, linen, and silk gowns and petticoats. With a solemn finger I rubbed handmade lace and velvet ribbon.

I put everything back where it had been. I did not lock anything. There was no point to it, since I was the person from whom all must be hidden and there was no need for that any longer.

I covered the picture with a sheet, blew out most of the candles, and took a candlestick with me when I made my way to my own bedchamber. Airig was waiting for me, sitting by my fire. Wordlessly she handed me the posset she'd kept warm on the hearth and turned back my bedcovers.

As I sipped, she unlaced the back of my bodice. She asked, "Will I stay with you, my lady?"

It was the first time I had been called so, and the significance of the phrase caused my breath to catch and my stomach to lurch. "No. I'll be fine. I just need to sleep. Airig?"

"Aye?"

"How do you say 'my blackbird' in Gaelic?"

She knew about the nickname. The slight hesitancy before her answer told me so. "*Mo lon-dubh.*"

I remembered.

She helped me remove my clothing down to my chemise. I slid between the sheets she had warmed and curled myself into a ball, covering my aching head with my hands. Thankfully, Grizel's sleeping draught was potent, and I did not suffer for long.

Nae mair we'll meet again, my love, by yon burnside...
Nae Mair We'll Meet Again (Trad.)

Chapter Thirty-Eight

The day of the funerals dawned. I thought of the old song I knew, about the blackbird.

The birds of the forest they all flock together
  The turtle has chosen to dwell with the dove.
And I am resolved in fair or foul weather
  Once more in the springtime to seek out my love;
He is all my heart's treasure,
  My joy without measure,
Oh, love me, my love, for my heart is with thee,
  He is constant and kind
And courageous of mind,
  And I'll seek out my blackbird wherever he may be.

In other days I might have been charmed with the words but not so now. The blankness hung with me still and the underlying pulse of fury was more insistent. My view of the world about me was skewed.

Evidently everyone knew the truth about me. Sandy, whose eyes had lost all life, expressionlessly kissed my hand. Anne embraced me in contrasting delight. To folk who came from far away to attend the funeral and the feast I was introduced as Lady Kirthgarran, and they all curtseyed or bowed with deference in return.

Ewen Drummond, who seemed to have aged years in the past days, approached me ceremoniously and placed a fistful of chilled earth in my hands. "Kirthgarran and its lands are yours," he said. "When the solicitors come I'll show you where the charter is kept. It is yours now, the charter to Kirthgarran. No one can take it from you."

I closed my fingers over the earth.

People arrived by the dozens. I stayed clear of those with whom I did not want to speak, namely the foster sons, Andrew, Lachlan, Coll, and Alistair. I could hardly bear to look at them. Their lies were all mixed up with truths and I did not know how to sort the falsehoods from reality. They had used me. They had not considered me a feeling, thinking human being at all, but a tool through which ownership of Kirthgarran could be achieved. What accomplished actors they all were. They had missed their calling. They should all be in London, on the stage.

Mairi arrived from Rathdale. "Dear Keeley," she said woefully. "The ruse is over and done with. How I wanted you to know. But Lord Kirthgarran would not have it. Now we can speak of things I dared not before. Your mother! I raised her as my own when she lost her mamma, and can tell you everything about her. And Lord Kirthgarran, your grandsire. Do not be callous with your thoughts, lamb. He loved you so."

She was beside me constantly. I fancied she saw herself as my shield. "They've told me of their schemes, and the trickery with Alistair," she said. "How will you ever forgive them? I do not ken if I can."

Toward her and the others—Sandy, Grizel, Airig, Ewen—I could not feel much animosity, for their silence had been held out of respect to Lord Kirthgarran's wishes and they had no part in the plan. Though I did not wish to discuss the details of my enlightenment with Mairi, I knew she had questions and further judgments to share. In time, perhaps, I would invite her to say them. Eventually I would also ask her about Mamma.

The only inquiry I could pose that day was about Coll's wound.

"The festering continues," Mairi replied. "But Sandy is persistent with his poultices and decided to bleed him this morning. It was done a few hours ago."

People came from Kirthgarran, Rathdale, Strath Gruachan, Blair Atholl, lands east and south of Loch Rannoch, and more. Grizel and other women had been cooking for days to prepare for the feast. For most of the afternoon I sat beside the bodies of my husband and grandsire. Andrew tried to talk to me once, but I had nothing to say and he turned away in disappointment.

I knew Coll watched me. Whenever I raised my eyes it seemed I saw his scarlet coat—across the great hall—by the fireplace—by the door. It did not matter. He followed me with the eye of a falcon.

Alistair—Davy—watched me as well. I sometimes caught myself staring at him for reassurance that I did not dream. When he stood beside his brothers I noticed they were of the same height. The planes of Alistair's cheeks were like Coll's, his hair fairer than Andrew's but still brown.

I studied him in stolen glances but I could not talk to him. All he had told me had been false. Someday I would reconstruct what had taken place between us but today, today and tomorrow, memories were to be avoided.

Reverend Cameron arrived, his usual jocular countenance subdued. Andrew drew him aside to tell of Lord Kirthgarran's secret and of my title.

I was introduced to Mairi's sister and her husband. They had come from Caiseal Àlainn, home of the Hamiltons. Molly was much like her sister, a little older perhaps, but bonny still. She embraced Mairi and wept at the loss of her nephew and felt no shyness at doing the same with me. She told me she remembered my mother, and had loved her.

The Fergussons of Lund came directly after and I became

known to my distant relatives. James Fergusson was a man of about forty years with a square jaw and curling black hair. He recognized my likeness to my mother immediately and kissed my hand as Ewen had done. His wife, sons, and daughters were named and brought forward, and in desperation did I try to recall all the fine points of graciousness and hospitality.

I could not help but regard every person I saw with a measure of suspicion. The person who had killed Rab still walked freely. Was he amongst us? Did he mean to shoot me?

Whilst the castle thronged with mourners there were cheeses, breads, ales, and whisky brought out, and a score of clay pipes plump with tobacco placed at the ready. Newcomers came into the great hall to see Lord Kirthgarran and Rab and to touch them. They were the objects of a great many toasts, and loud voicings of their fine qualities carried throughout the hall. Lord Kirthgarran's many achievements were listed and admired.

Sometimes there were laments, and hushes fell in the castle. The silences allowed me to ponder my exasperation and frustration, and in my head I demanded of the earl, "Did you not know how I loved you? Why did you not tell me the truth?" I wished I could speak with him about the past and Mamma and the future. I did not understand why he had delayed telling me. Now I could not ask him.

I sipped the ale in my hand and gazed at Rab as well, and tried to imagine how it would have been to have known the truth whilst he had been alive. He had expected to be recognized as the husband of the Countess of Kirthgarran one day. He had envisioned renting the estate lands to Mr. Baird. Evicting the tenants. Taking me to Edinburgh and London for balls and concerts and spending frolics. The money the wool brought in and his status would have been prizes he could not have visualized for himself as a lad. The same feelings with which I regarded his brother and their kinsmen stirred within me, but they were stained heavily with shame, for how blasphemous it was to think ill of the dead. In any case, the sight of him lying upon his board reminded me too much of his last moments, and the feelings were not easily replaced by the stabbings of wrath.

Contemplating the great hall, and understanding that it was mine, were endeavors beyond my ability. I would give up

Kirthgarran gladly if it meant the earl could come amongst us again. And Rab. The two were entwined, would always be entwined now.

And still, the questions on everyone's lips were, "Who killed Rab?" and, "Why?"

The drinking continued throughout the afternoon. At times Reverend Cameron sent prayers to our Maker in both English and *Gàidhlig*, asking for solace for the mourners.

At two o'clock the coffins were brought into the hall by the joiner. Everyone except the closest family members left the hall for the kisting, when with great care the earl and his foster son were placed inside their boxes and covered in their linen winding-sheets. With a small pair of scissors I cut pieces of hair from each of the men and small corners from their sheets in which to enfold the locks, just as I had done when Mamma had died.

Even after all of these days I had not grown accustomed to seeing the two men thus. They were not themselves, not my husband, not the earl. Rab seemed young, his cheeks smooth— one of them bruised—lips at rest, dark brown hair combed and the fringed whiskers in front of his ears neatly clipped. Lord Kirthgarran seemed youthful as well, for we had bound his silver hair at his neck as he had worn it in his portrait, and the puckers of disquiet and tension about his eyes and mouth were relaxed, eased.

They slept peacefully in this state that was not slumber but the halted moment between breaths. I wanted to embrace them both but could not tolerate the knowledge that their arms would remain still in return, and so, grasping their locks of hair, I turned away.

Our guests returned to give a final farewell. The lids of the boxes were nailed shut and mort-cloths of elegant linen draped over the tops. Men hoisted them on their shoulders and in groups of eight began the lifting and the procession out the door, whilst one by one all the curtains at the castle's windows were pulled open.

At the bottom of the wide steps stood Douglas Hamilton. The procession paused and an unnatural silence fell. The man's eyes traversed the crowd, the coffins. When he caught sight of me he bowed slightly, and, still mute, stepped back to allow the bearers to continue.

I went to the entrance hall with the rest of the women whilst the coffins were carried away. As I stood upon the top of Kirthgarran Castle's wide stone steps, I felt a pull at my skirts.

Iain stared up at me with his huge, brown eyes. I could not hear what he was attempting to say and I sank to the step beside him. "What is it, dearie?"

Being face to face with him allowed me to be swallowed up by those eyes. With his wee lips he said, "The puddock, Mrs. Rab." Pools of water slipped down his satiny cheeks, making crooked tracks through the grime.

"The puddock?"

"I killed them because I brought in the puddock."

My own eyes filled. "No, no, Iain! Such a thing as bringing in the frog was only a sign," I stumbled. "A sign. Like when you see the black clouds in the sky and ken it means rain is to come. You do not make the clouds come. You do not make the rain fall. It just happens. The puddock—it was just a foretelling, for those who look for signs."

He rubbed a wrist over his eyes. His fingers gripped two twigs of rowan.

I touched his fist and said, "Did you gather these?"

"For the graves. To keep them from harm. Like we did before."

I took the sticks. When I rose I found Sandy beside me and pressed them into his palm. "Take these," I beseeched him. "They're for the graves, after. I wish to place them there."

He regarded the twigs and agreed, folding his fingers over them. He said nothing but he had not said much to anyone since Rab's death.

I watched as he followed the others down the steps. Iain remained uncertainly before me. I placed my hands on his shoulders, finding relief in the touch as together we gazed upon the long line of men strung from the castle to the shore of the loch where bright torches burnt. I had never before heard the sound of pipes falling over the hills like tears down a man's cheek, but I did then.

By the water the Reverend spoke, though I could hear none of his words. Whilst the boat was loaded with Lord Kirthgarran's coffin and Donald played "Flowers of the Forest," I brought Iain away with me into the great hall. This was to be the last journey for the earl, across the water to the burial ground, but he would lie in honor forever amongst his ancestors. Rab would be interred there as well, for he had been revered as a foster son and belonged with the Fergussons of Kirthgarran. Besides, he had been my husband.

For hours men would be ferried back and forth to the isle whilst the women waited. Inside, the food was already prepared for the meal, and when all returned there would be merriment, feasting, dancing, and drinking until early morning. I was asked about allowing my mother's bed to be used by folk who would be staying overnight, and although I wanted to keep her bedchamber untouched by strangers, it seemed inhospitable to be so selfish and I reluctantly consented.

I settled Iain down in a chair with food and drink. I paced the great hall, wanting a glimpse of the loch from a window, but dared not ignore the old adage of risking death by doing so. At last I fled outside to the garden where I could watch, alone.

Where Rab lay bleeding days before, a small cairn had been erected in his memory. He was murdered and nothing would ever grow in this spot where he had lain losing his life's blood. The pointed pile of stones was a gesture of love and honor.

The lament of the pipes was unending. Donald piped "Lochaber No More," and on and on went the pibrochs, telling stories and painting pictures in music. Words came unbidden: pride, courage, love, bravery, strength—and sorrow. They floated in the air as sunset burst in the sky, flooding the streaked clouds and the waters below with crimson, gold, and mauve. The colors bled together and reached as far as the eye could see, a tapestry as rich as any painting, dark and bright at the same time with shades that changed as the sun lowered, turning blood red to vermilion, pink to rose, and violet to scarlet. I watched as Rab's coffin was rowed across to the isle and mourners joined him there to say farewell.

Mairi appeared beside me. We put our arms about each other as we gazed at the shrinking boats. The warmth of her body was unexpected, yet soothing. She said, "I always thought there could be no greater pain than the pain I felt when Christopher died. But I was wrong. Hearing that Walter and Hugh both perished, far away, those lads for whom I'd cared as my own, made me think the world had ended. I thought then there could be nought else that could cause a hurting so deep. But oh Keeley, I was wrong again. So wrong."

The boat bearing the coffin bumped the rocky shore of the island. I laid my head against Mairi's.

"I do not know," she said, "how to live without them."

Silently our hands clasped together.

When it was dark and the palette had burnt into inky black, the men came back. Together Mairi and I reluctantly returned to the hall where torches, candles, and the log fire now flared. Platters of mutton, kail, and cabbage were spread on the long table and trestle-tables alike, competing for space with cheese, biscuits, cooked goose, pullets, and potatoes. The kitchen at Rathdale was of great help; that morning Andrew had brought with him two garrons laden with fare.

Douglas Hamilton was nowhere to be seen, but there were numerous conjectures about his state of mind and how deeply he must have respected the earl.

When folk had taken their fill, the fiddle music began and dancers claimed the center of the floor. Brandy, claret, whisky, and ale flowed freely, and the relief of bearing the earl and his kin to their resting places, as well as the knowledge their souls now had crossed into the beauty and grace of God's company, brought everyone great ease.

Except me. I wished not to talk, or sing, or dance. Even Mairi's presence became too burdensome. I made excuses, wandered, swallowed a glassful of whisky.

I felt nothing when Isabel looked at me and burst into tears. She wept where she stood, motionlessly, silently, but her visage was dark with anger. An older woman put her hands on her shoulders and drew her aside.

I had to get away. There was nowhere to go but outside. At the kitchen door I let Kit re-enter the castle. She had been banned ever since the deaths, for no one desired to become blinded by looking at a cat that might have leapt over one of the bodies in the hall, and no one, indeed, wished her to be overtaken by demonic spirits. Superstitions—again. As she bounded into the kitchen, I imagined she was happy to escape the eyes and deadly talons of the falcons in the courtyard. She rubbed against Grizel and patted at her skirts, begging for a tidbit of the steaming fowl being lifted, dripping, from its roasting pan.

I crossed to the stable. Inside was the familiar fragrance of hay and oats, manure and horseflesh. MacNeil was tending to tack and feed in the newly mucked-out barn, for the horses residing tonight at the castle and in the paddock beyond were many.

"You're not wanting to ride, Lady Kirthgarran?" the stableman gasped.

"No," I said, my finger idly tracing a line across the edge of a loose box. "Just wanting to be away, from everyone. For just a bit. Is Greyfriar here, or is he out on the grass?"

"He's here. Every box is full, but he's there, in his usual spot."

And he was, beside Dominie and McKay. For a moment I stroked McKay's neck, knowing the horse would miss Rab's voice and his exuberant handling. I hoped Lachlan would take him to the race-meetings in Kinloch Rannoch, or at least gallop him across the hills as fast as the wind as Rab had loved to do.

I went to Greyfriar and ran my hands along his nose, smoothed the long fur on his rounded jaw. MacNeil left me to my musing as he dragged sacks of oats and corn into a corner far away.

It was so simple to be with animals, I thought. They accepted, forgave, trusted. And they did not lie. With my fingers I combed Greyfriar's white mane, beginning at the point where the hair grew from his neck.

I could not have been in the stable for more than five minutes before I found Coll standing beside me.

The interior was dim. MacNeil could be heard grunting whilst he rearranged sacks and barrels out of sight, and his bent body became etched by the lantern's light when he moved near Greyfriar's box. The groom's glance was caught by Coll's. A wordless request must have taken place, for MacNeil abandoned us, walking out into the night and leaving us alone. One of the horses blew through its nostrils, another shifted its position, the sound of its hooves muffled. Muted, from far away, came the reedy strains of Donald's pipes.

"The earl and my friend from childhood are buried," Coll said in his low voice, the voice he had used to sing with me, and tell me he loved me. "Your grandsire and your husband. God has them now. And they are with your mother. It must be a comfort."

I nodded, my fingertips lost in white silken hair, my voice lost in anguish.

"I do remember her," he said. "She had laughter like the burn rippling over its stones. Hunting with the falcons was a passion with her, for she loved the peregrines and had her own. She was fond of telling stories. Rabbie and I listened to her, for hours, on summer nights when the sun did not know enough to go to bed and neither did we."

Greyfriar twitched his ears, blinked his great eyes. I wished I could have said something.

"Delicate hands she had, I mind. With long, pointed fingers. I was always in awe of them. She liked to use them as she talked, told her tales. It made her words all the more picturesque. I watched her paint with those lovely hands. And play the clarsach. I mind that well, Keeley. The first time I heard you play, I was taken backward over twenty years to my childhood when Lady Nóra sang for us. There's much that's unclear, for as Andrew said, I was but a lad when she left us, but I remember a few things. Her stories, her hands, her songs..."

I turned my eyes to him then, almost swept away by the deep, velvety voice coming quietly in the stillness of the night. His back was to the light and I could not see his features well. He seemed tall in the vaulted stable, and threw a long shadow across the golden, hay-strewn, cobbled floor. The left arm of his coat hung slack, for his arm was held against his chest by a sling. A little of the white linen peeked out from his chest.

"So many times I wanted to tell you," he said. "Especially when you talked about her, missing her. I wanted to tell you she'd grown up here and had been happy. It was she who showed me dragonflies hatching from their papery skins and drying their new wings in the sun. She who laughed like a demented demon behind her hands when once I fell off a pony into a knee-deep puddle of glairie."

"But you did not tell me," I said at last.

His head moved slightly to one side. "No. I did not."

"Because it was a promise to Lord Kirthgarran."

"A promise," he agreed, "that I could not be breaking. During those last few days I was trying to convince him to tell you himself."

My mind, being as sore and wounded as it was, could not wholly contemplate or trust anything. My lips parted, and into the hollowness between us I said, "Of course you would say that now."

A pause. A breath. A shake of his head. "You do not believe me?"

"I find I have difficulties believing aught you and the others say to me."

For a score of heartbeats there was no response. "I'm not surprised by it, I suppose," he conceded, yet his tone remained perplexed. "But this is different. Can you not see I wanted the earl to tell you about your mother, and quickly? I wanted it all to be told. You had to know before I left. I said to you that in a day or two we could speak better about what could be done. If you knew you were Lord Kirthgarran's heiress you could make a decision. I never expected you'd want to come to me in India once you knew, nor would I want you to. And certainly Rab would give you difficulty. I was not sure he could be convinced to let you go. But knowing, understanding why I could not ask you to leave Kirthgarran, surely would have made our separation more bearable. You would not have me, but you would have a grandfather, and a title to inherit, with lands to match and the duties and privileges that went along with them. And you would finally understand that you were not a specter nor a wraith, but merely the image of your mother who many remembered."

His head lowered. "I had nought to offer you. Nought, but myself. In truth, Keeley, I knew, and know still, I could never be as important as those other things. My only fear, especially after that last night, was that Rab would continue to mistreat you and I did not think I could live with that. I was not sure I could leave you with him. It rent me in half, knowing you belonged at

Kirthgarran, but wanting you with me, safe. I struggled between greed and guilt. Told myself I would bide by whatever decision you did make, myself be damned, and try not to influence you. And all the while I begged the earl to tell you the truth."

Greyfriar's nose nudged my back but I ignored it, struggling to discern the face before me. "And how was your request taken?" I asked him. "Did he not agree it was time?"

He rubbed his eyes as if weary. "He knew it was time. I even told him about the letter from the emigration agent. But he balked. He began to be plagued by headaches. Finally he agreed, and I suffered because of how strongly I had to press him. I told him you must know soon because I was going to leave, and for the truth to be told before that—would mean a great deal to me. What I did not tell him was that I needed to be forgiven by you for a deception far more appalling than his."

"It was a risk you were taking, then."

"It was a risk I must take, with no choice about it. I was guilty. Am guilty. Myself just as badly as the others."

"Because you are all as one."

"In the beginning we were, yes."

"Forgive me," I said in a mocking tone that did not sound like me at all. "But for how many deceptions am I expected to pardon you?"

"What do you mean?"

I could feel the wrath welling up of its own accord, threatening to escape, and it frightened me even as an unknown, untested part of me welcomed it. "We could label them if you like. The First Deception. Not telling me who my mother was, who I was. The Second. Sending a lad to me—*your brother*—who did all in his power to make me fall in love with him. The Third. Having Rab rescue me, marry me, bring me here, to begin a life all based on lies. It's incredible, is it not, that you lied to me before I even met you."

"For all of it, aye, your scorn I deserve."

It hurt again, hearing him say that. His acceptance of the charges brought against him proved how true the story was. His acknowledgment proved, as well, how foolishly I still tried to dismiss everything as a worthless nightmare. "And yet the worst of all, the worst of all is The Fourth. You told me you loved me."

His eyebrows drew together. "You cannot possibly think that a lie."

"How can I tell where one falsehood ends and another begins?"

"Falsehood? Is it false how we have felt about each other? Have I pretended to be in anguish? Do you think I pretend to care for you so?"

"Do you not? You, who kept the other truths from me so perfectly? Why would this be any different?"

He said, with a sudden ire of his own, "Just how callous do you think I am?"

"I do not know! I must not know you at all. You and the others contrived to have me shamed and taken away from my home merely because you wanted to be assured of a share of Kirthgarran's coffers. First there was Alistair who pretended to care for me—then Rab—then you. Was I to be passed round to all of you, in turn? Who was to be next? Andrew? Or would it be Lachlan?"

His free hand became a fist at his side. I was stricken by what I said, but the words had been seeping through my mind since the night before.

In a strangled voice he replied, "I am worthy of contempt for bringing you here under connived circumstances, but do not stand in front of me and tell me I am lying about how I feel."

"I will tell you about *my* feelings. All I can think of is a day in Melrose when I discovered a wild apple tree. In the grass below the boughs were the most beautiful fruits, fallen in ripeness. There was one, larger and bonnier than the others, all shining and golden. Surely there'd never been such an apple, I thought. I admired it so, and lifted it up, but when I turned it over I saw the decay, the blackness, the ugliness that had been hidden. I am reminded of it now and cannot forget it. Nothing is as I thought it was."

"Except for what is between us. What will convince you are wrong about that?"

"There is nothing you can say."

"Even to tell you I can resign my commission? There's many who would be eager to buy it. It might be understood, with the deaths of Lord Kirthgarran and Rab here. Murray could take my recruits. I would do it, risk dishonor even, to remain here with you."

Cruelly I interjected, "Because all of your futures are once again uncertain? It's clear that owning and sharing Rathdale is not enough for any of you. Is it that you'd marry me? To become the husband of the Countess of Kirthgarran and bring everything back into the hands of you and your kinsmen?" I waited, finding my voice deepening when I added, "I would not be such a fool twice in one lifetime."

I might as well have struck him. He took a step backward. He whispered, "May God help us. What are you doing?"

Looking at him, tracing the shape of him in the dark, brought forth a bubbling mass of memories of all our intimate encounters. He had known Lord Kirthgarran was my grandsire. From the beginning he had, with the others, planned my meetings with Rab and Alistair and caused everything that had befallen me. "I'm asking you to go."

He seemed puzzled.

"I cannot bear this anymore," I went on. "I cannot bear seeing you, and remembering. Do you not understand? You cannot stay. You must go with your regiment, and let that be the end of it."

His voice came low, unrecognizable. "Do you ken what it is you're saying?"

"That I never want to see you again? That you must go and I'm hoping you never come back? Yes, yes, that is what I am saying."

I fancied he held his breath. As I watched him in the lantern glow something in his face closed. So long did he gaze at me I thought he had become a statue, engraved in cold, hard stone. Finally, in a murmur hardly audible, he said, "This is what we've done to you. This is what I have done to you. Oh my love. Love of my heart. I do not think God can help either one of us."

When he strode away I remained unmoving, caught, breathless, bloodless. My words to him ran through my mind like unwanted music that would not be put aside. They had been what I had meant to say. They had been rising and sinking in my throat all the night long, all the day long.

But having been spoken, their comfort was taken away. Further, the words were wrong. The air turned them black, evil. They had fallen on a man who did not deserve them. I had told him I no longer loved him. I had spoken phrases that could be interpreted as death wishes to a soldier preparing to depart for war.

I called his name, a mere breath coming from my throat. I was such a fool, such a hypocrite. I had accused him spitefully of being a liar when, for a reason I could not completely understand myself, I had just spoken the darkest untruths I had ever uttered in my life.

There was the desire to hurt him as I had been hurt. But having attempted to do so brought me not relief but a deepening of agony. This was a revelation to me in the silence of the stable, and he was gone—the man I loved and had cursed.

I called his name again, and realized how foolish it was. He could not hear me now. I tried to move my feet and found they had been nailed to the cobbles. I nearly fell to my knees in my desperation to reach the door. I stumbled toward the opening, grasped the framework, searched the courtyard. He was nowhere to be seen.

I had to look for him. I had to find him, to explain.

I yearned for nothing else but to touch him, to put my arms about him and feel his arms come round me. I knew well his feelings were genuine. I needed to tell him so and assure him nothing he could do would ever prevent me from loving him.

I ached to hear his stories about my mother. I needed to see his wounded arm and find out for myself that the infection was not worse. I longed to share my grief with him and talk about Rab and Lord Kirthgarran and the estates and all that the future entailed; to convey to him that in spite of my hurt and continuing disillusion he was forgiven.

I searched everywhere. I skirted the great hall, swept through the wings, and looked into every part of the castle: the dining, sitting and drawing rooms; the library. I went to his bedchamber only to find it cold and empty. Up and down the passages I went, checking in desperation the nursery, the whisky cellars, the stable once more, and even the garden. But he was gone. He had disappeared into the air like smoke into mist, not wanting to be found.

The wrath inside of me had long ago burnt away and I trailed from chamber to chamber in misery, wanting him and becoming more anxious with every step.

In the end there was nothing to be done but to sit, hoping he would come. I waited in the smoky hall and listened to the singing and watched the dancers who followed the rhythm of the fiddle. An hour passed with my heart pounding in my throat and mad wings beating inside my head. I ignored Airig who came to me and I wandered away from her, not answering her questions. I returned to Coll's chamber but nothing was changed.

I comforted myself by chanting aloud that as soon as I found him I could convince him I'd not meant what I had said. His very essence lived here in his room, another kind of comfort. I touched his leather coat draped on a chair and took it into my hands. I rubbed the rough hide and smelt the musky scent of him. On the dressing table were carelessly left his gauntlet, whistle, a half empty glass of whisky, a few sheets of blank paper, a quill, and pot of ink. Beside them rested the feather bonnet of the 74th, ready to be taken on the journey to Argyll. How many days were there before he was expected to leave? I had lost count. I furtively numbered my fingers, fumbled, and started over three times. Was it fifteen? Fourteen? He had said he could resign his commission...

I could not go to bed. I would not be able to sleep. I left Coll's wing and went back to mine anyway, seeking my bedchamber, not knowing where else to go. I placed my candle down on my commode and stood, my mind churning as I attempted to decide what to do. Perhaps, after all, if I waited in Coll's room he would return to it sooner or later. I did not particularly care if others discovered I was there or not. No one else mattered. My reputation did not matter.

I turned to leave, but my eye caught on the bed. My feet came to a halt. I felt my scalp contract as my hair lifted. My clarsach had been placed on the forest-green coverlet, on its side. I had not put it there. And there was something wrong with it.

I took a step forward and stood at my bedside to view it better. With a shaking hand I brought the candle closer. Someone had hacked at the taut strings and broken the highest, thinnest ones; someone had struck again and again at the honey-colored wood, scarring and splintering and permanently disfiguring the polished surface. The medieval designs inspired by the Books of Kells and Durrow and lovingly carved into the oak were now chipped and sliced. The dragon, or dog, on the bottom was now neither, only a welter of notches and punctures.

Embedded in the sounding box, abandoned by the hand that had wielded it, was a plain, heather-wood-handled knife from the kitchen of Kirthgarran.

The sight took the life from my limbs.

That someone could have harmed an instrument meant for giving pleasure was mystifying. That someone had meant the knife to lie in my throat and not the clarsach's was a possibility that was terrifying.

It could not be, I told myself. But there it was in front of me, and with cold clarity, fear crept into my soul, and stayed.

Dae you see yon high hills all covered wi' snow
They hae pairted mony's the true love and they'll soon pairt us twa.

Bonnie Glenshee (Trad.)

Chapter Thirty-Nine

W went down to the hall in the morning, went down to join the others when all I wanted was seclusion.

I stood at the bottom of the mural stair and looked at the people who had slept on the floor or in chairs, and said aloud, "What would you do, Lord Kirthgarran, were you in my place?"

There was no answer. None that I could hear, at least, over the drone of voices.

Bannocks, oatcakes, ale, and whisky made their way to the long table. From every corner people were waking, shrugging off the effects of last night's frenzy, seeking sustenance. They would be here for days.

Through the shifting mosaic of people, Andrew's head and shoulders became more pronounced. He came to me and bent his head. *"Madainn mhath,"* he said. "You're up early."

Was it your hand? I asked, though nothing at all came from my lips. Your hand that left the knife in my clarsach?

"My lady? You're looking peculiar."

"I'm—it's nothing. You're up early yourself, if you've come from Rathdale."

He continued to appraise me, but said nonetheless, "Like you, I cannot sleep. I thought I'd bring some eggs from our hens at Rathdale. The folk here have voracious appetites."

"I should see Grizel. I have no idea how she's managing."

"She has the maids fearful for their lives, but she herself seems to have things well in hand. I'll send over more provisions from our larder in a few days."

"You'll not strip your own. I could not be happy, thinking you and Anne and your mother were going hungry." And Alistair, I reminded myself. "They are well, are they not? Anne seemed spent yesterday, and of course Mairi is too distraught..."

"Annie's recovering, thinking of the bairn, and Mam, well, Mam. She was abed this morning when I left. When we returned home last night she had a difficult time. She needs to sleep, to rest."

"I'll go to her. Perhaps tomorrow."

"She'd like that, I'm thinking."

I was unable to prevent myself from casting about in the sleepy crowd.

"You're looking for someone," Andrew said.

"I was hoping I'd see Coll."

He explored the faces himself. "I've not seen him at all this morning."

I believed him, but it was with difficulty I brought my attention back to the figure beside me. "I'm uneasy. About his arm."

"As are we all. But we must trust in Sandy's judgment. I've never known him to be neglectful, especially where Coll is concerned."

I compressed my thumbs in my fists.

"It's too soon to ask for any kind of forgiveness," Andrew

said. "But I hope that we can speak later about Kirthgarran, the estates, and all. You may find it a solace. Lord Kirthgarran had ideas and plans and you may wish to follow them, or you may have your own. He had confidence in you. We talked at times about how it would be when he was gone. I can tell you what he said, what he hoped for."

"I wish he had told me."

"If he'd known what was to come, he would have."

"I'm overwhelmed, Andrew. I cannot think what to do about anything."

He nodded. "Luckily the estates exist, they sail along, they support themselves, and can do so for quite some bit of time before looking to anyone for decisions. All, from the privy rakers to the factor, see to their tasks still, as they have for years. But when it is time for changes to be made or problems to be solved you ken I will be here for you."

I could tell him about the clarsach, I thought. Asking for assistance would have been what Lord Kirthgarran would have done. The earl would have raised a cry at the castle, shown the harp in its sorry state, and begun accusing, questioning, threatening. Andrew would help me find the aggressor and protect me in the process. I parted my lips. "I need you. I do need you."

"Ewen will do all he can, as well. What you must mind is that none of your holdings depend solely on you. There are others to help you. We have years of experience amongst us and you need only ask for it to be shared with you."

"Andrew," I said, reaching for his sleeve.

Someone spilt an ale-caup and amber liquid flooded over the table and spattered to the floor. Whilst others rushed to assist I realized that anyone here could have been in my chamber last night. Someone meant me harm. Perhaps he was also Rab's murderer.

The madman might be James Fergusson of Lund with his black and curling hair, heir to Kirthgarran upon my death if the Crown favored him. Or the bent man with broken teeth who blamed me for the clearing and the sheep coming, who could barely walk let alone lift a knife in rage. Or even Mr. Cameron, our minister, who prayed alone in an alcove.

"Andrew," I said again.

He turned his face to me. He was kind, questioning, eager to hear.

"Lady Kirthgarran," said Ewen Drummond at our backs. "How does this morning find you?"

We revolved to face the baillie. He was smiling but there was wretchedness in his eyes.

I said, "I will never become accustomed to that title."

"Then we must use it often, for it's a title you deserve and will hold with great pride," Ewen replied.

"The title," Andrew said, musing. "My lady, Ewen has not yet shown you the charter."

"The charter," Ewen echoed. "Aye, you must see the charter. Hold it in your hands. The solicitors arrive today, like as not, but is there a reason, after all, to wait for them? We can go to the library now and present it to you."

"The countess has not yet broken her fast," Andrew said. "Nor even had a cup of tea, I'm guessing. Is it not so?"

I shook my head, grieving for the moment when I could have told Andrew.

"By all means sit you down and have your meal," Ewen said. "You should not be so slighted. We must make changes here, Andrew. There should be a lady's maid for her, tending her. Airig? Ròs? Someone new? And then there's the other posts. The earl was not in favor of rearrangements but mayhap the time has come. Your mother cannot continue her duties as housekeeper, not greeting as she is and living at Rathdale. Airig would be more suited. And there's room for more housemaids, and a footman and butler, and enough money to pay them with wages being as cheap as they are. There's no reason we cannot fit out the castle as well as other grand houses, especially now that we'll have the means to do so."

Andrew addressed me. "We will have the means, with the income from the land-rent that begins in spring. You can live quite comfortably then and afford the help. Have you a preference? For a lady's maid, that is?"

"I'm very fond of Airig, but she will—I mean, she is more familiar, I think, with the housekeeping..."

"It is for you to choose whom you want," he said. "Airig will serve you well in either manner."

"I must think on it. I never thought I would have someone serving me so."

"Of course," Andrew said. "Speak to Mam about it later, if you will. She'd be helpful to you, I believe. But for now we must get you your breakfast. Ewen, join us?"

I was swept away to the dining room, surrounded by Andrew, Ewen, Lachlan, James Fergusson, and others who scooped eggs, fish, and cheese into their mouths as well as buttered bannocks and scones dripping with marmalade. I chewed a corner of toasted barley bread and drank tea into which Andrew insisted throwing a dash of whisky. The morning was gray and burning candles stood like sentinels amongst the dishes. I surveyed the heads about the table. Coll's was not amongst them.

When I could no longer pretend interest in my food, I accepted Ewen's invitation to accompany him to the library. From the unlocked Chinese cabinet he drew a long, wooden box. The panels and straps were hand-painted with floral designs, and wood and leather alike were shiny with lacquer. His hand shook as he fitted a key into the ornamented brass plate and released the latches on either side. He lifted the cover on its leathern hinges, releasing a musty odor. Inside lay a roll of creamy white parchment.

He hesitated, looking up at me. The long hairs in his eyebrows quivered. "It is yours. Take it, my lady."

"Do," Andrew urged. "For you are the eighth to own it, in the line of Fergussons of Kirthgarran. Yours are the hands in which it rightfully belongs."

I was unable to obey at first. I gazed at the scroll. *Coinneach Fergusson, Laird of Strath Gruagach,* I could hear the earl saying. *Cousin of James the First. He was given the title of Earl, and the lands of Kirthgarran, for repayment of loyalty. And James gave them by letters patent. Royal charter, lass. Sheepskin.* I lifted it as though it were pieced together of butterfly wings, liable to crumble into dust in my fingers.

A nod from Andrew encouraged me to unfurl it.

The skin lengthened into a rectangle. Words covered the top two-thirds: Latin words written in brown ink, small and close and carefully ruled. The first letter was an *"I"* for James, Iacobus, three inches tall and superfluously embellished.

Ewen eyed the meticulous lines of script and said, "I could translate it for you, but in essence what the writing puts forth is that he, James I, second Stuart on the Scottish throne, does grant lands to his kinsman for unquestioned loyalty. That Coinneach will be Earl of Kirthgarran, and in turn so will his progeny. That into his and their hands is put the responsibility and obligation of caring for the beloved mountains, glens, and valley that surround Loch Seàrr." At the foot of the page was a waxen seal and long, parchment tassels hanging in a curling, twisting fringe.

I held the three hundred year-old document and mused about my ancestors holding it before me. They might have stood here on this spot, in the midst of these hills, and experienced the same reverence.

"Yours, my lady," Andrew said. "Yours."

"Lord Kirthgarran told me of it. He was proud of it, and gave me the story about the first earl. I never thought, never imagined, I would hold it so."

"No one can take it from you. It is yours, to pass to your own son or daughter."

My own child.

Something in my expression seemed to prompt Andrew to quickly add, "Forgive me. I did not mean to upset you. Of course you cannot think of the future, not yet. I merely meant the charter safeguards Kirthgarran for you and any descendants that might follow you."

Ewen said, "Safeguards, aye. The lands and the castle are yours. But be aware that this parchment can be a bane as well as a blessing. You may do anything you will with Kirthgarran, except sell it. The solicitors will explain it to you. With the joys of ownership come the curses. And mind, the tailzie exists still. If you yourself have no heirs, all will pass to the Crown upon your death."

"Ewen," Andrew protested. "Let's leave it at that."

"Time enough for the particulars later, I suppose," the baillie admitted.

I painstakingly rolled the charter into its former shape and laid it inside the kist. I smoothed some of the tassels underneath and tucked them in like coverlets about a child in its cradle.

Ewen held out the key. From it dangled a faded purple ribbon. "You have a key to this box," he said. "'Tis one of those Andrew gave you, together with the ones that open your mother's chest. This is one Lord Kirthgarran gave me years ago."

"Then you must keep it."

"The earl gave it to me but that does not mean his successor must entrust it to my safekeeping as well."

"I want you to keep it." I was adamant. I closed the lid.

"Lord Kirthgarran dreamt of handing you the box, and saying 'This will be yours one day,'" Andrew told me. "I can nearly imagine him here with us, smiling because he knows Kirthgarran is safe, because he knows you will love it as he did."

"As he and his children did," I said.

My duty was to be hostess to our guests. There was food and drink and tobacco to provide, music and dancing to initiate. I sat in the great hall and tried to collect my thoughts as I replied to well-meant inquiries. I was slow and without wit.

The solicitors arrived in the afternoon and were treated to nourishment and its extravagances. The two men were young, inexperienced partners, sent by their elders to officially preside over legalities that were all but sealed and neatly filed. Together with Sandy, Ewen, Andrew, James Fergusson of Lund, and his wife I scrutinized documents and was shown Lord Kirthgarran's will.

True to his promise, the earl had left the house at Rathdale and its three small farms to Andrew. I had inherited everything else.

"Although it was Lord Kirthgarran's wish for me to have my father's house," Andrew said to me. "I want you to know that I do not accept it."

"But why?" I asked in disbelief. The others eyed each other and then me.

"The arrangement we held with Lord Kirthgarran meant that we lived here, at the castle and at Rathdale, and were obliged to serve as factors," Andrew said. "He offered us incomes but we chose to turn them back into the estates. In light of what you've learnt in the past days," he said with some hesitation, "you may, well, to say it plainly, you may not want the same arrangement. And I do not deserve Rathdale. Not after what I—what we—have done to you. I want to give the house and lands back to you. Certainly I will stay long enough to help you, as I promised, but..."

The solicitors bunched up their eyebrows, clearly puzzled.

"Andrew," I said, grasping the table edge. "You cannot think I want you to leave."

"*You* cannot think that Lachlan, my brothers, and I take it for granted that we live on the bounty of Kirthgarran, or that I myself expect to benefit by taking away an estate that by rights should be yours."

"My grandsire desired you to have it. When he lost Walter and Hugh, when he hoped my mother would be found, he still meant you to have it."

"If he knew my deceit I wonder if he would still feel the same."

I stumbled for words, saying finally, "What you have given is beyond measure. How could Kirthgarran have endured without you all! Do you believe I could ask you to give up Rathdale, you and Anne and Mairi? It was your father's home. The earl went against what Eleanor wanted, but I will not go against what he wanted. And the castle. It is your home as well, home to you and the others."

"You could lease the house at Rathdale and bring in a fine profit from it."

"Why would I ever want to do that? Rathdale is yours," I said. "It will always be yours."

He glanced at me with skepticism and shook his head a little. "It is not right."

"I understand what it is costing you to suggest this. But pray, do not continue."

"I will stay if that is what you choose. Mind, you do not have to make the decision the day. I know what misery we've caused you. When the loss of Rab and Lord Kirthgarran has lessened, you may think on our situation differently, and we'll accept what you determine. All of us."

"The only change I want to make, hope to make, is to force each of you to accept the incomes you refused from Lord

Kirthgarran."

He sighed.

Ewen nodded in agreement. "Aye," he said. "When the sheep come."

"Never again speak of forsaking Rathdale—or of leaving," I told Andrew. "I beg of you."

He nodded a little, and we looked long and hard at each other. The solicitors seemed to breathe easier despite their confusion and got on with their shuffling of papers. The others sat quietly, too polite, I supposed, to inquire about Andrew's mysterious guilt.

Thus, the meeting I once pictured as being traumatic and cold, with papers drawn up restoring the ownership of Kirthgarran and Strath Gruachan to King George III, was merely a formality to ascertain that all was bequeathed to a legal heir after all. Short and perfunctory. A boring task to be performed by fledglings barely divested of their apprenticeships.

"We're done then," said one, scratching his nose and turning red when he discovered himself doing so. He hastily clasped his hands together. "Have you any more of that fine claret?"

Sandy took them away whilst James Fergusson and his wife congratulated me and made me promise to one day visit them.

I wandered through the great hall, speaking with those who had ridden great distances to attend the funeral, urging all to enjoy their stay before returning home. In Gaelic I exchanged brief words with cottars, trading their polite sentiments for welcomes. I said the same words over and over, finding it impossible to think. I was safer, I was convinced, being amongst many people rather than a few.

A fiddler played jauntily; dancers enjoyed a fast reel. When Andrew was free of the lip-licking, young solicitors, I promised myself, I would tell him about the clarsach. I stood alone for a moment, wearily contemplating the legion of people before me. I studied heads, faces. And realized I stared at Coll.

He sat on a stool, loosely holding a half-empty glass. Sandy stood beside him, momentarily snared by a dialogue with someone else. The bodies between us ceased to be. The music and the murmur of many voices became whispers. He was here.

His hair was disheveled, loose about him, spiraling in kinks down his back. His shirt was not of army issue but his own coarse homespun. The sling was gone. Leather breeks covered his knees. He raised the tumbler to his lips, swallowed, put his elbows on his legs, and let the glass hang from his fingers.

He looked up. I wondered if he could sense me, across the hall, caught by the sight of him. It seemed he could. Our eyes connected.

Everything I had wanted to say, all the apologies and phrases of forgiveness, crowded in my head at once. He was here. I had only to walk across to him and touch his haggard face and let all my self-reproach fall from me, and our hurts would be healed. I took a step and became trapped by a person in my path. Coll's shadowed eyes followed me.

My movement seemed to decelerate, become timeless. I watched as his eyes widened and searched mine. There was a question in them. He was asking, "Have you forgiven me after all?"

And I allowed mine to say, "Yes, and I love you and I am so sorry, so sorry..."

I moved behind another body, my eyes still linked with his, and the seconds continued to slow to a crawl, and he was expectant, waiting to see what I would do. I tried to pull cohesive words into my mind and plan what I would say when I reached him. He blinked and it was as though a whole minute passed.

Without warning, a vision of my clarsach intruded and thrust itself before me. The lacerated wood. The ruptured strings. The gashes. I felt my eyes constrict. The vision expanded to include a hand squeezing the handle of a kitchen knife and thrusting downward. He had been overwrought when he had left me in the stable the night before. Impassioned. Inflamed. Thinking I wished him dead.

I could not breathe. I felt my face stiffen. I pictured Coll's hand holding the knife.

I had put the harp away in my cupboard after my discovery of it, unable to withstand the sight of its mutilation. Yet I knew it was there, perched behind the cupboard door like an injured animal, hurt and without hope of recovery. I had hidden the knife away in my writing desk, shot home the bar on my chamber door, and cringed in my bed all the night, dreaming, whenever I did fall asleep, of a shapeless, faceless stranger trying to grab at my throat. This morning before coming downstairs I had sent Airig away and locked the clarsach in a cabinet in my mother's old room, thus leaving it where the terror of it seemed far removed.

What must have shown on my face whilst I thought of it was unknown to me, but Coll's reaction was clear. His eyes blinked again, opened, and looked away. When his eyes returned to me they were hardened, eyelids and brows both drawn down. He was infuriated. He turned aside.

A man was in my way. We turned left, right, and left again in an effort to get past each other. I sought Coll once more, but he was interested in me no longer. He hurled a swallow of drink into his mouth. Sandy bent down to his ear and seemed to ask a question, for Coll nodded. With some hardship he got to his feet and followed Sandy. He did not look back.

I tolerated the company of the folk whilst I waited. I was convinced Sandy was ministering to his arm, and once lint and bandage were renewed Coll would return.

An hour later I glimpsed Sandy climbing the steps by the piper's gallery. I rushed over to him and called his name. He paused with a hand on the balustrade and I said, "Where is Coll?"

"Away to Rathdale."

"He's gone?"

"Aye."

"He went to see Mairi," I said.

"Gone to stay with Mairi," Sandy corrected me.

"Stay..." I repeated. Sandy's face was impassive and revealed nothing, but his eyes investigated mine coolly. I would have liked to talk to him about Rab, but thus far the appropriate moment for such confidences had not materialized. And this particular moment, when I was overwrought by concern for my lover, was certainly not right at all. Embarrassment and shame swelled within me. I did not think I was able to hide either one.

Nonetheless I was driven to ask, "But his arm. How is it?"

"No worse, thanks be to God."

"Then it's getting better..."

"It's no worse."

I found it difficult to stand still. My feet moved a little and my hands clamped on my arms. "And you say he's gone to stay with his mother. Did he say for how long?"

He shook his head. His eyes narrowed. "Possibly until he's off to Argyll."

I stood a moment longer but could bear it no more. I backed away and crossed the hall, plunged down the mural stair, and went out into the courtyard. Rain spattered my head as I bounded for the stable. The postern gate was closed. I flew into the open stable doorway, caught myself on the post, and said to Kenneth who was rubbing down a saddle, "Coll. Have you seen him?"

He stilled his hands in surprise. "Why, he's just left, Mrs., I mean, my lady."

"Where did he go? Did he say?"

He shrugged. "He did not say much. He told me to saddle Dominie, that he was bound for Rathdale, and not to expect him back."

I saw the naked truth in his face, heard it in his words, and watched as his expression turned from perplexity to distress. "What's amiss, Mrs.? I mean, my lady? Will I ride after the Captain?"

I went back out, darted for the gate and swung it open. Beyond, the countryside was quiet, bare, stung by sheets of cold December rain. The loch was leaden, its surface pitted. The pebbled path glistened and led away into mist that thickened as I watched.

Kenneth was at my side. "I'll go for you, if you've a message," he offered again.

"No," I said. "No."

Together we looked out at the gray mountains as winter dusk fell. After a while I felt sorry for the lad's shivering, and allowed him to accompany me back to the castle.

Coll left an emptiness behind him. It deepened by the hour and grew into an ache as heavy as the white vapor cloaking the hills. Night dissolved into another morning. Nothing interested me but the path that followed the shoreline. Few of our guests had packed their belongings, and as I watched, only two or three of the mourners departed and took to the track. White plumes rose from the loch like wisps of smoke, forming clouds that drifted away, and later when a breeze stirred and became stronger, it swept the air clean. For as long as I waited Coll did not appear and my heart rebelled against what my mind already knew.

The one person I wished to stay said farewell to the folk behind me. Mr. Cameron, man of God and head of our parish, was needed elsewhere. As I turned from the window, forsaking the barren path, I caught sight of him patting the heads of a half-dozen children. He had had a good meal, had collected his Bible and hat, and only needed to bestow a few parting words upon his flock.

"When is it you'll be returning to us?" I asked him when he prepared to leave at last.

"Oh, a fortnight, I'm thinking. That is, if Providence sees fit to render kind weather. I'd not go now if Hamish Black's wedding was not on the morrow, but it seems I have little choice."

"I'll watch for your return."

From the entrance hall I glimpsed MacNeil leading the reverend's horse to the front of the castle and there they waited, whipped by forceful gusts. Mr. Cameron took my hands and pressed them between his warm, dry palms and shook his nose at me.

"A bride and a widow in the space of a few short months. You've a right to greet. And to lose a grandsire you did not know you possessed! There's a great deal for you to mourn, my lady. But there's many besides me to offer you comfort, and you must not refrain from the asking for it. I am but one man, and there's God to keep you, besides the families that surround you here."

Does God want to keep me, I thought, when I have sinned so badly? "I've no right to ask aught of God," I said with vehemence.

He sat me down on a settle. He tucked his bag next to a bolster and lowered himself beside me. "And why do you say such a frightful thing?" he asked.

I stared at his black shoes and the small, dull buckles. "It was because of me that they died."

He did not reply at once. "Both of them? Rab and the earl together? Why, how can that be so, lass?"

"I left my clarsach in the garden. I left it, when I should have remembered to bring it in."

"None of us is perfect, are we. Who amongst us has not forgotten something, at some point in our lives?"

I could not tell him the reason I had forgotten it, that I had run away to fornicate with my husband's kinsman, and the excitement had caused me to forsake it.

"Here, here," the reverend cajoled. "You're forgetting the manner in which Rabbie died. He was murdered, by a madman, in the quiet of a night. Such a man would have found his opportunity, whether it was that particular night or no."

"Perhaps there never would have been another opportunity."

"Taking the responsibility for your husband's murder is too large a burden for you to hoist to your shoulders. God would never ask you to do that. He has His own plans, He does, and it is no business of ours to take pride in what comes to pass, or to assume guilt."

I allowed my head to come up and I saw the compassion in him. "But if Rab had not offered to go out, to fetch the clarsach for me..."

"My lady," said Mr. Cameron. "Did you mean for your husband to be killed?"

"How could you think..."

"I do not think. And neither does God. In the Bible Daniel says, *'To the Lord our God belong mercies and forgivenesses.'* But in this case I'm thinking you must forgive yourself, not expect it from Him."

I searched his face, wanting to believe him, until I remembered my adultery and knew that such forgiveness, from me or our God, would be a long time in coming, if ever it did at all. My gaze fell once more and yet somehow I found the words to say, "It is not something I can easily do."

He leant forward. "But do it you must. We could spend our lives wondering what would have happened had we done this, or not done that. It's too complex a matter for us to understand, and sometimes there are no whys or wherefores to aught. The best we can do, the most we can do, is be true to our beliefs and the teachings of the kirk, and to learn from our mistakes should we err and forget. God forgives us. We should be as kind to ourselves."

"I promise I'll think about what you say."

He let a long breath whistle out through his nose and seemed reluctant to be on his way. When he rose to his feet it was with a groan. I took his offered hand and rose also as he said, "And though 'tis not pleasant to remind ourselves of this, it seems you must be made to recall that Lord Kirthgarran was fortunate to have as many days as he did. Five years ago, if someone had prophesied that the earl would not succumb to a seizure before this, I would have called him an idiot. It was only a matter of time, was it not? Feel sorrow if you must, but I forbid you, with all the power I possess, to take any guilt of any sort into your heart when you think on your grandfather's death."

"I will try very hard to heed your words," I said.

"Well then. It's time I was off. Bide you well, Lady Kirthgarran, until we smile on each other again."

I nodded, and he gave me a hopeful grin before he ventured out the door and down the steps. The wind flapped his cloak and blew the hairs that peeped out from the curled periwig he wore. MacNeil held his horse's head whilst he clumsily mounted, and he was away, a scion of reason and peace amongst men of passion and hatred who killed and threatened.

I should have told Mr. Cameron about the clarsach. He never would have gone, leaving me alone with someone who had threatened me. Perhaps the visitor to my chamber had been Rab's murderer. Perhaps I was the next quarry.

Coll would not have gone either, if he had known I was in danger.

Resolutely I hurried upstairs. Airig was smoothing fresh linens on my bed. I gave darting looks into the corners of my room and tried not to dwell on the table where the clarsach had once lain.

"Were you wanting me?" she asked as she floated the coverlet over the sheets and allowed it to settle.

"No. I came to change. I'm going to Rathdale."

"Oh! Mairi will be glad of that."

I shook out the skirt of my riding habit and reached for the jacket in the clothes press. I would see Mairi, yes, and Alistair as well, which caused me some dismay, but I could not linger on that thought. I closed the door and began to unfasten the laces of my gown.

Airig was behind me, assisting. "There's others going with you, of course," she said lightly.

"Why, no, I'd not thought of arranging anything. I just want to ride over, for an hour or two. Before dinner."

"Are you not afeart of it?" Her fingers stilled and at her mere mention of the word, I did feel afraid.

"Of riding to Rathdale alone? Why should I be? I have done so, a number of times." Perhaps she was right, though, and I wondered if she knew about the clarsach or even noticed it was missing.

"But the fire. They've not discovered who it was, and it might be that he's wandering about on the moorland. I'd not like to think you'd come across him. Although he probably means no one any harm, and is, most likely, away by now. But still, it does not seem right, you, the Countess of Kirthgarran, riding off without a groom or an escort. I cannot help but remember that death comes in threes. How I wish the man who shot our Rab would come forward and claim what he's done..."

"Airig," I interrupted. "Please stop. What fire?"

"Surely you've heard?"

"Where was there a fire?"

"Did you not learn of it this morning? A cottage burnt, on Rathdale lands."

I turned to face her. "Was anyone hurt?"

"The family emigrated, some time ago. The house has been empty for months."

"Then how..."

"Aye, how could an empty cottage burn? Tam Lovey saw the smoke early this morn and went to see, and told us when he brought in the milk."

I concentrated on her face as pinpricks assaulted the base of my spine. "What cottage was it?"

"I would say halfway betwixt here and Rathdale House. A bonny wee house, set in a hollow. There were yews and honeysuckle planted round. It was lucky it was off by itself so it did not threaten others. But then it was not lucky, was it, for it was too far to be noticed and saved. It's odd you were not told. And yet perhaps no one wanted to distress you. And now here I've done it..."

I fought the urge to sink to the chair. I cleared my throat, shook my head. "And do they not know how it started?"

"They think it must have been a wanderer or a beggar intending to harbor there for the night, lighting a fire and not being careful with it. But whoever it was is gone. They did not find a body." She wrinkled her nose. "It was a fine house. Such a shame it's a ruin, with none of it left but the stone walls."

I stared at her a moment longer. I said, when I could speak again, "I must go." I did not wait for her to help me. I began to pull my gown over my head.

My abruptness must have surprised her. She helped me with the habit, but said nothing until I stamped my feet impatiently into my boots. "Ask Lachlan to go with you," she begged. A glance at her solemn eyes made me promise.

In the great hall I searched for his shaggy head, even looked in the drawing room, but I had no time to waste. Knowing I was foolhardy, and unable to prevent it, I sought the stable alone.

Kenneth found me leading McKay out of his box. "Losh, Mrs.! It's that one you're wanting?"

I did not reply. I ignored Kenneth's gaping mouth and bulging eyes and reached for a bridle.

He seemed to become aware of my urgency and came forward to help. McKay was saddled and stood snorting, as fidgety as I. The lad boosted me up onto the tall beast's back and gowped at me with an air of consternation. "McKay is..."

"I ken," I said, tightening my grip on the rein as the horse took his customary sideways steps. "Open the gate for me, will you now?"

"Surely you're not off alone with him?" he said, glancing about.

"There's nought to worry over."

"No, no, no, my grandda will tear my limbs from me if I let you go alone. A minute, just a minute, and I'll be alongside of you..." He flung himself away.

I opened my mouth to protest but stopped. Restlessly I urged McKay toward the postern gate, willing to wait for the stableman's grandson but begrudging his company all the same. I let myself be distracted by the incessant wind that threatened to pry the hat from my head. It blew cold across my eyes, stinging them, bringing forth tears that I rubbed away in irritation. McKay lifted his nose into the full force of it, widening his nostrils and prancing fretfully.

Kenneth opened the gate and McKay and I cantered through. The steely loch was in frantic motion. Long rows of waves teemed to reach the shore, their sharp ridges cresting at times into forelocks of springing, white curls. Amongst the boulders by the stone arch they crashed, sending sprays of water into the air that were whisked away by the wind. Along the pebbled shore the waves clawed and churned.

Kenneth leapt into his own saddle. I held back not a second longer and kicked McKay into a gallop down the path. As we drummed over the well-known meadows and moors, I told myself that the burnt cottage was not the same one in which Coll and I had met. There must be two white houses that fit the same description. Kenneth did not ask for our destination but followed me in silence, he and his mount becoming a grim shadow that relentlessly kept pace with McKay. I gripped my horse with legs and fingers that felt nothing, and endured the reckless gallop with a fear that could not begin to compare with the trepidation of what I would find on the moorland.

At last it lay before me, the wee cottage where Coll and I had loved and lain, the haven of safety. It was now a blackened husk with gaping, broken walls. Tendrils of smoke still rose from the rubble in the center and disappeared in the wildness of the wind. The bonny bushes were charred skeletons. Everything of beauty was gone.

The fire could not be a coincidence. The burning came too close on the heels of the clarsach being ruined. As I sat the heaving McKay and stared at the sooty mangle I tried to think, but my thoughts coiled in the form of jumbled questions.

Who else knew we had come here? Was this a warning of some kind, to me, to Coll? Or was it the vindictive eradication of a symbol, a memory that was no longer wanted?

It was not possible that Coll had set fire to the cottage to tell himself—and me—that the love we had shared was over. His state of mind could not be so troubled.

I did not want to ponder it. I did not want to believe he had done it. The culprit had been a traveler, a beggar, a careless man who had built up a fire to warm himself and then thoughtlessly left it to be fanned by the growing wind. Or perhaps flames had spread from the hearth and sent sparks shooting to the stool and the bracken-stuffed bedding, and the poor wretch who had kindled it had fled, unable to put out the monster he had unwittingly created.

McKay snorted, danced on his eager hooves, and still I gripped the rein and stared at what was left of the cottage. There was nothing of any consequence remaining to remind me of the happiness I had felt here or the dream I had once envisioned. Whether the dwelling had been engulfed by accidental flames or purposeful ones, my response to its destruction was the same.

"Is it Rathdale we're going?" Kenneth inquired, shouting over the roar of the wind.

I pulled McKay's head about and began to walk him away, back the way we had come. I shook my head, unable to speak.

Wordlessly we rode back to Kirthgarran.

The frost wind soon will sweep away
That luster deep from glen and brae.

Norah's Vow (Trad.)

Chapter Forty

I stood up straight, weak and lightheaded and yet strangely tranquil after having vomited my breakfast tea and bannock down into the dark hole in the garderobe. A hand planted on the cool stone of the wall brought back a sense of solid well-being. Though my vitals seemed locked in a knot still, the urgency of illness was abated since the offending items were now gone down the chute, and I breathed easier, ready to resume life again.

I was confused by the hunger that gnawed, for it was a sensation that merely masqueraded as hunger. Clearly my stomach did not want any food. I turned my back on the chilly draughts and reentered the passage, determined to find further relief. I could make a brew of chamomile myself and need explain it to no one.

A new day spread itself before me and hope budded in my mind. I had slept better the night before, having locked my chamber door and trusted in the bolt's tenacity. I had shrugged away Airig's mystified expression when she had come knocking with a breakfast tray. The world seemed less menacing with a few hours of deep sleep and my brain was now busy with planning. I would drink a medicinal tea and ride to Rathdale with renewed courage. I must see Coll and put an end to this discord between us. I must enlist his aid in discovering who was attempting to frighten me. Seeing the burnt cottage was a blow yesterday but I would not allow myself to remain a victim of my own cowardice.

I snatched my riding hat from the press and impatiently pulled free the listless black feather. I tossed it into the fireplace on my way out, and strode down to the kitchen.

I was unprepared for the number of people I found there, however, and made my way amongst women bearing trenchers and platters bound for the tables above and others restocking the larder and bringing in pails of milk and cream. At first I did not see Sandy seated at the oak table. He was surrounded by a group of young lads of various heights and ages.

"I'm only after some chamomile," I reassured Grizel who was turning bannocks on the hot girdle.

"I'll fetch it for you."

"Nonsense. I can do it myself. Carry on with your cooking and I'll not get under your feet."

I found the jar of herbs, and whilst I stood untying its leather bonnet I glanced at the semicircle of six or seven lads, with their black heads and dark eyes.

One of them caught me looking and smiled, bobbing his head. "Lady Kirthgarran," he said.

His greeting brought other heads up, including Sandy's. "My lady," the steward said impassively. His attention returned to his hands.

"Do you ken," said another lad to me, "that my da's off to war with Captain Fergusson?"

"And my da, too!"

"They're all brave men," I replied.

"My brother's away as well," put in one. "I wish I could go." He must have been all of twelve years old.

"But you'll want to stay home and be of help to your mother," I said.

"Aye, but I wish I could go across the water and fight the infidels."

The other lads nodded their heads in unison, agreeing fervently, before their gazes fell once more to the table.

"My da says when I'm grown enough I may go," said another. "And I will. I'll be just like the Captain and I'll have a sword and a dirk and a pistol."

My fingers stilled when I saw that Sandy was holding a pistol. It was one of Coll's, one of the brass-fitted Doune flintlocks Lord Kirthgarran had entrusted to him long ago. Its twin rested on a rag beside a bag of flints and shot, a gallipot of oil and oiling feather, and other cleaning implements.

"Are they not bonny?" a lad purred, noticing where my eyes were drawn. "I want a pair just like that."

I examined all the youthful faces. They eyed the weapons with ill-concealed envy, as if they had never seen a pistol before.

I looked back at Sandy's hands. His fingers lovingly caressed the muzzle of the weapon, smoothing the engraved metal with his fingertips. He must have found fault with the texture, for he chose a twist of linen and polished the steel with methodical strokes. A sharp, new flint was grasped in the vice at the top of the mechanism and oil glistened on the brass.

"If he must go," Sandy said without looking at me, "then he'll go with arms that will do him justice. His life will depend on them."

I admired Sandy's diligence but I could hardly behold the pistols dispassionately, for Rab's death was too recent. I would never be able to forget the blood that had poured from him, taking his life with it, a result of someone having fired a pistol similar to one of these.

A lad said, "My da's to be given arms like that."

Whether ordinary recruits were issued pistols or not I was not sure, but his boast brought to mind the fact that pistols were not commonplace at Kirthgarran. Arms had not been needed since 1746 and had been illegal until only recently, and what need, indeed, did a grower of oats or a herder of kine have of them? The reverence and curiosity shown by these lads from the glen told how rarely such instruments were encountered.

I became transfixed by the sight of the elegant firelock in Sandy's grasp. He put down his rag and lifted the pistol to his eye to sight along the barrel.

They all must have forgotten my presence. The lads were intrigued by Sandy's movements and Sandy himself was absorbed by his task, deftly handling the pistols as if they were his own. It was a quiet picture they made at the homely kitchen table. But my mind was anything but quiet.

I knew that the crowner had questioned Coll about his whereabouts at the time of Rab's murder just as he had all the others. My memory of the King's coroner was vague but I had been aware of his arrival, had suffered his indifferent questions, and had watched him ply everyone with queries and receive answers with disinterest. He was a man who was inspired by one matter: to discover if the murdered victim was a person of means whose lands or money could be absorbed by the government.

Once it had been ascertained Rab possessed nothing, the crowner had put forth perfunctory inquiries and taken his leave, with a last-minute wish flung to us over his shoulder. "May luck be yours in finding the lout responsible," he had called.

Coll had been with Kirstie when Rab had been shot in the garden. They had heard the discharge together and Coll had come running to the castle. I remembered how he had looked when he'd seen me on the ground with Rab. He had been stricken.

He had been wearing his uniform. I tried to recall what he had worn at supper that night, what he had removed when we'd met at the Rathdale cottage earlier. I had seen the pistols at the cottage, I was certain. If he had been wearing them then, thrust into his belt, he might have been wearing them later.

My hands trembled as I turned away and shook dried chamomile into my palm. I took a long while putting the leather cap back on the jar. My eyes slid to the hearth where only days ago Rab's body had lain.

Lachlan was convinced the ball of lead he'd found had come from a pistol. Who else at Kirthgarran owned one? There were Brown Bess muskets with their long, narrow barrels and mahogany stocks, but I'd never seen pistols except for the brass and silver pair Coll had taken to America and brought back for the earl to see. Others must have wondered about it, must have thought of Coll, but none had done so aloud. "A man who loved Rab as Coll did would not murder him," they must have said to themselves.

Images remained with me. Coll's sword crashing without restraint against Rab's, the blade eventually hanging over Rab's head. Fury blistering in Coll's eyes as he considered what my husband had done to me. The northern lights rippling in the night as Coll said perhaps there was something he could do, after all, to lessen our sorrow.

I squeezed the jar in my fingers. Coll was not a murderer. The man who loved me could not fire a ball of lead at another's back and coldly conceal the fact. There were other folk who owned pistols and had hidden them during the harrying of the glens.

In spite of my resolution not to look again, my eyes slipped back to the table. Both pistols now lay on the rag, glinting in the light of the cooking fire. Women moved back and forth in front of me but I was hardly aware of them.

I thought, was not Coll a murderer indeed, having been a soldier in the King's army, ordering others to kill on command, killing with his own hand when battles became close affairs and captains could not withdraw to safe borders? His accounts of piercing enemies with bayonets until the blades became corkscrews came into my mind in stunning detail. The cool rationale behind such killings must surely make a mark upon a man's mind, or inure it in such a way that one more death would be of no great moment.

If he had wanted to rid us of Rab he had only to wait for a good opportunity. He possessed the arms. He had long ago mastered skill in their use. And he had made a promise that he would never let Rab hurt me again.

I made my tincture and yet I did not think I could drink it. Sandy rose and organized the pistols, the leather case of flints, the bag of shot, and the flattened, engraved powder horn whilst the lads hung on and conversed in rapture amongst themselves amid a cloud of dreams.

"Is it something that just came upon you?" came Grizel's voice.

I stared at her with no comprehension.

"Your insides," she explained. "Are they paining you much, my lady?"

"It's nothing at all, just enough to bother." I compelled myself to swallow half a cupful of tea. Over Grizel's shoulder Sandy's eyes met mine. The warmth of the room faded in the chill of his blue gaze.

I found myself walking Greyfriar away from the castle, following the burn. His feet trod slowly on the track, and I turned him north when the path forked and led to the houses beyond. The Drummonds' cottage, lime-washed stone with a neat, thatched roof and a chimney, came first. Second was that of Donald Fergusson, piper to the Earl of Kirthgarran. It was white as well, but edged with scarlet ivy.

I bid the garron to become still and Kenneth, who seemed to have adopted the role of personal groom, halted his as well. One of Donald's sons—I could not remember if it was Douglas or Fergus—was bearing a stack of peats through the doorway. He nodded to us and reappeared empty-handed, brushing his hands against his shirt.

"Good day," he said in English, bowing as I dismounted. "Is it our da you're looking for? He's at the castle, or at least he was."

"He is, but—I was hoping to find Kirstie. Is she at home?"

"Aye." He grinned. Kenneth was beside me and reaching for Greyfriar's bridle, and I gave up the rein though my sudden wish was to bound into the saddle and gallop away.

I followed Kirstie's brother into the house. She must have been aware of my arrival for she came into the front room, as fair as ever with her brown ringlets and glowing cheeks.

"My lady," she said and curtseyed. "I was surprised to see you stopping."

"I only thought to stay for a moment. I wanted to thank

you for helping the women at the castle. Grizel said you were invaluable during the funeral, serving the meals, aiding with the cooking..."

"I had to do something. The tragedies have struck all of us. I cannot imagine how it must be for you. Will you sit? Will you have some refreshment? I've shortbread and a wine cordial I could pour for us. Fergus, fetch the glasses on the top shelf of the dresser."

She indicated a wooden chair with a worn cushion on which I might make myself comfortable, and I lowered myself to the edge. I was conscious of my fingers gripping one another and wondered if my face betrayed as much guilt at my deception as my hands. I unwound my fingers and tried to keep them still on my lap. I should have protested about the wine and pastry. Kirstie placed triangles of shortbread on a chipped china plate and offered them to me whilst Fergus poured wine into fluted glasses. He brought me one glass and gave his sister another, but took none himself.

"I'll be off, then" he told her and nodded respectfully at me.

Kirstie smiled after him and settled herself on a stool opposite my chair. With delicate fingers she brought her glass to her lips and took a small sip of the purple cordial.

I could not refrain from picturing Coll here as he must have been in years past: a welcomed visitor and suitor treated to wine and cake and Kirstie's warm smiles, and possibly a stolen kiss at the door. Sometimes he had shared suppers with her and her family, and I looked across the room at the wide table by the window where they most likely sat at their meal, eating, talking, and laughing. The piper's house was a home indeed, with curtains at the window and a hot fire burning. Plate and napery, cracked and mended though they were, appeared clean and neatly arranged. With a father and four brothers for whom to care, Kirstie was a diligent housekeeper, but her presence made itself not only known by the unfinished mounds of knitting and the jars of preserved fruits on the dresser, but by touches that could only have come from her hand. A pewter pitcher stood on the mantel, filled with dried, blossomed heather; a colorful satin-piece featuring the figures of a mother, bairns, and the name

"Kirstie Fergusson" was framed and hung on the whitewashed wall.

I could imagine Coll here in this house and understand his affection for Donald's daughter. I appraised my own fingers grasping the wineglass and critically judged their apparent innocence. Kirstie did not know that they had touched the man she loved. She did not know their owner was capable of cold deceit.

"How is Coll?" she asked me as if she could peer into my thoughts.

My glass began to tremble and I hastily set it down on the stand beside us.

"He's gone to Rathdale," she went on, looking down. "But perhaps you've had word. Is his arm any better?"

"Sandy assures me it is not worse. I've heard nought more than that, so we must both believe it is beginning to heal."

"It must heal," she pronounced. "It must."

"I am sure Mairi tends to it with loving persistence."

She put aside her own glass and considered it for a moment. When she raised her eyes to me they were brilliant and her nose was red. She blinked and put a brave smile on her lips. "I am sure, as well. Will you—do you think you will see him soon?"

"I had thought to ride to Rathdale this day, to see Mairi."

She blinked again and nodded, her eyes falling away. "She is not well, I hear."

"Andrew says she greets sorely. I have no delusions that my visit will help her."

"But there is the tie between you and Rab, and the earl. She'll know you share her pain."

The deceit hung thick about me. I go to see Coll, not Mairi, I wanted to say to her. And I sit here, not to offer gratitude and share hospitality, but to seek answers to horrible questions. Instead I replied, "There is no relief for any of us."

"How bereft you must feel," Kirstie said, looking up at me. "To lose your husband, and the man who suddenly became known to you as your grandsire, both on the same day. What a wonderful story it would have been. Rab searching for you and falling in love with you, bringing you home to Lord Kirthgarran. One day the earl would have told you about your mother and made you so happy."

"He was happy knowing who I was, even if I did not."

"My father guessed. Not that you were his granddaughter. But he was sure there was a kinship. He said you resembled Lord Kirthgarran's daughter who fled the glen all those years ago."

"There were some who believed I was her ghost."

"I heard it whispered that you were."

"Did you believe it?"

She smiled a little. "I've always thought spirits are like smoke, that you can barely see them. You seemed very real to me."

"At least the folk seem to have accepted the truth."

"It must be a relief to have the story told and all knowing that there is a reason why you are here, with Lady Nóra's visage upon you."

"It is."

"And yet the wonderful story is spoilt by the ending." She seemed to hear her own words and stopped. "Oh, I am sorry. I cannot be helping your grief with my ill-chosen words."

"It is of no matter. You speak only what is true."

Her mouth became a crooked line. "Although Lord Kirthgarran was not my grandsire, and Rabbie was not my husband, I miss them both dreadfully. I thought, one day, Coll and I—that we would be—but it's not to happen. Still, I thought Rab would be like a brother to me. That you and I would be as sisters. Now all is a nightmare. The earl is gone, and so is Rab, and Coll will soon be away to Glasgow and beyond, and the homes in the glens will be destroyed to make way for the sheep."

"Not yours," I said quickly. "Your father's house was never meant to be one of them."

"Perhaps not, but what cheer will there be in the end? My brothers speak of leaving, of selling themselves so they can go to America. They cannot forever live in this house, wanting wives and families of their own and land to farm. They will go when the rest go. And so—everyone will be gone. Everyone." Her eyes grew moist once more.

We were both silent. A hundred possible replies presented themselves to me. I studied her face. There was a small mole above her upper lip. Her eyelashes were long, dark. We were nearly the same age, Kirstie and I, but I began to feel older as I watched her, as old as a worn, bent woman who can no longer straighten her spine.

"As soon as I am able, as soon as my head is capable of thinking again, I must speak with Andrew and Ewen," I told her. "There must be something that can be done."

"Despite his decision to clear the land, Lord Kirthgarran was distraught. My father knows that, and so do my brothers and I. I hope you understand I am not speaking ill of him, or of you."

"You're very kind. You do not need to explain. Let me assure you that you are not alone in dreading what is to come."

She drew a breath, attempting to restore herself, I thought, and I realized the moment had come when I must decide how dearly I wished to keep her friendship. I wavered. I pressed my lips together, hoping I would not begin what I had come here to do. But the need was too strong. I felt my mouth open, heard the beginning sentence come out and fill the air between us. "Of course, everything seems worse because Rab and Lord Kirthgarran are gone."

"Oh aye. Both of them at once. It's been a double blow," she said.

"Sometimes I think about the man who shot Rab. He must still be amongst us."

She said nothing. Her eyes left mine.

Into the silence I said, "The crowner has urged us to raise a hue and cry. And to offer a reward to anyone who discovers who the man was. Andrew is trying to gather everyone's memories of that night. I know others have asked you. Will you tell me, though, what it was you heard?"

"Is it not too painful for you to relive it all again?"

"Perhaps you saw something—someone—you have forgotten."

"I saw no one."

"You were with Coll. He said you were walking outside, on the track."

Brown eyes came back to question me, but they were wary. "He was here, aye."

"It is distressing to you to mind it, as well, but I ask you because you might think of something, something you saw or heard on that night. You were so near the castle. You might have seen someone."

"If I had seen anyone I would have told."

"I would give anything for Rab's murderer to be found. He was responsible for Lord Kirthgarran's death, too. He must be a dangerous man. If he were to lose his self-control again someone else's life might be in danger."

Kirstie paled. Her breathing quickened.

I forced myself to say, "Coll saw no one either?"

"He would have told. Rab was his dearest friend."

"But you both heard the shot."

"We were on the track, where it curved and led up to the castle. It was difficult to see very far because of the mist."

Coll would have been telling her he never meant to wound her heart and that he was sorry he could not find it within himself to marry her. "And when the shot came…" I said with a dry voice.

She hesitated. Her lips were quite white. "Coll and I looked at each other and he said, 'It came from the castle,' and he took me home and started running along the track."

I wondered if my face seemed as disconcerted as hers. I heard myself say stiffly, "It is true, then, that you were together when the shot came."

Her eyes filled and her mouth began to quiver. She rose from her stool and stood looking down at me, and when she spoke it was in a whisper. "What are you asking me?"

I rose also. "To please tell me that the shot came when you were together, not after he left you."

"You cannot mean to be thinking…"

"Please. Tell me he was indeed with you."

"You think Coll killed Rab!"

"I do not want to. It's why I'm asking you, to be assured…"

"How can you even doubt him? You must not know him as I do. You are calling him a murderer. There is no one less likely to aim a pistol at a man's back."

"You mistake me if you believe I want it to be him."

"We were together," she said louder. "We heard the discharge together. No one else disbelieves that. Why is it that you do?"

I had no answer for her. I suffered her condemnation of me in silence.

"He told me he did not love me," she said as tears crept down her colorless cheeks. "He told me he was sorry for it, but he felt he must be honest. He kissed me on the forehead and held me close and I wept, and he tried to comfort me, and he said it was for the best he was going to India, that I could find someone else and not be reminded of him by the sight of him, and then we heard the firing of the flintlock. It came from near the castle, probably the garden, muffled by the mist but clear enough to figure. He said, 'It came from the castle.' He embraced me one last time and said, 'I'll take you home, Kirstie, back to your house,' and he did, leaving me at the door, and he began running down the path. That is what happened. That is everything we said, everything we did. I tell you the truth, my lady. Coll is not a murderer. How could you suspect him? How could you?"

I remained silent. I could not say to her, "Because Rab was between us."

She said, "I have known Coll all of my life. Have loved him, too. You wrong him greatly. And by asking me to repeat what he himself must have told you, you wrong me as well."

"Please do not take offense."

"I do not understand you. Is this why you've come here today? To examine your suspicions and test your theories? Are you thinking even now, 'Poor Kirstie, who loves Coll and strives to protect him, perhaps even lies for him, and look at how she is falling apart under the strain of it all?' I tell you I would lie for him if I had to. I would do anything for him. But Coll Fergusson is not the murderer you seek. We were together when he heard the firing of the ball that killed your husband. I will swear it in front of God and the kirk and the King if I must. He did not kill Leslie Hamilton and he did not kill Rab."

"Oh Kirstie..."

"There is nought else to tell you."

"I beg of you, do not blame me for trying to discover the truth."

"I can say nought more," she cried and turned her back to me. Her shoulders shook as she brought her hands up to hide her face.

Somehow I made my way out the door and across the frozen grass to Kenneth who held our ponies.

I saw nothing else round me. My throat was too tightened by shame to speak. Kenneth helped me up into the saddle.

Of course Coll would not have killed Rab. I was demented to even consider it.

I nudged Greyfriar into a gallop, hoping the bitter wind and the spittle it blew would clear every vestige of the terrible interview with Kirstie out of my brain. I urged the pony round the loch, to the place I should have gone days before, to Rathdale.

"But there is, Glenlogie, a letter for thee."
The first line he read a low smile gi'ed he,
The neist line he read the tear blindit his e'e,
But the last line he read he gart the table flee.

Bonnie Glenlogie (Trad.)

Chapter Forty-One

Anne welcomed me at the door. "Come, come," she entreated, gesturing to the drawing room within. "I'll fetch Mairi. She'll want to see you."

"How is she, Anne?" I asked, removing my hat and gloves.

"A bit better. She began hemming a blanket for the bairn this morning, and we spoke about names that have been used in my family and Andrew's. Do you not think that's hopeful?"

"It is." I gave her my cloak and she shook rain droplets from it before she hung it on a peg behind her. I said, "And how are you?"

"Better as well. Andrew says to think of the bairn and so I've been trying to eat and rest and do all I should. I've wanted to come to the castle but Andrew will not have it. The smoke makes my eyes water and there's no place to sit. Although—we might all come again, to see the guests before they leave. For Rab and Lord Kirthgarran's sake."

I nodded, and hoping my voice would remain neutral, asked, "And Coll? The festering..."

"Mairi's been poulticing his arm and the wound seems to be healing. I only hope he tends to it on his own now he's away."

One of the old stones that used to thud about in my stomach announced itself with vehemence. "He's not here?"

She put her arm through mine as we began to walk. "He decided to go to Strath Gruagach, to look for men to list. I wish he'd not gone, but he said he could not sit still any longer. He's not been himself. Perhaps he's right, and it is such a journey he needs."

"It appears you must settle for my company," said a male voice beside us. I looked up and there was Alistair.

Anne turned from me to him and back again. "Alistair. I thought you were writing letters."

"There's not much to say." He threw himself down on a settle and interlinked his fingers.

The incongruence of the scene was unexpected and for a moment I stared at him. He was Davy, who long ago wore dust on his wrinkled waistcoat and fine stubble on his chin; Davy, who kissed me lightly and put flowers behind my ear. He was sitting comfortably, clean and bright and educated, unmindful of the wreckage he had once caused.

Anne squeezed my hand and peered at me with worried eyes. "Perhaps you'd be more at ease in Mairi's room. We could go to her there."

"And deprive me of redeeming myself at last?" Andrew asked.

"I'm sure the countess will speak to you when she's ready. I do not believe I could ever face you again. Not after what you did. What all of you did, including my husband." She grew red-faced when she said this but her skewering of Alistair was unyielding, and he did not dispute her. I glanced at him and saw a muscle tighten in his jaw. "Will you not go and write another letter?" she asked him.

"If my lady wishes me to disappear, I will."

"It matters little," I said. Coll was gone, most likely for days. I sank to a chair and found it difficult to look at either Anne or Alistair. I promised myself that before I left today I would discover when he was expected back, and I would return tomorrow or the next day or whatever day it might be. At least his wound was indeed healing, and for that I was thankful.

"I'll fetch Mam," said Alistair at last.

Anne sat beside me and attempted to regain her cheeriness, asking me about the guests remaining at Kirthgarran, inquiring if we had enough to feed them.

"We sent some cheeses and barley bread this morning," she said. "And venison. I hope it will help. I've saved some to take with us when Andrew and I go to my parents in Camghouran in a week's time. Mamma and Papa crave the cheese we make here. We go twice a year to stay with them, sometimes for a fortnight. I've a younger sister and brother and I miss them all, and always look forward to our visits. You must miss your father, too, aye?"

The question caught me by surprise and I said, "I miss nought of my old home but my horse."

"Oh. Well, I do understand. I suppose I am fortunate, to have had a happy childhood and memories of a home I treasure."

"When did Coll leave, Anne?"

She paused before she answered. "This morning."

"He wanted to travel in this spiteful weather?"

"I pled with him not to go, but my words fell on his deaf ears. I'm thinking he wants to be away with his regiment as soon as he can. He may leave a few days early, once he returns. He's been forlorn, my lady."

And so have I, I thought.

"He's been sitting alone, talking to none of us, not sleeping, not eating. It's troubled me so. Even his mother cannot approach him. Finally he took himself in hand and announced he was going to find the last of his recruits."

"And when—when will he return?"

She squinted as she counted. "'Twill be the Monday next, I'm thinking."

"I must see him. I cannot bear the thought he'd leave for

Argyll without coming home first."

"Certainly he'd not go without a farewell. You did get his message?"

"Message?"

"I saw a letter he wrote last night, with your name on it. He told us to include it with the next lot of provisions. We gave it to the lad this morning before he left with the garron, and told him to deliver it to you."

I was about to ask at what hour the lad left when Mairi and Alistair appeared.

"My lamb," Mairi murmured. I embraced her and she took my hands as we sat together on the settle. "How kind of you to come. How have you been?"

"I am well. But I feel oppressed by all the folk at the castle, even though they mean well."

"A few more days. Then they will go."

"I doubt the void they'll leave behind will be any more pleasant," I said, realizing that I would be living alone with only Lachlan and Sandy and the servants. My voice threatened to break. "I cannot imagine how silent the castle will be."

"Come to us here as often as you must," Anne said.

Despite the warmth of my hostesses I was eager to be on my way. For perhaps an hour we sat in the drawing room. Frozen rain sprayed the windows. Alistair said little but I could feel him contemplating me even when I turned away from him. Repeating itself in my mind was the thought, there's a letter from Coll—waiting for me at home.

"I must go," I blurted when Anne mentioned something about refreshments.

"Will you not warm yourself with a cup first?" she asked in surprise.

I could conjure up no excuse, so sat for half of an hour more whilst the tea was brewed and cups were brought. Politely I sipped from my saucer and attended to the conversation, but my gaze kept straying to the window and the pattern of melting crystals on the glazing.

When at last I donned my cloak and pulled on my gloves, Alistair said, "Bide a moment, Keeley."

I turned. Anne was glowering at him.

"I said this in jest before, but there was an earnest wish behind it," he said. "I was hoping to have a word with you. Alone, that is."

I faltered, stammering, uncertain of how to reply.

"She's not ready," Anne said.

"Are you not?" persisted Alistair, looking at me. "Should we not speak of what is betwixt us rather than allow it to grow and worsen with time?"

"Perhaps you are right," I said.

Mairi and Anne exchanged glances. Anne said, "Very well, but we'll not be far."

I had been dreading this moment and had thought about it a great deal during the past days, trying to envision what we would say to each other. He seemed relaxed, and as the women retreated he perched on the edge of the marble-topped table and folded his arms. For months I had considered him a dead person, dead to me at least, never to be seen again. His face had faded in my mind since the summer but now here he was again, alive and jaunty and real, splendid in a gold brocade coat and lace-edged shirt, well-rested, well-fed.

"There was a time," he said, "when you were overjoyed to see me."

"Now I do so only with a remembrance of pain. And you treat it with jocularity."

He seemed abashed. "It may seem so, but you must realize it's a shock for me, too, to see you again. The only difference is I knew that one day I would. I was not prepared, though, for the effect you'd have on me. I watched you in Kirthgarran's library soon after I returned from Oban. I stood behind the door and saw you writing, and thought how bonny you were, and I minded how happy I'd been when we were together in Melrose."

I watched him, baffled.

"The last time," he continued. "Do you mind it? In the pasture, when you told me what your housekeeper had said?"

"How could I forget? Afterward, when you did not come for me, I went over that morning again and again, trying to find anything I could that might explain why you left without me."

The remainder of his exuberance faded. "You cannot ken how sorry I am. 'Twas a role I played, like an actor in the theater.

It had to be done. And the pain I caused you, well, I regret it with my whole heart. I never thought it would crush you so. If I had known—but then how could I? And what could I have done? I was not alone in the arrangement. The point I wish to make is that you should be aware of the effect you had on me. I began the acting but I did not count on the affection I began to feel for you."

"I do not understand."

"No? I felt like a soulless wretch walking away from you that day. You must believe me. I never bargained I'd come to feel such tenderness toward you."

"But walk away you did. Without a word." I was there again, in the pasture with the sheep, forcing myself to return to Gilchrist House and Mrs. Taggart and an unknown future.

He regarded me intently. "There were actual moments when I forgot I was playing a part. It was refreshing, at first, to leave my Nancy at home and take to the roads, to become a lad I thought you'd like. You were kind to me, were you not? Bringing me rations of food. Reading to me. I gave you things in return, hoping you'd regard me with favor, until I neglected to fix it in my mind it was all a deception and I nearly became the figure I pretended to be. I allowed the pretense to go too far. Aye, I regretted at last that 'twould not be me you'd finally wed. I became very fond of you. I mind it well. Meeting you in the hollow between the hills in the cool evening, walking together..."

"Please stop."

"It was difficult to restrain myself. Do you ken there were times after our meetings that I needed to leap into the river and stand in its current, cooling my blood? I let you become too free with yourself. Rabbie warned me and ordered me not to touch you. He would have killed me if..."

"I cannot listen to this."

"I only want you to realize I am not unfeeling. I made a great mistake by letting you come to care for me. I could have fulfilled our plan in far less time, before your affection—and mine—became so deep. Certainly a few meetings betwixt us would have been enough. But no. I began to enjoy your company and could not stop myself from seeking more of it. Finally I had to force myself to follow the end of the plan. Rabbie was growing impatient, beginning to disbelieve me that I'd not defiled you. So I did what I was told. I wrote the letter to Reverend Andrews that incriminated you, and sat back to see how it would all come about. And hence my part in it all was over. But seeing you last week—I feel I've been knocked on the head. The time we spent together in Melrose has come back to haunt me. I regret so much."

"I'm sure it is not more than I do."

"I did hate leaving you. It was a foul trick."

I felt compelled to reiterate what his deceit had cost me. "Leaving me was just a part of it. You lied about who you were. You invented stories about a mother who died to stir compassion in me. Leaving me would have been hurtful enough but you asked me to pack my belongings and wait for you to come and fetch me. You and I began to plan a future. You said we'd marry. It was all I could think of, you and our plans, and how perfect it would be."

"I had to be sure you'd stay in one place. The design we'd conceived would not have succeeded had you not remained at home and been reproved by your father."

"Did you ever consider I might follow you—to wherever you had gone?" I asked him.

"I did not think you'd have the courage." He said it sadly, but it still hurt. "At any rate, leave you I did, because it was part of our scheme. I do regret it, though, as I said. How simple it all would have been had I not already had a wife. I sometimes wish I'd never met her."

I shook my head, not wanting to hear any more of his sentiments. "I watched for you, and was beaten by my father, and disowned. That was part of the scheme."

His voice lowered. "We only intended to cause your father enough disappointment in you that he'd welcome Rab's second offer for your hand."

"You underestimated him. My soiled reputation was not a disappointment, an irritation. He was too concerned about how it would reflect upon him. He wished me dead, and barely held himself back from bringing it about."

"No," he replied. "That we did not foresee."

"When I discovered you had left Melrose without me, I was sorry he showed that fortitude."

He tilted his head to the side. "You had Rab to comfort you."

"When all I wanted was you."

His sorrowful eyes wandered over my face. He reached out a hand as if he would stroke my head and he said, "Your father did this? Cut your hair?"

I stepped backward, unwilling for him to touch me.

"I loved it well, your bonny hair."

I pulled my cloak together and began to walk past him.

"Keeley, wait."

I stopped.

"You do not know me. Not Alistair Fergusson."

"And who is he?"

"I will tell you, if you'll listen. I am Davy, in many ways. There are only a few variances. I told you I could not read, but I can. I am not a smith but a farmer, who toils to keep Kirthgarran and Rathdale and Strath Gruagach from the talons of greedy bankers. I carve wood into lambs, and etch horn with dragons, and will listen to tales and stories by the hour. You taught me the names of flowers and I remember them. And I loved your grandsire, and your husband, and grieve for them both just as you do."

For a moment I was drawn in by his words.

He said, "I was not alone in the plan to have you brought to Kirthgarran. When you forgive the others, then forgive me as well. I beg it of you."

"Is that what you want of me?"

"That, and to see the hostility in you go away."

"But why? None of you are homeless. You all have what you wanted."

He allowed a small smile to return. "I want to make peace with you. I want us to accept the past and let it rest. Can we acknowledge what we felt for each other, and look to the future?"

"What is it you expect from this future?"

"Lachlan makes his home at the castle. Andrew has Rathdale. Coll will be gone soon. But what about me?"

"It would seem you have everything you need."

"I've been gone from Kirthgarran these past months but now I want to come back. I want to retrieve my Nancy and take up my life again. At Kirthgarran."

I pictured him living at the castle with his wife. I would never be able to forget everything, but his presence there would sting my senses, cut my composure to tatters. "No," I said. "No."

"It is my home," he explained, his smile weakening.

"It is *my* home. I say who abides there and who does not. I cannot have you living there. I just cannot."

He struggled to find a reply, and in the silence that followed I could suddenly see the resemblance to his older brother Coll, and it tore at my heart.

"It is too much to expect," I said as soon as I could find my voice. I did not wait to put on my hat. I fled into the passage and strode through the door. Sleet stung my cheeks.

He called after me, "I'd not be unwilling to resume our alliance, to be the man you once wanted."

I whirled about so that I might see if he were serious, and found that he was.

"I could thaw your heart," he said in the doorway, Davy once more, with the mixture of sweetness and gravity that had been his forte. "I could make you forget all you went through."

I gave him one last look and ran to the stable, slipping on the slick earth.

I went in search of Sandy as soon as I entered the castle.

"Is there a letter for me?" I asked him. He was lighting torches in the great hall and paused with a sputtering fir root in his hand.

"Aye." He thrust the spur into a sconce and led me into the drawing room. Guests rose and greeted me and I had no recourse but to acknowledge them. The steward retrieved a folded paper from the gate-legged table and held it out. The edges were sealed with a heavy swirl of red wax.

I took it and turned it over. "Lady Kirthgarran" had been written across it in a fearless hand.

I'd not yet removed my cloak and I was wet from the ride from Rathdale. I wiped a drop of water from the paper and said,

"Why was this not given to me earlier?"

"The lad did not arrive until after you'd gone."

I cracked the seal and spread open the leaf to find a few lines of writing streaking across the top half, but before I could read them my eyes slid to their end where Coll had signed his name. I glanced up at Sandy.

"All is well at Rathdale," he said. "Is it?"

"It is." I refolded the page. My fingers fumbled. I attempted to put the letter back together as it had been, but the folds were impudent and refused my coercion. "Thank you." I was sure his eyes followed me as I strolled toward the great hall, absorbed by the uncooperative paper. I took to the turnpike stair, and after I had climbed a half-dozen steps I abandoned my leisurely pretense and began to hasten. I did not stop until I reached my room, closed the door, and pressed my back against it.

The paper, now crumpled, sprang open once more in my hands.

I needed to read the contents twice before comprehension seeped into my head.

"6 December.

"Dearest Lady Kirthgarran,

"It is soon I must go. Less than two weeks remain. I find myself reliving what came before. I cannot bring myself to come to you, to see rejection in your face. Once before I asked a woman to follow me to war. I will not do it again. But if I thought there was hope, if I knew you cared for me, we would find a way to be together one day.

"You must tell me if I am being a fool. Too many people linger still at Kirthgarran, too many eyes and ears surround us. I will wait, Monday night, under the arch at the lochside. Come at eight o'clock. If you choose not to meet me there, it will be understood. You will not have to say the words and I will not have to hear them. I'll merely take my leave of the glens, and allow this letter to be my farewell to you.

"Coll."

The letter had not been simple for him to write. Some of the words were crossed out and rewritten. One whole sentence had been inked over. It did not matter. His meaning was clear. I forgot my conversation with Kirstie; I drove away the sound of Alistair's voice. The joy that filled me was pure and overpowering.

My happiness was joined by impatience. We had both been distressed but our true feelings could not be denied. I wished he had not gone north in search of recruits. I must live through two nights and three days before I could tell him there was indeed hope.

At first I did not know how to occupy myself because the hours stretching ahead seemed endless. I need not have worried, though. When Andrew arrived at Kirthgarran on Saturday I made use of my new exhilaration and optimism and took him aside.

"There is a matter of the gravest nature which I must examine with you," I told him.

"What has happened?"

"Lord Kirthgarran is barely in his grave and I'm thinking of making changes. Is it wrong of me, Andrew? Is it too soon?"

"I suppose I cannot answer until I understand of what matter you speak."

"I'm thinking of the sheep. Of Mr. Baird and his mill and his sheep. I am not certain what I want to do, except that I must talk to you, and Ewen, and Lachlan. I wish the solicitors were still here."

Clearly he was curious and begged for a few minutes to fetch the others. We all came together in the sitting room. Andrew closed the door and stood expectantly. I could not sit but paced the carpeted floor and finally came to a halt, clenching my thumbs in my fingers.

"What would happen," I said, "if we changed our minds about renting the lands to Mr. Baird? If we wrote to him and explained we were no longer interested in the arrangement?"

The men glanced at one another, unwilling or unable to speak. Ewen's eyebrows met at the center of his face and locked.

"Or what if we decided to let him rent only some of the land?" I continued.

"Lord Kirthgarran was adamant the venture take place," Ewen said. "For your sake."

"I am not interested in money. I want Kirthgarran to succeed, to keep itself out of bankruptcy, but for the balls in

London and dozens of servants that Rab envisioned I have no desire. I know the earl wanted to keep me well provided for. I do not want to lose Kirthgarran. But I am not persuaded, I was never persuaded, that clearing the land was the answer."

The men shifted their eyes from me to one another once more and let long breaths escape them.

"Will you tell me," I pled, "about the cattle and the debts and the legal matters? Will you explain to me what the account books put forth, and tell me what the numbers mean, what they meant to Lord Kirthgarran? He never allowed himself to speak much of it with me. I heard all of you arguing. I heard Rab's voice, louder than the rest. But I do not ken if I am aware of everything. I'm not even sure if I can reverse Lord Kirthgarran's decision."

"You can," Andrew said. "You can do anything you like."

"Then help me. Tell me if I am being a halfwit to even consider this."

"There's much to debate," said Ewen. "Is it how you wish to employ yourself, in this your time of mourning?"

"The fog is clearing from my mind. There are others to think of. If Kirthgarran is mine, allow me to learn more about her, and perhaps reconsider what will happen to her."

Andrew sat down and leant forward. "Where do you want to begin?"

"10 December, 1787," I scribbled in my dairy.

"I am overjoyed. How wicked it seems to write it, to feel it. Only six days ago my husband and grandfather were buried, and though I doubt I will ever recover from the pain of it, my heart is selfishly gladdened.

"I have spent the last two days with Andrew, Lachlan, Ewen, and sometimes Sandy, searching these men's minds and souls. I have been studying the accounts and trying to dredge from my memory all the things I learnt about sheep from my father. He shared a great deal with me, when he thought I could understand and began to show an interest. He told me what was said during meetings of the British Wool Society. He took me with him to see the farms at Whitestone and Clary.

"I have been summoning forth those memories with all the energy I possess, and the men have been listening to me and conveying the concerns Lord Kirthgarran felt when he, too, tried to come to a decision about Mr.

Baird's land-rent offer. It has been exhausting. But today we created a compromise and sent word throughout the glen of Kirthgarran, and gathered the folk at the kirk to tell them."

I sat back, remembering it all with excitement. It had been cold in the kirk this morning. The farmers and laborers had come in and taken seats on uneven wooden benches worn smooth by decades of use. Breath had frosted the few glass panes set into the stone walls.

I eagerly resumed my writing.

"I stood at the front of them all. How did I dare? I cannot remember. All I know is that I wanted them to learn, as soon as possible, that they would not have to leave their homes. Andrew and Ewen stood on either side of me. What I said in English Andrew repeated in Gaelic and in a voice all could hear. 'There is an idea I want to put before you and to the people of Strath Gruagach and Rathdale,' I said. 'It is an idea that is new and hopeful. If you are in agreement with it I can be drafting a letter to the mill owner who hoped to rent the lands and tell him I am destroying the writ of promise.'

"I could not blame them their skepticism. They were polite at first and listened intently, but as Andrew translated my appeal they began to stand and look at one another. They asked questions of Andrew and received satisfying answers."

We did not know if the plan was a good one. I was not sure if such an undertaking was being attempted anywhere else. We encouraged the tenants to combine their farms and resources, hire shepherds of their own acquaintance, and together buy a flock of a few hundred Cheviots from the Lowlands.

"Part of your rents will be accepted in wool and mutton," Andrew told them. "The wool of Cheviots will bring you three times more pounds in a year than the selling of kylies."

There would have to be change. Most of the black cattle must go. Some homes would have to be deserted, land ownership restructured, and new cottages built where the sheep would not graze. There was an abundance of new agricultural practices to learn.

I did not want Kirthgarran to founder, or to deprive Lachlan, Coll, Andrew, and Alistair of income they easily deserved as replacements for tacksmen, but I was convinced there was an arrangement that could strike a balance between emptying the glens and continuing to farm the estates.

"We could start with perhaps one hundred rams and three hundred ewes," I suggested to them. "You'll not believe the difference between the Cheviots, and the Leicesters, the Lintons, and the wild animals you have known here. Their wool is thick and they are hardy. They'll be able to climb the hills with their short legs. We can consult the British Wool Society and discover the best prices."

The tenants listened to Andrew repeat my words in the kirk and pessimism began to fade from their features.

I wrote, *"I think we can do what Mr. Baird hoped to do. But instead of importing shepherds and dogs from the Lowlands, instead of flooding the hills with thousands of Lintons and driving the folk from their homes, we can start in a small manner and find what is productive and what is not. The wool the animals produce will be our own, with no need for a seller betwixt us and the mills. There can be meat sold as well, meat that will add a few shillings to the farmers' pockets and help them to pay their rents. It will take longer to free Kirthgarran from debt, and no doubt Lord Kirthgarran would be dismayed to see my disloyalty to his decree, but my conscience is unfettered.*

"And there must be more we can do. I have not forgotten what Coll said about the income from the whisky. If Kirthgarran has customers for it then we must produce it. If we can increase the amount we make and sell jars of it without having the stills discovered or paying heavy fines, our creditors will be paid all the sooner."

I could not wait to tell Coll of my decision. He had never wanted the land to go under the sheep. I imagined the joy that would appear on his face when I told him the folk had agreed to talk about raising Cheviot sheep. If they were willing they would not have to be evicted.

He and I could begin talking about our own plans. He might take his recruits to Argyll but he could resign his commission. Together from the roof-walk we would watch the comely, new sheep grazing on the hillsides and the plumes of smoke rising from the houses just as they had for centuries.

The man who had killed Rab and caused Lord Kirthgarran's death—and defaced my clarsach instead of attacking me—would be just a memory. We would discover who he was, or he would disappear from our lives forever. My prayer was for him to be found and compelled to pay for his crime, but certainly my life could not be in danger any longer since the folk were not being cleared from the glens. There was no reason for retribution or anger.

I ended my entry for the day by writing, *"The tenants left the kirk with eagerness in their voices and sparks of light in their eyes. It was astonishing to see. They will go and tell their wives and their kin and the word will spread through the estates. They are sure to agree to this idea. In a few days I will be writing the letter to Mr. Baird and ending our contract.*

"The only blemish on the day was seeing Isabel, who came with her father. Her strange eyes were fixed upon me the whole time we were in the kirk. She hates me because I was Rab's wife. He is gone but the resentment exists still. Perhaps it is only her grief. She must have genuinely loved Rab. I could not speak to her, though, and I wonder if I will ever be able to do so."

For a second her face flashed before me, but I could turn away from it with little hesitation. I blew the sand from my writing and thrust the paper inside the desk. The thrill of this morning's success still surged within me, and there were only a few hours left to pass before Coll would wait for me under the stone arch. Beyond the window the heavens were packed with clouds the color of forged steel and the lands about the castle were becoming dim and indistinct.

"Please hurry," I told the invisible sun as it crept toward the horizon.

Once you wrote me, well I min',
That you'd come and mak' me thine.

The Sailor Laddie (Trad.)

Chapter Forty-Two

scrutinized the hands of the Jeremiah Johnson longcase clock for as long as I could bear it and listened to the ticking and the chimes until they echoed between my ears. When the ornate brass needles proclaimed the hour to be quarter to eight, I made excuses to the few of our loyal guests in the drawing room, hinting I had an aching head and no appetite for supper, and quietly retired.

Moments later I slipped out into the courtyard. Snow had begun to fall. Feathery clusters as round as sovereigns materialized out of the black night, fell in silence, and melted into the earth. I passed through their midst as if dividing perpetual curtains but there were no interruptions in the vertical folds. I drew wool over my head and tread with careful toes over grass and shiny pebbles. There were few sounds in the muffled air.

As soon as I left the gardens I tried to peer through the snow and detect the old wall. He must be there already, I thought. I hurried toward the water's edge. Eagerness prompted me to charge the last few feet and I rushed under the arch.

I was alone. The night was ink, dotted with plummeting star-shapes. The quick rhythm of my own breaths was so loud I removed my hood, yet I sensed nothing but the shy whisper of the snowflakes as they struck cloak and stone.

I was early, I suspected. But he would come. I would find his shape, tall and black, blocking out the snowfall, looming larger until he was beside me. Our hands would reach out and grasp. His would be cold and hard but they would bury themselves in my clothing as he pulled me toward him. We would hold each other in relief and passion, and his voice would come at last, murmuring into my ear, his breath warm against my cheek.

The loch was a dark mass, a creature that stretched before me with no beginning and no end. I stepped back two paces, allowing myself to be more fully protected under the ceiling of lichened blocks, and took a measured breath. Childhood memories of the black cellar at Gilchrist House seized me.

I thought I heard a noise at my back. I was about to turn when a shock unlike anything I had ever experienced reverberated in my skull. My knees buckled beneath me. The points of half-buried boulders rushed up to meet me. One of them caught me between my hips.

All fell into darkness.

I coughed. My lungs were on fire, and I was cold, so cold that my skin seemed to be on fire as well. I thought my eyes were open but I could not tell for sure if they were. I thought I was awake but I was not certain of that, either.

I shook so violently I could not move. I coughed again and thunder beat inside my brain. I did not want to breathe. There was water in my mouth. I tried to lift my hands and could not locate them. I wanted to move my head but it was in a vise.

Eyelids parted and there was no change in the blackness. The need to cough intensified and I was taken over by its fury, and then there was vomit in my throat and I began to choke.

I discovered I could turn on my side. Diffused light shone through a blur of white, telling me my eyesight had returned, but I could make no sense of what I saw. The slow realization came that I was lying in the water, and my hands were sliding on the gravel, barely allowing my head to remain above the surface. With a heave I righted myself, and on knees and elbows retched whilst sparks shot about in my head.

Something was wrong about being in the water. The light from far away came into focus and I decided it originated from a castle window. It illuminated the edge of the arch on the shore—and a dark figure. Someone hurried away. Grew smaller. I raised myself up on shaking arms but the figure disappeared.

I was tempted to remain where I was, to stop struggling and to give in to the murky netherworld that crept about in my head, beckoning, subsiding, overtaking reason. But I was convinced it was wrong to be in the water. I brought my knees forward and inched my reluctant body toward the shore.

I could not tell when I was out of the loch. The rocks and the arch were there before me and I thought I must have been successful. I curved my form into a ball and no water filled my mouth or my nose. My mind drifted and it was sleep I sought.

The world became sharp about me once more and I thought, I will die here in the cold. I clutched a boulder with fingers that felt nothing and pulled myself to my feet. My skirt wrapped itself about my legs. I took a step and fell. I followed the process over and over. Sometimes I did not know how long I lay on the ground before I forced myself up again.

The great door of the castle chose to admit me after a struggle with its latch. The vacant hall suggested people were at supper. I crawled up the rear stairs by the piper's gallery and stumbled along the passages. The darkness consumed me from time to time and I was surprised when I recognized my bedchamber. My bed grabbed me by the shoulders and refused to let go—but I had no further strength to fight and let it take me where it willed.

Ròs's face materialized out of the dusk. "Losh, my lady!" came her voice. She disappeared. I could not stop my shuddering.

Airig's face came. She and Ròs struggled to take my wet clothes from me. Blankets appeared in great piles and buried me in my bed. The light in my room grew brighter as flames in the fireplace crackled and roared, and I could see the deep green of the canopy curtains above me as well as the rafters of the ceiling with their painted ivy leaves and cherry-red blossoms. I turned my head away from the hot dish of tea and the movement brought glitters of red behind my eyelids.

They would not let me sleep and it was sleep for which I hungered.

"Speak," begged Airig. "Speak to us. Tell us where you went, and why."

They did not seem to realize my tremors would not allow my mouth to move. I wanted to hide under my mountains of blankets, wanted to lie like one of King Arthur's knights under the Eildons, but the women would not suffer it.

Andrew floated over me. "I'll send for Mam," he said. "She'd want to be here at your side."

I am sleeping, I told myself. This is all a dream.

Warm stones wrapped in wool were tucked in beside my waist. Airig dried my hair. Whenever I opened my eyes I watched the whimsical shadows dancing in the corners of my chamber. I listened to more voices, as if they came from afar. I tried to raise my head to see.

"Do not move now, lamb," Mairi said. "You're in your own bed, and we're all here to make sure you recover. Rest now. Just rest."

I was able to say, "I am feeling better."

She smiled and behind her came a murmuring. I focused beyond her shoulder and saw gliding faces. One by one I gazed at them. Anne was here; Andrew, Sandy, Lachlan, Airig. And Coll.

Mairi put a woolen cap on my head. "You did not rub her hands or feet, or her limbs?"

"Oh no," Airig said. "We dared not damage them. I do not believe her fingers or toes have frozen, thanks be to God."

"She'll be restored. She'll come back to us," Mairi said, smiling at me again. She touched my chin with a fingertip, as if examining a bruise, and I felt again the impact of a boulder there.

"I am better," I said, between shivers.

"What happened to you, lambie? Where did you go?"

I sought Coll's face. His features were made of stone yet his eyes were burning. I believed they would set me on fire and I tore mine away.

Mairi leant closer. "Your clothing was sodden, my lady. How did it happen? Did you fall into the loch, or the burn? Why did you go outside?"

I swallowed. "I cannot remember."

"How did you come back? Did you not ask for help?"

"I saw no one."

"How long were you outside, dear?"

"I do not know."

"How long were you in the water?"

"I do not know."

"They tell me no one knew you went out. They said you had an aching head and came here to rest."

I said nothing.

"But then you went outside?"

I twisted my head away. I could remember it all. But I said nothing.

Mairi withdrew and turned to whisper to the others. I sensed them stirring and taking their leave. She came close and said quietly, "I've sent them all away, all but Anne. We'll stay with you the night, keep you warm. There's no need to say aught. Just stay still, and close your eyes, and tomorrow we'll try to put this behind us."

I nodded a little. There was an unusual note in her voice I could not identify.

She said, "Will I send Airig to fetch you a warm drink? They said you refused the tea. Would you take hot milk? It would be well to have something heating you on the inside."

"Aye."

She smiled but it was marred by woe. "My sweetheart. I had no idea. I suppose I've been too indulgent of my own pain. I should have seen it. I should have known."

I was confused but she let her words fall away.

I awoke in the night. Anne was sitting beside my bed. A candle was burning on the table and the fire was ravenous, consuming wood and emitting waves of heat. I was no longer cold. It was a relief to stretch out my limbs and draw the blankets to me.

Anne touched my hand and felt my cheek. "You're not shivering," she said happily.

"I did not fall into the loch," I told her.

Her smile faded and her hand squeezed my fingers. "We all guessed you did not."

"You ken what happened?"

"So much grief has come to you in such a short time. Losing Rab, though he became your husband by fraud, losing Lord Kirthgarran, who was your grandsire. Oh my lady, do you not see how dear you are to us?"

"What are you saying?"

"Perhaps the realization that Kirthgarran is yours—it is too much, despite the changes you want to make about the land-rent. We all thought you were content with that. But it could not mend what came before. The scheming that Andrew did with his brothers and Lachlan and Rab cannot be undone, and certainly talking to Alistair must have reminded you of it all. You've been distraught and none of us saw the depth of it. How could I not see it? I blame myself."

"You think I decided to take my own life," I said. I watched her face and felt a sinking in my stomach. "It is not true."

"Why else would you pretend to seek your bed and then leave the castle, alone?"

"I went to the lochside," I began.

"To—to freeze to death," Anne said with a trembling mouth.

"No. No..."

"Andrew thinks you went into the water to hasten it. Did you have second thoughts? Did you come out and wish you'd not done it? I'm so glad you did. I could not bear to lose you."

"I did not intend to drown or die from cold."

"I wonder," she said dismally, "if Coll's leaving has not affected you as well. How dearly the two of you have come to hold each other. I, too, dread the day he joins his regiment. Perhaps I should not be telling you this, but he's terrified by what's happened. It's reminded him, and us all, of the other time."

"What—other time?"

"When Coll was about to leave for North America. Leslie Hamilton died by her own hand. It is too much like that. Coll about to go off to war again, and a woman taking her life."

"Annie, please listen to me. I did not try to harm myself."

"Then why did you go into the water?"

"I was put into the water. I was standing by the arch and something struck me. The side of my head is sore where I was hit. When I awoke I was lying in the loch and knew I'd die if I did not come out. So I did. I came back to the castle. Because I wanted to live."

Doubt puckered her face as she sat thinking and trying to follow what I said. "Who would want to hurt you so?" she asked.

"Perhaps the same person who hurt Rab."

"But we thought Rab was murdered because of the threatened evictions. 'Tis not the same now. Who would want to do such a thing to you? To *you*?"

"I do not know."

"But why did you go out at all? In the dark, in the snow? Sandy said you left your company and wanted no supper and came upstairs."

If I told her I went to meet Coll, there would be more questions and I was not certain how to answer them. He was here at Kirthgarran, downstairs perhaps, and his eyes were full of fire. I did not understand what it meant. I could not tell Anne what it meant when I did not know myself.

Coll had not mentioned his plan to meet me, it seemed. Neither had he followed through with it. If he had been near the stone arch he might have seen who had knocked me down. If he had come at all he would have found me in the loch or crawling toward the castle. For some reason he had sent me a letter asking for hope, and then changed his mind.

She was waiting for me to reply but I had nothing to offer, and her golden head bowed. She said with compassion, "Perhaps you went outside to think, and tripped on a rock by the curtain wall."

She did not believe it herself. It was a story one would use to cloak the behavior of a poor creature bent on self-destruction.

"We can talk of it tomorrow, if you wish. Perhaps your memory will be better then. I'm only thankful that Ròs came up to see if you needed aught. If you'd not been found in your wet clothes with the fire so low and all, oh, I cannot bear to think of it."

I wanted to leave my bed. I needed to be brave and ask Coll why he had not kept his word to meet me by the ruins. Mairi and Anne stayed with me all night and morning. By midday I was recovered and feeling well, but Mairi was inflexible and would not have me forsaking my chamber, arguing that any small chill might prove ruinous.

"Bide here by your fire with plenty of hot tea and rest," she commanded.

"If you think I should, but..."

"Andrew told your guests you were ill and they all conveyed their sympathies and went home, so you've no need to worry about hospitality. Grizel has the kitchen in order. Airig and Sandy are in command of the household and I told the lads to remain away."

"Are you going to stay?" I asked her.

"I will if you need me, lamb. And so will Anne."

Anne appeared pale and I did not think staying awake all night had been healthful for her or her bairn.

"I promise I'll keep myself warm. You must go home and find your own rest," I said.

"You'll be lonely. No, I'm thinking we should remain and provide company for you," Mairi replied.

She did not want to leave me alone. Perhaps she believed I would try to end my life again. The two women took turns napping and sitting with me at my fireside, and at times I found them contemplating me as if they thought I might jump up and leap through the window. If only Coll would come upstairs, I thought. If only I could think of an excuse to go down. I was quiet as I watched the flames and tried to make sense of what had happened to me.

In mid-afternoon I began to feel uncomfortable. I shifted

in my green chair. Twinges rippled through my abdomen and spread to my lower back. I pushed them away, out of reach of my consciousness, until their insistence could not be ignored and my bowels became queasy.

I said to Mairi, "I think I'll take to my bed for a while."

My flesh was tender where I had fallen on the stones, and when I brought my knees up and lay on my side, I warily pressed my fingers to my middle. I was certain the malaise was just a reaction to the trauma.

When the pain grew worse instead of subsiding I began to wonder if my courses were coming upon me. I could not decide if I felt happy or sad. I had dreamt often of a child but the future was uncertain, tremulous. I turned my face into my pillow. I was overcome with sorrow. The weeks I had spent wondering if I were with child or not suddenly seemed absurd. A visit to the garderobe confirmed that my courses had begun.

Airig arrived with broth on a tray and some sweetmeats Grizel had put aside just for me, but whilst she stood talking to us, further spasms gripped me. I was able to hide them until Mairi asked me if I would mind if she went to bed. Anne had already gone an hour or two before but it was nearly eleven o'clock.

"I'll stay with you, if you like," she added. "But my eyes are going to close whether I'm standing or sitting." She peered at me and seemed to sense all was not well.

"Just pains," I said. "Normal pains."

"A visit from the French lady?" she said and smiled, but her hand was cool on mine. "Nought else?"

I shook my head, forgetting about the ache this action caused.

"Send Airig for me, at any hour, if you want me," she said before she left.

I dozed but there was to be no respite. The flow of blood began to worsen. An obscure knife was lodged inside of me. I sat up in bed to call out and Airig was beside me at once. I clasped her hand. "I'm afraid," I told her.

Mairi came to me wearing her bedgown and plaid and carrying a candle. Her hair fell over her shoulders and her eyes were enormous in the dark. I felt little embarrassment whilst she looked beneath the sheet and felt my body, for the alarm was too great in me. Her voice came low and soft when she paused and caressed my arm. "Keeley. Are you with child?"

I could not answer at first. The fire hissed and sputtered, engrossed in its own ambitions and oblivious to human distress. I said, "I was not sure—cannot be sure—I do not know..."

I saw her exchange glances with Airig. "I think," Mairi said, "you cannot be much more than two months in it, aye?"

I knew I wept. I could taste the tears.

To Airig she gave instructions I could not decipher.

I said, "But a woman does not bleed unless..."

"I greatly fear something is amiss, Keeley. I'm not a lying-in-wife but I've seen this sort of thing often enough. You must be prepared, lamb. I think you are losing the bairn."

The sorrow I had felt earlier was nothing compared to what swept through me at that moment. I lay back on the bolster and a noise came from my throat. Rab's bairn—or Coll's. It did not matter whose it was. "But you're not certain," I murmured.

She had no answer for me. Then.

I did not know the hour. My shivering had returned. It might have been midnight or early morning when Mairi said, "I want to wake Sandy."

I put out a hand as if I could stop her.

Gently she took my fingers. "I'm thinking the best thing will be to bleed you. I could send for the lying-in-wife, if it's her you want. But I must tell you that Sandy knows the art of blood-letting better than anyone."

"Must I be bled?"

"'Tis proper. Most likely we should have done it before this. You've a fever. Any midwife will tell you it's a half a pound of blood that must be taken when..."

"You think it is true then, that I am losing my child?"

It appeared she could not bring herself to say it, but the shimmer in her eyes was enough. Behind her Airig concurred. "Sandy is the best one."

Another cramp bore down on me and I clenched Mairi's fingers. I did not want Sandy near me. Sandy, who was aware of every thought that crept through my head. I did not want any man near me. "No one else must know," I begged them. "Promise me. You'll not tell anyone about the bairn."

"You must be bled," Mairi insisted.

"I leave it you. You decide who will do it. But beyond that one person, promise me you'll not tell another soul. No one, no one at Kirthgarran, no one in the family. Not even Anne."

"I promise," Mairi said reluctantly, and so did Airig at her side.

Sandy came into my bedchamber, a foreign profile that emerged from darkness into the light of candles. He closed the door behind him. Beside my bed he put down the Argand Burner and a copper bowl half-filled with sawdust. "My lady."

Mortification had been growing within my breast and when he touched my forehead with a hard, dry hand I closed my eyes.

"Aye, there's a fever," he muttered.

"She is beside herself with pain," Mairi told him. "But she's full of fright as well."

"I'll be quick."

I was forced to lie flat. Mairi came beside me and my fingers grew slippery in hers. Sandy ignited the lamp and drew it close so that the light of seven candles brightened his face, his grave eyes. "The arm," he said.

Mairi nodded to me and I extended my left limb. My skin, sensitized from fever, recoiled at his touch though he could not have been more gentle. He expertly rolled the sleeve of my chemise upward. Airig grasped my hand whilst he took a bandage from his waistcoat pocket and placed it about my lower arm near the elbow. He tied it tightly. He put a knitting wire through the knot and twisted it, making the ligature painful. With two fingers he tapped the skin near the knot. The lancet appeared in his other hand, glinting in the flaring light.

His thumb stroked my arm an inch below the bandage and he said without looking at my face, "Ready yourself."

He brought the lancet to my skin. Airig held my arm firmly on the copper basin. I could not watch as Sandy made the wound but I felt the cut, felt him loosen the bandage, and heard my blood drip against the metal vessel when it missed the sawdust.

My hot fingers slid in Mairi's and Airig's and I gripped them again.

My heart, pounding in my ears, was a clock. On and on it ticked. My eyes were closed but I felt the edges of my vision constricting and dizziness sweeping upward from my very feet.

"Is that not enough?" Mairi said at last.

Sandy's hands came over my arm. Pressure was put on the opened vein and Airig released me. I widened my lids and watched as a new bandage was tied about the wound. Sandy bent my elbow and placed my hand against my shoulder to rest.

They took the pillow out from under my head and rearranged my bedding.

"One rug only," Sandy said. "She should not be overheated. Tomorrow some cold oat-gruel, or cold broth. I would think now a decoction of calcined hartshorn."

"I'll prepare it," Airig offered.

"And bring her some barley-water. Or perhaps a half a drachm of powdered niter in a cup of water-gruel. Aye, that would be better. Give her some every five or six hours."

I wondered if that was what had been offered to his wife, who had lain dying so many years before.

He bent his head to me and for a moment I allowed myself to look at him. He said, "Lie quietly now. Mairi will fetch me if it needs to be done again." And then: "I am very sorry—about the bairn."

It would have been his grandchild. If not by blood, perhaps, at least in name. I said, "I am sorry, too, Sandy, just as I am about your son."

Alone, with Mairi sitting silently at my bedside, I finally knew how my mother had felt every time The Fairies had come and taken her bairn.

Three dawns came and melted away. One morning I awoke to find Sandy at my bedside staring down at me, his face unreadable. I thought at first he had been summoned to bleed me again and my fists tightened on the coverlet as I looked into his eyes, seeking evidence of his intentions. But he shook his head and put a tumbler of water down on my bedside table. He bowed his head, and disappeared.

On the afternoon of the third day Anne and Mairi returned to Rathdale, leaving Airig in charge of my convalescence. Anne and Andrew were bound for Camghouran for a fortnight winter visit to her parents, and Mairi, judging my difficulties behind me, offered to help them prepare for their journey. It seemed my desire for secrecy had been honored, for Anne spoke of my despondency as being a combination of despair from my recent losses and the physical chill I had suffered from my foolhardy effort to release myself from the grip of that despair.

"Keep well," Anne begged, kissing my cheek.

Mairi embraced me, saying, "Keep to your bed. I'll return to you in two days' time." She had spoken little since I had lost the child.

I stayed in the vault of my room, protected by the engraved, arched door and the stone walls. I did not know what I would have done without Airig, though she was but a shadow.

On the afternoon of the fourth day she came to my bedside. "'Tis the Captain," she said. "He begs leave to come to you."

I raised my eyes. I could not think of what to say. But I need not have bothered to ponder it, for Coll came inside my chamber, stood by the opening, watched me.

"Mam can be formidable," he said. "She said no one must harry you. But now she's away and I'm relying on Airig's mercy." He was not smiling. He had not shaved for some time and beard darkened his face. "Will you have a visitor? Or am I intruding, as my mother predicted?"

For dark is the night and the road is o'er lang...
The North Highlands (Trad.)

Chapter Forty-Three

The flames in his eyes seemed to have dissipated since I had seen him last, but he was wary. Airig hovered, unusually dubious.

"It is a long while since we spoke," I said. I lifted a hand to my throat, overcome with both thankfulness and foreboding at having my prayer answered.

He seemed little interested in the state of my room or Airig's presence, and strode toward me. "Will I bide here for a bit?" He took my lack of reply for acquiescence, and sat on the oak chair his mother had used during the previous days. "Your mistress might wish for tea," Coll said to Airig.

Uncertainly she sought my approval and yet all I could do

was agree. She said, "I'll find Ròs—and wait outside."

We were by ourselves, my lover and I, though I could not remember the last words of love that had passed between us. If I could have but reached for him and felt his body against mine, I believed the last week would disappear in my mind forever.

I sat up higher, drawing bedding to my chest whilst he bent his head and looked at his hands resting on his knees. He cleared his throat and his voice came low. "I'm told you're not ill. Merely being cautious."

I nodded and the movement caught his eye; he looked more fully at me. His face revealed little expression. A week's worth of stubble gilded upper lip, cheek and chin with tarnished gold, and grooves seemed to be engraved between his brows. His mouth parted as though he delved for what he might next say, and for a moment I was transfixed. My hands ached to touch him. My heart was full of a thousand questions.

"I need to know," he said, "how you fare."

The unison of our thoughts was unexpected. "My heart is heavy. You must know it is."

He dipped his head in affirmation, and his eyes, as gray as the rain yet beleaguered by red inflammation, bore into mine. "I do not have the luxury of many hours left, nor do I possess a temperament at this point that allows me much patience. Therefore you must forgive me my bluntness, my discourtesy perhaps. This—misfortune that befell you. It was not unplanned, was it." His face seemed to swim in the poor light. I shook my head, trying to keep his eyes in focus. He went on, "Did you intend for me to find you? Can you be that cruel after all?"

"Are you asking me if I meant to take my life?"

"What else could I be asking?"

"You believe that I tried to punish you?"

"It would seem to be a fair conclusion. The others believe you sought such an end, and I have not dissuaded them."

The idea was so ludicrous I could not even think how to defend myself. I clutched coverlet and blanket without mercy and pressed them against the pulse in my throat. I said, "You know why I went outside."

"I know what I've been told."

"But you sent me the letter. I went to meet you."

"Did you? I was there. I left the arch after thirty minutes or so because you did not come. I began riding back to Rathdale. Lachlan overtook me on his way to fetch Mam and told me what you'd done."

"I do not understand. I waited for you."

"If you had, I would have seen you."

"Do you disbelieve me?"

"I believe you went outside. I believe you walked into the loch and meant to die there. For me to find you hours later. But then you lost your courage and came back inside."

"No! It was not that way at all..."

"Was it not meant to be a vengeful joke? I told you about the other lass. She took her life as well, before I left. For it to happen again..."

"No." Confusion muddled my mind, left me unable to choose the best words. "How can you think I would do that?"

He leant back and observed me, and shadows deepened beneath his eyes. "The proof of it lies before me. What better measure for repayment is there than the one you chose? But you did not succeed. You changed your mind. Or was it in this bed you planned to die?" His severity was not born of anger but coldness, and I felt as if I were once more enveloped by the frigid waters of the loch.

"You were there," I said finally. "And you saw no one?"

"Who else would be foolish enough to venture out on such a night?" he replied evasively.

"There was someone else there. At least, I think there was."

He did not respond.

"Were you there, exactly at eight o'clock?" I asked. "Why did I not see you?"

A pause. "It was at the hour of ten I asked you to meet me."

"I went out just before eight."

Another pause. "To allow time to do its work, it would seem. Two hours in the freezing cold, with wet clothing upon your back, and I'd have found you dead at my feet when I came to see you. A perfect answer it may seem. But for some reason it did not happen the way you hoped."

"In your letter you wrote eight o'clock."

"You are mistaken."

I searched for a fissure in his aloofness and could find none. "I will show you your letter," I insisted. "It is you who are mistaken." With arms that felt as cumbersome as oak trees I pushed my coverings aside and inched my legs over the edge of the bed.

He stood and I came to my feet beside him. The room tilted back and forth. He reached out a hand but I resisted it, knowing that if he touched me I would be lost.

I crossed to my writing desk and after two attempts withdrew the velvet-lined drawer. I had placed his letter on top of all my other papers but it was no longer there. I sifted through the pile, once, twice, three times.

Coll stood behind me, watching.

I lifted my papers to the top of the desk and traced the contours of the drawer with my hand, the pile of the velvet smooth and cool against my fingertips. The letter was gone. And something else was missing as well: the knife I had removed from my clarsach.

I had to sit down. I took some steps to the wing chair by the ingle, and after finding it with my hands in that spinning room, sought its safety. "It is not there," I said. "Your letter is not where I put it."

"You should get back into your bed."

"Someone has taken the letter."

"Lie down, my lady. Clearly you are not well."

"Why do you not remember what you wrote?"

"I mind well what I wrote."

"There were some things you crossed out."

"Aye."

"Did you not change the time?"

"No."

I looked up at him. "It should be my memory that is faulty, not yours. I was struck down that night. I was pulled into the water."

"And who do you accuse of this most shameful act?"

"You think I am lying." The word hung between us like a deadly thing. How bitter it was that only a short time ago he had said much the same to me, in a pool of lantern light whilst far away Donald's pipes sang their sorrow. "I've told no one," I said, "about us. I told no one what your letter said."

"I admit I did not expect you to."

"And I went to meet you. Does that not tell you what was in my heart?"

"I see no more than I did before I walked into this chamber. You do not have to invent these tales for me or anyone else. 'Tis all plain to me—and what I hoped to discover I suppose I already knew."

"I am not inventing tales! I read your letter and waited for you and was struck on my head and dragged into the water. I was left to die there. I saw someone walking away from me when I awoke. I came back inside and lay on my bed until Airig found me. By then it was probably ten o'clock."

"Then you think I am lying. Again."

My gaze fell away from him. For one who dreaded the threat of another's suicide he seemed obstinately convinced of its actuality, or at least he intended it to be accepted as truth.

When he spoke again I could hear the vexation in his voice. "Take to your bed. I've done nought but champion your defenses." At my reluctance to move he said, "Airig will have your tea by now."

Thoughts remained half-formed. Emotions welled up within me. Relief from his imminent departure conflicted with desperation to delay it. And as I struggled with these pieces, he thrust my counterpane to the side of the bed in an impatient bid for my compliance in crawling beneath it, and left me.

I sat in the stuffed chair unaware of any physical sensation. He wanted to believe the worst of me and for others to believe it as well. I sat staring at nothing at all.

My surprise was sharp when Coll came back carrying an earthenware cup. "I've made you a posset and told Airig to forgo the tea," he stated. "You mind I sometimes mixed them for Lord Kirthgarran. This is the same, for sleeping."

"I do not need it."

"You've never appeared more ill. Drink it." He handed me the cup and remained beside me as if waiting to see me tip it between my lips.

I was apprehensive but could not seem to trace the reason why. "It is too hot."

"But you will take it." It was a demand.

I solicited his eyes, fearful of what I would see in them, and met with an intensity that had not been there before.

"Do drink it," he said. "Let it be my last duty to you. You have my promise you'll not set eyes on me again." He left me once more and this time I knew he would not be back.

I held the cup until all trace of warmth left it. I stared at the milk and tilted the vessel, observing the liquid welling up beneath the skin that had formed across its top. There was no such protective skin in my mind, nothing to keep away the memories of a lost bairn and a vengeful lover. The afternoon light was dying and soon it would be winter night, and nighttime was the worst time for me in any case, when all energy for inner self-protection seemed to fall away. Coll's words prowled back in forth in front of me. They were joined by Ewen's. I pictured the baillie standing in the rain, staring white-faced at Coll.

A farmer's lad discovered one, and his father the other, came his voice from inside my head. *Who'd more reason to do away with my brave dogs, than you?*

The wrinkled film of the milk in my hand mocked me.

Ewen's voice echoed again. *But you were all I could think of. You, and the vengeance you might have had inside you.*

Unsought came the vision of Coll when Ewen had accused him. Brows drawn, lips narrow whilst water streamed down his face. It was the same visage that had been here in my bedchamber only moments before, without the rain but with the same ferocity.

When Airig brought my dinner to me she was dismayed at my state.

"Now! What are you thinking? Should you not be taking better care of yourself? Here, you must come back to your bed and stop your shivering. You've not drunk the draught!"

She took the cup from my unresisting fingers and peered curiously inside. "Come now. I've your broth and a nice cut of beef. And it's just as well I've brought you another posset. He said he did not think you'd take it."

"Coll?"

"Oh, I was not to say. The Captain told me not to press you for fear you'd balk, but he wants you to take the sleeping draught. He made another just to be sure, and you must drink it, my lady, for it's as he said, you do appear unwell." She plunked down the cold cup on the writing desk and beckoned me to my bed.

"I want nothing, Airig."

"Still, it would do no harm for you to have a good, long sleep. The afternoon is growing dark already with a miserable night before us. It looks to be a cold one with the wind, and it's bringing a heavy snow. Ewen is downstairs and claims his knees say 'twill be a dreadful storm. Oh, I do hope Andrew and Anne are well-sheltered within her father's house by now."

The food appealed not at all to me. I followed her listlessly to the bed and allowed her to spread the coverlet over my legs. My fingers were cold when they pressed against my aching forehead.

In an eerie imitation of Coll's voice Airig urged, "Do drink it." I looked up and found her watching me. She steadied the tray on my lap and remained waiting until I enclosed the warm posset in my hands. She strode to the window and pulled the curtains closed with sure snaps of her wrists, retrieved the old cup, and appraised the waning fire. "I'll be back," she said. "Kenneth needs to bring more firewood." Before she took herself away she looked back at me. "Drink it, now," she charged.

I raised the vessel to my mouth and she disappeared.

I wavered. My lips were less than a half-inch from the rim and the steam from the milk wafted into my nostrils. I was behaving as though the people I cared for most in the world were trying to poison me. I was deranged. My mind was unbalanced. I must drink this warm, healing remedy that Coll had made for me out of concern and love, and find beneficial sleep to restore peace of mind and bodily health. I must take the foxglove, the *lus a bhalgair*, noted for its ability to bring drowsiness.

The foxglove, able to bring death, Mamma had prophesied, if not handled with care.

I put the cup down.

A war was raging inside my head and there was no relief

from it. I tried to convince myself I had been hysterical ever since Rab's and Lord Kirthgarran's deaths. I must have slipped near the curtain wall and fallen into the water as Anne had theorized, for certainly I was a threat to no one. I must have imagined in my groggy condition that I had seen someone walking away. I must have read Coll's letter wrongly and gone too soon to meet him. I had mislaid the letter. The Rathdale cottage had burnt by accident.

I was slowly going mad. The process had begun with Rab's murder and had since been abetted by the revelation of Coll's complicity in a manipulative plot, our subsequent quarrels, the strain of learning about the link between Mamma and Lord Kirthgarran, and the loss of my child.

I put my tray aside and climbed out of bed. I slid on my slippers and drew my plaid over my chemise. I had difficulty remembering in what sequence everything happened. Perhaps I had even imagined the knife in my clarsach and no such thing existed. No one had touched the harp after all.

The passage floor was swept by a chill current, reminding me of Airig's talk of a storm, and as I stole into my mother's old room I allowed myself a glance at the window. Pellets of snow were being driven against the castle. I lifted the key from my pocket and embedded it into the lock of the walnut cupboard. With eyes closed I pulled open the doors. Warily I parted my lids—and there was the clarsach, just as I had left it, with its sides scarred and chipped and its tiniest wires cut. I ran my fingertips along the roughened surface of the soundbox, and with the feel of the ravaged wood came back recognizance of the truth. Someone had cut my clarsach. I had pulled out the knife and hidden it in my writing desk and had later placed Coll's letter beside it, but they had been taken away. Someone had set fire to the house where Coll and I had loved. Someone had tried to kill me, either by drowning or by exposure to the cold. And he had killed my bairn as well.

Whoever was responsible showed a vengeful nature. Whoever had poisoned Ewen's dogs had possessed a vengeful nature. And then there was Rab's murder. There must be a connection. As unwelcome ideas clashed I found it impossible to remain still. I left my mother's room and took the steps upward to the lightning-struck tower. I stood at the rectangular window oblivious to the wind and the snow that burst in, and gazed out over the loch as Fergussons must have done for hundreds of years. As I focused on the lochside curtain wall with its arched opening, and at the dark thread of a rowan stick protruding from the snow-covered grave of a dog, a story began to form in my mind.

The tale began years ago. Leslie Hamilton had professed her love for him, but when she had withdrawn it she had died. They said she had killed herself, leaping from her tower window. But Coll had gone to see her and not returned until morning light. He could have remained at Caiseal Àlainn or slipped back later and pushed her. Perhaps he'd not meant to. Perhaps there had been a violent row.

He had mourned her, of course, but then sailed to America and buried himself in a profession that encourages a man to kill. He came back to Kirthgarran and resumed his life, but when Ewen Drummond's dogs tore his own apart, revenge took place again. There might be other instances of reprisal of which I was not aware.

Then there was me. We fell in love. He removed Rab, a barrier to our future together, but in the end I rejected him. In a rage he struck at my clarsach and the Rathdale cottage, the relative coolness of his exterior belying the seething emotions within. Now it was time to fully avenge himself against me just as he had done with the unlucky Miss Hamilton.

The lure to the water and my immersion in it had failed. My suicide would have been believed but I had survived, and something must be done whilst I was weak and considered feverish. I suspected there was something awry with the draughts he made, yet if I did not drink them he would try something else. He need only make it seem that I had taken my life, a possibility the others were already more than ready to believe. He had stolen away his letter and the knife, perhaps even as I had lain in the water, so there could be no physical evidence of his involvement.

I needed to support myself against the cold, unyielding wall. My eyes no longer saw the snow blowing across the darkening sky.

Could it be that it was not I embracing madness, then, but Coll? Was there a cold, vindictive executioner somewhere within him who would stop at nothing to ease his own hurts? If that was true I was in danger because I had wounded him, and only a few days remained before he must leave Kirthgarran with his recruits.

His voice, his beautiful, sonorous voice, seemed to caress my ears. I could hear him saying, as if he stood beside me, *I cannot imagine how I can leave you at Kirthgarran with Rab.*

If he was the one who had killed Rab, if Kirstie was lying to protect him, he was an unstable murderer with no conscience. The story I seemed to be weaving would not be a myth or a fantasy, but a nightmare.

It could not be true. I must not believe it. The man I loved would not have killed Leslie, or poisoned Ewen's dogs, or aimed his pistol at the back of his lifelong friend. I had constructed a fabrication from unrelated puzzles in order to incriminate a thoughtful, caring person who was not deserving of such infidelity.

I pushed myself away from the stones. I could not do this any longer. I loved him and I would not permit myself to continue this fantastic inventing. I did not understand his ferocity of late or his drive to purposefully misunderstand me. My bewilderment was causing me to fear him, but how ridiculous it was. There was a reason why he had not told the others about our intended meeting by the loch, and it must be a significant one. It was my trust he should have, not my suspicion. Like Kirstie, I would defend him or I would never know peace.

My feet were freezing and all I wanted was my warm room. To prove to myself that my story was indeed a spurious one I would drink Coll's posset. I would welcome the quiet easement into sleep and the serenity it promised. I would accept everything he told me as truths and toss away the mysteries as I lay my head down and dreamt. When I could think clearly I must talk to him again and tell him everything.

My slippers made no sound as I retraced the path to my room. I halted before I could turn into the doorway. Coll's tense voice bellowed out from within. "Where have you looked?"

"In the garderobe," Airig said. "Rab's room. Lord Kirthgarran's.

She cannot be far, for I only left her a few moments, and her clothes are here..."

I clamped my spine against the wall of the passage.

"Find her, Airig. At once. Do you hear?"

"I have been looking."

"Look again. Look everywhere. Pretend you're doing something else if you're asked."

"And when I find her?"

"Bring her to me. No one else. Do you understand? I'm not going to wait. This is the end of it."

"Forgive me, Coll. I did not think she'd leave her bed."

"Go on. Go on!"

I could not remain where I was. I slid into Rab's room and secreted myself behind the door. Airig's footsteps clattered away, along the passage. I listened, but for as long as I pressed my head against the wall I did not hear Coll's ring out after her.

I brought an eye to the crack between door and post and fixed my vision on my room opposite. I could only discern the edge of Coll's body, compelling me to discover a better angle. At last he became clear. He was ramming a short rod into a pistol. He stuffed a bag of shot into a pocket. The rod was fitted back into place and the hammer was cocked with his thumb.

I retreated and forced my head back against the wall.

The man I loved was not a murderer. But there he was, armed. It might be me he wanted, or it might not, but I could not afford to sway back and forth between assumptions.

When he strode out of my bedchamber he did not follow Airig but pursued the opposite end of the passage. He did not return. I removed myself from behind Rab's door and looked into the vacant corridor.

After a moment passed I crossed to my room. I pulled the woolen skirt and bodice from the clothes press and dragged them on. I put my unyielding feet into hose and boots. I re-entered the corridor and followed Airig. I crept down the stairs by the piper's gallery.

I was about to step into the great hall when I heard footsteps and voices. I leapt into the gallery and shrank down to the floor.

"Search the northern wing," Coll said brusquely. "I'll look

yet again through the keep."

"I've sent Airig to the kitchen and the storerooms," Sandy replied.

They parted. My hands curled into fists as my heart raced. I was not sure I could stand and make my feet move again.

The pistol gleamed in Coll's fingers. I could not imagine who he meant to use it against—other than me.

I must not go to Airig. Or Sandy. From my lair I could hear Ewen talking in the drawing room, perhaps conversing with Lachlan. I levered myself upward and grabbed the balusters. I tried to consider where I might go for safety. The chilling truth was that I trusted no one, not Ewen or Lachlan, not Airig, Grizel, or Ròs. Must I stand and fight my battle with Coll, taking the chance that he was not my foe? Or must I run in order to stay alive?

I fled down the steps, out the front entrance, and entered the world of cutting snow.

I had not realized how treacherous the weather had grown. My face and fingers were bitten by cold. In defiance I held my face up to the slanting snow as if urging clear thought to come, and ignored the burning of my cheeks and the pulling of the water from my eyes.

I picked up my skirts and ran round the castle walls to hide behind the bushes in the garden. Through the diagonal lines of snow I saw a bent MacNeil coming back from the paddock leading a horse with each hand. I let myself through the postern gate and sidled to the edge of the wall. There was no movement in the courtyard. I dashed to the stable door and found a horse rug within, crushed it against me, and went back the way I had come.

I watched until MacNeil and the horses disappeared. As I drew near the paddock I realized there were only two beasts left in the blowing snow. One of them was Dominie.

I whistled to him as Coll was wont to do and the noble ears swung about and found me. We met at the fence and I urged him to come through the gate. I climbed on the dyke-stones beside him, and though I slipped occasionally I was able to squirm to his back and wind my fingers through his snow-frosted mane. He was patient as I covered my head and shoulders with the rug, but tossed his nose and rolled an eye as if to ask me, "What strange business is this, now?"

I would be grateful, I thought, when the snow melted from his back and the heat of him warmed me also.

A kick of my heels sent his hooves beating through the drifts, and I clung to his shock of black hair hoping the rug would not fly from my back. The afternoon light was dying but Dominie and I both knew our way to Rathdale, and we had no trouble following the lochside path.

When the track became roofed by the first pines, I drew the horse's head up and looked back at the castle. Sheets of snowfall obscured the shapes of keep and bartizans. Yet there was movement: a shape not so easily shrouded because it moved away from the walls and approached the flat expanse of the loch. A horse and rider.

My feet pounded Dominie's sides. He circled once in confusion and bowed his head low as he dug his hooves into the slippery snow. The trees enclosed us as we galloped over the unbroken footpath that led round the edge of steely water.

To the marches of Rathdale we flew. The horse rug held little warmth and my feet and hands were stiff. I could not perceive anything in front of us. With the trees gone and the moor before us, our landmarks were withdrawn, and still I bid Dominie on, uncertain of the trueness of our bearing and hoping we did not make a circle.

I stopped him when I could not see in any direction, for the wind blew the snow horizontally now, unhindered by wall or tree or hill. My eyes probed the stratums of white behind us, watching, gauging. And I thought I saw it again—the dark gray shape that moved. I lingered, squinting as if it would aid my vision. There was no mistake. The shape was still in our wake.

Again I kicked Dominie into a dead run. I could not sense my fingers in his mane any longer but they were not inclined to uncurl. I pivoted my head and realized the horseman was gaining. With a lunge I pulled Dominie's muzzle to the right.

We traveled over the snow-filled heath until I had a blurry sense of where we were. I turned Dominie once again. The shattered bulk of the burnt cottage coalesced against the dimming sky and quickening snow.

"Come, lad," I wheedled the black horse, pushing and pulling him into the quadrangle of scorched walls. If I sent him away our pursuer would be apt to follow him, but I had not the courage to finish the remainder of my journey on foot over the pitiless moor, neither did I dare subject Dominie to the possibility of foundering, though I suspected he would find refuge far more quickly than I. I hugged his neck and urged him more fully behind the cottage wall. Above me the wind dove downward, sending clusters of snow into the ravaged house like sprays of grapeshot.

Dominie swung his head and sent air through his nostrils.

"Hush now," I whispered to him, laying my hands against his hot neck. It would not do to delay for long. His sweat would cool him too fast in this frigid air. Once more I considered forcing him on and remaining hidden alone.

"Only a few minutes," I said, pressing myself against him. "Our tracks will be covered, and he'll not know where we've gone."

I listened to the wind and the snow and Dominie's blowing, and tried to still my own breaths as if the sound of them alone would call the hunter to our asylum. I tread from foot to foot, watching through a corner of the crooked window. No gray forms emerged from the whipping white curtains. I pulled ice from the horse's mane. Watched again as my brain counted seconds, minutes. There was nothing on the moor.

I gathered the rug to me, shaking snow from the folds. "We'll go, Dominie. Come now, just a wee bit farther." I lifted a hand to clear rimed hair from his eyes.

Another hand appeared and grasped my wrist. My middle was caught by an arm. The horse snorted, frightened.

"You've led enough of a chase," came a man's voice in my ear.

I wrenched my arm backward but his fingers were bound in place. I could not turn though I tried to fling myself round. "Who?" I was able to mouth. "Who is it?"

He did not answer, but I felt his hold slacken. I tried to turn myself about once more and came face to face with the man. His eyes sparked in the dusk light.

"Sandy," I said.

"What madness is this, my lady? To be abroad on a night such as this?"

"Why do you hold me so, when I have done nought to threaten you?"

His grip loosened as my weak words dwindled in the air between us, but he did not release me. "I am threatened by your flight."

"Then cease your chase of me, Sandy, that I might go where I will in peace."

"But it is your going that puts you in peril. To ride over the country at breakneck speed in the midst of such a storm! Do you blame me for wanting to save you from it?"

Attempting to save me was not a possibility I had considered, nor did I entertain it now. My hand writhed in his, and the manacle of his fingers relaxed. The arm about my waist slid away. "Let me finish my journey," I said.

"And where is it you fly to?"

"Rathdale."

"You must come back to the castle. I'll take you."

"I do not wish to go back to Kirthgarran. It is Rathdale I want."

His face, struck by handfuls of sharp snow, showed no emotion at all. "When MacNeil found a horse gone, Coll and I set out to find you. We're to meet—at the castle."

"We're closer to Rathdale," I replied, reaching for Dominie's back. "I'm chilled and so is he. Be merciful and let us go. Take me there, if you wish to help. But the castle, no, I'll not go back there. I will not go back."

He did not move.

I turned my back on him, expecting to feel his restraining hands reattach themselves to me. And they did. They came about my waist. I peered at him with one eye, panic closing my throat. He inclined his chin toward Dominie and encouraged me to leap. His hands lifted me up high enough so I could scramble onto the beast's back.

"I'll take you to Rathdale," he said, pulling the collar of his greatcoat closer at his throat.

I wanted to thank him, wanted to pour out my relief, but his eyes would not meet mine and he strode through the drifts to the door.

Side by side our horses began plodding east. Darkness was encroaching at last. I found my eyes closing against the blast of the wind. Before long I realized Sandy was in front of me, leading the way, and I did not know where I was.

He stopped. I lifted my head and called out, "Are we there, Sandy?"

The top of his tricorn was white, revealing an edge of black about his frozen hair. "I think we've gone too far south." He stared at the horizon though land was indistinguishable from sky. "This way," he shouted.

He moved his horse forward and Dominie followed. I huddled under the rug, and soon found myself lying prone on Dominie's back, hugging his neck, seeking his warmth. The journey was taking too long. "We are lost," I said faintly, and I watched Sandy's figure through the flying snow, trying to see beyond him, trying to find recognizable points. Soon I could not even see Sandy.

I was aware when Dominie halted. The muscles beneath me ceased to move and the world stood still. My father-in-law was at my elbow and he said, "Come down."

I allowed myself to fall into his arms. "Where are we?"

"Rathdale."

I raised my head, saw the lights of the house glowing in the windows, let my gaze follow their gleams as they stretched toward us over a courtyard of unbroken snow.

Sandy helped me limp forward. "I'll carry you," he said, "if need be."

I shook my head. We crossed the buried lawn.

The servant lass who met us at the door sputtered in surprise and entreated us to come inside and remove our outer garments. Whilst we did so, she went off in search of Mairi. I found my fingers could grasp nothing as I attempted to shed my rug. Sandy threw logs onto the fire in the drawing room and came back to aid me. We moved to the fireside where our clothing began to drip, and I held my hands near the flames.

Mairi appeared, holding a black shawl to her breast. "What has happened?" she asked. The joints of her fingers were white.

"I have come to you, Mairi. I will explain."

She accepted this, nodding her head a little. "You are ill. You can explain later."

I gave myself up to her capable hands.

Oh my bonnie bonnie Highland laddie,
When I was sick and like to die
He rowed* me in his Highland plaidie.

*wrapped
Hieland Laddie (Trad.)

Chapter Forty-Four

I was taken to a small bedchamber upstairs. A fierce fire was built and all my clothes were taken from me. They were replaced by a dry chemise and a quilt, and whilst my bed was being warmed I sat shaking on a chair by the hearth.

"You're fever has returned," Mairi accused. "If we do not take precautions you'll become very ill indeed."

"Has Sandy come back from the stable?"

"No. I do not think so. He's been over-long, has he not?"

"He promised he would come in as soon as the horses were cared for." I looked round at the rose-colored walls, trying to stem my shudders and think clearly.

"You must calm yourself, lambie. There's something terribly wrong but there'll be time for us to contend with it later. First you must think of your health. Are you feet warming now?"

She tucked the quilt more tightly about me, and though I was reluctant to be treated like a bairn I leant back and rested my head. Counterpane and curtains alike were the color of briar roses, and for a moment I let my eyes close as the soothing stillness of the chamber reached out and enveloped me.

The room was spinning, however, and I could not rest wondering where Sandy had gone.

"I'll fetch some dry woolens for your feet," Mairi said. "And tea. Then you can tell me what's amiss."

I nodded weakly.

I was alone for a long while. I listened to the wind trying to come in the window, and the hiss of the fire. My boots by the ingle began to steam. Mairi had left candles burning and I supposed the room could be regarded as a cheerful, comforting one, but the aesthetics of my environment were my least concern.

"Drink this, my sweet," Mairi said softly at my back.

I turned and took the hot cup and saucer of fine china from her.

"Do you mind," she said, sitting on the stool at my feet, "how I brought you tea on the first morning you ever woke at Kirthgarran? That seems a gey long time ago. This should help you just as that did."

I considered taking a sip, but I could not manage it. My suspicions of hot possets had ingrained themselves too deeply. I gave the cup back to her. "Thank you, but I cannot."

"It will do you so much good."

"Perhaps later. Not now. Mairi, I must explain."

"You must only if you feel well enough."

"Did Sandy come in? He promised he would."

"I'm afraid Sandy has gone. I sent Deirdre to the stable to urge him to come in but he was not there. Neither was his horse, and a lantern's missing. It appears he's gone back out into the storm."

To fetch Coll. I sat up and glanced at the window, at the pattern of snow stuck there. "I do not know what to do."

"You came to me for help, I'm thinking. I'll do all I can,

but I'm fearful for you, especially since—what happened a few days ago. Nought will happen to you here. Rest, do. I forgot the stockings but I'll get them now. When I'm satisfied there's nought more I can do for you I'll sit and you can tell me everything."

"Andrew and Anne went to her parents?"

"Aye. They probably arrived this afternoon."

"And Alistair? He is here?"

"No, dear. He left for Oban on the Monday. He's gone for Nancy, to bring her home."

"I see."

"I ken he brings you unwelcome memories. 'Tis best he's gone, at least for now, aye?"

I was not sure. I would have felt more secure with Andrew and Alistair at Rathdale House. She went in search of stockings and as I waited I tried to think of how I could tell her about her son Coll. No words came to mind but I must try to find them, even if they were clumsy ones. I bent my head, concentrating on the heat bursting from the fireplace. I did not realize she had returned until I felt something small and hard, pressed against the side of my skull.

I tried to move but the pressure increased. I saw her blue gown out of the corner of my eye. I said, "Mairi?"

"Sit still, lamb. It will be best." A hand touched my hair, smoothed it.

"What is it? What is it you have?" I tried to move my head and the hard object was pressed more firmly against me.

"It was my Christopher's," came her voice. "I found it here, after he died." I heard the click, and knew. A hammer had been engaged, ready to strike flint.

"This is the perfect time," she went on. "Sandy is gone. I sent Deirdre home to her family for the night. There's no one else here. You could not have chosen a more perfect time to come."

"I came," I said haltingly, "because I needed you..."

"A brutal irony. I do not know why you came, but aye, it is an irony." She shifted her weight and retrieved the cup and saucer. "You'll drink the tea. And then 'twill be over, all over. Now, here, take it. You must drink it, Keeley, or I'll be forced to fire, and I will have to invent a new tale."

I did not doubt her. There was a note in her voice that was not softened by sweetness or mother-love. I took the tea she held out in front of me. The hard knob left my head. I turned my eyes to see.

The size. The shape. It was identical to Coll's pistol except there were scrolls engraved on the brass plates. The smooth muzzle remained pointed at me. Mairi's finger was hooked over the trigger.

"I do not understand," I said, horror grasping my entrails and brain.

"Do you not? Do you not ken you must die?"

"I cannot believe this is happening."

"I cannot believe aught has happened as it has. I might have forgiven you, and tried to live with the way things were. But not after what you caused. You were responsible. It was because of you."

"What did I do?"

"You killed Rab."

I stared at her. Her eyes were filled with tears. "No," I said. "I was in the kitchen. With Grizel."

"It was supposed to be you. But you stayed inside. It would have been you lying in that coffin instead of Rabbie if you'd come back to the garden." The pistol glinted, but far more threatening was the faraway cast of Mairi's eyes. "Do you not see what happened? I was in the garden. I heard the two of you quarreling. I'd come to wait, with this, as I sometimes did, and I'd seen your clarsach on the settle, and knew sooner or later you'd come to fetch it. But both of you came and I listened. It was dark and the mist was thick and I wept because of what you said to each other. You'd ruin the life of Rab, and my son. I thought I'd lost my chance to frighten you, or wound you, or kill you, for you went into the castle together. But you forgot the clarsach. I knew you'd be back. I waited for you. My eyes were not clear. Someone appeared in the garden. Someone sat on the settle. Someone plucked a string of the clarsach. I fired at you." Her lips trembled and yet her hand was steady. "Do you not see? I thought it was you. I fired and fled before I knew differently, and a bit later Lachlan came here and told us Rabbie was dead. Rabbie. Do you ken what it did to me to realize that I had—Sandy's son..."

He had offered to fetch my clarsach for me. He had sat down in the garden before going to the stable, thinking about our quarrel perhaps, and he had absently fingered a string. The note had been his death knell.

Mairi struggled to shake herself and I watched as anger crept over her. "But in truth it was you who killed him. And because of it, Lord Kirthgarran died. That, too, is on your head. After the funeral I went to your room but you were not there. I had a knife. I saw your clarsach and plunged the knife into the wood instead of your neck. If it had not been for the clarsach—if he had not touched it—but it was too late. Nought could bring back our Rabbie."

"It has been you, all along, wishing me dead."

"You never said aught to anyone. I wondered why." We gazed at each other. "Nor did you say aught about the letter," she said.

"The one Coll wrote?"

"I found it on the table downstairs. I crossed out ten o'clock and wrote eight, and put it back so it could be taken to Kirthgarran later. By the time he would find you that night, I thought you would be dead."

"Then it was you, you who I saw..."

"I was waiting beside the ruin, and you came looking for him. I used a stone to knock you down and I pulled you into the water. I tried to keep your face down but you recovered and began to beat about. I was afraid you'd become alert enough to draw me down into the loch with you, so I left you alone and hurried away, thinking the cold would be the end of you instead of the drowning. I went to the house of a family at Rathdale. I'd been nursing the man the night before and thought if I went there, and changed my wet shoes and stockings to sit at his bedside for a bit, no one would have any doubts about where I'd been all the night. When I at last came home, believing I'd have word that you had died by your own hand, Lachlan arrived saying you were alive and well but needing me."

"You came to me then—and pretended you were distraught?"

"I could do little else. I was too closely watched. I thought, in the days I spent with you, that I would find the chance to make a powerful draught for you, but I was never alone long enough. 'Twould have been easy, lamb, far easier than it is now. I should have made more of an effort, fed you the powdered lorchel or put the destroying angel in your gruel. But Anne was always with me, or Grizel or Airig."

The more she spoke, the greater the blow of truth struck me. "And whilst I lay, you thought of these things…"

"I did until you lost the bairn. And then shock overtook me, and I could not think at all. Rabbie's bairn. Or was it Coll's? Do you know?"

I could not answer her. The impact of the truth was too crushing. Mairi had been responsible for my child's death.

"It does not matter," she went on without expression. "Although if I'd known of its existence, I think—I think I would have waited. It might have been my grandchild."

A gasp escaped my throat.

"I've not done this well at all," she said. "Until now."

I became aware of rage surging up through me. "Tell me, then, why you went to the garden that night, with a pistol, watching for me."

Her chin lifted and she gazed at me with eyes half-hidden by their lids. "You came betwixt them. They almost killed each other because of you. And you were causing my Coll to go."

"I did not want him to go."

"You do not ken how I suffered whilst he was across the sea the last time. I awakened in the night, every night, from nightmares. I could not bear to think of him dying, or lying wounded. He was Christopher all over again." Her free hand pressed the oval locket against her chest. "I could not bear to think of losing Christopher more than once. He'd loved me so, as no one else could. I gave him sons when his wife could not. I gave him Coll, who was just like him. It was before Coll was born that Christopher said to me, 'I'll take you away. You and our sons. We'll go far away where we can be a family.' He meant to. He would have, eventually, if he'd lived. And we would have had all our sons round us. Especially Coll. Dearest Coll." Her eyes widened. "But you came and could not be faithful to your husband. You made Coll fall in love with you and because of his honor he believed the only thing he could do was leave. He was going to cross the sea again to fight. I was going to have to spend years again with those nightmares, always praying, always hoping, missing him, wanting him safe, loving him as issue of the man I still love. He might die—and it would be because of you."

"I did not force Coll to accept the commission. I did not force myself to care for him, nor him to care for me."

"It matters very little. Because of you he was going. But now with you gone, he'll resign his commission and stay."

"I think if you kill me, Mairi, he will still go."

Her hand lifted the pistol higher. "You made me murder Sandy's son. You'll not live when he's denied life. And it is even clearer to me now. You've hurt Coll. He's been inconsolable. You must be held accountable, as others have, for causing Coll despair."

"Others..."

"You are going to drink the tea. No doubt it's cold now but it does not matter. 'Tis the less painful way. If Sandy had remained I'd not have dared to put in the deadly nightshade. He would have kept too close an eye on you. But when he or someone else comes from Kirthgarran in the morning he'll find that the past week has been too much for you. Tonight you'll be dizzy and nauseous, perhaps have trouble seeing, and your heart will beat fast and you may rave a bit, out of your head. Tomorrow you'll be overtaken by weakness and sleepiness, until your lungs no longer allow you to breathe. You'll die as from cold and illness. I will weep but the deed will be done, and Coll will remain at Kirthgarran, safe." She nodded toward the cup and saucer in my hands.

Everything seemed distorted. Mairi appeared to be far away and very small.

"It will be painless at the end," she assured me. "But if you'd rather, this pistol will be held to your head and the others will learn that in your delirium you found Christopher's pistol here in the bedchamber he shared with Eleanor, found it on the dresser where it had been left. I will tell them you put an end to your unhappy life. That you were successful at last."

My fingers gripped the china.

She said, "The poison will be less painful. 'Tis why I used it with the dogs."

Her face wavered before me in the rose-colored room. "The dogs that hurt Coll's and caused him grief."

"I'm so tired of watching. I watched for the dogs and discovered them alone and fed them meat soaked in a tincture of nightshade. They could not go unpunished for what they did. Just so I have watched for you. I watched you and Coll together. I followed you with the spyglass Christopher had brought from his home by the sea. I saw you sometimes, going into the cottage not far from here. Sometimes I watched at Kirthgarran, hidden, when Andrew and Anne thought me here in my chamber greeting for Rab and Lord Kirthgarran, or visiting the home of a sick bairn."

"You set fire to the cottage, did you not, Mairi?"

"I lost my composure after Rabbie died. I thrust my knife in the clarsach, I burnt the cottage. All out of anger. I've grown so tired, waiting, watching, trying to put an end to this horror. I must be rid of you. Coll must be rid of you. Somehow, somehow I will persuade him to stay."

"He did not stay last time."

Her head moved a little to the side. Her eyes took on a stranger light. "Leslie! She was like you. She hurt him. She decided she'd not have him. He was devastated and I'd have done aught to have saved him from that."

"Then the death of Leslie Hamilton was at your hands also," I said. The ridiculous story I had invented in which Coll was featured as a murderer snaked through my pain and taunted me.

"Christopher was gone. Gone! And Coll was going away, too. Because of her. Losing the two of them so close together— I could not bear it. I knew he went to see her. He came back at dusk, told me what she'd said to him, told me how she'd laughed at him. He took himself off to be alone with his sorrow. I watched him go. And I walked all the way to Caiseal Àlainn, and crept into the castle during the betrothal gathering. I knew the rooms because we had often visited my sister there. I went up to Leslie's chamber and waited. I looked through the things on her dresser. There was a box, with brooches and that. And there was the Luckenbooth Coll had given her. She came to her chamber after midnight, sat on her stool, gazed into her mirror. And I came behind her with this pistol and struck her. She was dazed, like you at the waterside, and I pinned Coll's brooch upon her breast where it belonged, and with little trouble I pulled her to the edge of her window and put her through."

Sickness pulled at my stomach. My fingers slipped on the saucer. "And you let Coll go off to war thinking she had changed her mind and wanted to die."

"It was far better that she paid for what she had done. With her gone, he could begin to forget."

"What if he had been blamed as her murderer? Would you have let him go to the gallows for you?"

Her face turned as pale as linen in a bleachfield. "Not then. Not now. If ever it comes as close as that I'll not hesitate to claim my guilt. For Coll. Do you not comprehend? I would do aught. If it seemed he was guilty of Rab's death I would have confessed. If it seemed he had aught to do with your death in the loch, I would have confessed. I took the letter he wrote you, and the knife you foolishly kept—to protect him. I am not a fool, Keeley. I've tried to be careful, and sometimes the anguish has been too much and I've not been able to control myself as I wished, but I'm better now, more cool-headed, and can recognize an opportune moment. Tonight, with you here and Coll at Kirthgarran, there'll be no cast of suspicion upon him. Or on me. With the tea, or with Christopher's pistol, it will be done and no one will question how ill you've been, in body and spirit. 'Tis time to finish it. He'll forget about you, too. He'll forget the hurt you caused. Everything will be different. Perhaps the Crown will give Kirthgarran to James Fergusson of Lund. Coll will find a way to resign his commission. Andrew and Anne will have their bairn. Alistair will return with Nancy and take up his life again. The families will stay together and there will be no more hurt, for any of us."

I said, "I think, Mairi, you have lost your reason."

The muzzle of the pistol came once again to my head. "You ken nought of a mother's love for her child! Everything I have done has been for my Coll."

Deliberately I let the dishes fall from my hands. They

crashed at our feet, shattering, and the tea laden with the lethal belladonna flew everywhere. "What you have done has caused only more despair. And as for love for a child," I added, "I have no child because you have taken it from me."

I pushed myself away, and heedless of the porcelain slivers underfoot, I ran. I did not care if she fired her pistol. I sought the head of the stairs.

In the passage I heard a voice calling "Mam? Keeley?" It was Coll.

I ran to the top of the staircase.

He was there on the first floor, beginning to climb up the steps, his hair and the shoulders of his black greatcoat encrusted with snow. I took a step downward and his eyes found mine.

Her voice came behind me. She cried, "Even he cannot save you!"

My foot was sliding down to the next step when I heard the whoosh and crack of gunpowder. My left shoulder was pounded from behind, heaving me off-balance. I found myself thrown against the wall, where a hole burst open in the wood with a violent spray of splinters. I was unable to stop from falling sideways. I felt Coll's hands seize me, lose their grip. Down and down I went. It seemed such a long way to the bottom. But Coll was there, calling to me.

He lifted me and pressed me against his body. "What have you done?" came his voice.

"You do not have to go," Mairi cried. A metal object clattered down the stairs. "Can you not see? With her gone there's no reason for you to go. She bewitched you, and Rabbie, too, and would have been the cause of death for both of you if I'd let her."

"You want her *dead?*"

"I've wanted her gone for months, ever since I saw the effect she had on you. And when Rabbie died, when it was her fault, I knew it must happen. I want you to be happy, Coll! That is all I ever wanted. Those who've brought you such pain as she has— Leslie, those four-legged De'ils of Ewen's—they don't deserve to live. I want you safe and happy and free from harm. Coll, I am your mother! There is nought I would not do for you!"

"What is this?" Coll said, clutching me closer. "What are

you telling me?"

"I do not want to lose you..." Her voice thickened. "I would have done it for Andrew, for Alistair..."

"Damn your wants," Coll roared. "There's no time for this! If she dies, I swear, Mam, you're the one I'll curse to hell and beyond!"

"No..." she exclaimed, and the word became a moan.

Everything was strangely blurred. Coll's anxious face came near mine and grew dim; I could not answer a question I was sure he was asking me. When I heard Mairi begin to beg something amidst her wild sobs, I let myself glide into sleep within the circle of Coll's arms.

I thought I was in a boat. I was lost at sea. The boat rode up and down upon the waves. Sometimes the mist was so thick about me I could see nothing, but I was afraid to cry out.

Voices came and went. At times I knew someone was with me and I felt safe because then the sweat that poured off my body did not frighten me, nor did the beating in my head, nor the searing pain in my shoulder. Nonetheless, the boat still rocked and the waves carried me on and on, and I was wary of moving lest the rocking become too severe and the bodily agony too sharp.

I had lapses into consciousness. Sometimes the fever did not seem so great and I realized Airig was beside my bed, pressing cloths of cool water to my face, and just as often there was Coll, with his taut fingers covering my own. I did not speak, but it seemed to be unimportant; he was with me and that was enough.

Once I awoke from a hot, distorted dream to feel the pain in my shoulder. Coll was there and I felt I had to speak to him. I had to tell him something but I could not make myself understood.

He said, "Hush," and tenderly held me. In a voice low and soft he began to sing.

> *Wheesht, wheesht, my ain love-lowe,*
> *Wheesht, wheesht my love.*
> *Thou art winter-shadit*
> *As the wind forever blows.*
> *Wheesht, wheesht, my bonnie lassie,*

> *Wheesht, wheesht, my love,*
> *Sleep beneath my rawchan,*
> *Sleep sae doucely.*

I listened to the soft timbre of his voice and as he coaxed me I forgot what had troubled me and fell into a quiet, dreamless sleep.

Another time I woke to hear him talking to me. He was watching me uneasily, holding my hands, telling me about Lord Kirthgarran's and Rab's funeral and how dismayed he had been by my wrath, how critically he had blamed himself for my disillusionment. He had seen the pain in my eyes across the hall the following day and blamed himself for putting it there. He had gone away to Rathdale and tried to forgive himself, but it had not been forthcoming, especially when the Rathdale cottage had burnt. He'd been convinced I'd destroyed it.

He had hoped I would meet him by the loch when he returned from his recruiting as he'd written in his letter, but when he could not find me that night he'd become despondent and had started back to Rathdale. Lachlan had later overtaken him with news of my attempted suicide. He had ridden back to Kirthgarran. Suffered whilst he waited. Become convinced that I had tried to end my life. He had been even more assured of it once he'd been able to speak to me alone. But my words had confused him, and when he'd had time to sit by himself and think them over, he had realized something was wrong. He came to believe that someone had indeed struck me and pulled me into the water.

"And then you were missing, gone from your bed, and all I could think of was that the same person had lured you away, taken you, hurt you. I was not sure of who to trust. I bid Airig and Sandy to help me find you, and when MacNeil claimed someone had stolen Dominie, Sandy and I rode out to look for you. I knew you were running from me, and I could not understand it. But I thank God Sandy found you, my dear heart. Thank God he came back to fetch me. If only I'd been a few moments sooner. If only I could have stopped her..."

He lowered his head and his voice was on the verge of breaking. "I love you so. You must get well, Keeley. Stay with us."

I opened my lips and tried to tell him that I wanted to, more than anything. I yearned to remind him that I had gone to the lochside because I loved him, and in spite of all my fears I had never ceased to love him. But nothing came from my tongue.

He seemed to realize my struggle and held me closer. "Not now. You must not waste your strength. We've given you quite a strong tincture and the fever is still with you. Here, have a drink of this water. Lay your head back down."

I wanted to say I forgave him, and that I never wanted us to be parted again but my voice was nonexistent. Exhausted, I lay my head against his arm and closed my eyes.

One morning I awoke with my mind surprisingly clear and my body damp with perspiration. I saw the rose-colored bed curtains and knew I was at Rathdale. My boat-dream melted away. I discovered that a bandage swathed my shoulder and I probed the length and breadth of it with my fingers. My feet had been wrapped as well.

I was in Christopher and Eleanor's old chamber and today everything looked brighter, sharper. There was a fire burning in the fireplace. Unhampered white sunlight streamed through the narrow window. I looked up and there was Anne at my side.

She smiled. "Oh aye," she said. "Andrew and I have returned. I'm with you, now."

I tried to smile a little and found that I could.

"I'm glad to see you awake," she said. "You do look better."

"I can talk."

"That is good news! You'll recover quickly now. I've been frightened, but Airig never gave up hope, and she and Coll tended you tirelessly. He sent word to us and there was no question but that Andrew and I must return."

Later she brought me clear broth and fed me small spoonfuls. As she dipped the spoon she said, "Andrew says you must stay here at Rathdale for as long as you wish."

I looked up at her. "There is so much, so much I wish I knew."

"If you've the strength for it, we can talk a little."

"I must know, above everything else, what has become of Mairi."

She sighed and her lips began to droop. "We discovered what she did, to you, to Rab. You must have been terrified. None of us could believe what has been going on in her mind—for years! She told Coll everything. But with the telling she realized he was becoming wild, and his fury seemed to turn her mind for the worse. He told her if you died he would never be able to look at her again. She's not mended from that blow. She's retreated into the past. She does not know me when I go to her."

"Is she quite mad, then?"

"Quietly so, I'm thinking. She minds nought of the past few years. She believes Christopher is still alive, gone for a visit to his isle and bound to return soon."

"Oh, Anne."

"I cannot abide to see her very often. She's at Kirthgarran. Her sister has come to stay with her until it can be decided what must be done, and Andrew has been to see a friend of his, a solicitor, to talk in confidence about what could happen."

"What do you think will be done?" I asked, finding I could not take any more of the broth. The memory of her holding Christopher's pistol to my head was coming back to me with swift lucidity.

"Andrew says it will be up to you to decide. In the eyes of the law she'll be considered dementit. If she's turned over to the courts she'll be found unfit for trial, and a place for her to be sequestered will be sought. If Andrew's Aunt Molly is willing, Mairi can be given into her care instead. There would really be no need for an examination or a trial. Mr. Bain says his advice is to send her away where she can do no more harm, to live out her life in this state of fantasy she seems to have created for herself. Unless..."

"Unless?"

"You desire her to be arrested and taken to Inverness, where she'll be questioned and then sent to be cared for by strangers. But you must not think of it now. Wait until your head is clear. She is protected the now, and cannot harm anyone. Yet, the upheaval she's caused is unbearable. I ask myself, what must her life have been like to bring her to this insanity? She loved Christopher perhaps too intensely."

"You must know everything, then, even that Coll and I—

that we..."

"Aye," she said. "I do know now. And I suppose it is not difficult to understand. You were fooled into wedding Rab. And your heart chose someone else. Another day, when you're stronger, we'll talk of it, I promise."

I nodded, uncertain. "I was not a good wife to Rab. Mairi was not wrong about that. It was because I wounded him, and Coll, that she wished me gone." I glanced at Anne. "Perhaps you blame me, as well."

She frowned and shook her blonde head vigorously as she leant forward. "No, no, no, you'll not get far on that path. Be quiet now, and throw those ill thoughts from you! I love you, Keeley, and am so glad you're alive. If you think I blame you for caring for Coll you are very much mistaken. How could anyone have predicted what Mairi would do?"

I lay back weakly. "I have so many questions, and there is so much to tell..."

"Another day," she insisted. "We'll have plenty of days, you and I, to examine everything."

She was right. I drew a breath and tried to loosen my shoulder, which had begun to burn.

I felt better the next day. I began to take an interest in my surroundings. Andrew came to see me and expressed his distress at my wounds and subsequent illness that his mother's unsound mind had caused. I was relieved I could finally face him with all of my suspicions removed. At last there were no more secrets to haunt me.

I did suffer unspeakable guilt, however, when I thought about how I had wronged Coll. Now that I could put coherent thoughts together and voice them, I wanted nothing more than to explain to him why I had turned from him as I had. He had poured out his heart to me when he thought I was about to die, but I had not been able to console him.

When Anne came to see me in the afternoon I said, "Do the people in the glens know about Mairi?"

"They do. They shake their heads and greet for her. And yet they cannot understand the workings of her mind."

"How does she fare at Kirthgarran? Does she remember

her sons? Do they visit her? Has Coll forgiven her?"

"She sits at the window, waiting for Christopher. Andrew visits her and she talks to him as if he were a young lad. And Coll—he cannot forgive her, no, cannot even see her, but mayhap with time..."

"Anne, where is he? He did not come yesterday. Did he come the day before? The days run together. I cannot remember."

Her reluctance to answer forced me to rise a little in my bed. She appeared to bolster her courage. "Coll has been gone for almost a week now. He's joined his regiment."

I had not considered that time stopped for no one.

"I did not want to tell you until I thought you strong enough," she went on. "And he made me pledge to wait until you asked."

I tried to sit up straighter. "He did not say farewell."

"He did. I left him with you, but it seems you do not remember. He stayed until the last possible moment, putting off bringing in his recruits for as long as he could. He was fearful for you, but he saw you improving, and knew you were no longer in danger. He's told Lachlan to fetch him if you grow worse again."

"But he's gone—to Argyll?"

"It must be a shock. I am sorry. But he could wait no longer. There was not enough time to do aught else. They expected him in Argyll and the regiment is going to Glasgow. He had men to bring in. And he thought, oh dear, he thought you would feel sad, but he said it's for the best, that after all, he and the others used you and there's no forgetting that. 'The best thing she can do,' he said, 'is to start anew and be the Countess of Kirthgarran, and put all of this behind her.' He said for you it must be the fifth deception, that Mairi tried to kill you. I'm not sure what he meant by that. He said it was something even he could not pardon, something done by his own mother. How could you ever forgive her, or him? Later I did try to assure him he was taking on a guilt he had no right to, that what his mother did was no fault of his. But he turned a deaf ear and took on the blame, and forced himself to think of his duties toward the regiment. He had the look of a man facing the gallows. I hated to see him go. Even Andrew's pleadings to reconsider his commission made no difference. He kissed your closed eyes and joined the men waiting outside."

I'd not yet told him I had forgiven him. And he thought there was another offense I would add to my list. How troubled he must be to believe I would blame him for something about which he had known nothing.

Anne crossed the room. "He left you something. He told me to give it to you when you asked after him." She went to the mantle and reached for a small object. She placed it in my hands.

I knew what it was. I unwrapped the circle of brass from the fragment of leather. I could hear him talking to me. My unsteady fingers caressed the texture of the thistle, the crown, the words. *"Quicquid Aut Facere Aut Pati,"* they professed. Whatever is to be performed or endured. Coll was saying, "Endure."

The room faded round me. My head was throbbing and so was my shoulder. I lay back as my fingers gripped the bonnet badge. The words were wrong. He was wrong. Losing him: that was something I could not endure. "I cannot," I said aloud. "I cannot."

And Anne held me whilst I grieved.

And they looked sae braw as they marched awa'.
The drums they did rattle and the pipes they did blaw.
Which caused poor Mary for to weep and say,
"I will follow my Hieland soldier."

The Hieland Soldier (Trad.)

Chapter Forty-Five

"Where is he now?" I said out loud. Dawn had arrived and sounds of activity rose from Rathdale's kitchen. I could picture him in his uniform surrounded by others like him, men whose conversations revolved round battle readiness and arms and the subcontinent. Perhaps he was leading his men on a march. Perhaps he was in Glasgow, billeted in a tavern or someone's home. But what might be in his mind I could not imagine. He had left his home thinking I could not forgive him. He had left behind a mother who had killed, for him.

Before breakfast I asked Anne for pen and paper and stubbornly struggled with the task of writing. At first I could not make the words sound as I wanted them, and wasted valuable time until I resolved that it did not matter how refined they appeared.

On a new sheet of paper I finally scrawled the barest message possible. I had forgiven him as soon as I had lashed out at him in the stable that night. Mairi's subsequent attempts on my life had so frightened me I had been unable to confide in him, or anyone. But I loved him—and somehow we must not be parted unless it was his wish.

I sealed it and gave it to Airig who promised to leave then and there for Kirthgarran. She was to put it into Lachlan's hands and implore him to find Coll.

I waited. It seemed forever I waited. Now that I felt myself mending I chafed because it was not rapid. My shoulder was healing but I was weak. Anne and Airig placated me but I was not content with sympathy, and every day I attempted to rise a little and eat heartening foods in an attempt to restore myself. I viewed my recuperation as disappointing, but it was only so because I wished it to be instantly accomplished.

I dreaded those afternoons when Airig bathed the cuts on the soles of my feet. Even worse was when she changed the dressing on my shoulder, putting in fresh lint and wrapping it with linen soaked with oil. The wound throbbed and sent burning tentacles up and down my neck and arm. I would always have a ragged scar beside my shoulder blade but I did not care. There was only one matter of any importance in my life.

I watched a little snow fall. Several days passed and Lachlan did not return. I was able to stay up for longer periods and I spent them at the window, watching. I wanted to go to Argyll myself. I counted the days, several times a day.

A fortnight after his departure Anne rushed into the room. "It's Lachlan," she said breathlessly. "Should he come up?"

"Help me with my dress and I'll go down." My feet had healed considerably and I was able to walk without much pain. I ran down the stairs. My heart was touched when I saw Lachlan. He was unkempt and windblown and frost glittered on his moustache.

"I came here first," he said. "I knew you'd be waiting."

"Did you give him the letter?"

Lachlan did not reply at once and I sat heavily on the settle. The jarring reached my shoulder though I had anchored my arm with my hand.

"I could not give it to him because I could not find him."

"Was he not in Argyll?"

"I learnt as soon as I arrived that the regiment had marched on to Glasgow. I decided to follow, since their pathway was clear. They'd been taking on recruits as they'd gone, and leaving disappointed lads too young to join moping along the waysides. I reached Glasgow, too late. They'd had orders to march to Grangemouth."

"So soon!"

"From there they were to sail to England, to Chatham. I went to Grangemouth. But again, I was too late."

I said the terrible words. "They have sailed to Chatham."

"And from there to the East Indies," he finished.

"It is too late."

"Everyone is in a hurry. The regiment was not up to full strength, but they sent it on in any case, leaving only a recruiting company behind. It was never even reviewed. There are about four hundred men in the detachment. I checked the manifests again and again, and aye, Captain Coll Fergusson was indeed dispatched with his regiment."

"And even if you went to England..."

He shook his head. "'Twould be useless. They are on the seas already."

Anne came to me. My body had gone numb and I barely felt her anxious touch. The final truth came clearly. I had lost him. We had lost each other.

How slowly the months went by. January gave way to February. Reverend Cameron brought us word that Charles Stuart had died in Italy, ending hopes for all lingering Jacobites. The Bonnie Prince would not be returning to wrest the crown of the British Isles from the German usurper; his brother had joined the Church; there were no more descendents of James.

Sometimes I thought about Mairi.

I visited her once, before her sister Molly took her away. I had been warned of her decline but I was unprepared for the change I saw in her. With courtesy I greeted Molly, her constant companion behind the locked door, but my concentration was stolen away by the white-capped figure at the window.

Beside me, Andrew said, "Mam. There's someone to see you."

The face that turned to me was gaunt. Unfocused eyes gradually beheld my own and I realized how absurd had been my trepidation at seeing her again, at being in the same room with her. This was not the same woman who had threatened me and spoken of death. A smile spread on her lips and she rose from her seat. "Lady Nóra!" she cried. "I've not seen you or your father for days!"

I found it impossible to move or take the hands she offered me, but she did not seem to notice. She beckoned me farther into the chamber and glanced through the rain-speckled window.

"I was waiting for Christopher. I thought he might come today. I've been sewing a great deal but it seems to be bothering my eyes, so now I'm contenting myself with watching the path along the loch, and waiting. You look fine, lamb, and I've missed you. Come, come sit with me and we can talk about your drawings. Have you any new ones to show me?"

I caught Andrew's eye and saw the sadness there. He had not envisioned his mother mistaking me for my own. For a few moments I sat with her and pretended, answering questions simply and with compassion. She was serene in her fantasy and chatted complacently, becoming agitated when she mentioned Coll's name.

"I'm thinking Alistair has been keeping himself occupied with his books, under Master Anderson's nose. 'Tis a joy to know he's applying himself so. And I'm thinking Rabbie is off racing the earl's horses. Lachlan has been for tea, and so has Andrew, though I tell them I must stop being indolent and check the aumries and the larders, and tell Lord Kirthgarran to look at the beams in the nursery, for I've noticed woodworm there. But Coll has not come. Have you seen him? Perhaps it's foolish of me to expect him. Is he at the university?"

"I'm sure he will come when he can," I said.

"I thought he was home from St. Andrews. I forget sometimes. I wish he was home. He'd like to see his father. And

Christopher—Christopher will be here shortly."

She turned back to her casement, twisting the locket at her bosom. Her expression was puzzled. After several minutes I knew she had forgotten me.

When the door was shut and Andrew and I walked away, I could not hide my distress. I had thought I would remain angry and vengeful, but just the opposite was true. I said up to him, "We cannot bring charges against her. How would she survive a court with advocates and judges pelting her with questions? I think we must listen to the advice of your friend, and send her away with her sister if indeed Molly is willing to take care of her so."

"Are you certain about this?" he asked, slowing his steps. "Mind what she has done."

"Nothing will bring back those who have suffered at her hands. And there is an illness within her, something that affects her mind. For how many years has it been there, I wonder?"

"'Tis impossible to ken. If Molly and William keep her, she will be safe, you can be assured."

We had reached the drawing room and I turned to face him. "We must tell Douglas Hamilton that she is the one responsible for Leslie's death. And get word to his parents in France. It will end years of blame toward Coll."

"Of course. I'll attend to that at once."

The truth would be a blow for them but provide healing in the end. They would be able to bury their innocent Leslie where she belonged, and her ghost would no longer wander her castle's passages in anguish.

I sighed. "Where will Molly and William take her?"

"If you're willing, to a cottage in Strath Gruagach. One that's been empty for over a year. William has saved a little and he and Molly could take her there, perhaps grow some corn and keep a few cows. Would you be averse to that idea?"

"She would be close enough, and yet removed."

"Until the end of her days, my lady. I cannot think they will be happy ones for her, but if she is not aware, if she believes she is waiting for our father, then they will not be that much different from those of her youth."

"You will visit her. That will bring her happiness."

"I'll visit her, as I do now. But I envy her, I suppose. She alone has been able to forget that she has slain two people."

More than two, I told myself. "One can hope, for her sake, that her forgetfulness will continue. And you are not the only one," I went on, trying to keep my voice even, "who envies it."

Alistair came back from Oban with his wife. I left him the freedom of Rathdale House and returned to Kirthgarran Castle where I received him once, a brief moment in the banqueting hall when I was introduced to his Nancy, a pouting, auburn-haired young woman who could not do much more than curtsey and glare at me with suspicious eyes.

"Andrew tells me," Alistair said politely, "that Mam destroyed your clarsach."

I did not expect such a statement. I nodded.

"Is it beyond repair? May I see it?"

Sandy retrieved it from its hiding place for me and Alistair drew his fingers along the chipped soundbox. He turned it at every angle and squinted as he examined it. "Let me have it for a bit. You mind how canny I am with a blade."

I thought of the gifts he had carved for me in Melrose. Undoubtedly they had been doomed by Mrs. Taggart's prophecy of fire and no longer existed. I had misgivings about turning the clarsach over to him but there was no reason to keep it as it was. I gave it a last glance and turned away.

February faded into March. I slept in my old chamber and Airig and Ròs kept me company during the daylight hours. Grizel cooked the meals and Lachlan busied himself with affairs on the estates. There was much to be done now that the farmers had agreed to buy a flock of Cheviots, and the men spent the early spring planning for their purchase, transport, and arrival. But how empty Kirthgarran Castle seemed. How quiet the passages, the hall, the drawing room, and library. I tried to take an interest in my lands and tenants. I helped Ewen write letters to the British Wool Society. My mind wandered, though, when I listened to the men discussing seeds and planting and how well the black cattle had fared through the winter months.

I survived. Yet every day I held Coll's Fraser badge in my hands and envisioned his ship sailing farther and farther away.

The days were very much like one another. Once upon a

time I had looked forward to spring, that season when the earth comes alive once more. March was a month of hunger when stores ran dry and one wondered if there was enough feed for the cattle, sheep, and horses. It was the time when as I child I had listened for the green plovers—the teuchats—whose return predicted the storms of rain and sleet that could kill new lambs overnight.

But it was the beginning of the end to winter, an interval of transition when I usually awaited sprouts of green from the earth and the appearance of birds: oystercatchers who flew noisily about overhead as they vied for territories or posed and preened comically on the ground; blackheaded gulls soon to display brown heads and crimson beaks and legs. Mamma had loved the curlews, I remembered. They always came one at a time, and eventually gathered into flocks at eventide. As soon as they paired and built their nests they seemed to float in the sky, calling with cheerful, musical voices. Before long April would make itself known. The hawthorns would begin to show more than just a blur of green and the birks and geans would burst into leaf. Spring would be upon us with summer at its heels. This particular summer, if all had gone well, I would have been delivered of a son or daughter.

Mamma and I had always embraced the rebirth of the world, leaving the house and everything behind to revel in it. And now I sat at Kirthgarran and welcomed nothing. I did not care what the days brought. My ears could not hear the comfort Mr. Cameron offered, my eyes were unable to find it any book.

It was with this feeling I looked up from my chair in the drawing room one night and discovered Sandy standing before me. He was holding a woolen-wrapped bundle.

I could not regard my father-in-law without being reminded of our losses. Since my return to Kirthgarran he had gone about his daily responsibilities with a resolute but drained appearance. I was aware that he had sat with Mairi every evening before her uneventful exodus to Strath Gruagach, and though he'd said not a word to anyone about her, the experience had been difficult for him.

The week before, he had caught me standing in Coll's forsaken bedchamber, holding the worn, leather coat the

Captain left behind. He himself had come to gaze upon Coll's belongings, I did not doubt, and for a number of moments we had both stood, accepting each other's presence, remembering, and praying.

"I would make my peace with you, Sandy," I had said, putting Coll's coat on the back of a chair.

He'd shaken his head and answered, "Your sins, or lack of them, are betwixt you and our Maker. Rab wed you out of trickery and could not leave the women and the drink alone. Do I blame you for all that happened? How could I?" He had bowed and left me, but I had felt oddly soothed, and since then I had found my embarrassment in his company beginning to wane.

He held the bulky parcel away from his chest. "Alistair has brought this back and wishes me to give it to you."

"It's the clarsach."

"Aye."

For a moment I could not move. "Is he here, Sandy?"

"He gave me this and said he was away home."

I lifted my hands a little and he placed the instrument on my lap. A part of me did not want to look beneath the wool to see what changes had been wrought to my old friend, though I knew nothing could be as hideous as the cuts left by Mairi's knife.

"I'm afraid to have even a keek at it."

"He's very particular, our Alistair. He always had a fondness for wielding his knife through a stump of wood or a length of stick, and spent many an hour perfecting the skill. If he's returned it, it means the result has satisfied him."

I held my breath. I pulled away an edge of gray wool to reveal the oak beneath. Corner by corner I unwrapped the shape until the wool hung over my knees and the clarsach lay gleaming, completely disclosed.

How Alistair had managed it I could not envision. Where gouges and nicks had once textured the bonny wood there was now a polished, silken surface. The carving of the beast underneath was clarified, reshaped, chiseled, with no doubt remaining that it was a dragon that dwelt there. From some secret source Alistair had procured new strings, and the brass stretched like threads of gold from soundbox to pins.

Sandy was examining it in admiration as well. "Aye, he's done a fine job of it. Will the sound of it be changed, do you think? He's taken away some of the wood."

I plucked a pair of strings and the resulting discord was acute. "It must be tuned. But I cannot think how I can be disappointed. See how he has carved away the ugliness. He has done it lovingly, and kept the character of it. I must thank him. In some way tell him how astonished I am, and how grateful."

"'Tis a small price for him to pay. Do not be too free with your gratitude."

I rested my fingers on the familiar pegs and said, "I would think you'd be eager for me to absolve him, as I seem to have absolved the others."

"It is for you to say, in the end," he admitted. "But my loyalties to Mairi's sons have never blinded me. Take your time with this one. He'll not be the worse for it." A corner of his mouth lifted in a roguish grin, and I could not repress the smile that crept to my own lips.

It stared at me, the clarsach did. It glared at me from its tabletop in my room as it never had before. Proud in its new skin, it taunted, "Play me. You have wanted to. Here I am now, waiting for it to happen."

To silence its acerbic mocking, I took it onto my knees one day. I turned the key on every one of its pins. I drew my fingers across the strings, played a scale, and dropped into a hesitant version of "The Wee Cock."

For two hours I played. The music both consoled and devastated me. Behind the chime of the strings I could hear Coll's whistle weaving in and out like a silver filament capturing notes as if they were pearls, binding them together. Sometimes I could hear his voice singing with mine.

I made the mistake of playing the song I had written about our afternoon by the waterfall and was conveyed back to the top of the hills where the linn splashed into the pool and the pines spread their red branches overhead. The longing I felt was intense and I could not continue.

"Mamma?" I called. I pulled the clarsach away from my

shoulder, hazily aware of the ache of my healed wound. "What am I going to do?"

I tread the muddy tracks on the hillsides. I knelt beside the graves of Lord Kirthgarran and Rab on the wee island. I turned the pages of the Fergusson Bible and re-read the names of those who had lived and died.

I tried to think what my mother would have said to me. I attempted to visualize her beside me as I stood at the edge of the garden and watched the March drizzle soak into the idle earth. "What should I do?" I said aloud into the rain.

There was a voice in the dripping air. "About what?"

It was not Mamma's, but wee Iain's. He stood behind me, studying me with bright eyes and pink cheeks. He was carrying a porringer of grain for the geese.

I lowered myself to his eye level and wiped a smudge of dirt from his chin. "I'm feeling lonely, Iain. I miss Lord Kirthgarran. And Rab. And the Captain."

He nodded with the wisdom of an aged man.

"I wish I knew what to do. To stop myself from missing them," I rambled.

He smiled, showing his new, half-grown front teeth. "I miss Captain Coll, too. But he told me if I did, I was to tell Sandy, and he would write it in a letter for me, and when next Mr. Cameron came to the castle he would take the letter away and it would go half round the world to find him wherever he was."

"Then perhaps that is what I should do."

"The Captain said he'd write back to us, and that he'd write a letter just for me. The others cannot write letters, not Rabbie nor Lord Kirthgarran. But Captain Coll can. He promised he would."

"It is true. The others cannot write."

I stood, thinking of his words. I could think of nothing in the following days but those words.

I collected Andrew, Lachlan, Sandy, and Ewen in the drawing room. I drew myself up before them and spoke the words that would change my life. "I am going to India."

Four pairs of eyes enlarged with astonishment.

Andrew, seeking to comprehend, said, "You want to find Coll."

"I must."

He shook his head. "It is not done, my lady. A woman alone—a land of savagery—it is impossible. Why not a letter..."

"I've made the decision. I have to find him."

"You cannot," Ewen fumed. "Just as Andrew says, a woman alone cannot do such a thing. And think of the estate. Kirthgarran's future will be in the hands of the Crown if something should happen to you."

I said emphatically, "I ken you mean to show your respect and affection toward me, but hear me, all of you. I am asking for your approval, aye, but I will go without it if I must. Now that I have decided, nothing will hinder me."

"You take the risk of giving up all of this," Ewen said, "for going after a mere man, for listening to your heart instead of your mind? You intend to put yourself in danger and imperil all our lives here, merely to ease some emotional quandary?"

"You must not do this," Andrew said.

"I am going to do this. I will find the money and leave the estate in your capable hands. I am going without delay, and there is nothing that will change my mind. If I die this day Kirthgarran will go to the Crown, aye. If I die in fifty years, Kirthgarran will go to the Crown because I will still be a widow, I will still be childless. There is no one for me but Coll."

They thought me mad perhaps, as mad as Mairi who clung to a love that no longer existed. Yet I did not care. I made plans. I visualized going to the headquarters of the 74th in Glasgow to find out exactly where the first detachment was placed in India. I imagined selling my wedding ring, my mother's brooch, the ruby and pearl necklace, and the silver brushes—anything I could without jeopardizing Kirthgarran's financial state. I wondered from whence the next ship would depart for the East Indies, and how soon. They would have to lock me within the castle walls to prevent me from leaving. I contemplated their set faces, drawing strength from my own stubbornness.

Sandy raised his head a bit. "You cannot go, Lady Kirthgarran."

"I am going. To Coll."

"Not alone. Not without one of us. I'll go with you, if you've no objection, but you cannot, cannot go alone."

I was unable, at first, to grasp what he was saying. He returned my look steadily and I realized at last he was my ally, my only one at the moment. I also knew that, having decided to give me his loyalty, he would never waver.

"We will find him," I said fervently. "Alive and well. We will, Sandy."

"I've no doubt of it," he said.

My farewell was a poignant one. As I stood round my family, servants, and friends, I was struck afresh by my love for Kirthgarran and the inhabitants I was leaving behind. I had no qualms about placing Kirthgarran in Andrew's care, but it was a part of me now, and I was not sure when I would see it or any of the folk again.

Anne and I clasped each other and I urged her to write to us as soon as her bairn was born. Airig, Ròs, and Grizel took turns grasping me unashamedly amongst great sobs, and wished us a safe journey and luck in finding the Captain free from harm. The others, Kenneth, MacNeil, Gordon, Donald, a gathering of Fergussons from the glen—even Ewen Drummond, with his long eyebrows twitching in suppressed irritability—called out humble parting wishes.

Isabel stood by the ruined stone wall, and when I glanced toward her she turned her head and walked away.

I found it awkward meeting Kirstie's eye, knowing how fervently she wished herself to be in my place. We had not spoken alone since my visit to her house.

"God go with you," she murmured, pressing my hand with hers. "May He keep you safe, you and the Captain both."

Wee Iain at my knee deserved a special embrace, and I knelt on the ground to bind him to my breast and dab the tear from his dark eye. "I will write to you," I told him, "and it will be your own letter, just your own, not meant for anyone else. And so you must learn to read, to prepare for its coming."

"I will," he said in a bit of a voice.

"I have something for you. But first you must guess which hand it is in." I withdrew sweeties from my pockets, held out my fists, and chanted words my mother had spoken dozens of times to me.

> *Neive-neive-nick-nack.*
> *Which hand will ye tak'?*
> *Tak' the richt, tak' the wrang,*
> *And I'll beguile ye if I can.*

A smile barely broke on his lips. He pointed to my left hand and I opened it to reveal a half-dozen sugared almonds. I gave him the four that were in my right palm as well.

Andrew and Lachlan waited patiently. They were the most difficult to leave.

With sudden ardor Lachlan crushed me to him and I became breathless, squeezed in his massive arms. "I should be the one to go with you," he said.

I pushed myself away to shake my head at him. "But to whom else can I entrust my castle? You must stay, to keep the towers and battlements safe from marauders, to keep the lands together and free from plunder. I commit my holdings to you, dear Lachlan, for I know you will keep them as your own." I was horrified to see that his eyes were over-moist.

Andrew's embrace was hard but quick. "Are you certain you'll have enough money?"

"I think so. From the few things I have to sell and the two garrons, we're hoping to collect at least 500 pounds Scots. That's the fare for two berths to America, and so it cannot be much more than twice that for the voyage to India. Sandy has some savings, which will help."

"The bank would not be averse to extending some credit, I'm thinking."

"I'll not add to that burden. Diminishing the stable is as far as I want to go."

Solemnly he nodded.

"Say goodbye to Alistair," I urged him. "Perhaps when we return I'll feel differently about his banishment. Some time must pass, I think."

He nodded again, and stepped away.

There was no reason to linger. Kenneth helped me mount the waiting pony and Sandy heaved himself to his own. I refused to consider selling Greyfriar, so he was remaining behind. I had rubbed his nose this morning in a gesture of farewell, and stroked McKay and Dominie. Even the falcons and the cat had not gone unnoticed. I was aggrieved to leave my clarsach as well, but I assured myself that holding it once more upon my return would only add to my joy. For a moment the significance of all I was about to desert rose up and blotted out the knowledge that it was for Coll I was making this journey. When I turned the pony's head southward, the path was obscured by the tears in my eyes. I twisted once, to wave to the figures standing as still as the stones on the banks of the loch. Their arms lifted in answer.

I could not refrain from stopping on the other side of the water. Sliding on a path of March mud that cut through the flattened bracken, I finally gained the leafless shore where once Rab had brought me to point out his beloved home.

Sandy came beside me and together we looked past the isle to the opposite shore.

Sheltered by the hills of blue, the ancient oaks and rowans, and the slumbering, sculptured parkland was the tower of the castle with its bartizans and gabled wings. Traceries of ivy from the green, winter-hardened shrubbery at its feet twisted upward to the sienna chimneys.

I always enjoy looking at it from here, Rab had said. *The castle belongs there across Loch Seàrr, with the pines and the blue bens beyond. It's how I remember it when I'm not here.*

It was how I would remember it.

Finding myself once again in a room at The Black Horn brought a tumult of memories. They joined those conjured up by the sight of the Eildons and Melrose Abbey, and the Tweed banks where Mamma and I had once wandered.

"Before we go," I had told Sandy from the beginning, "I want to see Mamma's grave, and to say goodbye to Mrs. Dundas."

Together we walked from the inn to the lying-in-wife's wee house. The roads of Melrose seemed the same, yet different, as though it had been eight years since I had walked over them, not eight months. I was drawn into Mrs. Dundas's home as though she had always been keeping a place for me. It was a relief to find her unchanged, with her plump face still cheerful beneath its lap-eared cap.

Her brown eyes grew brilliant with amazement whilst I related my account of the deception fashioned by Rab and his kinsmen, Mairi's disturbed mind, and the tragedies her compulsions had brought about. Though Mrs. Dundas was amazed by these events, it was the story of Mamma's past and birthright that stunned her the most.

"Never a word," she repeated again and again. "Never a word to me of it all. I had no idea. Oh, the poor lass."

"I'm going to the kirkyard to see Mamma's grave. It may be the last time I ever go there. I do not know what will happen if—or when—I find Coll in India."

She nodded. "I go myself, from time to time. To clear away the weeds and to brush the stone clean. It does not occur, I do not think, to your da."

At the mention of him, I drew a long breath.

She tilted her head. "You'll find changes at Gilchrist House. Mrs. Taggart has begun keeping mostly to her bed with rheumatise. And he himself stays at home, and is no longer an elder. He goes to his mill from time to time but he's not the same. His hair is disheveled and he's forsaken his wig. The whiskers stubble his chin. He hasn't been seen in his gig for months. It's since you left. I think he misses you, dearie. Have you thought, that is, do you suppose you'll call on him whilst you are here?"

"I do not know." I looked away, avoiding her gaze and Sandy's. "Perhaps."

"I cannot believe he'd not welcome you."

"I must think about it," I said, too overcome to even begin to understand Father's behavior.

She did not press me. Instead, she poured ale for all of us and brought out freshly made barley bannocks, the delicate ones, with butter spread over the top, the kind that folded into crunchy tiers in one's mouth.

"Tell me," Mrs. Dundas said as she herself took a bite and sat back in her chair. "Tell me more about Kirthgarran, and this soldier you've come to treasure."

In the morning I went to the kirkyard alone. Before my imprisonment in my father's house I had been a faithful visitor to the little stone that proclaimed Mamma's name, keeping the bushes at bay and pulling the grass. I was thankful Mrs. Dundas had continued the task with loving hands.

I sank to my knees on the frosty ground, touched the chiseled letters that spelt "Caitlin Allanson," and knew that she was not truly here but in my heart. "Your father loved you," I told her. "He wanted you home again. He hated himself for what he had done to you. If only you could have known."

I thought of what Mrs. Dundas had suggested to me, that my own father might be suffering regrets.

Visions of the old days besieged me. Father, throwing a bird across the garden and taunting Mamma for her shortcomings. Father, striking Mamma because she played music with a stranger. Father, burning all of her belongings because I had disgraced him in the eyes of his neighbors. And the most bitter of all: his demand for my mother's obeisance. He had felt a need to punish her, which had perhaps cost her her life.

If I went to him, if we could talk as adults, we could accept each other for who we were. He had made mistakes, just as Lord Kirthgarran had. Possibly contrition was creeping upon him, bringing him misery just as it had my grandsire. My difficulty lay in determining just how much I could accept.

I walked alongside the river, I sat in Melrose Abbey, I galloped my garron over the meadows I had known since my infancy. All the while I imagined my mother beside me, not the woman my father had married, but Lady Nòra Fergusson, daughter of the Earl of Kirthgarran. I saw Melrose and the pastures and the birk woods through her eyes, as she must have viewed them after a happy childhood at Kirthgarran and the misfortune that befell her during her seventeenth year.

It became obvious to me what I must do.

Sandy and I rode to the gate of my old home. I suffered constricting pangs as I looked down the drive and studied the graywacke walls, the faceted windows, the steep roofs of slate. My old room faced us; there was the casement where once Young James had nailed boards across the shutters.

"This is Gilchrist House," I said. "It's where my mother came when she married my father."

"'Tis a fine place," he said.

"She believed she would be content here. She loved my father. At least, she did at first."

Sandy must have been thinking of the lass he had known, the daughter of Kirthgarran Castle. This was where she had spent the rest of her life. For a long while he said nothing as his eyes took in the pleasant house and gardens. "If Lord Kirthgarran had begun his search for her only a few years earlier he would have found her. Do you think she would have minded?"

"She would have gone home."

Sandy urged his pony to come round in a circle so he could face me. "Why have we come here, Keeley? It is not just to show me the house."

"No."

"Will you call on your father? Is that what you're meaning to do?"

I could not answer at first. I let my eyes roam over the walls, the roof, and the spreading trees that framed all. "I've come to say goodbye."

He must have understood. He remained still.

"It is God's turn," I went on, and heard my voice disintegrate as I finished, "to forgive."

I sent the last of my love to my father within, and turned my back on the house and lands by the river. It was the last time I ever sought them.

Edinburgh. A city of grime, smoke, and wonderment.

For hours Sandy and I trod upon cobblestone streets lined with towering buildings of blackened sandstone, seeking buyers for my treasures of silver and gold. The roads, wynds, and closes of the city teemed with folk from all walks of life and brought just as many odors to our noses. The cry of gulls merged with the voices of merchants, owners of street stalls, beggars, soldiers from the Castle, jugglers, noblemen, fish sellers, gentlewomen and their escorts, and obvious criminals. Whenever I came face to face with one of the latter, I thought of Rab's clasp knife in my purse. The recollection of the knife's presence, however, was always accompanied by a shriveling of courage, not a bloom of confidence.

At the western end of the Royal Mile we huddled under our

cloaks and added figures in our heads.

"Do we have enough, do you think?" I asked, disappointed at the meager number of coins in my purse.

"Let us consider," Sandy said. "If we can sell the garrons for two hundred and fifty pounds each, we'll have over seven hundred and fifty pounds Scots. The innkeeper thinks the ship fares to India will be about one thousand pounds Scots. We've no idea what lodgings, meals, and travel both here and there will cost us, but do you believe perhaps another two hundred and fifty pounds is reasonable? That would mean we need at least five hundred pounds more. We'll have to convert it to pounds sterling in England."

I brought my fingers up to my forehead in order to think. "Where are we ever to get that much?"

"There's auld friends of Lord Kirthgarran's in the city, men who'll probably lend you gold if you ask."

"They'd just be new names on a list of creditors. I could not bear the imprudence of it."

"We must return to Kirthgarran, then, and take more time finding things to sell. The silver. The longcase clock. The horses. McKay would fetch a handsome purse, and so would Dominie."

"No. I'll not take away any more from the estates."

"If you were not in such haste you could take your share of the profit from the new sheep. But that's a year away, or more. You could let Rathdale House in the meantime, and have enough by next summer. Or perhaps your kinsman of Lund will lend you the money and be more than patient with its repayment."

"I have one other hope," I said hollowly.

He crossed his arms against the wind. Mud from the wheels of a passing wagon sprayed our legs. "And what is that?"

"My half-brother, Malcolm." I was dismayed by my idea, but I could not force it away.

"I'll take you back to the inn," Sandy said after a moment. "You're exhausted. I'll go about and ask folk for his whereabouts. If I'm lucky I'll have the address by supper and we can call on him tomorrow."

I agreed. I pulled my hood over my head, hoping to hide my apprehension. We trod the curved roads down to the

Grassmarket where we were met by a fresh wind laden with the ubiquitous scents from Candlemaker Row. When we reached the north side of the square I gazed up at Castle Rock. The silhouette of Edinburgh Castle was studded with shimmering lights. The hour was nearly five o'clock; dark clouds had been gathering all afternoon and the black smoke from countless chimneys added to the gloom. I yearned for our rooms in the public house where I could enjoy a short-lived escape from the noise, the warring aromas, babble, and turbulence of this vital but terrifying city.

"If Malcolm refuses, we'll be away and think of other ways to raise the money," Sandy said as he aided me across a trench choked with dung, dead rats, and offal.

"I almost wish you'll not be able to find him at all."

He was silent until we stood before the painted door of the inn. "We'll have some strong tea, my lady," he said. "And then I think 'twill be time for you to tell me all about this half-brother of yours."

I would I were the snow-white swan
That wings the sky above me;
Then I would fly o'er sea and land
To tell thee how I love thee.
O, Tell Me Where She Rests To-night (Trad.)

Chapter Forty-Six

The courtyard we entered the next morning featured tall, gabled houses emblazoned with sculptures and doorway inscriptions. They were typical of Edinburgh, but unlike other tenements that housed rich and poor alike, the domiciles of Byer's Close seemed to hold only judges and lawyers.

We climbed steps to the third storey of one in particular and entered an elegant flat. Our feet sank into deep carpeting. Expensive books lined the walls. Sandy reassured me that his inquiries the night before had revealed Malcolm Allanson to be an advocate of irrefutable prosperity. So successful was he, Sandy had discovered, that he had lately begun to display political ambitions.

A dignified clerk allowed us to gain admittance. Two other writers looked up from their high desks and eyed us brazenly. We were asked to wait until Mr. Allanson could find a moment to receive us.

My inclination was to cringe in my chair and grasp my thumbs, yet the sight of Sandy calmly sitting opposite me was heartening enough to straighten my spine and still my hands.

I heard his voice before I saw him. When I turned my head and rose, there he was, imposing in his English-cut coat of slate and flawless, snow-white cravat. Beneath the tilted brows, Father's dark brown eyes took stock of us.

"It is you," he said, coming forward and bowing ceremoniously. "My clerk gave me your name but I hardly thought it would be my dear sister come to call."

I gave him a small curtsey, not daring to let my attention fall from his face.

Malcolm regarded Sandy and dipped his head again. "Sir. I do not think we are acquainted." His eyes came back to me and there was a glint in them. "Keeley. Where is your new husband? Surely you've not forsaken him for another?"

The heat was instantaneous in my cheeks and I stumbled with my response. "I am a widow now. May I introduce my late husband's father, Mr. Alexander Fergusson?"

"I'm sorry," he said, but he meant it more as a question. "Malcolm Allanson," he added, bowing to Sandy. He held out a hand, entreating us both to enter his study.

I am a lamb, I thought as I followed him, being led to slaughter inside the den of the lion.

"Will you have some brandy?" Malcolm asked, reaching for a crystal bottle as we settled ourselves in chairs slippery with varnish. I declined and so did Sandy. Malcolm poured one for himself, reclined in the chair behind his neatly arranged desk, and nonchalantly put an ankle across one knee. "I must be honest, Keeley dear. I thought never to see you again once you wed your braw Highlander. And now that I do, I am overcome. Mrs. Taggart's hodden gray has gone by the wayside it seems, and you've grown into an enchanting woman."

The heat was spreading to my neck, my chest. I could feel it creeping onto my limbs. "I ken you must be curious about what has befallen me since last we were together," I said. "But it's a dreary tale, and I do not presume you have the time to listen, or perhaps even the interest. I've come to ask you a favor."

"Oh no, do not presume anything so discourteous. I would love to hear your tale."

Drawing a quick breath, I began a story severely limited in detail and scope, leaving out all mention of Mamma's background and my inheritance. I finished with an abbreviated account of Rab's death at the hands of an unidentified man, and said, "He's left me with some business interests in India. I'd like to go there myself and attend to them. I'm not sure I'll ever return."

"You said you have a favor to ask of me," he replied before he took another sip from his glass.

"This is a time of need for me. I would like to borrow five hundred pounds Scots. I do not know if I can repay it, but I would like to try. I've no one else to whom to turn." The words I had practiced with Sandy seemed to slide effortlessly out of my mouth.

He raised one brow and placed the wee tumbler on his desk. With a smile that revealed his uneven front tooth, he said, "I'd have thought you would ask Father before me."

"He has disowned me. You apparently made it legal."

"Hmm." He tapped one finger and said, "True. So. You have come to me. That's quite a sum, five hundred."

"The price of a horse and gig."

"I was not planning to buy a horse and gig this year."

I leant forward and glanced at Sandy. If he had not been beside me I would have flown long before this. I said to Malcolm, "I'll not beg for it. I'm here merely to ask. As a kindness, as a gesture of friendship due to our familial bond, you might have said yes. But I can see it is not something you want to do. So I wish you good day. Remember me to your sweet wife."

I rose, but he scowled and planted both feet upon the floor. "Have patience, now. I mean to ask you some questions." He put his elbows on the desk. "Is this money to be used as an investment of some sort?"

"No. For travel only."

"Are you in difficulties? A dispute with the law?"

"No."

"Will you be traveling alone?"

"Mr. Fergusson has graciously offered to accompany me."

He bowed his head and watched me with some amusement. "I'm inclined, I think, to grant you this favor."

I thought it a trick at first and studied his face. "As I said, I cannot guarantee repayment."

"I have appointments until late this afternoon. I'll go to the Bank of Scotland then."

He was solemn. I said in a softer voice, "Could you put something on paper, to make it lawful? Can you write that there is no date by which I must recompense you, and that if I die the debt will be pardoned?"

He plunged a quill into ink and scratched a few words on a paper. "A missive. With a resolutive clause. I'll have two copies made and we'll both sign them. Is that what you want?"

I nodded, struck with amazement.

"Here is an idea," he said. "Let me take you to a late supper. There's a tavern in town that offers exquisite oysters. Have you heard of the poet Robert Burns? He's been staying in Edinburgh lately and is sure to be there tonight, though I hear he plans to go home soon. I can introduce you."

I was tempted by the idea of meeting the poet, but only for a moment. "Thank you, Malcolm, but it is not possible."

"A pity, that. It would have been a unique evening for both of us. Well, so be it. Tell me where you're lodging and I'll bring the money to you."

I hesitated. "We can return here tomorrow..."

"I'll be in court all day tomorrow. What is it? Do you not trust me? I give you my word I'll merely bring you the papers to sign, and the money."

I peeked at Sandy as my face flamed. Malcolm sighed noisily.

"So. There is a limit to our familiarity. You're minding too much of the past, Keeley. If you dread my presence in your rooms I'll send a clerk. Will we say seven o'clock?"

"I hope you're not offended."

"Where will my clerk find you?"

A final hesitation. "The White Hart."

"Well then. It seems our business is finished. I cannot interest you in a dram after all? Mr. Fergusson? It would be an agreeable way to seal our affairs."

Politely we took the proffered liqueur, and I stammered my thanks to the sibling who had done nothing but plague my life since the day it began.

Mr. Smith, one of the haughty clerks we had encountered that morning, arrived punctually at the White Hart Inn at seven o'clock. I signed the missives, gave one back to him, and was rewarded with a sheaf of over forty pounds sterling as Malcolm had promised.

"Look," I cried, showing it to Sandy. "We have enough. We have enough!"

He was as pleased as I. We shared an exultant supper of our own in the hostelry and made plans to rise early for the journey to Glasgow.

I curled up in my hard bed and found I could not sleep for all the expectations I had. The hazy future gaped before me. To realize that in a few months I would be traveling over a hot, dusty land in search of Coll filled me with excitement tinged with dread.

The grinding hours took their toll and I drifted into an irksome state between wakefulness and sleep. I was fading away at last when a tap came at my door.

I listened and it came again. I called "Yes?" in a reedy voice.

"May I come in?" whispered a masculine voice through the gap.

"Sandy?"

"Just for a moment."

Soundlessly I crossed the floor, pulling my plaid about me. As I drew back the bolt I said, "I almost did not hear you..."

The tall form of Malcolm stood before me, resplendent in fine clothes and the familiar cologne. I began to push the door back but it was no effort for him to slide into the chamber and shut it himself.

"How do you dare do this?" I protested in alarm.

"I have the same mettle as you, coming to see me today."

"You promised you'd not come."

"I've been regretting that." He was smiling. I backed away from him when he reached out a hand. "You should have joined me this evening. I sat thinking of you, have not stopped thinking of you since I saw you. We need to renew our acquaintance, Keeley. Have I not always said I find you tantalizing?"

"You must go. I warn you—you must go."

"I like what time has done to you. You're far more intriguing than when you left. Do you not want to tell me more of your story, share your adventures?" His eyes moved to the rumpled bed in the corner. "But I've disturbed you. Well, I'm sorry. It is late. I'm tired myself." His eyes came back meaningfully.

I retreated toward the bed. "Go, Malcolm."

A brighter smile appeared in the darkness and he shook his head. "Ah no. Not this time, I do not think. You're a poor widow, and I'm a man who would comfort you. And ease the wants of us both. All day I've been thinking of it and I am gyte with cravings for you."

"You're my half-brother."

"Who else can know you better? Who else could love you better?"

He advanced and I recoiled. I bumped into my feather mattress. I reached back with both hands and found what I sought under my bolster. "Will I not scream?" I said. "Will I not call out for someone?"

"The only one you will call for is me." He lunged, caught me, and pulled me to him. When I tried to twist away we revolved in a circle and my bare toes hit against his boots.

I had no air within my lungs to speak. With revulsion I saw his head coming down. Every memory from childhood assaulted me—even the suffering of my mother at the hands of our father—and the old sickness that had often risen in my throat surged again. Outrage and hatred gushed together and I brought up my hand. Malcolm became still. I pressed the point of Rab's open knife under his chin.

"De'il swarbit on you!" he cried, taking care not to move. "What are you about?"

"I'm not afraid to plunge it in, Malcolm."

He began to lift a hand and I pushed the blade upward. A

bead of blood ran down its surface, tracing a line of black in the dimness.

"Will I tell you what I'm thinking now?" I said, fighting for breath, remembering that day in our father's library when he had taunted me so.

He was silent.

"I'll bring you to your own courts with charges of rape and incest," I said. "For a man who makes his living cleverly discharging laws, how can you be so ignorant of the consequences? They still hang men in the streets here."

"Take that thing away. Wedding a savage has made you one as well."

I did not move but my thoughts were anything but still. He was a well-built man and his strength had never suffered from the years of reading and study to which he had subjected his body. He could have knocked my hand away and swept me to the floor as easily as flicking away a bee. But he did not. He was a coward. He had always been a coward. The revelation left me reconsidering all the times in my youth when I could have ended his hold over me by merely taunting him with this truth. The sudden rush of cold reason and contempt I felt for this weakness sent new courage rushing through my veins.

I said, "I have heard the story of Major Weir, the man who lived not far from here with his sister. He was strangled and burnt at the stake for what you want to do."

"That was one hundred years ago, damn you."

"But the statutes have not changed. God's law has not changed. You have goaded me my whole life and I cannot abide it! By God, I will bring up the charges."

"You've no evidence."

"I have a tongue. And you have much to lose, even if there is only a rumor. Think what the accusations will do to your wife. To your political hopes. To Father."

There was no response.

"This is the end of your consanguinean ventures," I told him. "You may demand your money back if you wish. You'll take it and go."

"I could break your wrist," he muttered.

"You'll have to do more than that to silence me," I said,

and another droplet trickled down the blade. "And there is no stuffed rabbit to hurt this time."

A voice came from the doorway. "For aught you do, Mr. Allanson, there is a witness to it."

I said without moving, "Sandy..."

"You're doing well, lass. Do not move, until he promises to take himself away."

The breath in Malcolm's nose whistled as he angrily suffered his humiliation.

"You will go, then?" I said.

"Have I a choice?"

"You are shrewd, Malcolm. You'll take what dignity you have and leave me in peace."

"You infernal witch."

"It is the Countess of Kirthgarran to which you speak," Sandy warned. "Is it your practice to address a member of the peerage so?"

I wished he had not said this, but the effect upon Malcolm was instant. His eyes widened. His hands fell away from me. "How can that be?"

"I'll give you the names of my solicitors if you wish to discover the wherefores of it. But now, tonight, I have had enough." I drew away the knife and stepped back. He stood looking at me with confusion as I veered sideways to join my steward at the open door. When Malcolm did not say anything I asked, "Do you want back your notes, and for me to destroy my copy of our agreement?"

He refused to answer. With a fist he wiped blood from the underside of his chin. Ignoring the state of his hand, he strode toward us and we gave him space for his exit. I could hear his boots pounding away down the corridor to the rear stairs.

"Sandy," I said, exhaling. I dropped the knife. "You came."

"Do you not ken I am always near, as a good steward must be? I heard something and lay awake, but was not convinced all was well. When I tried your door there you were, with a man at the end of your blade."

"A man. My brother..."

"Lord Kirthgarran would be aye proud," he said. "You've the blood of your forefathers in you, and the valor to match."

I took it with shy pleasure, this, the greatest compliment he could have ever bestowed.

We went on to Glasgow, reaching it at nightfall and luckily obtaining a pair of rooms at a hostelry where I changed my clothes and washed my face. Sandy went out to visit the Headquarters that Lachlan had sought over two months before.

He came back visibly excited. He marched into my room and cried, "You'll not believe the news I have. It is an unexpected stroke of luck!"

"Tell me..."

"Coll's detachment may still be in Chatham."

"But they were to have left in January."

"The East India Company and the Government have been embroiled in a terrible quarrel. It appears the affairs in India have not been as desperate as everyone dreaded. The French have not been sympathetic with Tipu Sahib's emissaries and they've sent no troops. The Directors of the Company have decided, in a calmer state, to be content with their own army and have informed the Government they do not want the King's troops after all. Is this not absurd? The Government paid for the raising and the upkeep until now, but it wants to turn the four regiments over to the Company. It wants it to pay for the transports to India and all future expenses. It has no wish to burden British taxpayers any longer."

"It's a question of money? What is the outcome? Has aught been decided?"

"The troops have been delayed in Chatham whilst the quarrel's been going on. The East India Company has not acted outside the law, but in order to resolve everything Pitt has had a Declaratory Bill passed through Parliament that states if any troops are needed for British security in the East Indies, the costs of raising, transporting, and keeping them are to come out of the revenues from the East Indies. Therefore, aye, the quarrel is at an end. The detachment has been waiting further orders and I was told tonight they've just been sent. The four companies in Chatham have just been ordered to embark."

Just been ordered. All of this time he had been close, and I had been such a laggard. I said, already in unbearable haste, "Do you think they'll still be there if we hurry to catch them?"

"From what I can tell the men are probably boarding now and the ships are being made ready for sea. If we hurry—if we hurry..." He was at a loss.

"We must go to England. We must start at morning's light."

He concurred, but my excitement and apprehension were so deep I could hardly sleep at all, and I was ready before the first streak of dawn.

The boat on which Sandy secured passage for us to travel from Grangemouth to England could not sail fast enough for me. Already too many days had passed to suit and I prayed that when we reached that seacoast town on London's periphery it would be to find the 74th Highland Regiment of Foot still waiting to board the East India Company transports. It did not seem possible that the regiment had been delayed in such a manner. I would never have wasted all these weeks if I had known; I would have attempted to reach Coll even before my shoulder had healed properly. I wondered why he had not written to us.

I spent the short voyage viewing the North Sea and the changing coastlines of Scotland and England with very little fascination or pleasure. I was obsessed. I was driven with the desire to attain Chatham and to discover if Coll had yet left the country.

Sandy, knowing my thoughts only too well, said, "Even if they've already sailed, all will not be lost. We'll find another East Indies-bound ship and follow. Trade is brisk and there'll surely be another soon."

I nodded, but my patience was thin. An extra day, even an extra hour, seemed too vexing.

I had no interest in Chatham. As soon as we arrived we found rooms and set out to discover the whereabouts of the 74th. In one dockside tavern after another we asked questions of men who did not yet appear too far gone with drink. The places were rife with press-gangs looking for men who would make likely sailors, and bronzed, worldly seamen who smelt of rum and debauchery. Sandy bought a draught of ale and held it up high to examine the glass bottom of the tankard.

"If I drink this and there's a shilling in it," he told me, "it means I've accepted the King's money and I'll be taken aboard ship and pressed into service in the navy."

I begged him to be careful of finding the King's shilling being thrust upon him and of wandering into the path of roving bands of sailors. In turn he admonished me to keep close to him and avoid the wandering hands of strangers.

I was losing hope until Sandy entered into conversation with an ageless sailor who seemed to understand what was being asked. We entreated him to come outside with us where the noise of revelry was decidedly muffled.

The man scraped a hand across his stubbled chin and smiled, revealing brown, misshapen teeth. He appeared pleased he could impart information that was of the utmost importance to someone. "There's three East Indiamen. The *Bridgewater*, the *Triton*, and the *Lord Macartney*. Good ships they are," he digressed in a slow, English drawl. "Built to carry merchandise as well as passengers. Eight hundred tons each of them, strongly made of English oak..."

Respectfully I interrupted, "I understand, but..."

"Square rigged, with a good number of guns. I used to be a seaman aboard one of the Company's ships, just like one of those. They pay is good on a Company ship. My mates and I were sailors by trade, and fighting men, too, when it came to pirates and the Dutch and French. Those soldiers will fare safely unless they drink too much of their rations of rum and brandy and fall down hatchways..."

Sandy nodded. "We wish to know, more precisely, if those three East Indiamen have sailed."

"They've taken the regiment aboard. They're out in the estuary."

"They have sailed?"

He shook his head and his small eyes ceased to blink as if he knew he was making us happy. "In the Downs they've put down anchor, they have. They're waiting for the wind. Just waiting for the wind."

The jolly boat cut through the salty sea air and swelling water. With my bag at my feet I sat beside Sandy and watched our hired men pull at the oars. I had no eyes for the scenery about me except for the rigged masts that grew taller as we approached them. In time, when the wind came at last, the sailors aboard would climb the ropes and unfurl the massive sails, and the ships would glide out onto the green sea.

A line from "The Blackbird" rang in my head: *"And not the wide ocean can fright me with danger."* A woman who sought her love, as I did mine, felt no fear. My only dread was hearing Coll say he would not allow me to accompany him.

"There's the *Lord Macartney*," one of our boatman said as he pointed with a dripping oar held aloft from the water. "And the *Triton*, I believe," he added.

"It's the *Bridgewater* we want," Sandy reminded him. Early this morning Sandy had met with an ensign who had been able to tell us which ship Captain Fergusson had boarded. It was supposed to be the largest of the three with room enough for two companies, with cabins for the officers and their wives.

At the sound of Sandy's voice I considered a loss I had not foreseen until several days ago. If I sailed with Coll to India we would be leaving Sandy behind. I must say goodbye to my father-in-law who had been a faithful companion and confidante these past weeks. During our trek we had shared stories about my mother and the childhoods of Mairi's sons and his, and the closeness between us had ripened to such a degree I suspected the sudden loss of him would be abysmal.

"That's the *Bridgewater*," said the same boatman, and I found the sturdily built East Indiaman, larger than the other two, floating at anchor with its three masts reaching for the sky straight and true.

My anxiety increased in those last few moments. As our boat made its way toward the weighty ship that reduced us to diminution by comparison, I was not sure what I would say to Coll. I did not know if he would welcome me. I had found him, and my anticipation was intense, but my future beyond this point was unformed, uncertain. My hands clenched the edge of the boat. After days of haste this was the finish.

I was not prepared for what occurred when we bumped alongside the massive hull. Soldiers ranged along the length of the ship called to me. Our leading oarsman had informed us that visitors to the anchored ships were not unwelcome, especially female visitors. I scanned the faces of the men banned from visits ashore whilst they waited for their lengthy voyage to begin. They mistook my purpose in coming.

Sandy asked for permission to come aboard as a sling was lowered down. He was hoisted up into the many waiting arms above, and I followed. The boatmen and my bag waited below, bobbing in the water.

On the crowded deck I looked about me uncertainly. Sandy was speaking to a ship's officer. Soldiers near me smiled, winked, offered comments, asked questions. I heard Sandy saying, "Lady Kirthgarran," and, "An officer aboard," and my eyes roved the faces, searching.

All at once I saw him, across ship, his back toward us as he stared out to sea. He seemed to be oblivious to the commotion my appearance had caused.

I began to push toward him and the men let me pass, turning aside as if they read what was on my face and in my mind. I recognized some of them, for they were recruits from Rathdale and Kirthgarran.

The cold sun shone down on Coll's burnished head. His hair had been shorn and blew fretfully about his ears in the fresh wind. The pleats of his kilt rippled as did the tails of his red coat. A pair of calling gulls circled about the tops of the masts above us, and as if he slowly became aware of being watched, he turned. His expression moved from sternness, to shock, to disbelief.

I said, "I was not sure I'd find your ship before it sailed."

"Dear God."

"I was unaware you were still in Chatham. I sent Lachlan after you but we thought you sailed months ago. I would have come sooner if I'd known about the affairs between the East India Company and the Government, but you..."

He took a step toward me. "You're not ill. Your wound..."

"It bothers me little. And yours?" I looked at his arm.

He shook his head as if it were of no importance.

I said, "I had to come to you. I had to see you."

"After everything I did to you?"

"I tried to tell you. I thought I did, before you left, but I must have only imagined it. There's so much you must not know. There's so much I need to tell you. You must understand, first, that I forgive you of everything. Everything."

Would that we were not of interest to Coll's men who looked our way and waited with growing curiosity. Sandy held them at bay, urging them to give us a moment's privacy.

Coll's gray eyes held mine steadily despite the crowd on deck. I almost forgot what I had meant to do. I slid my fingers out of the pocket of my cloak and presented my fist, palm upward. With difficulty he brought his gaze down and watched my fingers open. In my hand lay his brass Fraser badge.

I said, "You gave me something to keep for you. But I do not want it. The words mean nothing. Not without you to read them to me."

Several seconds passed. I forgot the soaring gulls and breaths of sea wind and the men behind us. I was not aware of anything but Coll's face before me and the intensity of his gaze. I felt his fingers touch my own. He did not take the badge but closed both our hands over it, hard.

"Then I'm glad you brought it back to me," he said, and the love I had craved for months was warm in his eyes and voice. He tried to speak further but could not. He raised our hands to his mouth and crushed his lips against my fingers. He closed his eyes and brought my fingers to his forehead and pressed them there, overcome. Blindly he pulled me to his chest and held me with the all the power he possessed—as if daring God and the entire British army to part us.

We were wedded, Captain Coll Fergusson and I, by the army chaplain on 4 April, 1788, the day before the first two East Indiamen sailed from the estuary.

A week later the *Bridgewater* lifted anchor and followed her sisters.

The only blight on our happiness was leaving Sandy behind. He had attended our wedding and drunk to our union along with all the sailors and soldiers on deck. Before he had taken leave of our ship he had promised to return Malcolm's loan and to reinvest the rest of the money in Kirthgarran. We had vowed to write letters to each other constantly.

"I'll be keeping your home warm and safe for you, my lady," he had said with forced cheer. "Until you and your husband return." He had placed a kiss on my cheek and gripped Coll firmly before his descent to the waiting jolly boat below. He left an inconsolable, vacant place in both our hearts.

Our voyage lasted four months and eight days, shorter than what had been foreseen but an eternity, nonetheless. Privacy was hard to find, and we were thankful for our cramped cabin where we could at least be alone at night. The rations of boiled beef and pease were monotonous and tasteless. Our vessel creaked and rocked ceaselessly upon the seas even in the best of the trade winds. There were compensations nonetheless, in my new friendships with the other officers' wives, in the dancing, singing, and storytelling on deck under exotic night skies when Pipie played his tunes and alleviated the overwhelming boredom, and in the companionship of those who had followed Coll from home.

There was time for us to consider what had happened to us after Lord Kirthgarran's death, and Coll and I spent countless hours unraveling the past.

Mairi figured largely in these exchanges. During the months the regiment had waited to receive its orders, Coll had examined the effects of his mother's secret reprisals. He had wondered throughout his entire life why misfortune always seemed to befall those who disappointed him. Some instances had seemed natural enough, such as when Ewen's dogs had been poisoned. He had believed Sandy was responsible for that. Other adversities he could never explain.

Since learning of the sickness in Mairi's mind he had come to terms with many of her actions, but he blamed himself still for what had happened to me. For this reason he had not sent a message to Kirthgarran informing us of the delay in sailing. He considered himself unworthy, and could not imagine that I had forgiven him. I was determined to convince him that I had, and I recounted the events, one by one, that had led up to the day I had sought his mother for protection.

I could not keep my miscarriage from him. He held my hands and wept with me when I related the story of my loss. It could have been his bairn. Neither of us would ever know.

"We will heal," I said when I regained my composure. "I was told that time changes us and our thoughts."

"Not even an eon can change the past."

"I believe what I was told. So far everything Mrs. Dundas has told me has come true. She said people mend and I no longer doubt her. Besides," I added, reaching into a linen drawstring bag and removing some items. "I have these." I showed him a horse hair strung with three, naturally pierced stones from the burn at Kirthgarran. "Airig forced me to take these elf stones. I do not ken if there are Fairies in India, but if there are, They'll not come near us now, nor be taking any more of my bairns." To reinforce this prediction I stubbornly planted my stuffed rabbit on my knees.

Coll looked at me quizzically, but my conviction seemed to be a beginning of comfort for him.

Our ship did not stop at any ports during the long journey. The fresh food on board dwindled away. The soldiers lounged listlessly in the canvas breeks they were allowed for the passage.

The ordeal ended when we docked at Madras, and then our lives began to center round the enigmatic country in which we found ourselves and the more familiar structure of Coll's regiment. I was indeed an officer's wife in a blistering, grimy, and bizarre place that bore little resemblance to the world I once knew.

We traveled to the cantonments of Poonamallee where a second detachment from Scotland joined us. The men were quickly trained, and Coll was one of those who defended the passes that led into the Carnatic from Mysore.

I could understand the pride he held in being one of the brave 74th, yet sometimes when I observed him riding away on a mission, or even safely reviewing his ranks of men on parade, the old stones tumbled in my stomach. I suffered every time there was to be fighting, such as when the 74th, in brigade with the 71st and 72nd Highland regiments, took part in the storming of Bangalore. I had to learn to be content with the consolation that at least we were together.

We lived in officer's quarters: a bungalow of our own on the border of the post with green shutters and a cool verandah. How different from Kirthgarran Castle it was with its high, whitewashed walls and gardens of vibrant flowers. A white frangipani tree grew next to the house and in the evenings the rooms were filled with its fragrance. I wrote lengthy descriptions in my diary of all the strange things I saw, wondrous and frightening alike: elephants, water buffaloes, and the Hindus' sacred cows; vividly-colored parrots that swooped through the trees; lizards, insects, and King Cobras; mangoes and guavas that dripped from our fingers whilst we ate them. I described the smells of the dust and the clay. The air was always filled with the scent of spices—cardamom, pepper, cinnamon, cloves, and nutmeg—and the rice, fish, and coconut from the cooking fires of the servants who lived behind the bungalows in the square. They cooked their chapattis on griddles held over burning cow dung, and the aroma joined the scent of jasmine, the sharp yet mellow bouquet of incense, and the stench of urine and sweat.

The women wore exquisite jewelry and saris in every color of the prism. Some men wore turbans. I loved to watch them and listen to the music they made with their unusual instruments. We were invited to gatherings where we were entertained by men playing two-headed, wooden drums called dholaks, bansuris—flutes fashioned out of bamboo and said to be Lord Krishna's divine instruments—and the complicated sarangi, carved from a single piece of wood and strung with forty wires. It buzzed and hummed as if it were a beehive. Despite the novelty of the sound, I longed for my gentle, melodic harp.

India was a fascinating and yet shocking place. We allowed ourselves to enjoy the pleasurable aspects but we could not escape the heat, the pests, or the diseases. Officers, soldiers, and their wives were insulated living on the post but it did not protect anyone from death. The bluidy flux, parasites, worms, and fevers were far more lethal to us than Tipu Sahib's army.

Coll and I often talked of home. Kirthgarran called to us in our dreams. Coll admitted that he did not want to spend the rest of his life on the subcontinent or even in the army. We both yearned for Scotland, hungering for the cool rains, the heathered hills, and our family. He wanted to take me back to my inheritance.

The calling grew more intense when our wee Graeme was born. India killed children. I had seen bairns die from inexplicable fevers and from nothing at all. The army doctors could do little to prevent it.

We kept Graeme away from the barracks children and hired a clean Indian ayah to attend him. We covered his wee cot with mosquito netting and made sure he did not become overheated. I often held him close, stroking his fair hair and thanking God for him, and begging Him not to take him away from us.

"We're going home," Coll promised. "I've already warned them. When the end of this turmoil is in sight I'm resigning my commission."

Tipu Sahib was defeated at Seringapatam in May of 1791, and six months later we boarded a ship bound for the British Isles.

At the end of April we halted on the bank of Loch Seàrr and looked across the water at the castle that had survived for centuries and would endure for centuries more.

There would always be a shadow over us—the memory of Rab, the shame of our wrongdoing, Mairi's damaging vengeance—but today the grass was green and the hills were dyed blue from the sun shining through the mist. We gazed at the sheep speckling the slopes and the fold of black cattle grazing beyond. Coll stood beside me and our young son bounced up and down in excitement at our knees. Another bairn within me kicked with tiny, adamant feet.

Coll looked down and smiled. "Graeme," he said as he put out a hand to catch our son. He knelt and brought his body against his. "Do you ken what that is, lad?"

"'Tis a castle."

"Aye. It is indeed. It's home. It's Kirthgarran."

He gave a little gasp. "Like in the stories?"

"There is no other."

"And are we going to stay there? Always?"

Coll took a moment to answer. "We'll never leave it again."

Wee Graeme, descendent of Kirthgarran's blackbird and the long line of Fergussons who came before, took his father's hand. He glanced upward in joy, and the earl's twilight-blue eyes danced before us.

Glossary

A chiall: (Gaelic) goodness!
ain: own
ance: once
an-seo: (Gaelic) here
Aon. Dà. Trì.: (Gaelic) One. Two. Three.
auld: old
aumrie: cupboard
bairn: child
bannock: Scottish pancake
banshees: female spirits who wail, warning of death
beild: a shelter
bens: hills or mountains
besom: broom
biggin: house
birks: birches
bluid: blood
boyne: washing tub
brae: bank of river or stream
brander: gridiron on which to cook
braw: handsome; excellent
breeks: knee breeches
bridie: meat and gravy pie
brogues: leather shoes
brose: porridge
brùid: (Gaelic) brute
burn: stream
busk: to make ready
but-and-ben: two-roomed cottage
cadge: carrying cage for a falcon

Caiseal Àlainn: (Gaelic) Beautiful Castle
camlet: fine silk and wool blend
canty: pleasant, cheery
ceilidh: (Gaelic) gathering
clachan: village
clarsach: wire-strung, Celtic lap harp
cog: wooden bowl
colcannon: potatoes and cabbage
collops: portions or slices of meat
coorie doon: snuggle down
corbies: ravens
cottar: farmer
crowner: coroner
cuirtan: fine, woven wool
curcuddoch: intimate
De'il: Devil
doocot: dovecote
dominie: schoolmaster
doucily: quietly, sweetly, gently
dowie: sad
drauky: damp, wet weather
dreich: dreary; hard to bear
drookit: thoroughly soaked
drugget: heavy cloth
drumlie: sad
ee: eye
fae: foe
farm-toun: farm town; village
feek-fike: needless bustle; small household job
flanched: flattered
fleerish: C-shaped bar of tempered, carbon steel which is struck against a

flint to produce a spark; a firesteel

forbye: besides

fou: intoxicated

foul-tak-me: devil take me

frae: from

Gàidhlig: (Gaelic) Gaelic

gallipot: small, glazed earthenware jar

garron: Highland pony

gastrous: monstrous

gawp/gowp: stare

geans: wild cherry trees

gey: very

ghillie: someone who attends to his employer; manservant

gin: if

glaikit: senseless, thoughtless

glairie: mud

glisses: glissandos

goun: gown

gowd: gold

greet: grieve

Gu sealladh sealbh ort: (Gaelic) Dear God, or my goodness

gude: good

gude-sister: sister-in-law

gudewife: wife, homemaker

greeting: grieving

haggis: pudding made of oats, onions, and sheep entrails

hairst: harvest

haud: hold

heid: head

hie: high

hodden-gray: homespun cloth

hoolets: owls

ingle: hearth, fireplace

kae-witted: hare-brained; half-witted

kail-yaird: kitchen garden

ken: know

kirk: church

kirn: feast to celebrate the end of harvest

kisting: placing a body in a coffin

laird: Scottish landowner

laithfu': loathsome

lav'rock: lark (bird)

leannan: (Gaelic) sweetheart

lime-harled: whitewashed

linn: waterfall

loch: Scottish lake

love-lowe: flame of love

lum-cheek: chimney-side

lying-in-wife: midwife

lyke wake: watch kept over a body until the funeral

madainn mhath: (Gaelic) good morning

mair: more

marbhphaisg ort: (Gaelic) curse you

maun: must

mawkit: dirty

meikle: much

mony: many

muckle: very large

muir: moor

neep: turnip

nippock: very small piece

nippit: short, scanty

nought/nocht: nothing

nowt-hide: leather

oorit: tired, looking sickly

ower: over
pedlar: peddler
pitleurichie: fuss, disturbance
potage à la reine: (French) a cream-colored soup made out of almond and mushroom or fowl stock
puddock: frog
puir: poor
quaich: low, silver drinking cup with two flat handles
rawchan: a man's plaid
reeving: high, strong
richt: right
sae: so
sair: sore
Salmagundi: a dish containing poultry or fish, chopped meat, eggs, and onions
Samhain: November 1
sark: shirt
sculting: striking with the palm of the hand
shieling: summer hut on hillside used when watching the cows
sneck-drawing: crafty, sly
stoup: deep, narrow vessel for holding liquid
strath: valley
Strath Gruachan: Valley of the Maidens
strykit board: the wooden board on which a body is laid until burial
suidh sios: (Gaelic) the command to sit
tae: to
tatties: potatoes

tauld: told
tinder box: a small box in which is kept a fleerish, flint, tow, and wooden splinters for starting a fire
tocher: dowry
tod: fox
tongue-tackit: tongue-tied
toun: town
tow: fine fibers
trews: trousers
trobhad: (Gaelic) come along
uisge beatha: (Gaelic) whisky ("the water of life")
unco: unknown, strange; extremely, very
wae: woe
wean: child
white house: limewashed cottage
widdershins: against the movement of the sun as it crosses the sky
winter-shadit: sheltered from the north, facing the south
wist: wished
wrang: wrong

www.ingramcontent.com/pod-product-compliance
Lightning Source LLC
Chambersburg PA
CBHW020452020726
47493CB00001B/6